COFFEE LOFT COLLECTION

ALL 3 DENVER EDGE HOCKEY ROM-COMS

Plus a Bonus Novella

KERRY EVELYN

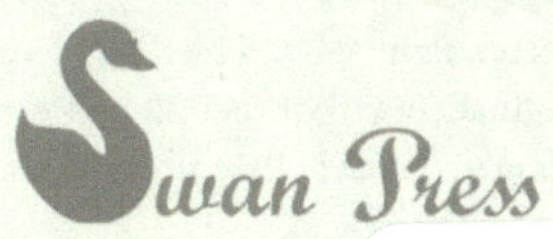

Paperback ISBN: 978-1-960412-33-1

Proofed by BookNookNuts and Jane Litherland

Contents

Welcome to the Coffee Loft! vii
A Note from the Author ix

THAT THING YOU BREW 1
PUMPKIN SPICE SPICE BABY 199
SEW MATCHA IN LOVE 449
SUN, SEA, & BLUEBERRY TEA 629

Recipes 734
Acknowledgments 753
Books by Kerry Evelyn 758
About the Author 760

For Heather Haughton,
my dear reader-turned-friend and the Coffee Loft's
most mug-nificent cheerleader!
God absolutely knew what He was doing when He connected us.
Your support, encouragement, and joy have carried me through more
"chapters" than you know. You have the biggest, most generous heart,
and an incredible talent for making our stories shine—
and for reminding us indie authors (usually right when we need it most)
why we fell in love with writing in the first place, and why quitting is
simply not part of the plot.
Thank you for your friendship, your listening ear, and for your
love for sweet rom-coms. I love you a latte!

Welcome to the Coffee Loft!

At the Coffee Loft, romance is always brewing.

Grab your favorite table over in the corner and be prepared to be swept off your feet! This multi-author collection features some of your favorite sweet romance authors that you already know and love, as well as a few new names you'll be rushing to check out.

From cold brews to cappuccinos and frothy frappes, there's something on the menu for every romantic comedy reader. Fake dates, meddling matchmakers, friends-to-lovers, and so much more; each stand-alone story is the right blend of sweet, guaranteed to warm your heart.

Happily ever afters coming right up! For full immersion, listen to the playlists to these books, you can find them here:

- tinyurl.com/ThatThingYouBrewSpotify
- tinyurl.com/PumpkinSpiceSpiceBabySpotify
- tinyurl.com/SewMatchainLoveSpotify
- tinyurl.com/BlueberryTeaSpotify

For all the Palmer City extras, sign up for my newsletter at KerryEvelyn.com/links to receive the password to the Freebies tab on my website.

For more access to me, a peek into my life as an author and homeschool mom, daily posts, games, takeovers, giveaways, and more, join my VIP Crew at Facebook.com/groups/CranesCoveCrew.

A Note from the Author

Welcome to Palmer City!

Thank you for "attending" the opening of the Palmer City Coffee Loft! I'm so glad you've come to visit this charming old Western town, where residents have been following their dreams for more than a century! In 1888, the Palmer and the Brewer families settled the land, dividing what would become a prosperous mining town into two equal parts. The details were decided by card games, and when the chips settled, the Brewers owned the land west of Snowpack Creek, and the Palmers had control of everything east to the Colorado Springs border, as well as naming rights.

Over the years, the Palmer family began to dwindle, and in the '90s—the 1990s—Quinn Brewer and his wife, Angie, opened a sports bar and grill across from the new arena and mall—on the Palmer side of Snowpack Creek. Quinn's mother was a Palmer, and, well, the sale of that land is a story for another time!

With the addition of the arena, an all-in-one-stop sportsplex popped up on the west side, providing a place for professional athletes and townies alike to learn and play. Featuring pro hockey players to Olympic figure skaters to world-class all-star cheerleaders, the Plex rivals the Creek Walk on a Saturday night for the busiest place in town.

Local businesses along the creek are owned by the kindest and quirkiest residents this side of the Colorado River. Rock on a swinging creekside bench or stroll along Restaurant Row to the town park, a magical place to find love and solace in all the seasons. Everything is light and peaceful here in Palmer City … mostly. With favorite destinations for locals and tourists alike, including a rustic wedding barn venue and the new Coffee Loft, you're sure to find your heart in this small town!

Find a cozy corner, settle in, and enjoy your visit to Palmer City!

XOXO!
Love, Kerry

DENVER EDGE ROSTER

2025-2026

#	POS	CTY	Last	First	Nickname(s)	Age	H	Hometown
1	G	DEN	Priest	Anderson	Priesty	32	6'1	Herning
4	LW	CAN	Allaire	Noel	Santa/ Ally	24	6'2	Toronto, ON
9	LW	CZE	Raffa	Antonio	Raffy	35	5'10	Havirov
11	D	USA	Emerson	Trask	Tiger/ Emmy	31	6'4	Charleston, SC
14	D	CAN	Schwann	Xavier	Swanny	24	6'5	Seattle, WA & Calgary, AB
16	RW	USA	Brewer	Kingston	Bruise	32	5'10	Palmer City, CO
18	RW	CZE	Rozek	Gage	Rosie	29	5'9	Frýdek-Místek
20	RW	USA	Houlihan	Quill	Quilly/ Hoo-Wee!	30	6'2	Colorado Springs, CO
21	LW	CAN	MacDonald	Kel	Kelly/Macky	27	6'1	Summerside, PEI
24	RW	ITL	Pesaro	Artem	Pezzy	27	5'9	Naples, Campania
26	D	USA	Chambers	Bryce	ChaCha	28	6'0	Piney Brook, AK
37	C	CZE	Kolar	Honza	Koley	25	5'11	Prague, Cechia
38	RW	RUS	Koval	Lukolo	Kovvy	27	6'1	Lipetsk
41	D	SWE	Adamsson	Gustav	Gus	29	6'3	Stockholm
A 43	LW	CAN	Moreau	Emile	Romy	38	5'11	Montreal, QC
57	D	GER	Goldman	Tomas	Goldie	30	5'10	Bremen, Lower Saxony
65	RW	USA	Landry	Flynn	Landie	27	6'0	Shelburne, VT
71	C	CAN	Rockdale	CJ	Rocky	28	6'1	Hamilton, ON
C 86	C	USA	Hathaway	Dean	Cappy	35	5'11	Dartmouth, MA
A 87	D	DEN	Marsch	Zaki	Marshy	32	6'3	Herning
88	G	USA	Dexter	Jason	Dex	33	6'2	Atlanta, GA
91	C	FRA	LaFleur	Etienne	Flower	34	5'11	Ivry-sur-Seine
98	D	USA	Trotter	Brendan	Goofy/ Trotty	28	6'4	Cloquet, MN

THAT THING YOU BREW
COFFEE LOFT SERIES
KERRY EVELYN

To my old friend Mike Valcy, the coolest Cat in the Territory! Thank you for the peeks into your world, your epic generosity, and putting up with my incessant texting during nail-biters and gongshows. ¡Vamos Gatos!

And to those of all ages who struggle with speaking: Know that you are loved fiercely. Never let any perceived weakness define you. You are extraordinary.

CHAPTER 1
Xavier

The slush-filled Main Street of downtown Palmer City the day after Christmas matched my mood: on edge, mushy, and anxious as a skater on thin ice.

The traffic reporter advised an alternate route to the Old Town Bridge, which would've been the most direct route to my destination. Taking Canyon Pass Road to the South Bridge only took a few extra minutes, so I didn't mind. I signaled to turn left at the church and onto Main Street, which was full of the same traffic I'd been trying to avoid.

So close. I could get out and walk. I was *that* close to the Bevvie Bar and Café. Around the corner just up Main Street past the church and Sundae School Ice Cream Parlor, I could ask my teammate and passenger Jason to get my coffee for me, but I was afraid that would alter my routine and backfire. I was already struggling after missing the last three games.

Denver Edge starting goalie Jason Dexter was along for the ride today, having spent the holidays with his wife's family in Palmer City, not far from my apartment. Jason lived on the northern outskirts of Elk Creek Falls, the neighboring town, about halfway to Denver. He kept looking over at me, concern etched on his face. I knew he was worried about my mental state, given my performance at practice and the imminent loss of my Opa. Jay wasn't usually a funny guy, but his impressions of my

grandfather were dead-on and hilarious, even capturing Opa's heavy accent and playful tone.

"Zavey-boy, ve got to get you a vife. All your smart hockey friends have vifes. Vhy don't you have a vife? Zeez muscles"—Jason poked my bicep—"Zeez muscles are strong. Your heart is big. Vomen like you. Pick one. Make Opa happy before he dies."

I laughed. "You even sound like him. He asked me to grant his dying wish—to get married."

Jason shrugged. "That's wild. Glad I could make you laugh. I've had plenty of practice reading to Lauren's students and to Quimby." Quimby, his niece, was four and a half years old and had her uncle wrapped around her finger. "It's been fun to play around with an accent. I must have read *The Nutcracker* at least a dozen times in the past month. And yesterday, I read the hockey alphabet book to the Bellies."

Both Jason's wife, Lauren, and her sister-in-law Lola were expecting baby boys in the spring and jointly referred to the boys as the Bellies.

"It sounds like good practice. You're going to make a great dad," I replied, surprised by the slight sting in my heart. Opa was getting in my head. He'd loved Oma so much and couldn't understand why I didn't want to be married—or even be in a relationship at this period in my life.

I *did* want to be married. Someday. But I wanted to make my mark in the NHL first and bank as much money as I could in case I fizzled out or got injured. I didn't have a degree like Jason. I'd only ever played hockey; it was all I knew. And so it was my priority.

I pressed my lips together and leaned back in my seat. Being one of the younger members on the team—especially one who didn't like to go out and party—I often felt like I was in a weird kind of limbo. I preferred hanging around with the older guys and their families or working out to spending nights barhopping and clubbing.

"I'm worried about you," Jay said. "When you're not laughing, you look like a peewee who had his championship goal taken away."

I forced a smile. "Jay, I'm fine, really. I was lucky to have over two decades with my best friend. And I got to say my goodbyes."

Jason *hmmm'd* like a teacher who didn't quite believe you when you claimed not to have instigated the latest recess shenanigans.

My fingers tightened over the stick shift. This red light was taking forever.

"He's a cool guy," Jason reminisced. "The few times I met him, we could have chatted for hours. And that castle—whoa."

"It's a *chateau,*" I corrected him for the thousandth time. The family chateau, tucked into a mountainside in the Bavarian Alps, wasn't as grand as the word "castle" made it out to be. The grounds were extensive, though, with several small buildings and cottages that once housed family and were now used as offices or were homes for employees who lived on-site. Located in the tiny remote kingdom of Alpintraum, south of Munich, it was small enough to miss if you didn't know to look for it.

Over the years, much of the chateau's main building had been closed off. Before Oma died, she'd worked to open parts of the chateau and grounds for interested tourists. It paid for the upkeep. But without her there to manage it, it had barely been sustainable. The staff was great, but it was a job to them. They weren't and never would be as invested as a family member might be. These last five years, Opa's health and broken heart had slowed him down considerably, and he refused to take money from my dad.

"Dude, 'Schwannenschloss' literally translates to 'Swans Castle,'" Jason stated, like this was new information for me.

"Castle of the Swans," I corrected. His smirk signaled I'd played right into his point. My jaw tightened. Of course my smarty-pants Harvard grad teammate would know that. "Just because you have a fancy Ivy League degree doesn't mean you know everything."

"*Two* degrees, thank you very much."

"Riiiight." He'd just completed a master's degree in data science to go with his bachelor's in applied mathematics. "Nerd."

I caught his eye and tried to keep a straight face, but neither of us could hold in the laugh.

Mine came forth from a deep place, and God knew I needed it.

Jason was a stats guy, and when I made it clear I didn't want to talk about Opa, he pivoted and began contrasting my performance playing on the road—dismal—to my numbers at home. They still landed me first in the league for defensemen, even though I missed the last few games. But there had been several awkward pauses, like he wanted to say something more but refrained.

Finally, I couldn't take it anymore. "Just say what you want to say. Please."

He took a deep breath. "I can tell you're only half listening to me. But … there's something you should know. There's a reason I asked you for a ride this morning—not just because I missed your ugly face."

I frowned and resisted the urge to reward his insult with an elbow to his bicep. This sounded serious. "Just spill it."

He gestured toward the coffee shop. "The news is all over social media. They announced it this morning while Montoya Construction was hanging up the new signs. The Bevvie Bar has been sold. I'm not sure what we'll find when we get there."

Penny. My first thought went to the barista who invented my lucky coffee. Was that what he wasn't saying? That Penny wouldn't be there?

I shook my head to clear it and focus on the facts. *Sold?* It had never crossed my mind that the Bevvie Bar might ever be sold. The businesses along Main Street hadn't changed as long as I'd lived here. I gripped the wheel tightly as I edged closer to the light, stopping just shy of the intersection as the yellow signal turned to red.

If I couldn't get my toffee coffee … I was toast. I didn't think it was magic, of course, but when something was going right, you kept doing it.

It's bad luck not to.

I wasn't Irish—half German and half First Nations—but I was born on St. Patrick's Day. I knew luck. And, as a rule, hockey players were overly superstitious. I was probably on the higher end of that spectrum.

I also hated coffee, but superstition dictated how seriously I took my pregame coffee routine, and I'd done everything possible in the last three-plus years to make sure I hit up the Bevvie Bar before each home game.

If I lost my streak, I could be bounced straight back to the minors. Then I wouldn't just be living in Palmer City, I'd be playing here again, too. Or worse, they could put me on waivers and trade me away if I cleared them. Who knew which team might pick me up?

I'd never been happier than where I was now.

Not that it was a bad thing to play in this close-knit small town. I still lived here, not minding the hour or so drive to Denver. But it was backward motion for a defenseman in his early twenties. I'd finally landed a full contract last summer after years of two-way play with the Voltage, filling in for defensemen on the Edge when they needed a D-man to fill a spot if one of the rostered players was out. The thought of being put on waivers so they could send me back to the minors made me physically sick.

Practice earlier this morning had been brutal. I hadn't played hockey in a week. Jet lag combined with anxiety and grief kept my body awake and my mind racing. Opa had taken a turn for the worse just before Christmas. He'd been ill these last few years, one thing after another, but the pneumonia over Thanksgiving had done a number on his lungs.

Needless to say, it hadn't been the happiest Christmas. My littlest sisters begged me to stay longer at the chateau, for Opa's last days, but he insisted I get back. I took the last flight out of Munich last night to be here for today's morning skate so I could play tonight, knowing he'd be watching online, maybe for the last time.

The season was almost half over, and this was crunch time for us if we wanted to make the playoffs. Management had been gracious enough to let me miss the road trip before Christmas, and they'd lost all three games. Those losses while I was away knocked us down to fourth place out of eight in our division and only two points ahead of Montana, who'd come out of nowhere in the last few weeks with a run rarely seen this time of year.

Opa was my biggest fan, and I was his. I knew he hated me seeing him in his condition and it troubled him that I was missing work on his account. He'd always referred to hockey as my job, which I appreciated. It was more serious than "play," as my dad viewed it.

I would have violated my contract in a minute if Opa asked me to stay, and he knew it. But that wasn't his way. Hard work and service were his way of life. He'd grown up wealthy in the chateau with expansive grounds and gardens—but you'd never know that if you met him on the street. Schwannenschloss was our fairytale family home, and it was especially enchanting at Christmas. But this year, I hardly noticed.

We played at home tonight, and I needed some good to balance out the bad. Once I got my toffee coffee from the Bevvie Bar, I'd be ready to go. I had a perfect record on the ice at home on the days when Penny, barista extraordinaire, was at the Bevvie bar to make my special drink. For the last few years, every time I'd drunk her custom-made pregame toffee coffee, I'd scored a goal.

Penny. Was her job safe? The beautiful, shy barista who played the harp during the slow afternoons, taught American sign language to preschoolers at the library, and …

And had barely said three words out loud to me in as many years.

We communicated through coffee cup messages.

A month ago, she'd written, *Get the 3 points you need to "edge" out the others for the Norris trophy! #14MVP2024*

The Norris trophy went to the best defenseman in the league. In that game, I'd scored once and gotten two assists. After that, the points kept coming, and I was way ahead now. For the last game I'd played before I left for Europe, she'd written *Hug your Opa.* She must have overheard me talking about him in line. I scored a goal in that game, a snappy wrister through heavy traffic during a penalty kill, and got an assist on a pass to our captain, who always found the net from the left circle.

Speaking of not speaking, I didn't reply to Jason. What was there to say? Instead, I drew in another deep breath and let it out slowly. The light turned green, and as I crossed the intersection and turned left, I glanced up the block.

What I saw made me take in another deep gulp of air.

"Never seen that before." Jason leaned forward in his seat. Three buildings up on the right, the Bevvie Bar was thronged on both sides by a crowd of people, some holding signs. Across the street, cars were parked bumper to bumper in front of Karta's Kitsch, the antique shop, and the bookstore. Only one parking space was available on the whole block, right in front of the coffee shop, but there were people standing in it.

As we approached the sea of people in the marked space, they parted, motioning for me to take the spot. I pulled up alongside a pickup and glided backward into the spot easily.

While I parallel parked, Jason read aloud some of the signs. "*Swanny, we love you! I'll make your coffee. Hashtag Bevvie Bar Forever! Coffee Loft Stinks.* Yikes."

I stared past him, through his window, to the old saloon-turned-coffee shop. A new awning and lettering on the door and windows matched the unlit logo on the front of the building. The crowd, a mix of ages, wore the royal blue, red, and silver colors of the Edge. Some in jerseys. Some with scarves. It looked like half the town had shown up to support the end of my toffee coffee.

I groaned, immediately recognizing a particular trio of twentysomething season ticket holders who sat a few rows up from our bench and were always trying to get our attention.

"Bubbles, Blossom, and Buttercup are here," I muttered. The trio had been so nicknamed after a jumbotron spotlight lookalike cam had likened these three to the PowerPuff girls because of their similarities to the blond-, red-, and raven-haired cartoon characters.

"We should go in." Jason unbuckled his seat belt and stroked his short-trimmed beard, reminding me I hadn't shaved this morning. I was sporting a scruffy anchor beard this season, and it was a little out of control. I'd need to fix that before the game tonight.

"Yeah." I pulled at my tie, loosening it just a little, and turned the car off. He reached behind him for our suit jackets and handed me mine. I slung it over my arm and opened the door to my Audi R5. The car had been a gift from Opa when I'd signed my contract. "Zave your money, Zavey-boy," he'd said in his thick accent. "I vant you to zave for vhen hockey cannot make you money anymore."

I loved the Audi, but it was a little too flashy for my style. I liked to fly under the radar, even on the ice. It was one of the reasons I chose to play defense. I'd send the puck to a scorer and be happy with the assist. But Coach Conway of the Volts saw that I was holding back and called me on it at the end of last season. "Swanny, you'd be in the NHL already if you didn't hold back. Play the two-way hockey. Score goals. Get noticed. You've worked hard. Show us all what you can really do."

So I did. We made it to the playoffs and won the minor league championship.

And I got noticed.

Press was everywhere. Fans were everywhere. Bubbles, Buttercup, and Blossom were *everywhere*.

Except for at my little coffee shop in the little town between Denver and Colorado Springs where my favorite barista strummed her harp and soothed my soul during lazy afternoons.

Oh, there were always a few fans to wave and greet me and ask for selfies on game days, but it was nothing like this. A couple of kids after school, a hockey mom with a van packed with mites or peewee players on the way to practice, the occasional retirees. This display today was a shy kid's nightmare.

I often employed the tricks I'd learned from the media training when I'd played in the World Junior championship. Slowing my breathing, I took my time, slipping my suit jacket on and extracting my six-foot-five frame from the low bucket seat. Jason did the same, and our doors slammed shut at the same moment as if choreographed. He waited by his door as I walked around the hood of the car, lifting my hand in a polite wave to the fans. We stuck out like sore thumbs in our high-end designer suits. Everyone in the crowd was dressed for a snow day in puffer jackets and jerseys over hoodies.

"Looking sharp, boys!"

"I wish my husband dressed like that!"

"Swanny! What will you do if they don't have toffee coffee anymore?"

"The team better do something about this! It could tank our season!"

"Dex, you better step it up!"

"Swanny! We're here for you!"

I flashed a smile and thanked the teenage fan who opened the door for us and followed Jason inside. The coffee shop was just as crowded, but being tall has its perks. I scanned over the people and through the Christmas decorations, looking to see if Penny was behind the counter. It was Tuesday afternoon, and though it was a holiday week, she should be working.

Her sister, Tasha, was at the register taking orders. Behind her, their cousin Gabby, who was engaged to Coach Conway's stepson and my sometimes teammate, Noel Allaire, puttered about, filling orders. Their rust-colored Bevvie Bar aprons had been replaced with white aprons featuring a steaming cup of coffee. A woman I didn't recognize, sans apron but wearing a name tag, was in a hushed conversation at the end of the counter with Adri Delicata, our local sports reporter, who had one eye on the woman and one eye on us.

Oh no.

I spoke low to Jason as Adri's cameraman turned in our direction. "I'm going to ask Tasha where Penny is. Block me from Adri?"

He nodded and stepped out of the line to make his way toward the left end of the counter. I skirted around the people in front of us and caught Tasha's eye. She nodded, handed her customer a receipt, and met me at the end of the refrigerated cooler.

Her eyes met mine expectantly. "You don't ever cut the line or ask for favors. What's up?"

I stuffed my hands into my pockets and nodded my chin in the direction of Adri and the new woman. "Trying to avoid a spectacle. Is Penny here?"

She averted her gaze, her eyes darting to the small—and empty—dais on the side wall near the entrance to the restrooms where Penny's harp sat during her shifts. "She's out back, in her car. Her anxiety can't handle this today. She blew another audition." Tasha clapped her hand over her mouth. "Oops. I shouldn't have said that."

Blew an audition? *Another* one? Penny was the most talented harpist I'd ever heard play. How many auditions had she blown? Opa was a symphony aficionado, hiring string players for all of his and Oma's events at the chateau. Only the best for Ludorf and Louisa von Schwann. But no one had ever come close to Penny's talent, if you asked me. Her fingers didn't fly over the strings; they fluttered like butterfly wings. Her posture was straight but relaxed. And when she closed her eyes, she smiled while she played, as if she, too, were enjoying the music.

I loved to watch her play.

Not in a stalkerish way. She practiced at the Bevvie Bar when business was slow and often took special requests. My favorites were the instrumental animated film ballads. Opa used to play those for my sisters when we visited. Penny was just as good—if not better—than he was. But the first time I'd heard her, she was playing Opa's favorite song, "Little Bird, Little Bird" from the stage musical *Man of La Mancha*. I'd choked up, hit with a powerful wave of homesickness and emotion that gutted me.

I could close my eyes while Penny was playing and I'd be in Opa's music room with him and Oma and my sisters and parents. Before cancer claimed Oma, before Opa's lungs began to fail, before I played professional hockey. Sitting on a plush sofa with my sister Daniella, with our little sisters Karina and Edyta on our laps and Mom and Dad getting cozy in a corner.

"Xavier!"

"Huh?" I'd gotten lost in my thoughts again. "Sorry. Where do I go?"

Tasha pointed toward the door to the kitchen, just a few feet behind her. "Sneak through the kitchen and out the back door. Jannell won't mind. See if you can get Penny to come inside."

"Jannell?"

"Our new owner. She and her husband, Marcus, are really cool. I was afraid when the Bevells retired that the new owners would let us all go and start fresh. It happened at the Long Island store. The new owner fired his whole staff on Christmas Eve! *Christmas Eve!* Can you imagine?" She shook her head.

"But the Riveras seem to want to keep most things the way they are, except for what's necessary and required for the franchise."

"The Bevells retired?" I didn't know why I was still talking. Jason could only keep Adri engaged for so long. Hopefully he was regaling her with stats. There was no interrupting him once he got going.

She nodded. "It was quite sudden. They only told us a few days before Christmas that they were selling the business and moving onto a cruise ship."

"A cruise ship?" I shook my head, catching the reporter in my peripheral. "Tell me later. Adri's on the move."

In a flash, I was through the swinging stainless-steel-plated door and safe in the kitchen. I navigated around the counters and equipment and outside into the winter sunshine a mere seconds later.

The back lot was just wide enough for angled parking spaces and a narrow lane that traversed all the shops on this block. Behind a grass-laden median, an apartment complex rose up three stories. I started with the cars directly behind the Bevvie Bar—er, Coffee Loft, and spotted Penny in a little blue Mazda hatchback. Her face was tucked into her arms over the steering wheel, but I'd recognize her waist-length sandy-colored braid anywhere. Behind her, the seats were down to accommodate the harp's hard case, which took up all the space in the back and under the hatch.

I didn't want to startle her. Tentatively, I knocked lightly on the window. She jolted upright.

Smooth, Schwann. I gave her what I hoped was an apologetic smile. But it fell as she turned her head, revealing puffy eyes and a makeup-streaked face.

Her eyes widened in horror, and she immediately hid her face again. Had I scared her? I suddenly felt an ache in my chest, as if I'd been checked into the boards during a game. It was real pain, dull but definitely there. And my gut began to burn as I wondered who had made her cry. Didn't they know how amazing she was? I wanted to check *them* into the boards and bang some sense into their stuck-up, snobbish—

"Please ... go." The muffled words from within the car hung in the air.

Going was the last thing I wanted to do.

I pushed my sunglasses onto my head and leaned down to speak at the glass. "Can I help?"

She shook her head. "Tasha ... coffee."

"I don't need coffee. Please, Penny, let me in? It's freezing out here." It wasn't really, and I liked the cold. You sort of had to if you played hockey.

After what seemed like eternity but was probably less than a minute, she nodded her head. I walked around to the passenger side and waited for the lock to disengage.

Thunk!

I pulled the door open and folded my oversize frame into the cramped seat, doing my best to angle my body toward her.

"So ... embarrassed," she murmured into her coat sleeves.

Instinctively, I reached out and placed my hand on her shoulder. She didn't recoil, but she didn't lift her head, either. "Tasha let it slip that your audition didn't go well. Whoever they are, they're stupid and don't deserve you."

"Ssss ... sym... phony. Sssaid I ... dd-didn't have wh-what it tt-akes."

I leaned in. "That's a load of garbage. Penny, I've attended some of the best symphonies in Europe, and you're the most talented harpist I've ever heard play. That includes my Opa, who played his whole life. And—" Dare I tell her she was beautiful to watch? I nodded my head, even though she couldn't see me. "And you're beautiful to watch."

"Th-th-anks."

We sat there for a few moments, neither of us speaking. I wondered how long we'd have until Adri found us. Hopefully she'd give up looking.

I glanced at the clock on the dash. I'd have to leave soon if Jason and I were going to make it to the arena on time.

After what seemed like an eternity, Penny sat back, pinning my hand between her back and the headrest.

I didn't mind.

"Sss-orry I ww-asn't there t-to … make your coffee." The last three words were rushed, and she looked like she was going to cry again. She wasn't sobbing, but her words came out like she was.

"It's okay. I'm more concerned about you. Want to talk about it?"

She shook her head. "Your … game? L-late?"

"Yeah, I need to get going," I replied. "But I wanted to make sure you were okay."

"I'm—" She took a deep breath and gave a quick, tight smile. "Fine."

I tilted my head, challenging her reply. She shrugged.

"Take my sunglasses?" I pulled them off my head and held them out to her. "Sometimes it's easier for me to speak when I can't see who I'm talking to or there's a barrier between us. Like my helmet's visor or a camera lens. It creates distance, and sometimes I even trick myself into thinking I'm someone else behind the glass."

Penny pressed her lips together and took the sunglasses, turning them over in her hands. Slowly, she slid them on and checked her reflection in the rearview.

I squeezed her shoulder reassuringly. "What do you think?"

She chewed on her lip, then turned her head towards me. "Cool."

I laughed. "The coolest girl I know."

She pressed her lips together again, and her cheeks flushed where her makeup had been rubbed away.

How could I make her smile? I glanced at the dash again. I had ten minutes if we were going to make it on time.

"You ssh-should go." She removed the sunglasses and handed them back to me. Her chin dipped into her chest. "T-Tasha can m-make coffee."

I studied her, and it occurred to me that this was the most she'd spoken to me in the years since I'd been frequenting the Bevvie Bar. She wasn't crying anymore or breathing heavily, yet she was stuttering. Did I make her nervous?

I retracted my hand and hung my head. I owed her an apology. She obviously wanted to be alone and was only being polite, letting me into her car and allowing my knight-in-shining-armor attempt to fix her problems.

I was always trying to fix people's problems. Mine, my sisters', my teammates. It wasn't until recently I realized that not everyone wanted solutions. Some just wanted a listener. I wasn't wired that way, but if that was what Penny needed, I'd be that for her.

I clutched the door handle. "I'm sorry, Penny. It's not my business or my place to offer help. But if you ever need anything—"

She laughed mirthfully and fixed her gaze on the back of the building. "N-not unless y-you c-can help me s-speak."

Memories of being pulled out of class in elementary school rushed into my mind, and an idea occurred to me. I chose my words carefully. "I had a speech impediment when I was a kid."

She turned her head and regarded me curiously but didn't speak.

"I had lessons three times a week. I remember them clearly. Maybe I could help?"

Penny shook her head. "N-not im-im-pedi-mment. N-nerves."

I sat back into the seat and tried to keep my expression open and neutral. If Penny's condition was due to nerves, that meant I was making her nervous, too.

Had she had this condition all her life? Was that why she'd become fluent in ASL?

I needed her to know she didn't have any reason to be nervous around me.

Shifting in my seat again, I turned towards her. "You're safe with me, Penny. I hate that I make you nervous."

Her face fell into her hands again, hitting the steering wheel. It let out an angry *honk!* We both jumped.

I wanted to laugh but held it in. She didn't react. I'd made the situation worse. *Way to go, dummy.*

"I'm sorry." I reached for the door handle, and her arm shot out to stop me.

"Wait … please."

Penny reached behind my seat and retrieved a small red purse. She dug around inside and pulled out a pen and one of those skinny receipts you get at a gas station. I watched as she wrote a message on the back of it, in a tiny, perfect script.

> *I blew the audition because I can't speak properly when I'm nervous or anxious. People I don't know make me nervous. Addressing a group, especially an interview panel, paralyzes me. And if I am able to get words out, they're rushed and undecipherable. I can perform and imagine them all away, but before the music starts and after it ends, I stutter. It's crippling and embarrassing and I'm so ashamed. I hate that you know my secret. But I hate living like this even more. So I'd like to try whatever you think might help. But I'm not hopeful. Fourteen years of speech therapy did absolutely nothing.*

As I read, that achy feeling in my chest returned.

I met her gaze and reached for her hand, clasping it in mine. Her gray-green eyes shone with fear and uncertainty. "I'd be honored to help. Media training taught me some great tips. And your secret is safe with me."

"Th-thank you."

I looked down at her thumb, admiring its perfect shape and manicured nail, painted a soft pink with an ivory tip. Connected to the same magical hand that strummed the right side of her harp.

She inclined her chin toward the building. "T-together?"

"Go inside together?" I repeated.

She nodded.

"Okay." I opened the door and jogged around to her side, making it there in time to pull her door open and offer her my hand. I was surprised and delighted when she took it.

Once she was out, I closed the door. She scooted over to open the back door and pulled out a tote bag and a white apron.

"Want me to get the harp?" I asked.

She shook her head. "N-not today."

I followed her to the back door and inside. She hung her tote on a hook, tied on her apron and went directly to a small sink and turned on the water. I watched as she wet the hem of her apron and mixed the soap in her hands.

I probably should've left the kitchen, but I stayed rooted to the spot as she washed the traces of makeup away, revealing her perfect fair skin with a light dusting of freckles.

I loved her freckles.

She patted her face dry with a paper towel and beckoned me to follow her out to the coffee shop.

"I'll get the door for you," I said, rushing ahead of her to push it open.

Penny took one step and her body went stiff. I followed her gaze.

Staring straight at us was Adri Delicata and the imposing circle of her cameraman's lens.

And dozens of phones pointed in our direction.

CHAPTER 2
Penny

Oh no. Oh no. Oh nooooo.

"Xavier! There you are! And Penny, too!" Adri flashed her trademark wide grin and fixated her eyes right on mine. "Perfect! Xavier, can you address the rumors that the Edge owners have made an offer to buy out the Riveras? Penny, can we get a shot of you making his toffee coffee?"

My day couldn't possibly get any worse.

Behind the reporter, Xavier's teammate Jason towered over Officer Douglas, speaking in hushed tones, but it wasn't doing anything to help the situation.

Xavier stepped around me, positioning himself between me and everyone else. Shielding me, becoming the barrier he'd spoken about. Like being a defenseman on the ice, he was wired to protect the goal.

I didn't know how I felt about that, but I was in no headspace to speak to reporters—or to anyone for that matter. I'd make his coffee and then maybe they'd all get out of here before I had another breakdown.

My cheeks flamed in shame. I couldn't believe I'd let Xavier Schwann see me that way or confessed my heavily guarded secret to him. What had I been thinking? When Tasha texted me that the place was a zoo, I should've gone home and called in sick.

But ... Xavier. His visits and my ability to strum my anxiety away on the harp were the only things that made working in a coffee shop tolerable. His dark eyes were the color of rich soil with golden flecks and reminded me of Palmer City's prospecting past. Tanned skin, high cheekbones and devil-may-care quiet confidence that made every girl swoon. His almost-black hair and close-cropped beard were usually neatly trimmed, but I also loved when he let it all grow out when the Volts made the playoffs and on days like today, when it was just a little long and scraggly. And his smile … a girl could get lost in it.

I spoke from experience.

Which was why it was best never to look.

But it was when he raised his thick eyebrows quizzically over those deep, soulful espresso eyes that made me weak in the knees. Higher in the center of his face, his eyebrows transformed his expression to part movie star, part puppy. A heart-melting combination of Flynn Ryder's smolder and the eagerness of Rexie, my grandparents' husky, when he was anticipating a treat.

I probably shouldn't compare Xavier to a puppy, but it was what it was.

And when he spoke with his gentle and kind Canadian lilt, my brain melted like the coffee ice cream in his to-go cup. How a boy from Seattle sounded Canadian, I had no clue. Was it because of his mom or all the time he spent playing with Canadian players? I didn't care. It was adorable.

Jason had told me recently that when I made Xavier's coffee, he scored a goal in the game one hundred percent of the time. When Tasha made it, only seventy-two percent. Gabby, fifty-three percent. And it dropped off from there. Surely if Jason told me this information, Xavier had to know, and after missing three games, I flattered myself by thinking he needed me.

So I'd driven to work. I couldn't let him down. Especially not this close to the trade deadline. It wasn't totally selfless; I needed to see him regularly for my sanity's sake and because making his coffee was the only way I was contributing positively to anything in this world.

Only today, the story had broken about the new owners. Probably because the signage had been changed. In a small town like ours, news traveled fast. Xavier wasn't just a player for the Edge, he was a part of our community. He'd lived here for three years playing for the Volts first and volunteering at local youth camps and events. There were always fans here on game days, but they were usually cool.

Nothing like today's crowd.

Besides, it wasn't like I was needed—or wanted—anywhere else. Thanks to my lack of a social media personality and unwillingness to be on camera for anything other than my music, I'd failed to get a spot in any of the local holiday performances. My classes didn't start up until the second week of January, and they were all online. I'd saved all the easier courses for last so I could do them on my own time and focus on auditions and getting into a grad program.

While I busied myself gathering the ingredients for Xavier's custom coffee, Adri fired off questions to him.

"I've spoken to the new owner, Jannell Rivera. She says they'll be transitioning to the Coffee Loft brand coffee. With the base ingredient of your personalized coffee changed, do you think that will impact your scoring?"

"Well, I don't know, Adri. I would hope not."

"You've shared in interviews that you're not a fan of changes during the season because you don't want to invite bad luck. You're a superstitious guy, Xavier. You said so yourself to your team's sideline reporter. And you've been adamant during your time here in Colorado that you make, and I quote, 'no big changes during the season' because it could bring bad luck. Correct me if I'm wrong, but your goal scoring percentage is nearly one hundred percent when you stop in here for your toffee coffee on game days." Behind her, Jason grunted. Our sideline reporter was his sister, Bailey.

"It's all in good fun," Xavier replied amicably with his winning smile, which could charm Scrooge McDuck out of his money. But I'd heard him speak enough to catch a nervous note to his assurance. When one has a speaking problem, one tends to pay more attention to the vocal patterns of others.

And I'd been paying attention to Xavier for a long time.

What he didn't know—and what I wasn't about to tell Adri—was that I'd emailed the Bevells asking for their supplier and had ordered enough of the same coffee to last him two more seasons —the term of his contract. After that, well, we'd see where we both were.

I'd hoped to be part of one of those European symphonies he'd mentioned by then, but reality was I'd still be here at the Coffee Loft. If I couldn't get a chair in a local or somewhat local orchestra—this last audition had been in Parker, just under an hour away—how would I ever build my résumé?

Certainly not with my short gig at the medieval-themed dinner show. I'd been let go due to their preshow "going in a different direction." Or the Renaissance Faire I worked a few weekends each summer. I loved that job. I didn't have to say a word, just sit there and play background music while the magician and bawdy singing groups took their breaks. I was especially grateful to the Bevells and Riveras for allowing me to play at the coffee shop. It was thanks to Tasha that I was working here. She'd vouched for me when I couldn't speak during my interview and even asked if I could practice my harp-playing during slow times.

Okay, time to put this thing together.

Coffee ice cream, butterscotch chips, light roast, whipped cream, sea salt caramel drizzle, toffee crunch bites.

I could make Xavier's drink in my sleep.

I secured the lid and hastily scribbled a message on the side of the cup while I walked back to Xavier, who was trying to reassure everyone his game was not threatened by the change of ownership.

He took the coffee from me, twisting it to read the message. A smile lit up his face, and I felt the blush in my cheeks burn hotter than a steaming pot of Joe. *Top shelf, right side.* The Edge were playing the New Orleans Crescents tonight, and their starting goalie had a blind spot.

How did I know? I followed a popular hockey guy on YouTube. He was a former goalie and spotlighted all the AHL and NHL goalies. Xavier probably already knew about him, but I felt it was helpful. And so far, well, everyone knew his stats now.

Xavier covered my message with his hand and tipped his cup to the fans behind Adri. "Thanks for coming today. We know you love our team, and we appreciate your support. And thank you,

Penny"—he turned to me—"for inventing the magic coffee that accelerated my career."

Oh my. My cheeks were on fire, and the stifling air had reached choking levels. I needed oxygen, STAT. I gave a quick double thumbs-up, smiled, and made a beeline to safety through the kitchen door.

The door swung shut behind me, and I sank to the floor beside it to try to get my heart rate down. *Breathe in ... Release ... Breathe in ... Release ...*

The door squeaked open, and Tasha squatted down next to me.

I lifted my head. "Too much."

She nodded. "I got you." I followed her gaze up and to the door. "I told Xavier to leave. Gabby texted her mom to encourage Adri to wrap it up. We should be clear of the crowd in a few minutes."

"Thanks." Our aunt was a weeknight news anchor at the same local station where Adri covered sports.

Tasha pulled me into a hug. "I hate this for you. I wish ... Never mind. It's not about me."

I squeezed her. "It's okay to wish. I hate this for me, too."

"Have you told Jannell yet?"

I shook my head. "I can't speak to her, either."

Tasha stood and offered her hand. I let her pull me up. "I can talk to her for you, if you'd like. Save you from the anxiety of a conversation or long, blabbering email where you give too much information and can't sleep for days agonizing over every word."

I laughed. That's exactly why I hadn't written one yet. "Thanks."

She grinned. "What are sisters for? Why don't you doomscroll for a bit to clear your head and I'll pop back in when the coast is clear?"

"All right. Thanks for covering for me."

"Anytime."

Tasha left, and I pulled out my phone. I wasn't much of a doomscroller, but I did want to get on Instagram and send Xavier a thank-you message.

Xavier's account was the sweetest thing I'd ever seen. For

every picture of him, there were twice as many of his sisters. He had three younger ones, all figure skaters. He was so proud of them, captioning their photos, videos, reels, and even some bloopers—photos going back to when he first started playing hockey, only about ten years ago. His father had played in the NHL, and his mother was a figure skater, and they decided all their kids would be figure skaters. His first post was a selfie of him as a young teenager, on the day of his first hockey game.

A few family pictures, some with his mom, some with his dad. Never a girlfriend or a girl friend. I wondered if he was dating anyone or had. All the fans speculated. Did he have a sweetheart back home in Seattle or in one of the cities he'd played in before coming here? It was generally believed that he was single, because how could you hide a girlfriend living such a public life, unless you never saw her?

I paused on a picture of his family's castle in Alpintraum. On the smaller side compared with the ones in the bookstore's wall calendars, it was still impressive and beautiful. I often imagined going back in time and playing on the balcony that overlooked the beautiful gardens instead of on a tiny pallet stage in a corner of the dusty Ren Faire lawn, my hands caressing my harp strings while Xavier looked on, dashing in embroidered puffed sleeves, pantaloons, and stockings.

His father had played hockey in Germany before he was drafted at eighteen years old by Calgary. Heinrich Schwann wanted to see the world, and he did. He'd also met Xavier's mom there during training camp. He fell hard and fast and proposed a week later, after he was assigned to their minor league team, so they could be together. He'd been traded to Seattle the next season. The family lived there during the hockey months, and he retired when his last contract expired and the team didn't have the cap space to re-sign him. He'd left the game instead of uprooting his family to play for another team.

It was amazing what you could learn and deduce about someone from social media videos and captions, Google, NHL commentators, and a little math.

Prep school in Seattle, summers in Calgary, Christmases in Alpintraum. I felt like I knew him.

That was ridiculous, though. You can't really know someone unless you spend time with them. Right?

I never tried. I couldn't even get a full sentence out to him without stammering.

The last photo was taken earlier this afternoon. Xavier and Jason, in their fancy game day designer suits, holding long overcoats in the crooks of their arms. They stood in front of a cozy-looking house by an outdoor pine strung with lights and dusted with snow. Jason's brother-in-law, Brady de la Tour, was tagged, so I assumed it was his house. Brady was the equipment manager for the Volts, and Jason was married to Brady's sister, Lauren.

The caption read, "Dex the Halls needed a ride to the game tonight so I volunteered to be his driver. He doesn't like his new nickname. If you like it, chant it when he takes the ice!"

I snorted. I loved Xavier's sense of humor. After a few more seconds of staring at his perfect face, I tapped the icon to open a message.

But the words didn't come. I wrote a few words and deleted them, repeating the pattern until I lost count.

Tasha popped her head into the kitchen. "All clear."

"Thanks."

I stuffed my phone in my apron pocket and squared my shoulders.

Back to work.

I'd message him later.

Maybe.

CHAPTER 3
Xavier

"Dex the Halls! Dex the Halls!"

Jason glared at me through the cage of his mask as the fans chanted his new holiday nickname. I grinned as I leaned against the tunnel wall nearest to him. We were waiting for our cue to take the ice for warmups. I was trying my best not to smirk.

That would be unkind.

But someone needed to fill in for the team's prankster, Zaki Marsch, while he was out with the flu. Why not me?

Jason was a serious guy. I was serious, too, but he was next-level. The dude graduated from Harvard. Both our dads played in the league, and we had similar work ethics. But sometimes he forgot to have fun.

Someone had to remind him of that.

I took on the role willingly.

"Ha!" Bryce Chambers, aka ChaCha, my defensive partner for tonight, joined me at the wall and held out his gloved fist. "Knuckies?"

We bumped our knuckles together as Jason continued to glare.

"Better be careful, Dex," Bryce warned. "Your face might freeze like that."

I snickered. "It'd be an improvement, for sure," I joked.

Did I also mention that good-natured chirping at my own teammates was one of my favorite pastimes?

"Nice one, Swanny." Bryce held up his fist for another tap, and I obliged.

I usually played alongside Zaki. He kept to the net and allowed me to play more offensively. Bryce and I had practiced together yesterday, taking turns staying close to the crease and alternating on the offense. As defensemen, it was our job to block and deflect pucks headed for the net, to protect our goal—and our goalie—at any cost. Scoring when the opportunity arose was our secondary goal, so while I had every intention of shooting at the opposing net tonight, covering our goal effectively with ChaCha was my priority.

"Go time." Our captain, Dean Hathaway, stepped behind Jason, who was already walking the few feet to the ice. Bryce and I waited while the starting offensive line followed him out. We stepped in line behind Dean, our center; left winger CJ Rockdale; and right winger and assistant captain Emile Moreau.

Bryce and I were starting tonight. Plagued with injuries this season, New Orleans didn't have a prayer of making the playoffs. We should beat them easily, so Coach decided not to start our best defensive pair, Brendan Trotter and Trask Emerson. I knew those guys well, having played with them on the Volts, and they both still lived in Palmer City, too.

One of my favorite parts of stepping onto the ice was knocking the stacked pucks off the ledge. With my (lack of) seniority, there were rarely any left by the time I took the ice. But tonight, there were three, and I beat Bryce to them.

"I left them for you!" he shouted.

"Sweet of you, man!" We skated fast, forming a circle on the home side of the ice, flying as our blades sliced through what we fondly dubbed winter's dance floor and taking shots at Jason.

Emile sent a puck sailing toward me from the other side of the ice, a perfect pass. I snapped it, sending it straight over Jason's left shoulder. It hit the back of the net, and I dropped to one knee, holding my stick in the air as I glided toward the boards to wave to the Wags and kids who had come out tonight.

"Nice wrister, Swanny!" I smiled and skated toward the high-pitched squeal of Trask's stepdaughter, Ryleigh. She loved to insult us with her A-game chirping, so a compliment from her was high praise and couldn't go unrecognized.

You don't want to mess with almost-eight-year-old girls. I speak from experience.

"Thanks, Ry." I nodded at Trask's wife, Kami, who was hugging their two-year-old son to her chest, facing out toward the rink. She smiled and adjusted his noise-canceling headphones.

"You're welcome." Ryleigh grinned wickedly. "You're *almost* as good as my brother with a mini stick."

And there it was. *Ouch.*

She crossed her arms over her chest and challenged me with a slight raise of one eyebrow. I held in a laugh and responded soberly. "Guess I need more practice, huh?"

She nodded. "You're slow. I hope you had your lucky coffee today."

I assured her I did, but the expression on her face told me she still wasn't impressed.

Trask glided up next to me. "These fans giving you trouble?" he drawled. He and Kami were from South Carolina and still had their accents.

"The worst!" I mock-complained. "This little lady says her brother is better with his mini stick."

"Aw … Well, she knows her stuff. I taught her myself." He beamed proudly, giving Ryleigh a thumbs-up, which she returned, before turning to Kami and baby Conner.

The toddler banged on the glass, laughing and gurgling as Trask made funny faces at him.

Butterflies the size of hawks started flapping in my stomach. I couldn't pull my eyes away from the sweet, wholesome scene on the other side of the plexiglass.

I wanted that. I wanted a wife and kids I could teach to skate and play hockey. Ryleigh was a local star forward in her age division. Kami kept busy driving her to games and tournaments for the multiple teams she was on. I wondered if I'd ever find someone who would enjoy the hockey wife life as much as Kami did. She'd had to put her career as an earth scientist on hold when Conner was born. She taught a few online classes for the local university, but she didn't do field studies anymore.

I shook my head. I never wanted to have to ask my future imaginary wife to give something up before she ever even had the chance to do it.

Trask skated away, and with a final parting insult from Ryleigh —"Keep your head in the game, number fourteen!"—I waved goodbye to the Emerson family and took off down the side towards the blue line.

I'd spotted a familiar-looking kid holding a sign with my name on it and wanted to get a closer look. *Swanny: Trade you toffee bits for your stick?*

Aw. Definitely.

The little boy's mouth dropped open as I neared the glass. "Hey, man! You know I can't resist that toffee candy crunch. Were you at the Bevvie Bar today?"

He nodded.

"Awesome. Thanks for coming out to show your support. Tell me your name?"

He just blinked at me. Adorable.

"His name is Isaac!"

"Hi, Isaac! This your dad?"

He nodded again.

"Hey Dad, can you lift him up to toss my toffee over the glass?"

Isaac squealed and dropped his sign. His dad handed him the toffee and hoisted him high.

"Bombs away!" Isaac pitched the bag over the glass.

I darted back and to the side, catching it in my left glove and holding it up. "Thanks!

"You're welcome!"

I grinned, happy he'd found his voice, and skated back to the wall. I lifted my stick high and over the glass. Isaac's dad reached up to ease it down until the boy had it in his hands.

"Thank you!" Isaac hopped up and down with excitement.

"Come by the Bevvie Bar before one of our home games and I'll sign it. You know when to find me!" I called.

I glided backward for a few feet, waving, then skated back to our team's bench for a fresh stick. I always taped up three as part of my pregame ritual, just in case I had the chance to give one away, and of course I needed a spare taped my way in case I broke one during the game. Making fans happy, especially the kids, was the best part of my job. Sure, scoring goals was fun, but making kids happy? It fueled me.

I missed my younger sisters. They weren't little anymore. Ten and eight years old already. I'd been away for so much of their growing up, just as Dad had missed much of my and Daniella's childhood. He'd retired three seasons ago, while I was still playing for the Volts. I'd always imagined us playing on the same team—or even against each other—for a season or two before he retired. He was still younger than some of the oldest guys in the league.

But he'd had enough. And when my dad decided something was enough, there was no reversing it. Like becoming a permanent citizen of the United States. We celebrated his and my mom's citizenship last year. My grandfather had been heartbroken and swore he'd disinherit my dad. "Heinrich! You break your old man's heart. Vhy you do this vhen you have beautiful home here?"

Dad tried to explain that he'd made a life for himself in North America. I think he *did* care but had instigated Opa's reaction on purpose to make taking the news easier, in his own weird way. He was happy in Seattle and grumbled every Christmas we spent in Alpintraum.

I'll never forget Opa's scathing words to him. "All the years this family has vorked to keep the Schwannenschloss intact and maintained! And you vould leave it?"

My dad had shrugged in his offhand way and replied, "My life is in America. We'll come visit."

I'll always remember how Opa's mouth had hung open, his eyes shining with unshed tears. "You break my heart, Heinrich."

"Don't worry, Opa," I'd said when Dad left the room. "The girls and I love it here. We'll make sure it stays in the family."

"Swanny! Heads-up!"

Too late.

Ow.

I'd caught a puck.

With my face.

It was wedged between my visor and my temple. Luckily, I'd made it to the ledge in front of our bench, so when it knocked me off-balance, I had something to grab on to.

I blinked and saw red. Half hanging over the ledge with my back to the ice, I eased myself to standing so the trainer rushing over could look at the side of my face.

Ryleigh's advice had been solid. My head *wasn't* in the game tonight.

The trainer gently pried the puck out from under the plastic and pressed a gauze pad to my face where the puck had been as I slowly lifted my helmet off. "That's a lot of blood, Schwann. Probably a dozen zips. Let's take you back and check for signs of a concussion."

"I feel fine," I insisted. "Just a bruise. My sisters throw snowballs harder than that."

"They put rocks in 'em?" Bryce asked, skating up to us. "You okay?"

"Just a bit embarrassed," I admitted.

"Is he out?" Bryce asked, concern in his tone.

"We're going to give him a thorough check," the trainer replied.

I sighed. "Fine." I followed him back through the tunnel. By the time the team returned from warmups, I had six stitches in my temple and had been cleared to play.

Somehow—and I think Jason was behind it—the crowd forgot about Dex the Halls, because when I scored five minutes into the first period, they chanted "Stitch-es, stitch-es!"

I'd take it.

I loved this game. I loved our fans. I loved my teammates.

When we left the ice at the end of the second period, our sideline reporter waved me over. Bailey Dexter Brewer, or B-Dex, as we all called her, was Jason's younger sister and a former hockey goalie herself. She loved the game as much as I did.

"Xavier, the fans on social media have questions." She held up her phone. I peered at the post. It was the picture Brady had taken of us on his lawn that morning. *Liked by RenFaireAspen and 643 others.*

RenFaireAspen was Penny. We followed each other.

My arms tingled, and my lips spread into a wide grin. "Whatcha got, B-Dex?"

"Well, first I want to know what ignited that grin." She peered at her phone and signaled the cameraman to wait. "You've got a thing for Penny," she whispered.

"What?" My heart raced. No. *Wait.*

Yeah, I guess I did. She was sweet, smart, beautiful, talented, and the reason I was in the big show.

How could I *not* have a thing for her?

"Mm-hmm. You should do something about that. We're live in 3, 2, 1 …"

I stared into the camera and tried to keep my expression neutral.

"Swanny, you started this game with six stitches." She paused and looked up at the crowd.

"Stitch-es! Stitch-es!" chanted the crowd.

"You did that on purpose." I lifted a brow.

"You pranked my brother." She shrugged but mouthed silently, *Keep doing it!*

I laughed. "It's all in good fun."

Bailey grinned. "We all know how superstitious you are. Your fans want to know what's going to happen with your toffee coffee when the Bevvie Bar officially changes their products over."

I opened my mouth to reply, but she didn't give me a chance.

"I have a reliable source that claims your barista has personally ordered a substantial supply of the special light roast the Bevvie Bar served so that she can continue to make your coffee exactly the way she's been doing it for the past three years."

Now both my eyebrows were raised. Penny had done that for me?

If that was true, I owed her big.

Bailey asked me a few questions about my goal and partnering with ChaCha, then I headed back into the tunnel.

We didn't have a game tomorrow, and I planned to go straight to the Bevvie Bar before practice, if Penny was working or able to meet. I wanted to make a date—er, time?—to help her with her speaking.

We won 5-3. I scored another goal, further proving to the fans that Penny's coffee was magic.

But deep down, I knew it wasn't the coffee.

It was the barista. *My* barista, Bailey had called her.

I liked the sound of that.

CHAPTER 4
Penny

I had every intention of watching the Edge game when I got home from work, but the excitement of the day had drained me. After a long hot shower, I curled up under the covers to read with a microwaved mug of soup and my tablet. Tasha would be home late after coaching her cheer teams, and I hoped to be asleep before she walked in.

First, though, I needed to see if the Edge won. I tapped the Instagram icon and typed @denveredgehockey into the search bar. A reel popped up of a puck sailing through the air and hitting a player in the face. The player dropped, grabbing onto the ledge in front of the bench. It was captioned, "Puck stop of the night."

I started to laugh, but then I realized it was Xavier. I scrolled in haste, looking for confirmation that he was okay, and let out a sigh of relief when I read that he not only was okay but that he'd scored two goals and the team won.

A headline from the sports channel caught my eye. "Schwann's At-Home Goal Streak Continues as Barista Orders Years' Worth of Special Coffee."

What? How could they know that? I scanned the article and watched his interview with Bailey. She'd been in the Bevvie Bar Christmas Eve morning chatting with Tasha. But why would my sister tell her that?

I watched Adri Delicata's interviews with Jason and Xavier and groaned at my own awkwardness. More headlines. "Is Swanny Sweet on His Barista?" and "Barista Is Schwann's Lucky Penny."

Oh, my.

And—*if only.*

I remembered wanting to message him earlier. Now I was glad I hadn't. Who knew who had access to his phone or social media?

I pulled up his timeline. He'd taken a selfie of his bandaged face. "Hazard of the job," he'd captioned it. "Six zips."

Hockey lingo. It made me smile. They had their own word or nickname for everything. Warmups were warmies, the puck was an apple, a goal up high in the net was top shelf, helmets were buckets, gloves were mittens, their hair was lettuce, and the goalie's pads were pillows. The list was endless.

A notification popped up over my message icon. I tapped it, and my eyes widened. It was from Xavier. He'd never messaged me before.

Hi. Sorry about today's madness. Are you free tomorrow?

I squealed out loud and quickly slapped my hand over my mouth, forgetting I was home alone.

Straight and to the point. I liked that. No pointless small talk or mention of the game or his injury.

Hi. I work from 10 a.m. 'til close.

As an afterthought, I added *'til 6 or so, and then we have a staff meeting.*

I have practice at ten. Can I meet you at the Bevvie Bar at 8:00? We could have breakfast and talk about ... you know.

Sure.

Sure? I smacked my forehead. Could I sound any less excited? Probably best. I didn't want him to know I'd had a huge crush on him since I made his first toffee coffee.

He replied right away. *Great! I'll see you then.*

I stared at his words. Instead of replying, I held my finger on his message until the emoji options popped up. Before I could chicken out, I tapped the red heart and closed the app.

THE NEXT MORNING, I arrived at the Coffee Loft at seven thirty. Our new owners, Jannell and Marcus Rivera, had taken the early shift this entire week to get a feel for the layout and meet the regular customers. We staff appreciated the chance to sleep in. The week after Christmas was insane.

The nineteenth-century building had originally been the town's saloon. It was renovated into a café in the 1920s by one of my great-grandfather's brothers. I forgot which one, as there were eight that lived into adulthood. It had changed ownership many times over the last hundred years, each new owner making it look less and less like its original vessel.

All that remained of the original furnishings on the inside was the dark-paneled side wall along the north-side wall and its matching countertop, which had been brought out of storage a few years ago and set up along the left-side wall for working customers so that they didn't take up a whole table while they sipped. The Wordsmiths' Bar, they called it.

The swinging door panels had been attached to the outside walls, and today a Montoya Construction employee was painting them Coffee Loft Red to match the new awning. Minor changes but bold. Definitely different. I waved to him and went inside.

The line was long with our regulars. I nodded and smiled and waved and prayed for the line to move faster. If the new owners hadn't been here, I would have slipped behind the counter and made my own coffee. I was still getting to know them, though, and didn't want to chance they'd fire me over something the previous owners encouraged, like eating stale cookies. The Bevells hated waste and refused to serve anything that wasn't fresh, so the employees benefited, for sure. Anything we didn't eat or take home was donated.

Behind the two registers, Liam Brewer and his wife, Beck, the owner of Montoya Construction, were installing a gigantic recessed mug cubby into the wall next to the kitchen door. It probably had an official name, but what else would you call shelving with individual spaces for mugs? Liam was our local architect, and Beck and her father ran the contracting business. They were doing all of the work to transform the Bevvie Bar into a Coffee Loft.

"Hi, Penny!" Marie, Jannell and Marcus's seventeen-year-old daughter, waved to me as she emerged from the kitchen.

I waved back and smiled. She was a sweet girl, an efficient barista and an exceptional person, training therapy dogs in her spare time. She'd even cleared out a cupboard under the counter to use as a doghouse for her newest trainee, Riva. I was thrilled we were going pet-friendly. Riva was a sweet dog, gentle, loving and obedient.

Finally, it was my turn to order. I stepped up to Marie's register and scanned the doughnuts in the case.

"You're here early. What do you think of the new mug storage?" Marie asked.

I smiled. "It's cool." No stuttering. Marie didn't make me nervous, and the crowd had dissipated. Maybe I'd be okay with Xavier when he arrived.

"I think so, too. Every summer, we go to this resort in Maine called the Cliff Walk. There's not one duplicate mug on the property. You never know which ones will show up in your cabin or what you'll be served with in the dining room. Mom loved that and wanted to do it here, too. For the regulars, mostly." She leaned over the register conspiratorially. "And the coolest part is you can use them to send a message."

"That's a cool idea," I said. "Passive-aggressive, but I can see how that can come in handy."

"Yup! Only bottomless for the dine-ins, though. I'd really like to send some messages to some of the to-goers, though, know what I mean?"

I chuckled. "Sure do."

She grinned. "What can I get you?"

"I'll take two toffee crunch doughnuts, a Lofty-size sea salt caramel Frodoughchino, and a Lofty Matcha Madness."

She peered at me through her glasses. "Meeting a *friend*, huh?" She winked and then giggled.

I laughed, too. Few people ordered the Matcha Madnesses,

among them, hockey players. In the week she'd been here, Marie had already served the matcha to a handful of Volts.

A cloud of nerves descended on me, and I pressed my lips together. What had I been thinking, agreeing to meet Xavier here? Especially after yesterday and all the speculation about him and "his barista." And I'd just ordered his food.

Well, why shouldn't I? He was going to do me a favor. If Xavier could help me lose my stutter, I'd owe him more than a healthy shake and doughnut.

It occurred to me that the doughnut and the matcha protein shake were at odds nutritionally. Maybe he'd save the doughnut for after practice.

Marie applied my employee discount and I paid for the order, tapped the thirty-percent tip option, and scooted down the counter to wait for it.

"Go find a seat. I'll bring it out to you." Jannell smiled and nodded toward the only empty table in the front corner of the restaurant.

Xavier's table.

"Are you s-sure?" I paused to concentrate on getting my next sentence out flub-free. "I can wait."

She shook her head. "If this Matcha Madness and toffee crunch doughnut are for who I think they're for, I want to say hi and thank him for his business."

I snorted. "Yes, m-ma'am."

I pulled a few napkins from the dispenser and headed toward the front of the café. Two large bay windows flanked the old saloon-style entrance. One side featured a seating area with small sofas. At the other window, small round tables and upholstered chairs filled the space.

I reached the corner table and adjusted the chairs so that my back was to the wall and Xavier's would be to the window.

Hmm. People might recognize his backside. The broad shoulders, the backward cap, and his larger-than-most frame would be noticeable to passersby, especially those who knew him.

I'd for sure know who he was at a glance. Plus, this was where he usually sat to listen to me play. He'd close his eyes, and a few times I thought I'd put him to sleep. Other times, I felt the heat of his stare on me. Once, I looked up and caught his gaze. It made me warm all over, and it took all my focus to pull my eyes away, like there was a strong supernatural magnet demanding our connection.

Dangerous. I'd tried really hard to avoid that happening again.

I untied the curtain and slid it just past his chair to block the view of his broad shoulders and biceps from the street and then moved the third chair to another table.

Just in case anyone thought it was open.

When everything was just right, I sat in my corner chair and checked the time. Seven fifty. Ten more minutes to get my mind set.

Jannell delivered my order, frowning at the empty chair. I shrugged and arranged the drinks and doughnut on the table, startling every time the bell above the door chimed. I hardly noticed it when I was behind the counter, but today was different.

I sipped my drink and scrolled Instagram, looking for more pictures of Xavier's face. From what I could tell, the cut was near his hairline, and if their trainer was any good, the scar wouldn't be too noticeable when it healed.

The door chimed again, and this time when I looked up, the face I'd been staring at on the screen was only a few yards away. *Xavier.* He paused just inside the door after it closed and scanned the room. His gaze landed on me, and I held it, unblinking.

As he approached my little table, I broke eye contact to take in his backwards Voltage cap with matching hoodie and running pants. I loved how he still lived here in Palmer City and supported his old team.

Should I stand up to greet him? Stay sitting? Say something? I was paralyzed, as frozen as Snowpack Creek this time of year.

What was wrong with me? He was just a guy. A guy I'd known—sort of—for *three years*. I was acting like the worst kind of fan.

Xavier slipped into the open seat and flashed a smile, though it didn't reach his eyes. Stubble dusted parts of his cheeks and neck that were usually trimmed. His bandage was barely visible under his hair and hat. Instinctively, I reached out to touch it but snapped my arm back when I realized what it was doing.

"Hey, Pen." He spoke low, in his usual kind tone, but something was different. I loved that he called me "Pen," but I couldn't celebrate it like I usually did.

Something was wrong. I knew it as sure as I knew how to make his coffee.

"D-does it h-hurt?" I asked.

He shook his head and reached for his matcha. "Thanks for breakfast."

"Of c-course," I replied. "W-what's wrong? Are … are you ch-changing your m-mind? It's ok-kay."

"What?" His head lifted, and his eyes locked on mine. "No. Not at all." He sighed. "I'm sorry. I should have canceled today. But it would have been last-minute and … and I didn't want to."

Oh, those eyes boring into mine.

Beautiful. Dark and soulful.

Pained.

Why?

I placed my hand on his forearm and tried to make my expression look supportive. I didn't trust myself to speak again.

"My grandfather passed away last night. Well, this morning. My Opa, in Europe," he added to clarify.

Oh, no. My heart cracked. There was so much I wanted to say, but it wouldn't come out.

Actions speak louder than words, right? I learned that lesson with my American Girl doll Samantha, and it'd always comforted me when I couldn't communicate verbally. How a Victorian nine-year-old who wasn't allowed to speak unless spoken to was able to give a compelling speech in front of a packed opera house was beyond my understanding. My parents had bought me the doll and set of books when I was in second grade, hoping Samantha would help inspire my stutter away at school.

It hadn't.

Actions. The poor man looked like he needed a hug. Badly. Before I could talk myself out of it, I rose from my chair and held my arms out.

Xavier stood, took one giant step toward me, and engulfed me in the hug I'd invited.

A hug I'd dreamed about for years.

Gosh, he was tall. Six-five, the stats said. He had a whole foot on me. Three inches taller and a whole lot thicker than when he'd moved to town to play for the Volts.

I tentatively wrapped my arms around his waist, and he pulled me even closer. Flush to him. My sweater to his hoodie. My head rested right over his heart. It thumped as hard and fast as mine did. And he was *warm*. It was freezing outside. How was this man a walking furnace?

I don't know how long we stood there like that. It could have been seconds or minutes. I was lost in his warmth and his faint scent of strawberry shampoo wafting down from the still-damp hair under his hat. Imagine! Xavier Schwann, world-famous hockey player, used strawberry shampoo!

Deep breath in, deep breath out, deep breath in …

When I heard snickering, I pulled away. Two teenage girls at the next table had their phones up, facing directly at us. I glared at them, and they quickly put their phones down.

Rude.

"Thanks," Xavier said. "I needed that."

I nodded. "W-welcome."

"So," he said, looking around. "I didn't think this through. I can see you're uncomfortable here." His eyes darted to the teens and narrowed to a glare. They quickly looked away, and he turned back to me. "Would going to my place be too weird? My roommate got traded, and since I'm playing for the Edge now, my pay is better, so I'm not looking to replace him. We'd, ah, be alone there."

Alone with Xavier Schwann? Um, yes, please! The fangirl in me wanted to jump for joy.

The practical girl in me was blaring a warning signal.

A loud, honking goal-horn blaring warning signal.

The empath in me scolded myself, reminding Fan Girl and Practical Girl about the loss of his grandfather.

I wasn't afraid of Xavier. I was afraid I wouldn't be able to keep my crush to myself.

"Th-that's fine." I swallowed. "W-when?"

His eyebrows lifted. "Tonight?"

The inflection in his tone sounded hopeful.

Nah. It was probably my imagination.

I nodded. "S-sure."

"We're home for the next week or so, then we have a road trip to the east coast." He sipped his drink, eyes cast down.

"Fu-funeral?" I asked.

He shook his head. "I want to be there, but Opa made it clear I shouldn't come back if it affects the team. I told him to hang on until the All-Star Break, but he said I'd be playing in it. Ha."

I smiled. "You w-will."

He shook his head. "It's not likely. There are much bigger stars on our team that have been around a lot longer than me."

It was my turn to shake my head. Vigorously.

He laughed. "Thanks." His cheeks pinked.

Xavier was blushing. He couldn't have been more endearing if he tried.

"T-tell me ... about h-him." I wanted to hear about the man whose loss had put a big hole in Xavier's heart.

He took a long sip of his matcha and smiled. "He was my best friend." Crossing his arms, he leaned casually on the tabletop.

I mirrored his position and waited.

"My Opa was the most generous, amazing guy I've ever known. He was equal parts stubborn and giving. Kind but firm. We spent every Christmas at his chateau. He visited us more than we visited him. Dad played in the league up until a few years ago, and we spent the summers with Mom's family on the Reservation in Calgary. I played a lot of roller hockey there as a kid. I loved it. But my parents—mostly my dad—didn't want me to play ice hockey. I was a figure skater for twelve years, but I hit a growth spurt in eighth grade and couldn't do the jumps like I used to."

I grinned widely. I knew this, of course, but to hear him say it was adorable. "T-too t-all?"

"Yeah. I was six feet at that point. Still, Dad resisted when I asked to play hockey. He said it wasn't a good job to have if you wanted to be a family man. When I turned fourteen, my grand-parents were in town for the annual Dads' trip. When Dad and

Opa returned, my grandparents decided to stay longer to watch us kids so Mom could attend some of the home games by herself and meet Dad at his next away game. Opa and Oma bought me hockey skates and equipment and paid for spring break camp while my parents were gone. I loved it. And by the time Mom and Dad returned, I was on a team. Opa picked my parents up at the airport and brought them to the rink to see me play. I never had to wear tight sequined pants again." He sighed dramatically, as if he missed his old costumes.

I giggled. "B-bet you w-were cute."

He waggled his eyebrows. "All the grandmas thought so."

I burst out laughing, picturing his Oma and her friends reaching up to pinch his cheeks and fawn over him.

The low buzz of a phone in vibration mode cut through my thoughts. I reached into my tote to check mine.

"It's me," he said. "It's been going off since 2 a.m."

I nodded. "No s-sleep?"

"Very little."

"Re-re-schedule?"

"What? No." He leaned closer. "I'll go crazy if I'm by myself. Please. Come over?"

"O-kay." I pointed to the clock on the wall. He needed to leave soon if he was going to make it to Denver on time for his morning practice. How did the last hour pass so quickly?

He turned his head to follow my finger. "Right. Thanks for breakfast and the hug." He pulled out his phone. "What's your number? I'll text you my address."

I held out my hand for his phone. He handed it to me, and I dialed my number. My phone rang in my pocket. I saved my number to his contacts and handed the phone back to him. "Th-there. Now I've g-got your number and you've g-got m-mine."

He grinned and pulled me in for another long hug-to-remember. "Did you really order a year's worth of coffee for me?"

I stepped out of his embrace and nodded, hanging my head and hoping he wouldn't see me blush. "T-two seasons' w-worth." Cautiously, I raised my eyelids to peek at his expression.

It was everything I'd hoped for. His full smile beamed down upon me.

"You're a dream, Penny. I'll see you again soon."

I watched him walk toward the front door, loving that he snuck a glance back at me as it closed.

The Bevvie Bar had never felt so empty.

But I was full.

Of hope, warmth, and ideas that I should never let cross my mind.

CHAPTER 5
Xavier

I took my time showering and changing after practice, avoiding eye contact with my teammates because I wasn't in the mood to talk. When I arrived, I texted the team group chat from the parking lot with the news about Opa. I asked them not to mention it, and they didn't, but I was the recipient of over two dozen encouraging shoulder pats before, during, and after our time on the ice.

Between Opa's passing and anticipating Penny coming over tonight, I couldn't keep my thoughts on the ice. And they were going easy on me, which was well-meant, but I didn't appreciate it at all. I needed to work hard and burn off my grief.

This was why I never dated during the season, or seriously, for that matter. Distractions threw you off and interrupted your focus. My dad could've been greater than Gretzky if he'd made hockey a priority. No major life changes, I always said. Opa's passing was the majorist of majors.

Instead, Dad had gotten married at nineteen—*nineteen!*—and he and Mom hadn't waited to start a family. A lot of hockey players got married young, often to their high school sweethearts, but that hadn't been my parents' story. They'd barely known each other. At least Mom's parents insisted they wait until she graduated college. She was three years older than Dad and on a full ride

to Mount Royal University. The day after she graduated, they eloped.

Instead of going home, I decided to stay for a workout. While I was tying my sneakers, Coach Sandquist dropped onto the bench beside me. "I want you tested again for a concussion."

I sighed. "I'm fine, really. Just distracted."

He stared at me hard.

There was no negotiating.

"Yes, Coach."

An hour later, I was cleared again and sprinting on the treadmill. I tended to go overboard with my workouts, but it paid off. My endurance was exceptional. I could skate a forty-minute game without slowing down. The team knew they could count on me in OT—overtime. It was extra things like that which could save a player when it was time for cuts or trades.

Our practice facility was state-of-the-art, but I missed the Palmer City Sportsplex. The Plex was like a town within the town, featuring everything from youth leagues to the Edge's minor league affiliate, the Palmer City Voltage. Olympic hopefuls trained there, and it housed every sort of business related to sports, from medical practices and therapies to equipment, and even a daycare and camps. Plus three rinks, two swimming pools, and countless courts and fields.

My favorite part of the Palmer City Sportsplex was the workout area. On the ground floor, it was open three stories high and featured a curved window wall that offered a stunning view of the mountains. I'd spent a lot of time there when I played for the Volts and still had a membership. There was no urgency for me to relocate to Denver. It was only an hour commute, and I was a small-town kind of guy.

No windows in this room at the Edge's facility. The walls were painted in our colors and decorated with encouraging phrases and motivational quotes interspersed with framed photos of past teams.

My favorite was *PUSH YOURSELF TO THE EDGE.* I'd pondered over the wording of it since I'd first seen it. The edge of what? Ability? Endurance? Was it meant to be punny?

After my run, I moved around the circuit, pushing and punishing myself until my body screamed that it was done. While the assistant trainer on duty filled my ice bath, I pulled out my phone to check my notifications.

Forty-two missed messages and eleven missed calls.

My chest tightened. I scrolled through but didn't open any, noting the majority were from the family group text. Six texts and three calls were from an unknown number with Seattle's 206 area code.

None were from Penny.

I checked the clock. It was nearing 5 p.m., so she was still working. We'd never set a time for her to come over, and I wondered if she'd have the chance to eat dinner. Would management provide it at the staff meeting? I didn't know how coffee shops worked.

I texted her to find out. *Will you get dinner at your staff meeting?* After I sent it, I realized I probably should've led with something less abrupt. I wasn't any good at small talk, but today I felt the urge to learn.

I tried to back up. *Hi. I hope you're having a good day. If you don't have dinner plans, I could cook for us.*

I rubbed my face and stifled a groan. That sounded so stupid.

I stared at my phone, waiting to see if she'd respond. When she didn't, I set my timer for seven minutes and slipped into the icy water. After the initial familiar sting of cold, I was alert and relaxed. Closing my eyes, I let my thoughts wander and they found Penny, the first time I saw her.

I smiled, remembering how I'd told Opa the story, over and over again. The initial time, when we visited for Christmas, and since then he always asked me to tell it at least twice when I saw him. To Opa, and to whoever he had over for company. *Zay-vyor,* he'd say to me, *tell zeh story of zeh coffee girl who plays the harp.*

I hated coffee. Still do. But being triple-dog dared by my teammate Brendan to drink it at the Bevvie Bar on a game day trumped any tastebuds. I hated avocados, too, but I ate them. So I'd pointed to a toffee crunch doughnut and asked if they had coffee that tasted like it.

Tasha told Penny to make it, and she got right to work. I couldn't take my eyes off her as she scribbled a message on the cup, scooped coffee ice cream, and added butterscotch chips. Then the light roast coffee—but not too much, only enough to melt the ice cream and butterscotch. Then a whole bunch of whipped cream, sea salt caramel drizzle, and crunchy toffee sprinkles—the same that were on the doughnut.

The same doughnut she'd bought me for breakfast this morning.

I'd told her she was a dream, and it was the truth.

Because she was in mine.

Daydreams, night dreams. Whenever I wasn't distracted, thoughts of her crept into my mind.

It wasn't until I got to the rink that first time that I realized she'd written more than my name on the cup. *Good luck! I triple-dog dare you to score tonight.* The team was going through a thing with triple-dog dares that week, and everyone had been the recipient of multiple. Stupid stuff, mostly. Wearing dirty socks, singing along to Taylor Swift on a reel for our social media channels, that sort of thing.

After a brief wave of panic at *two* triple-dog dares in one day, I focused.

And I got to work. I scored that night and had two assists.

And thus began the pregame Bevvie Bar tradition.

If I were any other guy, I'd have asked her out a long time ago. But I wasn't. I was Xavier Schwann, and I was focused on one thing: hockey.

This was my year. I'd signed a nice deal with the Edge last summer and made the roster after training camp. Without a no-trade clause, they could sell my contract to another team, or put me on waivers to see who might pick me up. If no one did, I'd be sent back to the Volts.

As much as I loved my old coach and mentor, and this town, I was determined not to let that happen. I'd worked too hard to blow it now.

If Penny and I were meant to be more than friends, it would happen sometime down the road. If we weren't, then … I'd just keep on doing what I was doing. You couldn't miss what you didn't have, right?

I was lying to myself, but it was necessary. I'd already missed too many games this season. No more distractions. Opa would be livid if he'd seen my performances at practice the last two days.

The timer went off, and I climbed out of the tub. After I showered again, I checked my phone to see if Penny had replied.

She had! A giddy, involuntary shiver vibrated through me.

One new message from Penny: *Staff meeting postponed since Tasha couldn't be there. Whatever it is, they want all of us. I can be at your place by seven. What can I bring?*

My whole body tingled with glee. I texted her back. *Just yourself. Do you have any food allergies?*

No, but I don't like mushrooms.

Me neither! See you at 7.

See you at 7.

I'd have to hurry to get home and get everything ready. I wanted to wow her with my cooking skills.

To make her comfortable, of course. So she would feel safe and not stutter.

Not at all to impress her.

Well, maybe a little. But I'd never admit it.

Bzzzzzzz!

I grabbed a dish towel, wiping my hands as I ran to the security console to press the button that would let Penny into the building. I had an app for that, but I'd been trying to avoid my phone. More messages from the family and the unknown number had come through, and I wasn't ready to read or respond to them.

Mountain View, the condo complex where I lived, was gated. I'd added Penny to my guest list, but I'd forgotten to give her the code to enter the building. My building was mostly hockey players and employees of the Voltage. With its proximity to the Plex and around-the-clock security, it was ideal. There were two to four units on each level, depending on the size, with garages on the ground level.

My unit was one of the bigger ones, with two smaller bedrooms and an office. Like I'd told Penny, I no longer had a roommate. I was in no hurry to get one, either. I liked having the place to myself, and I had plans to convert the second bedroom into a home gym that rivaled the Plex's.

On a smaller scale, of course. I didn't have three levels of windows facing the mountains. However, large bump-out windows in the dining nook and office provided a similar view.

I tucked the dish towel into the back pocket of my jeans and checked my reflection in the mirror over the table in the vestibule. Hair combed, check. Short beard trimmed, check. Fresh bandaging over the zips, check. Team logo polo fresh and unwrinkled, thanks to the dryer's fluff cycle, check.

I wasn't nervous at all.

It was totally normal and polite to look presentable for company.

I breathed in deeply and opened the door, letting my breath out slowly like I was benching heavyweights. Across the hall, the elevator light didn't change from "2," so I angled my body toward the stairs in anticipation.

I heard her before I saw her. Light footsteps and then she emerged. Her long wavy hair, usually piled on her head or braided, fell to her waist and was capped with a light purple pom-pom hat. A matching scarf was knotted around her neck and hung over a fitted ivory wool coat with oversize buttons that belted at the waist and stopped at her knees. Her denim-clad calves disappeared into fleece-trimmed camel-colored winter boots, and her black leather gloves clung to the strap of a dusty plum-colored tote bag slung over her left shoulder.

I knew a thing or two about fashion. I edited every one of my sister Daniella's fashion merchandising papers last year.

Penny had style. And I liked it.

But it was her smile that I lingered on. Her lips were tinted the same dusty plum as her bag, not too dark but vibrant enough to stand out. I forced my gaze up, taking in her pink cheeks, reddened from the December cold, and her clear green eyes, shiny and hopeful.

Hopeful. If I couldn't help her ... If I failed ... I couldn't live with her disappointment. There simply was no failing at this task. I knew in my heart that I had what it took to inspire her to overcome her anxiety. I just had to find a way to bring out her confidence and teach her the techniques that had helped me to relax in stressful situations.

I was a shy kid with a speech impediment. I'd had speech lessons as a kid and media training for hockey. There had to be *something* useful in my toolbox that could work for Penny.

She paused at the top of the stairs. "Hi."

"Hi," I echoed. I cleared my throat and quickly stuffed my hands into my pockets, not trusting they'd keep to themselves. "Uh ... thanks for coming."

My phone vibrated against the back of my hand, startling me. I backed up, tripping over my own feet. My hand shot out to grab onto the doorframe. I recovered quickly and made a show of leaning into it.

Women liked a good doorframe lean. Social media told me so.

She laughed. "You ok-kay?"

"Never better," I assured her easily. I straightened and made a sweeping motion with my hand toward the open doorway. "After you, my lady."

She giggled, dipping into a quick curtsy. "Thank you, milord."

Note to self: Use more Renaissance references. Her reply was stammerless.

I followed her in and closed the door behind me. "Can I take your coat?"

Penny nodded and held up a finger, signaling for me to wait, and reached into her tote bag. "I b-brought—" She huffed a frustrated breath and pulled out a wine-size cooler bag.

I reached for it and pulled out a bottle of Tia Gia's Lemonade. "This is perfect. I made grilled chicken alfredo."

Her eyes widened, and her mouth formed an *O* before transforming into a wide smile. "M-my fave-rite."

Yes! I was confident she liked it, since I'd seen her eating the dish one night with Tasha and their parents at Pasta Nacht's, a restaurant in town near the arena. It was German-Italian fare and owned by retired Edge player Roman Kubek and his family. Their tafelspitz was just like Oma used to make. Roman's wife, Gia, *the* Tia Gia, was New York Italian and sold an entire line of kitchenware, pasta, sauces, and beverages.

Penny stuffed her hat, scarf, and gloves into her tote bag. She set it on the floor and untied her belt. As she slowly unbuttoned her coat, revealing a form-fitting knit black turtleneck, I gripped the bottle of lemonade tighter.

I took her coat and hung it on an empty hook on the other side of the entryway. Neither of us seemed to be able to speak, but the silence wasn't awkward.

It was comfortable.

Easy. Natural.

Like we'd done this before.

Penny looped her tote over her shoulder, and miraculously I found words.

I gestured for her to move deeper into the apartment. "Dinner's ready. I just need to bring it out. You can sit anywhere you like."

The small round table sat four. Penny chose one of the two places I'd set and sat, letting her tote drop by her feet. I sprang into action and poured lemonade into the glasses I'd set out. "I'll be right back with dinner." I pointed to the French baguette on the cutting board in the center of the table. "Help yourself to the bread."

"Th-thanks."

I stored the lemonade in the fridge and quickly washed my hands so I could plate the chicken alfredo. As I carried it out, I noticed Penny rubbing her hands together. The faint aroma of vanilla-scented hand sanitizer warred with steaming cheese. It was a strange combo but memorable.

My phone had vibrated the entire walk to the table. At some point, I was going to have to answer it.

Later. When Penny left.

I set our plates down and settled into my chair. Penny was to my right but not beside me. Not too close, not too far away.

I supposed I should start the conversation. "So, um, how was your day?"

She smiled and gave me a thumbs-up.

Well, that backfired. I needed to get her to talk.

We twirled alfredo around our forks and spent the next few minutes eating. Penny's cheeks were still a deep rosy color, but I couldn't see any other outward signs that she was nervous.

When we finished eating, I cleared the plates and refilled our lemonades. Penny sat back in her chair and stared at her hands, folded in her lap. She looked like she wanted to say something but didn't know how.

I cleared my throat, and she looked up. "You said you've had all kinds of therapy, right?" She nodded. "What's worked the best so far?"

She pressed her lips together and tilted her head in thought. "D-deep breaths. P-pauses. N-not sp-peaking."

I chuckled softly at her joke. "Seems effective. Those things helped me, too. But it wasn't until I was confident enough in myself and didn't care what other people thought of me or what I had to say that I truly lost the stutter. I had to realize how great I was on the inside to not care what people thought of me on the outside. And I had to believe in what I was saying. Make sense?"

She nodded.

"Do you stutter around kids?" I asked.

She shook her head.

"People you've known all your life?"

"N-no."

"When you sing?"

She shook her head again.

"And there's nothing medically wrong?"

"N-nope."

I extended my arms in her direction and took both of her hands into mine. She shifted, turning toward me. "You can beat this, Penny. You just need to practice not caring so much."

Her eyes widened. "B-but I *d-do* care."

I squeezed her hands gently. "Because it matters to you what people think of you. Under it all, the root of it is fear. Fear stems from pride. You don't want to disappoint anyone. You have to let that fear and pride go. And then—bam! No more stammering."

Our gazes locked, and all that she couldn't tell me in words was there. She trusted me and was putting her hope in me.

That was a lot of pressure, but I was determined not to let her down. She could overcome this, I was sure of it.

A sudden loud banging on my apartment door jolted us apart.

"Xavier!" a deep, unfamiliar male voice boomed. "Xavier Schwann, I know you're in there!"

I jumped up from the table, heart racing, and placed a finger over my lips, motioning for Penny to go down the hall. "Hide," I whispered.

She was out of her chair in a flash, and I walked slowly towards the door, scanning for something I could use for a weapon if it came to that.

Nothing. Note to self: Buy a baseball bat and keep it by the front door. Or bring in a hockey stick from the garage.

"Xavier! I know you're in there. Your lights are on, and your windows aren't covered. My name is J.R. Harlow. I represent your father, in Seattle. He gave me the access codes to your building. Will you please let me in? Time is of the essence!"

J.R. Harlow? The name sounded familiar. I pulled out my phone. So many messages. I scrolled to the unknown number and read his texts. I gaped at the screen. When he couldn't reach me today, he'd flown here from Seattle to meet me in person.

I cleared my throat. "If you work for my father, tell me our family code word."

"Is that really necessary?"

"Do it or I'm calling security," I ordered.

His exasperated sigh was audible through the door. "Fiiiiiine. Loopy doopy poopy schmoopy."

I snickered. My youngest sister, Edyta, said those four words over and over again as a toddler. Every time she spoke them, we all cracked up, which encouraged her more. We were all sad when she outgrew it, so we collectively decided it would be the perfect family phrase to indicate a stranger was safe.

I unlocked the door. A short, stout man in a long leather trench coat breezed past me, straight to the table. "You, sir, have forty-eight hours—minus the sixteen we've already wasted today trying to connect with you—to decide if you want to inherit Schwannenschloss or not."

I gripped the back of the nearest chair. "I'm sorry. What?"

He grumbled as he pulled a folder from his briefcase and handed me a single sheet of paper. "Your father was written out of your grandfather's will. You are the heir. The heir must be married to inherit. Some medieval clause, yada yada, that states the chateau, grounds, contents, yada yada, will go to the next male in the succession line, and your father didn't want it. Your grandfather knew this, and he knew he was dying, so he changed the beneficiary. It's my job, on behalf of the former Baron von Schwann, to ensure that the heir is in compliance with the terms."

I blinked at him. "The heir? Baron von Schwann? The chateau —the chateau is *mine*?"

"Not so fast. Halfway down the page. Read the highlight."

I swallowed. Was this a bad dream? I needed to read it out loud to believe it was real. "'If the next male in the line of succession is over the age of twenty and unmarried, he must find a bride by his next birthday. In order to ensure the heir takes this condition seriously, he must sign a contract within forty-eight hours of the death of the current Baron von Schwann promising his intentions to wed by said birthday.'"

My mouth hung open in disbelief.

"It's barbaric," JR spat. "I've never seen anything like it. Not in this century, at least."

I was still trying to process. Opa hadn't been joking when he'd ribbed me about my lack of dating. *Vind a voman, Zavey-boy. Be happy, like your Opa.*

That old schemer!

"So you're saying that unless I sign this paper in the next thirty-two hours, I forfeit my inheritance and my whole family's ability to return to the chateau? Who gets it if I don't? Why can't my sisters inherit?" My voice rose with each question.

"All valid inquiries. I have zero definitive answers for you. I'm here strictly to obtain your signature on this facsimile, one way or the other. Unless you want to go back to Schwannenschloss and sign the original."

"But this is insane!" I protested. "Who's going to agree to marry me in thirty-two hours?"

"I would." The strong, clear statement behind me was free of stammering and reverberated in the room like a song sent from heaven.

I whirled around.

Penny.

CHAPTER 6
Penny

What was I thinking?

That this is your dream guy and you want to help him?

But—marry him? By March?

See? You even know when his birthday is. You'd make a great wife!

But—I don't like people. Hockey wives are in the spotlight. And people follow him everywhere. He's on television. HIS FACE IS ON MERCH AND BILLBOARDS.

So what?

So … I can't live in the public eye. I can't even have a conversation with him without stuttering. How will I speak to the Wags or his teammates? The press?

The Wags will embrace you and rally around you. You know several of the wives and girlfriends already, including your cousin Gabby. Give them a chance. And you know Bailey, their sideline reporter. She's in the Bevvie Bar at least twice a week. She'll help.

I'll make a fool of myself.

Xavier's point exactly. Care less what people think about you, and relax.

"Pen?"

I love it when you call me Pen, I wanted to say.

I internally shushed the angel-devil banter in my head and squared my shoulders. "Y-you're h-help-ping m-me. I … w-want to h-help you."

Xavier's eyebrows did that thing that made my knees weak. I stayed rooted to my spot, begging my heartbeat to slow and every muscle to hold on so I didn't drop to the floor.

"There's your answer, kid." The man at the table looked at me. "You're the barista, right? Lucky Penny?"

I nodded meekly.

"Perfect. Saves me a trip to your place. This will make great press. I need to call—"

"NO," Xavier growled, cutting off the man. "No calling anyone." He turned back to me, his expression softening. "Penny, no. I'm helping you with your speaking so that you can follow *your* dream. I don't expect anything in return. If you marry me, you'll be stuck in *my* dream."

He truly was the sweetest, most thoughtful man. My feet began to move, and they didn't stop until I was next to him. I looked up into his shining eyes. He had to be thinking about his family and losing the castle—or chateau, as they'd called it. That was a lot of pressure. Plus, he was grieving for his best friend. And yet, he'd risk losing it all for my sake.

"P-plenty of t-time for all d-dreams," I said.

"You hear her, Xavier? Don't be foolish. The document doesn't specify how long you have to be married for. You can split up whenever you want. People do it all the time."

Xavier glared at him and squeezed my hand, breathing slowly through his nose. "I am not 'people' and neither is Penny. What you're suggesting is dishonest." He took both my hands in his and lifted them to his chest, facing me.

Our eyes locked.

I might die.

"What I'm suggesting is a solution to save your family's estate. If you don't take action, it'll likely be auctioned off to the highest bidder and you Schwanns won't see a penny of that profit —or your ancestral home—ever again. *This* Penny, whom you can see clearly, is willing to help to prevent that."

Xavier tightened his grip and didn't break our stare. "It's too much to ask."

"Then find a puck bunny. Or one of those powdery puffy girls or whatever they are that sit by your bench at every home game.

There are endless women who would jump at this chance. I can draft the prenup tomorrow."

Xavier shuddered. His vibrations jostled me, but I held my balance.

"No," he stated again. I should say something, but there was zero chance it would come out unjumbled.

I pleaded with my eyes when he turned back to me, hoping he could read them. I didn't want to let go of his hands. Here, standing like this with him, was as easy and as comfortable as the plush beanbag chair I had as a kid. Well, before Gabby and Tasha decided to use it as a landing mat for their tumbling.

Cheerleaders. Mom was still finding the little bean fillers from the epic explosion that ended the bag's rough life.

"Come on, kid. Be smart. Fake it."

"I don't fake anything." He angled his head down and spoke softly but quickly, as if he was in a rush to get it all out before he changed his mind. "Penny, I would only consider doing this if there was a chance to make it real someday, if we were playing for keeps. I think the world of you. We're friends, right? Could we be more? Do you think—do you think we could get to know each other and grow to love each other? Over time?"

What?

Did I *think?*

No.

I *knew.*

Because what I felt for him didn't feel like a fangirl crush. Did he have feelings for me, too? Why would he want to try to make this real if he didn't?

I was definitely dead. Because in my world, my very *real* awkward difficult world, this would never happen.

"Y-yes. E-easy p-peasy."

Xavier laughed, a fully belly laugh. The tension in his jaw relaxed, and he pulled me into his chest in one of his hugs-to-remember.

Yep. I was dead. As. A. Doornail.

He'd felt solid enough this morning through his hoodie, but through the thin fabric of his polo?

Sculpted. Solid.

Like one of those literary vampires, made of the finest, polished marble.

And safe.

Slow down, Penny.

What? No! Marry this man! He's perfect on the outside AND the inside!

You have a point. No argument there.

My inner angel and inner devil were in agreement.

This was new.

Xavier tucked my head under his chin. His arms were still around me, like a protective cocoon. His voice rumbled in my ear, strong and firm. "This is an incredibly selfless thing to do, Penny. I don't know how I got so lucky."

I reluctantly dislodged my head. "I l-like castles," I whispered, with a shrug.

He chuckled. "It's a *chateau.*"

I shrugged again and smiled up at him. "K-keep s-secret?"

He nodded. "I think that's wise, for now. We can keep it a secret until we're ready to tell the world. There will be a lot of publicity. Maybe wait until after the season ends? The sports media will have a field day. No one gets married this time of year, especially not a player on a playoff-bound team. It could be bad luck."

"Good th-thing I'm l-lucky," I quipped.

Xavier straightened. "What do we need to do, J.R.? And when?"

The lawyer grunted. I couldn't see him with half my face pressed into Xavier's muscley pec, but the noise sounded positive.

"Sign this doc first." He handed Xavier a pen.

Xavier placed the paper on the table. His eyes shone with kindness as he looked back at me for a final consent. I nodded, and he scrawled his practiced signature at the bottom of the paper.

I twisted away from him to add my signature next to his.

"Aspen Ethyl Palmer." Xavier spoke my full name slowly and grinned. "I like it."

"Eh. I g-got used … to it," I mumbled. "T-Tasha and I are b-both named for … flowers. Ethyl's m-my g-great aunt."

"She own the oddities store by the Creekside Inn?"

I nodded, tensing up as I waited for his laugh.

But he grinned wider. "I love that place. I tagged along with Noel and Gabby once and was hooked. She's got the best old books."

I relaxed. "Sh-she d-does."

"Yeah yeah, la-di-da. Chat later." J.R. was growing more agitated. "You two have a wedding to plan. License, venue, officiant. Courthouse or church?"

"B-barn," I blurted. Since Brenna Brewer had renovated their old barn into a wedding venue, I'd dreamt of getting married there. My dad's family might not be happy, but they didn't have to know. Or even come to the wedding, if we were going to keep it a secret. The Palmers and Brewers had been civil with each other for the last few generations, since Brenna's grandmother, a Palmer, married a Brewer, but there was still a whole lot of competition between the families.

"Brenna's barn?" Xavier asked, his brows furrowing. That puppy dog look would surely cause the second death of me.

I nodded. "J-just us?"

"If that's what you want."

Why did he sound disappointed?

"P-parents? T-Tasha?" I offered.

J.R. spoke up. "Xavier, your family will have to know. It'll be obvious when the property is transferred. I'd suggest you invite them. Your sisters might not forgive you if you don't."

"He's right," Xavier said. "Edyta has been training to be a flower girl since she was three."

"Sssshe's the y-y-y …" I paused, unable to get the word out and angry with myself.

"Youngest," J.R. filled in, glancing at Xavier. "She always stutter like that?"

Xavier's arm tightened around me. "*She* is Penny, and don't you dare disrespect her like that ever again."

"Woooo!" J.R. belted gleefully. "Already protecting your girl. Yeah, this will work. You've sold me."

My gut boiled with loathing for the man. He must be very good at his job because I couldn't fathom any other reason the Schwanns would trust him with their important matters.

Xavier spoke through his teeth. "Will that be all, then?"

"For tonight," J.R. replied. "I'll send the NDAs and prenup. Call me when you file the license."

I relaxed into Xavier, who hadn't loosened his grip. I felt like I'd just run a marathon. When the apartment door clicked shut, I dared to look up.

Xavier's gaze was fixed on the opposite wall. I twisted around to follow it to the cuckoo clock next to the door. I hadn't noticed it when I arrived, and it hadn't chimed since I'd been here.

"It's painted to match Opa's chateau," he said.

"It's b-beautiful. Is it h-hand-m-made?"

He nodded. "Opa carved it himself. He gave it to me when I signed my first pro contract. 'Zay-vyor,' he said, 'vair-ever zis goes, I go vith you.'"

Hot tears stung my eyes. "You m-must m-miss him so m-much," I said softly. All of my grandparents were still alive. I didn't know when his Oma died, but I assumed she wasn't alive anymore or there wouldn't be an issue with the property.

"I can't believe I'll never talk to him again." His words were laced with sadness and anguish. "I really want to go to his funeral. He'd be so mad if I missed more games. But I need closure, you know?"

I wrapped my arms around his waist. "You should go," I said firmly and clearly. "Bereavement leave."

His eyes widened. "No stutter," he said. "Does that mean you're comfortable with me?"

I shook my head. "P-probably n-not. M-maybe soon?"

"That would be a wish come true for me," he said. "I've been afraid to talk to you all these years. But yesterday … I don't know. Something kicked in and I knew I just had to find you and see if you were okay."

"G-glad." There was so much more I wanted to say.

"Me, too. Seems providential, doesn't it? The timing. The inheritance clause." Xavier's eyes bored into mine. A tear leaked out, and he brushed it away with his thumb.

I sighed and wished with everything I had that I could overcome this awful stutter.

Sooner than later.

I didn't want to muck up my wedding vows.

Wedding vows!

Oh my …

CHAPTER 7
Xavier

"I'm coming back for the funeral," I said to my father. After Penny left, I'd stayed up late looking for flights and called Dad at 6 a.m. Central European Time. "And I'm going to marry Penny to save the chateau because you don't want it. You can't stop me."

I rubbed my eyes and pinched my forehead. We'd been talking in circles for almost an hour. "This is exactly why I have stayed away." Dad's words came tight and fast, with notes of his former thick accent returning. "Your grandfather's manipulation has no boundaries. I want no part of it. You shouldn't play into it, either."

Suffice it to say, my father had not been supportive of my intention to bend to Opa's will—literally—and marry Penny.

"Well, then, you don't have to be part of it. I don't need your permission."

I *would* like to get Penny's father's blessing though. I tried to picture that conversation. *Hi, I'm Xavier. I want to marry your daughter so we can save my family's chateau. Oh, and I'm also a pro athlete who travels and will hardly be around from September through April, May, or June, depending how well my team plays.*

Yeah … if I was on the receiving end of that, the answer would be a resounding, booming, shotgun-holding get-off-my-property-and-never-come-back-here *NO*.

Maybe I'd skip that for now.

"Are you planning to move there? Ever?" My father's voice dropped an octave, and his accent thickened. "Who vill oversee it vhile you're living in America? What about your career? How you vanted to stay single because families are *distractions?* You don't think the upkeep of an estate that size on another continent von't be a distraction?" There was more than a little hint of sarcasm there but also pain. I'd judged him harshly for his choices, time and again.

He was right, though—I'd said that families could be distractions. Over and over, for many years, and to everyone. In private, in public, to the press. Xavier Schwann wasn't going to let a relationship distract him. I'd learned to cultivate a response that wasn't arrogant or judgy; I didn't want my teammates to think I thought they were making mistakes by getting married or starting families, and I didn't want a public reputation as ladies' man. No one who knew me would believe that I was, but rumors about Penny and me could ignite bad press, which would be a whole other kind of distraction. I'd always been shy around girls and avoided the ones who hung around the team, hoping to snag a player. I'd never imagined a scenario where I would focus on or care about anyone or anything as much as hockey.

This situation was different, but the fans wouldn't see it that way when the news got out. Penny and I weren't dating. We hadn't been high school or college sweethearts. Although, technically, Penny was still in college and I had taken some online classes.

This, for now, was a business arrangement. And I had the resources to hire a company to manage the chateau. As long as I didn't get distracted, I was on track for my performance bonus, and that would help, too. Perks for both of us. I get the chateau; she gets to visit it. She could even travel Europe to see all the great symphonies, at my expense, if she wanted. I'd help her with her speaking, and she could make my toffee coffee on game days. Maybe she could even teach me sign language.

I wanted Penny to have the chance to spend more time on her music. Married to me, I'd pay the bills. She wouldn't have to work at the Coffee Loft. She'd insist on it, because she wouldn't want to leave Tasha high and dry for rent and expenses. I'd be happy to take care of their rent for the next year—or longer, if she'd let me.

When this season ended, we could date. Travel. I could learn if the Penny I'd imagined while daydreaming in the café matched the Penny in real life.

And if she didn't, or if she couldn't fall in love with me, we'd split.

Split.

Why did just the thought of that little word feel like a stab to my heart?

"Vell? Are you even listening at all?"

"I am, and I can afford to hire help," I repeated for the umpteenth time.

"It's a money suck. You've vorked too hard to throw your money avay on a crumbling ruin from the past!"

"I guess we'll just have to agree to disagree." I didn't like the edge to my voice, but Dad was being impossible. The chateau was our history, our legacy. Just because he didn't want it didn't mean future generations wouldn't. Schwannenschloss had survived enemy raids, world wars, and wild weather. It meant something to Opa and Oma, and it meant something to me.

"I cannot and vill not." Dad was going to keep persisting until he wore me down. That was his method, but I wouldn't fall for it this time.

"Then I have nothing else left to say," I replied. "I need to get to the gym."

"This conversation isn't over."

Didn't I know it. "Bye, Dad."

The conversation with my father left me feeling heavy. I didn't want to wallow or feel guilty or get sucked into my own head. After tossing and turning for an hour, I did the one sure thing that always turned around a bad day or lifted me up when I felt low: the Sister Chat.

Karina had started the chat a couple of years ago when my parents had given her a phone to keep in touch with them while she was at the rink. With me playing in Colorado, Dani in college, and Dad playing in charity golf tournaments, Mom often had to leave Karina at the rink while she drove Edyta to dance class or whatever extracurricular she was trying out that year.

When Edyta got a phone this year, she was added to the chat, and the tone had changed from sweet I-miss-yous and wish-you-were-heres to bruh-when-are-you-coming-homes and TMI recounts of the latest happenings in her third-grade class.

Another addition from Edyta was her weekly Edyta Edict. She'd learned the word the first week of school and thought saying it out loud was hysterical, and so the next obvious step for her was to use it and overuse it.

This week's edict was "Read your sister a Christmas story." I liked that one.

Thinking about my sisters always made me smile. I opened the chat and typed out a message, taking a chance they'd be up early. *Guess who's coming back to Schwannenschloss?*

Karina was the first to respond. *Don't mess with me, bruh. If it's not you, that's mean.*

It's me. And hi to you, too. I added a crazy face emoji.

Oh good! Cause we're all super sad. I need Big Brother Hugs.

I know how you feel, kiddo, I thought. *No shortage of those, ever.*

Edyta's first message came through then, a GIF of a hairy-faced lumberjack peeking out from behind a tree. It was quickly followed by a GIF of a newscaster with the caption, "We apologize for the interruption." And still another, a toddler pulling on his mother's shirt and saying "Hey!"

You're good, Ditty, I texted back, bracing myself for her signature non-word communication.

A string of crying emojis followed by GIFs of crying anime characters in rapid succession.

Poor kiddo. I hadn't thought about how hard Opa's death might hit her. She'd cried when we lost Oma five years ago, but she didn't have much of a memory of it, nor our German grandmother, having been so young when we'd visited. Oma hadn't traveled more than a few times to Seattle. Mom's parents were closer in proximity, and the girls naturally bonded to them more. But in the last few years, as Opa's health declined, my parents had spent more time at the chateau and the little girls got to know him like Dani and I had when we were their ages.

It's going to be okay, Ditty. He's at peace now. No more pain, no more struggling to breathe. You'll see him again one day.

Rows of crying emojis.

Karina was able to get a message in before Edyta's next GIF. *Dani's here with us now. We're okay. But we're glad you're coming.*

I am, too. My heart warmed, and I was suddenly antsy. *Tell Dani I'll text her my flight info.*

I will, Karina replied.

Edyta sent GIFs of a smiling cartoon airplane, Carlton Banks dancing the Carlton, and Ridgie the Bear, our Denver Edge mascot, throwing confetti in the air.

I wondered if they knew there were GIFs of me.

Well, they'd know now. I typed my name into the search and selected the one of me scoring my first NHL goal. It was on a breakaway and I'd been clear to the net. It went in five-hole, through the goalie's legs, and as I dropped to one knee for my post-goal celly, I made the mistake of looking at my on-ice teammates headed my way to congratulate me—and I skated right into the boards—hard. They piled on top of me and then helped me up. Luckily no one got injured, but boy did I feel sheepish.

My family had teased me incessantly about it, so I knew it would make my sisters laugh.

I was right.

Laughing emojis and one final GIF from Edyta: A Ridgie the Bear jump-scaring me when I arrived for a home game earlier in the season. I'd panicked, run, and nearly spilled my toffee coffee.

I guessed they did know about my GIFs.

I WAS able to get on a direct flight later that morning from Denver to Munich. Dad sent an olive branch in the form of a driver to meet me at the airport, so I was hopeful my decision to accept the inheritance wouldn't permanently damage our relationship.

Opa's chateau was nestled in the Bavarian Alps, about an hour south of Munich on the way to Innsbruck, not far from the Austrian border. If you blinked, you'd miss it.

As the car turned off the main road onto the estate, I was hit with a pang of nostalgia as we neared Schwannenschloss. The memories I had here were out of a storybook. The well-manicured lawns and gardens, the clover field, the architecture, and most importantly, the images of my grandparents and the overwhelming feelings of love and security. Joyous celebrations with the extended family at Christmas, summertime exploring the terrain. Once, Dani and I wandered so far away we thought we'd never be found, only to spot smoke from a chimney. We made a run for the source and found the ski resort town of Garmisch. We'd wandered west all the way into Germany!

My mind raced, picturing Penny here, seeing what she'd helped to save and listing off the places I wanted to take her when hockey season ended.

June was a long way from the bitter cold of late December. The blustery mountain winds and cloud cover suited the somber tone of my visit. It was like the sun was also mourning for the generous, upbeat man who could—and did—find joy in everything. He'd also told me that every important decision came with a cost. Was the Schwann legacy worth putting Penny through a marriage of convenience that might or might not work out? Was it worth losing her if it didn't?

After years of watching her from afar, pining for her, and now finally getting to know her, I had a whole new set of fears.

At the top of the list wasn't losing Schwannenschloss. It was imagining the rest of my life without Penny in it.

CHAPTER 8
Penny

Today was the soft opening of the Palmer City Coffee Loft, and Xavier was on a plane from Munich to Denver. Our first wedding planning meeting was this afternoon, and we were having dinner at his place again tonight. It was crazy how much I'd missed him while he was away. How did I become so invested so fast? I'd made it through three years without seeing him every day. Why had that suddenly changed?

We'd texted the whole time he was gone but hadn't spoken over the phone. I was worried about him. I didn't know what it felt like to lose my best friend, but I could imagine the pain of the hole in my heart if something happened to Tasha—or anyone in my family, for that matter. We Palmers were close-knit and thick as thieves.

The café was buzzing with excitement and caffeine. Every staff member was working the morning shift, and it was a good thing. Despite the frosty morning, our loyal customers—and some new ones—showed up in force. Word had traveled fast that we had a freebie today, and whether it had to do with wanting to support a new-ish Main Street business, curiosity, or the free-with-purchase Coffee-Loft-branded travel tumbler, I couldn't be sure. I snagged one for me and one for Xavier when the supply started to wane.

By 11 a.m., we were almost out of the tumblers. I handed the last one to Montgomery Biddington, who never drank coffee, ever.

"Hey, Monty. Your usual iced chocolate?" He was Tasha's age, and I'd known him since I was in preschool. He was one of the people I could talk to easily. As the tag-along little sister, I was there for a lot of their competitive sparring. He, my sister, and Gabby had been on more than a few cheer teams together when they were younger, and all three had competed on the Plex's Worlds teams.

I was also there when Monty declined to be Tasha's stunt partner in favor of Gabby. And I was there when Tasha took a bad fall when she and her assigned partner attempted to do a new flip sequence which resulted in her breaking her leg and missing the Worlds competition her junior year of college. She hadn't cheered since, opting to use her sports fitness degree to coach instead.

Monty smirked. "Just a bottled water for today. Nana Booboo can have this." He turned the cup around in his hand and looked at it with disdain. The disdain deepened into a full frown when he looked up at the menu. "Pumpkin spice blah-tes in the winter? And 'Lofty-sized?' Isn't large big enough? Don't these people know how bad coffee is for you?"

"Pumpkin spice all year round now, and I'm not sure they care," I replied, pointing to the new refrigerator on the side wall, which Marie had restocked twice already this morning. "I certainly don't."

He rolled his eyes, and I hid a smile while he excused himself from the line to retrieve a water. Monty was a pumpkin spice hater and took every opportunity to remind us every fall, especially since it was Tasha's favorite. While I processed the transaction, his gaze swept the counter and tables.

"Looking for Tasha?" I asked. Antagonizing her had to be his favorite pastime.

"Actually, no." His lips curled into the arrogant smile that grated on Tasha's nerves. "I'm here on an errand. As you know, my parents host the annual Valentine's Day fundraiser. This year, they chose a Renaissance theme. And since *you*"—he waved his water at me in circles—"seem to like that sort of thing, they asked me to ask you to play during the dinner hour and fill in during the band's breaks."

I raised an eyebrow. The Biddington family's annual event was well-attended by people who knew people and local citizens of importance.

He hadn't mentioned payment. I waited for him to continue. When he didn't, I mustered up my nerve and took a risk. The Biddingtons had money. Lots of it. One of Monty's ancestors had won a good-size parcel of land gambling with one of my Palmer ancestors.

I pinned him with a hard stare and tried not to waver. "My fee is $100 per hour."

He snorted. "That's a joke, right? This is for *charity*."

"Is the band donating *their* time?" I knew my worth, and if I was ever going to make a living with my music, I had to stop playing for free.

He didn't answer.

"Take it or leave it," I pushed.

He rolled his eyes again. If Bumper from the movie *Pitch Perfect* was a professional cheerleader, he'd be Monty.

"Fiiiine," he said, dragging out the word with a dramatic sigh.

"This guy giving you trouble, Pen?"

I jumped as Tasha reappeared beside me. "Nah. Just doing business."

"You're holding up the line, Montgomery." Tasha *never* called him Monty. "Move along." She made a shooing motion with her hand. Monty's lips twitched like he was going to laugh or like he wanted to say something but hadn't decided yet.

"One more thing." He fixed his gaze on Tasha. His voice dripped honey and charm. "You're looking at the newest Ridgie the Bear."

Tasha's jaw fell open. She recovered, narrowed her eyes to slits, and shook her head. She was back in the kitchen seconds later.

"That hurt." Monty pressed a hand over his heart. "Truly, she wounds me. Not even a congratulations for her oldest friend."

Friend? More like *frenemy*. I sighed. "You really do love to rub salt in her wounds, don't you?"

Monty set his shoulders back, and the furrowed forehead and frown almost looked genuine. "Me?" he asked innocently. "What did *I* do?"

"You've known for years that Tasha has always wanted to be part of a pro team's Spirit Squad or dance team. Now you're the mascot of one of the best teams in pro sports?"

"Well, I'm too talented to just *dance*." He shrugged and leaned in. "And besides, tryouts aren't until July. This was a special audition. Invite-only. They're adding a third bear since the team is probably going to make the playoffs this year. I'll start out doing birthday parties, social media reels, and PR events, and then who knows? The current game day Ridgie is over *thirty*. He can't even tumble anymore."

"Tragedy." I glanced behind him. The line had grown even longer while he'd been bragging. Luckily, Marie, who was at the register next to mine, was fast and kept the queue moving.

Tasha reappeared with a bag of "Lofty-size" to-go coffee cups and shot Monty a blinding glare on her way down the counter to restock them. To my right, Jannell, Marcus, and Gabby filled orders. The rest of the staff was in the kitchen, baking and prepping food items.

"She should try out if she wants to be one of the ice girls. She'd make it," Monty said kindly, his gaze shifting to my sister. "She's, uh, engaging to watch."

Was he still talking? "Listen, Monty, you know she can't. Pro team dance squads pay less than she makes at this place, and there's no health insurance like her coaching job at the high school. Every one of those women has a full-time job or is in school." He should know this.

"Oh. Right. I forgot some people actually have to work to make money. Sad. Truly." His face fell, and I knew him well enough to know his empathy was genuine. Monty wasn't as stuck up as he sounded. He just liked to rile up my sister, and sometimes he forgot about his privilege as the grandson of an oil tycoon. He loved being the center of attention, yes, but he also loved kids. In addition to coaching three teams at the Plex, Monty spent a lot of his free time at the hospital reading to and playing games with sick children. The mascot job would be perfect for him.

"It's called adulting." I met his gaze. "Someday, you might grow up and learn the basics."

He shuddered. "I intend to live life to the fullest as long as I'm physically able." A shadow of a frown crossed his expression, but he recovered quickly. "Thanks for the water."

I paused, watching his retreating form as the next person in line stepped up. Monty's older sister had died when he was only eight. The loss had affected all of us, but it had really changed him. From the outside looking in, it seemed as if he was on a mission to remind us she was still here by trying to be just like her. In the process, he'd lost himself. The fun-loving rambunctious little boy had disappeared into the shell of a competitive Type-A do-gooder who shut everyone out of his personal life.

The rest of the morning flew by, and before I knew it, my shift was over. Xavier wanted to pick me up at work, but I suggested meeting at the barn instead. No sense in the crowd starting to speculate about us. Not yet, anyway.

Tasha and I shared an apartment in the complex located behind the Bevvie Bar—*Coffee Loft,* I corrected myself for the umpteenth time—so it was a quick walk home through a gate and across a parking lot to change out of my work clothes and into something more wedding-planning appropriate. I hadn't been to many weddings, but I'd seen them on television and surfed the Internet to absorb what I could about how to act as a bride-to-be.

I chose an ivory sweater dress and sage leggings and pulled a tendril loose from each of my two French braids. I wound the braids into a low bun and pinned them into place with bobby pins, then pulled gently at the strands to fluff them out. I finished the 'do off with a jeweled comb at the top of the knot and slipped my feet into my favorite fuzzy-lined boots.

Bride-to-be.

Maybe it would feel more real after this meeting.

I WAS a few minutes late to the appointment. On my way out of the store, Jason and Lauren's niece, preschooler Quimby de la Tour, was melting down over toast. Apparently, she'd overheard her parents talking about toasting at their upcoming New Year's Eve party, after she went to bed. Her pregnant mother was trying to explain that the "New Year's toast" wasn't actual toast, but Quimby wasn't having it. I'd popped a slice into the toaster, added butter, slid it into a doughnut sleeve and handed it to Tasha, telling her to ask Lola before she served it to her daughter just in case of allergies. "And her decaf Frodoughchino is on me," I added.

I loved kids. They were literal and simple energy-suckers and so much fun.

Once inside the barn, I jogged up the spiral iron staircase that led to the loft where Brenna's office suite was located.

Claudia, Brenna's assistant, sat at the desk and directed me to the love seat where Xavier was seated, across a coffee table from a pair of wingback armchairs. Brenna sat in one, her long blond hair and back to me. Fyvie from Sunflower Bakery occupied the other chair, sitting with one leg tucked up under her. Her tight auburn curls were piled loosely on her head and bobbed as she twisted around to greet me with a grin and a handful of eyebrow lifts.

On the table was a very large robin's-egg-blue bakery box. Cake?

I liked cake. I liked everything the bakery made, including the treats the Bevvie Bar hired them to stock for us. I hoped the Coffee Loft would continue that tradition.

"Sit down, sit down!" Brenna ushered us. "Xavier gave me the basics. Secret wedding because of PR craziness during the season. Don't tell Brendan. We can certainly keep all of this under wraps."

Xavier looked worse for wear. Grief and lack of sleep take a toll, but this—this was more. This was a massive pressure, one that sunk shoulders and made it look like a struggle to hold your head up. His family legacy was a heavy weight. I was glad he was amenable to me helping him share the load.

He offered me a weak smile. I joined him on the love seat and lifted his arm to cradle my shoulders. Settling in next to him, I marveled at how natural it felt.

I gave his knee what I hoped was an encouraging squeeze, and we turned our attention to Brenna, who took the cliché "grinning ear to ear" to a new level.

I'd known Brenna my whole life—my grandfather's favorite cousin married her grandfather, linking the Palmer and Brewer families after generations of rivalry. Brenna was married to Xavier's teammate, defenseman Brendan Trotter, who'd been the one to triple-dog dare him to drink a coffee at the Bevvie Bar years ago when they'd played in town for the Volts.

Small town life ...

She held a clipboard on her lap and pointed her pen at us. "I just knew you two would wake up one day and realize you were meant to be together! It's about time! Does Brendan know you've been secretly dating? Tell me all about it."

Xavier's arm tightened around me. I'd asked him to do as much of the talking as possible, so I waited for him to answer. I didn't usually stutter around Brenna, but Fyvie made me nervous, and I didn't know Claudia at all.

He shifted a little on the sofa. "He doesn't. We've, ah, been very secretive. I've been laser-focused on my career, and I knew that if I ever tried to get to know her, I'd be hooked. My grandfather died the other day, and ... life is short. And I figured, that was a major life change and I'm playing okay. Maybe another major life change won't hurt. And after three years of toffee coffees and sneaking in on off afternoons to hear her play, I just ... didn't want to wait any longer."

This was not the story we'd rehearsed.

He looked at me with such tenderness, my throat went tight.

Without breaking our eye lock, he continued. "One day, I finally got up the nerve to talk to her. I went to the Bevvie Bar for my pregame drink, and Penny wasn't there. My heart sunk, and I realized I wanted to see her more than I wanted the coffee. Tasha must have seen the panic in my eyes and sent me around back to find her. I thought I was just going to ask her to make my coffee.

But ... we had a moment." He smiled at me, and his shoulders relaxed. "And we've been having moments ever since."

Yeah, we did. And we have.

And *I* was having a moment now.

I smiled back and nodded for him to continue.

"I've admired you for years, Penny. Since the day I met you when you effortlessly and magically turned a doughnut into coffee. There's no one else I've thought about since. You're it for me." His hand squeezed my shoulder, and he looked at me so earnestly I was sure time froze.

In the background of my haze, I heard Brenna gasp. Fyvie mumbled something under her breath that I couldn't make out.

I continued to stare at him, struggling to keep my composure. *Don't cry. Don't cry.*

He'd spoken with such conviction—if his words were untrue, then he was a champion liar and should quit hockey this minute and take the next plane to Hollywood.

Fyvie spoke the words I couldn't, her Irish accent thick with her emotion. "I ... didn't come here to gurn my lamps out." She swiped her eyes and scooped up the box of tissues from the coffee table. "'E's a keeper, this one, Pen."

I couldn't hold my tears in any longer. "M-m-making m-me cry," I scolded her. She handed me a tissue, and I dabbed at my eyes.

"Why can't they all be that sweet and straightforward?" Fyvie lamented with a wail. "Wasted no time, this one. 'E should be a lesson fer them all."

Brenna and I laughed. We'd all watched Fyvie's love story play out, full of bumps and strife, but it'd eventually smoothed out.

Xavier closed his eyes and pressed his lips to my forehead. I melted under his touch. "I wasted *three years,*" he corrected. "I've been so focused on my game, and it's been going well, but ... something was always missing. I—I didn't know what that was for so long. And now I know what it was. It wasn't accolades or points or trophies. It was you, Penny."

He *sounded* sincere but maybe laying it on a little thick? This was fake, right?

This was supposed to be fake.

His pocket vibrated, and I jumped. "Let me turn this off." He slipped his phone out of his pocket to silence it. When he saw the screen, his eyes widened. "It's Coach," he said. I leaned over to look at the screen. Notification bubbles with familiar profile pictures began to pop up, coming in fast succession.

Congrats!

Norris trophy for sure!

Swanny! You did it!

I'm so proud of you.—Mom

I told you so, son. See you soon!

Opa would be so proud!

Eeeeeeeeeeeeeeeeeee! Way to go, big bro!

Yeah, bruh! <heart emoji> <hockey stick emoji> <star emoji> <hand-clapping emoji>

And from Edyta, seven GIFs of different pro hockey mascots throwing confetti.

"You should answer that call," I said, heart rate quickening in anticipation of what could only be good news. "And then read your messages."

"We don't mind, do we, Fyvie?" Brenna asked.

"Not a wee bit. Answer!"

Xavier swiped and lifted the phone to his ear. "Coach?"

The coach's answer was muffled, but I could make out a few words. *All-star. Seattle. February.*

It didn't take a genius to figure out his coach's news. Shock froze Xavier's face into the humblest expression I'd ever seen him wear. His eyebrows knit higher than ever. I wanted to jump into his arms and celebrate.

But I couldn't. We weren't in that kind of place. Not yet, anyway.

After the season. Be patient.

But … we were here to plan our wedding. Shouldn't I be more … affectionate?

I had a few seconds to decide.

He ended the call and met my gaze. "I'm an all-star."

I went for it. With a squeal proportionate to how big his achievement was, I launched myself at him, wrapping my arms around his neck. He tugged me onto his lap and leaned down, his face inches from mine. My heart pounded in anticipation.

My cheeks heated to boiling. Was our first real kiss going to be on Brenna's sofa?

No!

Just as his lips were about to touch mine, I twisted away from him and slid off his lap.

I should have thought this through more.

I smiled sheepishly at the women on the other side of the table. "S-sorry?"

"No apology necessary," Brenna insisted. "Let me get some champagne!"

"Thanks, but none for me," Xavier said. "It's a game night."

Brenna shrugged. "You can take it with you for another time, then. So, I guess that weekend is out. February is busy for Valentine weddings, plus there's the Biddingtons' Sweethearts charity ball, and I have several birthday parties." She scrolled through her tablet. "I can do any Tuesday or Wednesday in February if you don't mind the barn's interior in the middle of a setup. Or if you want to get married pre-Seattle and make a little honeymoon of it"—she waggled her eyebrows—"I can squeeze you in on January twenty-seventh."

"Definitely after," Xavier and I replied in unison.

And stutter-free. Whoa.

I wondered if his reason for delaying was the same as mine. Seattle was his home. I assumed I'd be meeting his family if he took me with him. Probably best to meet them before the wedding, right?

Was he thinking the same? Or was it something different?

Brenna looked from him to me and back to him.

He cleared his throat. "No more big life changes until after All-Star Weekend. It might, uh, be bad luck."

Brenna huffed. "You were just saying 'what's another major life change?' Nothing about Penny has ever brought you bad luck. I'll bet you have your best weekend ever. Toffee coffees before each event!"

Xavier gave her an easy smile. "I *am* looking forward to that, if she's willing." He turned his head back to me, and his smile fell away. “But I’m most worried about the PR. If she’s there with any kind of ring on …”

I’d thought about that. I expected wedding rings. But he’d said “any kind of ring.” I didn’t have an engagement ring. Was he planning to get me one?

We still had so much to talk about.

CHAPTER 9
Xavier

Saying goodbye—again—to Opa had been the hardest thing I'd ever done. It gave me the closure I was looking for, but it was at the expense of the finality the rituals signaled.

Before I left Alpintraum late Christmas night, our last conversation had been jovial and good-natured. *Zavey-boy, go find yourself a vife vhile you are young hockey star. Before you get old and fat like me and none of zee ol' ladies look at you tvice. And take your Oma's emerald ring. It's from Idar-Oberstein and has been in the family for generations. It's good luck. I have faith you'll give it to the right voman.*

I'd laughed along with him, until his chuckles morphed into a coughing fit. Then I'd sat with him, holding his hand until he slipped into a peaceful, medicated sleep, snoring softly. The image of him sleeping in his ornate bed with the curtains tied to the posts would be forever burned into my memory.

Oma's ring was in my drawer. I wanted to give it to Penny. It was the same color as her eyes, a deep green the color of the chateau's lawn on a warm summer day. I had to be sure she was one hundred percent committed to the long game as I was before I gave her a piece of my family's history.

Returning for the funeral had reminded me just how deep my Alpintraum roots went. With the chateau and grounds, Opa's title of baron would also be passed down to me. And with it, the traditions and trappings of an old noble family. Could I really expect to manage all of that and play hockey, too?

As for the funeral, only a big to-do would suffice for my Opa. His visiting hours and service had been grander and larger and longer than Oma's, him having known and affected hundreds of people over the years and her wanting a small, private event for family and friends only. Many locals had stories to share, and the tributes went on for hours. I learned so many things about him I hadn't known.

How he once sheltered and fed everyone in a five-mile radius during and after a blizzard. How he opened up the pond every January to the public and hired college kids to run it. How he sent a generous handwritten card every Christmas to every staff member, including the students earning service hours.

I had big shoes to fill … someday.

Thinking about all of this on the way home from the wedding consultation, I was glad Penny and I had driven separately. I wouldn't have been good company.

Claudia had ordered takeout for Penny and I from Brewski's Sports Bar & Grille, which Brenna's parents owned. Her brother, Drew, ran it over from the restaurant, which was located across the field from the barn. It was all Brewer property this side of town. We also took the cake samples with us.

Penny followed me home, and I set our food out on the coffee table. Sitting on the sofa to eat instead of at the table felt less formal. More comfortable. Maybe even more domestic?

J.R. had sent me a deck of getting-to-know-you question cards, and I suggested to Penny that we use them while we ate. I hoped she'd get more comfortable with me in the process. Then we could work on her speaking.

I pulled the first card off the deck. "The ideal number of children I'd like is …" I swallowed. Nothing like jumping right to the big stuff. "Uh, you don't have to answer that if you don't want to."

Penny held up four fingers.

"Really? Me too. Someday, anyway. I like having three little sisters."

She smiled. "I alw-ways w-anted brothers."

I laughed. "Sorry I can't help you with that. But I think you'll love my sisters."

"No d-doubt." She reached for the next card on the deck and scanned the words. "Early b-bird or n-night ow-owl?"

"Early bird for sure. I like to get up early."

"Me t-too."

I reached for the next card. "Share your deepest desires, both personally and professionally." I glanced up from the card to read Penny's expression. Pensive. Maybe writing it down would be easier for her, like that time in her car.

My coffee table had a little drawer under the tabletop. I pulled out the notepad and pen I kept there for list-making and set it in front of her while I answered the question.

"Professionally, I want to play at least until I'm forty. My dad played until he was forty-one, but he had a few seasons left in him. I want to be one of those rare guys who can play for the long haul. When I start to slow down, I can be a mentor to the younger guys coming up. And I don't care where I play." Penny jerked her head up, eyes wide. "Well, I want to stay in Colorado, of course. Because you're here," I reassured her. She let out a long breath. Relief? "But really, if the NHL doesn't work out, I'd love to play in the Swiss league or the Czech league. It's beautiful in Europe during hockey season."

Penny handed me the notebook.

I've always dreamed of playing my harp in Vienna, in a grand ballroom, while couples in fancy evening attire waltz to classical music. Realistically, I'd just like to be part of any symphony and teach children how to play the harp. If I could make a living doing that, I'd be happy.

I recalled her saying there would be plenty of time for all of our dreams, and a thought began to take shape in my mind. Opa had friends in Vienna and connections all over Europe.

Suddenly, helping her overcome her stutter became even more important to me. It was holding her back from great things.

I slid my hand under hers and brought it to my lips, placing a light kiss on her knuckles. She blushed and lowered her eyelids but didn't pull her hand away.

"I can see that happening. This summer? We can stay at the chateau and you can play for our tour guests. We could even have a party. A grand ball to introduce you to everyone."

She drew in a breath and fixed a gaze on me that was so full of happiness and hope, I knew for sure I would fulfill my promises and take her to all the places that filled her with joy.

I was still holding her hand near my mouth. I kissed her knuckles again, then boldly brushed my lips over the top of her hand, then her wrist. The knit sleeve of her sweater prevented me from going any farther. Reluctantly, I lowered her hand to my thigh and didn't let go.

I was falling fast and hard. I needed to slow it down or I'd fall flat on my face. We'd agreed to date *after* the season ended.

But today, the potential of six more months of stagnancy while the Edge chased the Cup felt like forever.

There was another part to this question. What was it? I glanced at the card.

Oh, right. *Deepest personal desire.*

I tore my gaze away from her perfect hand and met her eyes again. "I want a family. Those four kids we talked about. I want to have enough money so that we can travel the world but also spend time with Dad's family in Europe and with my mom's family on the Reservation, so they can learn about their First Nations heritage. I want to start a nonprofit to pay for the kids there to fund sports—and music," I added, as the afterthought presented itself to me.

That was a new idea, but it was important. From the approval in Penny's eyes, she thought that was a good idea, too. I continued. "And I want to be the best husband and father I can be. Supportive, loving, and always there for my family." I hung my head to voice the problem with it all. "But I don't know how to do that if I'm playing pro hockey. My dad couldn't. He retired early because he missed so much of me and Daniella growing up and wanted to do it differently for Karina and Edyta."

Penny squeezed my hand and spoke softly. "You'll find a way."

No stutter. I raised my chin to study her. Eyes shining, shoulders set. A confident pose.

Progress? I sure hoped so.

"What about you?" I asked.

Her chest heaved, and she let out the air in her lungs slowly. "I ... want ... all ... that ... too."

My chest was heaving now, and the thumping inside it was louder in my ears than the team collectively banging our sticks on the ice.

Penny turned away when I didn't respond and took the next card. "F-favorite holiday."

"Easy," I said softly, mourning how this most recent "moment" had gone cold. "Christmas."

She nodded. "Same."

I slid the next card off the top of the deck. "What are your dealbreakers?"

Penny leaned back into the sofa, her hand guiding mine to the cushion in between us. "Lies ... m-meanness. M-making fun of my st-stutter."

"I would *never.*" I had to make that clear.

"I know." She smiled. "You?"

"Fakeness." I laughed at the irony. "Not our fake marriage, but you know, when someone changes who they are to try to fit in and you don't know them anymore. I see a lot of that ... women trying every kind of thing to get our attention. Or thinking they have to become influencers and be perfect when they marry one of us. I see that, too. The guys don't like it. So many Wags look like Barbie dolls once they're Instagram-official."

"D-don't worry." Penny smiled. "I don't w-want to be b-blond. Or w-wear heels."

I laughed. "Good. Because I like you just the way you are."

The color of her cheeks deepened to that rosy glow I loved so much, and it looked like she was finally starting to relax.

She sat up and reached for the next card. "W-what ... makes ... you ... angry?" Penny set the card down and brought the notepad into her lap. Our hands were still linked, so I held the pad steady with my free hand and read while she wrote.

> *Not too many things make me angry. My stutter. I'm very hard on myself. My dealbreakers, for sure. Lying. Mistreatment of people and animals. Loud chewing and gum smacking. High-pitched giggles from groups of girls; it takes me back to middle and high school when I was made fun of. Wasted time—time we never get back.*

"All of that makes me angry, too," I said. "I'm sorry those awful girls were mean to you. It probably made you even more nervous."

She nodded. "N-needed th-therapy."

"Oh, Pen." I tugged her to me and let go of her hand so I could wrap my arm around her and dropped my chin to kiss the top of her head. "I hope they're all in dead-end jobs and marry trolls. And I hope they cry for days when they hear you landed yourself pro hockey's biggest stud."

Penny chuckled and leaned her head back to look up at me. "B-biggest stud, huh?"

I waggled my eyebrows. "You just wait. I've dreamed of playing in the all-star game my entire life. Just wait till the world sees what I've got planned for the Breakaway Challenge. All the women are going to go crazy."

"All the w-women, huh?" Penny's grin was wider than I'd ever seen it.

"Yup. But only one who matters. Well, and rubbing it in those mean girls' faces, of course. Revenge, bwahaha!"

Penny lost it, laughing harder and longer than ever, so hard she had tears in her eyes. I just grinned, loving the sound. The sound of her happiness was even more beautiful than her music. I wanted to make her laugh like this every day. I wanted her to be happy and stress-free and …

And I wanted to kiss her. More than anything.

As her laughter tapered off, she relaxed against me again, and I had an idea.

"Pen?"

"Yeah?" She shifted to look up at me again. I locked my eyes on hers, green as the emerald I wanted to give her. Makeup-free, her freckles were visible, dotting her cheeks and the bridge of her nose. Lips the shape of Cupid's bow just begged to be kissed.

"Do you think it might behoove us to, um, *practice* for our wedding kiss? So that it looks natural and not fake?" My pulse quickened. *Say yes, say yes, say yes.*

Penny tapped her chin thoughtfully with her index finger. "Hmm … *behoove.* Big word."

She was teasing me, and I loved it.

"It's one of Dex's I'm-smarter-than-you Harvard words."

A wide smile spread across her face. "I … like it. And … yes. P-practice is … important."

She said yes! A jolt of excitement buzzed through me. I'd never anticipated a kiss so much before. This one would mean something.

And I hoped, for both of us, it would be our last first kiss.

I better make it good.

Penny's eyebrows lifted in silent challenge.

Game time.

I sat up straight and pulled her onto my lap, which leveled our faces closer in height. Cradling her against me with my left arm, I brushed a wayward tendril off her forehead and tucked it behind her ear, then trailed the fingers of my right hand down the side of her face. Without breaking eye contact, I leaned slowly toward her, and she met me halfway.

Our lips connected, and the chemistry was instant. Her hands were on my face, both of my arms held her close, and we became one very efficient kissing machine.

I closed my eyes and let the euphoria take over. I wanted full immersion. The warmth of her breath mingling with mine, the vanilla scent of her face—like her hand sanitizer but without the alcohol sting—the strength of her arms that were now securing the back of my head, holding it in place in case I had thoughts of breaking the kiss.

Nope. I'd be like those characters at Disney who weren't allowed to be the first to break a hug. No way was I breaking this kiss.

Not even if my phone rang. Which it did.

The mood-breaker cycled through three rounds of the sound bite from the *Pirates of the Caribbean* theme before Penny pulled away.

I groaned. "Why you go? My lips are cold," I whined, grudgingly opening my eyes.

She grinned. "I wanted to kiss *you,* not Jack Sparrow. And that's all I could picture once your phone started ringing."

I stared at her, joy pumping through my veins. Had I heard her correctly?

"What?" she asked, her smile fading. "Are you … mad?"

I shook my head. "Pen …" I blinked, not caring that my eye wells were filling with water.

She tilted her head, and then realization marked her features. Eyes wide, she blurted, "I didn't stutter!"

I squished her to me. "This is the best day ever. It started off sad but pulled a one-eighty. I'm an all-star, I'm marrying the sweetest girl in the world, and she's lost her stutter with me." I rested my chin on her head. I loved the way her silky hair felt on my neck. "Do you think we should practice more?"

"Absolutely!" came the muffled reply.

We could finish the card game another time.

CHAPTER 10
Penny

Xavier's kiss had been magic. Almost as good—maybe better—was that I felt so incredibly free being able to talk to him without stammering or stumbling over my words. It was liberating.

But—*that kiss!*

We "practiced" until he had to get ready for his game.

I wasn't working the afternoon shift, but I didn't think Jannell or Marcus would mind if I popped in to make his coffee.

We still had to tell my family about our plans. It didn't feel right keeping something this big from them. I thought the best time would be after church tomorrow. It was New Year's Eve, and Xavier had a home game later in the afternoon, so the team had the morning off, which worked out perfectly.

He wanted to come with me to church, which filled me with joy on a whole other level. Our Sunday family traditions were important to me, and Xavier said they would be important to him, too. *Swooooon!*

Suddenly showing up with a boyfriend—or fiancé-to-be—was sure to cause a stir. But being that you were supposed to be quiet during church, it would give my family time to process our sudden togetherness in an environment they couldn't ask all the questions in. Then we'd head over to my grandparents' house for weekly brunch. Gabby's fiancé, Noel Allaire, would be there, too, so at least Xavier would know someone other than just me, Tasha, and Gabby.

Xavier and Noel had played together the last few years, starting the year Noel returned to the Volts after a season-ending injury. He'd taken a hard stick to his abdomen and needed a kidney transplant. After taking a year off hockey to recover, he currently bounced between the Volts and the Edge, depending on who the Edge was playing. Noel was fast and had a real talent for the game, but no one wanted to risk another critical injury playing against the more physical teams. Both the Volts and Edge had rallied around him, making sure opposing players weren't too rough. At any time, either organization's medical team could pull him from playing, and no one wanted that. Gabby told me he hated having his friends fight his battles, but facing a lifetime of dialysis was worse.

Brunch was lovely. My aunt put her interview skills to work—she was a local news anchor—and put everyone at ease. Xavier fit in easily with my family, and he even helped my grandmother and I clear and wash the dishes.

Good. We were going to need all the brownie points we could get.

We'd decided to tell my whole family and ask them to keep it a secret until after hockey season was over. Only Tasha knew the real circumstances. I'd filled her in that morning before church, and though she said all the right things, I could tell by her skeptical demeanor she didn't entirely approve.

Once we were all settled in the family room for what my grandpa liked to call the "post-brunch bunch and munchies," where we ate dessert and each of us shared how the previous week went, my nerves started to kick in. I didn't stutter with my family, and if I did, our news wouldn't be received well. If they thought Xavier made me uncomfortable ... well, that would be bad.

I was grateful Grandpa saved us for last. Rexie snoozed at my feet, and the presence of the old husky did wonders to calm my nerves. When it was my turn to talk about my week, Xavier stood and held his hand out for me. He tugged me up to his side and wrapped his arm securely around my shoulders and squeezed me to him gently. I glanced at each of my family members in turn and took a long breath.

"I, um, have a boyfriend," I said. Gabby squealed and clapped. Everyone was smiling. Before I lost my nerve and everyone got loud, I dropped my bomb. "And … a fiancé."

"What! Congrats, man." Noel stood up and crossed the room to shake Xavier's hand. Gabby was still squealing. Tasha was smiling, my parents were blinking, and everyone else was just staring at us.

Xavier was beaming. Like a kid at Christmas.

He was selling it like a boss.

"We're excited for you," my mother said. "It just seems … sudden. How long have you been dating? Are you sure about this?"

Xavier cleared his throat, and we exchanged a glance. I nodded at him to say his part. "It *is* sudden. My grandfather died earlier this week. He was my best friend." He paused for murmurs of condolences. "Thanks. I've had time to do a lot of thinking. About the way he lived his life, about the way I want to live mine. He loved my Oma more than anything and always said being married to her and building their life together was his greatest achievement and deepest joy."

He looked down at me and grinned. I smiled shyly.

"Penny and I … we've never defined the connection we have, not until now. I don't want to waste any more time. She is … She's everything to me. More than hockey. I want us to build a future, starting now. Well, February twentieth. We'd love your blessing and for you to attend."

"And—" I swallowed. "To keep it all a secret until the season's over. The team is very superstitious."

Noel narrowed his eyes. "It's bad luck to make any major life changes during the season. Why can't you wait?"

Xavier leveled a gaze on him. "I won't entertain that marrying Penny could be bad luck. And we don't want to take any attention away from your wedding. It's been years coming, and everyone is looking forward to it. As far as a major change, there's already been two this week. Opa dying and the Coffee Loft taking over the Bevvie Bar. This will be the third, and it's a *good* change. How can it possibly be unlucky when I'll literally have my lucky Penny by my side?"

The collective sigh from the women told me he'd won over at least half the room. *Phew.* I didn't think Noel was truly convinced, nor anyone else for that matter. But they were supportive. My grandfather sent Gabby's brother Jake to the pantry for a bottle of bubbly to celebrate.

When the drinks were poured, my dad raised his glass. "To Penny and Xavier and their happy future."

I couldn't wait to get out of there. Luckily, after the excitement died down, people started to leave.

We walked to Xavier's car, and I waved to Liam across the street. He was up on the roof, taking down the Christmas lights at his and Beck's house. He and his brothers grew up there, and Beck had lived next door to them. They were a little older than us Palmer grandkids, so we didn't play with them often. I made a mental note to message Beck to ask them not to mention Xavier was here today. Although him coming to church with us might start the gossip train. I needed to stress that we were just getting to know each other. It wasn't a lie.

Xavier opened the passenger door, and I slid into the low seat. Tasha was parked behind us, so we followed her back to downtown.

"That went well," he said. "They took it much better than my family did."

"It did," I said. "Noel seemed a bit irked. And Tasha isn't thrilled, but she'll come around."

"They'll work it out." Xavier made the turn into the parking lot. "Would you like me to come up?"

I shook my head. "Nah. I'd avoid Tasha for a few days if I were you." I flashed him a teasing grin. "She can be scary when she thinks she knows best."

"Noted. But I don't find her scary at all. Just protective. I'm sure I can win her over with time." He shifted the car into park in front of the lobby doors. "Do you think … we should practice kissing a little more often, you know, in public so that we can really sell it? We wouldn't want anyone to think we weren't crazy about each other. And ... it's New Year's Eve."

"Why, Xavier Schwann." I booped him on the nose with the tip of my finger. "I do believe you enjoy kissing me so much you just need an official excuse for more."

His eyebrows knitted as if to challenge me, but then his lips spread into a roguish grin. "Guilty as charged."

I laughed and leaned in, wanting to kiss that wicked smile right off his face. "You can kiss me whenever and wherever you wish. No need to ask. Ever." I closed my eyes and waited for his soft lips to touch mine.

Click!

He depressed the button at my side, and I chuckled into his kiss as my seat belt retracted toward the door. Our arms wrapped around one another, seeking the connection and security we both so craved.

A car horn honked behind us, and I reluctantly pulled away. "I'd better go. When will I see you again?"

"You could come to the game tonight. I forgot to ask you earlier." The back of his hand stroked my cheek, and he leaned his head to the side. "I got you a jersey."

"You did?" I asked.

He shifted, snaking his arm into the back to retrieve a reusable Denver Edge shopping bag with Zaki Marsch's likeness on the front. "They haven't made any Swanny bags yet," he joked.

"Surely they will next season," I assured him and took the bag. "You're their biggest star this year. Their *all-star*. I wish I could go tonight, but I promised Tasha some sister time when she asked if I had plans with you. We usually spend New Year's Eve together."

"That's true." He rubbed at his beard and smiled. "I still can't believe it. And Dex got the fan vote of all the goalies in our division."

"That's awesome! So you'll have a friend there with you."

"Would you want to come to Seattle? You can stay with my family. Get to know my sisters. They're going to love you."

I beamed. "And I'm going to love them." *Just like I'm going to love you,* I thought. "Yes, I most definitely would like to. I ... better go," I said quickly before I voiced what I was thinking. "Good luck tonight. Want me to meet you at the Bevvie Bar—er, Coffee Loft? At the usual time?"

He turned to look across the parking lot at the back side of the coffee shop and shook his head. "Nah. Better lay low today. I'm expecting a big crowd there again. If I don't score, it's okay. I'll still have the highest points of all the defensemen in the league. Spend time with your sister. Keep that tradition. For now," he added with a slow smile.

"Okay." A shiver went through me imagining what he might have planned for next New Year's Eve, if the Edge weren't away playing.

He got out of the car and came around to open my door for me. One last kiss before I floated inside, ready to face my sister.

No way could anything bring me down right now. Not even a stormy Tasha.

I took the stairs up to the second floor and let myself in. "I'm home!" I shouted, setting my purse on the counter and hanging up my coat on the hook by the door.

Tasha was ready for me, firing off questions quick and fast. "How are you going to pull this off? What if someone in his family leaks the inheritance clause? They paint you as a gold digger and you'll be canceled all over social media. Everything you've worked for ... Are you sure you want to do this, Penny? Can't he find someone else?"

"No, he can't," I insisted. "And yes, I'm sure. His family isn't going to leak anything. The lawyer has to keep it a secret or he'll lose his job and be disbarred."

"Is he old? If the lawyer is ready for retirement, he might be willing to sell his story. I can see the headline now: 'Edge all-star marries barista to save family castle.'" She shuddered and tossed a pointed look at me. "How can you trust him or Xavier, for that matter? You barely know him."

"I don't know." I sank into the sofa. "I just have to. And I feel it in my soul, this deep connection I can't explain. It's been building for years. It'll all be fine, really. It's not like there are any orchestras or grad schools banging down our door wanting me."

My heart beat a little faster. "And Xavier said I can play for guests at the chateau this summer." I sighed happily as I settled into the cushions, closing my eyes. "I'm already imagining it."

She plopped on the cushion next to me and leaned her head on my shoulder. "I hope he keeps his promises and the terms of the NDA. It all sounds too good to be true, Pen. If that man lets you down, I swear I will hurt him. Harder than an illegal cross-check into the boards without a helmet. I don't care how good the prenup is."

I laughed. "Thanks. That is super specific. I love you. And thanks for always having my back."

"Always," she replied, tight and firm. "Unless you don't invite me to the castle."

"It's a *chateau.*" I raised my eyebrows, and we both gave way to giggles. I was going to miss this. Living with my sister. Our time alone, just to ourselves, in our quiet apartment. Her inventive and always mouthwatering Crock-Pot meals. I'd keep my bedroom here, for when Xavier had away games, just in case I didn't want to be alone, and Tasha promised to teach me all her one-pot secrets.

But I had no intention of giving up on our marriage. Unless he turned out to be someone totally different than what he presented, I could see our entire future ahead of us.

And I wanted all of it.

AT NINE FIFTY-FIVE, my phone rang.

Xavier.

"Answer it," Tasha said. "I'm going to run down to the lobby's snack machine. I decided I wanted to ring in the new year with a Hershey bar."

I laughed. Tasha was supposed to be giving up all things milk chocolate as her New Year's resolution. "If you get it down by eleven fifty-nine eastern, I won't count it. Four minutes until they drop the ball in New York City."

She shook her head, but she was smiling. "I'm thinking I'll get two and stay up until midnight mountain time this year."

"Oooh, you rebel, you," I teased.

She snorted. "Be right back!"

I swiped to receive the call. "Hi," I greeted him. "Sorry you didn't score tonight. Good game, though. A tough win against Phoenix. We watched it. Glad to see Zaki Marsch is back."

"Thanks. Have I mentioned I love it when you talk hockey? It makes me want to kiss you." I chuckled as he went on. "Yeah, it's good to have the team prankster back, but I miss playing with ChaCha. That guy can read my mind. And Jannell's ratio of coffee to coffee ice cream was a little off. No big deal."

"I'll work with her to remedy that," I vowed, tucking my feet under me and readjusting my blanket. "Are you out celebrating with the guys?"

"Nah." His voice was low but upbeat, like he was teasing me.

"No?" I asked. I glanced at the timer on the television.

"Nope. Didn't feel like ringing in the new year with those clowns."

I laughed. "Three minutes until the ball drops on the East Coast. Tasha and I usually watch their ball drop and call it a night. We're lame."

"You? Nah. You're the opposite of lame. And someday, you'll be in a fancy orchestra ringing in the new year on stage."

I sighed. "Unlikely, but I appreciate your confidence."

"It'll happen," he said, but I wasn't so sure. I wouldn't bet the ranch on it. Well, if my Palmer ancestors hadn't gambled away and sold all our ranch lands. "How many minutes now?"

"Less than two. Happy New Year, Xavier." The line went silent. Had the call dropped? I checked my screen. Still connected. "Are you still there?"

"No," he said.

Huh?

The door opened, but instead of Tasha, an extremely handsome man in a wool overcoat and newsboy hat stood in my doorway. I gasped.

"I'm here."

I tossed my phone on the sofa and scrambled out of the blanket, hurrying into his open arms. He lifted me off the ground and kissed the top of my head before setting me back on my feet.

"Nice hat." I tapped the brim. "I like this look on you."

He lifted it off his head and set it on mine. "And I like it better on you."

I grinned like a dummy. I couldn't think of a thing to say.

"Tasha said it was okay to stop by." Behind him, the door to her bedroom clicked shut. I hadn't even noticed her reentry. "I texted her earlier. When I called you, that was the signal for her to come down and let me in."

"Wow," I said. Wow, indeed. She'd meant it when she said she'd be there for me, even if she was worried.

Xavier had passed the Tasha Test.

"So." He glanced at the television. "Thirty seconds. Can I still kiss you whenever and wherever I wish?"

"You better."

Xavier's fingertips lightly caressed my cheek, and then he bent toward me until we were forehead to forehead, nose to nose. The hat was bumped off my head, and neither of us bent to fetch it. As the last ten numbers counted down, we stared shyly at each other, grinning like Cheshire cats, anticipating the arrival of midnight in the east.

"Three! Two! One!"

Xavier didn't wait for the crowd in Times Square to shout *Happy New Year.* His lips were on mine, and then I was off my feet again, this time over-the-threshold style, but he was standing in place, holding me securely. I reached up to cup his face, his short beard soft under my hands. Parting my lips to deepen the kiss, all I could think about was how much had happened in the last few days and how amazing this next year of our lives could be, if every day felt like this.

When he pulled away, I opened my eyes. A dreamy look lit up his features, and I was sure my expression mirrored his own.

Too good to be true, Tasha had warned.

I pushed the thought away as he carried me to the sofa and sat, arranging me over his lap, legs to one side and cradling me to him like our first kiss-to-remember.

"Fifty-five minutes until the fireworks in Nashville." Xavier waggled his eyebrows hopefully.

"And one hour and fifty-five minutes until Denver and Colorado Springs light up the screen. You should probably take your coat off," I suggested.

"Only if we can ring in every year like this." His eyes shone with sincerity and promise.

"I'd like nothing more," I whispered.

CHAPTER 11
Xavier

Smitten? Yup. Me.

Distracted? One hundred percent.

Regretful? Zero percent.

January passed in a blur. Home games, away games, toffee coffees, harp afternoons, wedding prep, speaking sessions, and plenty of kissing practice. I'd even learned the ASL alphabet while attending a handful of Penny's library lessons.

We were having fun and getting to know each other, and the other day I'd introduced her to what my elementary school speech therapist called "see-food speaking." Penny had laughed so hard I decided we were going to practice it first thing once she got off work today. Talking with your mouth full of food, you couldn't stutter, and you had to take your time. I'd demonstrated with a peanut butter sandwich. When she tried it, she got the hiccups and we lost focus. Hiccups turned to laughs and laughs to kissing and, well … Lesson over.

Today, as I watched her strum her harp in the Coffee Loft—I still wasn't used to the place's name change—I thought about the progress she'd already made.

We'd started with some simple words and phrases and role-playing. I'd pretend to be a customer or a sales rep in a retail store. Then we moved up to talking about her music and practicing interview questions. She was killing it, but we hadn't

tested it out in a real-life situation yet. And she still hadn't attended one of my hockey games. With her final semester of classes starting and her job, all her extra time was spent with me. I wasn't complaining.

I had to get her ready to talk to my family. And for an interview at the all-star game. Management wanted to do a special feature on me and my family, since the game was in Seattle. A full hour-long special would air on Denver's sports network and streaming channel. Bailey would be there and said she'd try to arrange for her to be the one to interview Penny, but it was ultimately up to the producers. I told her Penny was nervous, and she'd sent a list of possible questions they typically asked.

Back in the corner by the Coffee Loft front window, at the table we'd sat at that first time together, I sipped a Lofty-size Matcha Madness and tried to clear my thoughts so I could get lost in her music. Someone had requested 1960s songs, and with my eyes closed, I could imagine myself back into the past.

I wished I had a professional recording of Penny's songs. Discreetly, I'd videoed her playing on my phone, and I played her songs while I was on the road and/or missing her. As the chords of "In the Still of the Night" faded away, I recited the lyrics in my head. They inspired me. We would be writing our own vows, and I wanted her to know I was serious about mine. I wanted to hold her tight, every night, and never let her go.

But how did we work up to that? With our team playing so well, it'd be another four months at least until we could get started on our relationship.

Unless … unless we *didn't* wait.

Brenna was right about one thing. Nothing about Penny had ever brought me bad luck.

The melody changed into a catchy, upbeat tune I'd heard before but couldn't place. I opened my eyes. One table over, Jannell was mouthing the words as she typed on her laptop while Riva, Marie's yellow lab therapy dog trainee, sat at her feet. Steam rose from her mug of coffee. I'd seen it in the cubby shelf earlier and wondered if she'd chosen the message for herself: *Most Likely to Need Coffee.*

"Excuse me." I leaned over, and Jannell lifted her head. "Sorry to interrupt your work. And you, sweet girl." I leaned down to scratch Riva behind her ears, and she gave me an appreciative doggie smile. "What song is this?"

She smiled. "'That Thing You Do.' It's from the movie by the same title. It came out in the '90s, but it's '60s-themed."

"Thanks." I vaguely remembered watching it as a kid with my mom. She was a big fan of musicals. "You said the movie was *That Thing You Brew?*" I asked, returning my gaze to Penny.

"*That Thing You* Do," she corrected. "Although we all know *your* story." I turned back to her, surprised. "It's Penny's *brew* that made you a star." She winked and tapped her finger on her chin. "I wonder if we can use that in marketing without getting sued?"

I laughed. "Maybe. I'm happy to be your ad guy. I've got the money to sue back."

The music ended, and I glanced at the clock above the restroom archway. Another forty minutes.

"She can go," Jannell said. "I know you're waiting for her. It's pretty dead here." She nodded toward the counter, where Gabby was hunched over a textbook. "If it picks up, I'll jump in and help. But I don't expect a busy afternoon. Not with Montoya Construction staging outside."

I turned to look out the window. Almost the entire sidewalk was blocked in front of the café.

"They'll bring it in as soon as we close. It'll take about a week to cut through the ceiling and attach the spiral iron staircase—like the one they put in Brenna's barn. Then we'll *really* be a 'coffee loft.'"

I grinned. "Can't wait. And I'm glad it's the week we're in Seattle. The timing is perfect for Penny to be gone."

"Yes, amazing how that worked out." She tipped her chin toward Penny, who was chatting with a few of the little kids who'd been dancing to her music. "Go help your girl pack up. And good luck All-Star Weekend. Brewski's is holding a watch party. Half the town is planning to be there."

"Thanks," I said. *No pressure.* I was looking forward to the game, of course, and with Bailey's help, I'd secured all the necessary pieces for the Breakaway Challenge.

It was going to be epic. I wanted to wow the crowd and the viewers but most of all, Penny.

After All-Star Weekend, it would be full speed ahead with games and wedding prep. My parents still refused to come, but I was hoping after meeting Penny, they'd like her and see how good we were together and change their minds.

Still, whether they were there or not when we said "I do," I was getting married in three weeks.

Three weeks!

I was falling hard and fast, and if I didn't catch myself soon, we'd be way ahead of our timeline. I didn't want to pressure Penny into anything she wasn't ready for.

"Welcome to Seattle," I whispered into Penny's ear. She was finally in my arms after we spent the last two days apart. I'd traveled with Jason, Bailey, and the team staff via charter plane and spent the last day and a half in interviews and traipsing all around Seattle for the player spotlight, plus all-star media shenanigans at the arena. Waiting for Penny to arrive this morning had been torture. "Your harp is safe at my parents' house," I added for good measure.

"Thanks." She stepped out of the hug and peered over my shoulder. "You must be Daniella?"

Right. My sister had driven me to the airport to pick up Penny. I grinned sheepishly. "Sorry, Dani. I forgot you were here." I rubbed at the back of my neck and hoped my expression was appropriately apologetic.

Daniella smirked. "You've got it bad, bro. It's wonderful to meet you, Penny." Her long, shiny black hair caught the sunlight streaming in through the windows on this unusually sunny day in the Emerald City. Or as I liked to call it, "Rain City." That nickname wasn't as popular, but it definitely seemed more accurate. I loved living in Colorado and found it amusing that Colorado had more sunny days per year than Florida did.

"I'm a big … fan of yours," Penny said to my sister, taking

only a short pause to get her words out. I felt my grin widen at her perfect sentence and at the revelation she knew who my sister was, aside from being related to me. "I love the way you transitioned from solo skating to pairs. You're even more beautiful to watch in the air."

Penny followed Daniella's ice skating? How did I not know this? And—two long, complete sentences, easy and natural.

Pretending I was my sister at our last "lesson" must have worked. Had it been the black towel I'd worn as a makeshift wig? Was Penny picturing that now?

It amazed and inspired me how far she'd come in such a short amount of time when years of professional expertise, intervention, and therapy had failed.

"Thanks." Daniella blushed. My hard-as-nails cynical-yet-sweet sister *blushed.*

Now I'd seen everything.

I shouldn't have worried about Penny fitting in with my family. If she had Daniella's approval, my little sisters would love her, too. I was sure it was only a matter of time before my parents came around.

I wouldn't hide my affection while Penny was here. I wanted them to see with their own eyes how serious I was about making this work long-term.

And how serious I was about Penny.

If they still disapproved by the end of the weekend, then I'd call them out on their hypocrisy.

I retrieved Penny's suitcase from the baggage carousel and followed them to Daniella's car. I'd brought something for Penny, just in case the timing presented itself while we were here.

Now seemed like a good time.

I loaded the suitcase and Penny's carry-on into the trunk and raced around her to open the passenger-side door, catching Daniella's approving eyebrow lift over the top of the vehicle. My sister was almost six feet tall herself, which was unusual for a figure skater, but everyone in my mother's family was tall. We'd started off as a pair, Dani and I, and when I quit skating for hockey, there were no boys our age tall enough to skate with her.

Sometimes, I still thought she harbored a bit of resentment for being forced to go solo.

Last year, she'd found a partner over six feet tall, and he'd moved to Seattle to train with her. Decent guy. I'd met him over the summer and watched them practice together yesterday when I showed up at the rink with Bailey and the Edge's video crew. They'd gotten a kick out of me in figure skates, trying to perform some of the jumps and spins that had come so easily when I was younger, lighter, and shorter. It was going to make great content and broadcast viewing. I was a bit of a shy guy and tended to avoid our social media manager, so the Edge fans would get to see more of my personality in the filmed special.

And they had definitely gotten a heavy dose of it yesterday. My parents had brought Karina and Edyta to the rink, and within minutes, they were giving the Edge staff skating lessons.

I folded myself into the back seat of Daniella's SUV. You'd think they'd make more leg room in the second row of these things.

As if reading my mind, Penny turned around in the passenger seat. "There's more room up here. Wanna switch?"

So thoughtful. I shook my head. "Nah. You need a front-row seat to the awesomeness that is Seattle." I caught Daniella's eye in the rearview mirror. "Can we stop at Kerry Park? The view of the skyline on a sunny day is a must-see."

"Of course." Daniella's eyes narrowed, understanding the veiled request we'd discussed earlier. The park wasn't on the way to our family home in Bellevue, but Penny wouldn't know that, would she? "And the arena afterward?"

Ah, nice. *Quick thinking, sis.* The arena was only a few minutes from the park, so we could pull this off as a bit of a tour. My parents weren't expecting us until lunch.

Daniella and Penny chatted the entire way to the park. I tried to get comfortable as I listened to their upbeat and friendly conversation.

All was going well. Penny hadn't stuttered or stumbled over her words once.

We pulled into the park, and I jumped out quickly to get the door for Penny. Taking her hand, I led her to my favorite spot overlooking Elliot Bay and the Central City. In the distance, Mount Rainier loomed large and powerful. The weather was unusually perfect.

Too warm for gloves, I thought. *Good.*

"What a stunning view." Penny shielded her eyes with her hand and leaned into me. "The skyline, the Space Needle, the mountain. Gorgeous."

"It's even better at night," I replied. "Tourists crowd this spot. The stars and ferries light up the water and sky. It's like a scene from a fairy tale."

"I'll bet," she agreed.

We stood there for a moment longer. My heart thudded in my chest as I mentally prepared for the next thing. It was important I did this right, because I only wanted to do it once. And I didn't want our future selves disappointed when we looked back. Because I had every intention of growing old with my lucky Penny.

Clutching the little box in my pocket, I pulled it out, flicked it open, took two steps backward, glanced at Dani to make sure she was recording, and dropped to one knee.

"Pen?"

"Mmm? Where did you go—*OH!*" As she turned, her expression changed from dreamy bliss to wide-eyed surprise, and her hands flew up to cover her nose and mouth.

I couldn't see her expression behind her hands. My throat constricted as I took her in, her long sandy-brown hair blowing in the gentle seaside breeze, framing her. Her green eyes shone like the precious gem I held out to her.

"Aspen Ethyl Palmer ... You have been a bright light in my life since the day we met. It's not the coffee I kept going back for—it was you. And I lied to myself for years thinking it was enough to stop in before games and sit and watch you play your harp on my days off. I know this is moving fast, but ..." My eyes burned into hers. I wanted her to know that I meant every word I said, even the next three. "I love you, Penny. I've been falling for you for years, and I was so glad I finally got up the nerve to talk to you. And now ... Now I want to marry you. I want us to be by each other's sides, for the rest of our lives, and help each other fulfill our dreams." Penny let her hands fall from her face, and I voiced my final plea. I dropped my gaze to her mouth, just briefly. I wanted her lips on mine. "Will you say yes, Penny? Will you honor me by letting me be your one person, your life partner, your husband?"

My question hung in the air for what seemed like ages. I held my breath.

"Yes … I … I—" She held out her hand, and I slid the ring on. "I …" With a frustrated huff, she grabbed a fistful of my hoodie, right over my heart, and tugged.

Before I could reach full height, her lips were on mine and my arms were around her. Was Daniella still filming?

I didn't care.

Penny said yes!

CHAPTER 12
Penny

Whoa.

Not whoa. *Wow.*

What was that?! Was it real?

It sure felt real, from the zing of shock to the pterodactyls in my stomach to the giant princess-cut emerald on my finger to that kiss-to-remember.

Which was still happening.

He said he loved you. You should say something.

But it was fake. This whole thing was for show.

Did it feel like it was for show? Why are you still kissing if it doesn't mean anything?

Normally, I'd have pulled away by now, seeing as we were in a public place and his sister was here. But I had big hopes for us, expectations that we would work hard to make our marriage stand the test of time.

I wanted this to be my only proposal, and if Daniella was getting it on video, even better.

When I started to shiver, Xavier extracted his face from mine. "You're cold," he observed.

"Not on the inside," I quipped. I searched his face, looking for a crack in the façade, but I didn't see any. "That felt so real," I whispered, wishing for him to confirm what I felt.

Xavier leaned down to whisper in my ear. "What makes you think it wasn't?" His voice was husky and strong, confident. His eyebrows knitted just for a second as he waited for me to reply.

But I couldn't.

I turned my face to kiss his cheek, his beard, his ear, and leaned my head against his. I didn't have any words. My actions would have to convey my message for now.

Daniella's voice cut through my euphoria. "I stopped recording. We need to go or we'll be running late for lunch."

Xavier's groan rumbled through me, and we parted reluctantly. He took my left hand and brought it to his lips, kissing my knuckles, the ring, and the top of my hair.

We strolled back to the car. Daniella handed Xavier the keys. "There's a few extra minutes if you want to take her around by the arena."

"I'd love to see it," I said. Xavier opened the passenger door for me. I would never get tired of that. For a secret-ish fake relationship, he sure was doing all the things men did in real relationships.

I was getting impatient for the end of hockey season. A part of me wished the Edge *didn't* make it to the playoffs so that we'd have a longer summer together.

Xavier drove around the arena and other notable places nearby. I wished I was here longer and we could go exploring. Another thing to add to my future Want-to-Do List.

We left the city, and Daniella gave me the must-knows about Bellevue, where their home was. When Xavier pulled into the driveway at their multimillion-dollar waterfront estate, I couldn't believe my eyes.

The house—if you could call it that—looked more like a castle than the family's European chateau. It was massive, sprawling at least the length of a hockey rink, with an oversize rounded bump-out resembling a tower on the left side and a six-car garage on the right. You could barely see the water in the distance. Separated from the house and covered in ivy was a small three-story building. A treehouse, perhaps?

The interior was elaborate and expensively furnished. Xavier held my hand as we followed Daniella through the entry rotunda —a rotunda!—past an open seating area with multiple configurations of couches and down a hall toward the rounded tower.

"Zavey!" Xavier's little sisters burst through the archway and into the hall. He gave my hand a squeeze before letting it go to rush toward them and scoop the eight- and ten-year-old girls into his arms, letting them knock him to the ground.

"Aren't you supposed to be in school?" he chided. I stepped away as they climbed on him and giggled as they all unleashed "tickle monsters." I caught Daniella's gaze, and we both smiled.

"Mom says it's a personal day!" Karina shouted, diving at his head to tickle under his chin.

When they seemed worn out, Xavier sat up. "Guess what?"

"What?" they screeched. He pulled them into his lap and looked up at me.

Karina's head turned in my direction. She smiled and shout-whispered to Edyta. "That's *her.* Lucky Penny!"

Edyta looked at me, awe painting her expression, and turned back to her sister. "She's so pretty!"

I held back a smile while Xavier shout-whispered to them. "She's the most beautiful woman in the world. But don't tell Mom or Daniella that I said so, okay?"

Daniella snorted, kicking off more little-girl giggles. Karina and Edyta scrambled off Xavier's lap so he could make his way back to me.

I glanced past the girls to the archway where their parents were standing. How long had they been watching?

Taking a deep breath, I pasted on my best smile and summoned all my confidence. Four new people at one time. I could do this. I fisted my hands in my coat pockets and waited for Xavier to introduce me.

His arm snaked around my back until his hand was at my waist. I mimicked his gesture, unclenching one fist, supporting him as he supported me.

"Mom, Dad, Karina, Edyta ... This is Penny." He bent to kiss my cheek, and the little girls squealed again and fired off questions.

"She's going to be our sister!"

"I want to be the flower girl!"

"No, *I* want to be the flower girl!"

"Can she sleep in my room? We can have a girls' night!"

"No, *my* room!"

"Girls!" Xavier's mother shouted quietly over the din. "Penny is our guest. She'll have her own room. And you'll only go in if you're invited."

"Okay."

"Fiiiine."

I grinned and gave Xavier a nudge toward his parents so we could close the distance.

"Penny, these are my parents, Heinrich and Irina."

I unclenched my other fist and held out my hand to his mother, who looked like she could be Daniella's older sister. "Hi ... great to meet you."

She shook my hand and smiled. "Welcome to our home, Penny. Heinrich and I are happy to have you."

I swallowed and said evenly, "Thank you."

Heinrich Schwann narrowed his eyes at Xavier, but they turned friendly when he set them on me. I shook his hand firmly. I got the impression he was the one we'd have to convince.

We entered the room, and it wasn't what I expected. The section of the tower that faced the front of the house was only a small piece. The rest of the view looked out over the bay, and I was surprised to see my harp and a stool set up in the arc of the windows overlooking the water. This would be a beautiful spot to play in.

Xavier had told his parents that I was shy, and so while they asked me questions over lunch, I wasn't the focus the entire time. The little girls were chatty, and for the most part, I felt comfortable. When dessert was cleared, I poked Xavier and pointed to my harp. He nodded.

"Mom, Dad, would you like to hear Penny play?"

"More than anything!" Karina shouted. "Will you teach me? Opa was going to but ..." She didn't finish the sentence and turned her head sharply toward the window. "Harps are pretty."

"They are," I replied gently, "and they sound pretty, too." My heart clenched. "I'd love to teach you."

"After she plays for us," Heinrich declared, then turned to me. "You play the little bird in the cinnamon tree song?"

I nodded, and Xavier and I exchanged a long, meaningful look.

This was a test.

He pressed his lips to my forehead, and I closed my eyes. The girls giggled. I couldn't help smiling. They reminded me so much of myself and Tasha when we were young.

"What a … beautiful view," I said, settling onto the plush velvet stool.

"We like it," Daniella said.

I smiled at her and looked over my shoulder at Xavier. He gave me a thumbs-up and I turned back to my strings. Closing my eyes, I took in a deep breath to ground myself in the moment, running my fingers along the strings to make sure the instrument was still in tune after its travels. It was, and I began to play Xavier's grandfather's favorite song.

When I finished, the room was silent. My heart pounded as I swiveled around to see their reactions. Tears streamed down Irina's and Daniella's cheeks. Karina stood next to Xavier, her head on his shoulder, wiping her eyes. His eyes were closed. Edyta was on her dad's lap, using the end of her sleeve to wipe *his* eyes.

Daniella recovered first. "Just like Opa." She sniffed. "Thank you."

"Truly," Henrich said, hugging Edyta close. "He was with us. *Here.* With my eyes closed, it could have been him playing. We—" He tipped his chin toward his family. "*You,* Penny, have brought us much joy today. I hope you will consider our home yours. Play anytime you wish. We are honored to welcome you to our family."

Stunned, I swiped at my own eyes. "Th-thank you."

Karina left Xavier's side and tentatively approached me. "Can you teach me now? Please?"

"Of course." I stood and gestured for her to sit. "The first thing to learn is proper posture … sit up straight. Shoulders back

... feet on the floor." I pointed as I named its parts. "This is the base ... the backbone ... the sound bar ... See these levers?"

She nodded. "Do those change the sound?"

"They do, by a semitone. When the levers are down, you get the natural sound of the strings. When they're up, it means the notes are sharp. Flat notes are a little trickier, but we'll get into that later. Now, let's meet the strings ..."

CHAPTER 13
Xavier

Lunch with my family couldn't have gone any better. I was surprised to see that someone had moved the harp from Penny's guest room to the breakfast nook, but it turned out to be more than okay. After Karina's lesson, I gave Penny a tour of the house and grounds.

"It's so beautiful here, even if it's cold." Clouds had rolled in. The sunny morning had given way to a gray afternoon. "That treehouse … how fun! I bet the girls love it."

"They do, especially since I moved out of it."

"You lived in there?" she asked.

"I did, for part of a summer, anyway. After my first season in Palmer City, I stayed for the youth camps at the Plex. Mom's brother and sisters and their families plus her parents were visiting from Calgary. We usually visit them for part of the summer, so it was a big deal that they came here. But I just wanted to be alone. Anyway, I was sore that the Edge didn't offer me a deal then."

"They should have. Noel said Coach Conway was even surprised you didn't get called up."

Her cheeks turned pink, and she looked away. I took the opportunity to tease her. "You were asking about me back then?"

She pressed her lips together, fighting back a smile. "Maybe. I saw you at the Ren Faire one weekend that summer. You tried to

get your teammates to sit and listen to me play, but they weren't interested. You stayed, but you had a frowny face the whole time."

"A frowny face, huh? That sounds about right." I'd sulked most of the summer.

Daniella's car was still parked outside, and she'd left it unlocked so I could retrieve Penny's luggage. When she reached for her carry-on, I stopped her.

"I got it," I insisted. "It wouldn't be right to make my secret fiancée carry in her own luggage."

"App-appreciated." She closed her eyes. "Your s-secret f-fiancée ... appreciates it," she said. Penny opened her eyes but averted her gaze. "I need to practice tonight for B-Bailey's interview. My n-nerves are getting the best of me."

"Hey." I let go of the suitcases and pulled her into my arms, cradling her to me. "Are you okay?"

I'd told her I loved her, and she didn't say it back. I assumed she didn't feel the same. But if that was so, why did she seem bothered now? If she didn't feel the same, fine. I had plenty of time—a lifetime, I hoped—to show her how I loved her.

I stroked her hair and gently nudged her chin. "You're going to do great." I dipped my head so that our foreheads were touching. "Remember the three things."

"B-believe in what I'm saying, re-rehearse ahead of t-time, and v-visualize. And if all else f-fails, f-fake it."

"You've got this, Pen." I pressed my lips to hers for encouragement. "And if you stutter, so what? You wouldn't be the first to flub on live TV."

She sighed. "True. But I d-don't want to think about that. Will you kiss m-me to m-make me forget?"

I caught a movement in one of the second-floor windows. "Even if we're being watched?"

Her eyes widened. "By who?"

"Edyta's in her window. Doesn't bother me."

"N-nor me," she replied.

I cupped her face in my hands and got to work kissing her nerves away.

IT WAS hard leaving Penny and my family. I had to be back at the arena by four o'clock and didn't get back until after midnight. I had a room at a hotel downtown, but I didn't need to be anywhere until ten o'clock tomorrow morning.

After parking Dad's Escalade in the garage, I texted Penny. *Are you still awake?*

Likely not, but a guy could hope. I should have texted her earlier. She'd probably gone to bed early, all peopled out from my sisters.

Yes, in Dani's room. Come by if you want.

My heart leapt. I *did* want. And I wanted a good-night kiss.

Coming up now.

I jogged to the foyer and took the grand staircase two stairs at a time to the second-floor landing, and darted down the hall. I knocked lightly on Daniella's door.

Here, I texted.

Come on in.

I slowly pushed open the door, and what I saw made my heart hurt.

In the best way. On the bed, against a mountain of pillows, my little sisters were asleep, cuddled up to Dani and Penny.

Penny beckoned me to her side of the bed. I squatted to hear her whisper. "I can scootch over a little if you want to watch *The Princess Diaries* with us."

I looked at the big screen mounted over the fireplace. "One of my favorites," I whispered back. With gentle care, she slid an arm behind Karina's back and the other under her knees, easily lifting her up and placing her down carefully closer to Edyta.

Dani gave me a wide smile. "Crashing girls' night again, big brother? You're lucky we like you."

"This is a regular occurrence?" Penny asked as I slid onto the bed next to her. She settled into the crook of my arm and looked up at me. "You're a repeat offender, huh?"

I grinned widely. She wasn't stuttering, and I loved her teasing me.

"Guilty as charged," I confessed, laying a soft kiss on her forehead.

"Hey, no funny business," Daniella warned. "Or you are o-u-t."

"That spells out," Edyta mumbled, her eyes still closed.

I snorted. "You talking in your sleep, Ditty?"

"I'm awake. Just my eyes are tired." She turned into Daniella's side. "Now shhhh, okay?"

"Okay," I promised.

This was absolute heaven. Extraordinary contentment. All my favorite girls, right here.

My family.

I would fight to keep this, no matter what it took.

CHAPTER 14

Penny

All that was missing was Tasha. She would love this. I wished more than anything that Xavier's parents and sisters would come to Colorado for our wedding. Tasha and I could have the girls over to our place. Our pull-out sofa and small screen wouldn't be the same, but we'd still have a great time.

Maybe someday.

When the movie ended, Xavier carried the little girls to their rooms. I hugged Daniella in the doorway. "Thank you for …" I gestured toward her room. "Everything."

"Thank *you* for marrying my brother and saving our family's legacy," she replied, her tone thick with emotion and sincerity. "My parents … they're happy here. They don't feel the same way about Schwannenschloss that the rest of us do. It's our magical fantasy escape. My sisters and I—in our eyes—you're our hero, Penny."

Stunned, I could only stare at her. "I d-don't know what to say." Where was Xavier? I needed to get back to my room before I bawled my eyes out.

"Just say 'I do.'" Daniella wrapped her arms around me. "I'm so glad he chose you."

I felt Xavier's presence behind me. His big heavy arms encircled the both of us. "There was never anyone else," he whispered.

FRIDAY CAME FAST, and amid all the buzz and excitement over the events and rehearsals, there was time carved out for a family skate. I arrived with Xavier's sisters and mom; his dad had a reunion thing to do, so he'd left earlier that morning. There were so many celebrities and athletes, current and retired, milling about, and it was hard not to get caught up in the excitement.

I'd transferred my emerald to the ring finger on my right hand, just in case someone recognized me. It would be easy to put the few pieces together, especially after tomorrow. Bailey was going to interview me before Xavier's Breakaway Challenge. I told her I was nervous, so she promised to stick to the script.

She also told me that the production team would likely seek me out afterward, so if I didn't want to speak with them, I should scurry back up to the Schwanns' box.

I would *scurry* like an Olympic runner, I assured her.

Having been focused on music my entire life, I hadn't spent a lot of time on ice skates. Karina said it was only fair that since I was teaching her to play the harp, she could teach me how to skate.

We agreed to terms—I'd get to skate close to the wall at all times—and she would challenge me according to my ability level.

"That sounds pretty involved," I said. "How do you determine my ability level?"

She shrugged. "I just know."

"All right then."

And so began my skating lessons. I was even skating backward a little bit by the end of the session.

Xavier had shared his time between me and his sisters, hoisting them into the air and spinning and all kinds of tricks, clowning around. It was great to see him having so much fun.

Up in the stands, several of his teammates had arrived with their families. I recognized the Trotters and Lauren Dexter. I blew a kiss to Gabby. She and Noel had flown up with Noel's mom,

Gemma, Coach Conway, and their new baby. I didn't see Coach, though. Probably with some former players somewhere.

It was all wonderful and overwhelming at the same time. I didn't want to leave, but I needed some quiet time to play before the events tonight.

When we returned to the house, I went straight to my harp. The day was overcast, and a blustery breeze created whitecaps on the water. I watched the Schwanns' two boats rise and fall with the waves before turning to my instrument.

I loved my old thirty-four-string folk harp. Made from black walnut, it had been carved from a pew in Palmer City's first church by an ancestor of mine. My grandfather found it when he and his siblings cleaned out the attic in their parents' farmhouse after their mother died. It had been a decoration in my grandparents' living room until I started strumming it as a preschooler.

I set the keys and started with a scale to warm up, and soon the pads of my fingers were moving on their own accord, dancing and plucking and performing soothing, calming melodies. I'd chosen a selection of ballads; the slow tempos always helped to tamp down my nerves and lower my heart rate. Something I loved about the harp was arranging music. A harpist couldn't play the composer's every note on orchestral pieces since there were fewer strings than notes. You could purchase other harpists' arrangements, but I enjoyed composing my own.

I didn't know how long I played. When twilight set in, I stopped so that I could leave the room before dinner. I gathered my tote bag and water tumbler and turned to leave.

I jumped, startled to see Xavier's father leaning against the archway.

"My son has chosen well. And your playing is lovely. Thank you for teaching my daughter. Perhaps you can help me choose a harp to buy for her?"

"Of ... course. Th-thank you?" Of all the things Xavier and I had rehearsed, a one-on-one conversation with his father wasn't among them.

"Thank you, Penny, for all you are doing for him. He is lucky to have found you. It saddens me that it is only temporary to save Schwannenschloss. We like you very much."

I took a deep breath. "T-temporary?" I repeated. My heart crashed at my feet. Had Xavier told him that?

He raised an eyebrow. "Is it not?"

I shook my head. "I hope not. I … c-care about your son very much. We b-both want to make it last."

His brow furrowed. "J.R. said … never mind. So … you want to be part of our family permanently?"

I nodded. "V-very much so."

His worried frown spread into a wide smile, and his whole face brightened. "Welcome to the family, then, Penny Palmer. It is our honor to gain such an outstanding new daughter-in-law." He held his arms out.

The tension between us lifted, and I walked into his hug. Now that he knew how Xavier and I really felt, maybe I could convince him to come to our wedding.

After all Xavier had done for me, I wanted more than anything to fulfill his wish that his family attend our wedding.

CHAPTER 15

Xavier

The Breakaway Challenge was the event I always looked forward to watching the most. It wasn't held every year, so the fact that they'd chosen it this year—and me to participate—was another dream fulfilled. Other all-stars would be competing for fastest skater or most accurate shooting. As a defenseman, I didn't get as many opportunities to shoot; my main job was making sure the opposing skaters' shots were blocked. When my dad finally acquiesced to my playing, he taught me how to be a two-way player and how to play offense without compromising defense. His guidance had definitely played a huge part in my success.

This event was about showmanship. In past years, all-stars had pulled all sorts of hijinks, crafting skits and fancy tricks to shoot the puck at celebrities or retired goalies. It worked out well that my team's netminder had been fan-voted into the Central division's all-star team, and it would make my exhibition even more spectacular.

After I rehearsed the routine in secret, the event coordinator decided I should go last. That was fine with me—leave the audience with something to remember.

I fidgeted on the bench as the other guys executed their shenanigans and tapped sticks with them as they returned.

Dante Leinecker, representing Tulsa, was the second-to-last to

skate. He was one of those guys who treated you like garbage if he thought you could be a threat to him. And he was shady. He knew how to hide illegal hits from the officials.

I watched as he executed his routine, dressed as a football player—sans cleats—clutching a ball under his left arm, holding his stick in his right hand. The Tulsa dance team members were cheering him on, scattered on the ice that was lit up green to resemble a football field. He weaved around them like they were rushing opposition, took possession of the puck and skated it towards the goalie who was defending the right end of the net. At the last second, he slid left. The goalie made a move to cover the other side of the net, and the puck glided in between his pads.

Five-hole goals were always crowd pleasers, and this was no exception. The crowd roared as he dropped his stick and slammed the football into the ice, celebrating like he'd scored a touchdown. I did my best to keep my eyes from rolling into the back of my head. The judges held up their scorecards—three nines and a ten. He gloated all the way back to the bench.

"Beat that, Schwann." He dropped into his spot beside me and didn't bother to hold up his glove for a fist bump. He knew better. "And nice skates. You borrow them from your sister?"

I pinned a hard glare on him through my visor. "Don't mention my sister again—any of them—unless you want to drop gloves." I stood up and fired one more retort. "Let me know how it feels to come in second." I was confident I had a better act. Why else would they have saved me for last?

Now to execute it.

Stick in hand, I skated to the host at center ice as the announcer introduced me to the crowd. The ice crew appeared to sweep the surface and began sweeping the ice with their specialized shovels. I couldn't help smiling at the last three—especially the mini-size final two.

"Xavier Schwann! You've had an incredible year." Karter Padieux, a retired goalie and well-known podcaster and influencer, was the master of ceremonies this year. He was a player I'd looked up to as a kid. He'd been on the Seattle team with my dad when they'd won the Cup and was still a hometown hero.

"It's been memorable, for sure, KP," I replied into his mic. It was hard to see the fans in the stands with all the lights shining in my face. I squinted up toward the box my dad and some of his buddies had sponsored, looking for Penny.

Karter addressed the crowd. "You all may not know this, but I once babysat for Xavier and his sister Daniella. Little Swanny here was a figure skater back then. Hence, what he's got on his feet now. You want to tell us about your skates?"

I grinned. "Thought I'd change it up a bit. Give my ankles a bit of a workout," I joked.

"Can't wait. Speaking of, hold that thought. They're talking to me in my earpiece."

I regarded him curiously. We hadn't rehearsed this. Was something wrong?

"What's that, B-Dex? You do? Sweet! Of course." He flashed a grin at me, then addressed the cameras. "If we could all turn our attention to the right-side tunnel. My associate, Bailey Dexter-Brewer, has brought a good luck charm for Swanny."

Good luck charm? Karter's choice of words threw me off guard.

The spotlights swept over the ice to the gate opening at the entrance of the tunnel where Bailey was standing. "Thanks, KP. We all know I'm a big fan of Swanny and the Denver Edge." The crowd laughed. "And not just because my big brother is an all-star goalie. Or the fact that I work for the team. No sir, no bias here." She gave a slow exaggerated wink and the crowd went wild.

I laughed. I'd known Bailey for years. She was an Olympic gold-winning goalie, and the crowds and cameras loved her. If this bit she'd planned would help me beat Leinecker, I was all for it.

"Swanny, I've got something special for you," she taunted in a singsong voice. "Why don't you skate on over and see what it is?"

I looked at Karter. He shrugged and gestured for me to go.

Bailey stepped onto a small red carpet that had been set down at the edge of the ice and continued to address the crowd. "We all know Swanny's secret to scoring is a toffee coffee from his favorite barista, so … I brought her with me. Please welcome, all the way from Palmer City, Colorado's Coffee Loft, the one and only Penny Palmer."

The crowd roared as Penny stepped out from behind Bailey, wearing my Edge jersey and holding a to-go coffee cup.

Elated, I dropped my stick and gloves and flew toward her. I wanted to pick her up and spin her around, but this probably wasn't the best time if we were trying to still be secretive about our relationship. Forgetting about my toe-pick, I stumbled the last few feet as I came to a halt at the edge of the carpet.

I couldn't get my helmet off fast enough, nor take my eyes off Penny as she handed me the drink. She wore her emerald on her right hand. *Smart*. "Thanks, Pen." On impulse, I leaned in and kissed her on the cheek. "You're amazing," I whispered as I pulled away.

The crowd began to chant, "Kiss! Kiss!"

I grinned, sipped my coffee, and waited for further instruction. Bailey wore a smug expression, and I had no doubt she'd orchestrated this whole thing. She and Brenna were thick as thieves, and both loved to play matchmaker. I trusted Brenna hadn't told her our plans, but I wouldn't be surprised if she'd cooked up this scheme or hinted to Bailey that we were her next "project."

Bailey smiled at the crowd. "Calm down, calm down. Let's not get ahead of ourselves. But maaaaaybe if Swanny wins this competition, Penny *might* consider rewarding him with a kiss?"

Bailey was pushing it now. She held her mic out to Penny, who looked surprisingly unruffled and calm. Had *they* rehearsed *this?*

Penny's eyes locked with mine. "I might," she spoke clearly and flawlessly into the microphone. "Why don't you go win this thing and find out?"

I wanted to win before. But now—there wasn't a snowball's chance I wouldn't give it my all. As the crowd cheered me on, I removed the lid and chugged the coffee.

Penny reached out to wipe some whipped cream from under my nose. "Good luck, Xavier."

"My luck is standing right in front of me." I handed her the cup, replaced my helmet on my head, and skated back to Karter, collecting my gloves and stick on the way.

"Well if that wasn't the most wholesome and heartwarming little gesture." Karter slapped me on the back. "She is pret-ty," he intoned. "Think she'd like an old guy like me?"

I narrowed my eyes at him. "Don't even think about it."

The crowd laughed. I was growing impatient. I'd already taken twice the air time as the other guys, which was an unfair advantage, even if the time was being used by the ice crew to smooth the surface. And now Karter was trying to get a rise out of me?

Nope. I would not play into that.

Karter sighed. "Fine, fine. Are you ready?"

"KP, you of all people know I was born ready for this." The crowd cheered, but I saw only Penny. She'd spoken in front of millions of people—perfectly—to support me. That meant more to me than winning this challenge.

But I still wanted to win. Any and all kisses from Penny were prizes.

"I guess I do! Take your mark, then," Karter instructed. "And good luck."

As I skated toward the dry ice cloud masking the entrance to the tunnel in the opposite corner from Penny, all I could think about was that I wanted us to start our relationship *now*.

Forget about bad luck during the season. I'd already had enough good luck for a lifetime. Penny was marrying me, and that made me the luckiest guy in the world.

And it had nothing to do with coffee.

I was engaged to the woman I loved. Yes, *loved*.

And I couldn't wait to tell her so, in a way that left no doubt that I meant it, unlike the proposal Daniella recorded. Did Penny wonder if that had only been for show or for posterity's sake? I couldn't blame her if she did. I needed to convince her I spoke the truth, from my heart.

She hadn't said "I love you" back to me.

And more than winning this challenge, or the Norris trophy, or even the Cup, I wanted Penny Palmer to tell me she loved me.

More than anything.

I'd earn her love, no matter what it took.

CHAPTER 16
Penny

"You did great!" Bailey assured me.

"Th-thanks." My hands were still shaking. If Xavier won this, he was going to kiss me—*really* kiss me—on live television, streaming all over the world.

There would be speculation.

"Do you know what he's doing for his number?" Bailey asked. "They wouldn't let me into the rehearsal."

I shook my head. "No idea."

The lights dimmed, and a spotlight shone on the dry ice cloud in the left-side corner of the ice. "Officiating for Xavier Schwann's Breakaway Challenge, Coach Zaaaaaaaaaander Conway of the Palmer City Voltage." Xavier's former coach and mentor skated out through the cloud, clad in the black and white stripes of a referee, complete with orange armbands. I grinned, loving that Xavier's mentor could make it with his own team's schedule and all-star festivities.

"And now, introducing your starting lineup for Xavier Schwann's Breaaaaaaaaaaaakaway Challenge!" My eyes were glued to the jumbotron to see who'd come out next. "Xavier has put together his own all-star lineup. Join me in welcoming some familiar faces. At left wing, Atlanta Suns Hall-of-Famer and five-time all-star Liiiiiiiiiiiincoln Dexter! At right wing, retired Denver Edge forward and three-time all-star Roooooooooman

Kubek! At center and holding the record this season for the most points, your current captain and two-time all-star from the Phoenix Wolves, Tristaaaaaaaan Dexter! Keeping it in the family, on defense, Boston Whalers four-time all-star and Hall-of-Famer Harrisooooooooon Dexter! Also on defense, retired Seattle Evergreens captain and three-time all-star Heiiiiiiiiiiinrich Schwann! And in goal, facing off against Swanny, your 2024 Central conference fans' choice all-star and his Denver Edge teammate, Jaaaaaaaaason Dexter!"

I grinned as Xavier's "starting lineup" skated to the red line. He'd stacked his act with family hockey celebrities and his favorite coach. Next to me, Bailey was grinning, and I wondered why she wasn't out there, too. Several women's league and Olympic champions had participated in some of the events this weekend. Why not her?

And ... where was Xavier? I didn't see him anywhere on the ice.

"Ladies and gentlemen." I looked back up at the screen. "The opposing team has pulled their goalie, allowing a sixth skater on the ice!" A familiar tune began as the lights came up, and I recognized the score from *The Mighty Ducks*. I'd played this tune on several occasions for the hockey kids at the Bevvie Bar.

I watched in awe as the men on the ice glided into a vee formation on the far side of the center red line. Xavier explained to me that it was one of the most unrealistic plays in hockey for a bevy of reasons, yet being part of a flying vee had nonetheless been something he'd always wanted to do. Tristan skated backward to form the point of the vee, and a puck appeared at his feet. They skated in formation toward the goal and Tristan passed the puck forward to—Xavier!

What was happening?

Xavier sprinted from the bench and raced to the center of the ice, catching the puck on the tip of his stick. He darted left, right, then left again, setting up for a shot. His stick rose above his shoulders and fell sharply. The puck flew into the air, sailing over Jason's shoulder into the back of the net. *Yes!*

Instead of dropping to his knee like he usually did when he celebrated a goal, Xavier dropped his stick, tossed his helmet and gloves as he skated toward the other guys, high-fiving them and —passing through them?

A spotlight appeared on the other side of the red line, where three of the ice crew were waiting, one adult and two—hold on a hot minute! His sisters!

Karina and Edyta held their arms up while Daniella looked on. Xavier scooped them up, one under each arm, and spun them around. As the spin slowed, the girls touched down and pulled at his jersey and shorts, tearing them away and revealing—*oh my!*

OH. MY.

I lost it. The audience lost it. I was laughing so hard I was crying, vaguely aware of the tears streaming down my face.

Wearing sparkling tight-fitted skating pants and a matching collared shirt with the Edge logo on the back, Xavier picked up speed as he circled the rink, arms extended, on his way back to Daniella. She caught his hands, and they skated as a pair back to center ice, where he lifted her into the air and spun in a slow circle.

I watched in awe as he gently let her back down to the ice and lifted her up again over his shoulder. She gripped his hands as he pushed her up, and her legs stretched out to the side in a split. They skated past the judges in that position, and then Xavier lowered his arms while Daniella brought in her legs and sat on his left shoulder. He wrapped his arms around her shins to secure her and glided back to where Karter was waiting for him.

The ladies in the stands behind me hooted and whistled and screamed their approval.

"Ten! Ten! Ten!"

Karter's face appeared on the jumbotron as the music faded out. Daniella sat coolly on Xavier's shoulder as if she'd been doing it for years, and I remembered she probably had.

"Swanny." Karter looked from him to the spectators behind me. "What was in that coffee?"

The arena erupted in laughter again. This guy should do standup.

Daniella waved at Karter, and he aimed the mic up at her. "KP, I think that coffee had more than luck in it. I think it was made with—dare I say it?" She furrowed her brow for the cameras, in the same way Xavier did. They really could have been twins.

"Say it, say it!" the crowd chanted.

KP shook his head. "Ladies and gentlemen, my former babysitting charge, the beautiful and incomparable national figure skating medalist Daniella Schwann. And what do you think was in that coffee, Dani, if not luck?"

The decibels this crowd was reaching! I needed earplugs.

Daniella turned her head toward the tunnel. "Karter, I think that coffee was made with *love.*"

I stared open-mouthed at the jumbotron.

Bailey tapped my shoulder. "Be ready for that kiss!"

Oh wow. Oh gee. Oh no.

Deep breath, deep breath, deep breath!

Karter nodded his head. "Mm-hmm. I think you're right. Swanny, why don't you go and show her some love with that kiss she promised?"

"Well, I haven't won yet," Xavier said smoothly, his brows lifting and his expression turning into one of sweet concern.

He was so cute when he made that face. I couldn't look away from the screen.

"Let's see what the judges have to say," Karter said. The camera panned the celebrity judges as they raised their scorecards one at a time. "Ten, ten, ten, and a ten plus one to make eleven." Karter turned back to the camera wearing a smug expression as Daniella slid off Xavier's shoulder to the ice.

She gave Xavier a little shove, and he spun on his skate. I pulled my eyes down from the jumbotron to the ice as he neared me. Bailey's videographer hoisted his camera into position, and its red light blinked on.

"Kiss her! Kiss her!" The crowd was relentless.

I stepped to the edge of the little carpet and waited. Xavier slowed to a stop gracefully this time and held out his hands. Goodness, he had to be well over six and a half feet tall with his skates on.

I placed my hands in his and lifted on my toes as high as I could. He leaned down, and our lips met in a chaste kiss. I teetered trying to catch my balance, and the crowd gasped. Xavier gave me a gentle tug to tip me his way, and in one smooth move he scooped me into his arms in that threshold carry he seemed to be a pro at.

His eyes locked on mine, and I forgot all about the cameras and Bailey and the crowd. I reached up with both hands to cup his cheeks and pull his face to mine, indulging both of us and our worldwide audience in a lingering kiss.

Karter was saying something about going to a commercial, but I hardly heard him.

Nor did I care. I was insatiable for this man, and at the moment, right now, we were creating another moment, and I didn't care if the whole world knew it.

Xavier had won the Breakaway Challenge and the hearts of everyone watching what they hoped was the beginning of our love story.

But it was already well underway.

The question was, did he realize it, too?

CHAPTER 17
Xavier

The only good thing about the end of All-Star Weekend was that I didn't have to play on the same team as Dante Leinecker anymore. Who taunts their own teammate? Luckily our celebrity coach for the three-on-three game noticed the tension between us and changed up the lines so we didn't have to play on the ice at the same time. Penny delivered toffee coffees, and I scored in each of the two three-on-three exhibition games.

Penny had become the sweetheart of the weekend. In addition to the coffees and kisses, she'd filled in for the ASL interpreter during the games when he slipped on the ice and broke his arm during rehearsal. I'd never been so proud of her. I could picture her signing at some of the Edge games in the future.

Each night Penny was in town, I skipped the hotel and went home to my parents' house. I didn't want to party or celebrate. I just wanted to be with her and my family. On Saturday, I checked out of the hotel on my way to the arena. There was no point in the team paying for a room I wasn't using for two more nights.

In past years, all-stars were drafted onto four teams. For this year's games, players were separated into our divisions to make up the teams, and then the best Western Conference team would play the best Eastern Conference team in the final.

Our Central division team beat the Pacific team and then advanced to play the Atlantic, who'd edged out the Metro division

by one goal. We'd won that game and the million-dollar prize, but I already felt like a winner. And Jason, with the most saves among the eight goalies, won a hundred grand, which he promptly donated to Beats & Eats, Lauren's philanthropy that fed inner-city kids dinner while high school band members played for them.

Later that night, I kissed Penny at her door and went to find my dad. I owed him an apology.

I paused in the archway of the breakfast nook. Dad was at the window, standing next to Penny's harp, facing the bay. Lights from the ferries and skyscrapers mingled with the twinkling stars to pepper the darkness like the fairy lights I'd hung in my little sisters' rooms.

I cleared my throat to alert him to my presence. He lifted his hand and waved me over.

We stood there a moment, silence hanging thickly between us. Before he could say anything, I needed to tell him how my perspective had changed about his and mom's rush to marriage and how I felt about Penny.

"I get it now, Dad. I get why you married Mom so fast and quit the game before you had to. I—I think I'm in love with Penny."

"I know you are." He patted my shoulder and pulled me into a side-hug. "Your mother told me. She said, 'Heiny, that boy looks at Penny like you look at me.'"

I dropped my chin to my chest and smiled. When I was little, I hated it when Mom called Dad "Heiny" in public. It was awkward and cringy, but Dad was so in love he didn't care.

"Yeah, I do. She's just ... perfect, Dad. Perfect for me. And ... I regret the three years we could have had together if I hadn't been so bullheaded and had asked her out when I first met her."

"Don't regret time lost, son. Regret time *wasted.*"

I looked out at the bay, wishing it was summer and that Penny and I could be married here. "What's the difference? It's all time I can't get back."

He shook his head. "It's not the same. Time lost is unintentional. Time wasted is when you intentionally pass the time with things that do not matter. For me, I wasted time playing hockey when my heart was somewhere else. The game was always a means for me to leave Europe. That life—it wasn't for me. I wanted to pave my own path, build my own castle and little kingdom, not be bound by medieval rules and traditions or my parents' expectations. But that is me. And we—you and I—are different. Just as my father didn't understand me, I am afraid I have failed in trying to understand you."

"Dad, I—"

"Let me finish. You have never done anything with less than one hundred percent effort, or unintentionally. I know that in my heart. I also know that I must let you set your own course, and support it, or you will resent me like I resented my father. I don't want that for us. I don't want you to ever dread coming home. So you and Penny have my blessing. And if you still want us at your wedding, we would be honored to be there."

"Wow ... yes." I was stunned and thrilled and couldn't wait to tell Penny. "Will you be my best man?"

"I would be honored. But—" He sighed dramatically. "I have one condition."

"What's that?"

"Can you please tell Edyta and Karina they can *both* be your flower girls? They've been pestering me for days, and I can't take it any longer."

I laughed. "Of course."

He pulled me in for a hug and patted my back. "Congratulations, my son."

"Thanks, Dad."

I WAS glad to get back to Colorado. The producers of the player spotlight sensed the chemistry between Penny and I, so they asked her if she'd be all right with them filming me arriving for my pregame coffee before our next home game. To my delight, she'd agreed, and we ran through some possible questions they might ask her. Neither of us wanted a repeat of that first time.

The renovation of the Coffee Loft took a few days longer than expected, so we didn't get to film until the eighth of February. The producer thought it would be sweet for me to ask her to be my Valentine, so I'd asked her in advance if that would be okay. We hadn't gone public with our relationship. She wasn't ready to be put in the spotlight, but I didn't want to hide her anymore, either. A Valentine was sweet and common and low-key enough. She'd agreed to that as well.

The day of the filming, I was so giddy I couldn't stand it. Wearing a new suit with a pink tie and armed with a bouquet of pink roses and baby's breath from the flower shop on Main, I pushed open the door to the Coffee Loft and sauntered in.

The place was crowded, but the line wasn't long. The new space on the second level was full. From what I could see below, it looked cozy. Penny said they were taking donations of books, Little Free Library-style. I loved that concept.

I fist-bumped a few kids as I stood in line, catching Penny's eye only about every other blink. By the time I reached the counter, her cheeks were as pink as the roses, which I made a show of dramatically "hiding" behind my back before the camera started rolling.

"Hi," she said, giving the camera and the producer a side glance. "Your usual?"

I nodded. "Yes, please."

She grinned. "Coming right up!"

Gabby rang up my order, and I dropped a twenty-dollar bill in the tip jar. I wanted to leave more, but that's what I'd left that first time, so I couldn't alter the ritual.

I couldn't tear my eyes from Penny as she wrote on the cup. It dawned on me that I might not want to share the message with the camera crew. *Coffee ice cream, butterscotch chips, light roast, whipped cream, sea salt caramel drizzle, toffee crunch bites.*

"Here you go." Penny always handed me the coffee instead of setting it on the counter in the pickup area.

"Thanks." I took the cup, arranging my palm over the message, and held it up to my nose, breathing in the subtle aroma of coffee beans softened by a cloud of sugar. "Perfect. And —" I paused, pulling out the flowers from behind my back with a flourish. "I wanted to thank you for traveling to Seattle to bring me luck there. As you know, I won the Breakaway Challenge and scored twice in each of the games my team played."

"You were amazing," she agreed.

"You're the amazing one." I held up the flowers. "Will you be my Valentine?"

Penny accepted the flowers. "I'd love to."

A cheer went up around us, making Penny jump. I think we both forgot there were people around.

"Here, let's get a quick selfie." I leaned backward over the counter. "For us," I added.

"Okay." She held her flowers to her chest and smiled.

"Got it?" I said to the video guy.

"Got it. Great moment."

I turned back to Penny. *"I'll text you,"* I mouthed.

She nodded and waved goodbye as I walked out. I turned around at the door to blow her a kiss. She caught it in the air and lightly touched her lips.

Yes!

I snuck a glance at the message on the way to my car. Penny had drawn three hearts like those little candies with the messages on them, and written on each: BE MINE, ALL IN, and HAT TRICK.

Challenge accepted.

Twelve more days, and we'd be living together. I couldn't wait to have her by my side and in my life as much as possible.

Both Dad and Penny had opined about wasted time, and they were right. You never got it back.

Three years was long enough to languish.

It was time to thrive.

Together.

As I celebrated my third goal with my linemates at the final horn of the game, hats raining down on us, I thought of Penny first, how she challenged me to be my best in the kindest and most encouraging ways.

Penny was more than the source of my luck.

She was my everything.

CHAPTER 18
Penny

Valentine's Day

Xavier had Valentine's Day off, and I was a little bummed that I'd already agreed to play at the Biddingtons' Sweethearts Ball. But I reminded myself where that money was going and that in a week's time, I'd have all the time with Xavier I wanted.

So we'd had a romantic indoor picnic at his place instead, in the office, which he'd emptied for me to use as a music room. He'd also moved all his workout equipment and desk to the smaller bedroom, leaving the larger one with an en suite bathroom for me.

Xavier kissed me goodbye at my door, and I promised to call him before I went to bed, no matter how late I arrived home. With any luck, I'd be home by eleven, since I could leave after my last set.

I'd earn five hundred dollars tonight, and I planned to give it all to Tasha to help with expenses. The landlord had sent us a letter the other day, thanking us for paying off the balance for the rest of the *year.* We suspected Xavier was our benefactor, but he didn't 'fess up, likely because he knew we'd try to pay him back.

I took one last look in my full-length mirror. I'd braided my hair while it was wet last night and only just now combed out the waves. A faux-flower circlet with long, streaming ribbons sat atop my head, and I'd applied just enough makeup to highlight my features in photos. When I arrived at the venue, I'd cinch the flowy bell-sleeved summer gown with an embroidered vest and add a pink overskirt and my wine-red velvet cloak to stay warm if there was a chill on the stage.

"How do I look?" I poked my head into Tasha's bathroom. She was getting ready for a Galentine's night with her single cheer coach friends.

Her eyes flicked to me in the mirror as she held her curling iron in place. "Stunning, as usual." She smiled as she released the hair on the barrel and wound the next section. "Too bad Xavier won't see you tonight. You'll have all the men's attention on you, for sure."

I frowned. "Maybe I'll leave the cloak on, even if it's hot, then." I'd often had hecklers and propositions at the Ren Faire, but security didn't let anyone near me. I was sure the Biddingtons' event would be the same, but I certainly didn't want to appear provocative.

"Oh, nothing like that," she assured me. "You'll be fine. Trust me." She quickly looked away, back to the mirror and her curling.

That was a curious reaction. "Okay … Well, thank you. I guess I'll be going now. Have fun?"

"I'll try."

Tasha hated Valentine's Day, and I felt bad to skip out on her this year, but I needed that money for her—and to ease my guilt. Marrying Xavier would ensure I had no financial troubles, and Tasha would still struggle. She took the job at the high school for the benefits, which even when added to our parents' health insurance still left a big chunk of monthly out-of-pocket expenses to keep her systems working properly. It felt like she'd always gotten the bad deal our whole lives. I was born a year and a half later and didn't have one health problem to speak of. I didn't count my stuttering in the same category as Tasha's issues.

I gathered up my costume bag and accessories and tied on the heavy cloak. The harp was already in my car. Monty had assured me someone would be waiting when I arrived to help me lug in all my stuff.

The ball had a different theme each February, and the venue always complemented it. This year, the Biddingtons were raising money to fund the renovations of a historical Tudor-style home in Elk Creek Falls on the Colorado Springs border. When the work was completed, it would be open to the public for tours and lodging.

Monty's parents had donated the funds to get the ballroom, electrical, and plumbing ready for the event. Donors and guests were free to don hard hats and roam the building and grounds if they desired to see for themselves where their money was going. A separate silent auction, set up by Monty, would benefit the children's oncology wards at hospitals in the area.

A stage had been built at one end of the ballroom, theater-style, with curtains and everything, and included access to a green room where I waited with the other performers. The band would arrive later, after the dinner entertainment was finished, and I'd get this room to myself while they played.

It was almost like an episode of *America's Got Talent*. Dancers, a singing group, a comedian, a puppeteer, a dog with a ruffled collar who did tricks with his trainer, and to my surprise and delight, The Great Howdidhedini, the magician from the Ren Faire. His bunny was in a basket with a cage-like door on the top, like one might see on the side of cat carriers.

"Penny! Oh, thank goodness you're here!" Howdidhedini waved frantically from his corner. "My wife and son are lost. Can you watch Abby Cabunny while I go find them?"

"Of course. Will she be okay if you're not back by the time I have to play the national anthem?"

He pursed his lips. "Ugh ..."

"I can help," the dog trainer, overhearing our conversation, offered. "It's no trouble."

"Oh, thank you both! I'll be back as soon as I find them."

"Good luck," I replied. "Abby Cabunny will be fine."

I knelt before the basket and peered at the bunny through the opening. "Hey, there, Abby Cabunny. Long time." I held my fingers out for her to sniff. Her little nose pushed at my fingers, nostrils flaring as she took in my scent. "Good girl. It's nice to see you again, too."

I checked my phone as the clock ticked toward the start time of the event. Howdidhedini hadn't reappeared by the time I had to leave to go on stage.

"I've got her. Don't worry," the dog trainer assured me, lifting her out of the basket and cradling her to his chest. She promptly clamped her chompers down on his pocket square. "See?" he asked, gently tugging the fabric out of her mouth. "We're already friends."

"All right. I'll be back in ten minutes or so." With one last look towards the bunny basket, I left for the stage.

On the other side of the front curtain, the emcee was interviewing Monty's parents, who were thanking the donors. I settled onto the stool and waited for my introduction.

The curtains began to separate. I set my shoulders back and closed my eyes as the host asked everyone to remove their hats and stand. "And now please welcome harpist Penny Palmer playing the national anthem."

I could play this song in my sleep. I kept my eyes closed to shut out the distractions. It was just me and the strings until the song ended. After the last note, I opened my eyes and stood to curtsy.

Polite applause punctuated with loud whistling from the back caught my attention as I turned. I wobbled into the curtsy, but kept my balance. My eyes sought the source of the whistles and hoots.

There!

Half a dozen men dressed as Musketeers—in blue tunics in the style from the '90s film version—cheered from a table in the back corner. As I rose, their faces became clear, and I smiled widely.

Xavier and his friends had bought a table! And wow, did they look dashing. Next to him, and the source of the whistling and hooting, was his teammate, Bryce Chambers, pumping his buff arm and wearing a ridiculously fake handlebar mustache. The other teammates had brought dates, and their appreciation was more subdued. Noel and Gabby, Jason and Lauren, Brendan and Brenna, Trask and Kami. They'd all come out to support me on their night off, on their Valentine's Day, at the Biddingtons' stuffy annual gala.

I lifted my hand in a small wave before exiting the stage. I was glad I hadn't opened my eyes; I might have been too nervous to perform.

Once I was out of sight of the audience, I hurried back to the green room to check on the bunny. Surely, Howdidhedini should have returned by now.

But he hadn't, and as the cocktail hour wore on, and performer after performer left and returned from the stage, he still hadn't arrived.

Neither had the band, but they weren't scheduled to set up until dessert.

The event coordinator hadn't had any luck contacting Howdidhedini or his wife, or his mother, who was his emergency contact. We hoped they were okay, but there wasn't anything to be done—and no spare staff to watch the bunny, who was getting restless in her basket.

I'd have to take her on stage with me while I played during dinner. She was quiet and well-behaved, at least from my observations at the Ren Faire and tonight. Maybe my harp would even lull her to sleep. And if not, I'd let her run around a bit in the green room while the band played their first set.

I searched on my phone for what bunnies eat and asked an event staffer to bring me a bowl of water and a plate of lettuce, cucumbers, and carrot tops. There was room in her basket, and if she was eating, she would be less likely to fret.

Ten minutes later, the staffer returned, and I hurried to prep the basket. "Are you ready for a front-row seat to my show, Abby?" I arranged the food and a lowball glass of water from the bar securely into the hay-filled basket.

She blinked her big dark eyes at me and got right to eating. I closed the lid, making sure the latch was secure, and hoisted the basket into my arms.

"Here we go, girl," I whispered as we reached the wings. The main curtain was still closed while the emcee chatted up the crowd. I placed the basket on the side of the stage where I thought the front curtain might cover it from view. Behind my harp, the middle curtain was closed to allow for the band to quietly set up while I played.

The front curtains parted, but this time I kept my eyes open and held my breath.

"Once again, Ms. Penny Palmer to delight you with her soft ballads while you enjoy a feast fit for a king."

The retracting curtain stopped just short of the basket. *Good enough.* I turned to the audience and smiled in Xavier's direction before closing my eyes and letting the music take me away.

I played a variety of Celtic melodies, instrumentals of modern ballads, and mixed in a few lullabies. The hour passed quickly, and when I finished, I was greeted with an even more boisterous response from the table in the back. Many of the attendees rose to their feet, and I curtsied to a standing ovation.

The curtains closed, and the stagehands arrived to move my harp and stool back into the wings. I raced to the bunny basket and carefully crossed back to the other side of the stage, in front of the band and into the wings.

"Are you ready to let loose?" I asked Abby as I entered the green room. "I bet you're stiff and stuffy from being cooped up for so long."

"Oh, I definitely am," said a low, husky, masculine voice. I startled, gripping the handles of the basket tightly.

I knew that voice!

"Xavier!" Just inside the room, he leaned against the wall like he was born for leaning. The man took my breath away. "How did you find me?"

"I bribed Monty with an additional donation." He grinned and bowed deeply, holding on to his hat with its ridiculously large feather. "At your service, milady."

I set the basket down on the floor and opened the hatch. "I want to hug you, but I'm bunny-sitting. Meet Abby Cabunny."

Xavier squatted by the basket. "A pleasure to make your acquaintance, Miss Cabunny." I giggled as he reached in and gently pulled her out. "Bunnies wear diapers?"

I smiled as he set her on the floor. She hesitated briefly, then began to explore. "This one does. Not when she's performing, of course. Just for travel."

"Smart." He scanned the green room. "Besides Abby, are we alone?"

"We are." I stepped toward him. "Thank you for coming and bringing your friends. That was really nice."

He smiled and took my hands, guiding them up, up, up until they were around his neck. I leaned into his tunic and lifted on my toes. Our lips met in a dreamy kiss.

He pulled away too soon. "I was hoping my bride-to-be might want to dance with me to music by my favorite harpist."

I regarded him curiously. "How?"

"With a device from the future called the cell phone, milady." I laughed as he pulled his phone from the folds of the tunic with a flourish. My performance of "(Everything I Do) I Do It for You" filled the room. Our eyes locked as he tightened his arms around my waist. "I thought we needed a song, but then I heard this, and —this is my song, for you."

My eyes stung with unshed tears and my throat was burning, but I needed to speak. I wanted to tell him I loved him.

"Xavier, I—" But I still couldn't voice those three words. Instead, I asked, "How did I get so lucky?"

"That's my line, Lucky Penny." He buried his head into the curve of my neck, and we swayed to the music.

Chicken, I scolded myself.

Tell him at the wedding or whenever. You want a lifetime, right? This man is so smitten, he'll wait forever.

It won't be forever, I argued.

These angel-devil-on-my-shoulder conversations were getting old.

Definitely by the wedding, I promised myself.

CHAPTER 19
Xavier

An alarm went off somewhere inside Penny's skirt, taking us both out of the euphoric cloud we'd been dancing in for the last hour, in between playing with the bunny and me making sure Penny ate some dinner.

"Almost time for my last set," Penny whispered. "Help me wrangle Miss Cabunny?"

"For a kiss." There was a sturdy-looking chair a few feet away. I wasn't confident it could hold me and all Penny's layers—her skirts had to be around fifty pounds by the look of them—but I sashayed us there anyway and pulled her onto my lap.

"Smooth," she praised. "Well, get on with it, Sir Zavey, so I'm not late."

"'Sir Zavey.' Has a ring to it. A proper name for a Musketeer." I decided to try out my really bad British accent. The Musketeers were French, but so what? "I shall defend ye's honor to the death!" She giggled. "Call me Sir Zavey again? I really like it." I batted my eyelashes against her cheek for cuteness points.

Penny grabbed a fistful of my tunic, forcing my head up.

"I love it when your forehead crinkles and your eyebrows do that puppy-dog lift," she breathed. "Kiss me, Sir Zavey."

"As you wish, milady." My mouth closed over hers, and our kiss deepened, heating up with a passion we'd had yet to seek or

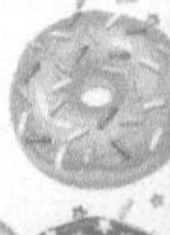

explore. I ran my hand down the length of her silky hair, careful not to knock her flowers out of place.

Six more days.

Six more days. I would do anything for this woman. If she asked me to volunteer at the Ren Faire, I'd do it. If she asked me to buy her the moon, I'd find a way. And if she wanted to play the harp in Viennese ballrooms, I'd spend my life making sure it happened.

The alarm trilled again, and I pulled away with a sad groan. "The lady leaves her admirer for an audience. Lucky audience."

Penny laughed and slid off my lap. She planted a kiss on my nose. "Aw, he doth be jealous! Try to hang on, Sir Zavey. In a week, when my harp is at your place, you'll be my *only* audience. Now round up the bunny while I reapply my lipstick."

"As you wish, Lady Penny. Lady *Lucky* Penny," I amended.

I found Abby Cabunny asleep, snoring lightly, her head resting on the plate of lettuce. She'd eaten all the vegetables. I lifted her carefully so as not to wake her and placed her into the basket.

"Are we supposed to change her diaper?" I asked.

Penny shrugged. "Does it need changing?"

I'd changed my sisters' diapers when they were little. "I don't think so. It's not sagging or stinky."

"I'd leave it for now, then." Penny slid the lipstick tube into her pocket and smoothed out her skirt. "Would Sir Zavey be so kind to carry the bunny basket to the stage? Lady Lucky Penny shall reward him with another kiss if he obliges."

I grinned and bowed deeply, sweeping my arm dramatically and stealing a line from *The Princess Bride*. "As you wish." I picked up the basket and waited for my next direction.

She beckoned for me to follow and led the way through the curtained passage to the wings. Two stage hands were positioning her harp and stool between the front and middle curtains as the emcee gave an update on the money raised and reminded bidders that the silent auction would be closing.

Penny walked past the harp and pointed to a spot for me to set the basket down. I placed it carefully and drew her into my arms, brushing my lips softly against hers so I wouldn't smudge her makeup.

"I'll meet you in the green room at ten thirty," I promised.

"You better," she whispered.

I jogged across the stage, looking back once to flash her a grin. She blew me a kiss and sat on her stool, turning her back toward me. I made it back to the table just as the curtain was opening.

Bryce snickered as I sat down. "What?"

"You're supposed to be my date. Yet you disappear for an hour and a half, lose your hat, and your hair looks like you just rolled out of bed." He leaned in closer, twirling one side of his ridiculous press-on moustache. "Are you seeing someone else?"

I snorted. "Sorry?"

"You've got it baaaaaaad," he drawled with a grin, drawing the end of his mustache into a point. Bryce was from a small town in Arkansas and had held on to his accent, unlike Jason, who'd grown up in Atlanta. His lazy cadence was sometimes singsong, and he often got away with a lot more than most of the guys because even his mean chirps sounded nice or complimentary.

But I knew better.

I sighed, wishing I could tell him everything. "Is it that obvious?"

"Don't need a Harvard education to figure that one out." Brendan tipped his chin at Jason and patted my shoulder. "Or any education," he joked, turning to Brenna. "Ready for more dancing, Bren-naa? This harpist plays the *dreamiest* slow songs." He stood and gave Brenna an exaggerated wink. A smile played at her lips as she took his hand. I caught her gaze, wondering if she'd told Brendan anything about us, and she quickly looked away, tugging him toward the dance floor before he could say another word.

I sighed and settled into my seat. The other couples at the table all headed for the dance floor, leaving Bryce and I to wallow in our singledom.

"You should pursue her, man," he said. "This feeling, watching all the happy couples—it stinks like a hockey bag when your washer's broke."

"But … it's the middle of the season. Past the middle."

"Dude, we're eight points ahead of everyone else in the West. We'd have to totally fall apart to not make the cut. Don't risk yourself falling apart from pining or loneliness for our sake. You're not the only guy on the team, you know. Coach could pull you and we'd be fine. At away games, anyway."

"Thanks a lot," I grumbled. I still had terrible stats at away games. I hoped that would change once Penny and I were married. I wondered if I could convince her to fly out for some of them. Especially during the playoffs. If we stayed in first place, we'd have home ice advantage in the playoffs, so we technically could lose all our games on the road *if* we won all the home games.

But who wanted to take that risk?

"Just giving it to ya straight," Bryce said.

"I know. Hey, you don't have to sit here with me and be miserable. That redhead a few tables over has been giving you the eye."

He shrugged. "Maybe later."

"Okay then." I swiped my phone to record and closed my eyes as Penny's melody changed to a familiar animated movie ballad. I'd watched *Tangled* with my sisters at least a handful of times and knew all the words to "I See the Light." I sang them in my head as she played, feeling every lyric.

Penny had shifted my world, lifted the fog I'd been living in, and warmed me up to what my life could be like with a significant other that fit with me, how and who I was. I'd been blind, and she'd opened my eyes to the light that was *love*.

One question remained. Did *she* see *that* light, as I did? Was it crystal clear to her that we were meant to be together?

A collective "aaawww," followed by a shriek from the direction of the stage, snapped me out of my thoughts. The music stopped, and I jumped to my feet to make sure Penny was okay.

The diaper-clad Abby Cabunny was center stage, hopping this way and that and obviously terrified. Penny fell to her knees, crawling slowly toward the bunny while onlookers did nothing to help.

I raced out of my chair toward the stage. How had this happened? I'd closed the basket and—I groaned. Had I latched it?

I think I knew the answer to that question.

The scene unfolded slowly. The couples on the dance floor

gasped as the bunny hopped off the stage. Penny's look of horror spread across her features, the same reaction as that day Adri Delicata shoved a microphone in her face.

Except that day was about *my* career. This bunny on the loose was messing up *her* performance and could have serious ramifications. People talk, especially in wealthy circles, and I could imagine the last thing she wanted to be remembered for was being the harpist whose performance was ended by a bunny.

A tiny boy in a tux ran out onto the stage. "That's my bunny! Abby! Abby Cabunny, come baaaaack!" He started to cry.

Where'd he come from? And where was Whotheheckdoneitdini or whatever his name was?

Penny looked between the boy and the bunny's jumping-off spot. "I'll get the bunny!" I shouted. She nodded and held her arms out toward the boy. He ran into her arms as the couples began to disperse, forming a wide circle around the bunny.

A man wearing a modern top hat and cape over his historical costume shouted above me on the stage—was this the missing magician?—berating Penny for letting the bunny escape. She didn't say a word, just rocked the crying boy in her arms.

My Musketeer brothers appeared in the circle, evenly spaced, and I signaled to them to tiptoe toward the bunny, slowly. We closed in, and I lifted my tunic away from my body, ready to use it as a blanket to capture her.

The poor thing was quivering so violently I was worried she'd go into cardiac arrest. "C'mon, little Abby." I held my hand out. Her nose twitched, her eyes darted, and she leaped.

I caught her in my tunic and pulled it snug around her. Bryce whooped, and the crowd applauded. I glanced up at the stage, where security was pulling the irate magician offstage. The little boy clung to Penny, tangled himself in her hair—

Tangled.

I caught her gaze and twisted my face into my very best attempt at a smolder.

She didn't smile. Instead, she stood, adjusted the boy in her arms, and darted offstage.

My heart plummeted to the floor. I tightened my grip on the

wiggly bunny as I reached the stairs at the side of the stage. I paused to let Gabby cut in front of me as she took off after Penny.

Bryce and Noel waited for me by the stairs while I returned Miss Cabunny to her basket behind the curtain. This time I made sure the latch was secure. Instead of following Penny to the green room, I went back down the steps and joined my teammates.

On stage, Penny's harp was being carried off, and I could hear the band's movements behind the middle curtain. I guessed she was done for the night.

"Nice job catching that thing." Bryce tapped a finger on the basket. "You'll be okay, little bunny-boo. Where did it come from, Swanny? I don't remember a magician."

"He never showed up." I didn't care that my voice had an edge to it. "He left Penny to bunny-sit, and she didn't want to leave Abby here alone in the green room. I'm the dummy that didn't latch the basket."

"Ah. Well, if you don't need me anymore, I guess I'll take off. Good luck." He clapped me on the back and bro-hugged Noel.

"Coming with me?" I asked.

"Yeah." Noel followed me out of the ballroom and down the hall to the green room's door.

I nodded to him to open it, and we entered. The magician was arguing with security, Gabby was securing the harp into its case, and Penny was in a corner with the boy, rubbing his back.

"We are going home! With the bunny!" The Great Whatshisnamedini shouted at the two police officers and fixed an angry glare on me. I set the basket down by the door and hurried over to Penny. She whispered something into the boy's ear, and he left her lap to go check on the bunny.

I offered a hand to Penny to help her up, but she shook her head, using her fingers to comb out the knots in her hair. Her eyes were red and puffy.

I wanted—no, needed—to kiss all of that sadness away. I squatted beside her. "What can I do?"

"N-nothing, th-thank you," she whispered. Her face contorted like she was going to cry again. She looked past me, and I turned to see Gabby standing above us, her hand extended toward Penny. Penny took it, and Gabby hoisted her to her feet.

The snub stung. No one in the ballroom could possibly know or think that Penny was at fault for what had transpired. From my view, it was all the magician's doing.

"Pen?" I asked, pleading for her to let me comfort her or help.

"Xavier, p-please, I … have to g-go. I'm s-so em-emb … barrassed."

"Penny, I'm so sorry. This isn't your fault. I didn't latch it, and the magician—"

"I kn-know. B-b-but I—puh-please. All th-the ph-phones … re … cording. I … L-let me g-go. I … need … to b-be al-lone."

"I got her, Xavier," Gabby said from behind me. "Penny? Let me drive you home."

Penny nodded and turned away. I wanted to fix this, make it better. She was stuttering again, and it was all on me. I'd taken a perfect day and turned it into a bad memory.

Noel got the harp, and I gathered up all her other stuff, plus my hat from the floor behind the chair. A heavy sense of dread descended upon me as we loaded it all into her car.

Penny avoided looking at me as Gabby backed out of the parking space. I lifted my hand to wave anyway and watched the car get smaller until the taillights vanished into the night.

"She'll be okay." Noel clamped his hand on my shoulder. "Just text her that you love her and give her time to respond."

I turned to him in surprise. "Love her?" I was surprised to hear that from him. He'd known me well enough to know that Penny and I hadn't been secretly dating like I might have implied when we announced our engagement to her family. Lucky for me—and I thank the emerald—he didn't push me for an explanation.

Noel shook his head with a short laugh. "You two couldn't hide it if you tried. I don't know what your story is, but the feelings are there, on both sides."

"Thanks. It's quite a story and not one we're ready to share."

"No problem from me. I need to go get Gabby's stuff. See you at morning skate."

I shuffled to my car, feeling sorry for myself. We had a home game tomorrow. Would she show up to make my coffee?

If she didn't, then I knew we were in real trouble.

She wouldn't back out of marrying me, would she?

I honestly didn't know. The bunny incident didn't seem like a deal-breaker, but if she thought it could harm her reputation as a musician …

I had to fix this.

ASAP.

CHAPTER 20
Penny

Luckily, Tasha wasn't home yet when Gabby and I arrived. The last thing I wanted was to hear her harangue me about how all guys were awful and then proceed to list how her exes had done her wrong, coming full circle to all the ways Monty had annoyed her since childhood.

As annoying and rude as Monty was, he'd sat with and stuck by his Nana Booboo (so dubbed for fixing all his boo-boos as a rough-and-tumble toddler) and pushed her wheelchair out onto the dance floor, where he entertained her with his corny moves. When the bunny escaped, he'd quickly maneuvered her out of the crowd to safety. From what I could see, he was only ever rude to Tasha. Whatever was wrong between them ran deep, and I didn't have any intention of getting in the middle of it.

After a long shower and combing out my tangles, Tasha *still* hadn't arrived home. I hoped she was having a nice night. I picked up my phone to text her a good-night-stay-safe message and saw a whole bunch of texts from Xavier.

I sighed. I should have expected him to want to make sure I was okay, but I still wasn't used to being one half of a loving relationship.

Loving.

I sure hadn't acted like I loved him when everything fell apart tonight.

His carelessness had caused the chain reaction that ended my performance early and on a bad note. And then Howdidhedini lashed out at me—that wasn't right, either, but his wife and son had been in a car accident. She'd broken her arm and was still at the hospital. I couldn't blame him for being so upset. Luckily, their little boy remembered me and had let me comfort him. I'd offered to bunny-sit, but the boy was already so distraught, all he wanted was his Abby Cabunny.

I texted Tasha, then scanned my messages.

Gabby: *I texted Jannell. She's okay with me opening tomorrow if you want to take my afternoon shift. Let me know so I can set my alarm.* I texted her back yes, and thanks.

Xavier: *I'm so sorry about tonight. I ruined a perfect Valentine's Day, and I wish I could make it up to you. I love you, Penny. Please tell me I can fix this.*

I sank onto my bed. I'd almost told him tonight that I loved him. I wished I had when I had the chance. After tomorrow's home game, the team was leaving for a road trip and wouldn't be back until late on the nineteenth. We wouldn't be alone again until our wedding night.

Our wedding night.

Six nights from right now. I looked around my room, and the reality hit me like the stone wall Mrs. Howdidhedini had skidded into.

My life was about to change drastically. I didn't feel ready to leave Tasha. I was still in college. How was this going to work?

We'd made all the plans, but were we really ready to live as a married couple? Neither of us wanted to fake it, and with the way we'd grown to love each other, a business arrangement was out of the question.

But was I—were *we*—ready for … well, the *wedding night*? And other things.

I wasn't.

Suck it up, Penny. You committed. That ring you're wearing on the wrong finger—remember that?

Oh, leave her alone. She's confused. Give her time to process. It'll all work out.

"Will it, though?" I asked my angel-devil voices. "How can you be sure?"

Silence.

I sighed and swiped at my phone to text Xavier back.

Nothing to fix. I'll see you at the Coffee Loft tomorrow. Text me when you're on your way.

I'M ON MY WAY.

My heartbeat kicked up a notch as I read Xavier's text. He was early today.

Be careful, I replied. *It's raining pretty hard.*

"Is that him?" Gabby asked.

I nodded. "I'm going to make his coffee now and sneak him into the kitchen for a minute when he gets here. Cover for me?"

She grinned. "You bet."

I'd brought my calligraphy marker with me and took my time writing today's message on the cup. *Lady Lucky Penny* ♥*'s Sir Zavey 4-eva*

I quickly covered the message with my palm and set to work. *Coffee ice cream, butterscotch chips, light roast, whipped cream, sea salt caramel drizzle, toffee crunch bites.* Done.

I'd also packed him a little red box with some of our toffee sugar cookie fudge for his road trip. My hands full, I scooted behind Gabby toward the kitchen.

The outside door opened, and Xavier ducked his head in. The troubles of being six feet five. His feet must hang off the bed, poor guy.

Don't go there.

I took him in from head to toe before he noticed me. His newsboy hat was perched on his head, and the collar of his overcoat was turned up to keep his neck dry. A convention of hummingbirds fluttered in my stomach, stealing my breath as his gaze swept the counter and finally found me.

I nodded towards the door behind me and backed into it, indicating he should enter the kitchen.

He grinned and was through the door in a few giant steps.

"I remember this place." He leaned toward me and then caught himself. My shoulders sagged. I must have done quite a number on him last night if he was scared to kiss me in private.

"I ..." My breath whooshed from my lungs. Where were the words I wanted to say? They were in my head last night. I willed them to come back.

Frustrated at myself, I handed him the coffee. "Read."

The eyebrows did their lifty-magic, and the hummingbirds turned to lava. Why did he affect me like this?

Because you love him!

And he loves you!

The voices in my head taunted me as Xavier turned the cup to read the message.

His eyes widened, and then *he* sucked in a breath. "You love me?"

I nodded. "I do. I love you. It feels so right to say that out loud. I—I'm sorry it took me so long to say. I wanted to say it ages ago."

"You did?"

"I did. I am madly in love with you, Xavier, and it scares me a little."

He took the coffee and package from me and set them on the counter. Then he cupped my face in his hands and pressed his lips to mine. His hat slid to the side and off his head, but as per our usual fashion, neither of us made an attempt to catch it.

I wasn't in charge of my hands anymore. My fingers found his silky black hair and laced themselves deep within it. *So soft.*

When I felt like I couldn't breathe anymore, I turned my head and burrowed into his chest, not caring that his scratchy wool coat was rough like sandpaper on my cheek. I needed to breathe and I needed to be in his arms and I needed to tell him I loved him again.

Our breathing synced, then slowed.

"Five days," he said thickly. "In five days, we can kiss as long as we want to. You should up your cardio so you can keep up. I can skate a forty-minute game, you know. Once we're alone, I promise to kiss you for *much* longer than that."

And there went my heart rate again. A thousand beats a minute, for sure.

"You better." I picked up his hat and stretched to set it back on his head.

He pressed his lips to mine one more time. I handed him his coffee and fudge and backed into the door so he could leave, then rushed to safety behind the counter and waved goodbye.

Gabby leaned in to me and spoke quietly into my ear. "Your hair's a mess, and your lips are swollen."

My hand flew to my face, and I dashed back into the kitchen, her laughter ringing in my ears. I hoped no one else noticed that I'd been kissed so … thoroughly.

CHAPTER 21
Xavier

I was getting married.

Today.

To my lucky Penny, who'd hardly spoken to me, in the three-plus years I'd known her, until two months ago.

How was that possible?

Because she's the most remarkable person you've ever met.

That was true, one hundred percent.

And my family was here. Penny had won them over, and they were *here*. My father went from "dragging that sweet shy girl into a life she never asked for" to "welcome to the family."

There was one person missing, though, and his absence was a glaring hole. I had no doubt Opa was looking down on us from Heaven, quietly smirking. He'd been speaking to me in my head since I woke up.

See, Zavey-boy? It all vorked out. You commit to your voman and you vill have someone other than yourself to play for. Next level of success. You are not like your father. You vill balance hockey and family because you love both.

I did. I loved hockey, and I loved Penny. With everything I had. I'd make it all work.

And I'd start by being her Renaissance fantasy guy. The fire in her eyes wasn't lost on me when she saw me in my Musketeer tunic and hat.

If I knew Penny as well as I thought I did, her dress would be historic or historically inspired. She'd told me she only wanted to do this—get married—once. I took a gamble and left my tuxedo in my closet and bought a costume instead, paying extra for the rush job from a Renaissance vendor in Denver. When Mom texted me pictures of Karina and Edyta's dresses, I was confident I'd made the right choice.

Now to wow Penny like I knew she was going to wow me.

The ceremony was at 9 a.m., two hours before Brewski's opened, so there shouldn't be any traffic in the vicinity, except for the restaurant staff. Luckily, Brenna's wedding barn was set far back from the road.

I'd barely slept three hours, but I was confident my adrenaline would carry me. The power nap on the flight back from Tampa would have to be enough. We'd won, and I'd contributed with two assists. I still hadn't scored in a road game, but at least I was racking up points.

"You look ridiculous."

I grinned into the mirror. My dad stood in the doorway, and he'd been shaking his head with every piece of clothing and accessory I'd added to my ensemble, all in different shades of blue. The tights, the striped poofy short pants, the pirate-style shirt. The embroidered brocade vest. The cape over one shoulder. The codpiece. I'd skipped the ruffed collar. I needed freedom to move my head so I could kiss Penny properly.

"Don't forget your sword." He handed me the saber and burst into laughter.

I couldn't hold a straight face and joined him.

"If my father could see you now," Dad roared. "Zavey-boy!" His impression of Opa gave me chills. "Zavey-boy, you make your Opa proud. Unlike my vayvard son, running off to America and forgetting all I taught him."

"Aw, Dad. Opa was proud of you, too."

He shrugged. "Maybe, maybe not. Still, a man has got to live his own life. And you are doing that. I'm proud of *you*."

Dad wasn't supposed to be the one choking me up today. "Thanks. I'm so glad you're here."

"Me, too. You ready?"

"More than ready."

In an effort to further ensure the secrecy around the wedding, I'd hired two stretch Escalade limos, one black, one white. The first would collect me, Dad, and Penny's extended family in one of the outer parking lots behind the mall. The other limo was at a resort in Colorado Springs where my family was staying. Mom and my sisters, along with Penny, Tasha, and their parents, would arrive twenty minutes after the rest of us. I'd also rented large privacy screens for each side of the barn doors to ensure no one with binoculars or a wide lens could see who was climbing out of the vehicles' jet doors.

Just after eight thirty, our black limo pulled up to the screens at the barn entrance. I was the last person out and hurried inside ahead of Dad, who fell into step behind me. For a small wedding in between other events in the middle of the week, I wasn't expecting the degree of elegance Brenna had coordinated. Sheer fabric swooped in arcs from the beams above us, chandeliers sparkled, and each table had a floral centerpiece of roses in pink and red tones. Only two tables were fully set, one on each side of the long white carpet that led to the dais where Penny and I would say our vows and exchange rings.

I took my place next to Brenna's father, Quinn, who was a licensed officiant and knew how to keep a secret. He assured us he'd performed more than a few secret weddings over the last few years. We posed for Claudia who was photographing and recording the ceremony.

"They're here!" Brenna announced.

Dad waited at the door to escort Mom and Daniella to their seats and then joined me on the dais. "You're sweating," he observed, pulling a handkerchief from his pocket. "May I?"

"Thanks. I think it's the hat," I joked.

"Sure." He dabbed my forehead and the back of my neck as the music began. Penny had chosen a recording from a string quintet she knew from the Ren Faire.

Edyta was first through the doors, dramatically stopping to pose and raise her arm every few feet and let the petals flutter to the ground. Trailing her, Karina opted for a more traditional petal toss, sprinkling them as she walked. Each wore a circlet of white flowers over their long dark hair, ribbons trailing down their backs. Their white satin dresses featured light blue ribbons that crisscrossed from the neckline to the waist and tied in a bow. The wide, bell-shaped skirts brushed the carpet, and I held my breath, hoping neither would trip.

Karina went to her seat next to Daniella, but Edyta climbed up the steps to the dais and dropped a handful of petals at my feet.

"For good luck!" she explained. "Why are you dressed so funny?"

"Thanks, kiddo. I'll explain later." She grinned and hurried to her seat. Tasha was halfway down the aisle, wearing a long-sleeved sheath dress with puffed sleeves in the color of my sisters' ribbons.

My blue-tone ensemble had been a good choice indeed.

Tasha climbed the steps, her eyes sweeping me from head to toe, smirking as she turned left to take her mark.

Yeah, I looked funny. So what? All that mattered was what Penny thought.

The music paused, and I immediately recognized Penny's rendition of "(Everything I Do) I Do It For You." She must have recorded it while I was away.

Everyone stood, and I took the opportunity with their backs to me to rub the water from my eyes. The barn doors slid open, and my bride stepped inside.

It took all my effort not to break down weeping.

Good thing Claudia was taking pictures. I needed all the pictures. In frames, all over my apartment. Durable frames for travel. Prints to tape to my sticks and inside my helmet.

I wanted to tattoo the image of Penny in her wedding dress to the inside of my wrist so I could have her with me and kiss her for good luck before every game.

I forgot about my watery eyes as she neared me. Penny's long hair cascaded in thick spirals down her back, under a crown of flowers and a sheer veil. The corseted top flared out from her waist to the floor, and her long, lacy sleeves trailed up her arm to satin poofs like a fairytale princess's.

Her parents met her a few feet from the dais, and each took an arm, guiding her the rest of the way to the steps.

Mine. Gimme.

I didn't even bother to scold my inner caveman for his uncouth nonsense.

Penny shifted her bouquet to her left hand. Her dad took her right hand in his and brought it to his lips before holding it out to me. In one giant step, I was at the stairs, with her hand in mine, holding it tightly as she climbed the steps.

Not to be outdone, I also kissed the top of her hand. Penny passed her bouquet to Tasha, and I quickly captured her free fingers in mine. *Mine.* I brought both of our joined hands to my lips and kissed each of her knuckles. *Mine.* I liked this version of *knuckies* way better than fist-bumping my teammates.

And I kissed her emerald. For good luck, of course. It was back on her right ring finger, just for the ceremony, she explained. That way the wedding band would be the closest ring to her heart when she returned the emerald to the left ring finger.

Penny smiled up at me, and I dropped my forehead to hers. "I love you," I whispered. "You … You're stunning."

She turned her head to whisper in my ear. "I love you, too. And you're … I don't know … Handsome doesn't begin to describe how dashing you look, and there's a burning in my belly I've never felt before."

I turned my head quickly to capture her lips in a pre-vow kiss. She laughed quietly, and we settled back into our forehead-to-forehead position.

I didn't care if I got a crick in my neck from stooping.

The song faded out, and Quinn began the ceremony. "Dearly beloved, family and friends, we are gathered here to witness Xavier and Penny pledge their love to one another and seal their commitment spiritually and legally. Marriage to the one you love can be the most fulfilling promise one makes in their lifetime. Matrimony is a commitment of the heart, of time, of resources, and of trust. It is a promise to yourself and to your partner to work every day, side by side, to create a life together and thrive in it. Today, Xavier and Penny will commit themselves to love the other and to receive that love in return.

"The bride and groom have written their own vows. Xavier,

this will be one of the only times it is not proper to let your lady go first."

Quinn gave an encouraging nod, and I turned my head to Penny. I couldn't remember a word of what I'd written. I squeezed my eyes closed, fighting the old fears of stage fright and willing my carefully crafted words to come back to me.

I felt my hands rising and opened my eyes to find Penny drawing them to her lips. She kissed each knuckle, giving me time to find my thoughts.

The words rushed forth like a skater on a breakaway. When her lips touched my last pinky knuckle, I gently tugged our hands back in my direction and laid them over my heart.

I took her in.

Beautiful wasn't adequate. She reminded me of a winter fairy, an angel from my dreams. Her grace, the way she carried herself, the kindness in her eyes, the generosity of her spirit, so willing to take a chance on me to save my family's legacy.

I was lucky indeed.

"Penny. My lucky Penny." My breath stalled in my throat, and I gulped for air. The feelings I had for her were real and tangible, and I needed to get through this without crying. Forcing down the softball-size lump in my throat, I began again.

"You are the melody of my soul, a song that has inspired and enriched my life in ways I never anticipated. As we embark on this journey together, I promise to cherish and honor you and celebrate the unique harmony we create together. With each beat of my heart, I promise to love you more deeply than the depths of the ocean and higher than the tallest mountain peak."

There. I did it. All the words. All the feels. All the … everything.

Penny began to speak, as clearly as I'd ever heard her. "Xavier … my dashing Musketeer in troubadour's clothing … My protector, my encourager, my biggest fan. You chose me, Xavier, and I made a promise to choose you back. Today, tomorrow, and for every day to come. Through the good times that bring us closer, the hard times that threaten to break us apart, and all the ordinary days in between, I'm all yours."

Not one stumble. No pauses needed. Her words flowed mellifluously, smooth and sweet like honey.

"The rings, please," Quinn requested. My dad handed them to him and Quinn held them out to us. "These rings symbolize eternal love. They are a physical reminder of the commitment and love between Xavier and Penny. May they also be symbols of the vows they have made to each other and a source of comfort and strength."

I took Penny's ring from Quinn and slid it on her finger. We'd written this part together, she and I, but I'd added something to the end. "Penny, I give you this ring as a token of my love, as a promise that I choose you forever. All that I am and all that I have, I offer to you with joy and fidelity. With this ring, I thee wed. With this ring, I promise that from this day forward you will not walk alone nor ever lack for love ... or an audience to your soul-lifting music."

Penny slid my ring on and recited the words. "Xavier, I give you this ring as a token of my love, as a promise that I choose you forever. All that I am and all that I have, I offer to you with joy and fidelity. With this ring, I thee wed. With this ring, I promise that from this day forward you will not walk alone nor ever lack for love ... or a toffee coffee in your time of need."

My grin widened. *Perfect.*

We looked at Quinn. "By the power vested in me by the state of Colorado, I now pronounce you husband and wife, Baron and Baroness von Schwann, and as I've been advised by the bride, Sir Zavey and Lady Lucky Penny." I laughed. Penny must have added that part. "Xavier, you may kiss your bride."

"Baroness?" she whispered.

"Mm-hmm."

"Right. Well. That's going to take some getting used to."

"You've got your whole life," I whispered, lowering my mouth to hers. I dipped her into a Broadway-worthy kissing pose and took my time amidst the "aws" and applause below us. Then, hand in hand, we stepped down to the floor to take pictures and accept congratulations.

Brenna and Claudia had set up a hot breakfast buffet. Dad gave a mimosa toast, and Tasha had us in tears with her touching big-sister speech. Not to be outdone, Edyta asked for the mic and told everyone just how great her big brother was, including the time I'd taken care of her when she'd had food poisoning.

"I pooped all over him and he didn't even get mad!" She looked over at me, and I grinned back at her. "Hey, Mommy!"

"Yes, sweetheart?"

"Everyone here is family now, right?"

Uh-oh. I was pretty sure I knew what was coming. I caught Brenna's eye and tapped my ears.

"We'll cover our ears!" Brenna shouted behind the buffet table. She and Claudia made a big show of placing their palms over their ears.

"Okay. Since you're family ..." Edyta twirled a lock of hair around her finger and looked at each of the Palmers—and Noel—in turn. "I have to tell you our secret family words. In case there's an emergency."

I looked at Penny, and she lifted her bouquet to cover her face. My parents and Daniella also covered their mouths with their hands. Karina seemed unbothered.

"Are you ready?" Edyta leaned forward. "I'm going to whisper it, okay?"

Everyone nodded their encouragement.

She whispered into the microphone. "If there's an emergency or a stranger with a message, you know it's real and safe if they say these words." She paused and took a breath. "Loopy doopy poopy schmoopy."

Silence. Then a giggle from Karina. Edyta began laughing, and then everyone was joining in. "I'm serious! Ask my mommy!" More laughter. She rolled her eyes and turned toward me and Penny. "Can we have cake now, please?"

We'd opted for a tower of sea-salt-caramel-filled toffee-crunch-topped cupcakes from the bakery, a nod to my favorite doughnut and the coffee that had brought us together. Feeding each other cake was a tender moment, and suddenly I was anxious to leave.

All that was left was the bouquet toss. Despite the intimate gathering, Penny insisted, and our sisters and Gabby gathered on the dance floor, Daniella and Tasha standing way back and looking unimpressed. The little girls stood at the front, and I'd assumed Penny would throw to one of them. Or, if she couldn't decide, to send it toward Gabby, who was marrying Noel in June.

"Ready?" I held Penny's hand as she climbed up on the chair Claudia had set out. "One! Two! Three!" She slid the ribbon holding the flowers together off the stems and one bouquet became two. Twisting around, she tossed one straight to Gabby and hefted the other one at Tasha.

My little sisters groaned, and both Gabby and Tasha promptly gave up their bouquets to the girls. I didn't miss the exchanged glances between Penny and Daniella, though.

This toss had been premeditated.

Shady.

I liked it.

I reached up to gather Penny in my arms, cradle-style. It was our thing. "Sneaky move, Baroness."

She giggled and tapped me on my nose as I set her onto the floor. "I don't know what you're referring to, milord."

I leaned closer to whisper in her ear. "Call me that again when we're alone?"

She snorted. "Maybe."

I leaned in. "You ready to get out of here?"

"More than ready."

"Time for the send-off!" As if she could read my mind, Tasha signaled to Karina and Edyta. They ran to their flower girl baskets and pulled out little bottles of bubbles, passing one to each guest and shooing everyone toward the barn doors.

A bubble send-off?

I looked at Tasha in confusion. This wasn't part of the plan.

"We're all squeezing in one limo because ..." She sang, then gestured for my dad to finish her sentence.

My dad appeared beside her and handed me an envelope. "You two have reservations at the Honeymoon Tree House at the Top of the Falls Resort."

"No way!" Penny squealed. "But—I have to pack!"

"No, you don't," Tasha said. "I raided your moving boxes. Your suitcase, with everything you need, plus a cooler of snacks, is already in the white limo."

"And I may have raided your closet last night before you arrived home," Dad told me. "Your suitcase is also in the white limo."

"Thanks, Dad." I was touched.

He patted my back. "Your schedule is rough, kid. Be sure to take a proper honeymoon when the season ends, okay?"

"Deal." We shook hands, and he pulled me into a hug. "Love you, Dad."

"I love you, too, Zavey. *Baron* von Schwann." He patted me on the back. "Now get out of here."

I laced my fingers through Penny's and brought her hand to my lips. "Yes, sir!"

CHAPTER 22

Penny

The Honeymoon Treehouse above Elk Creek Falls was everything I imagined it'd be.

Even in winter, the views were stunning, the sunset was magical, and the company ... perfect. Cuddled up under a heavy blanket in the cozy window seat in my fleece leggings, oversize turtleneck sweater and fuzzy socks, I wanted to take in every detail, minor to major, and imprint it in my memory.

We'd had a lovely afternoon smooching over board games, and a surf and turf dinner of steak and lobster had been delivered after sunset. I'd destroyed Xavier at Scrabble, and he'd sunk all five of my battleships before I could get one hit on his. We were pretty evenly matched at Scattergories and abandoned the game when we tied it up over a music category that led to a slow dancing marathon that led to an even longer kissing marathon.

A storm was coming in overnight. The resort manager had delivered personal-size premade breakfast casseroles we could warm on the gas stovetop, in case the power went out or the four stories of steps to the road below were buried.

While Xavier stoked the fire, I waited for him to return to me. The side wall had temporarily replaced him as my lean-to in the window seat. Snowflakes fell from the patchy cloud cover, gliding down into the darkness, catching light from the moon and stars as they disappeared into the water and treetops. It was chilly in the window, but I wasn't ready to lose the view—or the moment.

I leaned forward to allow Xavier to retake his spot behind me. I relaxed into him, secure in the snuggle and wishing this night could last forever.

"They've altered the forecast. Twelve to eighteen inches up here," he said.

I shifted to look up at him. "Do we need to leave? What if we can't get out tomorrow? You'll miss practice."

I was sure he'd thought of that, but just in case.

"Not a chance. I'll pay the fine." He kissed the top of my head. "You are my only focus right now, and I intend to spend every moment here until we get shoveled out fulfilling that promise I made to break our longest kiss record."

"Oh really?" A thought occurred to me. In the regalest Renaissance-y accent I could summon, I challenged him. "Sir Zavey … Baron von Schwann … *Milord,*" I emphasized, knowing it would kick up his heart rate a bit. I kissed the pulse in his neck to confirm my hypothesis and leaned back to lock my eyes on his. "The Lady Lucky Penny wishes thou to cease speaking and bestow upon her lips all the promised kisses, at once."

I'd never heard a primal growl such as the one that left Xavier's mouth before it covered mine. I submitted to his kisses until all of my energy was expended.

Contented, I closed my eyes and welcomed the ascension into dreamland. In the window, in his arms, to the harmony of the waterfall's serenade and the steady breathing of my equally contented husband.

Beds were overrated. This window seat was where all the magic was.

"PENNY?" Xavier shifted underneath me. "Penny?" Nope, I wasn't answering. "Penny?"

I pressed my lips together and fought to keep my eyes closed.

I didn't want to wake up from the coziest, most perfect dream I'd ever dreamed and face the day of going back to real life.

My next thought was fleeting, but for a few seconds I legit couldn't wait for the end of hockey season.

No no no, you don't mean that! Xavier could win the trophy for best defensive forward this year!

I know, I know! And once my classes end, I will be at EVERY game, including some away games, with a toffee coffee to ensure he breaks his away game scoring drought.

Atta girl! And then when his beautiful body is broken and battered from playoff hockey, you can nurse him back to health as you travel to all the pretty places!

Staaahp. You make her sound like an opportunist.

Only stating the reality. He travels every summer to Canada, and he said he'd take you to the chateau.

Truuuuuue.

"Penny? You're missing the sunrise."

"Mmmm." I briefly opened my eyes to catch the sun rising over the falls as I twisted to bury my face in his ... coat? The soft team-branded hoodie had been replaced by the scratchy wool overcoat.

Slowly, I sat up. The cabin was dark and cold, but the fire was going strong. A handful of candles flickered light around the room.

Xavier brushed my hair to the side. "Power's out. I woke up a bit ago after dreaming I face-planted into the ice. Turns out, it was just your face."

I raised my eyebrows and tried to hold a straight face. But that was funny. I favored him with a snort.

"There it is," he said. "I could wake up to your smile and laugh every day." *I* could wake up to his rumpled hair and his morning voice every day. It was a bit gravelly, deeper, and comforting.

"Ditto, Baron von Schwann." I'd forgotten about his title until Quinn Brewer mentioned it yesterday. Me, Penny Palmer, a real live baroness. *The baroness barista,* they could call me, if they knew. "My nose *is* a little cold," I admitted.

"Allow me to remedy that, Baroness Lady Lucky Penny von Schwann."

"Eh. We'll have to work on th—" His mouth covered my nose in a big, wet kiss. I laughed, and soon we were kissing again. Neither of us seemed to care about morning breath.

That was love, right?

Love.

We eventually unfolded ourselves from the window seat and moved to the small sofa facing the fire. Until Xavier's stomach growled. I traded my blanket for the puffer jacket Tasha packed for me and pulled on my sherpa-lined boots. On the bed, our wedding clothes were laid out, waiting to be packed back into their garment bags. I'd mentioned how much I loved his costume, and he'd joked that he might wear it weekly, just for fun. I'd swatted him and followed up with a *yes, please.*

Xavier warmed up breakfast while I made coffee. My sister had thought of everything, hand-packing his preferred light roast into little pods and putting together a cooler bag of all the ingredients for his toffee coffee, including the coffee ice cream. Never mind that he didn't have a game today or that there was no power for the single-serve coffee maker. I gave it my best effort with the boiling water, pouring it over the coffee in the pod and hoping for the best.

"I hope it's not bad luck to have this on a non-game day." I set the coffee on the table and slid into the seat across from him.

"We'll see. I don't think I'm making it to practice, so no harm." He nodded toward the door. "The road below still isn't plowed. If we're not dug out in the next hour, I'll call Coach."

I grimaced. "Will you really get in trouble?"

He shrugged. "Might have to do extra laps or pay a fine if I'm the only one who doesn't make it. Not afraid of that, either."

"Oh no?" I teased. "Then I'm afraid I must impose a penalty of my own."

Just as I'd hoped, his eyebrows drew together into his curiously cute expression. "Ohhh ... Let me guess. A volunteer position at the Ren Faire?"

"No. I like that idea, though. But I probably won't be working it this year."

"No?" he asked. "Why not?"

I tapped my chin. "There's this thing called the Stanley Cup final, and it sort of overlaps with the beginning of the Faire. And the Faire is every weekend in the summer, and I kind of want to spend that time with my husband, if he's amenable to that plan."

"One hundred percent amenable," he said quickly. "You think we'll make it to the Cup final?"

"How can you not with endless toffee coffee?" I teased.

"Touché," he agreed. "So, my penalty?"

I laughed. "Right. After lunch. We need to brush up your medieval and Renaissance history. Robin Hood was late twelfth century, so the Bryan Adams song, while lovely, and now ours, is medieval. Your Musketeer costume was right on but just only. They were founded in 1622. *The Princess Bride,* nope. While it may seem Renaissance, or even medieval, there's a reference to prisoners being sent to Australia, so it would have to take place after 1788. The Renaissance ended around the early 1600s. However, I do love it when you say, 'As you wish,' so that transgression is forgiven."

He let out a long dramatic *whew!* "Thank goodness. I do like saying that. As for you not working the Ren Faire, are you sure? That's been such a big part of your life."

"And miss the chance to meet both sides of your family and stay at Chateau Schwannenschloss? Not a chance." I hoped I was clear enough, with the stress on meeting his family.

"I better start planning now." He smiled and set down his fork. "You still haven't said what my penalty is."

"Oh ... Well." I swiped my phone and selected my favorite ballads playlist. "An hour slow dancing to some of my favorite songs should do it. Don't you think?"

"As you wish." I giggled and quickly pressed the play arrow for "All for Love" as he came around the table and drew me to my feet. "I think that's a light punishment and I might need more than an hour of penance."

"I'll have to reassess after the last song," I said. "But yeah, probably more than an hour."

XAVIER DID MISS PRACTICE. The power returned around noon, and we were dug out a few hours later. I was sad to leave when the rideshare arrived but also excited to go to my new home.

Home.

That would take some getting used to.

Xavier's apartment was nice. While he helped me unpack, he asked what I thought about staying here or buying a house.

"I thought you liked it here?" I asked as I hung a dress.

"I do," he said, coming up behind me and wrapping his arms around my waist. "For now. But … it's not very family-friendly."

I twisted to look him in the eyes. "You're thinking long-term, right?"

He was quiet for a minute. "I'm thinking that we made a plan and it changed in a matter of weeks. What if our revised plan changes, too? What if we decide we want to be parents sooner than later?"

Xavier's question surprised me. "Like, how soon?"

He shrugged. "Whenever." His eyes searched mine, and he leaned in to kiss my neck. "I want you all to myself for as long as possible. And we both have dreams to work toward. But when you're ready, I'll be ready. And a home with a yard would be nice. Especially if the yard is big enough for an outdoor rink."

"I like homes with yards," I agreed, pulling his head down for a kiss and resting it on my shoulder.

"Are you sniffing my hair?" he asked.

"Guilty," I cooed, taking an overly dramatic breath in. "I love your strawberry-scented shampoo."

He trailed his lips along the curve of my neck. "I love your vanilla lotion. Tastes like cake. Makes me want to—"

I pressed my fingers to his lips. "Let's not get ahead of ourselves, Sir Zavey Baron von Schwann. Kisses only for the lady —for now."

"As you wish," he grumbled, swooping me up into his arms.

Our lips found each other's once again. At this rate, it might take me weeks to unpack.

CHAPTER 23
Xavier

St. Patty's Day. My birthday. Our twenty-sixth day of marriage.

The last few weeks had been like that cliché about living in a dream, except I was awake. Penny had settled into the apartment, and we were settling into a routine. On the mornings she woke up early to open the Coffee Loft, I woke up early to drive her.

She had the idea to leave her car in the lot of her old apartment building to try to hide that she was living at my place. After work, her mom or Gabby would bring her here or I'd pick her up if I was in town and had a night off. I taught her how to drive my car, so when I traveled, she used it. But the black Audi was pretty recognizable to fans, so we'd let people think she was having car trouble.

The deception was taking a toll on her, even though she wouldn't admit it. We both had our reasons for not letting our secret out, but they were starting to wear thin. I'd gotten to the point where I didn't care what the fans thought about what I'd said when I was younger and stupid and not in love. And Penny hadn't stuttered in weeks. She'd come home on Thursday all smiles from an admissions interview for a master's in music program in Denver.

It was Sunday, and I'd woken up before my alarm. No practice today, but we had a big game tonight, and I wanted to get a

workout in before church. I pulled on my gym pants and old Volts hoodie and sneakers, thinking about how cute Penny looked when she used my resistance bands when we spent time in "my office" together.

She was still sleeping. Tomorrow kicked off her spring break, and she'd stayed up late last night to finish a paper so that she could join me for away games this week. It was an easy week of opponents that were below the playoff line, so Noel was back playing with us since these teams with no chance of making it tended to be less violent and slower and thus less of an injury threat to him. So Gabby and Penny would meet us in Nashville on Tuesday night and follow us to New Orleans and Dallas.

Another routine I loved … watching Penny sleep. Every night, she braided her hair and piled it on top of her head, then cocooned herself in the blankets.

I still couldn't believe she was here.

That she was *mine.*

Mine, mine, mine. My love for her had me sounding like a lovesick pelican.

And I was hers.

"I know you're watching me." The mass of blankets with the crown of braids shifted, and the top half of her face poked out. "C'mere, birthday boy."

"As you wish." I probably overused that phrase, but as long as it resulted in laughter, I felt no need to vary it.

Her muffled giggles were my siren song, leading me to her as she rose to sit. I wrapped my arms around her and rocked her in a long hug-to-remember, as she called them. It was my first birthday as a married man, and I felt incredibly fulfilled and happy.

"You going for a run?" she asked.

I shook my head. "Just some circuit training. You wanna join me?"

"Nah. I've got a cake to finish." She grinned and pressed her lips to mine. I held on when she tried to pull away, and we fell to the mattress. I hovered above her, then eased myself down to place a soft kiss on her forehead, then as many freckles as I could until she playfully pushed me away. I grinned. "I don't need a cake. Sleep in."

"Not a chance, husband. You just wait. It's a good luck cake," she taunted.

"In that case …" One more kiss. "I'll leave you to it."

THE CAKE TURNED out to be a giant sheet pan of the Coffee Loft's Irish Cream brownies. They were topped with a layer of liquor-infused frosting and green and orange sprinkles. Penny remembered that I bought a bunch every March. Her touching gesture was exhilarating.

By the time we arrived at the Coffee Loft for my pregame coffee, I was walking on air, and there wasn't anything that was going to bring me down. Not even that jerk Dante Leinecker. We were playing Tulsa tonight, and I was going to take a page from Dani's book and pretend he didn't exist.

I dropped Penny off at the back door and circled around. As I suspected, there were more fans than usual waiting. It was a Sunday, and my birthday, and a holiday. The trifecta of reasons to show up where you knew one of your players was sure to be.

I steered into the spot they were saving for me and got out of the car slowly, scanning the people behind my dark sunglasses. Left side, Bubbles, Blossom, Buttercup, and a group of guys naked from the waist up and painted blue, each with a silver letter that spelled GO EDGE. On the right, a handful of kids I'd coached at the Plex's summer camps and one familiar little guy holding a stick that used to belong to me.

I pulled a permanent marker from my jacket and waved to the left siders as I turned right and walked straight to the kid I'd met in December, fist-bumping the camp kids on the way. "Hey, Isaac. Great to see you again, bud."

"You remember my name?"

"Swanny remembers *everyone's* name." A taller kid behind him lifted his fist for a bump.

I grinned, giving him knuckies as I took the stick from a shocked Isaac. "Hey, Gordie. How's your new team rolling?" Gordie had been a member of the Plex's Flying Stars team and Jason's buddy when he was a Volt, as well as a student of Lauren's when she taught at his school in Colorado Springs. Jay still worked with him, when he had time. Gordie had been born without his left hand and was killing it as a goalie on his club team.

"Just above the playoff line. Is Dex starting tonight?"

"As far as I know. You coming to the game?"

"Oh yeah. He got me and my mom a five-pack of tickets this year. We can't miss your birthday, and I can't wait!"

I grinned. "Be sure to come down for warmies. I'll tell him you'll be waiting, okay?"

"Okay!"

I signed a few pucks and jerseys, then went inside and stepped into the line. Penny was behind the counter, holding my coffee, but I'd wait my turn.

In front of me, Monty Biddington was bent over his grandmother's wheelchair, talking to her heatedly. "Nana, I am not getting that for you. It's poison. Full of sugar and even a bit of alcohol. You're not going into diabetic shock on my watch."

My lips twitched.

"Montgomery, I am an old woman, and if I want a treat on a Sunday, I'll have it. So there's Irish Cream in the frosting. Big deal. The alcohol content is surely less than the glass of champagne I had with my midnight snack."

"Nana! You didn't!"

"I most certainly did," she huffed.

I smiled, imagining Penny as a nana and hoping we had grandkids that cared about us as much as Monty doted on his Nana Booboo.

Nana got her way, and Monty wheeled her to a nearby table as she bit into her Irish Cream brownie.

I stepped up to the counter, and Penny grinned at me while Marie rang me up. "Guess what?"

"What?" I tapped my card to the payment terminal. "You're out of birthday doughnuts?"

She laughed. "Nope. Got yours all boxed up and ready."

I raised my eyebrows as I replaced my card in my wallet and took out a twenty-dollar bill. "You're coming to the game tonight?"

"I am, but you know that."

"You're wearing my jersey?"

"You knew that, too." Penny handed me the coffee and doughnut box. "The bagpiper canceled."

"The bagpiper?"

She snorted. "Yes, the bagpiper the Edge hired to play the anthem tonight. He's got the flu."

"Sorry for him. So?"

"So Bailey is already at the arena and was there when he called in, so she called me. She asked if *I'd* play the anthem! Me! In front of nineteen thousand people!"

I blinked at her. "You?"

"Me!"

"Wow!" I scooted out of line toward the end of the counter. She ducked behind Marie and met me at the kitchen door, pushing it open just before I got there. I slipped inside behind her, set my coffee and doughnut down and lifted her into a hug. "I'm so happy for you! You're going to be amazing!"

"I'm so excited! I almost didn't answer because I was just about to make your coffee, but you were tied up outside, so I figured I had a few extra minutes. She'd asked me about signing, but I haven't been able to do it with my school and work schedule. But tonight—everything lined up perfectly."

"Need help getting your harp out of here?"

"Nope. Marcus already carried it through the kitchen to the back door."

I set her on the ground and pressed my lips to hers for a proper kiss. "Meet you around back in a few minutes?"

"I'll be there."

IT WAS GAME TIME. Almost. We were lined up in the tunnel while the crowd got hyped up. On the ice, Trask's stepdaughter

Ryleigh skated our logo flag around the arena with Ridgie the Bear. It was a neat tradition, choosing a kid from a local hockey program to skate in the opening ceremony. Even neater when it was a team kid.

Even cooler was that my girl—my *wife*—was playing the national anthem.

"Dude, you're a giddy mess. Don't make me miss my cue." Jason tapped my shoulder with his blocker. "You already cost me my stick tonight."

I laughed. "Please. You'd have given Gordie your pillows if he asked."

He tilted his head to the side and tapped his pads. "That's true. I've been thinking about getting new pads, anyway. These should fit him after that crazy growth spurt. Thanks for the heads-up he was going to be here. I also slipped him a five-hundred-dollar Visa gift card so he could bid on my lucky leprechaun jersey."

I shook my head. As usual, our holiday-themed warm-up jerseys were delightfully hideous. Tonight's featured orange-and-green-striped sleeves and a caricature of a leprechaun diving into a pot of gold with the league's sports betting sponsor's logo on it. On the back, our numbers were made of a holographic material that reflected rainbows in the light. Definitely not practical for game play.

"Thirty seconds, boys!" Dean gave us our final warning, tapping his stick to our helmets as he passed us. Another tradition. "Time to hunt Foxes! Allaire, Johnson! Get your ugly mugs up here with me!"

Noel grinned at me as he passed by. The guy was practically my family now.

Family.

Penny was here tonight and would be playing her harp on the ice, just feet from where I'd be standing for the anthem. I was so proud of her. She'd only had a moment to decide whether to accept the invitation, and she hadn't hesitated. She knew she was likely to be interviewed after the splash we'd made during All-Star Weekend, and she'd told me she wasn't worried at all.

It was my birthday, Penny was here, and we were projected to win. I hadn't been the recipient of Zaki's game day prank. Poor ChaCha had found all his equipment stick-taped inside a bundle of towels. He'd had it coming though, since he told Zaki to "bless his heart" when he bested him in a drill yesterday.

A perfect day, indeed. I didn't even care that I wasn't starting.

BOOM! BOOM! BOOM! BOOM! The drumbeats from our intro song reverberated in the tunnel. Jason's cue.

Our goalie led us onto the ice while "Livin' on the Edge" played for the fans. We hit the surface and skated a few circles on our side of the red line. When I came to a stop at our bench, I blew a kiss to Penny, sitting on her stool just a few feet away on the carpet. It was dark, but she knew to expect it, and she was looking. She caught the kiss and touched her fingers to her lips. I was purposely the last guy into the box so I could be as close to her as possible.

That was my girl. Wearing my jersey. In my arena.

Going home with *me.*

Mine.

The music faded out, and the announcer named our starting lineup. Banging on the glass behind me caused me to turn. Gabby and Brenna waved at me and pointed to the empty seat between them. I grinned. My lucky Penny would literally be behind me all night.

I turned back to the ice while the Air Force representatives presented our nation's colors. They were followed by two Desert Storm veterans, twin brothers, who were thanked for their service. They saluted the fans, and then Penny and her harp filled the screens of the jumbotron.

"And now, to perform the anthem of the United States of America, renowned harpist and composer Penny Palmer."

Composer? I grinned. Another of Penny's secrets to discover.

Her back was to me, and she'd braided her hair into a thick, single rope so that *Schwann* was clearly visible on her back. Since hearing her play the theme from *Tangled,* I thought of that song whenever she wore her hair like Rapunzel.

I looked up at the screen as the camera panned from her closed eyes to the short and sparkly blue fingernails that weaved in and out of the strings. I'd never heard the arena so quiet before. The closeup of her hands reminded me of our wedding rings, at home in their velvet boxes. The emerald, on her right ring finger, was the only jewelry she wore.

When the song ended, the place erupted into applause. My teammates whistled and howled and banged their sticks. I slipped out of the box to hug Penny as her harp was carried away.

"You were amazing! Did you hear that applause?!"

She laughed and tapped my helmet. "Will you get in trouble if I try to kiss you?"

"I don't care."

She pushed my visor up and pressed her lips to mine. "Did you read your message?"

"I did. As you wish." And I had a new goal song picked out, just for tonight. Most teams had the same song for every goal, no matter who the scorer was. But on a few teams, like us, Winnipeg, and Montana, players were given the chance to choose their own. It had taken a bit of convincing to get it changed, but since it fit with tonight's theme, it was happening. And it was worth every chirp my teammates were going to give me.

She grinned. "And I got your back."

"Seriously, Schwann? You dating the barista?" Dante taunted from the Foxes' bench.

"Shut up, Leinecker!" I snarled.

He howled. "That's so rich. Like, *gold digger* rich."

I'd been mad before. I'd been in fights before. But I'd never felt the degree of rage that pulsed through me at that moment.

I let Penny go and turned to face my nemesis. "Do not EVER disrespect my wife like that again or—"

"Your *wife?*" He let out a string of unfavorable expletives, and I lost it.

I dropped my stick and lunged at him.

It took four guys to pull us apart. We were lucky to get only five minutes each in the penalty box. Coach was not happy to start the game four-on-four, but that was the least of my troubles.

I couldn't get Penny's expression out of my mind. Shock, betrayal, fear. It was all there.

I'd slipped up, big-time. Not only had guys on the benches heard what I'd said, but so had everyone on the carpet, too.

Including Bailey and our social media team. And Leinecker made sure everyone within shouting distance got the scoop as he was pushed toward the Foxes' penalty box.

Penny didn't get to her seat until the first period was almost over. Every time I looked behind me, Brenna shrugged and gave me a sad smile. Wherever Penny was, Gabby was with her, and I felt even worse because this was a big night for Noel and she wasn't in her seat for the first nineteen minutes.

Penny and Gabby finally returned during the last minute of play, but it was my shift, so I spent most of it on the ice. When I saw an opportunity to steal the puck from Leinecker, I swooped in and sent it airborne to Noel. He caught the saucer pass and took it around the net, scooped it onto his blade and inserted it top-shelf around the pipe and into the net, lacrosse-style—a Michigan goal! I fist-pumped the air and skated over to him to celebrate.

I skated back to the bench behind him, and he made a show of taking his helmet off and kissing the glass between him and Gabby. What a nut. I hung back, avoiding Penny's gaze and wishing for a moment like that for us.

During the intermission, I found Bailey in the tunnel and pleaded with her to help me control the narrative. She assured me she was already on it and to just do my best to score tonight so that I didn't break my toffee coffee record.

Whatever she had planned, would it be enough? I'd let Penny down in the worst way.

And I hated myself for it.

CHAPTER 24
Penny

After the initial shock and a chat with Gabby in the private bathroom of the family suite, I felt ready to face the public. Bailey had texted, asking for an interview toward the end of the intermission, and I'd agreed. Despite the surprise mention of our relationship status and the concern that keeping our marriage a secret would hurt people we cared about, I was okay with it and more than ready to put an end to the charade.

After the dancers performed and Bailey talked stats with the commentators, she and her cameraman met me in the aisle behind the empty home team bench.

"Are you ready?"

I nodded. Gabby squeezed my hand.

"Three … two … one … I'm here with everyone's favorite barista and brilliant harpist, Penny Palmer—or should I say, Penny Schwann?"

Bailey grinned encouragingly. She had one of those smiles that was so catchy, you couldn't help but return it.

"It's true," I admitted. "We thought it might be better luck to keep it a secret. Have you heard that hockey players are superstitious?"

She laughed. "I miiight know a thing or two about that." The fans laughed. "Well, congratulations are in order then. We're thrilled for you and Swanny. Any chance you might be joining us for any away games? He could use some luck in that department."

I laughed. "As a matter of fact, I'll be at all three games this week, and I fully expect his away-game scoring to improve." The crowd laughed. What was so funny about that?

"Awesome! You heard that, folks! Lucky Penny, aka Mrs. Swanny, is going on the road! With the regular season coming to an end, this is amazing news for Edge fans. Back to you in the studio." The crowd went wild. I looked over at Brenna and my empty seat. There were some rowdy fans around us. Maybe I'd stay in thc family suite at the next game.

"That was perfect," Bailey assured me. "I'll see you after the game?"

I nodded. "Wherever you want me."

She left, and Gabby towed me back to our seats. The guys were returning and filing onto their bench, banging on the glass and shouting congratulations and other well wishes. I waved to Xavier as he slowed to a stop at the gate. I hoped he heard the interview. He needed to know I wasn't mad at him.

He came straight back towards me and pulled off his glove. He raised his hand, palm out, and tucked his middle and ring finger in, making the sign for *I love you.*

My breath caught, and I returned the sign and bent to press my lips to the glass like Gabby had done earlier. Xavier whipped his helmet off and did the same.

I didn't care that the glass was dirty. Or that the camera caught us and started a whole kiss-cam segment.

All I cared about was that we were okay.

Our secret was out. And it was okay.

XAVIER SCORED a goal on his first shift in the second period, and the chorus of Amy Grant's "Lucky One" blared into the arena. Gabby and Brenna discussed how badly the guys would make fun of Xavier while I tracked him on the ice like a lovesick fool.

The Edge won the game 5-1. I smirked as the Foxes slunk off the ice. That Leinecker guy was awful.

Xavier had to stay for the press conference. Everyone wanted the scoop on us, but he wasn't talking. He only confirmed what they already knew, and I appreciated that. We needed to talk about what to say together.

Gabby and Noel waited with me until Xavier was released. His long strides brought him right to me, and he took my hand.

"Your harp?" he asked.

"Already in the car."

He squeezed my hand, and we walked through the building, waving and saying goodbye to the staff and others who wished us well. At the car, he opened my door for me, and I climbed in. I'd never seen him quiet like this before.

He didn't start the engine. Instead, he closed his eyes and leaned his head back against the headrest. "I messed up. I'm so sorry I let you down."

I twisted to face him and turned his cheek to look at me. "I'm not sorry."

He turned to me. "You're not? Pen, I saw your face. I never, ever want to see that expression on it again. It was soul-crushing. And to know I caused it … I'm so deeply and truly sorry I let that guy get to me."

"You were defending me. That's your job, Xavier. And it's my job to defend you. We promised to take care of each other, remember?"

He nodded. "But—"

"Sure, I was surprised. Shocked, even. But it's okay. Isn't it? That the whole world knows we love each other?"

"He said you were a gold dig—"

I covered his mouth with my hand. "You know that I'm not, and that's all that matters to me."

"Really?"

"Really. I found the cups." Xavier had kept every single to-go cup I'd written a message on. I'd been on the hunt for something to transport his birthday cake in when I found them in a high cupboard. "I can't believe you saved them."

"I guess I always knew you'd mean something more to me one

day. I didn't know what or when, but if anything, it seemed lucky to keep the cups. Kiss and make up?" He waggled his eyebrows.

I laughed. "I love it when you do that." I kissed each eyebrow, his nose, and his lips. "Nothing to make up."

"There's one thing." He pulled out his phone and scrolled, stopping on the selfie we'd taken at the Coffee Loft on Valentine's Day. I watched as he uploaded it to Instagram with the caption, "Swanny14 🩶's RenFaireAspen forever." "Now we're Instagram official."

He was so funny.

"It appears we are. But just so you know, I still don't have plans to go blond," I joked.

"Good." He leaned in for a kiss and murmured into my ear, "I've never much been into blondes anyway."

We laughed, then went quiet. Just staring at each other … not awkward at all. His scar had lost its pink tinge and was barely visible—his only imperfection and a reminder that he'd been thinking about me. I felt peace, security, and relief that we didn't have to hide anymore. After a few minutes, I remembered where we were headed next. "Now, are we going out to celebrate or what?"

"Celebrate?"

"Your birthday, us, your Gordie Howe hat trick? Pick one or all three. Brenna said the function room at Brewski's is available. And maybe we can stop at home first to pick up our wedding rings?" I lifted my hands and made a show of transferring the emerald from my right ring finger to the left.

He grinned. "Definitely. Gordie Howe, huh? A goal, an assist, and a fight. I love it when you talk hockey to me."

I booped him on the nose. "Noted."

He brushed a tendril off my cheek and leaned in for a birthday kiss-to-remember.

Epilogue

PENNY

I loved the word maelstrom. Merriam-Webster defines it as 1) a powerful, often violent whirlpool sucking in objects within a given radius, and 2) something resembling a maelstrom in turbulence.

And it perfectly described the last few months. I, along with my family and friends, had been sucked into Xavier's world, willingly and thoroughly. As the Edge chased the Cup, I was at every game, home and away. Jannell and Marcus had given me all the time off I'd needed and allowed me to come in on home game days just to make Xavier's toffee coffee.

The team had made the Coffee Loft one of their official partners (I think Xavier had paid for that, but I didn't have proof, and I wasn't asking), and on game days, the staff wore his jersey under their aprons. Even little Riva had a doggie version.

Because the final round of the Cup championship overlapped with the Ren Faire, I hadn't planned to return. But after my performance of the national anthem at the Edge game—and the subsequent follow-up invitations to play during the playoffs, plus other gigs—the entertainment director practically begged me to return for at least one day as a guest performer.

So I had, and that was where we were today, after being home for just two days from Xavier's mom's family reunion in Calgary. I shared the tiny wooden slatted stage with the Great Howdidhedini one more time before we left for Schwannenschloss. Xavier's parents and sisters were here, watching me play under the makeshift tent, which provided minimal shade. And in a small-world twist, Daniella had run into Beck and her father in town and recognized them as the contractors who had renovated the baron's chambers to make them accessible at Schwannenschloss. Beck's father had been in the Army, and they'd started free-lancing with Montoya Construction when he'd been stationed in Munich.

Xavier, in his wedding ensemble, sat off to the side with Abby Cabunny, supervising an improvised meet-and-greet during my second set. A bunch of his friends from the team were here, including Jason, cradling his new baby proudly against him, arms protectively around the bundle despite the cast on his wrist.

After the final game, the injury report had been released, and the world learned that a handful of Edge players were playing with fractures, Jason among them. He'd taped his wrist and hidden his injury and fooled us all. Xavier had a few cracked ribs, Brendan a broken foot, and Trask a torn rotator cuff. He'd had surgery a few days later and wouldn't be back playing until October at the earliest.

It amazed me what these guys would do for each other, and I had no doubt that they'd go just as far next year. As for winning the Cup, the Miami Ice Cats would continue to be a threat. They were bigger and faster but also older, and some of their players were slowing down. The Edge had a new crop of Volts ready to step up and add depth, so we were all looking forward to what next season would bring.

Most of my family was here, too, except for Tasha, who was strangely absent. As I greeted my audience—something I'd never been able to do until now—I noticed Monty in the back with his phone up, recording. He was staying in my old room at Tasha's for the next couple of weeks while Nana Booboo's house was being renovated.

I prayed they both came out of the experience alive.

After a few songs, Karina joined me for "Somewhere Over the Rainbow." She'd advanced quite quickly in four months, and it was evident she loved to play. After learning she had dyslexia, I'd recommended a harp with rainbow-colored strings to help her learn. It'd been invented by a dyslexic harpist who had originally put color-coded stickers on her harp.

When I finished playing, I hung around to greet my friends and family and well-wishers. Monty hung back, and it was obvious he was waiting to speak with me. I hoped everything was okay.

When the last person in line turned away, I signaled Xavier to pack up my harp and excused myself to cross over to where Monty waited off to the side under a trio of aspens.

Lifting my heavy skirts in the front, I hurried over. Concern was etched into his features, and it wasn't the overly dramatic intentional face he often put on for emphasis. No. I'd known him long enough to know this was genuine.

And it scared me.

"Is Tasha okay?" I blurted.

"I don't know." He wrung his fingers together. "She says she is, but she sent me out. She told me to record you and tell you she was sorry and—hold on, I need to make sure I get this right. She made me take a note." He pulled out his phone and tapped the screen, then turned it to face me. "I don't know what this means, and she hasn't come out of her room since early last night."

I read the words on the screen. "Tell Penny I'm sorry I can't make it. She'll understand. She cannoli imagine what I'm going through."

Oh man. Poor Tasha. She was having a flare-up. Cannoli was our code word for Italian food, which wreaked havoc on her systems.

"Monty, what did Tasha eat yesterday?"

"Eat? I don't know what she had at work, but I ordered dinner in for us from Pasta Nacht's. She had the gluten-free dairy-free Alfredo." He shuddered. "What's even the point? How do you have Alfredo without milk, cheese, or flour?"

A line began to form behind him. I'd never gotten this much attention in past years. People were asking for my music, which had never happened. And my tip basket had more money in it after three sets than I used to collect in a weekend.

As I suspected, Monty had no clue about Tasha's ailments. "She can't eat those things. I think the food might have had some cross-contamination."

His jaw dropped, and his eyes bugged out at me. "Is she going to be all right? Should I have left her? Do I need to call an ambo? I didn't think anything was wrong when she decided to go to bed right after dinner. What if she dies?"

Monty's panic surprised me, but then I remembered about his sister. I laid my hand on his shoulder to comfort him. "Yes and yes. She likely just wanted to be left alone right now. I'll call her and see how bad it is."

"Thanks. She's been working so hard getting her high school team in shape. And we're co-coaching the Worlds team this year, you know."

"Yes, I know. With your tumbling and her choreography skills, we all expect a win."

He grinned, but then it quickly faded. "How can I help her, Penny? I can handle the team if she's sick into next week, but she won't even open the door and poke her head out. How do I know she's not getting worse?"

"You don't. But trust me, okay? I'll keep in touch with her and let you know if you need to bust her door down. And I'll send Mom over to sit with her if she's still not better tomorrow. Okay?"

He nodded, then shook his head. "I wish she would trust me. I could help her."

I crossed my arms and forced his gaze to mine. "You've got a lot of years to make up for if you want to earn her trust, Monty. You should definitely start now. Bring home a twelve-pack of grape Gatorade. It's not much, but it's a start. Keep me posted, okay?"

"I will. Thanks for the tip." He sighed. "See ya, Penny."

I turned to walk back to the little stage. Howdidhedini and his little guy were setting up for their last set. I walked past them right to Xavier. His backside was to me as he chatted with Jason. I didn't want to interrupt their conversation, so I wrapped my arms around his waist and waited, careful not to dislodge my flower circlet.

His warm hands covered mine, and he said goodbye to Jason and turned around. "Well, hello, wifey." He bent into a deep formal bow. "Sir Zavey Baron von Schwann, at your service."

I giggled. "Lady Lucky Penny Baroness von Schwann requests your assistance to transport her instrument to her new carriage."

As he rose from his bow to his full height, his eyes narrowed, and he waggled his brows. "As you wish, milady. I'll be happy to see to the safe passage of your instrument to the Palisade. And may the Baron relay a request as well?"

"The Baron may state his request in between kisses. The lady requires payment in the form of affection, your lordship, no exceptions." I tapped him on the nose. "Commence kisses now, then state your request."

He grinned and then his mouth was on mine. Someone hooted and whistled behind us, but I didn't care.

I made a pouty face when he pulled away, but per our agreement, I let him speak.

"Sir Zavey Baron von Schwann wishes for the Lady Lucky Penny Baroness von Schwann to bestow her favor upon him and escort her on his arm to the castle courtyard for tonight's Masquerade Ball."

"Hmm." I tapped my chin, pretending to consider the matter carefully. "Perhaps you should bestow more kisses before I make such an important decision."

"As you wish."

I would never get enough of his kisses. "The Lady Lucky Penny Baroness von Schwann has decided to grant your request."

"Excellent," he whispered, trailing kisses from my ear down the curve of my neck. "I'll get our masks, too. Meet me there?"

"As you wish," I replied. He grinned and spun on his heel, headed for the harp.

While Xavier brought the harp to my new SUV—an early birthday present—I took the leisurely off-the-beaten path route to the back of the fairgrounds, where the ball was to be held in a gigantic event tent. I'd made a lot of memories here over the years and a lot of friends. I'd look back fondly on my time as a Ren Faire harpist, but it was time for a new chapter to begin. I spoke to Tasha briefly, and she insisted she was all right.

When I arrived at the tent, Xavier was already there, standing in a group of our family and friends. I was bummed Tasha was sick; this was the only part of the Ren Faire she had looked forward to. Monty was also missing, and I hoped he was on his way home to make sure she was all right, despite my advice to him to leave her alone.

As I approached, Xavier looked up, and our eyes locked. He straightened to his full height and bowed.

I would never get tired of that.

I said hello to everyone, and we all lined up.

"Penny? Erm, Baroness von Schwann?"

I turned around. It was one of the footmen from the queen's entourage. "Hi, Neil. Everything okay?"

He bowed. "Her Majesty wishes that you and the Baron allow me to escort you to the *other* entrance."

"Oh!" I exclaimed. "Wow. Um, sure." I tugged on Xavier's arm, and we followed him around the tent to the back, where the guests of honor entered, to be paraded in front of the Ren Faire royalty who sat on stage, watching their subjects.

The footman gestured for us to line up behind the courtiers, in front of the duke and duchess. "When you enter, walk to the right of the dance floor and line up facing the couple in front of you." He opened the gate.

I couldn't see over the heads in front of me. "Xavier!" I hissed. "Tell me what you see!"

After a few seconds, he leaned down and spoke low. "Trust me, this is something you don't want a spoiler for."

I groaned. "Okaaaaay."

As each couple was announced and entered, we stepped closer to the open gate. As the pair before us entered and turned left, we hurried to the entrance.

I shivered delightfully when the announcer welcomed us as Baron and Baroness von Schwann. We stepped forward and turned to the right. The king and queen sat on their thrones and smiled down at us. I gasped at the painted sign that hung over the stage.

FARE THEE WELL,

BARON & BARONESS VON SCHWANN

Xavier held on to me as I tripped on my skirt. I wanted to laugh and cry and cheer and—all the things. But most of all I wanted to dance with Xavier. We'd been working on a courante, and I prayed that would be the first song tonight to open the event.

We took our place at the edge of the dance floor. I looked around us for our family and friends. I spotted them at the tables close to the stage. Xavier had bought up three tables' worth of seats.

We all bowed or curtsied as the king led the queen from their thrones down the steps of the stage to the center of the dance floor. The music began, and they turned, one step at a time, until they were facing the gate.

"It's the pavane!" I hissed. "It's super easy. Just follow the others, okay?"

"As you wish, milady." He took my hand, and we stepped forward with the other couples. "They're hopping."

I giggled as we stopped just short of the center and a circle began to form around their majesties. "Just go with it!"

"I've no choice not to, milady."

I laughed again, and it was over soon enough. We declined the queen's invitation to dine on stage, something I'd dreamed about that didn't seem nearly as glamorous or prestigious now as it once had, in favor of the seats we'd purchased with our loved ones. Many of them would join us at the chateau in a few weeks to celebrate my birthday and graduation, since playoff hockey didn't stop for a proper party, as Xavier had called it.

Bless his heart, though. Xavier had flown into Colorado Springs for the ceremony after playing in a Round 2 game against Dallas and then had to fly back out again at lunchtime for a team meeting. Gabby and I had taken a later flight and then a rideshare to Addison Airport to meet up with Madison from the Coffee Loft in Tyler, Texas. She was a pilot and had taken one of her dad's Cessnas to transport the toffee coffee ingredients. A secret hockey fan, Madison had been happy to trade the ingredients for a pair of tickets to the game.

The dance ended to resounding applause. True happiness, I thought, was loving and being loved by someone who loved you and the things you loved. Xavier didn't have to understand my fascination with or affection for the Renaissance, and I didn't have to understand his passion for a sport that was rough on its best days and straight-up violent on its worst.

But we loved each other, and that would never waver. We'd continue to support each other in whatever captured our hearts.

"Before we go to our table," Xavier whispered, "how about we sneak out of here for a few moments for some kissing practice? I'm afraid I've been feeling a bit rusty."

"Oh, you most definitely are," I assured him. "That's a brilliant idea."

He offered his arm. "Shall we, then?"

I slipped my arm in his. "As you wish."

Bonus Epilogue

XAVIER

The slight chill of the starlit Alpine night didn't seem to bother any of the guests standing around Penny as she played her harp on the stone veranda at Schwannenschloss. During a short pause when the sun began to descend, I draped her cloak over her shoulders, and she'd regaled us with melodies for almost another hour.

It was her birthday and her dream setting for sharing her music.

In the mix with our families and friends were members of Opa's favorite ballroom orchestra. Penny had joined them for a few songs earlier in the night, and now, she played her own concert to a captivated audience.

When Penny finished her last song, I was waiting with my hand outstretched. She placed hers in mine and rose to her feet. I kissed her knuckles and then let go so she could curtsy to our guests.

"Thank you all," she said. "And now I'll leave you in the capable hands of Fraulein Karina von Schwann as you gather your things to say good night. We're so glad you came and ..." She looked over at me. "Thank you for the most amazing birthday."

Not a stammer, no skipped words, just perfect.

After the ball ended and the chateau was quiet, I offered Penny my arm. "A midnight stroll amongst the clovers, milady?"

She slipped her arm into mine. "That sounds lovely, milord. I know it's my birthday, but *I* have a gift for *you.*"

"You do? How very intriguing, Baroness." She laughed, and I led her down the old stone stairway. Our footsteps crunched along the gravel pathway lined by clover. Antique coach lights set on posts about ten feet apart lit our way as we strolled deeper into the grounds. "You know, I've never found a four-leaf clover. Being born on St. Patrick's Day and seeing them everywhere, promising luck, it's pretty disheartening to a kid who can't find one."

"I suppose one would be on the lookout for other lucky charms, then," Penny said, her tone teasing. "Like coffee, for instance."

"Your coffee got us to the conference final. I'd say that was pretty lucky." We'd gone all the way to play for the Cup this year, with a heartbreaking loss to Miami after seven games. Which meant a shorter-than-usual summer. I'd won the Norris trophy for the league's best defenseman. Then Noel and Gabby's wedding, a few weeks in Calgary, a memorable Saturday at the Ren Faire, and we'd topped it all off with a few amazing weeks here at the chateau.

It just kept getting better. We'd be heading home in a few days to get ready for training camp and Penny's first semester toward her master's degree in music performance.

"I'd say so," Penny agreed.

"About those four-leaf clovers," I continued. "I used to think, if I could just find one, I'd have all the luck in the world. But I found you instead."

"Aw." She leaned her head against my upper arm. "That's very sweet."

"You are." I stopped just past a light and turned to face her, taking her hands in mine. "I … did something today."

She regarded me with interest, smiling up at me with just a slight lift to one eyebrow. I let go of her hands and pushed up the sleeve of my left arm, turning my hand palm up, revealing a clear strip on the inside of my wrist.

Penny gasped when she saw the clear wrap. "Oh my gosh!"

"I'm not hurt," I rushed to assure her.

"It's a tattoo!" She leaned over to inspect it and smiled. "A three-leaf clover with a letter on each leaf. *A, E, S.*"

I'd asked the artist to draw *her,* but none of his sketches came close.

The moonlight shone on her face, and her expression conveyed awe, gratitude, and love. Everything I was feeling. "Aspen Ethyl Schwann, the love of my life, my lucky Penny, my everything."

"Oh, Xavier …" She placed gentle kisses just below the bandage and trailed her lips onto my palm before looking up to meet my gaze. "And you don't even like needles."

"Nope. But now my lucky Penny is with me everywhere I go, even when we're apart, and I plan to kiss her—the tattoo—before I put my gloves on, at every game."

She raised her arms. I caught them and guided them up and around my neck, "That is the sweetest thing."

Our lips met, and then I remembered she said she had a surprise for me. "So, it's your birthday …"

"It's my birthday."

"And you have a surprise for me?"

"Mm-hmm. If you want to know what it is."

"I want to know what it is."

She batted her eyelashes. "If you're sure …"

"Tell me what it is."

"I'll show you." Her hand disappeared into the pocket of her skirt. "Tasha smuggled this in for me. But I wanted to wait for you so we could, um … be surprised together?" Her uncertainty and thoughtfulness were charming and sweet.

A zip-top bag emerged from her pocket. She rotated her wrist and fanned out her fingers, revealing a—

"A pregnancy test?" I whispered. "Penny, are you—are we—is there a baby baroness?" My excitement grew with each word.

She smiled. "Or a baron. There might be. I haven't done the test yet. We're in this together, right?" I nodded. "We've both remarked about how … off I've felt these last couple weeks. I know we didn't plan this—"

"Pen?" I pressed my forehead to hers. "Either way, we've got this. If it's our time to be parents, we've got this. If I have to fly across the country in the middle of the playoffs to be there for you, we've got this. If you want me to be a stay-at-home-dad so you can play all over the world, we've got this."

She placed a soft kiss to my lips. "No way are you quitting hockey. Key word there: *We've* got this. If there *is* a 'this.'"

"I think we both know." I kissed the side of her neck, and she shivered. "Ready to go find out?"

Penny pulled my head down to her shoulder to whisper in my ear. "Sir Zavey Baron von Schwann, would you give me the pleasure of joining me in the baroness's chambers tonight, tomorrow, and for always?"

Oh yeah. Pleasure was guaranteed. But first, the test. My pulse raced, and I scooped her up, threshold-style, into my arms. "As you wish."

COFFEE LOFT SERIES
PUMPKIN SPICE SPICE BABY
EDGE
KERRY EVELYN

To Roxanne, my forever cheer bestie. Go Bears!

CHAPTER 1
Tasha

Mid-May

I tapped my toes on the mat, the light *thump thump* of my cheer shoe muffled by the surrounding din. The team announcements were well underway, and my coaching partner hadn't arrived yet.

The cheer gym at the Plex is large and loud. And on Team Reveal Day, the sound within the vaulted ceilings over the four cheer floors and tumbling area reached record decibels on the Screaming Girl O-Meter.

Having been part of the sport of cheerleading since I was a preschooler, I was neither surprised nor bothered by the racket. I was even the one to start it sometimes. But today, I was preoccupied with Nate's absence. This would be our second year coaching together, and we had a title to defend.

What could be keeping him? I lifted on my toes to peer at the staff door for the umpteenth time.

It was opening …

There he was! *Phew!* Nate caught my gaze and waved as he squeezed along the wall toward me, absently high-fiving as he waded through the athletes and parents between us.

Wait a sec.

A few feet behind him, another guy was easing his way

through the crowd of athletes of all ages, dressed in the same FireVolts tee and red shorts as Nate. His familiar blond hair and bulky build took my Nate-is-late anxiety to a whole other level.

What was Montgomery Biddington doing here? And wearing *our* team's official shirt?

I was sure he said he'd be here less often this year. Due to his new job as Number Three Ridgie, the backup to the backup mascot for Denver's NHL team, Monty said he didn't have time to coach cheer teams anymore. Private tumbling lessons only.

"Hey." Nate arrived by my side, breathing easy. "I was—"

"You're late." I shook my finger at him. "Our team is two away."

His cheerful expression dropped. "About that ... I found out this morning I got the internship with one of the physical therapists here at the Plex."

"For the fall?" I asked. That was a big deal, but his tone was suspect. I lifted my chin and forced myself to smile. "Congratulations!"

Nate shook his head. "I start next week."

I pulled my lips into my teeth and waited for him to say more.

He squirmed a little. "It's full-time."

"Great!" I replied. "No more money worries, and you can still coach at night."

He blinked, then turned his head back toward the crowd. I followed his gaze. Monty was getting closer to where we coaches stood behind the popup stage, waiting for the emcee to announce our teams.

"Tasha, I ..." Nate began. I turned my head to look at him. He was frowning. Not a good sign. "The hiring manager said that my schedule would be erratic, and he recommended that I not coach a team this year. So ... I had to give up my position coaching the Worlds team with you."

I was the one blinking now. "You're serious?"

He nodded. "They want me to work with the trainers for the Voltage."

My mouth dropped open. The Voltage was the Denver Edge's minor league hockey team, and they were based here in our hometown of Palmer City. Their practice rink was at the Plex—a hop, skip, and a jump from where we were standing.

"So you can miss some practices," I suggested. There had to be work-arounds. "I can take the athletes to the comps by myself. We'll make it work."

He shook his head. "I suggested that. This is an all-in or all-out opportunity. I'm so sorry, Tasha."

"B-but," I stammered as his solution seeped in. "Who—" I paused as he turned his head toward Monty. *"No.* Uh-uh. Not him. Anyone but *him."* The hairs on the back of my neck stood up, and I suppressed a shudder.

Nate swallowed, his Adam's apple bobbing while he chose his words. He squeezed his eyes shut, then opened them, locking his gaze on mine. I saw the sympathy and regret, and I honestly felt a little bad for the guy. He knew about my past with Monty. There really *had* to be no other option.

"Tasha, he was the only one available ..." He let his sentence trail off, unable to retrieve any additional words that might pacify me.

"Not *entirely* available." Monty stepped into place next to Nate and crossed his beefy arms over his muscular chest. "But *someone* had to get you both out of this bind. We can't be canceling our Worlds team. Not when we're defending champions. Wouldn't want to disappoint the athletes, you know? I worked too hard getting their tumbling skills almost as good as mine over the last year."

I rolled my eyes. Humble he wasn't.

"We're grateful to you, Monty. For sure," Nate said.

"Speak for yourself," I mumbled.

Monty's full lips spread into a wide grin. "It'll be like old times, Tasha. We can play Good Coach/Bad Coach just like when we used to run the summer camps."

That was forever ago, back when we were friends.

I cleared my throat and let my voice drip with sarcasm. "Sounds like a blast."

"That's the *spirit,"* he chimed. "Oh, and we'll have to tweak the practice schedule. I have forty-one home games plus NHL All-Star Weekend and other team obligations. Plus Nana Booboo's rehab. She'll be at Mountainview Manor's rehabilitation facility for some time, and I like to be there for her therapy appointments. I'm a busy guy. You understand."

I softened my expression out of respect for his Nana Booboo. Monty's grandmother had suffered a stroke recently, but the doctors were confident she'd make a full recovery. I hoped so, with all my heart. She was *his* nana, but she was *our* cheer nana. Monty had started the sport not long after I had, and Nana Booboo had brought him to every camp, practice, and competition until he could drive himself.

It was at the Plex she got the "Booboo" tag to her name. Monty was always pushing himself to be the best. Every time he hurt himself, he'd run to Nana and cry, "Nana! Booboo!" and she'd kiss it better. At some point during that first year, we were all calling her Nana Booboo and asking for get-better kisses. She was always happy to oblige.

Nana was also a frequent customer at my day job, the Coffee Loft. I credit Nana for my addiction to pumpkin spice lattes. She encouraged me to apply there when I was looking for my first job, and I've been there ever since. These days, I worked the opening until midafternoon shift, then drove to the high school to coach the varsity cheerleading squad. And two nights a week, I was here. This past year, I'd coached two competitive cheer teams here at the Plex, four nights each week, and it had been too much on top of everything else. The Worlds team was relatively easy; the members were older, mostly college students and cheerleading lifers, and they took direction like pros.

"Our turn." Monty gave my bicep a gentle nudge with his elbow. "C'mon, work wifey."

"I am *not* your work wifey." I shot him a glare and focused on the emcee.

"And now, on to our final team, the FireVolts, coached by Tasha and Monty! Defending their Worlds Championship this year will be ..."

The heads of the veteran FireVolts, gathered in front of the stage, swung to Monty. I noted surprise on their faces, and rightly so. We all expected Nate to be their coach again.

Monty and I jogged up the steps to the stage as the athletes' numbers were called. About two-thirds were veterans of last year's team. Two were newcomers from a rival gym, and a few had moved up from the senior teams. Nate and I had been super selective while also recognizing potential and coachability when we were choosing the members. No bad attitudes or drama allowed.

Nate worked his way through the group that gathered around us, sharing about his new position and confidently endorsing Monty as just what the team needed to level up. Most of them knew him already and welcomed him with open arms.

But Monty wasn't experienced enough to coach a team at this level. Sure, he could tumble and partner-stunt his way to first place with my cousin Gabby, but he'd never coached a whole team of athletes around his own age, in their early to mid-twenties. We'd turn twenty-five in January. Our Worlds team featured men and women ages eighteen through twenty-seven, and they deserved a coach of their caliber to ensure their winning streak remained intact.

I snuck a glance at Monty, chest out, shoulders back, practically oozing confidence, and sighed.

"You owe me big time," I mumbled to Nate.

"You'll be fine, Tasha. And maybe you two will become friends again."

"Unlikely." That would require Monty earning my trust back.

Never. Gonna. Happen.

Nate laughed. "So there's a chance. Good." He leaned over me to get closer to my ear. "I think he needs something like this to get his mind off his grandmother's recovery. I got the sense she's not doing well."

My eyes widened, and I whipped my gaze over to my archenemy. I might not like *him* anymore, but Monty's Nana Booboo was one of my favorite people in the whole world.

If coaching a team with him could help her in any way, I'd get through it.

I might even try to be civil to him.

Might.

CHAPTER 2
Monty

Mid-June

The strong powerhouse I knew as my Nana Booboo had never seemed so small and weak, covered to her chin by her favorite quilt—a patchwork of my old cheer tees and uniform shirts. I struggled to believe this was the same woman who pulled me out of sunrise-to-sunset (as she called it) preschool and took over my daily care while my parents worked and traveled.

I scooted the plastic and metal visitor's chair as close to the left side of the bed as was possible and lifted the blankets by her hip to find her hand. It was tiny and cold, so I kept it under the covers and gave it a gentle squeeze.

Her eyelids fluttered open, and the left side of her mouth curled up into a smile. "M-my boy," she whispered.

"I'm here, Nana. Did you have a nice nap?" I squeezed her hand again, and this time she squeezed back and the side of her mouth twitched with effort to form a smile. Her face was lined from years of smiling and laughing—and probably smirking from getting her way. I longed to see those lines deepen again.

As if exhausted by the effort, she closed her eyes and sighed.

It had been a month since her stroke, and except for a brief cursory visit from my parents to set up her health-care plan, I'd been her only familial visitor. Her siblings and their families had all moved out of Colorado decades ago, and my late grandfather's family was far too busy living their high-society lives to check in on the woman who had grown his business and their money when his father struck oil all those decades ago. Their son, my dad, was their only child, and after my sister died, I became their only grandchild.

"How's ... the h-h-how-sss?"

"The house is fine, Nana." Her speech was improving each week. It had terrified me in the days after the stroke when the side of her face drooped and all she could muster was moans and grunts.

I'd moved into her sprawling Victorian out by Lake Moonshine after boarding school. Scandalizing my parents when I chose coaching over a business career, I'd taken classes at the local university instead of attending an Ivy League school. What was the point? I had all the money I'd ever need, and I for sure didn't want my dad's life.

"D-Dr. sa-says ..." She closed her eyes again and pressed her lips together. The left side of her face scrunched in determination. "Says I need ... acc ... acc ..." She sighed.

The door to her private room squeaked open. I glanced over my shoulder and greeted her doctor, a fit man in his mid-thirties who resembled a grown-up Harry Potter, circular eyeglass frames and all.

What a chump.

"Nice to see you, Montgomery." He pushed at the center of his frames. As they slid up his nose, he cleared his throat. I'd told him countless times to call me Monty, but he hadn't. Like calling me by my full name gave him an air of authority.

"How's she doing?" I asked.

"Working hard. She's strong, but it'll take time."

"The rehab my parents set her up for—can she do that at home?"

"I'm glad you asked. I was telling Nancy here this morning that we can't release her until her home is accessible."

I frowned. "What does that mean? It has an elevator." My mind flashed back to the old house. It had been through dozens of renovations over the years. The elevator was added when her diabetes made it hard for her to walk up the stairs.

He schooled his expression into what he probably thought was kind, but it came off smug and his explanation condescending. "It means an extended ramp—the one you have isn't up to code—and a bathroom renovation. An entire bathroom must serve as a shower, with a drain in the floor. Grab bars in the others." My eyes widened as he went on to list even more extensive modifications her house would need.

With seven bathrooms between the house, garage, and pool, it would probably be cheaper to build Nana a new house.

"What's the timeline for her coming home?" I asked.

The doctor explained the benchmarks required for her to leave the rehab facility. I held on to her hand as he went over the requirements that were even more extensive than the house renovation list.

"And she'll need twenty-four seven monitoring until we're confident she can be alone safely," the doctor finished.

"N-no babysitter!" Nana barked out, and I laughed. It sounded more like *nah baybahtah,* but we both understood clearly what she meant.

"Don't worry, Nana. It's just a formality to keep you safe. We'll hire a nursing agency. You'll make some new friends and be waited on hand and foot, like you deserve. Teach them how to watercolor." Nana was a masterful watercolorist, and since her dominant hand hadn't been hampered by the stroke, I assumed she retained her ability to paint.

She harrumphed in objection, but her lips twitched, so I could tell she didn't totally hate the idea.

"As for when she's going home, it's hard to say. The stroke was extensive, but she's strong and has made significant gains. It will all depend on how she continues to progress. Get the renovations done, and then we'll talk." He turned on his heel and strode out the door with an air of self-importance.

I rolled my eyes at Nana, and she gargled a laugh.

"I don't like him," I said. I leaned forward to place a kiss on her forehead. "But I love you, so I'll do what he says. What color tile do you want in your fancy new bathroom?"

THE DENVER EDGE had made it to the playoffs and advanced all the way to the last round in their quest for the Stanley Cup. The first of the two teams that won four out of seven possible games would win the hardest and most difficult trophy in sports.

They lost Game 5 in Miami, so they were back in Denver for Game 6. It would be their last home game of the season, so I was called in to don the third Ridgie costume and visit the private boxes for photo ops. The backup Ridgie was outside working the pavilion and greeting fans, and the main bear would be on the ice and in the stands during the game. Our handlers were all in touch so that no two—or three—Ridgies were seen at the same time.

Jared, my handler, and I were able to catch some of the game from inside. Our team was literally on its last legs. After a nasty shove into the boards, one of our best defensemen, Brendan Trotter, had to be escorted off the ice on one skate. His defensive partner, Trask Emerson, had left the game in the first period and hadn't been back. When Jason Dexter, our starting goalie, missed a fifth shot, his blocker fell off his hand, revealing a heavily taped wrist. He'd left the game and hadn't come back. And from the way Tasha's brother-in-law, Xavier Schwann, was skating, I wouldn't be surprised if he had some cracked ribs. And those were just the guys I knew personally.

Hockey players were nuts.

They were probably the most skilled and strongest athletes of any team sport—except maybe all-star cheer, of course—and yet they continued to push their bodies day after day and year after year to the breaking point for a trophy. And they were underpaid —the entire team together made just over what the starting center for Denver's basketball team earned.

I kind of understood their drive, though.

I'd trained to be the best in my sport, and I didn't care about the money. I donated all of my earnings from coaching and sponsorships.

If this team didn't turn this game around fast, they'd be done tonight.

It wasn't looking good.

With eight minutes left on the clock in the third period, the Miami Ice Cats called a time-out. The crowd noise increased, but I couldn't make out what they were saying. I sipped my water and almost spit it out when the cameras zoomed in on Ridgie Number One, chasing a pigeon on the landing between sections 102 and 202. From what I could gather by watching the replays, it hadn't been a problem until it had flown down to the ice and almost got smashed by a stick. The refs had chased it off the ice and up into the stands.

Up steps, down steps, back up. Jumping, swiping. Just as I was thinking he was going to hurt himself, he tripped down the steps of 202, rolling at least three times before coming to a stop on the landing behind 102's accessible seating.

"Ridgie Number One down!" Jared's radio squawked. "We need Number Three to 202 STAT. We have crying children!"

On the screen, Ridgie Number One was loaded onto a stretcher. His handler lifted a bear paw to wave at the cameras as the paramedics rolled him into the hall and out of sight. The camera then panned the crowd. Kids were crying, and the place was in chaos.

Jared assisted me in attaching my bear head, and then we booked it to 202, where I emerged to thunderous applause. I waved, took a bow and did a standing back handspring to ensure the crowd that Ridgie the Bear's booboos were all fixed.

"Rid-gie flip! Rid-gie flip! Rid-gie flip!" The crowd chanted their request, and who was I to deny them? Before anyone could tell me no, I motioned to the yellow-shirted arena staff to keep the path clear on the landing.

Then I took off.

Back handspring into a back tuck, punch front to a cartwheel, two more back handsprings and a half twist, landing clean. I raised my arms, pumping the air and clapping my paws.

The game was still on hold since the pigeon's first merry jaunt over the ice. Continuing to fly free, it had made it down to the ice again. The refs chased after it, and from the looks of it, they were trying to direct it toward the tunnel.

I remembered a prop I'd seen in the mascot closet: a giant butterfly net. I jogged into the hall, motioning for Jared to come with me.

We entered the elevator. I pressed the button to take us to ice level and told him my idea. "Ask one of the other handlers to get the oversize butterfly net and bring it to me in the tunnel."

"You think you can catch that thing?"

I shrugged. "Probably not. But me trying will provide comedy until a bird catcher can figure out what to do."

"I'll get your skates." He bolted out of the elevator, and I headed to the tunnel to wait.

A few minutes later, Ridgie's skates were on and I had the net in hand. I walked to the opening and waited for the cameras.

The announcers called attention to me, and I raised my arms, waving the net for dramatic effect.

"And there's our Ridgie the Bear! Will he succeed where everyone else has failed? Let's cheer him on!"

I skated out to center ice, where the refs were still trying to corral the poor bird. I stopped just short of them and covered my bear mouth with a paw, mocking their attempt. The crowd ate it up as the Benny Hill theme song filled the arena. The comedic tune provided a laughter-inducing soundtrack for my plight.

The refs parted, and I closed in on the pigeon, swiping at it with the net but not really trying to catch it. Farther down the ice it went, until it was right in front of the goal.

If I could trap it in our net … my thoughts raced as they formed an idea. Slowly, I glided toward the bird, legs spread apart and arms out to the side, trying to appear as big as possible. The bird saw me and hopped back … then back again until it was just inside.

I skated into the net and plastered myself across it in a big bear hug. The fans went wild. I couldn't see the bird, but I didn't need to. The announcers were still giving a play-by-play.

"And Ridgie effectively traps the pigeon! The little fella could escape through the bear's five-hole, but he seems content to stay in the corner, folks. Here come the referees and linesmen to assist. It looks like they're going to try to trap the pigeon in an ice bucket! Yes, ladies and gentlemen, that's exactly their plan!"

I glided backward to allow them access, and two of the officials went into the net, one armed with a bucket and the other with a poster from a fan. The bucket closed over the bird, the poster underneath the bucket, and it was trapped.

I took a victory lap around the ice, waving and pumping my fists to keep the crowd excited.

And I threw in a few back handsprings for embellishment. I'd probably get in trouble for those—and for upstaging Ridgies Number One and Two, but so what? This crowd needed a pick-me-up, and so did the team.

Play resumed, and Xavier scored, making it a 5-4 game. With three minutes left, the backup goalie was pulled, and team captain Dean Hathaway tied it up with a minute left.

The Edge won in overtime, 6-5, and we would be going to Miami for Game 7.

CHAPTER 3

Tasha

June

I breathed in the aroma of my pumpkin spice flavored coffee, letting the steam warm my face and penetrate my pores. A few years ago, I'd changed up the ingredients for max health benefits—for me—and minimum digestive issues. I mixed my own blend of spices, subbed out the two-percent milk for oat milk, and nixed the pumpkin puree and whipped cream.

Three more minutes until I'd unlock the front door to the Coffee Loft and turn the sign to "Open." I liked these early morning shifts. Setup was quiet enough that I could visualize my day, and once we opened the door, the steady stream of customers kept me busy until it was time to go to the high school to coach the varsity squad. School was out for the summer, but my job wasn't done. We had tryouts and fundraising, cheer clinics, camp, plus new routines to plan—it was never-ending.

Having three jobs could be tedious at times, but it paid the bills.

And I had a *lot* of bills.

I pushed that unpleasant thought out of my brain and thought of Monty's Nana Booboo instead. Never one to follow rules, especially when caffeine or treats were concerned, she'd been the one who'd gotten me hooked on my favorite beverage, having handed

me hers during a water break at a hard practice when I was eight. I'd fallen several times already that day, having hardly slept the night before due to a stomachache. She'd told me to take a sip, and I did. Then another and another before she could pry it out of my hands. It was the caffeine jolt I'd needed, and the three sips became a before-practice ritual every fall until I could buy my own Lofty-size pumpkin spice latte.

Co-coaching with Monty had been going well, so far. As he'd suggested, we brought back our old Good Coach/Bad Coach shtick, and everything was coming together.

"It's time!" my cousin Gabby called out from behind the counter. Riva, the owners' yellow Lab therapy dog trainee, trotted out to join me on my walk to the door. The pup loved to greet guests and had a little doghouse built into the counter.

I set my Coffee Loft branded travel mug down and opened the door, peering up and down Main Street to see if any of the regulars were heading our way. The street was unusually quiet for a Monday. I shrugged and pulled my head back inside, closing the door behind me.

"No one's here yet, Riva." I picked up my coffee and bent down to pet the pup with my free hand. We crossed the store and split off, Riva disappearing into the recessed doghouse, and I joined Gabby and the owner, Jannell, behind the counter.

I loved this place: the aroma of the beans, the sugary sweetness of the treats, the bustle of locals in and out, and the new second level, an actual loft accessible by a spiral iron staircase in the center of the café. Cozy reading areas and tables provided the best atmosphere for losing oneself in a book or playing board games with friends.

In the front of the store, two large bay windows sandwiched the old saloon-style entrance. A seating area with small sofas created a comfy space by one of the windows, and on the other side, small round tables and upholstered chairs gave a cozy feel. Along the side wall opposite my station, the original mahogany bar was now lined with barstools and served as workstations. The rest of the first floor had your standard tables and chairs to seat the max capacity.

Customers began to arrive, and we fell into the familiar

morning rhythm of taking and filling their orders. My sister, Penny, arrived just before one o'clock. She used to work here full-time before she married her hockey player husband. Living with Xavier erased all her bills and gave her time to focus on her music studies and harp playing.

Gabby had cut her shifts as well. She was engaged to Noel Allaire, one of Xavier's teammates, and both she and Penny had been busy supporting their guys during the playoffs.

It was rare that the three of us had a shift together anymore, and I had a feeling come next season both of them would quit entirely. Gabby and Noel were getting married later this month when hockey ended. Why would she work here if she didn't have to? At least Penny had a reason to come in; she made Xavier's good-luck toffee coffee concoction before home games. He scored a goal every time.

During a brief lull, I refilled my coffee and snacked on a slice of Sunflower Bakery's gluten-free bread. I had to be careful with my intake; the right amount of caffeine helped my systems to function. Too much would cause my IBS to flare. I also had celiac disease and dairy sensitivities. Lucky for me, Jannell kept the shelves stocked with treats I could eat and also decided pumpkin spice would be available year-round. Before that, I brought in my own coffee in the offseasons.

"One more day!" Gabby sang to Penny. "Are you packed for Miami?"

My ears perked up, and I suddenly became engrossed in my coffee. They were excited about their guys' team making it to Game 7 of the Stanley Cup final, as they should be. They weren't purposely trying to leave me out of the conversation. The series was tied 3-3, and Game 7 would be in Miami. All the significant others and their families were traveling there for this game.

"Mostly," Penny said. "I'm glad to have you and Brenna to room and navigate with. It seems like a big ordeal."

"Because it *is* a big ordeal. I just hope Noel will get some play-time. In Round 3 he was a healthy scratch every game, and he only got a handful of shifts in Game 4 this round."

"I'm sure he will," Penny assured her. "The coaches probably just wanted to make sure he didn't get hurt. He's only got one kidney, you know."

Gabby laughed at Penny's quip. "Yeah, I know."

The bell over the door chimed. I tipped my chin up and sighed. Of course it'd be Monty.

He sauntered right up to my register. I set my coffee down and peeled myself from the back counter.

"Hey, Monty!" Gabby greeted him. "Are you going to Miami?"

"Hey, Gab. I am. Thanks to my extraordinary performance in Game 6 and Ridgie Number One's broken bones and subsequent retirement, I have officially usurped the incumbent bear and achieved the position of Ridgie Number One."

"That was epic, by the way," Gabby praised. "I'm glad you're coming. You can help me calm Penny's nerves."

Huh. She hadn't suggested *me* to calm Penny's nerves. I was Penny's sister, for goodness' sake. Why would she ask Monty and not me?

Oh, right. Because I wasn't going.

Just another item on the list of Ways Gabby Annoys Tasha.

Whatever.

I tapped the tips of my short cheer-friendly nails on the counter as I waited for Monty to stop talking long enough to place his order. Finally, they finished gushing over the trip and he turned back to me.

"Key lime protein shake, please."

My eyebrows lifted as I punched in the order. Like Gabby, Monty had always drunk iced chocolate since we were kids and still preferred it in the afternoons. But during one of our cheer competition trips to Orlando, he'd gotten hooked on a particular key lime and vanilla protein powder shake. He'd made a deal with the previous owners to have key limes shipped here after he decided the drink had everything to do with his best performance to date. "A little late in the day for your morning go-to," I observed, adding a hint of sarcasm to my tone.

"I was with Nana," he retorted. "Some things are more important than the time of day I drink my protein."

My heart twinged. I softened my tone. "How's she doing?" I asked as he tapped his credit card to the payment device.

"Fine." He glanced over at Penny and Gabby. "Do you have a minute to talk in private?"

"Private?" I stepped back, surprised at his request.

He rolled his eyes. "You know, like me and you, alone. Where no one else can hear us talk."

"I know what *private* means," I shot back and flipped my ponytail over my shoulder. "I'm just surprised. We could talk at the gym. Why here, why now?"

He huffed. "Just—yes or no?" The impatient response was very un-Monty-like. I'd rarely seen him lose his cool.

"Fine. Follow me into the kitchen." I turned and called out to Gabby to make his drink, telling her we'd be right back.

Monty followed me through the kitchen to the refrigerated room. I held the big heavy stainless-steel door until he was inside and slammed it shut behind me.

"That's not locked, is it?" he asked, concern flashing across his features.

"Nope. The last place I want to be is locked in a freezing closet with *you*," I assured him.

"Same," he drawled in his deepest register, but he was smiling.

Huh.

"So, why the clandestine meeting?" I crossed my arms and tapped my foot.

His gaze lowered to my sneaker. "I'll make it quick. You have an extra bedroom. I need a place to stay while Nana's house gets up to code so she can come home."

My heart pounded in my chest. He couldn't be serious. "I'm sorry, what? You want to move in with me?"

"I don't *want* to," he replied dryly. "But it makes sense. We can even carpool to practice."

I shook my head. "Can't you stay with your parents? Or with one of the guys? Penny and Xavier have a guest room." *Anywhere but my place.*

"No. Nana specifically suggested you because she'll know Parfait le Chat will be well cared for if I have to travel."

I gaped at him. "And your cat, too?"

"*Nana's* cat, officially," he corrected. "My parents are pet-free.

The guys all have their own pets or will be traveling for the summer. And Pen and Gab have enough going on to worry about caring for a pet."

"And I don't?" My voice rose at his implication that I wasn't busy. "Three jobs, remember?"

He tipped his head back and sighed dramatically. "Name your fee."

"My fee?"

"I'll pay your rent all summer."

"It's already taken care of." I didn't have proof, but I was sure Xavier had paid the rent for the rest of the year when Penny moved out.

"I'll pay you anyway."

"Nope."

"C'mon, Tasha. There must be something you want. And are you really prepared to turn me and Parfy out on the streets?"

"Pet-friendly hotels exist, you know."

He met my gaze and held it. I shivered. Darn near-freezing temp in this fridge.

Connections.

The word popped into my head, and I stewed over it. Monty now had access to guys my age that made big money. Big bankfuls of money that wouldn't even be dented by my medical bills. Nice, hard-working guys who had good enough insurance they only had to work one job instead of three. Guys who appreciated eating healthy and weren't averse to dating cheerleaders.

Surely, I could hit it off with one of them. Fall in love, get married, and relax for once in my life? I was more suited to being an athlete's wife than my sister was. Penny didn't even wear makeup, and her idea of styling her hair was braiding it.

"There is *one* thing …" I let the sentence trail off and narrowed my gaze, still locked on his.

"Name it."

"I want to be your plus-one for all Edge-related events." His eyes widened. "Don't get excited." I rushed to explain. "I want to date a hockey player. Help me get into their world. We can start with Gabby and Noel's wedding."

He didn't speak for a minute. I waited as he pressed his lips together, chewed on the inside of his cheek, and squinted back at me.

"Deal." He stuck out his hand. "Shake on it?"

I shook my head. "Didn't mean anything the last time."

His jaw dropped, and he pulled his hand back as if stung.

Good. I spun on my heel and stalked out of the fridge before he could invent an excuse or apologize or—

I didn't care. The past was the past.

It was time to plan my future.

A future where I didn't have to work so hard to merely survive.

CHAPTER 4

Monty

Move-in Day.

After a brutal Game 7 loss in Miami, I was back in Colorado and ready for the reno to begin so it could be over.

"Mew!"

Parfait le Chat, protesting vehemently from his soft-sided pet carrier, was my last trip. I'd set up the mackerel tabby's bed, toys, food, water, and litter box in my room and bathroom. "Almost there, boy. Just up these stairs and … here we go."

After my sister Mindy died, Nana decided I needed a cat. My parents wouldn't allow pets at our house, so Parfait—named after Nana's favorite dessert at the time—lived at her house. Tasha and I spent a whole practice brainstorming silly nicknames. Parfy, Barfy, Parfait the Cray, Parfetta the Chetta. All ridiculous, but it was the first time I'd laughed in weeks.

"Nana says his name is Par-feh luh Sha." I stroked my new kitten and winced when he bit me." But I can read and it says Par-fate-lee-chat. So dumb."

Tasha giggled. I was pleased that I'd made her laugh.

"Well," she said. "We'll just have to give the little fuzzball a nickname. How about Parfy?"

"Or Barfy!" I hooted. We collapsed into giggles as the kitten ran around us jumping and scratching and hopping like a bouncy ball in one of those lottery boxes.

"Parfait the Cray!" I could hardly get the words out I was laughing so hard.

"Parfetta the Chetta! Like cheese!" Tasha squealed.

Warmed by the memory, I couldn't help chuckling as I pushed my key into the lock and opened the door. Tasha's apartment was just off Main Street, separated by a parking lot from the back of the Coffee Loft and its neighboring businesses. It was a good ten-minute drive from Nana's, and Parfait had cried the full duration.

Montoya Construction would start the accessibility renovations on Monday. I figured with the wedding this weekend, it'd be better to move in on Friday than on Sunday. So I'd been in and out all morning while Tasha worked at the Coffee Loft. She was home now. Nowhere visible, but the aroma of something cooking gave her away.

I toed off my shoes under the entry table and slid my feet into the fuzzy slippers Tasha had given me for a high school cheer secret Santa gift. They were worn out like a well-loved teddy bear and a little too small. Trusty, dependable, broken in, a little withered and dulled by age but functional and far superior to a stiff brand-new pair. My toes peeked out the open front, but the worn-in softness and familiar comfort far outweighed the minor size deficiency.

I settled Parfait in my room and shut the door, closing him in. Best to let him get adjusted to a smaller space before overwhelming him with the full layout. I snorted. Tasha's entire apartment was smaller than Nana's master suite. The cat would be fine, but I didn't want to press my luck just yet.

I crossed the living space to the open kitchen to inspect the permeating scent. A Crock-Pot sat on the counter, and I lifted the lid. "Mmm." It was some kind of chili with veggies.

"Drop that crock cover or I'll shoot."

I glanced up, furrowing my brow as my brain registered the sight before me. Tasha, in a belted satin robe, her sandy hair in long, sculpted waves, held a squirt bottle. I couldn't help chuckling.

I replaced the lid on the pot and held my hands up in defense. "Wouldn't dare mess with your dinner. Why *are* you making dinner? Don't they feed you at rehearsals? And what's in that bottle?"

She glared at me. "Water, for the cat. If he goes where he's not allowed."

That elicited a full belly laugh, deep from my gut. "First of all, a cat is going to go where a cat is going to go. Second, and lucky for you, Parfait is old and lazy. Ancient by cat standards. And he only jumps if he's highly motivated."

The muscles in her face relaxed, and she lowered the bottle. "Fine. It's chicken and veggie chili. Gabby forgot about my dietary restrictions, and the kitchen couldn't accommodate tonight on such short notice. So, I'll eat before I go and probably when I get back. It's fixed for tomorrow, though," she added.

Tasha had always been a picky eater, and as an adult, she'd become a weirdly healthy eater. She was always refusing food at events; this had gluten, that had dairy, the other thing had cross-contamination.

"Why are you still looking at me?" she asked.

Was I? I guess I was.

"Uh ... your hair looks nice." It did. I was used to seeing her in a ponytail.

"Stop it," she gritted through her teeth.

"Stop what?" I asked.

"You don't need to be nice to me because I saved you and your cat from being homeless."

I held back a laugh and pasted on a smug expression. "Noted. You've got a blob of lotion on your cheek."

"I—" Her free hand flew to her face. "Uh!"

She spun around and stalked back to her room. I chuckled. It was fun ruffling her feathers. It came naturally.

After Nana's stroke, I made a list of my regrets. Not monitoring her sugar intake as stringently as I could have. Wasting years and effort trying to get my parents to notice me. Breaking my promise to a four-year-old Tasha that I'd be her stunt partner forever.

But it wasn't enough that I'd broken our partnership after sixteen years. It was my choice for her replacement that had rubbed salt in the wound, though that hadn't been my intention, and I'd regretted it almost immediately. There was a lot of work to be done if she was ever going to forgive me. I wanted to earn her trust again as much as I wanted Nana to make a full recovery.

I just didn't know how.

Maybe that path would be revealed to me while I was staying here.

I spent the next few hours unpacking and petting Parfait. I figured I'd stay in my room until Tasha left for Gabby and Noel's wedding rehearsal and dinner. Once I finished, I relaxed on the bed. The old cat climbed onto my chest, turned in a circle, plopped down, and fell into a deep sleep.

Knock knock. I glanced at the clock. 5:07. Parfait was still snoring. "Come in," I said lightly.

Tasha opened the door slowly, revealing herself one inch at a time. Her long waves were held back with a glittery headband, and she wore a fit-and-flare yellow sundress that set off her tan. She looked like … a ray of sunshine.

Very un-Tasha-like.

I tried not to react.

Because of the cat, of course. Didn't want to disturb the old guy.

Le Chat. I laughed internally at my own joke.

"Montgomery! You're not dressed. Aren't you coming?"

"Huh?"

"To the rehearsal."

"I'm not in the wedding," I reminded her.

Tasha's forehead knitted in confusion. "Gabby didn't invite you to the dinner?"

"She did. But I figured I'd stay here and help Parfait get adjusted. No one will miss me."

She tilted her head and frowned but recovered quickly. "That's true." But it didn't land with the usual vitriol. Was she disappointed I wasn't going?

Impossible. The girl hated me. I was only here because our arrangement was mutually beneficial.

"Help yourself to the chili. Bye."

The door clicked shut behind her, and I stroked the cat thoughtfully. Tasha had been almost civil. What was that about?

TWENTY-SOMETHING HOURS LATER, the wedding reception in Brenna Trotter's barn venue was well underway. The wedding party dances had been danced, the cake had been cut, and now it was time for my favorite part.

Line dances.

This reception was stacked with former cheerleaders and current hockey players, none of which were on the floor yet. They'd get rowdy later, but I'd be on my way home by then. I positioned myself in the center of the dance floor behind Tasha's grandmother and great-aunt as The Hustle got underway. DJs always warmed up the crowd with that one. It was old and got the Boomers on the floor. Then they'd play the Electric Slide, and the Gen Xers would join in. Depending on the event, the Achy Breaky Heart was next. Then the Macarena, the Cha Cha Slide, the Cupid Shuffle, and finally the Wobble.

I knew them all. I put my own spin into each of them. As did Tasha and Gabby. We'd been doing most of them at cheer camps since preschool.

I looked for her over the dancing septuagenarians. She stood by the dessert table, speaking to a waiter, probably asking for the ingredients. The sign *said* "Gluten-free Chocolate Cake," but as I learned from her, that didn't necessarily mean it was true, especially if it was made with or on the same equipment as the gluten-full desserts. When she turned away from him, I waved. She rolled her eyes and shook her head.

The next time I faced her direction, she'd moved, and I located her back at our table, chatting with Brenna. I waved again and caught Brenna's attention. She said something to Tasha, then pulled her to her feet.

They were coming my way. The song faded out, and most of the Boomers left the dance floor, making room for the next generation and a handful of Millennials and Gen Zers who knew the Electric Slide.

There was room in this line dance to change it up. Tasha had been the one to teach me that. One year at cheer camp, we had to choreograph our own variation. She was a born choreographer. She not only did hers but mine and Gabby's, too.

I loosened the tie around my neck and rolled up my sleeves as they stepped into place to my left. I'd ditched my jacket as soon as we arrived at our table.

"Let's see what you got," Tasha challenged, stepping into the grapevine and turning in circles instead of sliding.

Classic Tasha.

The next move was to lean back and twist your body to the right, then roll forward to punch at the ground. This was the part where she'd had me do a back tuck and then punch forward. But I didn't have room for that here. Instead, I busted out my pop-and-lock moves and flat robot hands.

Giggling behind me encouraged me to continue that way, and by the end of the song, I'd broken a sweat. Tasha patted my back. "The kids loved that."

I lifted my brow and waited for her opinion, but of course it wouldn't come. Straight praise wasn't our thing anymore. Not for a long time. Not since—

I kept my expression neutral as more guests crowded onto the floor. Tasha danced beside me through all the dances until the Wobble ended. The DJ slowed it down with a '90s ballad, and that was our cue to head back to our table. Neither of us got into the slow dances. They were awkward and … feely.

I didn't want any feels.

"Hey," she hissed, pulling at my elbow as we waded through the lovey-dovey couples to get to our table. "Who's *that* guy?" She tipped her chin with appreciation toward a tall, pale blond deep in conversation with Xavier. But he wasn't looking at Penny's husband.

His gaze was fixed on Tasha.

"Vlad?" I asked. "Noel's friend from some European league," I said dismissively. "Signed with the Edge last week."

"So he's local. Introduce me?"

I studied her face, flushed from dancing. Exerted, Tasha was at her friendliest. Endorphins made her nicer.

Without a word, I led her over to the guy.

Xavier saw us coming and waved us over. "Vlad, have you met my sister-in-law, Tasha?"

He shook his head. "Vlad Ivanov. Pleased to meet you." He spoke carefully and deliberately, almost robotically as he held out his hand for Tasha. She lifted hers for a shake, but he raised her arm and brushed a kiss against her knuckles instead. Her left arm was still hooked into mine, and I felt her whole body shiver at his touch.

I already hated the guy.

"Vlad's Russian and working on his English," Xavier explained. "We're all helping him learn words."

"Nice of you." I turned to Tasha. "Enjoy your conversation." I smirked. I peeled her arm off mine like it was poisonous and sauntered back to our table, plopping into my seat next to Penny.

"What do you know about Vlad?" I asked.

She fussed with the baby's breath tucked into her waist-length braid. "Not much. Xavier likes him. Why do you ask?"

I thumbed over my shoulder. "Tasha likes him, too."

"Aw, are you looking out for my sister?" She smiled and patted my knee. "I knew you didn't hate her."

"Hate her?" I blinked. "I don't hate her. She's the one who froze *me* out."

"I know. But you hurt her pretty badly when you chose Gabby as a partner over her that summer before she broke her leg."

"I had good reasons."

"I'm sure you did. But it cut her deep. Especially after your pledge to be 'partners forever,'" she air-quoted. "And then she fell and broke her leg ..."

"We were *four.* Little kids make all kinds of silly promises. And most don't remember them and hold onto them their whole life."

"It wasn't silly to her, and you know it. She trusted you, Monty. It's very hard for her to trust people; always has been."

"I know." I squeezed my eyes shut. The memory of preschool me and Tasha spitting on our palms and shaking on *partners forever* haunted me. "I never dropped her, not once."

"She knows that. And I think that made it hurt even worse, especially after she fell." Penny sat up straight as Vlad and Tasha passed us, hand in hand, toward the dance floor.

"And now she slow dances," I mumbled, incredulous.

"So go cut in," Penny suggested.

I shook my head. "Doesn't bother me."

She cast a pointed look at me and patted my knee again. "Keep telling yourself that." Xavier appeared behind her, and she stood. "Don't be so stubborn," she advised me. I averted my gaze as they made their way through the tables to slow dance to whatever lame song was playing.

Time to put in a request.

It took a fifty-dollar bill to convince the DJ to play "The Chicken Dance," especially since it was on Gabby and Noel's banned song list. Who banned the most iconic dance?

Gabby, that's who. I wish I'd had my phone ready to snap a picture of her face when it began to play. I knew it irked her, but I didn't request it to make her mad. I requested it to get Tasha's attention. Those two had been in competition since they were born.

They were both super smart and great athletes. But Tasha could also ice skate, and Gabby, despite years of lessons as a kid, was still a bender. She'd improved a bit since dating Noel, but there was zero grace in her slide. Tasha, on the other hand, could have gone into figure skating instead of cheer if she'd decided to. And with her natural ability to choreograph graceful and compelling routines, she was fun to watch on or off the ice.

I joined the guests forming a circle on the dance floor and snuck a glance in Tasha's direction. She was six people down from me, and I watched and listened while she taught Vlad the moves.

"Gabby *hates* this song!" she shouted over the music. "I had my tenth birthday at the ice rink, and she couldn't skate. But Monty and I pulled her out for this song because we thought we could hold her up. We couldn't. She fell more times than we could count!"

Vlad just smiled. Probably couldn't understand a word she was saying.

Probably didn't care, either, from the way he was looking at her.

It irked me.

I glanced at the glowering Gabby, and I smiled at the memory. Guess she never got over it. While I flapped my arms, I scanned the circle. A few people down from me were Brenna and her husband, Brendan, then Nate and his roommate, Leon. Across from me, Gabby's brother Jake and two of his college buddies were paired up with a trio of girls from the Worlds team, some hockey players next to them. Then Noel, Xavier, and Penny. Behind them, Gabby was at the DJ's booth, probably reminding him in the kindest way that he wasn't supposed to play this song.

When she looked up, I flashed a grin as I shimmied into a squat. When I wiggled back up, she was shaking her head and laughing.

Gab was a good sport.

But the joke was on me. "The Chicken Dance" ended, and another ballad began.

How I loathed weddings.

Couples getting cozy, singles on the prowl. Except for me. I didn't have time for a relationship. Since Nana had been stuck in a wheelchair, she'd been my top priority. I'd yet to find a woman who was okay with that. It was tiring, dating. And there was always that small part of me that wondered if they were more interested in my money than me. My trust fund was substantial. I drove a high-end pickup truck. I lived in Nana's Victorian mansion. And I had no plans to ever move out.

I'd given up looking for someone who was okay with all that.

I passed Tasha and Vlad as I exited the dance floor, trying not to be a creeper. He was a charmer. She was flushed, giggling, and batting her eyelashes. It was hard to tell if she was being genuine —because, endorphins—or playing it up because she so desperately wanted a hockey boyfriend like her sister and cousin. Xavier and Noel were great, but she sure was narrowing the field. There were only a handful of single guys on the Edge, and she'd managed to catch the eye of the newest most eligible bachelor.

"Monty!" Penny waved from the table where she was standing with Xavier. Seated at it were an older couple, probably his parents, and who I assumed were his three sisters. "Have you met the Schwanns?"

I offered my hand to Xavier's dad. "Montgomery Biddington. Nice to meet you."

"Heinrich Schwann and my wife, Irina."

"He's cute!" the middle daughter whispered loudly to the youngest. I grinned at the preteens but pretended not to hear.

The oldest, who I knew to be in her early twenties from Penny talking about her, shushed them and smiled. "I'm Daniella. These silly girls are Karina and Edyta. Nice to meet you."

"Pleasure." I shook their hands and kept my face neutral as Penny used her index fingers and mouthed *she's single* in Daniella's direction.

Time to go.

"Pen, can you make sure Tasha gets home? I need to check in on Nana before visiting hours end, and I don't think she's ready to leave." I nodded toward the dance floor, where she and Vlad were swaying. He was wearing a perma-smile, and I don't think he blinked the whole time I stared at him.

What a meathead.

"Sure. Say hi to Nana Booboo for me and tell her we miss her at the Coffee Loft."

"Will do. Thanks, Pen."

I weaved through the tables to my chair, retrieved my jacket, and was out of there before the song ended.

CHAPTER 5
Tasha

One week later

I should've known better.

My stomach seized again, and tears eked out of the corners of my eyes. The projectile vomiting had ceased around 2 a.m., but my gut was still revolting from being violated.

Monty ordered food last night from Pasta Nacht's, a restaurant that was usually safe for me. I ordered the same gluten-free dairy-free fettucine alfredo every time, and it was fine. They knew me and my food issues. And just in case, I personally called in the order every time to make sure they knew it was for me and reminded them of the consequences if any of the ingredients were cross-contaminated.

Foolishly, I let Monty place an online order. I typed in all the special requests myself, and when our food arrived, the delivery driver assured me they'd been honored, pointing to the extra-long receipt with all my instructions printed on it.

Ha. What did he know?

I should have called and spoken to the manager on duty.

Instead, I'd spent the night regretting every single bite, and now I was housebound and would miss Penny's only performance at the Renaissance Faire this summer.

I *hated* not showing up for her. When my sister's fingers

touched the strings of her harp, I relaxed. She used to play it in the Coffee Loft, but now that she was working there hardly ever, the harp stayed at her and Xavier's apartment. He'd even made her a music room.

She deserved it. Every bone in Penny's body was nice. Sweet like the coffee she made for her husband. His hockey season was over, and next week they'd be leaving to visit his family in Calgary. I probably wouldn't see her again until her birthday in August, when Xavier flew all of his and her relatives to his family's castle in Europe. He'd inherited his grandfather's estate and title—Baron von Schwann—making my sister a baroness. Pretty much European royalty.

I pulled my legs up to my chest and texted Monty. *I'm sick. Are you going to the Ren Faire? If so, can you record Penny's performances for me?*

He responded right away. *I was just about to text you. Sounds like an animal is dying behind your door.*

Ha ha, I texted back.

For real. I need to see your face. Penny will ask why you're not there. I need proof that you're alive and it's not an imposter messaging me.

I shook my head. *Not gonna happen. So, you won't go, then?*

Maybe. If you ask me nicely.

I rolled my eyes. Normally, I wouldn't cave to such demands, but I needed this text conversation to be over so I could lie down and close my eyes again. *Will you PLEASE go to the Ren Faire and record Penny for me?*

I think I can squeeze it in. Send me the details. And text me if you need anything from the pharmacy or grocery store.

Thanks. And please let Penny know I feel terrible I can't make it. She'll understand. Tell her I said she cannoli imagine what I'm going through.

Cannoli was our code word for Italian food. Different cuisines wreaked different havoc on my systems. She'd know by the use of the word I was sick as a dog with digestive issues. I tapped out all the pertinent information and attached the Ren Faire map to my reply, then stretched out on the bathroom rug, bunching a towel under my head for a pillow and praying for sleep.

No sense in going back to bed. I'd just be back here once the current bottle of water I drank processed.

Mercifully, sleep overtook me. When I woke up, the sun had shifted. It's light no longer shone at full force through my window and the bathroom was dim. Groaning, I sat up and felt around for my phone.

4:47 p.m.

I swiped to check my texts. A few from Penny, plus a missed call and voicemail. And a whole bunch from Monty. Recordings of Penny's performance alternated with questions about my welfare.

I groaned when my phone rang.

It was him.

I closed my eyes and swiped to answer it, tapping the icon for speakerphone and laying the device on the floor by my head.

"Tasha?" Monty's deep voice dripped heavily with concern.

"Yeah?"

"Can you unlock your door?"

"No."

"I have grape Gatorade for you."

Tempting. But I couldn't muster the energy to get up and go to my bedroom door even if I wanted to.

I tried to sound like my normal self. "Put it in the fridge."

"If you don't open the door, I'm going to pick the lock. Penny said you're probably dehydrated. I'm not playing, Tasha. I *will* call EMS if you don't let me in and drink this stuff."

Ugh. I wanted to curse into the phone and tell him where to go with his Gatorade. But I couldn't, because the truth was, I was weaker than I'd been before my nap. I needed electrolytes, but for now, Gatorade would suffice.

I kicked the bathroom door closed. "Fine. Bring it in and leave it on my desk."

"Aren't you going to open the door?"

I squeezed my eyes shut. "Can't," I breathed, admitting defeat.

There was no scuffle at the door; Penny had probably told him we kept the keys to our rooms on top of the doorframes, just in case of emergencies. I pulled my knees to my chest and prayed he wouldn't try to bust into the bathroom.

I couldn't let him see me like this.

"Tasha!"

Well, I guess higher powers had other ideas. I didn't have to open my eyes to know he'd pushed open the bathroom door. And I didn't need my eyes to tell me when he fell to his knees on the ground next to me.

And I didn't need my eyes to feel his arm snaking behind my shoulders and gently guiding me into a position conducive to sipping liquid.

I couldn't have been more mortified if I'd had a wardrobe malfunction at the top of a cheer pyramid. I'd never felt so exposed as I felt in this moment. Sweaty, disheveled, stinking like vomit and whatever else … I'd never live this down.

"Tasha." His voice cracked as he pulled my head into his lap.

"Your … thighs are harder than the floor," I gritted out. "Please go away."

"I'm not going anywhere. Drink."

I closed my mouth to protest.

He prodded the rim of the bottle to my lower lip. "And of course my thighs are hard. I work out five days a week."

"You're supposed to have rest days, dummy."

"Rest is for the weak. No drinky, I call nine-one-one."

I parted my lips in defeat. He hated me enough to follow through on the threat.

The cool grape-flavored liquid coated my tongue. I swallowed slowly, not wanting to incite another round of dry heaves.

Still with my eyes closed, I fumbled to swat the bottle away with my hand. "Enough."

"Open your eyes."

"No."

"You can't pretend me away. I'm going to help you get to your bed, and you should have your eyes open."

"No."

He sighed. "Fine."

Before I could respond, he maneuvered me so that one of his arms looped behind my back and another was under my knees. As he stood, my stomach groaned loudly.

"Down," I whimpered. "Please."

"In a minute," he cooed.

As Monty carried me to my bed, another wave of nausea hit.

My head spun, and I used every ounce of strength I could summon to keep my mouth closed. My cheeks puffed out with each burst of air from my stomach, but I succeeded in keeping the Gatorade on the inside.

Monty set me down gently on my bed, and I rolled to face the wall so my back was to him. "Please go," I whispered hoarsely, once the heaves had passed.

"Yeah ... no. Bucket's behind you." A creaking sound signaled he'd found my desk chair and was leaning back in it. "Penny would kill me if you died on my watch. You're my patient."

If I had the strength, I would've rolled my eyes, even if he couldn't see them. "I'm not going to die, and I'm not *your* anything. So, go."

"Right now, you're a pain in my backside," he retorted. "Pretend I'm not here. I'm going to read on my phone and pretend I'm anywhere else."

"Don't make me your pity project," I said through gritted teeth.

"Hard not to pity you. You look miserable. I wouldn't abandon a sick animal, even if it roared at me or unleashed its claws. So why wouldn't I sit here and get verbally abused by you?"

My stomach groaned again, and my eyes stung. I didn't answer his question. Why did it have to be *him* that was here?

Right. Because I had no one else.

Penny was at the Ren Faire. Gabby was on her honeymoon. I didn't really have any other friends. Over the years, my friend circle had shrunk to them and a few former-friends-now-acquaintances in the high school group chat. But I knew they had another chat that I wasn't a part of, for when they made plans to go to places I couldn't eat food at. For the longest time, I'd eat before I left to hang out and snack on celery and water at dinner. I guess after all the times I said no, I couldn't eat there, they listened. And stopped inviting me.

I *considered* calling my mother, but she'd overreact and baby me. I was a grown adult with a bachelor's degree in sports fitness and a master's in nutrition. I wasn't the type to call my mommy every time I had a hangnail.

I could take care of myself. I knew how my body worked. I knew what upset it, and I knew how to fix it.

It would just take a few days. I could rest until Monday, and if I had to call in sick to the Coffee Loft then, Jannell would understand. School was out, and the high school squad didn't start formal practices until the end of July. The FireVolts practiced on Tuesday and Thursday nights.

My digestive system would be back to normal by Tuesday, I was sure of it.

I must have dozed off again. When I woke up, I was curled up and facing the other direction, under the comforter. Blinking in the darkness, I waited until my eyes adjusted to the sliver of moonlight peeking in from between my curtains.

The desk chair was empty. Good.

My stomach growled a complaint. I should try to drink again. The small bottle of Gatorade was in an ice bucket on my desk, just out of reach on the other side of my nightstand. Tentatively, I swung my legs off the bed and pushed myself up to a sitting position. Taking a deep, steadying breath, I lowered my feet to the floor.

"Ow!"

"Mrow!"

I retracted my legs immediately and peered down. Monty sat up, rubbing at the hip I'd tried to stand on as Parfait shot out of the room.

Evening my startled expression and raising my eyebrows, I snorted. "Really? That hurt?"

"You're heavier than you look."

I tilted my head to the side. We both knew that he was capable of lifting girls heftier than me into the air, fully extended, in one hand. "Are you going to move, or should I attempt to leap over you?"

The moonlight reflected in his eyes as he scooted leisurely out of the way for me. "Glad you're feeling better," he mumbled.

"Yep, no need for you to play hero—or nurse. I can drink my own Gatorade, thank you very much." I clutched my stomach as I walked the few steps to the desk. I had to pretend I was fine so he would leave. I'd need to use the bathroom when I finished the bottle, and I didn't want him here for *that*.

Monty's hands beat mine to the Gatorade. He twisted the cap off and held the bottle out to me. I took it and used my other hand to brace myself on the desk. I sipped and stopped. Sipped and stopped. Sipped and—

"Excuse me." I set the bottle back into the ice and spun around, hobbling toward my bathroom.

The Gatorade was coming up, and there was nothing I could do this time to hold it back.

CHAPTER 6

Monty

I scooted across the floor to the closed bathroom door and leaned against it. I wanted to give Tasha privacy but also be there in case she needed help. A few minutes later, when a harp rendition of "Somewhere Over the Rainbow" drifted out from under the door, I surmised she'd placed the end of her phone next to it, speaker pointed toward me, to mask any sounds coming from within.

Deciding she was probably okay for a few minutes, I got to my feet and plodded to the kitchen. Last night, I'd found her binder of recipes and thumbed through it, selecting one for an everything-free chicken soup she'd tabbed and labeled as "Recovery Option #1." She had all the ingredients for it in the freezer, most in Ziploc bags with the same label, so I dumped them all in her Crock-Pot, clipped some cilantro and parsley from the pots by the window, and turned the setting to low.

The entire time I worked, Parfait lounged on the bar. He was a counter connoisseur and particular about his flat surfaces. Since he wasn't near where I was prepping the food, I allowed it. It was a laborious effort for him to jump from the arm of the sofa to the nearest barstool and hop up. He would continue the routine if I put him on the floor. And if I shut him up in my room, he'd mew at a surprisingly loud volume and disturb Tasha, so that was out of the question.

I moved to the sofa an hour later, and Parfy shifted his position to face Tasha's door. I was able to coax him off the bar with a handful of treats, and I pulled him into my lap.

They didn't call it a slow cooker for no reason. As the ingredients mingled, the aroma teased my nostrils and airways, and by hour three I was salivating for it. I fed Parfait, washed my hands, and checked on the soup. When I lifted the cover, a cloud of steam hit me in the face.

Should've expected that.

I returned the lid over the soup and came to the conclusion I was looking forward to trying it. Usually, the way Tasha described her unusual food combinations sounded weird. But having lived with her for a couple of weeks now, and having snuck bites and tastes of her leftovers, I was discovering they weren't half bad.

I wouldn't admit that to her, though.

In a lower cupboard, I found a stainless-steel container with a lid and ladled some soup into it for Tasha to consume when she felt ready. I also scooped some into a mug for myself, my curiosity getting the better of me. I wanted to taste this concoction of bone broth, chicken, carrots, cilantro, ginger, turmeric, egg noodles, and other things I'd never considered to be included in a recipe for this American family staple.

Parfait joined me on the floor next to Tasha's door, dropping a hair tie onto my fuzzy slipper and curling up into a ball in my lap. Serenaded by another harp melody, I ate the soup, careful not to drip any of the hot liquid onto his fur. He'd already been traumatized once this morning.

Besides checking on Nana, I didn't have any plans today. I usually took her to church on Sundays, but she wasn't ready for an outing outside of Mountainview Manor yet. Maybe I'd bring her some of Tasha's soup if there was any left.

I plucked the soggy hair tie from the slipper and rolled it between my fingers. It was one of those special ones without the metal band that held the two ends together. Years ago, Tasha had switched, claiming they stayed in place better. I'd shrugged. As long as her hair wasn't in the way of my hands, I didn't mind what she did with it.

Well, I *did* like it when she wore her hair down, in soft waves over her shoulders. The competitive, persistent, and perseverant version of her softened. Even her voice changed to a lighter, kinder tone. Less about business and more … human? Tasha was a machine in the gym and a bustling barista behind the counter. When she had time to relax, she allowed the personality traits she masked to come forward.

I liked both versions of her. She was kind and caring but not a doormat. She got things done and always put forth her best effort.

There was no one else like her.

And I hated that she was hurting. I wanted to understand why, what was wrong with her, and how to fix it. I knew about her gluten sensitivity now, and I noticed that she never ate dairy products or drank cow's milk or used it or real butter in her cooking. But she'd never confided in me why, even back when we were still friends.

I wanted to know more so I could help her and support her. My life was better with her in it, and I wanted her to feel that way about me again.

I had to find a way to get our friendship back.

No matter what the cost to my ego.

CHAPTER 7
Tasha

Like I predicted, I was feeling better by Monday but not well enough for the morning shift. I was able to switch from my opening slot to the midafternoon hours so I could rest a bit longer. Tuesday was better, and I made up my missed hours at the Coffee Loft before FireVolts practice.

Monty was already there, head-to-heads in conversation with our team captains, Amelia and Evan. They were former teammates of ours and three-time veterans of the Worlds team. Amelia coached a tiny team and a mini elite team, and Evan was on the cheer staff at the local university as a tumbling coach.

The rest of the members were standing on our designated floor. I clapped my hands, the loud sound echoing over the low buzz of athlete chatter in the gym. "Five laps. Let's go!"

All heads turned in my direction. I lifted my chin and nodded in the direction of the vulcanized rubber track that outlined the perimeter of the four cheer floors and tumbling area.

Monty wrapped up his conversation and sauntered over to me. "We still had three minutes."

I shrugged and crossed my arms over my chest.

"You know, you don't *have* to take on a bad coach role," Monty continued. He cleared his throat, and my eyes snapped up to meet his gaze. "You know what they're calling us?"

I didn't care.

He didn't wait for me to answer, probably guessing—correctly—that I wouldn't.

"Coach Monsha."

"So?" I asked.

"Sounds an awful lot like 'monster.'"

"So?" I asked again. I wasn't sure how I felt about that, but I didn't really care. "We have a job to do and a title to win. I don't care if they love me or hate me."

"Hmm." He pressed his lips together and averted his gaze, waving to our captains as they passed the starting mark. "Four more, team! Pick up the pace. You've got this!"

"They're not five, Montgomery. They don't need constant affirmation. Tell them what to do, and they do it. That strategy won them the title last year."

"So bristly today. Prickly, like a cactus."

I glared at him, silently challenging him to tell me I should've stayed in bed.

He tapped his chin with his index finger. "Like the taciveria flowering succulent you were named after."

I rewarded him with a look that could freeze fire.

"No? All right, like a hedgehog cactus then. All cute on the outside, but get too close, reach out to pet it, and ouch! Stung."

"You're not even making sense. A hedgehog cactus doesn't look like a hedgehog."

He shrugged. "So? You know what I mean."

Yeah, I did. But I didn't care.

Much.

I turned on my heel and strode to the edge of the mat at the lap mark. "Bring it in!" I pointed to the center of the mat, directing the athletes to turn as they completed their run.

Amelia and Evan led the team through stretches and warm-ups while I went over the choreography portion of the routine on my tablet. We had a week of extra practices set aside in late July to learn the entire section, but until then we'd play with bits and pieces of it. They'd learned six eight-counts of it at tryouts, and I plugged that portion into the end of the number. Nate and I had needed to see who could dance and who should be tumbling or stunting during the segment.

"We're splitting into three groups. Group One will go to the far side of the mat with Amelia to perfect and personalize the final dance segment, complete with ending pose. Group Two will follow Monty to the tumble mats to work on elements he wants to add to the big finish. Group Three will stay here with me to construct the final stunting component. Any questions?"

From the back, I caught, "Does she ever smile?" from a new member of the team. The girl he whispered to had the good sense not to answer.

"Five more laps for you," I called back to him. "To answer your question, it's not my job to smile. I'm not performing; *you* are. Get your positivity cup filled from Coach Montgomery or volunteer with a younger team."

The kid's eyes widened, and he mumbled a "yes, ma'am" as he bolted to the track for his laps.

Monty cleared his throat and shot me a grin. "I've seen her smile. It could happen."

I cast another glare at him, then turned back to the team. "Don't get your hopes up."

"Did you hear that *click,* team? New life goal unlocked." Monty turned to me with a smirky grin, but his eyes seemed ... kind. Like he actually wanted to make me smile.

Recovering quickly, I retorted, "You think too highly of yourself, Montgomery. Keep on smiling like a cheer floor jester."

"A clown, huh?" He waggled his eyebrows at me and turned back to the team, who were all watching us with amused expressions. "New life goal, point two: Unfreezing Tasha's ice face and making her laugh."

"Good luck with that." I stepped away from him to start calling the names for the groups, wanting to get this practice underway so the time would pass and I could go home and crash.

Monty must have sensed I wasn't one hundred percent, because I caught him sneaking glances at me throughout the practice. Each time, I'd narrow my eyelids to slits and look away. I hated that he'd seen me sick. Luckily, it hadn't been anywhere close to the worst I *could* get.

I prayed to all the heavens *that* wouldn't happen while he was staying with me.

One more week, the contractor estimated when she stopped in to the Coffee Loft after work today.

I was counting the hours.

Mercifully, the time passed at a rate I could handle. With twenty minutes left of practice, we brought the segments together and marked their places as a group. We ran through the routine a few times, and when I was satisfied, I called them in. Monty gave them a pep talk, and we dismissed them right on time.

I watched them file out in small groups, and I let out a long breath, allowing my tense shoulders to relax.

"You could have stayed home, Tasha," Monty said quietly. He was standing just off my shoulder, so his breath was warm on my neck.

My body gave an involuntary tremble as my hairs pricked up. "No, I couldn't. We have a fixed number of practices until the showcase. Every single one of them is planned out, and I refuse to let a little digestive issue mess with my schedule." I took a step toward the door that led to the coach's hallway, but he caught my wrist. I spun around, ready to lash out verbally. But again his expression was kind.

Concerned, even.

"I know what happened is an annoyance to you. And you're used to it. But—" He paused and looked down at his hand and its firm grip on my wrist. "Sorry. I— That was scary, Tasha. If I hadn't brought you Gatorade, you might have gotten worse. You might have *died.*"

I shook my head and reined in my tone. "I'm sorry I scared you. But honestly, that was like a three on a scale of ten. If I let every flare-up stop my life, I wouldn't be living."

His eyes widened to the point where it was almost comical. But I knew he'd been genuinely concerned, so I held back from laughing or making fun of him. It was comforting to know he had a nurturing side. I'd seen him care for Nana Booboo as her health declined, but he'd still been the same arrogant jerk to everyone else.

Well, mostly just to me.

I probably deserved it for the way I treated him. But he'd hurt me. Deeply. How did he think I'd react when he broke his promise and rejected me sixteen years later when he'd requested Gabby to be his partner?

Penny always said he must've had a good reason. I was sure he did. And if it was due to the reason I suspected, it was even more hurtful than just simply being rejected.

But maybe he'd grown up a little since then. Making sure I was okay, bringing me Gatorade, and cooking my Recovery Soup weren't requirements in any roommate agreement.

Not that we had one. Hypothetically, of course.

I gave him a nod and continued on to the door that led to the coaches' office, conference room, bathroom and shower facilities. He followed at a safe distance, and I gave in to the urge to put as much space between us as possible. Once I grabbed my purse, I all but sprinted to my car.

As I sat behind the wheel, my headlights lit up enough of the lot to silhouette Monty's exit and trek to his truck. I shifted into reverse and backed out, refusing to acknowledge the streaks of tears ribboning down my cheeks.

CHAPTER 8
Monty

I tried to get to our local hospital at least once a week to visit with the kids in the pediatric oncology unit. Each day, a different activity was planned for the patients who were well enough to walk or be wheeled to an activity room that also served as a parents' lounge.

I'd spent a lot of time in that room when I was in first and second grades.

Every time I entered this place, the memories hit like a truck colliding with a brick wall. I'd wrongly assumed it'd get easier over the years, but it never had. The ghost of my sister would forever haunt this ward. I crossed the hideously patterned carpet to the floor-to-ceiling windows and gazed out at the mountains.

Mindy had been thirteen when she'd been diagnosed with leukemia. At the time, she'd been a straight *A* student and at the top of her cheer game. A flyer on the Senior Level 4 team, she could also have easily been an elite gymnast. The things she could do in the air! She defied all gravity and flexibility expectations.

I wanted to be just like her.

When her leg started hurting, everyone assumed it was a cheer-related injury. But she'd never fallen. Melinda Biddington *never* fell. Even when her stunting partners dropped her, she was always able to twist in a way that landed her on her feet or in the back spot's arms, like a cat.

When the injury progressed enough that it caused her to limp, her coaches refused to let her practice until she'd had it x-rayed and brought in a physician's note that she was all clear to resume activity.

But the x-ray led to more tests, and a tumor was found. It was surgically removed, and we all celebrated. She resumed practice, and a month later, her team took first place at Summit in Orlando.

Then our parents sat us down. Things were never the same after that.

Sure, the tumor was gone, but Mindy's battle was just beginning.

It hadn't been the only tumor. But it was the only one that was operable. Removing it had allowed her to finish the season.

But now she needed radiation and chemotherapy.

Me, at seven, had heard loudly and clearly what they hadn't said: Without the cancer treatments, she'd die.

I decided then and there I would spend every minute I could with my sister. My dad's driver would pick me up at school and bring me here. I'd do my homework while Mindy napped. The cafeteria would deliver dinner for both of us. When Mindy was awake, I'd tell her about school and cheer, and she'd give me tips to improve my tumbling. My parents would take turns stopping in after work, and whoever stayed the latest would bring me home.

Nana was always here when I arrived, and she would leave just before dinner. Sometimes she'd stay longer if Mindy was having a good day. Sometimes, she'd stop knitting and pull me into her lap, and we'd sit like that for hours, watching animated movies while Mindy slept. Sometimes, on the really bad days, we'd each hold one of Mindy's hands and pray for a cure.

On days I had cheer practice, Nana would drive me. She'd sit in the balcony overlooking the Plex's cheer floors, sipping her pumpkin spice latte from the Bevvie Bar—now the Coffee Loft—and watching me flip all over the mats.

She took great care of me.

And once I was old enough, I'd vowed I'd take care of her.

"Monty's here!"

I spun around and grinned as the kids began to file into the room. First in was Britlynne, an eleven-year-old who'd beaten the disease, only to have it return two years later. She reminded me a lot of Mindy at her age, even if she was a dancer instead of a cheerleader.

A few long strides brought me to her wheelchair. I stuck out my fist and she bumped it. "You good today, Brit?"

"Slaying." She scrunched her nose. "I see you looking up at Nurse Trey to confirm. Believe me"—she twisted in her seat to look up at the twentysomething—"I'm beating this thing. Right?"

Trey grinned and nodded. "Never seen a fiercer fighter," he confirmed.

"Awesome," I said. "Save me a seat?"

She nodded, and Trey wheeled her off as four-year-old Anson entered the room, carried by his dad. His mom worked for the mayor of Colorado Springs, and they'd decided she'd keep working because her salary and benefits were better than his self-employment income. She visited as much as she could and reminded me a lot of my mom, back in those days.

Anson's dad, however, was nothing like my father. My dad only showed up when he felt obligated to and if it fit in with his client dinners, golf "meetings" and business travel.

"Ans, my man!" I held up my hand, and he high-fived it. "You just wake up?"

He nodded. "Wanna go back to bed." He turned his face into his dad's shoulder.

Anson's raspy whisper caused my throat to tighten. "Rough day?" I asked. I normally wouldn't ask such a personal question, but the man's tired eyes and several-days-old scruff tugged at my heart.

"We got through it. He keeps asking for his mom. I know it's killing her not to be here. But we need her benefits."

I nodded, wishing circumstances were different. Our family had enough money to enable our parents to be with Mindy twenty-four seven, but neither wanted to. And here was a family making impossible sacrifices so their child could receive treatment.

It wasn't fair.

Nothing about any of it was fair.

More kids, parents, and sitters filed in and gathered around the stage in the back corner. Today's activity was a puppet show. I sat by Britlynne, and we laughed at the puppeteer's corny jokes. I was there while he was setting up, and he'd asked me if I'd be willing to be part of the show. I agreed, as long as it was within the first three quarters of the performance so I had time to change into my costume before the hour was over.

At thirty-five minutes past the hour, a cat and a dog puppet were arguing over which was the best pet, and I wondered if my part was coming. I had to leave in ten minutes.

"I think we need to ask the audience which pet is better!" the cat suggested.

The dog's face scrunched, and its eyebrows lifted. "Okay. Hey kids, who thinks dogs make the best pets?"

The kids with dogs hooted and cheered. The cat asked the same question about cats, and the noise level was pretty even.

"Hey you!" The cat pointed to me. "The super big giant kid!"

"Who, me?" I asked in a forced high-pitched voice.

"Yeah!" The dog woofed. "Which pet is better?"

I scratched my head. "Well, I have a cat ..." The cat kids cheered. "But—I don't think my roommate likes him. Very grumpy roommate." I shook my head like it was the saddest thing.

The cat puppet gasped. "What kind of person doesn't like a cat?"

"I think my cat annoys her because he acts like it's his place, not hers. We're guests while my house is being renovated," I explained.

"Your roommate is a *giiiiiirl?* Oooooohh!" he teased. "Is she smart? Is she pretty? Do you liiiiiiiike her?"

I snorted. "She's both of those things. And my friend."

"Oooooh!" teased the dog. "Hey, kids, maybe we can help Monty's roommate not be so grumpy. Who's got an idea?"

All of the kids raised their hands.

None of them waited to be called on.

"Do the dishes!"

"Fix something!"

"Bring her flowers!"

"Tell her she's beautiful!"

I grinned sheepishly. "Thanks, everyone. I'll try some of those things."

The puppets moved on to the next topic, and Brit leaned over. "Make her dinner and bring her flowers. When my dad does that, it makes my mom so happy she's in a good mood for a week!"

"Noted. Thanks."

"Oh, and clean up your mess. Otherwise, she'll forget the nice things when she's cleaning the mess."

"You are wise beyond your years," I said and thanked her. "I'll be back," I whispered.

I slipped out and hustled to the nurse's station. Jared was right on time and chatting up two of the younger nurses. I slapped him on the shoulder and lifted my chin to the ladies. "Need me to take out the trash?"

They giggled, and I grinned. Jared's expression turned from flirtatious to annoyed, but I didn't care. I didn't need or particularly want his friendship.

I led him to the break room and quickly changed into the mascot costume. Jared was a college kid whose aunt worked in the Edge's front office. He was pursuing a degree in physical education, so this job was a good fit for him both because of the schedule and the opportunities to work with kids.

And he was good with kids. A natural. When I got promoted, one of my asks was that he remain my handler. Ridgie Number One's current handler wasn't happy being demoted to Number Three, but I needed someone with me who was comfortable and animated and kind to children, even if he was sometimes a stick in the mud when it came to rules.

The puppet show had just ended when I entered the room, and Jared corralled the kids into a semicircle that enabled me to easily move from one to the next. He passed out mini Ridgie bears with royal blue bows tied around their necks.

I was glad to see Vali had made it to the show. She was

newish, having started treatments about a month ago, eight years old, and hard of hearing. I'd attended many of Penny's American Sign Language classes for kids at the library over the years—most recently as Ridgie, of course—and asked Penny to tutor me privately in ASL so that I could communicate better with kids who were deaf and hard of hearing.

And since Ridgie couldn't speak out loud, it was pretty special that Vali—and others like her—got a little bit of extra communication.

Hi, I signed. *Are you having a good day?*

Her eyes lit up, and she straightened in her chair. Her mother fussed over her, readjusting her blanket.

Better today. And you?

I can't complain. I pointed to Jared. *Except about this guy. He snorts way too loudly.*

She giggled. *Can you hug me? I left my teddy bear in my bed, and this new bear is too small.*

I stepped closer, bent down, and held my arms open. Vali reached up and wrapped her thin arms around my waist.

She hung on longer than usual, and a muscle in my back began to spasm. I'd have to spend a little more time on it in the gym later, but I wasn't about to push her away. My rule was, I don't let go first.

When she slid her arms back into her lap, I patted her on the head. *See you next week?* I signed.

Vali nodded. *I'll still be here.* She sniffed and rubbed her eyes. *I'll probably be here until I die.*

"Valentina!" her mother gasped. She skirted around to the front of the chair and signed. *You are not going to die. The treatments are working. You will beat this! No more negative talk!*

But I'm so tired, Mama. And the doctor said it would be a long battle.

They were both crying now, daughter in her mother's embrace. Not for the first time, I was glad they couldn't see my face.

Because we all knew the truth: Lots of kids *didn't* beat cancer.

What would I have said to Mindy if she'd said something like that? Probably something similar to what Vali's mother signed.

Maybe I could give her an incentive. I placed my paw on her shoulder.

Her mother backed away, and I began to sign in fervor.

You hang in there. Be strong. When you feel better, I'll get you and your family special tickets to an Edge game. Just tell me when. You can hang out with me before the game, and I'll get you free snacks. Deal?

She laughed. *Deal.*

I squeezed her shoulder and patted her mom's back, hoping I'd left them encouraged and hopeful. I wasn't doing my job if I didn't.

Brit had positioned herself at the end of the line. When I reached her, she pressed an envelope into my hand.

"It's an invitation to my birthday party," she told Jared, who took it from me. He opened it and pulled out a pink rectangle. "For Ridgie and your friend Monty." She giggled. "It'll be here, after activity time, in a couple weeks. My little sister misses you since she's in daycare now and you always come during the day. Mom is letting her stay home from school that day."

I hadn't ever considered that the siblings would need a visit from the mascot. I nodded my oversize head emphatically and clapped my hands, ending with a thumbs-up so she'd know I'd put it on my calendar.

As I drove to Mountainview Manor after the visit, I thought about all the ideas I wanted to propose for Ridgie. More community service, more social media, more goofy meet-and-greets. Photo ops and fundraisers with the other pro sports mascots in the area. We had the power to make people smile, and I wanted to expand our audience and fanbase. If it wasn't in the budget, I'd finance it. I'd even pay Jared more than what he earned from the team.

I needed to do everything in my power to put more happiness in the world.

Because the world could be a very sad place.

And if we weren't laughing, we were crying.

Well, maybe that was just me.

CHAPTER 9
Tasha

A week after the flare-up, I was feeling great and back to my normal schedule, which meant on Tuesday at 5:20 a.m., I was chopping vegetables for the slow cooker before my shift at the Coffee Loft. Parfait had followed me to the kitchen, mewing his demands to be fed. I dished out some kitty salmon, cued my phone up to my morning playlist—on low volume so it wouldn't wake Monty—and got to work.

I hummed along to the upbeat music, dicing carrots and cucumbers, chopping zucchini. Did I want to add steak or chicken to this one?

Definitely steak. I'd had enough chicken in my Recovery Soup last week. I set my knife down and turned toward the fridge.

"Oof! Sorry, Barfy!"

"Mew!" he protested.

"Well, don't try to trip me on the way to the fridge!" I stooped down to scratch his chin and run my hands along the sleek striped fur on his back. "Who's the ugly old kitty?" I asked in a deep, silly yet condescending talking-to-pets voice. "It's you! You're so ugly. Yes you are, yes you are!" I touched my nose to his as he purred like a car motor. "Old fat ugly kitty!"

"His name is *Parfait,* and he's not fat *or* ugly." Monty's groggy voice carried over the kitchen island to where I was squatting on the floor.

I scooped the cat into my arms and stood to face him, momentarily frozen as I took in his morning Monty-ness. Tousled hair, sleepy eyes, minty fresh vapors strong enough to inhale two feet away. Fitted tank over his monstrous muscles.

I raised my eyebrows and glared at him while I tried to get my words to work. What was wrong with me?

I was watching too many cheesy Christmas in July lovey-dovey movies, that's what. Had to be.

I swallowed and lifted my chin. "So? He has no idea what I'm saying, do you, boy?" I rubbed my face in Parfait's neck, inciting deeper purrs. "He loves me. Always has. Right, Barfy?" I kissed him on the head between his ears. "Good boy!"

"Hmm." He blinked away his heavy-lidded gaze and cleared his throat. "Sounds like I need to have a chat with him about wolves in sheep's clothing." Monty's grogginess fell away a little bit with each word, and by the end of the sentence, his normal, arrogant tone had replaced the kinder, just-woke-up voice.

"Aren't you supposed to be moved out of here by now?" I asked. He skirted around the island and reached out to rub Parfait's head. His pale toes peeked out of his beat-up discount store fuzzy slippers like a turtle poking its head out of its shell. The sight of them took me back in time to when we were inseparable, both irking me and warming my heart. Why had he kept them all these years when he could afford the best slippers money could buy?

"Beck said by the end of the week. There was a delay on permitting to knock down the wall around the toilet. They'll be starting that today." He held out his arms, and Parfait scrambled into them.

Good. The clock was running down on this roommate thing. Then I could blast my playlist again.

I washed my hands and collected the steak and a homemade gluten-free marinade from the fridge. Monty's gaze never left my knife as I cubed the steak.

"You don't have to wait until I'm finished," I said. "There's plenty of room in here for you to make your protein shake."

He shrugged. "I figured I'd just stop by the Coffee Loft once it opened."

I pressed my lips together, wondering why he would bother with the morning rush when he could make it himself here in the peace and quiet. I much preferred to drink my coffee at home.

I glanced at the mug of pumpkin spice that I'd been sipping. Yeah. Much better to drink here in peace than at the café.

But to each his own.

In a rare burst of kindness that even surprised me, I said, "If you come over with me when I leave, I can make it for you before the rush."

Monty lifted his head, and his eyes locked on mine. His lips parted, then closed, as if he'd decided not to say what was on his mind.

"Or not." I shrugged at his rejection. Wasn't the first time. Wouldn't be the last. Not like it was an olive branch or anything. I was just trying to save the guy the time and hassle he was setting himself up for.

"Maybe another time." He avoided my gaze and slid off the stool, setting the cat on the floor. "I, uh, have some work I was planning to do there today."

Work? What kind of work did he do?

"For the charity," he added. He must've read my thoughts. "Several Edge players want to donate to the auction this year, so I need to figure out what I want from them."

I'd forgotten about his charity. Each year, his parents held a Valentine charity gala to raise money for whatever organization was trending and needing financial support. Several years ago, Monty added a silent auction to the event to raise money for the kids in the oncology units at local hospitals. This past year, Penny had played her harp at the event, and Xavier had attended with several of his teammates. They'd left inspired and wanted to contribute. Some of them had even joined Monty during his Ridgie visits at the hospitals.

I didn't say anything as I opened the drawer that held the various types of kitchen bags and wraps. What was there to say? I couldn't razz him over that. I dumped the meat into a large Ziploc bag and poured in enough marinade to coat the pieces. I'd run home from work on my break and add them to the pot once the marinade had time to seep in.

There were a lot of perks to living so close to work.

Montgomery Biddington being within walking distance wasn't one of them.

I cleaned up my mess and washed my hands again.

5:57.

"See ya," I said with a wave, grabbing my purse as I rushed out the door. I didn't turn around to see if he waved back. I took the stairs faster than usual, my heart pounding.

Why was it pounding?

No need to dwell on that. I took a few long breaths as I exited the building and crossed the parking lot to the strip of buildings that lined Main Street.

I punched in the code and slipped inside the back door of the old saloon-turned-cafe and into the Coffee Loft's kitchen just as the big digital clock over the bulletin board changed from 5:59 to 6:00.

Right on time. I hung my purse on the coat rack, tied on my apron, and pushed through the swinging door to the front of the shop.

With both Penny and Gabby cutting their shifts to support their guys during the playoffs, Jannell had to hire on additional staff. Betty was one of those new hires, a mother of three in her early thirties, back into the workforce after being a stay-at-home mom for eleven years. Her three kids were spending the summer with her husband's parents in New England, and she'd wanted something to do during the day so she wouldn't miss them so much.

Betty was one of those people who made you feel at ease the moment you met her, and by the end of the first week, she'd eased into working at the Coffee Loft like she'd been here all along. She quickly learned all the specialty drinks, could fix any tech problem that arose, and upsold at least half of all the customer purchases, offering shots of espresso or a cake pop to go, or the addition of food-grade essential oils into non-coffee drinks. She was brilliant, likable, and most important, not annoying.

True to his word, Monty arrived just after Jannell unlocked the door and entered the queue, which was already about twenty people deep with our morning regulars. Betty and I worked the registers, writing orders on cups while Jannell, her husband, Marcus, and their daughter, Marie, made the drinks.

The way the line went, Monty was next up for Betty, but he gestured for the man behind him to go ahead. I handed my customer her receipt, and Monty approached my register.

"Your usual?" I asked.

He nodded. "And a Lofty-size pumpkin spice blah-te for Nana."

I tapped in the extra item, surprised at his change of plans. "I thought you were staying here to work today?"

"I'll be back. Nana's therapy was rescheduled to 7 a.m., so I thought I'd soften the blow with one of your poisonous coffees to sip on all day."

I rolled my eyes. "They're not poison. There are a lot of health benefits to coffee. Coffee beans are actually—"

"I know, I know. Coffee cherries. From the coffee cherry plant." He waved his hand flippantly. "Antioxidant, heart healthy, can prevent cognitive decline, et cetera et cetera. Whatever. There are better ways to stimulate the brain in the morning."

Yeah, if it was only my brain that needed stimulating in the morning. But I wasn't about to say *that* out loud. Monty didn't need to know anything more than he'd already gleaned about my digestive system's inner workings. He paid for the order and moved down the counter.

The next few hours flew by, and I found myself glancing at the door every time it chimed to signal a new customer.

Astoria Brewer arrived during one of the short lulls after the initial rush. She stepped up to my register, and I greeted her warmly.

"Hey, Astoria! What's new in the hockey world?"

She grinned. Hockey was one of her favorite subjects. She'd played on the Olympic team, and her dad was an NHL legend who'd played for both the Voltage and the Edge. We'd known each other since we were kids.

"Lots of fan hearts will be breaking this week. Restricted free agents can start signing contracts July first," she reported.

"What does that mean for the Edge?" I asked, genuinely curious.

She frowned. "We'll likely lose a favorite or two that are worth more than what the team can pay them. Including Dean Hathaway. They haven't been able to agree on numbers with him yet, and other teams are calling with some significantly high offers."

"But he's the captain," I said. "Wouldn't they try everything they could to keep him?"

"Maybe if they'd won the Cup." She shrugged. "But they didn't, so they'll be aggressive in making changes over the summer to build a team that's better prepared to beat Miami and whatever other teams might be in their way."

"Oh wow," I said. I hoped none of *my* favorites were leaving.

"Don't worry about Xavier or Noel," she said. "They're safe. And so is Brendan."

I let out a sigh of relief. "How can you be sure?" I asked.

"I can't tell you. But don't worry, okay?" I nodded. She handed me an envelope branded to Pasta Nacht's. She co-owned the restaurant with her dad.

"What's this?" I asked.

"A gift card and an apology. I heard about your, ah, *reaction* to our cross-contaminated fettucine alfredo. I feel awful. I know the promise of more uncontaminated food can't make up for the agony you were in, but I hope you'll give us a chance to make it right."

My cheeks flamed. Who had told her about that?

I tried to hand it back to her, but she wouldn't take it. "I'm fine," I insisted. "It happens. No need for this. Can we never talk about it again?"

Astoria tilted her head and tucked a long blond wave behind her ear. "Only if you keep it."

I sighed. "Fine. Thank you." I slid the offending gift into my apron pocket. "How did you find out, anyway?"

She glanced to her left and right, then leaned in over the register. "Penny called Brenna and asked her to check on you, to see if you were at work Monday morning. I happened to be here in line with Brenna when she called, and I heard the whole conversation." Her eyes widened as she realized what she'd said. "I wasn't trying to be nosy or overhear, promise! And I haven't said a word to anyone. My nephew has food allergies; he's the reason Brewski's turned allergy-free. I saw him react once and—" She blinked as her eyes began to water. "I never want that—or anything like it—for any of my customers. *Especially* friends and family. You trust us. We broke that trust."

I sighed. Small-town life. Everyone knew someone who knew your business. "Happens all the time," I said. "You can't ever make a kitchen one hundred percent safe because you can't control what's on the hands or clothing of your employees. But I appreciate the gesture. Thank you."

She nodded. "I know. I hate that for you. And for Benji. And for everyone else affected by it."

"Can I get you your usual?" I asked, anxious to change the subject before any of my co-workers overheard.

"Umm …" Her gaze landed on the framed chalk menu between my register and Betty's. "Yes, but a small. I'd also like to try your Summertime Splash."

I rang in her salted caramel Frodoughchino, a frozen coffee inspired by our salted caramel doughnut, and the new Citrus Twist, a lemon-lime juicer infused with one hundred percent certified pure citrus essential oils. She paid for the order and scooted down the counter.

How embarrassing.

The door chimed again, and Liam Brewer entered. *So many Brewers in this town!* As a Palmer, it was annoying. But the Brewers were all so *nice,* it was hard to dislike them.

Liam turned his head, scanning the tables as he walked up to the counter. I stepped back so Betty could take his order, but he walked straight to me.

"Is Monty here?" he asked, pointing upward to the loft seating area on the second level.

I shook my head. "No, but he's due back soon. Said he was coming to work after Nana Booboo's therapy."

He pressed his lips together and nodded as he pulled out his wallet. "I have some bad news for him. What can I get him to soften the blow?"

My heart rate kicked up. "What bad news?" I might not like Monty, but bad news was never a good thing. "About the house?"

Liam rubbed the back of his neck. "Beck found a bad pipe."

"So? She can replace it, right?"

He shook his head no, then nodded yes. "It's a little more complicated than that."

What he wasn't saying was that Monty probably wasn't moving out next week. "How bad is it?" I crossed my arms over my chest. Liam was an architect, and if he was worried, I was worried.

The door chimed, and Monty strode in, straight toward us. "I got here as soon as I could," he said. "What's the issue?"

Liam looked from him to me and back to Monty. "The whole house needs re-piping. And we can't start until at least September first because the plans and all the permitting for something this extensive have to be approved through the town's Historic Preservation Board. I'm sorry, Monty. But it's good she found this now, before the winter. Those pipes are in pretty bad condition. They've been rotting for decades."

No no no. Another two-plus months of living with this guy?

I could kick him out.

Couldn't I?

I totally could.

But that would be mean.

I probably shouldn't.

But … I looked at Monty. His eyes were fixed on me, waiting for my answer.

I closed my eyes and dragged my hands down my face. "Fine," I acquiesced. "Stay as long as you need to."

He let out a long breath and nodded and, for once, didn't add a snappy or insulting retort. I rang up their drinks and handed Liam his receipt.

How was I going to get through almost three more months of Monty?

CHAPTER 10
Monty

Jannell handed me the small iced chocolate Liam guilt-bought for me, and I followed him up the winding iron steps to the loft above the café.

He explained the difficulties and intricacies of re-piping a historic home like Nana's, and thirty minutes later I was driving back to the rehab facility to break the news to her that she wouldn't have a home to come home to until fall. It had been almost two months now since her stroke, and I wanted to bring her home more than anything.

I found her in the dining room, sitting across the table from ninety-one-year-old Clarice, our town's retired librarian. The two were deep into a game of Rummy 500 when I approached.

"Hey, Nana." I dropped a kiss to her cheek and pulled a chair from the next table over and straddled it backwards. I winked at her and leaned toward Clarice like I was making a play to look at her hand.

She smacked my shoulder good-naturedly and grinned widely, her eyes closing and almost disappearing in her wrinkled face. "Monty, how many times do I have to tell you cheating won't even help your Nana beat me?"

Nana humphed. I knew for a fact she lost on purpose because she legit beat me every time we played in her room. She spoke slowly, her speech still slightly impeded from the stroke. "N-nope, there's no hope for me. This old b-brain just isn't what it used to be."

Clarice laid down a set of aces. "Sixty points! Doesn't take brains to get a good hand." She wrote her score on the notepad in front of her. "But maybe next time don't put an ace in the discard pile if there's already one there."

I couldn't stop my lips from twitching, so I pressed my teeth together and covered my mouth with my hand, thinker-style, and pretended that was the best advice I'd ever heard.

"Brilliant point, Clarice," I agreed, stroking my chin. "Nana, we'll have to work on your Rummy skills next time I come by."

She heaved a sigh as she drew a card from the deck on her good side. Her weaker hand, positioned against a small rice-filled pillow, held her cards. Thanks to the best speech therapist money could buy, her stuttering and pauses were almost completely gone. I was so proud of her perseverance and progress. "I suppose it c-couldn't hurt." She added the card to her hand and set down the king of diamonds. Two cards down was the queen of the same suit, and three over from that was the jack. "How is our dear Parfait le Chat? Have you found a way to sneak him in to see me yet?"

I shook my head as Clarice gleefully swept up the cards. "Not yet. He's good. But I have some bad news about the house."

"Bad news? What could be worse than me losing to Clarice *again?*"

"Jack, queen, king, plus I'll take that five of clubs to finish this set." One at a time, her mouth spreading wider with each card, she placed the three, four, five, six, and seven of clubs on the table. "Fifty-five points!"

"Hmm." Nana frowned and slid the top card from the deck. "Ha!" She placed it on the table and slowly used her left hand to extract two cards from her right hand. "Three tens! That's … ten, twenty, thirty points!"

"Glad to see your math is still sharp, Nancy. Now we just need to work on your observation skills." Clarice spoke with an air of authority as she recorded Nana's points. She pointed to me. "What's your bad news, Monty?"

I turned to Nana. "Beck's crew was re-piping the bathroom

and discovered the pipes were significantly rotted. She was going to just replace the ones that were bad but decided to take a look at other piping throughout the house that was relatively accessible. It's not good, Nana. She said we're one or two winters away from a disaster of epic proportions."

"Pipe-ageddon!" Clarice shouted, then whistled. "You have the dough to fix it, right?"

I nodded. "It's going to be expensive, but the worst part is since the house is a designated historic home, permitting is going to be a process. We'll have to get the approval of the Historic Preservation Board. They meet once a month, and a review can take time. And even if it didn't, Beck has another project coming up with her plumber and can't start on our house until September first at the earliest."

Nana tilted her head in thought. "We've dealt with them before. Not so bad. I like it here. It's kind of like an all-inclusive resort. Plus, I need to keep Clarice busy. She's *old,* you know. Might not have much time left."

My eyes widened, but the ladies just laughed.

"Oh, Monty, don't look so scandalized," Clarice scolded, taking a card off the deck and discarding it right away. "I've outlived everyone in my family, including my kids. And some of their kids, sadly. I'm ready to go whenever the good Lord takes me."

"Hopefully not before the end of this game." Nana took the card she discarded and set down the other three jacks. "We're almost tied up!"

"Not quite," Clarice corrected. "Plus, I'm one hundred twenty-five points ahead from the last two rounds."

Nana shrugged and shot me a grin. "I haven't beaten her yet!"

"We-ell," Clarice dragged the word out as she considered Nana's observation. Ever the upbeat encourager, she softened. "You're doing okay, considering your stroke wasn't that long ago. You'll probably win a round soon."

"I appreciate the sentiment," Nana replied. I shifted in my seat so I could see her hand as she took the top card from the deck, which she immediately placed in the discard train, missing the opportunity to set out a five-card run.

This time I couldn't hide my smile as Clarice swept it up mirthfully and laid out the rest of her cards with a flourish, ending the game and leaving Nana with almost as many points in her hands as her total on the scorepad.

"One more round?" Nana asked.

"Hold on, doing the math." Clarice hummed as she counted the value of her cards and Nana's and did the calculations. "Yes, I'm afraid so." She chuckled. "Just one should do it. I'm ten points from five hundred. You, on the other hand ..."

"No need to tell me how bad it is," Nana interjected, using her good hand to push her cards to the center of the table.

"Can I shuffle?" I asked.

Both ladies nodded, and I gathered up the cards, pulling them into a tight pile. Nana had taught me to shuffle when I was a preschooler, and by kindergarten I was executing moves like a Vegas dealer. Once, I considered moving there to do just that. But I couldn't imagine living that far from Nana, especially after my grandfather died.

She'd taken care of me my whole life, and I'd promised her when I was young that I would take care of her when she was old and in a wheelchair.

How prophetic those words had been.

A few years ago, her sweet tooth had caught up with her, and complications with her diabetes made it too hard for her to walk. Installing an elevator in the house had been a Band-Aid to the problem, but even having to use a wheelchair hadn't dissuaded her from her desserts. One good thing about her being here at the facility was that all the desserts they served her were sugar-free, and the security made it nearly impossible to sneak in sugar-rich foods. Even birthday cakes had to be preapproved and monitored by staff so that the recipient didn't inadvertently—or purposefully—share it with a patient with dietary restrictions.

I handed the shuffled deck to Clarice.

"So," Nana said as Clarice dealt the cards. "I assume you'll be staying with Tasha until the work is done? She doesn't have a new roommate lined up, right?"

I shook my head. "Nope, she doesn't. She wanted to keep the extra room open for Penny to stay over when Xavier travels. He said I can stay at his place on those nights, if I want. I might just sleep on the sofa, though."

"They might like their girls' nights male-free," Clarice said.

I hadn't thought about that. "Good point."

Clarice beamed. "Just common sense."

CHAPTER 11
Tasha

By the grace of God, July flew by. Monty did his best to avoid the kitchen when I was in it, but I'd often spy him taste-testing my Crock-Pot creations when he thought I wasn't looking. With him eating half the leftovers, I had to cook more often, but I didn't mind.

It gave me more chances to experiment. Monty made up for eating my food by regularly having groceries delivered, which decreased my trips to the wholesale club and farmers' market, and there were always more than enough ingredients in the orders for whatever I wanted to make. I suspected he'd raided my cookbook. How else would he have known to order some of the obscure items I regularly kept on hand, like specific gluten-free snacks and rice paper wraps?

One Saturday in August, I was in the kitchen chopping veggies when he walked through the door juggling multiple empty boxes I'd just unpacked and set in the hall for my next trip down to the dumpster. A huge smile was plastered on his face. He let the boxes fall to the carpet as Parfait ran to greet him. He scooped up the cat and carried him to the bar that separated the kitchen from the living area.

"*Do not* let him on the counter," I warned. The cat liked to drink from the running faucet. I'd given up trying to train him

not to, but I drew the line when his fluff was close enough to shed on my food.

"Wouldn't dream of it," Monty said in the bored tone he liked to use with me.

"And *why* did you bring the trash back in?"

"I had an idea for a project. What are you making today?"

Monty was always collecting odds and ends the kids at the children's hospitals could use in arts and crafts projects. "I thought I'd try out a chicken curry recipe. One that's not too spicy."

"Sounds good." He tipped his chin toward the bundle of carrots next to the cutting mat. "You ever going to open up that restaurant you dreamed about when we were kids?"

I stiffened. That dream had died long ago, and it hurt to think about it.

"Palmer City has enough restaurants," I said tightly, increasing the pressure on the knife. A carrot tip went flying across the counter, causing Parfait to paw at Monty's arms to let him go so he could chase it. But Monty held on, his ridiculously big biceps twitching ever so slightly.

I looked away. From the muscles, and from the man whose pitying gaze was fixed on me.

"None of the restaurants in Palmer City are *safe* restaurants, though," he said softly.

I shrugged. "The world isn't safe. When my time is up, it's up. Like I told Astoria last month, no restaurant can be completely *safe.*"

"But the food can. Have you thought about opening a meal prep service?"

Had I thought about it? Only every other day.

I shrugged again. "Yeah, but I don't have the startup cash. Never will."

I pushed the diced carrots to the side of the mat and snuck a glance up at him. He looked thoughtful, watching me as I pulled the chives into my cutting space. I hoped that meant he was done speaking.

When I got to chopping the fresh coriander, I couldn't take the silence anymore. "What?" I asked him.

"Huh?"

"You've been staring at me."

He adjusted Parfait so the cat's front paws were over his shoulder. "I like watching you work. You're so good at it."

Compliments from Montgomery Biddington were few and far between.

I almost smiled.

But my cheeks heated, and that was enough. He couldn't know that the compliment affected me deeply.

"Thanks," I squeaked out, my head still down.

He was quiet for a few beats, then blurted out, "I want to invest in your business!"

My head jerked up. "What business?"

"Your safe meal prep business. You have to do it, Tasha. People need it. And you're the perfect person for the job. I bet you could put together the most amazing sugar-free dishes and desserts for Nana that wouldn't send her A1C through the roof."

I laughed. He really had no clue what it was like for anyone who didn't have money coming out of their ears. "Montgomery, I can't *ever* own a business. I need a job with insurance. Right now, my only dream is to pay my medical bills so I'm not dependent on my parents forever. They work too hard to work for my digestive problems."

The look that crossed his face was one of confusion, then pity. "Well," he said, "if that isn't one of the most depressing things I've ever heard."

"Yep, it stinks," I said through my teeth. "But I don't want your pity."

"I don't pity you," he said in a surprised tone. "I admire you."

"Yeah, sure." I waited for the rest of the statement, the part where he would leave a jab that was worse than the first part.

But it didn't come. I continued prepping the food for the Crock-Pot and tried to ignore the tension in the air.

"What if we were partners?" he said slowly. "I can invest the initial startup costs, and then, once your business takes off, you'll be making enough that you won't need insurance and can pay cash for all your expenses."

My heart warmed at his confidence that I could ever make

enough money to cover my expenses. I had more medical debt than college debt at this point, and the only way I'd ever erase it was to marry a millionaire.

I shook my head. "It won't be enough."

"How much money could you possibly need? Let me take care of it. It's the least I can do for you letting me live here."

I gaped at him. "I'm not a charity case! I don't want to be another of your pet projects."

Monty set his shoulders back in defense. "My Cheerdanas have made me enough money to retire *and* fund Christmas gifts for pediatric oncology units at three hospitals." He spoke plainly, not bragging. I could tell he was both proud of his achievement and wanted to keep private about its success.

I set the knife down and met his gaze. His sweat-wicking, stretchy, and easily folded bandanas were perfect for cheer athletes and stayed put through the most grueling practices. "That's wonderful for you. I love that you've made your own money and aren't dependent on your parents. That must be ..." I swallowed and fought back the lump forming in my throat. "Such a relief and ... freedom."

I averted my gaze, not wanting any more of his concerned look casting on me. Some people were born with silver spoons in their mouths. Others weren't. It didn't matter that my ancestors had founded this town. Their fortune was gone, and I was on my own.

"I can help you get that, too," he said softly. "What's the point of having all this money if I can't help my friends?"

He considered us friends? I turned away, not wanting him to see the water that was rimming my eyes. I walked to the fridge and did some rearranging, calling over my shoulder in as cool of a voice as I could muster. "I appreciate your offer. I do. It's generous and kind. But I just can't accept."

"If you change your mind—"

"I won't!"

I closed the fridge and straightened up, setting my shoulders back and taking a deep breath, steeling myself to continue the conversation.

But Monty wasn't at the bar when I returned to my cutting station.

And, if I admitted it to myself, I was kind of disappointed he'd given up on persuading me so quickly.

CHAPTER 12
Monty

Mid-August

I shook my head and pulled Parfait into my lap. It was just us in the apartment. Tasha had been in Europe for the past week, celebrating Penny's birthday at Xavier's family's castle. They'd invited me, too, but I declined, citing Ridgie engagements. I could have rescheduled them, but the truth was, Tasha needed space from me. I could sense it from the ways she went out of her way to avoid me and barely spoke to me directly at FireVolts practice.

She was due home tonight, and I'd reached out to Fyvie from the bakery to help me make gluten-free dairy-free alfredo that would be ready when Tasha arrived. I figured she'd have to be starving. What airline could accommodate her food issues? And if they could, was the food even edible?

Fyvie had moved here from Ireland permanently a few years ago after a stint with her college's exchange program. She ran the bakery now, and though that was primarily breads and sweets, they always had a booth at community events, offering various savory items and hand-crafted chocolates. I knew she could make a mean shepherd's pie. Surely, she could follow Tasha's recipe, so I hired her to come to the apartment and help me create it.

"Ye couldn't've done this yerself?" She stared me down,

wiping sweat from her brow and winding a loose strand of curly auburn hair back into the messy bun atop her head.

"Why take the chance?" I needed this to be perfect the *first* time. I only got one shot.

She shrugged. "Ay. Well, 'appy to take yer money." She patted the counter. "It's good ter go."

She'd left an hour ago, right after we'd added the noodles into the mixture of plant butter, oat milk, and broth. The trick was not to add them too soon or they'd become overlarge and mushy.

My phone buzzed. I pulled it out of my pocket and swiped to open the international chat app.

The message was from Penny. *They're on their way.*

I'd asked her to text me when her parents and Tasha left the airport so I'd have an ETA. I thanked her and dumped Parfait off my lap and onto the adjacent sofa cushion. "Sorry, boy."

Originally, I'd planned a big, fancy welcome-home dinner at the dining room table. But after I'd set it up, I realized it might send the wrong message, and I didn't need Tasha hating me again, especially when I felt like we'd made great strides to repairing our friendship over the last two months.

Instead, I'd arranged two place settings at the bar and trimmed a dozen peach carnations, her favorite, arranging them inside a large mason jar I'd found in the pantry.

Informal, but slightly zhuzhed up to indicate this wasn't any old dinner. I was glad she was back, and not just for coaching reasons.

I'd missed her.

I would never admit that to her, but Parfait and I had felt her absence. While she was gone, I also had a cleaning service come in and detail the common areas and bathrooms. I appreciated her taking in Parfait and me, even though I was the last person she'd ever wanted to room with.

When her key clicked in the lock, I pulled Parfait back onto my lap and pretended to scroll my phone, looking as bored as I could muster.

"Hey," I said as she pulled her suitcase inside and closed the door. "Dinner's on the counter."

I raised my eyelids only enough to catch her expression.

Surprise crossed her features, but there was something else there, too.

Exhaustion.

"Thanks," she murmured, turning toward her room and stopping abruptly. "What"—she pointed past the dining table to the collection of boxes stacked in the corner—"is that?"

"That," I announced proudly, "is Parfait's new cat castle."

"You made it out of product boxes from Costco?" she asked, bewildered.

"I did. Thirty-seven of them." The boxes stretched out from the corner and lined the back and side walls for about three feet in each direction.

She blinked at the structure and sighed. "It's ... nice."

I pushed Parfait off my lap and stood. He mewed in protest. "Sorry, boy." I crossed the room in long strides to get ahead of her. "Stop."

Tasha narrowed her eyes. "I don't have the energy to fight with you. Please, move."

I shook my head. "Eat. I'll shlep this to your room. Want it on the chest at the foot of your bed?"

She pressed her lips together, considering, then nodded. "Yeah, thanks."

When she let go of the handle, I stuck my arm out for her backpack. She shrugged it off her shoulder and turned toward the kitchen.

After setting her suitcase on the bench and the backpack on her desk chair, I joined her at the bar. A scoop of fettuccine was on her plate, but she wasn't eating.

"It's safe, I promise." I slid onto the barstool next to her. "And Fyvie oversaw the whole process so I wouldn't mess it up."

"Fyvie was here?"

I nodded, spooning a heaping portion of noodles and cheese onto my plate.

"Did she bring the flowers, too?"

I shook my head. "Nope, that was me." Taking advice from Britlynne, but I left that part out.

Tasha regarded me curiously, and her cheeks pinked just enough for me to notice. Then she gave a half smile.

Would you look at that? I thought. I'd have to let Brit know the flowers worked.

Tasha turned back to her food and picked up her fork. Slowly, she wound the long noodles around the tines. "Penny's pregnant."

I swallowed my food and watched her carefully, not wanting to say the wrong thing. She was hunched, shoulders slumped. Her words carried a happy tone, but her body language told a different story.

"So, you're going to be an auntie," I said lightly. "Congrats."

"Thanks." She brought the fork into her mouth and chewed her noodles for what felt like a long time.

I did some mental calculations. "May?"

"May you what?"

"No, May. The baby's due in May?"

"Oh. Yeah. Right during the playoffs. They didn't plan it."

I believed that. I hadn't been in the hockey world long, but even I knew players and their wives did their best to plan summer births to avoid the playoff madness.

"She won't be able to travel to away games if the Edge make the playoffs this year."

I wound up a section of noodles for another bite. "And there's a good chance of Xavier missing the birth if they do."

"Yup." She popped the *P.* "But Auntie Tasha will be here. Or wherever I'm living at that point."

"You won't be here?" I asked.

She shrugged. "Depends if I find another roommate. But I was thinking it might be better if I moved home. Not having to pay rent is helping me make a dent in my bills."

"College loans?"

"Those are almost paid off. It's the medical bills. As long as I can manage to stay out of the hospital, I should catch up in about two or three years."

I was sure my eyes bugged out. "Two or three *years?*"

"What can I say?" She shrugged. "This body"—she used her free hand to make a sweeping motion from head to toe—"is expensive to maintain."

I struggled not to show my utter surprise. "And that's with insurance?"

"Yup. Mine from the school and my parents'. But that runs out the day I turn twenty-six."

Which wasn't that far away. I didn't know what to say, so I took another bite of noodles.

"Thanks for making dinner," she said. "That was nice of you."

I nodded. "You're welcome. Your recipes are really great." That gave me an idea. "What about a cookbook?"

"Huh?"

"If you can't open a restaurant or meal-prep service, what about writing a cookbook?"

The corner of her mouth lifted. "What, and sell all my secrets?"

I nudged her side lightly with my elbow. "I bet it'd be a bestseller."

Tasha's lips pulled into a full smile, but it didn't reach her eyes. "I love the confidence you have in me."

Her smile fell, so I spoke candidly to entice it back. "I've known you almost our whole lives, Tasha. You've always accomplished every goal you've set. Why *wouldn't* I have confidence in you?"

The smile didn't return, but she lifted her noodled fork and stabbed the air in my direction. "You forget I lack the trust fund to get any monetary dreams off the ground, and I don't have any connections in any industry—except cheer—to even have a chance."

"I can handle that part. Honest. And—" I nudged her again. "I'd work for free."

She stiffened. "I told you already that I don't want to be your charity project."

"But—" I tried to think quickly. "I'm not supporting *you,* per se. I'm helping to get a service or a tool into the hands of people whose lives your knowledge could improve. Why *wouldn't* you say yes to an opportunity that could help thousands of people better their lives?"

I had her there.

Tasha gathered the last of her noodles and twirled them onto her fork. "I wouldn't even know how to start."

I pointed to her recipe binder on the far counter, nestled between the microwave and knife block. "Type that up. Take pictures of your food. Put it all in a doc. Then give it to me on a thumb drive. I'll keep it safe and make sure only the right hands have access." I spoke that last sentence in a teasing tone, hoping to lighten the very big offer I was making.

"You're serious?"

"Cross my heart."

"And hope to die?" she filled in with just a smidge of snark.

"Let's not go *that* far." I ran my fingers through my hair and made a show of patting it all into place. "The world needs Montgomery Biddington alive and in studly form, thank you very much."

Tasha rolled her eyes, and I let out an internal sigh as she slid off her stool and carried her plate to the sink. She hadn't said yes, but she hadn't said no, either. Not *really*.

"Are you done?" she asked, turning the water on and rinsing the fake cheese off her plate.

I looked down at my dinner. One forkful left. I twisted it up and handed her the plate. Parfait hopped up onto his vacated stool and leapt onto the counter, beelining straight for the running water.

"Your cat has the rudest habits." She took the plates to the dishwasher and loaded them in with her fork.

I joined her in the kitchen and slid my fork into the utensils basket. "I got the cleanup. Go wash off the airplane ick and get to bed. We have Saturday practice tomorrow."

She groaned. "Right. At least it's at noon. Jet lag is going to be awful."

"Lucky for us, the team can nearly coach itself."

"Nearly?"

"They could probably stunt okay without us. But no one can choreograph like you, and none of those tumblers could touch me on the floor."

"Yet. It won't be long before the students surpass their teachers. Like we did ours." Tasha gave a small smile. "Thanks for dinner, Monty."

She turned and set off toward her room, leaving me stunned.

Tasha hadn't called me Monty in *years*. Did she even realize?

Probably not. She was beyond exhausted. Her brain likely reverted to its original setting.

I rubbed the back of my neck and watched her until she closed the door. My mind started to spin with ideas for how I could keep up the level of camaraderie we had tonight.

I missed the old us. For sixteen seasons, we were stunt partners and best friends. When I chose Gabby as my stunt partner over Tasha, I never for a minute even dreamed I'd lose her friendship. Our rivalry heated up after that, and it was in the process of trying to outdo each other that she'd gotten hurt. Her stunt partner hadn't known her like I had. Couldn't anticipate her moves and quirks like I could, and he hadn't had the experience to improvise quickly if something was off.

All these years, I blamed myself for Tasha's fall and subsequent departure from competition. I knew she blamed me, too. And it was easier for both of us to act like it didn't matter.

But I knew it did. To both of us.

I wasn't sure if I could ever make it up to her. Not with investing financially or even helping her coach her team to another championship. But I sure would try with all my resources—and heart—to get my old bestie back.

It didn't take long to scoop the leftovers into a container and load the cookware into the dishwasher. Her model was older than Nana's. I read the faded instructions on the inside of the door, loaded the soap, and pressed start.

Sleep came fast and was filled with flashbacks from our childhood. I woke up smiling.

Until I registered the banging on my door followed by Tasha's angry voice.

"Montgomery! You get in the kitchen NOW!"

CHAPTER 13

Tasha

What. An. Idiot.

I spun on my heel and stalked back to the kitchen with my phone to my ear. "Thanks," I told my landlord. "We'll have the bubbles cleaned up by the time the plumber arrives."

Nothing like getting an early-morning call from your sweet elderly downstairs neighbors about a ceiling leak in their kitchen on the rare morning I could sleep in. I'd quickly apologized, run to the kitchen and ended the call with them to dial the landlord.

"What happened?" Monty sauntered out of his room, bare-chested and sleepy-eyed, wearing those beat-up slippers.

"Floody bubbles! Go put a shirt on and grab all the towels in your bathroom. This better not make us late for practice! And where are all my hair ties?!"

I glanced up the bar. Parfait lay on his side, licking his paw like he had no care in the world.

Just like a cat.

"Barfy! This isn't funny!" I marched over to him and ran my hand underneath his massive belly. He pawed at me but didn't move out of the way. "Aha!"

I pinned him with a hard stare and retrieved three of the covered elastics while he glared at me like I was a lunatic.

Sighing, I pulled my hair into a ponytail and Parfait resumed licking his paw, completely uninterested in my frustrations.

It was only a little bit past eight. We had plenty of time, and we could always shower at the Plex if we needed to. But I didn't want to.

The kitchen was a good two feet deep in sudsy bubbles. The dishwasher was running, which wasn't good, especially if Monty had started it last night. In my urgent rage to get him up, I'd been too overwhelmed with panic that I hadn't thought to turn it off until now.

I placed my phone on the bar next to an annoyed Parfait, whose food dishes were drowning under the suds, and waded through the bubbly clouds to turn the machine off.

But the blasted bubble maker had its own ideas and continued to ooze no matter which button or combination of buttons I pressed.

"Come *on,*" I pleaded with the button. "Turn off!"

This dishwasher was a bad listener and needed a time-out. Maybe Monty could figure out how to end its production of suds. Although, from the appearance of things and the familiar scent of my Tia Gia's limoncello dish soap, I didn't have high hopes since it appeared he couldn't tell dishwashing soap from dishwasher fluid.

Frustrated and wet, I swatted the clinging suds off of me and carefully stalked across the slippery floor to the carpet and my room to get my own towels.

Back in the kitchen, I immediately set to work on my hands and knees on the tile. Lucky for us, it hadn't reached the rug in the living area.

"Whoa." Monty let the word drag like a surfer impressed by a bodacious wave.

"'Bout time you showed up!" I growled from the sudsy mess. I craned my neck to find him standing barefoot on the carpet at the edge of the tile, armed with a load of pink towels Penny left behind when she moved out. He'd donned his FireVolts Dri-Fit tee and pulled track pants on over his shorts.

Good. Still, my traitorous eyes lingered too long on him for my liking.

Wordlessly, he knelt beside me and imitated my movements. I was just doing my best to move the bubbles and trap them. If there was a better way, I didn't get the memo. We moved side by side, corralling and popping the bubbles as best we could toward the offending machine.

Over and over, I pressed the now soaking-wet towel over the bubbles to tamp them down. Bubbles popped and suds flew, and soon I couldn't see Monty, who had to be close by. I looked behind me at the clear path we forged and decided to venture back to the rug for a fresh towel. Carefully, I rose to my feet and traversed the slippery floor.

When I turned back, dry towel in hand, I hit a Monty wall. My feet began to slide … slide … slide …

"Eep!" Strong hands closed around my upper arms, but it wasn't enough to keep me from going down … down … down …

It all happened so fast.

I slid.

Monty slid.

He twisted me around as we fell. We hit the floor—hard—and slid across the tile, coming to a stop, Monty's head first, against the fridge and sending most of the suds we'd corralled in every direction.

For a fraction of a second, I registered my cheek coming into contact with his full lips; not a kiss, but a quick brush of featherlight contact. I immediately snapped to attention, mindful and mournful of the loss of the warm and unexpected caress.

My first aid training kicked into high gear. "Oh my gosh! Are you okay?" I pressed my hands to his chest and pushed myself up, trying not to think about the fact that I was straddling him in a very inappropriate position. But it gave me the best trajectory to examine him for a concussion.

His bright baby blues blinked up at me. Then a disembodied arm appeared through the suds and his hand found the back of his head. "I think so."

I leaned in closer and held up my index finger in front of his face. "Follow my finger." I traced the air in an arc.

He sighed and did as I asked. "I'm fine. Just a little bump." He narrowed his gaze. "No concussion protocol needed. Are *you* okay?"

"Yeah. Though my pride has taken a hit. Thanks for, um …" I gestured wildly. "Breaking my fall."

He grinned. "It's been a long time since I was there to catch you. And been in this position. Kinda miss having a mat under me, though." Monty rubbed his head and grinned again.

So much grinning.

Stop the grinning! Stop being so nice! Stop being so un-Monty! I don't want to like you!

Cheeks flaming, I sprang to my feet. At a loss for words, I held out my hand as he sat up. He didn't need my help to get to his feet, but he placed his fingers in mine anyway as we both stood up.

Monty didn't let go of my hand, and the strangest zingy tingles shot up my arm and raced through the rest of me, like I'd been shocked by a faulty electric outlet.

Our gazes locked. He was so close.

I gulped for a breath of air.

Why was I reacting like this?

Monty squeezed my hand, and I hastily let go, stepping back from him instinctively. His arm shot out for the second time to stabilize me as I found my footing a good arm's length away.

I covered my face with my hands. *What a disaster.*

"We should, um …" I slowly peeled my hands off my face and gestured to the floor.

"Yeah, let's finish this up," he agreed. "When's the plumber due?"

I glanced at the clock on the stove. "Nine o'clock. We're her first stop."

It didn't take much longer to clear the rest of the suds. The dishwasher continued to pump out more, but at a slow enough rate that made cleanup manageable. When the doorbell rang at nine, we were soaking wet from head to toe, and the dishwasher was continuing to pump out suds.

"Come on in, Yvonne." I pulled the door open wide for the plumber, an old friend from high school.

Her eyebrows lifted as her gaze swept me from head to toe. "That bad, huh?"

I gave her a weak smile. "We couldn't figure out a way to turn it off without cutting the power or busting a hose, so it's still oozing bubbles like one of those fake snow machines you see in Florida."

Yvonne snorted. "I'll take care of everything." She patted my shoulder and looked past me to where Monty was standing next to the bar. "Wow, he's aged well. That's your old partner, right?"

"Yes," I said tightly. "We're currently coaching together, unfortunately." Yvonne was single, so it shouldn't bother me that she was appreciating Monty.

Why *did* I care?

I swallowed. "Still single, too," I added, loud enough for Monty to hear me. "But he's a preener. Thinks he's hot stuff. Super annoying. Counting the days till his house is done and he can move out."

She chuckled as she tracked him. "He *is* hot stuff. Let him preen. He obviously works hard to look that good."

I needed to end this conversation *now*.

"Kitchen's all yours." I stepped back for her to have a clear path to the mess.

"Does it come with him?" She winked. "Just kidding. Hey, Monty."

Monty waved at Yvonne and skirted around her on the way to his room. I felt a twinge of satisfaction that he hadn't taken the opportunity she'd so clearly presented to chat or get her number.

"Go get changed," Yvonne said. "Then scoot out of here if you need water and electricity. I'll be playing with both sources for a bit."

"Thanks." I sighed. Guess I was showering at the Plex.

Fifteen minutes later, wearing dry clothes and armed with my toiletries, makeup, and hair supplies, I headed out with Monty.

He handed me his keys. "I'll drive. Start it up while I pick up our coffee order?"

"*Our* coffee order?" I asked.

"Was I wrong to assume you didn't get to make your morning pumpkin spice blah-te?"

"No, I—"

"I'll be at the truck in a jiff." He flashed a smile and jogged in the direction of the Coffee Loft.

Shaking my head in disbelief at his kind gesture, I lifted my hand to my brow to shield my eyes from the sun while I scanned the parking lot for his vehicle. Our apartment came with two reserved spaces, but he'd told the trio of elderly sisters downstairs they could have his spot. Elaine, Janice, and Joy had been elated and left him a batch of jellied thumbprint cookies at our door. The next batch that arrived had come with a note: *Monty, Tasha's recipe substitutions made these even better! We hope you both like them. With love, Elaine, Janice, and Joy.*

That was sweet of him to share my recipe and the cookies. And further confirmation he was poking around in my recipe binder again.

I located his truck in the back and trekked across the lot. After starting it up, I settled in the passenger seat to text Penny.

Monty used the dishwasher for the first time last night. I attached a picture of the kitchen in the state I'd found it when I woke up and hit send.

The driver's side door opened, and Monty climbed in, balancing a drink carrier laden with two to-go cups and paper bag in one hand.

"That was quick." I dislodged the hot cup from the tray and set it in the console's cup holder, then did the same with his plastic cup.

"Thanks," he said, lifting the bag and tossing the empty drink carrier into the back seat. He pulled a wrapped cylinder from the bag and held it out to me. "I ordered ahead. Bacon and avocado in a fried egg wrap?"

"Yes, thank you," I said, taking the proffered food and unwrapping it. This man's generosity and memory were next-level. He'd make a great husband.

For someone.

Someday.

"It's the least I can do after the Great Dishwasher Debacle."

I almost chuckled. "Is that what we're calling it?"

"To call it anything else would reflect badly on me, so yeah."

I shook my head. "And we wouldn't want *that.* My gosh, if the people knew you were only human ..."

A funny look crossed his face. "You're being awfully gracious about this. I disrupted your morning and probably lost you your security deposit." He paused, and the sincerity in his expression nearly undid me. "I emailed Yvonne to send me the bill."

I shrugged, doing my darnedest not to react to another kindness from the man I had to keep reminding myself I was supposed to hate. "Management—and I—appreciate that. Thanks."

He nodded and turned back to his breakfast, same as mine, and quickly wolfed it down. And two more after that.

The cheer coaches' locker room/bathroom was co-ed, which normally no one minded, as the shower and changing stalls featured eight-foot-high walls and doors with double bolts. Today, after the tense morning with my unwanted house guest, I was both aware and on edge to be getting ready three stalls down from him.

Always one to put his talents on display, Monty treated me and the coaches who popped in to his rendition of "I Hate Myself for Loving You" while he showered and dressed.

"Behind my back you wanna mess around … so not jealous but he's a clown. You're on my mind ev'ry night and day, stealing my heart and pride ah-way-ee-ay-ee-ay-ay-ay."

It only got worse from there.

"Hey, woman, it's not right, and you know that I missed you last night. C'mon over and we'll drink some Sprite …"

The effort might be endearing if it was *anyone* else. He could sing, but he really should learn the lyrics if he was going to bust into song in a public place.

"Hating myself for my love of you, there's no breakin' free from chains to you … can't walk away so I tumble to you …"

The words ended, and he hummed the rest of the song. When he joined me at the sink to brush his teeth, the quiet in the room was both welcome and … unsettling.

"Terrible rendition," I announced. "Those aren't even the words."

"So?"

I rolled my eyes, and when I glanced his way, he caught me looking. With his best Finnick Odair smirk impression, he found my eyes in the mirror as he inserted the high-end electric brush into his mouth.

I almost swallowed my toothpaste under the intensity of his stare.

I quickly looked away and finished up, anxious to dry my hair and get out from under the weight of his presence.

Aware that he'd stopped brushing his teeth and was watching me section my hair and clip it up, I found myself wishing he was singing again, if only to keep me distracted from watching him watch me.

Why *was* he watching me?

"Why are you watching me?" I clipped the last section and reached for my hairbrush to smooth out the strands of hair I'd left loose. "You're creeping me out."

A muscle in his jaw ticked, and he seemed to remember he had a mouthful of toothpaste. He bent at the sink to spit it out and turned on the water to rinse it away. "I don't know, Tasha. Sorry." He zipped his toothbrush into his case and pulled out his shaving gear. "Want me to do this somewhere else?"

I suddenly felt bad. Had I spoken too harshly? If so, he should be used to that. But he was acting as if I'd hurt his feelings. He hadn't even offered a snappy comeback.

Monty was being very un-Monty-like today.

It was unsettling.

As he shaved, I dried my hair one section at a time, trapping each long lock between the brush's base and the barrel of the hair dryer.

The air was thick, and not just with humidity.

Monty and I snuck glances at each other as we did our morning rituals, but neither of us spoke. Getting ready next to him felt intimate yet comfortable, despite the fact that I was growing increasingly *uncomfortable.* With anyone else, I probably would have taken them up on their offer to shave elsewhere.

But I'd known Monty since we were four years old. We'd been the best of friends and respected and taken care of each other. And these last few years, even though we hadn't gotten along because he'd hurt me deeply and I hadn't been able to forgive him, he'd never disrespected me or ogled me in the ways other guys had.

I hadn't realized how much I missed what we'd had until this moment.

"That's an awful lot of work for cheer practice," he commented quietly after I turned off the hair dryer. "Looks nice."

I shrugged, not sure how I should react to his compliment and still keep a cool head. "It's Saturday."

"You've rocked a pony on Saturdays before." He pointed to the FireVolts cheer bow clipped to my backpack.

"I might go out later, and it takes a flat iron to smooth out a ponytail bump. If we don't have electricity—"

"Ah. Right." He ran his fingers through his damp hair. "You have plans tonight?"

"No, but I might." It was none of his business, but I answered him before I thought.

"Well," he said slowly. "If nothing comes up, would you like to join me and Nana for dinner? It's steak night at Mountainview. And they can accommodate any food requests."

My throat tightened at his offer. I'd missed seeing Nana in the Coffee Loft and was sure he knew it. "How do you know?"

"I asked."

Now there was a lump in my throat. Had he been planning to ask me before this moment? Why else would he have inquired about dietary options? Unless Nana had more issues than I knew about?

I breathed in through my nose for a count of ten before I answered. "Okay, then. Thank you for the invitation. I'd love to see Nana Booboo."

Well, that hadn't come out as chill as I'd hoped.

"Great." He settled back on his heels and tried to play it cool, but I knew him well enough to tell that he was pleased I accepted his invitation. "We'll stop home after practice to change and then head over. That work for you?"

I nodded. What in the freshly ground beans was happening between us?

CHAPTER 14
Monty

Dean Hathaway, captain of the Edge, held a Back-to-Hockey gathering the Saturday before training camp started each year. All the players, prospects, coaching, medical, and front office staff were invited to his mountainside resort of a home outside Denver.

Nana's house was bigger and more tastefully decorated, but I digress.

Per our arrangement, Tasha attended as my plus-one. Xavier and Penny waved to us from a bank of six lounge chairs on the upper deck on the far side of the pool. I followed Tasha around the perimeter and up the steps, carrying all of our stuff, as Zaki Marsh, one of the alternate captains, welcomed everyone from the mic at the DJ's booth.

"This party almost didn't happen," Zaki was saying. "Our GM wanted to lowball our captain, and that's not right." A boo went up from the guests. "I couldn't let that happen. Mostly because *I* don't want to host these parties. Luckily, he and I and Dex have the same agent, and since we all have more money than we could ever spend, we settled for team-friendly contracts to keep him here for another year." Zaki swept his sculpted, tattooed arm in an arc in front of him, gesturing to all the guests. "You're welcome."

He bowed theatrically to the applause and cheers, but he wasn't done yet. "On Dean's behalf, I'd like to say—hey!"

I turned to see what had interrupted him. Dean's wife had taken the mic. "Dean can talk for himself, when allowed." She smiled and shook her head at the younger man. "Welcome to our home, everyone. Have fun, be careful, and if you need anything, ask this guy." She poked Zaki in his bicep. "Now, let's give a big cheer for Cappy, my man and everyone's favorite forward!"

While Dean gave his welcome speech and preseason pep talk, Tasha and I reached the upper deck. Noel and Gabby had arrived a beat before us, taking chairs next to Xavier and Penny and leaving two chairs open on Gabby's other side. Tasha pulled her sundress over her head, revealing an apple green tankini, and tossed her dress on the lounger adjacent to her cousin's. She shot me a look that was hard to read. Was it a reaction to the way I was looking at her?—I hoped not—or was it a stick-it-to-me for forcing me to an outside chair instead of the one next to my former partner?

I set our bags down, shook off my slides, and pulled my Fire-Volts tank over my head.

Time to remind us both that we were supposed to hate each other.

I padded to the edge of the decking. There was about four feet of brick pavers jutting out below.

I could make it.

After making certain the deep water was clear, and any potential child copycats weren't paying attention, I walked back to my chair and spun on my heel. "Watch this," I said to Penny.

With a wink to Tasha, I hopped in place, ready to execute a move she was familiar with from years past.

"DO. NOT," she warned. "This is not a diving platform!"

I shrugged. "It can be."

With that, I was off and running. I cartwheeled into a round-off and vaulted myself off the deck and into the air, revolving into a full twist before I hit the water feet-first.

I surfaced to loud cheering and waved to the unsuspecting audience.

Ryleigh Spencer, Trask Emerson's stepdaughter, dove into the pool and swam up to me. "Can you teach me how to do that? I play hockey now, but I cheered when I was little."

When she was little? The girl was maybe fifty pounds soaking wet and, at most, eight years old.

"Please?" she pleaded. "You see that *boy* over there?"

I followed the trajectory of her finger to a kid about her age standing, arms crossed, with other boys at the side of the pool.

"Yeah, I see him. Friend of yours?"

"Nope. We used to be teammates, but he moved up to the U10 team. *I'm* still in U8." She said it like it was the worst thing in the world.

"Are you even ten?" I asked.

She shook her head. "No. But neither is he. I'm eight, and he's nine. But his birth year is the one before mine. Stupid December birthday. Mine's in the spring, so he moves up first. *So* unfair."

I loved her competitiveness. Too bad she didn't cheer anymore.

"Can you do a round-off back handspring?" I asked.

"*And* a standing back tuck," she said proudly.

I was impressed. That was a big skill for an eight-year-old.

"Okay," I said, and she brightened. "But *only* if your mom says it's okay, *only* on the lower deck, and *only* if you let me spot you."

Ryleigh nodded and held out her hand for me to shake. "I agree to your terms!" I shook her tiny hand lightly, and she swam away, leaving me shaking my head and hoping I wasn't breaking any big rules by offering.

I swam to the side and pulled myself out of the pool. A scrap of fabric landed on my head. I pulled it off and looked up.

"You're scaring the children!" Tasha adjusted her hat as she leaned over the side.

I grinned and pulled the tank over my head. "You just can't take all of this!" I flexed my biceps and ran my hands in the air down the sides of my body.

"More like I can't take your blinding paleness!" she retorted.

I snorted. I wasn't pale. I spray-tanned year-round, and she knew it.

Now things felt back to normal. "Can you toss down my towel?"

I caught it just before it landed on my head and laid it at the edge of the pool, smoothing out the air pockets and wrinkles so Ryleigh would have a non-slippery spot to launch from. But first, I'd stand on it and toss her in, just to make sure she was capable of doing everything she claimed.

"Mr. Monty?" I turned to find her at my side. "Mommy said yes, but Daddy Trask said if I get hurt, he'll body-check you so hard they'll need to find another new Ridgie."

I glanced over to her parents. Trask was bouncing her two-year-old brother on his knee. He lifted the baby's sippy cup in the air with his good arm and grinned. Poor guy was just out of a sling from fixing his torn rotator cuff. Well, I was happy to throw his kid around until he was up to the task again.

I waved and bent down to Ryleigh. "Well, it's a good thing that's not going to happen. Trask is one tough guy."

She set a hand on her hip and appraised me from head to toe. "You're bulkier. You could take him."

Bulkier? I loved this girl. Delivering insulting compliments like a pro.

"Let's start with a standard backflip into the water." I linked my fingers together and squatted down to her height. She placed her hands on my shoulder and counted down from three. I tossed her up, over the water. On her first attempt, she circled fully around and her feet slid into water like a pro diver.

She was back at my side in seconds. "Can I try the twist now?"

I nodded and explained the technique. She managed to twist 180 degrees on her first attempt.

"Not bad," I said, holding my hand out for a high five. I gave her another tip to straighten out her form, and the second one was perfect. Next, I talked her through the round-off on a wet surface, making her promise not to try this without a trained professional in a controlled situation. After one round-off back tuck into the water, I determined she was ready for the twist.

"Let's get you some extra height on this one." I glanced over at the boys, who'd stopped laughing and pointing and were now watching with their mouths hung open. "Put it all together. Do you think you could round-off into my hands?"

"I was waiting for you to ask me that! Let's do it." She turned away to take her mark for the running start, tossing a glance at her adversary on the way.

Ryleigh was a natural. "Why did you quit cheer?" I asked after her second—and perfect—dive.

"Mommy said I had to choose 'cause she's only one person and club hockey and elite cheer are both full-time jobs."

I laughed. "That is true. What about tumbling in your spare time? I could help you perfect the full twist, add a kickout or whatever else, and by next year you can *really* wow those guys."

Her eyes widened. "I like that idea!"

"Great. Tell your mom to call the gym and we'll get it scheduled."

"Cool!" She tipped her chin toward the boys, who were now cannonballing and whatever else into the pool. "Can I go one more time?"

"Sure," I said. Most of the other kids of impressionable age were near the zero-entry end of the pool or using the waterslide. "How about two more times?"

"Yes!"

Off she went. As she swam back to the side, I caught a familiar accented voice above me.

Vlad.

I stiffened as I listened to him greet Tasha, Penny, and Gabby. Then, instead of talking about hockey—or anything else—with Xavier and Noel, he commented on *me.*

"He is good with the children, no? Makes a good bear."

"*So* good," Penny replied. "Not only has he coached kids at the gym, but he's visited the kids' cancer wards in local hospitals for years."

Good ol' Penny. If I ever needed encouragement, I knew who to call.

"One more?" Ryleigh called.

"Definitely," I said, leaning in conspiratorially and dropping my voice. "They're looking again. Make it good."

She nodded. "It's not hard. They look like a bunch of kids playing around compared to me."

I laughed. That was exactly what they were.

She set off and this time twisted a perfect 360 degrees on her way into the water. I shook my head. There was so much confidence and natural talent in that little frame. I hoped she did take me up on my offer for tumbling coaching. She reminded me so much of Tasha at that age.

Ryleigh waved and swam toward the waterslide. I turned toward the stairs and did my best to overhear Vlad, but he was speaking too low. From his perch at the foot of Tasha's chair, he regaled her about his summer overseas.

Chump.

I flopped into my chair and made a show of digging my earbuds out of my bag, making sure he noticed me putting them in.

I didn't turn them on, though.

Was that wrong? Probably.

But someone had to look out for my roommate. She was doing a terrible job of it herself, and her family didn't even seem to notice. I adjusted my chair and leaned back.

"Your date is giving me—how you say it?—the evil eye," Vlad observed. His upbeat tone and stilted English grated my nerves further.

"Oh, him? He's not my date." Tasha glared at me.

I winked at her.

"Then, what? You were at a wedding with him. You are here now."

"I danced with you, remember. Monty and I are just friends."

Friends, huh? Progress!

"Friends who date?"

I coughed. Tasha glanced over at me before shaking her head vehemently. "We're not even friends, really. We just work together."

Ouch.

"And live together," Vlad observed.

"Temporarily." The word was spoken with emphasis.

"He is quite a showman, no? And handsome."

Right on both counts, Vladdy. Was he really that thick he had to beat the subject like a dead horse? Tasha had made it perfectly clear she had zero feelings for me.

Tasha smiled sweetly at him. "I promise you, there is nothing-nada-zip"—she popped the *P*—"going on between me and Monty, now or ever."

Yes! She called me Monty.

Out loud. In public!

And she didn't refute my good looks like she was prone to do.

"Well, that is good. Because Vlad does not like to share."

You've *got* to be kidding me. He was referring to himself in the third person?

How tacky. I wished I'd thought to put my sunglasses on so I could hide my eye roll.

But Tasha was giggling like it was the funniest thing she'd ever heard.

Vlad had charm, I'd give him that.

"So then—it is okay I ask for your number?"

I could actually *hear* the breath she sucked in.

Give. Me. A. Break.

"Fine by me," she squeaked. Vlad's mouth widened into a smile. For someone who'd claimed not to know a lot of English only two months ago, he sure had the pickup convo down.

Tasha pulled her phone out and handed it to him. He took it and tapped the screen. Gabby looked over, and I caught her gaze, then inclined my head toward Vlad, who was now asking Tasha to accompany him to the buffet.

Gabby frowned as Vlad stood and offered Tasha his hand. When their backs were to us, Gabby slid over to Tasha's chair. "What's that about?"

I shrugged. "It's time she dated again. But *that* guy?" I shook my head. "He looks like an untanned Ken doll, and you can barely understand a word he says."

"Xavier likes him. Noel hasn't decided yet."

"Well, *I* think he's a chump."

She laughed. "Monty, you've thought every guy Tasha has ever dated was a chump."

I shrugged. "That's cause they were."

"*All* of them?" she challenged.

"All of them," I confirmed.

She settled back in the chair. "I'm going to need more than that. What was wrong with Sam?"

"He chose baseball over her."

"Marner?"

"Let her split the check."

"That was probably her request."

"A real man would have found a way to pay the whole bill."

She rolled her eyes. "Rafael?"

"How can you take anyone seriously who was named after a Ninja Turtle?"

"We don't know that for sure. His parents are artists. That all you got?"

"He had a unibrow. Bugged her to no end."

Gabby snorted. "I remember. And he said he'd never pluck it because society wasn't going to tell him how to groom himself."

"See?"

"Okay, what about DJ?"

"I didn't have a problem with him. Until they started dating."

"Broke the Bro Code, eh?"

I whipped my head around to her and scowled. DJ had been my so-called best friend from prep school. He began dating Tasha following our falling-out. "No. We would still be friends if I didn't have to hear all the sordid details of their dating life. Ew. She was like a sister to me."

"Uh-huh." She swatted me with her magazine. "Keep telling yourself that."

I would.

I *had* to.

Or I'd go crazy.

CHAPTER 15
Tasha

Sunday morning after the early service at St. Mary's, I hummed to myself as I boxed up the sugar-free dirt cake I'd baked for Nana Booboo. I'd had a glorious morning to myself, choosing to skip family brunch at my grandparents' house. Monty had left early, leaving a note behind that he was going to the Plex to work out before his private coaching sessions.

Good for him. He'd been irritated since yesterday afternoon. I sometimes wondered if the reason he was so built was because of vanity or working off steam. When we were younger, the more his parents neglected him, the more time he spent in the gym.

Maybe it was a mix of both.

And he didn't seem to like Vlad. Surprising, because the whole team seemed to love him. Zaki hadn't even pranked him.

"Stay away, Barfy!" I yelled to the cat, who'd moved from his perch at the bar to the counter where my frosting bowl sat unattended while I'd been boxing up individual slices of cake for Nana and her friends.

"Mew!" he protested as I gave him a squirt with the spray bottle. "Sorry, but chocolate isn't good for cats. Even the fake kind."

He glared at me and jumped down, flicking his tail in defiance as he sauntered around the counter and into the living room.

"You'll thank me later!" I called after him.

Cats.

Funny little things. I wouldn't admit it to Monty, but I loved his cat. Always had. I even left the door to my room cracked at night sometimes. He slept with Monty all night long, but shared the love. I kind of liked being woken up early with a wet nose pressed to mine.

I sighed. I was dying for physical affection. Maybe Vlad would work out. But if not, Parfait was here for at least a few more weeks.

There had been another delay on the house. The repiping wasn't scheduled to start until late September now.

It was fine.

Everything was fine.

Twenty minutes later, I checked in at Mountainview's reception desk. I handed the woman a list of the ingredients in the cake. She smiled and escorted me back to Nana's room.

The Biddington wealth had bought Monty's grandmother a private corner room at the back of the building with a breathtaking view of the mountains. I slid my tote off my shoulder and set it on the chair so I could have both arms free to show her what I brought.

"I'm g-glad you took me up on my offer to v-visit. And not just because … I knew you'd bring me … *treats.*" She grinned, her smile noticeably lower on her weak side.

I returned her smile and peeled the plastic cover off the top container. Her speech was almost back to normal. "Sugar-free dairy-free gluten-free nut-free dirt cake."

"Did Fyvie … make this?"

"Nope," I said. I set the other containers down on her dresser and retrieved a plastic spoon from my tote bag. "But you'll have to tell me if it tastes like hers. I got this recipe from the Creekside Inn. Bailey Dexter-Brewer mentioned Tabbi was the original creator of the bakery's version, and that she created a sugar-free version for a diabetic regular, so I went over there and asked Tabbi if she wouldn't mind sharing it. I tweaked it a little, though."

Nana waggled her eyebrows. "Mission accepted."

I stabbed the spoon into the cake and used the side of it to push off a small bite-size piece. "Open up."

"I can … feed myself," Nana protested. She grabbed for the spoon, and I guided it to place it in her fingers.

"Of course you can," I replied softly. "But why should you when I can do it for you?"

Her hand shook and I gently took it back before she could drop it. She sighed in defeat.

"Let me get it for you this time. I can tell they worked you hard this morning. This isn't a therapy session, and *you* are a queen. Let the peasant serve you."

The side of her mouth twitched. "You are … far from a … peasant."

"Well, thank you," I replied, holding up the spoon. "Ready?"

I was happy that she complied. I carefully placed the spoon on her tongue and kept it there until her mouth closed firmly around it, then scooched it to the left to pull it out on her stronger side.

She chewed slowly and swallowed. I set the container on the rolling tray, then held her glass of water out to her to rinse it down. She sipped at the straw, waving me away after a moment.

I returned it to her side tray. "What's the verdict?"

"Can't tell the difference … between that and the real thing."

"Really?" I cocked my head to the side.

"Yes. You should … put it in your … c-cook … book."

"I'm not doing a cookbook, Nana." But I was flattered that Monty thought it was a good enough idea he'd told his grandmother about it.

She set a hard look on me. "I will … invest."

"That's sweet of you." I picked up the container of cake. "More?"

"D-don't … try to … distract me."

"That's exactly what I'm doing. Open up."

She pressed her lips together.

I chuckled. "C'mon, Nana."

She shook her head.

I sighed. "Okay. I'll think about it."

"Good." She opened her mouth.

I smiled. While I fed her, I told her about the Back-to-Hockey gathering, including getting to know Vlad and detailing Monty's antics with Ryleigh.

I held the last bite poised while she sipped her water when Monty entered the room with a new backpack slung over his right shoulder. It was ... moving?

He shushed the bag and closed the door behind him. "Nana, I finally found a way to—Tasha, what are you feeding her?"

"Dirt cake," I said, placing the spoon inside Nana's mouth.

His eyes widened, and his face turned really red, really fast. "She can't have that! She's diabetic! You know that! Why would you—" He pressed his hands to the side of his head and took two long, deep breaths. "Why would you bring that?"

I looked at Nana, who was trying not to laugh, then back at him.

"Quiet, you'll make her choke," I chided him.

"But—"

"It's sugar-free, and I got it approved." I smiled, satisfied. "She likes it so much she wants to back my cookbook. Isn't that nice? I didn't even know I was writing one."

"She—you—Nana?"

He was almost cute, the way he pulled at his hair and looked to Nana to confirm my words. I did love that he was so protective of her.

"Monty." Nana pointed to him with her good arm.

"Yes, Nana?"

"A-pologize. Now."

"I'm sorry, Tasha. I—shouldn't have assumed." He unzipped the backpack and turned back to Nana. "I, um, brought the cat."

Nana's face lit up with glee. "Puh-puh ... Parfait!"

"Mew!"

I slid off the bed to make room for Monty and the cat. He sat the old kitty on the bed, and Parfait immediately set to work sniffing every inch of the bed and Nana before putting his paws on her chest and rubbing his cheek against hers.

It was a sweet reunion. When Nana teared up, so did I. As far I knew, it had been months since she'd seen her cat.

Someday, when I was old, I hoped I had a grandson—or granddaughter—who loved me as much as Monty loved his Nana. This grown man not only loved her deeply, his actions exemplified that love.

I walked around to the other side of the bed. “I should go. It was great seeing you, Nana. I’ll come by again next week.”

She smiled up at me as she stroked Parfait’s back. “You have ... a good time tonight ... on your date.”

I smiled. “Yes, ma’am.” I bent down and placed a light kiss on her forehead. “Bye.”

With a wave to Monty, I skirted back around the bed, collected my tote, and scooted out.

I had a date with a gorgeous and sweet hockey player to get ready for.

Why didn’t that excite me as much as it should?

CHAPTER 16
Monty

Later that evening, cat in lap, I was dozing off to *Air Disasters* when the door to the apartment opened. Parfait raised his head.

"Time to go to bed, Montgomery," Tasha sang. "It's past your bedtime."

I regarded her warily. "You're the one who has to be at work in six hours." It was almost midnight.

"What can I say? Long date."

"You don't sound smitten."

She shrugged and sat on the far side of the sofa. "He's nice. But his English is limited."

"Huh. Seemed pretty fluent yesterday." My tone held an edge of cynicism.

Okay, a *lot* of cynicism.

"Maybe," she conceded.

"So, did you have a good time?"

"Why do you care?"

Good question. "Because you're keeping me up late."

"Aw, you can't go to sleep till I get home? How *parental* of you."

"Yeah, well, I have to make sure you remember to lock the door and all that."

"You sound like my dad. Kinda look like him too, with those plaid flannel pajama pants."

"What's wrong with my pants?"

"They're *so* last century." She pulled a throw pillow into her lap and hugged it. "I'm a big girl, Monty. I've been taking care of myself for a long time."

That I knew. And she did a great job of it.

"I googled him," I announced. "Did you know his mother's last name is the same as a suspected spy family? I'm tempted to hire a private investigator."

She rolled her eyes. "'Night, Montgomery."

Soooo we were back to using my full name. I sighed, then masked it with a stretch, and before I said something too sentimental, I nudged Parfait off my lap and stood up to make a show of checking the locks. "'Night, Tasha."

"Mew!"

Parfait trotted behind me. Once on the other side of my closed door, I sank into the desk chair and opened my laptop. After Tasha left the facility yesterday, Nana had told me she seemed open to the cookbook idea.

But Tasha had very little free time. Earlier this evening, I'd brought her recipe binder into my room and started typing it up. I figured it would be harder for her to say no if the big part of the job was done and I presented her with a document to edit in her leisure time.

But she had so little of it. The high school team had already been practicing daily for weeks, and her Friday nights or Saturday mornings were shot because of the weekly football games. Her *only* full day off was Sunday, but after church and family brunch, it didn't leave her much time for a passion project.

I'd returned the binder at nine o'clock, wrongly assuming her dinner date would be over and she'd be home for bed by her usual turn-in time of 10 p.m.

How wrong I'd been.

But at least I'd had the foresight to snap pictures of a bunch of recipes. I pulled up the first one on my phone and got to work.

There was no way I'd be sleeping anytime soon.

Maybe not at all.

MASCOT MEDIA DAY was a league-wide event, and the Edge's social media team had set up some wild and wacky photo and video shoots for me. A little groggy on my five hours of sleep, I sucked down the last of my second key lime protein shake after I parked at the practice facility in Denver. Jared and I would start here and drive to the arena after lunch.

He pulled in next to me and waved. I sighed at the realization of being stuck with him all day. I stretched my lips into a smile over my pressed-together teeth and saluted him.

It wasn't that I didn't like him. I did. I just hated that he was a rule-follower and was constantly reminding me of what Ridgie could and couldn't and should and shouldn't do.

Lunch was provided, and when Jared took off to find his aunt, and probably someone to schmooze about a better job, I parked myself on a bench in the training room and zeroed in on Vladimir Ivanov.

In the most nonthreatening way, of course.

I had to send him a message that I would protect my roommate at all costs.

Xavier was spotting him on a weight bench. When they looked my way, I held up my chicken Caesar wrap in acknowledgement. Xavier leaned down to speak to the chump, and I smirked when he added additional weights to each side of the bar.

If he was trying to exert dominance, he'd need to lift more than 225 pounds.

The chump struggled with his tenth rep, and Xavier had to help him replace the bar on its rests. I made a show of yawning and feigned surprise when Vlad waved at me. I held my hand up and quickly looked away, as if he was the least of my interests.

Xavier moved on to a leg press, and I was annoyed to find Vlad striding straight for me.

"Don't drip your sweat on my lunch," I warned as he sat—too close—to me on the bench.

He pointed to my wrap. "Looks good. No carbs for me. Hurts definition."

I lifted the bottom of my shirt and sucked in my abs to show him *my* max definition. "Doesn't affect me any."

His eyes widened. "Perhaps you might share your secret?"

"Perhaps," I mumbled, then took a bite. It was no secret. I just ate a balanced diet and worked out.

A lot.

"What?" I asked. I didn't like the way he was staring at me.

"Tasha—you care about her."

"I *look out* for her," I corrected. Firmly.

"She ... We have a hard time communicating. My English is not well."

I raised an eyebrow. "Sounds fine to me. And you look good. Why do you need to open your mouth?"

He laughed. "I am not interested in being loved for body. Although ..." He curled his arm and flexed his bicep. "It *is* extraordinary."

I scoffed. "You say words like 'extraordinary' and expect me to believe you're bad at English? Do I look stupid?"

He shook his head. "No. I think you are very smart. Which is why I would like to ask your help."

"My help?"

He nodded solemnly. "To woo Tasha."

I regarded him with a hard look. "She can decide for herself if she wants you to *woo* her."

"Yes, but I have idea to move process along, and it requires, how you say, *finesse.*"

This guy's propensity to go from speaking well to broken English on a dime rubbed me the wrong way.

"And *no one* else can help you?" Surely, one of the guys on the team could help. Jason Dexter had two college degrees and read as much as a bookstagrammer.

He shook his head. "I asked Xavier. He said you were the guy, since you know her best."

"What exactly do you want me to do?" I pushed the last bite of the wrap into my mouth.

"I want you to translate—no, embellish?—my love letters."

My gag reflex kicked in. I grabbed my water bottle and took a swig before my choke was noticeable.

"Your *love letters?*" He couldn't be serious.

"Yes. You have never written love letters to woo a woman?"

"Heck no. What is this, the sixteenth century?"

A patronizing look crossed his face. "Dear Monty—"

"Don't call me that."

"Montgomery," he corrected. "Love letters work. Every time."

"Work for what?" And how many women had he written love letters to? "What's your goal?"

"With Tasha? Everything."

"Why?"

"Why not? She is beautiful, smart, talented, and citizen of the greatest country on earth."

And there it was.

"You want to marry her so you can stay here?"

He nodded. "Someday, perhaps. She is easy to love, no? And her sister is married to my friend. She is perfect."

"You don't even know her," I said, unhappy that a bitter tinge carried on my tone.

"I know enough to see that we could be good together. And make beautiful babies."

This guy was the Russian Gaston. Tasha was more than a freaking trophy wife.

"You're serious?" I asked.

He nodded. "Unless ... unless her heart lies with someone else?"

I shook my head vehemently. "She hasn't dated in a year. She's a bit prickly, if you haven't noticed."

His face lit up. "I like that about her. So, will you help me?"

"Can't you use Google Translate?"

He sighed. "It does not have personal touch that you, knowing her all life long, could add."

"And *why* would I help you?" I asked. This guy had nerve.

He regarded me curiously. "Don't you want your friend to be happy?"

I shrugged. "Not with the wrong guy."

"How do I become the *right* guy?"

"Seriously?" My face heated at the rate of an Instapot. "You either are, or you aren't."

A thought zipped to my brain just then. What if I *could* mold Vlad to be the guy Tasha needed? Maybe her ice would thaw and we could be friends again.

It couldn't be too hard. I'd rewrite his letters and add a bit of flair that would resonate with her.

I knew her favorite color, what flowers she liked. I knew she spent a small fortune every Easter stocking up and hoarding Cadbury Creme eggs, hiding enough of them in her room to last a year of stressful days, despite the fact that they turned her stomach. I knew now what she could and couldn't eat, even if she wouldn't share her diagnosis.

And I knew what *not* to say to her.

"If you want to win Tasha," I said slowly, "you have to do more than *woo* her. She's smarter than a puck bunny and won't be told what to do or how to live her life."

"Just what I am looking for. An independent voman!" Vlad grinned in a way that made me instinctively recoil. I didn't think he had nefarious intentions, but the guy seriously didn't know what he was getting himself into.

I *should* help him, for both their sakes.

Tasha deserved to be happy. She shouldn't have to live under the weight of her medical bills. If things went well with Vlad, maybe they'd get married and she could relax.

I wanted her to relax. She deserved to relax.

"Okay," I said. "I'll help you. But you can't tell anyone. It'll make us both look bad. I have a reputation I'm trying to build."

"Ah, yes. Best bear ever."

I cringed. "NO." I stood up and pretended to itch a spot on my upper abdomen so I could lift my shirt to remind him I was bigger and *bulkier,* as Ryleigh had put it. "As a helper. The bear is just the vessel. And you can donate a thousand dollars to the children's oncology unit for each letter I 'help' you with."

"Right. Deal. Do you have paper?"

I stared at him. He was awfully presumptuous. And what *was* this? The twentieth century? "Text me what you want me to translate."

While he went back to the locker room to grab his phone, I threw away my trash and tried not to regret what I'd promised. If Xavier liked the guy, that should be enough.

But still, it didn't feel right to me.

Tasha hadn't come home in that I-had-the-best-date-ever euphoria that women were prone to do. She didn't hum or smile or gush about Vlad. Maybe she did to Penny or Gabby, but I'd seen at the party how cool they'd been with each other: No visible chemistry *at all.* No secret glances, no heated stares, no private jokes or laughs.

It wasn't any of my business. But I'd help, see where it went. And be there for her when it didn't work out.

Because it never worked out. Because Tasha had a talent for only attracting chumps.

Vlad returned, and we exchanged numbers. Then he texted me what he wanted to say to Tasha. "I ran this in translate app, but it didn't convey the right tone."

I looked at the message. *My sweet Tasha. In cloudy sky, you are the sun, brighten and shine up my day and my path. You make my heart large with love every time I see you.*

I cringed. "How about this?"

In a cloudy night sky, 'tis you who light my way. The moon and stars are dulled by your shine, shining and sprinkling light on all that is dark in my world. Truly, my beating heart swells with every smile you bestow upon me. Your joy fills my soul and fuels my need to prove to you that I am worthy of your radiance.

Maybe I went a little overboard with the flowery prose, but Vlad wasn't likely to care if I got carried away, only that it was effective and hit the mark.

I didn't like the idea of Tasha being a *mark.*

Not my problem though. I hit send and waited while he read it, watching his smile widen each time his thumb flicked the screen to read more.

"This is perfect! *Shedevr!* A masterpiece! Exactly what I need." He wrapped his arms around me. "Thank you!"

I stood, slipping out of his clammy appendages. "I also sent you the link to my foundation. I expect two thousand dollars to clear before I translate another one."

"Yes, yes." He stood up and held out his hand for me to shake.

Against my better judgment, I took his proffered hand. "See you around."

"See you!"

I wanted to stay and scream at him that Tasha wasn't the kind of girl a man with an empty brain could woo with good looks, charm, and purple prose. But I'd play the game, and when she realized he was a fraud, I'd help her to rebuild her confidence, like every other time.

Well, except that last time. The DJ thing had been a hit to both of us. I'd put money on the fact that she also felt relief when he'd taken a job in California and we weren't running into him on a daily basis anymore.

Maybe things *would* work out with Vlad, like the pieces had fallen together for Penny and Xavier. Theirs had been a marriage of convenience, born out of a need for him to marry to save his inheritance. But they'd been friends first.

Tasha and Vlad didn't know each other.

I suited up with guilt, wondering if I'd just set my coaching partner up for the biggest mistake of her life.

CHAPTER 17

Tasha

"Soooo ..." Penny sidled up to me when I took my place behind my register Monday morning. "How's Vlaaaaaaad?"

I shrugged coolly at her teasing singsong tone. "Same as he was when I texted you last night, I guess."

"C'mon, Tasha." Gabby flipped her chestnut side bangs and leaned against the back counter. "Tell us about your date. Monty said you didn't get in till almost midnight."

"When did you talk to Monty—er, Montgomery?" Behind her, the long hand on the clock ticked to 6 a.m. Jannell hadn't even unlocked the front door yet.

Note to self: Think twice next time before arriving early to work.

Gabby's amused expression revealed she'd noticed my slip-up. "We were texting when you got in last night. He's got Mascot Media Day today."

"Right." He'd asked for my input on some of his ideas, which I freely gave while he watched me chop vegetables. He'd already spent a weekend in Florida to gather with some of the other mascots for what he playfully dubbed the 'Shenanigans Summit.'

"So? The date?" Gabby prodded. "Monty said you didn't give any details."

Gabby and Monty's close friendship had always annoyed me, especially once they began stunting together all those years ago.

Like we used to be.

Partner-close.

I didn't want to be bitter about it anymore.

Jannell unlocked the door and flipped the sign, and customers began filing in. I turned away from her to close the discussion and stepped up to my assigned register.

Brenna and Brendan Trotter were the first in the door this morning. I waved them over.

"Mornin', Tasha," Brendan said, then addressed Penny and Gabby. "Ladies."

They returned the greeting, and Penny frowned. "You're up early. Morning skate isn't until ten."

"I've got a baby shower brunch at the barn today," Brenna said. "We're heading over to set up so he can help me move the tables before he goes to PT." She and Penny locked eyes.

Now I was frowning. Brenna had never needed anyone to help her before. And Brendan was still recovering from the broken leg he'd sustained in the playoffs.

Penny's eyes widened, as if she'd just received an unexpected telepathic message.

Brendan squeezed Brenna's shoulder and cleared his throat. "My usual, please, Tasha, but decaf. Decaf for Bren, too."

"We're, um, trying to wean off caffeine," Brenna explained, as her hand splayed over her flat stomach. She quickly dropped her hand, as if the fabric was molten lava.

It wasn't my business to ask, but I'd bet my Crock-Pot the woman was pregnant.

Another Edge baby next summer.

I was happy for her and stretched my lips into a smile. "Montgomery finally got to you about how poisonous coffee is, huh?" I waggled my eyebrows and turned before she could confirm or deny. It was obvious they weren't prepared to announce their news yet.

I selected mugs for each of them from the cubbies that made up our mug wall above the back counter. *My Wife Is Hotter than Coffee* and *My Husband Is Hotter than Coffee* were a new fun set Marie had gifted to her parents for their anniversary. I didn't think Jannell would mind if Bren-squared used them.

Bren-squared. Why did every hockey couple have such cute nicknames? Way better than Coach Monsha.

Not that Monty and I were a couple.

I lightly affixed the printed order stickers to the sides of the mug handles and set them on the counter for Gabby or Jannell to fill, and we all continued with our routine. When I returned from my break after lunch, I was surprised to find Xavier and Vlad chatting up Penny at her register.

"There she is!" Penny gave me a light hip bump. "Our guys are here!"

She was already shipping Vlad and me? I snuck a glance to see how he'd reacted.

Vlad's blinding smile gleamed like the sun reflecting off an unspoiled field of fresh snow.

I smiled back and suddenly felt tongue-tied. It wasn't because I was smitten or crushing on him, but it wasn't a natural reaction, and I probably should analyze why.

Nah. He was here, he was smitten, and that was all I needed, right?

"Tasha! I am sad. I have just learned your break is over. I was hoping we could sit for a minute?"

I shook my head. "Sorry. Afternoon rush is about to start, and Gabby still needs a break." I signaled to her and nodded my head toward the kitchen door.

As she passed me, she squeezed my shoulder and winked.

Someone needed to tell her winking was creepy, especially from an elder Gen Zer.

Vlad pulled an envelope from the front center pocket of his hoodie. "For you, for later. I am looking forward to Friday night. My first American high school football game!"

I slid it into my apron pocket. "I told you, you don't have to come," I reminded him. "Your presence will make all the guys nervous and the girls giddy. Besides, I can't make it to your preseason game tonight."

"We'll be there Friday, too, Tasha," Xavier said. "Can't miss the first home game for Palmer City High. Some of my camp athletes play for the team. And Penny wants to see your timeout routines and the halftime show."

"I saw them practicing last week," Penny said as she handed Xavier his pregame toffee coffee. "It's going to be awesome!"

"I wish to as well," Vlad interjected.

Now I grinned for real. "My kids are going to knock your socks off," I said.

Vlad looked down. I peeked over the counter to find him wiggling his toes under the band of his team-issued slides. "Spider? Spill? Socks twisted?"

He shook his head. "Knock socks off?"

"It means to impress," Xavier filled in.

"Ah. English is weird."

I laughed. "That it is." I pointed down the counter. "Your order is up." I went back to taking orders and waved goodbye to them when they left.

Gabby returned from her break thirty minutes later. "Have you opened the envelope yet?"

I shook my head no.

"What are you waiting for?" Penny asked.

I shrugged. "Privacy so I can read it alone?"

"Pretend we're not here," Gabby said.

I rolled my eyes.

"C'mon, Tasha," Penny implored. "Aren't you dying to know what's in it?"

"I guess." I pulled it from my pocket. "Fine, I'll read it."

The flap of the envelope was tucked in instead of sealed, so the peach-colored card inside was easy to extract. I lifted the flap to find a note scrawled in loopy script.

My cheeks flamed with fire as I silently read each word. My joy filled his soul? Was he talking about me?

I was pretty sure *joy* wasn't a descriptor that anyone who knew me would use. I was cynical, critical, and sarcastic.

I cleared my throat and slipped the card back in the envelope, then met Penny and Gabby's expectant expressions. "Just a note. He seems to like me."

Penny clapped. "Yay!"

"Was it a poem?" Gabby asked.

I shook my head again. "The man barely knows English." But

the note was well-written. Maybe he ran it through an editing program.

"So what are your intentions with Vlad?" Gabby asked. "Dating, marriage, baby in a carriage?"

I shrugged. "Too early to tell, but it'd be nice not to have to work three jobs." I pointed at my sister and cousin in turn. "I'd still work here for funsies, like you two do."

Penny and Gabby exchanged a look.

"What?"

"Tasha, stop," Penny pleaded. "You can't marry a guy you don't know just for his money."

"Why not? You did."

Penny winced. "No, I didn't."

"Okay. For his castle then."

"Stop it, Tasha. We had a soul connection. We'd known each other for years. You don't know anything about this guy. He could be part of a criminal family. And he barely speaks English."

"Even better." I closed my eyes and sighed. "I can grow to love him. Just like you grew to love Xavier."

"I don't like it."

"You don't have to," I retorted, a little more firmly than I intended. "Sorry. But it could be mutually beneficial. I overheard him asking Xavier how long it took to become an American citizen. He doesn't want to go back to the KHL if it doesn't work out for him here."

Penny gasped. "Tasha! He could be courting you for a path to citizenship!" In a very un-Penny-like move, she snatched the envelope from my pocket and pulled out the card, her eyes widening as she read. "This is a love letter."

"Yeah? So?"

"Let me see!" Gabby reached for it, and Penny passed it to her.

I crossed my arms over my chest as they turned and locked concerned eyes on each other. "It's just words," I said.

"Very pretty words." Gabby's eyebrows lifted as she scanned the card. She handed it back to me, and I returned it to the safety of my pocket. "He has the soul of a poet."

"If he even wrote it," I said.

Gabby tapped her chin and turned back to Penny. “Maybe Xavier can verify that?”

Penny nodded. “I’ll see if he can find out without being so obvious.”

I shook my head. “Please. Let it go.”

“If you say so.” Penny shrugged.

I spun on my heel and retreated through the kitchen door to read the words again in privacy.

They were pretty words.

But did he mean them? And had he written them for me?

I really *really* hoped so.

CHAPTER 18
Monty

One of my ideas for the team's social media was jump-scaring the players.

Mean? Perhaps. Toronto did it, so the concept wasn't original, but it'd be fun. And if I got slugged, well, the league had good health insurance.

Health insurance got me thinking about Tasha. Tasha led my thoughts to Vlad. And wouldn't you know it?

There he was—walking in the building in his swanky plaid suit in autumn colors, complete with a coordinating fedora and matching plaid band, trying too hard to give David Pastrnak a run for his money this year as the league's fashion favorite.

What a chump.

I motioned to Jared with my fuzzy paw and scooted just inside the hall that intersected Vlad's path to the dressing room.

"Get your phone ready," he said to Mags, our new social media intern.

"Ready!" she called back.

"Now!" Jared hissed.

I launched myself into the hall, directly in front of the six-foot third-line center.

"Aaah!"

Vlad jumped and nearly fell to the ground as he tried to recover his balance.

That was satisfying.

"Got it!" Mags held up her phone.

I high-fived her. "Sweet!"

She laughed. "One down, twenty-two to go!"

Vlad's eyebrows knit together. "Scare everyone?"

Mags nodded. "It was Monty's idea. Great, right?"

I leaned against the wall and raised my voice to be heard through the bear head. "*I* think so."

Vlad nodded. "Fun."

Well, *that* was insincere. Where was the guy's sense of humor?

Down the hall, Xavier and our goalie, Jason Dexter, had just turned the corner and were fast approaching us. "Let's skip these two. If Xavier spills his lucky coffee, we're a goal down. And I don't want to mess with the netminder."

"Smart," Jared agreed. "Even if we *are* playing San Jose. You never know, they could have a lucky night. But why take the chance?"

We greeted them, and then I scooted back into the hall to get ready for my next victim.

"Trotter and Emerson just turned the corner," Jared said. "Ready?"

"Ready," Mags said. I gave a thumbs-up.

"Now!"

This time, I dove to the ground on my side and came to a rest with my head in my hand, elbow bent, like I was a model posing on a beach. Brendan and Trask hooted above me, but I wasn't able to see if they'd jumped in surprise.

"Great one, Monty!" Brendan praised. "You get Dexter yet?"

Jared helped me to my feet. "Not this time. Don't want to mess with the goalie."

"Wise," Trask agreed. "He's so serious. You know how he has all his routines to vibe with before a game. You should definitely get Marsch, though. Payback for all the pranks he plays on us."

Zaki Marsch was a known prankster and, from what I heard, had never been out-pranked, though many players had tried. But he'd retaliated and made them regret it.

I wondered if he'd retaliate on me?

Only one way to find out.

I slipped back into the hallway, and Jared adjusted the costume to make sure the head was secure. Mags decided to skip over all the players who entered before Zaki, just in case he walked in on one of the jumps.

"Here he comes! Right behind ChaCha." Mags tapped me on the shoulder. "Go!"

I waited until Bryce Chambers passed us, then turned with my back to the hall. I squatted with my arms straight out in front of me, and double back-handspringed directly into his path.

"What the—Monty?" Bryce must have turned around. "What are you doing?"

I lifted my arms in a shrug and called out to Mags. "Did we get him?"

"Eh. Not really. He did jump a little, though."

Zaki snorted. "Nice try, guys." He tipped his hat and continued down the hall, flinging a warning over his shoulder. "C'mon ChaCha. You can help me dream up some payback."

Bryce followed him down the hall, turning around to make a slicing motion at his neck. "Y'all are in for it now!" he drawled.

I shrugged and shouted. "Bring it on!"

"No!" Mags laughed. "Maybe we should avoid him completely going forward."

"Yeah, his pranks are legendary," Jared agreed. "I don't want to be in his crosshairs."

"Let him know it was all my idea, then. What's the worst he can do?"

"He put marshmallows in Moreau's wheel wells last year," Jared said. "His brand-new custom Mercedes SL 500 Grand Edition!"

"He posted a picture of Trotter's underwear drawer, open, with ragged tighty-whiteys he—Zaki—bought at a thrift store," Mags added.

"Okay, so I'll watch my car and not invite him over." They looked nervous. "It'll be fine."

"If you say so," Mags said. "Good luck."

If being the recipient of a Zaki Marsch prank was my penance for making Vlad look ridiculous, so be it.

"Let's do one more of these, take an early dinner break, then head outside to greet fans while it's still light out," Mags said.

"You got it, boss," Jared said.

She giggled, a little too giggly. Was she sweet on him? I looked between the two. He was grinning like she hung the moon.

How sweet.

Twenty minutes later, I retrieved my phone from my locker and grabbed my lunch bag. The team provided dinner, but Tasha's Crock-Pot braised beef and vegetables was far superior to anything I'd eaten here.

I was pulling it from the microwave when my phone buzzed in my pocket. I set the bowl on the counter and opened my messaging app to find a text from Vlad:

The roses are red and the violets are blue. Your pretty eyes are the ocean and I drown. Dying in your eyes would make me happy man.

You have got to be kidding me.

I thought about how I could rewrite it while I ate. Taking my food to an empty table, I inserted my earbuds to discourage anyone from talking to me.

This would take some work, but I was up to the challenge.

CHAPTER 19
Tasha

"You ready to go?" Monty leaned into the doorframe of my bedroom, arms crossed, sleeves of his FireVolts jacket pushed up on his forearms.

He was handsome, I'd give him that. And that casual doorframe lean would make most women swoon.

Not me, though.

"I need two more minutes," I said. I'd only been home for twenty, and I'd had to email several parents of my high school athletes to address questions about a competition I wanted to take the team to in the spring. It would require massive fundraising, but they were up to the task. And I had ideas for getting sponsorships, thanks to my recent connections to the Edge organization. Jason's wife, Lauren, was a fundraising superstar, and after chatting with her I had a plan and the administration's approval.

Apparently, he didn't take the hint. "You're still here," I said. "Why?"

"Did you eat?"

I shook my head. "I was just going to grab an energy bar. I'll eat when we get home."

He left, and I finished up the email, hit send, and closed my laptop. The peach envelope from Vlad was on a pile of books behind it. I smiled.

"'In a cloudy night sky, 'tis you who light my way. The moon and stars are dulled by your shine, shining and sprinkling light on all that is dark in my world,'" I quoted.

"Aw, that's sweet. And here I was, thinking you hated me."

I jumped in my chair, startled. Monty stood in the doorway again, holding my stainless-steel travel bowl. "You shouldn't sneak up on people!"

"Why not? You can hear the best things when people don't know you're listening." He grinned. "C'mon, you can eat in the car and fill my ears with more sweet nothings."

I shook my head, but I couldn't be mad at him. He was making sure I was fed, and that was nice. "That wasn't meant for your ears. Give me two minutes to change?"

"But I like you the way you are ... Womp womp!"

"Get out!" I shooed him with my hands. His grin widened, and he closed the door as he stepped out of the room.

As I changed into my team leggings and hoodie, it occurred to me that as annoying as Monty was most of the time, he had some endearing qualities. And I had to admit, after three months of rooming together, it was hard to remember sometimes that I was supposed to be eternally mad at him.

"So," Monty said as he turned out of the parking lot. "You writing poetry now?"

I shook my head and twisted my fork into the spaghetti squash and meatballs with marinara that had been slow-cooking all day. *So good.* He'd even scraped the inside of the squash for me. "I got a letter from an admirer."

"An admirer, huh?" Monty's eyes were fixed on the road. In the distance, the sun was setting behind the mountains.

"Yup."

"And you memorized a line?"

"All of it."

"Must have been good. Care to share more?"

"Mmm." I swallowed the forkful and twisted another. "'Your joy fills my soul and fuels my need to prove to you that I am worthy of your radiance.'"

Monty snorted. "Clearly, this is a man who doesn't know you

at all or loves to be verbally abused by someone who thinks your hedgehog cactus self is your version of joy."

I laughed. "Fair."

He stopped at a light and tapped the steering wheel with his thumbs. This was a Monty quirk he'd been doing since he got his license at sixteen.

"What's bugging you?" I asked. "The writing? It's actually pretty sweet."

He shook his head. "I'm not sure I like Vlad."

I sighed. "I'm not sure yet, either. But he sure is trying hard to get my attention." The light turned green, and Monty turned onto Canyon Pass Road. "That's the problem, I think. *Why* is he trying so hard? I mean, I'm a catch, but …"

Monty laughed. "Just be careful, 'kay? And let me know if he needs a good beating."

I smiled. "I will."

I finished the last bite of my dinner as we pulled into the lot. "Thanks for feeding me."

"Thanks for making amazing food day after day. I'm going to miss your cooking when I move out." He set the car in park and released his seat belt. "Have you put more thought into the cookbook idea?"

I shook my head. "No, but feel free to copy my recipes. I can sticky-note tab the ones Nana likes."

"That would be great. Thanks. Speaking of Nana, do you mind if we stop by her house after practice? I'd like to check on the reno progress."

"Sure. It's not too far out of the way. Do you think we'll be home by eleven?" Practice ran from seven until nine, and I liked to be in bed shortly after. Five a.m. came quick.

"I'll make sure of it," he promised.

Practice went well. The routine was coming along. We made adjustments, perfected what was working, and ran it over and over. We would be in great shape to perform at the gym-wide showcase in November.

Nana's house wasn't far from the Plex. I'd spent a lot of time here as a kid and teenager. She'd hosted all the team parties, and her doors were always open to Monty's friends. The Victorian mansion cut an impressive silhouette in the night sky, lit up by strategically placed lamps and recessed bulbs along the walkways.

"Beck's still here." I pointed to the Montoya Construction van in the driveway. "That's got to be expensive."

"Worth every penny," Monty said. "I may have added a few projects ..."

"Oh yeah?" We got out of the car. He waited for me at the hood. Instead of him opening the garage to enter the house, I followed him up the newly constructed walk to the front door. "I don't miss the stairs that used to be here," I admitted, "but these switchbacks will be a beast unless Nana has an electric chair. Couldn't she use the elevator in the garage?"

"The garage is full of construction materials," he explained, "and probably will be for months. Anyway, it was mandated. Jury's still out on whether Nana will get an electric chair. She can't be alone yet, and she likes to be pushed. And you know how she is with technology."

I laughed. "There is that." Since I'd known her, she'd always found a way to break or mess up phones, DVD players, smart TVs ...

"Tell me what you think of ... this." Monty opened the front door with a flourish and flicked a switch. The foyer came to life with light from a massive overhead chandelier.

I sucked in a gasp. "Wow," I breathed. "Beck did this?"

"Well, me and my crew." Beck appeared in the archway that led to the formal sitting room. "Hey, Tasha."

"Hey." I turned slowly in a circle, taking in the newly stained woodwork paneling that replaced the old mustard and ivory wainscoting below the chair rail, the matching grand staircase and banister, and the polished marble flooring. "This is ... this is beautiful work, Beck."

"Thank you." I turned in time to see her elbowing Monty. "I told you she'd like it," Beck hissed.

He nodded and caught my gaze. "What's not to like?"

I pointed to the wallpaper that covered the top half of the walls. "It's a bit outdated."

Beck grinned and stuck her hand in her pocket, pulling out a folded piece of paper. Monty held out his hand for it. "You were right. Here's your twenty."

He pocketed the bill. "She's hated this wallpaper since preschool."

"I don't ... hate it. It's just ... a bit hideous. It's like the artist wanted to see what art deco mixed with calico looked like. Pick one or the other. Well, for *this* house, anyway."

"What would you suggest?" Beck asked.

"I don't know," I admitted. "Anything else?" They laughed. "Maybe light peach or an ivory and pastel toile wallpaper. Hang a series of mirrors. It's a dark room, but a lighter color and mirrors could brighten it up, catch the light from the chandelier and the stained glass on the front door." I looked up. "That thing was made for a castle."

"Funny you should say that," Beck said. "It used to hang in Schwannenschloss."

My eyes widened. "Seriously?"

She nodded. "My dad and I did some work there a few years ago, when he was stationed in Munich. Xavier's grandfather gifted it to us, but I knew I'd never use it. Xavier didn't want it. When I saw this foyer, I knew it'd be perfect."

"It is." I looked up at it again. "It's going to be a beast to clean, though."

Beck laughed. "One of the reasons I didn't want it!" She turned to Monty. "Want to see the kitchen?"

Monty nodded, and we followed her through the elegantly decorated rooms to the back of the house, where the kitchen was located.

"We ripped out the wall you requested to create a more open space. The pipes here have already been replaced, so we're working on patching it all up now."

"Looks good," Monty complimented her. "Thanks."

I nodded my affirmation. My nose twitched at the dust that was still in the space, so I kept my mouth closed and pulled up my hoodie to cover the bottom half of my face.

Monty frowned. "What's wrong, Tasha?"

I shook my head and mumbled "Nothing yet" beneath the fabric. "I'll wait for you outside."

Monty stretched his arms out and blocked my exit. "Tell me."

My stomach began to feel queasy. I took a few deep breaths. "Gluten."

"Gluten? Beck, have you cooked here?"

She shook her head. "Nope. But there could be wheat in the drywall or insulation."

"Rip it all out." He lowered his hand and spoke softly to me. "I'll meet you outside."

I nodded and scurried out of the room, bolting for the front door and fresh night air.

Rip it all out? That would cost a fortune and extend the timeline. And it's not like I ever visited here anymore.

Monty and Beck joined me on the wraparound veranda about five minutes later and handed me a bottle of water. "Are you feeling okay?" he asked.

"Yeah." I turned to face them. "You don't have to rip it out. It's not an allergy, just a sensitivity. Minor reaction, promise. Doesn't even require Benadryl. It's just annoying. It shouldn't bother me when it's finished and covered up. And besides, it's not like I ever come here anymore."

"About that," Monty said. "Nana enjoys your visits. I hope you'll come here regularly again when she returns."

I opened my mouth to reply but lost my words. "Thank you," was all I could muster.

"I'm headed out," Beck said. "I'll see you tomorrow at our meeting with your Nana. Bye, Tasha."

We followed her to the driveway. The ride home was quiet, and I used the time to reflect on the history I had with the man sitting in the driver's seat.

I missed our friendship. I missed how easy it used to be between us. I missed our good-natured rivalry that made us both better, iron sharpening iron. And I wish I had the nerve to ask why he ditched me for Gabby.

That betrayal still felt fresh every time I thought about it. And the more time I spent with Monty, the more I replayed that day in my head.

CHAPTER 20
Monty

Mid-October

Opening night for the Edge.

By the time warm-ups started, I was a sweaty, exhausted mess. I'd been out on the pavilion for hours, then inside greeting fans and donors. Then back outside for the Kids' Club meet-and-greet. At least there was a chill in the autumn mountain air. I couldn't imagine how mascots in the South got through it. And characters at theme parks?

God bless them.

Jared held Ridgie's head while I shoveled spoonfuls of Tasha's latest experiment into my mouth. That woman could put the most bizarre ingredients together and it not only worked, it was always the best thing to date that she made.

Tonight's dinner was a beef and sweet potato chili. She'd added tomatoes, a bunch of spices, corn, and even a bar of dark chocolate. And somehow, it worked.

Well.

"Fourteen minutes," Jared warned, checking his phone. "You almost done?"

"Yeah." I covered the container and shoved it back into my travel cooler bag. "I'll finish it later."

Jared secured the bear head and followed me through the halls to a bench by the tunnel, where my ice skates were waiting for me. I sat on a chair and pretended to put them on while Mags filmed.

"Got it!" she announced.

Jared slid the skates on my feet and laced them up. I pulled on the paws and he helped me to stand.

"You good?" Mags asked. "The team is coming."

I gave her a thumbs-up, and she handed me a flag with the Edge's logo. We made our way to the end of the tunnel to wait for my cue.

The noise of the crowd was deafening. "Thirty seconds," she shouted.

Behind me, the team was lining up. The goalie always led the team onto the ice, but this team had a tradition where they picked a local youth hockey player to skate a lap with a smaller version of the flag I was holding. Because it was opening night, they'd decided to have me get the crowd going first.

"Ladies and gentlemen, please get on your feet and give a loud welcome to your fa-vo-rite bear, Ridgie!"

"Go!" Jared shouted.

I stepped onto the ice, holding the flagpole in front of me, taking a slow lap around the boards. When I passed the team's family and friends section, I let go with one hand to wave and blow kisses.

The fans ate it up, but I couldn't feel any joy.

Tasha was there with Penny, Gabby, and the other Wags and their families. I growled when I realized she was wearing Vlad's jersey, number fifteen. And on her face, she'd painted a crescent moon with dash marks around the opening to complete the circle. Which had nothing to do with the Edge and everything to do with a love letter Vlad had given her.

It made sense. We were up to four letters now, and I was just waiting on another grand to hit my bank account before I sent back number five. And he'd taken her out to dinner two of the last four Sundays.

But I didn't like it.

You fill my crescent moon to full.

Gag me. I thought she was too smart to fall for that garbage.

Apparently not.

I handed the flag to Jared and pushed myself through the players waiting for their signal. I heard the crowd quiet as the opening night video played and grow loud again when the kid skated out.

"Ridgie! Wait up!" Jared called, barely audible through the team's intro song, "Livin' on the Edge." "We don't have to rush upstairs yet! And you're still on your skates!"

Right. I wanted to get up to the platform so I could watch Tasha, but I'd break my ankles if I didn't change out my footwear.

Lucky for me, Mags had grabbed my shoes. I sat on the nearest bench and stuck a foot out.

"Diva," Jared muttered. I couldn't see his expression, but he didn't sound mad.

Once my sneakers were on, we rode the elevator up silently. I was sure they were confused by my quick exit, but I didn't owe them an explanation.

The doors parted, and I led the way to the platform. I waved to the crowd and danced, doing my best to sneak glances down to the ice.

But it was no use. It was too dark, the family section was too far away, and my giant head obstructed any chance of me viewing that section, even if the distance wasn't too far.

After the opening ceremony, Jared, Mags, and I retreated to an unused conference room, where I couldn't get my head off fast enough.

"Bruh, are you all right?" Jared asked. "Breathing okay?"

I thought back to Thursday night, when the drywall or insulation impeded Tasha's breathing. "Yeah. I'm fine. Just needed a break."

"Good," Mags said. "Because the game just started, so we're here for a good three hours. I've got a long wish list of content from my boss."

"We'll get it done," I said. "What's next?"

She scrolled her phone. "Second time-out shenanigans, mini Zamboni ride, T-shirt cannon, pics with our featured veteran and his family ..."

We got it all done, and when the final horn sounded, the Edge had won 3-2, with two goals from Xavier—almost unheard of for a defenseman in a first game of the season—and a five-hole goal from Zaki Marsch, right between the goalie's legs. Plastic and stuffed birds flew onto the ice at the buzzer—an homage to last season's pigeon incident—and I had a feeling there would be some bird-related bits in my near future. Thanks to fan demand, and an official vote, there were already talks of adding a second mascot, Percy T. Pigeon. "T" for "the." I hoped they came up with something more creative for its middle name.

It could be worse. At least they weren't dead birds—or fish. Nashville fans throw catfish; Detroit fans throw octopi ... shudder.

I waded into the crowd, taking pictures and posing for fans. It was fun, but my heart wasn't in it. I just wanted to get home and grill Tasha on her relationship with Vlad.

I arrived home just before midnight and wasn't surprised to see Tasha's door closed. I made sure Parfait's food and water dishes were full—they were, bless Tasha's heart—and I set my alarm for 5 a.m.

It came quickly. I dragged myself out of bed and shuffled to the kitchen, reminding myself that after she left, I could go back to bed.

Sometimes, it was good to be me.

But the realization made me feel worse, not better. Tasha *never* slept in, even if she could.

"What are you making?" I asked her.

She looked up from the cutting mat and smiled. "Barbecued pulled pork with carrots and cauliflower. What are you doing up?"

"Looks good," I replied. "It's Tuesday. Going to get in an early workout since we have practice tonight. Only four weeks until the showcase."

"Which we will rock," she said vehemently. "Taylor Brewer sent me a video of the Kalispell Worlds team. Our stunts are far more advanced."

"They always have been," I said, sliding onto a stool at the bar. "Just because they have two former national team members coaching their team, it doesn't mean the squad can actually execute the higher-level stuff." That was only true for *us* and *our* team.

"True," Tasha agreed. "But the team *has* improved tremendously since Taylor and Kane took it over. She can even compete, if she wants to. She demonstrates what she wants from the basket girls."

Taylor was local to Palmer City and a former athlete and coach here at the Plex before she married Brenna's cousin Kingston. He'd been traded to Montana a few years ago, and she now coached at the gym there. "I sent her portions of our routine to critique, and she admitted we were levels above them and most of the other big gyms. They're rooting for us, but we have to beat the Ontario team. They aren't giving any other team a peek at their stunts."

"We already knew that." I shifted in my seat. "Got any connections in Canada?"

She shook her head. "Nope."

"It doesn't matter," I said. "Evan could leave an Olympic gymnast in the dust if he went up against him in a floor routine. Your basket girls can do things in the air no one even dreamed about five years ago. And the FireVolts have the best coaches. How can we lose?"

She grinned. "They do, don't they?"

"One hundred percent," I agreed.

CHAPTER 21
Tasha

The Palmer City Harvest Moon Festival was an event I looked forward to every year. And this year, it lined up with OktoBrewFest, hosted by Brewski's, Brenna's family's sports bar and grill.

On Saturday, Brenna hosted a themed dance in her event barn after the family closed the grounds for the day. Xavier had bought out a full table: he and Penny; Gabby and Noel; Noel's mom, Gemma, and stepdad, Coach Conway of the Voltage; and me and Vlad.

I'd opted to meet Vlad here, on the OktoBrewFest grounds, instead of having him pick me up. It made sense; Monty dropped me off on his way to Nana's Mountainview Manor, where they were having their own version of the Harvest Festival. Xavier had invited him to join us—the tables were capable of seating ten—but Monty declined, citing his anticipation of spending his time with Nana weaving through the pumpkin patch behind the main building.

"There he is!" Penny hissed, pointing toward the entrance within the ropes.

I forced a smile and waved. Vlad was charming, good-looking, and thoughtful. And his love letters were straight swoon and fire.

But there was no chemistry in person.

Zero.

I read on a self-help site that you have to kiss someone to truly test compatibility. So I held out hope for that. Despite four dates now, he hadn't made a move. Xavier said it was because he wanted to be a gentleman and do everything right with me, but it still didn't *seem* right. If he felt as deeply and was as attracted to me as much as his letters claimed, wouldn't he feel compelled to at least *ask* me for a kiss?

Vlad hurried over and laced his fingers through mine, then raised our linked hands up to place a kiss on my knuckles.

I should have swooned, right?

Penny seemed on the verge, with one hand on her growing belly, her smile wider than I'd ever seen it and her eyes all googly and emotional.

"Hi," I said huskily, trying to sound enthusiastic.

"*Privet*. Hello." He squeezed my hand. "Shall we stroll through the corn maze?"

"Sure."

We separated from the group and entered the maze. He towed me down a path that led to a dead end. The moon shone on us. The mood evoked romance. And when he handed me a peach envelope, I prayed his words would flick a switch in my brain that had yet to spark.

Vlad shone his phone's flashlight on my hands as I removed the letter.

Dearest Tasha, it read.

WITH EVERY PIECE OF MY HEART YOU TAKE, IT RESETS AND EXPANDS EVER LARGER, FUELED BY YOUR BEAUTY, YOUR SMILES, AND YOUR CLEVERNESS. WAS THERE EVER A WOMAN SO PERFECT? I KNOW NOT. YOU LIGHT UP THE DAY AND THE DARKNESS WITHIN ME. MY ADMIRATION AND ADORATION GROW STRONGER EACH DAY, AND MY SOUL LONGS TO TELL YOU WHAT MY WORDS CANNOT.

I think I stopped breathing.

"Oh Vlad," I said, looking up to meet his gaze. "What beautiful words."

"Beautiful words for a beautiful woman," he said, angling his head toward mine.

Here we go, I thought. *He's going to kiss me.*

Finally.

I lifted on my toes, and our lips met.

It should have been romantic.

It should have lasted longer than a brief touch.

I shouldn't have felt the urge to gag.

There wasn't any good explanation why I ended the kiss, other than ... it felt wrong.

Very wrong.

I couldn't explain. I'd wanted this. For weeks, I'd wanted this.

And now that it'd happened, I realized ... I didn't want this.

I opened my eyes, and our gazes locked. I offered a weak smile and took his hand in mine. I needed time to process our lack of chemistry. "Let's get out of here," I said. Before he could misinterpret my words, I added, "The barn dance starts in twenty minutes."

A confused expression crossed his features, but he recovered quickly and squeezed my hand. "I shall woo you with my finely cultivated dance moves."

Finely cultivated dance moves? His English *had* improved since I met him, but not for the first time, I wondered about the discrepancy between his everyday speaking, his letters, and the phrases he threw out every now and again. Sometimes, it was hard for me to discern how all three versions of him came together.

Brenna had arranged for the hayride drivers to transport festivalgoers from the town park to the corn maze and to the event barn and back. We opted for the short walk along the lantern-lit path. The October chill had replaced the warm sun, and I pulled my cardigan closed with my free hand until we stepped into line to enter the building.

The OktoBrewFest-themed interior was decorated in blue-and-white-checked cloth and other German accents. Autumn photo backdrops for selfies and group pics were stationed around the perimeter. One featured a pair of wooden hedgehogs perched on top of a tall hay bale, which made me think of Monty and his silly comparison of me to a hedgehog cactus.

The barn dance was a blast. My concerns about Vlad melted away as he led me around the dance floor, through traditional folk dances as well as a waltz and even Monty's favorite, the chicken dance. My emotions were all over the place, one moment swoony and the other suspicious. When I excused myself to visit the ladies' room, I took the opportunity to sneak out the side door to catch my breath instead.

I pressed myself to the back of the barn and inhaled the crisp night air into my lungs. My thoughts wandered again to Monty. Was he home yet? Did Nana have a good time in the pumpkin patch?

I pulled my phone out from the side pocket of the exercise leggings I'd worn under my dirndl. Before I could think twice, I sent off a text.

You make it home okay? I asked.

I didn't have to wait long for his reply. It came through as I stared at the screen. *I'm just getting to my car now. These old ladies are party animals. You having a good time?*

I didn't know how to answer. It was fun, but I was still troubled, and I didn't know why.

Tasha?

I'm here. Just tired.

Want me to pick you up on my way home?

I didn't hesitate to answer. *Yes, please.*

Be there in ten.

I rushed back inside, told Vlad I wasn't feeling well and thanked him for a wonderful time. I kissed him on the cheek, made my excuses to Penny, and hurried out the main door. I didn't stop walking until I reached Brewski's.

I dialed Monty. "I'm almost at Main. I can walk the rest of the way home if you're not close."

"Stay put. I got you," he said softly. "You feeling all right?"

"A little queasy," I croaked. It was true but not for the reasons I was making him think. I felt like a fool running out of there the way I did.

"I see you. I'm going to pull over and get the door for you, okay?"

I nodded. "Thanks." Monty's white truck pulled up to the

curb like a legendary steed. He hopped out and ran around to the passenger side to open the door for me.

Unable to look him in the eye, I climbed up into the seat and buckled myself in as he shut the door.

"You're not okay," he observed, easing back onto the road. "What can I do?"

I swallowed the giant rock in my throat—hard—and shook my head. "Nothing," I whispered.

"Pharmacy? Urgent care? Your parents? ER?" His voice rose with each suggestion.

I shook my head vehemently, not wanting him to worry. "It's not a flare-up."

"What then? You look like you're going to be sick."

I drew my knees up to my chest and looked out the passenger-side window. "I feel like I might. But it's not food-related."

"Did Vlad—" He cut himself off. "Do I need to beat his backside back to Russia?"

Despite everything, I couldn't help smiling at the visual. I gave in to the chuckle that bubbled up. Monty kicking Vlad so hard on his rump, sending him sailing into the atmosphere toward Russia, was a funny thing to imagine.

"No. He was …" I thought carefully. "Perfect?"

"Then what?"

"I don't know."

Monty steered into the lot and pulled up to the entrance. "Go on up. I'll park and meet you inside."

"Okay."

I exited the car and tapped my keycard on the pad next to the door.

He must have found a close spot, because he was beside me at the elevator bank before the car reached the ground level.

"Come 'ere, fraulein." He held his arms open, and I walked into his beefy embrace, resting my head on his hard chest, just like I'd done after every breakup except that last one.

Was I breaking up with Vlad? Were we even together? I had no idea.

The elevator arrived, and we shuffled into it. Monty held me close while I tried to make sense of the thoughts in my head. When the doors opened on our floor, he walked me to the door, opened it, took my purse off my shoulder, and guided me to the sofa.

"Sit," he commanded.

I sat.

He snapped his fingers, and Parfait came running. "Up on the sofa."

The cat jumped on the cushion next to me, climbed onto my lap, turned in a circle, and began to purr.

I look up at Monty, surprised.

"He's an emotional support cat, remember?"

Unofficially, I wanted to say. Instead, I nodded and watched Monty hang my purse on the pegs by the door and move into the kitchen. He lit my trio of fall-scented candles, filled the teapot with water, set it on the stove, and turned the setting to high. Next, he left the kitchen and sprinted to his room, emerging a moment later with a box of … hot chocolate?

The teapot whistled. He switched it to another burner. My eyes didn't leave him as he emptied the premade powder into two mugs and poured the boiled water over it. He topped each mug with a splash of oat milk.

Since when did he drink oat milk?

Monty carried the two mugs into the living area and offered one to me. I took it and closed my eyes, letting the steam warm my face and hoping it would bring me some clarity.

When I raised my head, he wore the same expression I'd seen him set on his Nana when he wouldn't let her have a particular sweet treat at the Coffee Loft.

I sipped the hot chocolate and frowned. "This isn't—"

"It's certified gluten-free pumpkin spice hot cocoa."

"You steal it from your nana?" I teased. "I knew you were a closet PSL guy!"

"Nah. It's not sugar-free. I found it online."

"Huh. And you're drinking it?"

"It's not coffee," he reminded me and took a sip. "Think Nana would like it?"

I shook my head no. "Absolutely not. It's terrible." I watched his face fall into a frown, then added, "I'll have to drink all of it. To keep her safe from a major life disappointment."

He laughed, then his face grew serious. "I know a bit about that," he said.

"I know you do." I set my mug down on the table. "Mindy's anniversary is this week."

"Yeah. And as usual, my parents plan to go about the day like it's any other."

"People cope with grief differently," I said quietly. "I'm sure they'll be thinking of her."

"Maybe." He placed his mug on the table next to mine and rested his arm on the back of the sofa. If I leaned backward an inch, my head would be cradled in the crook of his elbow. "Nana's not mobile enough yet for me to take her to Mindy's grave."

"Oh, Monty." I looked up at his face. Water pooled beneath his eyes. I slid one arm between his back and the sofa cushion and wrapped the other around his middle. I gave a light squeeze and rested my head on his chest. "I'm so sorry."

A drop of water landed on the shell of my ear and traveled down to the lobe. I didn't make a move to wipe it away. I just sat there and held him till my eyes grew heavy and I fell asleep.

CHAPTER 22

Monty

Wednesday morning, I stayed in bed until I heard Tasha leave for work. For hours, I'd been awake while the last moments of Mindy's life played on repeat over and over.

She'd been going through treatment again, and I'd heard her doctor advise my parents against taking her home for Mom's big birthday bash. Dad had been adamant they sign off and even promised to hire a nurse. It was only for a few hours. What could go wrong?

Mom insisted it was fine; they could celebrate in the hospital and cancel plans or postpone her fortieth birthday bash. But Dad cut her off, reminding her there was a good chance this would be her last birthday with Mindy. Mom walked away crying, and the next day, we brought Mindy home. A nurse met us at the house and got her situated in a recliner in the expansive living room. After cake, Mindy asked to go lie down. The nurse took her into the first-floor guest room while Mom and Dad said goodbye to the guests.

Rain was in the forecast, so many of the guests opted to leave early. Me, at eight years old, played a video game on my Nintendo DS on the divan in the corner of the bedroom. At 9 p.m., the nurse left. Mom came in to lie on the bed with Mindy, holding her close and stroking her hair as she slept.

I must have fallen asleep, too, because when I woke up, Mom

was screaming at Mindy to wake up and for Dad to call an ambulance. I raced to the other side of the bed, and what I saw made my blood chill.

Mindy's eyes were closed, and she was struggling to breathe. Her IV was beeping, drained of its liquid.

"What's taking so long?" Mom cried. "They should be here!"

Dad got on the phone again and hurried out of the room. I ran after him, outside and into the storm. At the bottom of the hill, flashing lights blinked through the rain. The siren shrilled uphill to meet our ears.

"Stay in the house!" Dad ordered.

But I didn't. I followed him into the storm and down the incline to the bottom of the aspen-lined driveway, where the paramedics were trying to move a fallen tree out of the way just inside the gate.

"Fire rescue is on the way!" one of the men shouted. "Do you have a chain saw?"

Dad shook his head and joined the men trying to move the tree. I pulled at a sturdy branch, and together, the four of us moved the tree, inch by inch, just enough for the ambulance to get around.

The medics jumped inside and raced up the hill. Dad and I trudged back to the house, soaking wet, as they were loading Mindy into the ambulance. Mom climbed in after her, and they took off before we could reach them.

I never got to say goodbye to my sister.

By the time Dad and I got to the hospital, Mindy had slipped into a coma. Three days later, she was gone. And we were all changed forever.

My parents leaned on each other, and I had Nana. By the time I left for prep school, I was practically living with her. She was my rock, my everything.

I visited her pretty regularly, at the gravesite, but on the anniversary of her death, I liked to bring her sunflowers and a new cheer bow, which I hung on a sticky hook that miraculously had lasted through years of weather. She would have been a Fire-Volt if she'd lived, and I had no doubt she would have made Team USA if she tried out. Lucky for me, there was always a girl on the team who'd accept ten times what her bow was worth after competing so that I'd have a bow to give Mindy. I'd spend the whole day here at her gravesite, chatting about the things I thought a big sister might want to know about.

This year, I'd called Taylor to ask if she could make a special FireVolts bow, like Tasha's, but add "Honorary" in vinyl over the word "Coach."

Today wasn't much different than previous years, except I wouldn't be leaving to pick up Nana and bring her here to sit with me on Mindy's favorite blanket, a fuzzy worn-out supersoft flannel she'd received with a gold medal and championship ring at Summit after her last competition.

"Our Worlds team is going to win. I can feel it. Tasha is by far the most creative choreographer I've ever known. And I'm not just saying that because she used to be my best friend. She's incredibly talented, and I believe she should be on the team, too. She can dance circles around those girls. And I'm sure she could still do the stunt work. But she's refused to try ever since she broke her leg."

Soft footsteps padded on the walk behind me and came to a stop. I didn't turn around, but my heart knew who it was. I wondered if she'd been close enough to hear me talking about her.

"I'm so glad you suggested to Mom and Dad all those years ago that I go to 'baby cheer camp.' Even though I was mad it just was mornings and you got to go all day. But you knew it would be good for me. You *always* knew what would be good for me. And I met Tasha there."

I was ninety-nine percent certain it was Tasha behind me. Anyone else would have shown themselves by now or made a noise to alert me to their presence. All I heard was quiet breathing and an occasional sniff.

"I didn't know until I met her how desperately I needed a best friend. You were awesome, of course, best sister ever, but the five-year gap between us meant I didn't get to see you much. I'll never forget that first day of camp. It was pretty boring until the first water break. This girl with a long ponytail and enormous red bow tapped me on the shoulder and told me I was doing my forward rolls all wrong." I used a high-pitched voice to mimic four-year-old Tasha. "That's *not* how you do a forward roll. Watch me!' And right there, in front of all the other kids by the cubbies, she raised her arms, clicked her feet together, and demonstrated, telling me when and where to tuck my head. She stood up with a flourish and raised her arms in a triumphant *V.* It was pretty amazing."

Above me, Tasha snorted. I took that as encouragement to keep telling my side of the story. "She worked with me until the end of the water break and said, 'That'll have to do, for now. Stick with me and you'll be the best boy here.' So I did. Coach called us back from break and instructed us to pair up. Tasha scooted over to me, and I took her hand. I wanted to be the best boy so badly."

I closed my eyes, wanting to picture one of my favorite memories.

"We're going to try a basic stunt. Decide which of you will be the base and which will be the flyer."

"I'm the flyer," Tasha informed me.

That settled that. I didn't even know what that meant, but she did. She was so smart.

"Bases, you're going to kneel down and sit back on your heels. Put your hands out in front of you like this ... and tuck your head down in front of your knees to create a surface for your flyer. Flyers, you'll stand next to your base and place your inside foot on their bum. Raise your hands into a high V *and hold your position. Be very careful not to hurt or stomp on your base."*

Some of the kids giggled but not me and Tasha. This was serious business to us. I did as the coach instructed, and Tasha made a few adjustments. "Tuck your head like this. But not all the way because you might have to look up and smile for the audy-dance." Not very gently, she pushed my head into place. I felt her foot on my bum a moment later.

The coach came around to make adjustments but didn't touch either of us. "Great job, you two! No adjusting needed here. Look at me on three with your cheer face ... One, two, three!"

I popped my head up with my happy mask—that's what Mindy called it.

"Great job! Now hit your toy soldier positions for me. Awesome! Give your partner a high five!"

"We're the best girl and boy here!" Tasha said gleefully. "Will you be my partner forever?"

"Yeah! We're the best!"

Her eyes narrowed. "To stay the best, you'll have to work hard. Promise?"

"Yeah, I promise." Whatever it took, I wanted to be the best, like my sister.

"Spit on your hand and let's shake on it." Tasha spit on her hand and held it out to me.

I quickly did what she asked and clasped my hand in hers.

"Ew! You two are gross!" a girl said. "Why did you do that, Tasha?"

"Ignore her," Tasha said. "That's my cousin Gabby. She's just jealous 'cause I'm partners with the best boy."

"I'm not jealous!"

"Yes, you are!"

"No, I'm not!"

I stepped back, sure that they were about to fight, but the coach came over and Gabby stalked off before they could be reprimanded.

Tasha turned back to me. "Partners forever?"

"Partners forever," I promised.

A promise I'd broken epically.

I opened my eyes to find Tasha sitting on the blanket next to me. "Aren't you supposed to be at work?" I asked.

She shrugged. "It was slow. Thought I'd come out here and pay respects to the awesomest tumbler I've ever known."

"Hey, I thought I was the awesomest tumbler you've ever known."

She rolled her eyes. "Please. If Mindy were here today, she'd flip circles around you."

"Yeah, she would," I agreed. I turned my gaze from the gravestone to the woman beside me. "Thanks for coming by. It means a lot."

Tasha held my gaze and nodded. "I heard you talking about our first cheer camp. We totally rocked it." She smiled wistfully. It was considerate of her not to mention the part about me breaking my promise. "Remember the one before you went to boarding school in Denver?"

"How could I forget? We won the senior-level partner challenge." It stung to say the word "partner."

"The first of four straight titles." She smiled broadly.

"We totally deserved it. No one else was practicing lifts in the pool until lights out."

"And after." She snickered.

We might have broken a few rules over the years.

I smiled. "Then, after high school, we became coaches, and then it didn't matter if we were in the pool after lights out."

"We were dedicated, for sure."

"We were."

During that third summer of coaching together, between our sophomore and junior year of college, we'd devised new crazy stunts in the pool, and I began to see Tasha in a different light. She'd been struggling with some health issues, and I knew she'd been in a lot of pain. The way she fought through it made me admire her even more.

So much more, it interfered with my concentration.

My greatest fear was dropping her, letting her down literally and figuratively. I didn't think through my decision to partner up with Gabby, how it could hurt Tasha and have lasting effects years later. I figured it was best for the team because, well, because Tasha had become ... distracting.

She'd never asked me why I'd done it, and I was glad, because I'd never wanted to tell her. But sitting here, knowing she'd come here to support me, left work even, it felt like the old us—the old us before I broke our partnership.

I was feeling a growing need to explain, and she'd given me the segue to do it.

"That next summer, camp wasn't the same without you," I said quietly. "That whole year leading up to it, and every year since, hasn't felt the same. The FireVolts weren't the same without you. The national team wasn't the same without you." I turned to face her. "*I* wasn't the same without you. I'm so sorry I requested a new partner and broke us up. I'm sorry your new partner was a hack and dropped you. I'm sorry that drop broke your leg and ended your performance career. I *never* would have let you hit the ground."

She looked away, and I watched her cheeks twitch as she struggled to keep her emotions inside. "I wasn't upset at first. We had a new coach, and new coaches always liked to mix us up, try us out with other partners. But they always put us back together when they could see what we could do. But you stopped coming early. You'd arrive just on time and then rush out, leaving us no time to practice and show them what we could do. Then I found out you *requested* Gabby. That's what stung the most. You knew how competitive the two of us were."

"I was there when you found out, and I'll never forget the expression on your face. I ran into the bathroom to throw up. I knew instantly I'd hurt you and lost my best friend." I hung my head.

"The betrayal was unbearable," she whispered.

When I looked up, she was swiping at her eyes and staring off toward the church. An apology wasn't enough.

I owed her an explanation. "That was never my intention, I promise. You remember that last summer we coached at camp together? We were working on a new kick-out?"

She nodded. "I practiced it every chance I got. I wanted to be the first to master it."

"And I wanted that for you. Instead of the pool, one night we walked down to the lake and swam out to the floating dock so I could toss you higher over the deeper water. The only light was the full moon, and it was enough. We did it over and over and over again."

"We finally got it. We high-fived and decided to do it one more time. You launched me, and then you fell in, too." Tasha turned her head back to me. "We got tangled under the water and came up laughing."

I sucked in my breath. "We steadied each other. And then ..."

"It got quiet. And we just stood there." She tilted her head. "You were looking at me weird. A mix of pride, joy, and something else. What was that?"

I sighed. I'd almost kissed her. And it would have ruined everything. "It was ... something else. And it freaked me out. After that, I became more concerned with you not falling than I was with winning."

Tears welled in her eyes. "Is ..." She swallowed. "Is that why you broke up our partnership?"

I nodded.

"I thought ... all this time, I thought ... I thought ..."

She covered her face with her hands and started to shake. My heart raced. Did she understand what I wasn't saying? Did it repulse her? I wrapped my arms around her and pulled her to me. "What did you think?"

"It's too embarrassing!" She shook her head.

"It can't be more embarrassing than me admitting I ditched you because I was crushing on you. Spill."

Tasha stilled in my arms and sat back. "Promise me you won't laugh."

"I promise."

"I—I was having problems with my stomach that summer. I was on new meds, and I was very gassy. I know on more than one occasion I couldn't hold it in and—"

I *did* want to laugh, and it was hard not to. But I wasn't going to break any more promises to her. I pulled her back to me and tucked her head under my chin. "I noticed, and I didn't care. Not one bit. You were in pain, and I felt helpless."

"You didn't care? Really?" She pushed her hands against my chest. Her tear-streaked cheeks cracked my heart. Her eyes locked on mine and waited for me to answer.

"Really. Why would I? I actually thought it was cool. Made you human. I loved you more for it—Tasha's Standards of Perfectionism are hard to achieve. Piece of cake for me, though, of course."

"Of course," she mumbled. "Um ... That's why he dropped me."

"Huh?"

"That's why he dropped me."

I scratched my head and lifted my eyebrows. "I missed something. Why did he drop you?"

"I ... startled him?"

I knitted my forehead in mock confusion. "I'm not connecting the dots."

She pushed at me and laughed. "Don't make me say it out loud!"

"What? That you tooted your horn?"

"Oh my gosh!" She slugged me in my bicep and jumped to her feet, pointing and waving her finger at me. "Don't *ever* say that again!"

"What? That you broke wind? Cut the cheese? Dropped a bomb?"

"Aaaah!" She covered her ears, but she was laughing. "Stop!"

"On one condition."

"Anything."

"Come to the gym with me. Give us a chance to prove we're still the best."

Tasha took a step back and shook her head vehemently. "No way. It's been *years.*"

"It has. And it's time you got back up on your horse." I stood up and folded the blanket. "I *promise* I will not let you hit the floor."

"I ... um ... the high school team practice starts at three thirty."

"Plenty of time."

Her gaze swung toward Mindy's gravestone, then back at me. "Okay."

CHAPTER 23
Tasha

What had I been thinking?

If it hadn't been Mindy's anniversary, I wouldn't have let him talk me into it. Partner stunting after all these years? I doubt I could even execute a standing back handspring, never mind a flip in the air.

But I'd always felt safe with Monty. And I believed him when he said he wouldn't let me hit the floor.

We were partners for sixteen years. We'd worked through coaches who tried to break us up, significant others who couldn't handle our close friendship and the physical connections the sport required, and pushed ourselves and each other to our limits to be the best in the sport.

He'd failed me when he chose Gabby after our sophomore year of college. He'd broken his promise, and I'd written him off. And then my gassiness startled my new partner to the extent he stepped out of position for my landing and failed to catch me safely. It had been the end of my cheer career.

It was time to forgive Monty, and forgive myself. We were adults now, and if we wanted to repair our friendship—which I realized I so desperately did—it was going to take some work.

And kindness. And understanding. And grace.

The cemetery behind St. Mary's was about a ten-minute walk from our apartment building, and both of us had opted not to drive there. We jogged home to change into workout clothes, and Monty drove us to the Plex. On the way, he called Nate to see if he was available to spot us during his lunch break.

He was.

This was happening.

Oh my gosh, this was happening!

After warming up—and stretching extensively—we found an open spot by the tumble mats and deferred to Nate to instruct us.

"We'll start easy, basic." My former coaching partner looked past me to Monty, standing behind me. "Hands on her hips. Shoulder sit on my count."

Monty's hands closed over my hips, his thumbs pressing lightly into the dimples on each side of my spine. I closed my fingers around his wrists and exhaled. My heart was flipping at the rate of one of his tumbling passes. "Ready."

Nate counted. "Five, six, seven, eight!"

I prepped as he squatted, taking a small hop. My feet touched the ground for the second time, and then I was airborne, landing comfortably in a seated position on Monty's right shoulder.

"Like riding a bike." Monty held me in place securely. "Ready for something more advanced?"

"Let's see if I can nail the dismount first," I replied warily.

"Count it, Tasha," Nate directed.

"Five, six, seven, eight!"

Monty squatted, and I leapt off him, landing cleanly on my feet with my arms tucked tightly to my side.

"Lookin' good," Nate praised. "How about raising that sit up an arm's length?"

"Um ..." I looked at Monty. That would require his hand on my bottom.

"I'm a professional, Tasha." He rolled his eyes. "Your jelly isn't any different from anyone else's."

Nate laughed, and I scrunched my face. I wasn't sure how I felt about that. I stayed in shape and like to think my jelly wasn't very ... jelly.

"Whatever." I threw my shoulders back. "Let's do it."

We got into position, and on the way up, I let go of Monty's hands and raised my arms in a high *V* while lifting my right knee up into the liberty position. My bottom came to rest in his palm, and his other hand secured my straight leg.

I was back on the horse. And as cool as I wanted to present myself, I couldn't stop grinning. "Down in five, six, seven, eight!"

Monty bent and boosted me into the air. His hands found my hips again as I landed cleanly on the ground. I lifted my arms to high-five the guys, still wearing my cheesiest smile.

"Felt good, right?" Nate grinned. "Shoulder stand?"

I looked over at Monty. I had no doubt in his basing capabilities; his private clients consisted of everyone from girls on younger teams to college and national team members. But my balance? Would that come back the way I needed it to?

"I got you." There wasn't a hint of anything but determination in his tone.

"Okay." I looked to Nate. "Like riding a bike. I'll count." Same position as last time. Monty's hands on my hips. My hands on his wrists. "Five, six, seven, eight!"

Hop, jump, soar.

I tightened every muscle in my body on the way up and stared straight ahead of me. Monty held my shoes at his shoulders, then moved his hands to secure them around my calves, locking me in place. It was effortless, steady, and balanced like I was standing on the floor.

Secure.

It was like no time had passed. Monty was still the same partner who synced with me like no other ever could. When I was in his strong, capable hands, I was fearless, fierce, and focused, but more importantly, I felt like I could achieve anything. His touch instantly calmed me. In his grip or in his arms—there was no place I'd ever felt safer.

"Press to full extension!" I called down. "Monty, you count."

"Five, six, seven, eight!"

I held my breath and kept my body tight as I rose higher.

Breathe.

"I got you, Tasha!" Monty didn't have to remind me. I could feel it. From my vantage point, I could see across all four cheer floors and up into the balcony.

I'd missed this. The height, the freedom up here. After all these years, it was still a rush!

Nate called up to me. "Back to shoulders or full dismount?"

"How about a cradle?" I asked.

"Let's do it," Monty said.

I took in a long breath to fill my lungs. "Five, six, seven, eight!"

Down, up, down, catch.

But instead of dumping me out of his arms, Monty held me in position.

"Hey you." He pressed his forehead against mine. "You're amazing, you know that?"

Whew, he was so close I could feel the warmth of his breath mingling with mine. "Save your praise for something more advanced."

Monty tipped me forward and set me on the ground, holding on to my shoulders for a smidge longer than was necessary. He let go and cleared his throat. "How much more time do you have, Nate?"

"Fifteen minutes or so. What's next?"

"Cheese mat," I said determinedly. "I want to see if I can still flip."

Nate and Monty exchanged a look, then they said together, "We can spot you."

I laughed. "Okaaaay … No cheese mat." I looked forlornly at the giant wedge. "Looks like it'll be up to you two to get these legs around and back to the ground."

Monty smirked. "It's not hard. Watch me."

He took a step back, squatted with his arms straight out in front of him, and leapt backward in a textbook-perfect standing back handspring.

"Show-off," I teased.

"I learned from the best," he shot back. The man had the nerve to wink at me.

Oooh, he really knew how to fire me up.

"Whenever you're ready, Tasha," Nate said.

"Let me try a few back walkovers first and see where I'm at." I could still do a backbend; it was part of my stretch routine. But it had been years since I'd pulled my legs over.

I positioned myself between them. "Here goes." I fell backward, lifting my lead leg into the air. I pulled my core muscles tight as my hands flattened on the ground. Other than a light touch from Nate on my trailing leg, I got over and landed on my feet just fine.

The pride in Monty's eyes caused a warming in my chest I wasn't prepared for. He didn't need to say a word, and he didn't. But I was encouraged, and I suddenly felt invincible.

"One more time," I decided. "Then on to harder things."

Five minutes later, I'd perfected the back walkover, the standing back handspring, and a round-off back handspring.

It felt amazing. And from the look on the guys' faces, I knew it looked amazing, too.

"I've got to get back to the clinic," Nate said. "But we should do this again. You've still got it, Tasha."

"Thanks for coming down here." I turned to Monty. "And thanks for making me do this."

He nodded toward the trampolines. "Next time?"

"Yeah. I think you've revived an old monster."

"Monsha," he corrected.

We laughed, and he wrapped an arm around my shoulders as we walked through the gym and to his truck.

We were friends again.

We were *partners* again.

And if Nana's house was ready next week as projected, I was going to miss him as my roommate.

CHAPTER 24
Monty

I dropped Tasha off at home, then drove back to the gym at the Plex to work through all the unwanted thoughts and feelings our little practice session had brought to the surface. The fitness machines were on the ground floor and featured a floor-to-ceiling window wall that rose up several stories and presented a breathtaking view of the mountains.

Up until today, I could pretend I didn't care that she hated me. I could pretend I hated her. Our rivalry was working in the gym. Good Coach Monty praised and inspired; Bad Coach Tasha glared and demanded perfection.

I could pretend she wasn't the most beautiful and desirable woman I knew. I could ignore it when she lounged on the sofa in her tiny athletic shorts and tank top. I might have, on occasion, lowered the temperature on purpose to incite her to cover up so I wouldn't be tempted to stare.

Before this morning, I could pretend I didn't care about hurting her all those years ago. But now that I knew she thought I quit on her because of a health issue? I wanted to prove to her that I not only didn't care about her occasional wind breaking but also that I *did* care about the trials she'd lived through and continued to face with extraordinary strength because her gut was dysfunctional.

In another way, my gut was also dysfunctional. I should have

known that choosing Gabby over her would cause Tasha to write me off. They'd been competitive their whole lives. In retrospect, it had to feel like the ultimate slap in the face.

I'd just finished up on a bench press and was restacking the weights with a gym spotter when Nate came in after work. He'd changed into his FireVolts tee and shorts. My expression must have sent a signal I hadn't intended because he lifted his hands up, palms out, like he needed to defend himself. And now I was aware of my eyebrows and chin lifting.

My resting face needed some work. Was it possible to re-train your subconscious expressions?

"I'm not interested in dating Tasha," he said bluntly. "I swear."

I knew he wasn't, but why did he feel the need to state so?

I shrugged. "Neither am I."

Now his eyebrows were reaching new heights. "I was going to text you, but since you're here, I'll just say it."

"Say what?"

"She's fragile. "

I snorted. "If there's one thing she isn't, it's fragile. You saw her on the mat today, right?"

He nodded. "I've seen a lot of other things, too. I was here for your falling-out. I was ten feet away when she fell and broke her leg. I saw your so-called best friend DJ swoop in and try to fill your place in her life, just to prove he could. I was here six months after that, co-coaching with her, doing everything I could to encourage her to get back in the game. Which you did in less than an hour today."

I wasn't following. "Which, again, proves that she's not fragile." I crossed my arms, but my insides were glowing. He'd been trying for *years* to get her back into performing?

"Man, for a smart guy, you sure are dumb sometimes." He sighed loudly in frustration and looked up at the ceiling.

I waited.

Finally, he was done taking whatever dramatic breath he needed and locked his eyes on mine. "She's in love with you. She always has been. And she has no idea, will never admit it, and likely won't ever act on it. But if you hurt her again, it will *destroy* her, even worse than the first time."

I opened my mouth to reply, but it just hung open.

I'd never been so confused in my life.

I managed to find words. "What's your evidence? I need hard proof."

Nate closed his eyes and pinched the skin between his eyes, like I was causing him a headache. "Do you have all night?"

"Yup."

He shook his head. "Just take my word for it. Her pride is everything to her. She's tough on the outside, sure, but she breaks down, just like we all do. And a broken-down Tasha can be taken out by a toddler."

I thought back to her flare-up. How she hadn't wanted me to see her in her weakness. I didn't think an emotionally broken-down Tasha could even be a thing, but what Nate was saying made sense.

Tasha put up big, strong walls on the outside to protect herself on the inside.

Cliché and common, which was why it'd never crossed my mind. To me, she was invincible and above everyone else. To her family, she was the strength when they needed help. To her athletes, she was the iron coach, incapable of bending and unwilling to compromise, even under intense pressure. And she never got heated or lost her cool.

She was icy. Competitive.

Perfect.

And she was in love with *me?*

Nate was right; she'd never admit it. Because love me or hate me, she needed me in her life.

And I needed her.

"So … What do I do?" I asked him.

He shrugged. "Do you love her?"

"Since I was four," I said simply.

"Then only tell her if you're willing to propose forever. Or you'll lose her again, and this time, for good."

I DROVE by the high school on the way home. The varsity cheerleading squad practiced just inside the fence that separated the outdoor track from the road. The football field was inside the track, and the soccer field just beyond that.

I lowered the passenger-side window as I rolled past like a creeper. Under the lights, Tasha counted out a routine for her athletes, probably for a time-out at this Friday night's game. I glanced at the clock. Almost six o'clock. Practice was running late.

Could Nate be right? Could she have feelings for me that she couldn't—or wouldn't—acknowledge?

And all this time?

Nate's words shocked me like an errant spark from a bonfire, only the bonfire was within me in the form of a new anxiety I didn't know how to counter.

And what of Vlad? I'd concentrated my efforts on helping Tasha fall in love with him, but it wasn't working. Anyone could see they didn't act like a couple who were crazy about each other.

It was too much to believe that she had those feelings for me and that none of her previous relationships had worked out because her heart hadn't been in them.

But—what if it was true?

Back in the apartment, I took a quick shower and was setting the bar with plates and silverware when she walked in. Judging by the aroma, whatever was in the Crock-Pot was something different. I'd eat quickly and then go visit Nana until visiting hours ended.

I'd been by this morning, but I felt the urge to go again. I wasn't sure if I wanted to ask my grandmother about her take on Nate's theory or not, but I did want to just *be* with her. She was a calming presence, the only thing in my life that had always been steady and constant.

I lifted a hand to greet Tasha as she entered, hung up her team jacket, and disappeared into her room, reappearing without her backpack. She smiled at me as she passed me on her way into the kitchen.

"How are you doing?" She lifted the cover of the Crock-Pot and stirred the mixture with a large spoon.

"I'm good. Going to visit Nana after dinner. You?"

"Fine. You should take her some of this." She collected our plates from the bar and set them next to the slow cooker. "If it's any good. I had to modify her recipe."

"What is it?" I asked.

"A gluten-free dairy-free version of mac 'n' cheese with hamburger and peas." I stared at her as she set a plate of the mixture in front of me. "Are you okay?"

I shook my head and covered my face with my hands. Why would Nana give her *that* recipe? I'd told her when I was eight I never wanted to eat this stuff ever again.

"Monty, you're worrying me." She came around the counter and rubbed my back. "What's wrong?"

"P-peas and cheese!" I shook with grief.

"And meat," she added. "Are you laughing or crying?"

I let my hands drop so I could look at the food. Tasha used the end of her sleeve to wipe my tears. "It's Mindy's favorite," I choked out. "I haven't eaten it since she died."

"Oh, Monty." Tasha squeezed her arms around my middle. "Don't eat it, then. I must've misunderstood Nana. We were talking recipes the other day, and she told me this was your favorite. She probably didn't mean for me to make it for you, just add it to my collection."

"No, knowing Nana, this is *exactly* what she intended." I freed my arm from her hug and set it around her back. "Meddling old woman."

Tasha chuckled softly. "Silly Nana Booboo." She looked up at me and quickly looked away, sliding out from under me. "You better get eating so you have enough time to visit. Or do you want me to box it up for you?"

I shook my head. "Nah. I'm actually dying to try it. See if it's as good as Nana's."

"I wouldn't hold out hope. Those substitutions can be disappointing."

I waited until she returned to the bar with her own plate before I tried a bite. It was different but better in some ways. The rice pasta was a little mushy, even though she'd added it just three hours ago. She always added the pasta to whatever the mixture was before she left for her job at the high school.

"It's really good," I praised. "The cheese is a little different, but I think I like it better."

"Oh stop it. You do not." She tapped my bicep playfully.

"I do. And I'll definitely take some to Nana. She's going to love it."

"Now I know you're lying. That woman knows her food is the best of the best."

"And yet, she's never wanted to publish a cookbook of *her* recipes."

I had her on that. She blushed but didn't comment.

ON THE WAY to Nana's, I called Beck for an update.

"Everything is on schedule to be finished sometime next week," she confirmed. "If you can come by Monday for a walk-through, you can let us know if there's anything else you want. Is your Nana ready to move home?"

"She is. She's already planning a party."

Beck laughed. "Glad to hear she hasn't lost her spirit over there."

"Quite the contrary. She's like their queen, ruling over all the social events and game nights. I think she's going to miss it, actually."

"She might. But she doesn't have you or her cat there, so there's that. Oh!" she said excitedly. "I have an idea for the cat. I know he's old and fat, but what would you say to a custom cat tree in the sunroom? I've been itching to make one. I'll only charge you for materials."

I laughed. Parfait was so spoiled. "Send me the info, and I'll run it by Nana."

"You got it!"

I ended the call and pulled into the lot of Mountainview Manor. Halloween was next week, and they'd gone all out with the decor, inside and out. The walkways were lined with flood-lights alternating in white, yellow and orange. Candy-corn buntings hung off the roof, and twinkle lights lined the windows. A scarecrow held a sign that said "Candy This Way" and pointed to a series of booths lining the walkway on the side lawn. Kids visiting their grandparents could trick-or-treat with them all next week after dinner.

It was a chilly night, and I hurried inside. "Is Nana in her room?" I asked the receptionist as she read Tasha's ingredients list.

"Nope, she's holding court by the aquarium."

"Thanks." The "aquarium" was no more than a six-by-four-foot fish tank recessed into the wall in one of the common areas.

I heard Nana before I saw her, talking about her favorite subject.

Me, of course.

"And you should see him on skates! In that enormous costume. Graceful like a swan."

I snorted and wondered if her eyesight was going.

"Graceful as a swan, huh? Is he married yet?" An elderly man sat in a recliner near her wheelchair. She called him "Pauli Cracker" because he repeated what people said like a parrot.

Curious as to where this might go, I hid myself behind a column to listen.

"Nope, but he's sweet on someone."

"How can you tell?" Clarice asked.

Nana leaned toward her. "I saw his phone." She sat back into her chair with a smirk. "I was playing solitaire on it while he tinkered with my tablet—you remember the day I accidentally lost all my game apps?"

"I remember," Clarice said. "Go on."

"Well, a message flashed across the screen. It said, 'You are my everything. I wish every day was Sunday so I could see you more' or something like that."

"Ooh! Who was it from?" Clarice demanded.

"Who is it from? You should stay out of his business, Nan," Pauli advised. "Nothing good ever comes out of you meddling."

She ignored him and smiled at Clarice. "I don't know. He didn't have a name attached to the number, and I couldn't find the right screen to read any more of it—or catch the number so I could accidentally call it."

Clarice hooted. "You are too much! Remember when he used to get mad when people called you Nancy? 'Not Nan-*cee!* Nan-NA!'"

"The boy will be thirty before I blink. He's been lonely for too long."

Pauli snorted. "Too long! Isn't he only twenty-five?"

"Ish. January. And that's not the point," Nana said.

"Not the point. Maybe he wants to be lonely," Pauli said. "Women are expensive."

"Says a millionaire to a millionaire about a millionaire," Clarice pointed to him. "You old miser."

Pauli shrugged. "Miser! Whoever it is, make sure she signs a prenup."

"Sure, sure." Nana waved her hand. "But I really just want to see him happy and settled before I die."

Okay, that was enough. I emerged from behind the column and waved to the group. "Hey, Nana!" I said loud enough for all of them to hear.

"Monty!" Her eyes brightened. "We were just talking about you!"

"Uh-oh," I said, frowning. "Am I in trouble?"

Clarice giggled. "Maybe!"

"Shush," Nana shouted at her. "You too, Pauli. We don't need any of your negativity. Monty, will you wheel me back to my room? Whatever food is in that bag you're carrying, it's demanding to be tasted."

"Yes, ma'am." I handed her the bag and moved behind her chair. "'Night, Clarice. 'Night, Pauli."

I wheeled Nana back to her room and set her up in her recliner with the rolling tray so she could try Tasha's dinner while it was still warm. I sat on the bed and waited for her to comment.

"This is incredible! That girl has got some serious talent

turning yucky foods into gourmet delicacies." She pointed her spoon at me. "I might have more than a few bites. Don't rat me out."

I laughed. "Promise." I cleared my throat. "While you eat, I, um, need to come clean about something. I heard you talking about a message you saw on my phone."

She had the decency to look guilty, but I'd bet the cat she didn't feel one ounce of guilt. "And?"

"I don't have a secret girlfriend. I'm helping one of the foreign players polish his love letters to a girl he's interested in."

Nana's eyes widened, and her gaze flicked over my face. But I wasn't lying. She sighed when she realized I was telling the truth.

"That's shady business, Montgomery." She used my full name for emphasis. "It will come back to bite you in the butt. But what do I know? I'm just an old woman."

"Nana, it's fine."

She clucked her tongue. "Speaking of girls—you should ask Tasha to move in with us."

I choked on my saliva. "Wha-*what?*"

Nana chewed her food slowly, taking her time before she answered. "She told me she was moving back with her parents after Christmas because her lease is up and she's got bills. We have plenty of rooms. And I'd enjoy her company. And her cooking. It's better than anything Pru ever made."

"That's a fact," I agreed. Our longtime housekeeper cooked the most basic staples and rarely added seasoning. "But … that would be weird."

"Why?" Nana snapped. "Aren't you two getting along now? I haven't heard of any roommate issues from you *or* Tasha, and she told me yesterday she thought your friendship was well on its way to being restored." She lifted her spoon and stabbed the air to emphasize her point. "You, sir, have not been the same since the two of you had a falling out; don't try to convince me otherwise. And if you don't ask her to move in with us, *I will.*"

I blew out a long breath. "It's not a good idea, Nana. I—please, think about it first," I pleaded. As much as I'd miss Tasha when I moved out of her apartment, I *wouldn't* miss Vlad—or anyone else—picking her up for dates. Or worse—what if he—or whomever she got serious with—proposed to her on *my* porch or in *my* gazebo or—

"You look ill, Monty," Nana said. "Care to tell me the *real* reason you don't want her moving in?"

I just stared at her.

"Thought so., You don't have a good one, so it's settled. Now put this in the fridge, please, and press the call button. It's been a long, emotional day, and I'm ready for bed. Come give your Nana a hug."

I hugged her fiercely. "I love you, Nana. I wish Mindy was here with us."

"I love you, too, Monty. And you know I wish that, too, with all my heart." She patted my back. "Call me when you get home, okay? I'll wait up."

"I will. Good night, Nana."

"Good night, Monty."

CHAPTER 25
Tasha

Monty Move-out Day.

Now that it was here, I was surprised to realize I was sad about it. Since we were friends again, I was going to feel his absence. Twice a week at practice and the occasional pop-in at the Coffee Loft would hardly make up for all the time we were used to spending together.

The high school football team played on Friday this week, so I had a free Saturday. The Edge weren't playing tonight, so Vlad was taking me out to dinner, since tomorrow night the team was leaving for a road trip. They wouldn't be back until Thanksgiving. I wanted to try one more time with Vlad to see if there could be anything more than friendship between us, but deep in my gut, I already knew the answer.

Monty didn't have a lot of stuff to move out since he'd been able to access his house whenever he needed anything, like winter clothes or books, so he was able to fit everything in his truck. He'd insisted on packing it himself, and I counted seven trips while I prepped my latest Crock-Pot creation.

I hurried to open the door for him for trip number eight. "Don't forget your Halloween wreath." I pointed to the plum, orange, and peach circlet of leaves and mesh hanging on the door.

"Keep it."

"But—"

He shifted the box he was carrying to his hip. “It was made for this door. It’s *way* too small for Nana’s grand entrance.”

Just like Monty. Thoughtful but competitive and one-uppitive. Was that a word? If it was, there was surely a picture of Montgomery Biddington next to it in the dictionary.

“Thanks. I think.” I rolled my eyes, then flashed an apologetic smile. “What time are you busting her out? And would you like company?” I purposely didn’t offer help. He would insist he didn’t need it, like this morning when I tried to roll one of his suitcases to the elevator.

“Five o’clock.” He turned and walked out into the hall. “You can come if you want,” he tossed over his shoulder as he descended the stairs. “Bring some of that food you’re cooking.”

It would be ready by four, so I’d bring some for his and Nana’s dinner. Nana was throwing her own Welcome Home party tomorrow. She’d been planning it with Brenna for weeks.

Five minutes later, Monty let himself in and padded across the living space to the bar. He dropped a zip-lock bag on the counter. “Building access card and apartment keys.”

“Keep them.”

“But—”

“You’ll be back to steal leftovers.”

“Yeah, I will. About that—”

“Don’t you dare get mushy on me, Montgomery Biddington, or I’ll smack you and give you something to cry about.”

“Thanks for letting me stay with you, Tasha.” He pocketed the bag.

“You’re welcome. I’d say it was a pleasure, but …”

“You’d be lying.” He grinned, but then his smile waned. *“I’d* be lying if I said it wasn’t.”

“Aw, look at you being so uncharacteristically nice. I *almost* believe you.” I booped him on the nose with my index finger. “Take your cat home and get settled, and I’ll meet you at Mountainview at five.”

“I’ll swing by and pick you up.” He waggled his eyebrows. “Just to make sure you don’t forget the food. “

I shook my head, and he turned to go, blowing me an exaggerated kiss and waving as he closed the door behind him.

I sent off a text to Vlad, asking him to pick me up at seven instead of six, just in case moving Nana back in took more than three hours.

He texted back right away. *I have reservation for six thirty at Pasta Nacht's. Want me to cancel if no later time?*

I texted him back: *No, keep the 6:30. I'll just need you to pick me up at Monty's Nana's house instead. She's moving home today.*

Good news! We shall celebrate your free of bear home, yes?

I snorted. How could a man who wrote such eloquent letters also write "your free of bear home"?

It did cross my mind that he might be using AI to help him with the letters, but I didn't intend on asking.

The love letters were still coming, even though we hadn't been out together since the Harvest Festival. He'd brought them by the Coffee Loft on game days.

Vlad was a great guy, as far as I could tell, devoted to his sport, his family, and his teammates. He always seemed excited to see me, but I wouldn't say he was *crazy* about me. His kisses were quick pecks, and he was a hand-holder, not a cuddler.

Did I need that, though? Or was it just a luxury for people who didn't have to worry about medical bills or citizenship?

With the food in the slow cooker and nothing else for me to do since Monty had hired someone to clean the apartment, I decided to take a walk down to the Coffee Loft for a pumpkin spice latte. Being here alone was suddenly unnerving.

I took the long route, taking a left out of the front door to Prospect Road, and strolled past the dairy farm and St. Mary's to Main Street, where I turned right. This block was one of my favorite places in town. On my left, the businesses, including the antiques shop and bookstore, backed up to Snowpack Creek, and though it was cold, the creek hadn't yet frozen over. On my right was the church, ice cream shop, and the Coffee Loft, which was perpendicular to the entrance to the back parking lot. Just beyond were the fire department and diner, just before the next intersection at Cross Creek Road.

I pulled open the door and wasn't surprised in the least to see a full queue. I scanned the space for familiar faces. Penny and Xavier were at the table in the front corner, positioned just out of sight of the window, so I hadn't seen them when I walked by.

Their heads were bent together, and from their expressions, I could tell the conversation was serious. Penny had one hand on her abdomen. I hoped the baby was okay. She was recently out of her first trimester and just starting to show. The last couple of weeks, she'd been fighting severe nausea, so I was glad to see her out and about. Not wanting to interrupt, I decided to get my coffee and then check in on them.

"Tasha!" Brenna waved from the end of the counter, holding up her whipped decaf in greeting. She hadn't announced she was pregnant yet, but there'd been a lot of signs—like wearing loose clothing, a new, bigger coat, and allowing Brendan to carry her tote bag. They were too cute together.

"Hey!" I waved back.

She rushed over to me. "Get your coffee and then come sit in the corner with us. Brendan's on his way, and he says he's got some big news!"

I smiled. "Great!"

Betty took my order, and I moved down the counter to take my coffee from Jannell. I thanked her and waded through the people between me and the corner table. Xavier had pulled over extra chairs. I said hello and sat in the empty one between Penny and Brenna. I studied the drinks on the table. I knew their orders by heart. The guys were drinking tall green Matcha Madness shakes, a favorite of theirs since their years playing for the Voltage, and Penny sipped a Lady Grey decaf tea.

The chime over the door tinkled, and Bailey Dexter-Brewer, Jason's sister and the Edge's sports reporter, rushed over to us and sat in the vacant seat next to mine.

"So, what's the news? Any clue? You must know," I said to Bailey.

"Can't say or comment officially until the news goes live publicly," she replied. "But I *so* want to!"

Brenna grinned widely. "I have an idea, but I made Brendan make a call to see if he could squeeze more details."

"Sweet." I leaned over and whispered in my sister's ear. "Pen, are you feeling okay?"

She nodded. "Just some indigestion. The tea is helping. That's why we came. I wanted to get out of the house. And here we are, in the middle of breaking news." She forced a small smile.

"Here he comes!" Xavier reached to knock on the window.

Brendan was on the phone, but he looked up and smiled, rushing past us and entering the café. He unzipped his jacket and set Brenna's tote bag gently down on her lap as he said goodbye to whoever was on the phone.

"Is it done?" Bailey asked. She scrolled her phone and frowned. "Official?"

Brendan grinned and leaned his head in. "I shouldn't say anything, especially here, but rumors are going to start flying any hour now. And since Bailey's here, I can totally pin it on her."

Bailey snorted and shot Brenna a wink. "I dare you to."

"Don't dare him!" Brenna and Penny shouted in unison at her.

We all laughed. The players had a thing for daring one another and had gotten into some decent scrapes over the years. The best result came in the form of Xavier's pregame good-luck toffee coffee, the result of a triple-dog-dare from Brendan back when they'd both played for the Voltage. He scored that game, and the toffee coffee stuck.

Brenna's head whipped from Brendan to Bailey, who was grinning at her screen. "So it's done?" she squealed. "And it's what I think it is?"

"Not quite," Brendan warned. "From what I understand—and details are still to be finalized—there's a three-way deal in the works that will result in the Edge buying out the rest of Kingston's contract."

"My cousin is coming home!" Brenna shout-whispered.

Penny clapped. "This is awesome!"

"Agreed," Xavier said. "I hate playing against that guy."

We all laughed. I didn't understand how hockey contracts worked, so I asked. "So who's leaving your team?"

"No one that I can tell," Brendan said. "We have cap space for the rest of King's contract for this year if we send our third goalie back to the Volts."

"So who's the other team?" I asked.

"No idea. But whoever it is, they're giving Montana something real good. Otherwise, they never would have released Kingston."

"And they get what from you?" I asked.

"Probably a draft pick or future considerations." He shrugged. "It should all be finalized tonight, and King was told to meet us in Seattle tomorrow so he can play in the lineup in Monday's game."

"That's so awesome!" Brenna exclaimed. "I cannot wait for Monday Night Dinner! I'm going to call Gran and tell her to plan for us all to stay later to watch the game." She kissed Brendan on the cheek. "I'll be right back!"

Brendan watched her go, grinning like she was his sun. "I knew she'd be excited. They've always been close."

"So now all her family is back in Palmer City, right? He was the last one?" Penny asked.

"Yup," Brendan confirmed. "And the new contract is for eight years, so it's pretty much permanent as far as hockey goes."

"So will Taylor take her mindset coaching business fully online, then?" I asked. Taylor not only coached at the Kalispell Plex, but she was also a licensed psychologist specializing in sports mindset coaching and counseling for active and retired athletes—and still made cheer bows on the side.

"I'm not sure, but they'll figure it out," Brendan said. He nodded to Xavier. "You ready to go?"

Xavier nodded and leaned over to kiss Penny goodbye. "Call if *anything* changes. I can afford whatever fine they throw at me to get back to you."

She nodded. "I'm fine, really. Go to practice."

He left frowning, and when he and Brendan exited, Penny sighed. "It's just a little indigestion."

"Following 'just a little morning sickness,'" Brenna air quoted. "I understand why his protective mode kicked in. You had a bad bout that second month."

I turned my eyes on Penny. This was news to me. "Why didn't you call me? I could've helped. Did you keep a food journal?"

She shook her head. "I did, but it didn't reveal anything in particular. And there was nothing to do. Xavier took care of everything, and Lauren checked on me when they were traveling."

"But I'm your sister," I said.

"And you work three jobs and live twenty minutes away. She's next door, Tasha, and she has the same schedule as me. It's practical."

Another reminder I wasn't in their hockey wives club. Penny and Xavier had recently moved into their new home next door to Lauren and Jason. I sat up straighter and tipped my chin. "I've got to go," I said. "I need to figure out what I'm wearing on my date with Vlad tonight."

I didn't know if I was reminding them or myself that I was dating an Edge player.

"We'll see you at the party tomorrow?" Brenna asked.

I nodded. "Wouldn't miss it."

Once I was out the door, I turned right and stopped at the corner to wait for the signal to cross the street. I wasn't ready to return to my empty apartment, so instead I traversed the Creek Walk past Restaurant Row and all the way up to the town park, where I sat on a swinging bench.

The sun was warm, and I took off my jacket and held it in my lap as I rocked back and forth, watching the water rush over the rocks. Elk Creek Falls, just north of us, was the source of the creek water, and it occurred to me that I wasn't far from Nana's house. Behind the town park was the Brewer ranchland, which stretched north to the falls and west to Stagecoach Road.

Monty's great-great-great grandfather had won a chunk of Brewer land in a card game, and he'd sold off all but a patch of prime mountainside property where he built the Victorian mansion Nana still lived in today and Monty would inherit. With profits from the land sales, his oldest son—Monty's great-great-grandfather—traveled to Texas, where he purchased land and began drilling for oil.

He struck liquid gold and returned to Palmer City to try to buy the family's land back. But the proud business owners who'd opened shops along the creek wouldn't sell, so he was limited to what he'd kept. It was a beautiful piece of land, with unobstructed views of the Rockies and a stream fed from the falls that ended in a small lake. And the house? Extraordinary.

They were the richest family I knew, and yet no amount of money could've saved Mindy. And Monty couldn't make his parents love him. When Nana died ... I didn't even want to think about how that might destroy him.

Suddenly feeling the chill, I slid off the swing and pulled my jacket back on for the walk home.

Once inside the apartment, I wandered into Monty's room to see if he left anything. A cursory glance from the doorway revealed everything was in order, except for a stack of papers on the desk, bound by two binder clips.

I squinted at the bundle as I neared it. One third of the way down on the top page read simply, "Tasha's Recipes for Unique Dietary Needs," and he'd scribbled a note with the link to the document.

Heh?

I picked it up and thumbed through the pages. He'd typed up my entire recipe binder! It was all there, from the tried and true slow-cooker staples to the sugar-free desserts I'd Frankensteined for Nana. Plus, all the substitution recommendations and important reminders.

And he'd started each recipe with a quote like "Best mac; hands-down" and "You thought you needed real butter until you tried this," and "Gooier than gourmet."

I snorted. My brownies *were* unusually gooey.

What a thoughtful gesture! I needed to thank him.

I carried the manuscript to the kitchen and set it on the counter so I could text him.

I found the recipes. Thank you! You didn't have to do that. I still don't think anyone would want to buy a book of my hodgepodge creations.

It was nothing. I only have two jobs, so you know, lots of free time.

I laughed. *Yeah, us three-jobsters definitely do not have time to type up a recipe book.*

On the last page is Gia Kubek's email. She said she'd publish it as part of her line of cookbooks if you didn't want to produce it independently.

Oh my gosh, what? In addition to Pasta Nacht's, Astoria

Brewer's mother, Gia, known worldwide as Tia Gia, had a multimillion-dollar culinary line of products and foods.

Stop lying. She did not!

No cap, Tasha. Promise. She's expanding out of her Italian niche of products and thinks this would be a great addition.

Oh wow …

You're welcome. See what Gia has to say. I'm sure she's planning to advance you a hefty sum.

I don't know what to say, Monty. Thank you.

You're welcome.

I sank onto the sofa, stunned. How much was an advance? Enough to make a dent in that six-thousand-dollar bill at the top of the stack on my desk?

CHAPTER 26

Monty

I might have still had the key, but it felt more appropriate to knock on the apartment door instead of letting myself in.

"Come in!" Tasha called.

I opened the door. Her back was to me as she packed a grocery tote on the far kitchen counter.

When she turned, I had to blink twice. It took me a minute to process what I was seeing. Tasha's sandy hair fell in sculpted waves over a long white cable-knit sweater dress. The dress covered every inch of her, but it was *snug*. I wanted to toss her my coat and tell her to cover up. And her eyes … She hadn't worn eyeliner or done her lashes like that since she quit cheer.

"Stop staring. You're creeping me out."

Say something. Be rude. Insult her. Banter.

I reached for the right words, words that would both dig at and compliment her, and I came up empty. She'd rendered me speechless.

This did not happen.

Ever.

Where the heck was she going with Vlad that made her decide to get all prom-glam?

"Is it too much?"

"It's a little fancy for moving Nana," I said. "Better stay away from the old guys. You might cause a few heart attacks."

She groaned. "I was aiming for 'fancier than work … less than performance' face. I probably should have skipped the false eyelashes."

"It's fine," I assured her. "You've got that 'hockey Wag during the playoffs' vibe. Classy but not over the top. Sorry I made you think otherwise."

"Montgomery Biddington," she drawled, her smile widening into a grin, "I *think* you just gave me a genuine compliment."

"Yeah. I'm pretty sure I'm coming down with something. Maybe you should drive separately." I fisted my hand and brought it to my mouth, faking a cough. "Wouldn't want to get Vladdy sick before the big road trip."

Tasha laughed and handed me the bag of food. "Let's check to see if you've got a fever." She reached up to place the back of her hand on my forehead. "Hmm … a little hot—"

"Thank you."

She snorted. "Hot*headed.*"

"Aw, and here I was thinking you were giving *me* a genuine compliment."

"Maybe another time." She pulled her coat off the hook and slipped it on, pulling her hair free and carefully arranging it in front of her shoulders. "Thank you for typing up my recipes and pitching them to Gia. I don't know how to thank you for that."

"You don't need to," I said softly.

She smiled but didn't reply, so I gestured to the door. Once she was out, I locked it behind us and we headed out.

Nana was signing paperwork in the recliner when we arrived in her room. She looked up from the rolling tray when we entered and pointed her pen at her nurse, Marlene. "My two favorite people are here to break me free! It's been almost half a year, and if I wasn't so happy to get home to my cat, I might cry!"

The nurse was doing her best to hold it together. "You'll come visit, right, Miss Nancy?"

"Of course!" Nana waved at her like she was nuts. "Now that I don't have to live here, I think it's time I stop letting Clarice win at cards." She gave an exaggerated wink, and Marlene laughed.

"Take good care of her," Marlene implored of me. "And if you need anything, just call. The overnight nurse is scheduled to be there at seven."

"Count on it," Monty promised. "C'mon, Nana. Tasha made dinner." The nurse pulled the tray away and brought Nana's wheelchair over. I helped her stand and slowly pivot, then eased her down to the seat.

"Best grandson ever. I'm in good hands, don't you worry, Marlene."

"I won't. But I'll miss you. We all will."

I gestured for Tasha to push Nana so I could roll her bags. I'd been taking things from the room back to the house all week, so when we arrived, Nana's two suitcases filled with her remaining belongings were waiting just inside her door.

"Follow me," Marlene said.

Tasha complied, and I fell in behind them. When Nana turned the corner into the main hall, a cheer erupted. The walls were lined with residents and staff, clapping and shouting well wishes.

One of Nana's nurse assistants stepped forward and handed her a tiara. "For the queen," she said, and curtsied.

"Queen Nancy! Here, here!" Pauli shouted. He elbowed Clarice. "When you leave, they'll bring you a pointy hat!"

Clarice whacked him with a book. "And when you leave, we'll throw a party!"

Nana just smiled and waved like the queen she was until we were through the front door. "I think I might miss this place. Monty, you'll have to bring me here enough so that I remember why I'm glad to be home."

"Anytime, Nana."

Tasha parked the wheelchair by the passenger door and opened it. I loaded the suitcases into the truck and ran over to help Nana inside.

"I can lift you," I offered.

"Let me see if I can do it myself first." She turned her head to Tasha. "One of the things I had to do to get out of there was move from the chair to the commode without falling. Imagine if I fell and Monty had to help when I was bare as a baby from the waist down!"

"Didn't need that visual, Nana!" I called.

Tasha laughed. "You call me if you ever find yourself in that situation and your nurse is MIA. I'll leave wherever I'm at to help you."

Nana patted her hand. "I believe that. Thank you." She gripped the sides of her chair and pushed herself up. I watched as she eyed the running board on the truck "I got this."

Tasha hovered behind Nana with her arms out, ready to react in an instant like she was spotting one of her athletes. I was glad they'd stayed close over the years. I had to admit, if it hadn't been for Nana insisting I take her to the Coffee Loft several times weekly, I probably wouldn't have had the guts to face Tasha after she broke her leg.

Tasha made sure Nana was buckled in as I stowed the wheelchair in the back. When I pulled out of the lot, she twisted around to speak to Tasha in the back seat.

"I'd like you to move in with us."

I glanced in the rearview mirror. To say Tasha was surprised was an understatement.

"I couldn't—"

"Your lease is up at the end of December, right? We have nine bedrooms. You can have a whole hallway if you want. Or the turret room. You always liked hiding out there. I'm a lonely old woman, and I like you. And your food."

Tasha laughed. "I'm happy to cook for you. But I'm planning to move back in with my parents."

"I have a better kitchen."

"You definitely do. But I don't think—"

"Well, *do* think. Because it makes sense. Besides, Parfait misses you terribly, I hear."

"He's only been gone a few hours."

"Montgomery. A little help here, please?"

My eyes met Tasha's in the mirror. "We'd love to have you."

She blew out a breath. "I'll consider it."

"Good," Nana said. "Now tell me about this hot date you've got. Because I know you didn't dress up for me."

I held back a smile as Tasha's cheeks reddened. "She's having dinner with that hockey guy."

"Oooh. Vladimir Ivanov again, huh? He's hot. Tell me everything."

Tasha pressed her lips together to keep from laughing. "He's definitely easy on the eyes. We're still getting to know each other."

Nana questioned Tasha all the way home and while we got her settled. I learned more than I ever needed—or wanted—to know about that guy. I was actually relieved when he arrived to pick her up so I wouldn't have to keep listening to them.

CHAPTER 27

Tasha

Had I known Nana was going to grill me about Vlad for an hour and a half, I would've driven separately so I could leave. Or maybe I wouldn't have come at all.

I practically ran to Vlad's sports car when he arrived.

"Thanks for picking me up here," I said as I buckled my seat belt.

"No problem." He handed me a peach envelope. "Words I wish I could say out loud."

I smiled and opened the letter as he drove.

MY TASHA,
TRANSLATING THE FEELINGS OF MY HEART INTO WORDS IS TEDIOUS, FOR NO WORDS ARE SUFFICIENT TO ADEQUATELY ACCOUNT FOR YOUR BEAUTY, YOUR SELFLESSNESS, AND THE WAY YOU ENCOURAGE OTHERS. MY FEELINGS LIVE DEEP IN MY HEART, AND IT IS ONLY HERE I CAN CONFESS THEM, FOR I FEAR IF I SPEAK THEM ALOUD, THEY WOULD LOSE VALUE. CAN YOU FEEL MY SOUL REACHING OUT TO YOU? IT CRIES FOR YOUR LOVE LIKE A DESERT FLOWER CRIES TO BE WATERED.

ALWAYS YOURS,
VLADIMIR

"Oh, Vlad," I breathed. "You have the soul of a poet. How *do* you write such beautiful words in a new language?"

He shrugged. "It is heavily edited. But it is good, no?"

Heavily edited, huh? By AI or a human? I wondered. And to what extent?

I concurred. "It is good." But for the first time, I wondered if he even knew what he was writing. He seemed more excited about impressing me than advancing our relationship.

Astoria greeted us at the host stand at Pasta Nacht's. "You two look amazing. New suit, Vlad? Love the plaid. That rhymes! Special night? Birthday?"

I shook my head and looked up at Vlad. He did look good in plaid. But nothing about him gave me that fluttery feeling inside —unlike his letters, which spoke directly to my heart.

"No birthday," Vlad said. "Just a nice dinner with beautiful hard-working woman who finally has Saturday night off."

I poked him playfully. "Hey, now. You play on a lot of Saturday nights."

Astoria laughed. "I get that! Follow me." She led us to one of the small, private crescent-shaped booths in the back of the restaurant, set the menus down, and held her hands out for our coats. "Coat check number is fifteen." She winked at Vlad.

He grinned, and we slid into the booth from opposite sides, meeting in the middle. "Specials tonight are a filet mignon with traditional German rahm sauce reduction, served with steamed green beans and heirloom potatoes or over rice. Tasha, we can whip up a dairy-free version with plant butter and coconut cream for you if you'd like to try it. We've also got Maine lobster, served with beer-battered onion rings and coleslaw, and we can also sub ingredients for those. Oh!" She turned to Vlad. "And Keegan's debuting a new seasonal beer that he's featuring here. I haven't tried it because, well—" She patted her baby bump. "But it sure smells good!"

"Baby does not drink the beer, eh?" Vlad asked. "Just kidding!"

Astoria laughed. "Well, we do plan to name her Shandy …"

"Clever," I said. Astoria and Keegan had fallen in love over crafting the perfect lemon shandy for Brewski's. They'd used her mother's lemonade recipe, which featured lemons from the family's grove in Italy.

"Your server will be over in a few minutes," Astoria promised. "Let me know if you need *anything.*"

We thanked her and looked over the menus. I startled when Vlad's phone buzzed in his pocket, sending vibrations through the seat. He reached down to silence it, and I went back to reading the menu.

The server arrived, and Vlad's phone buzzed again as we were ordering.

And again when our drinks arrived.

"I think you should answer it," I said. "I don't mind."

"It is not as important as you," he said.

The phone buzzed again. "I really don't mind. What if it's family news?"

With a sigh, he pulled his phone from his pocket and swiped to check the screen. "Agent," he said. "I am not expecting call."

"Did he leave a text?"

Vlad scrolled his screen. "Da. Yes. He says must speak now. Urgent. I text him back to see how urgent."

His fingers flew over the screen, and then he set the device down on the table. The phone didn't ring anymore, but two short vibrations indicated he'd received a reply.

He pointed to our server walking toward us with our meals. "Eat first. Then I call, okay?"

"Okay."

While we ate, we swapped stories from hockey and cheer camps. He had a twin brother he'd come up with that still played in the KHL. They'd been competitive, and so I told him about how Monty and I sharpened each other growing up.

"Like brother, sister, you are. Work together. Competitive. But always support."

"Yeah," I agreed. "He and his Nana are pretty much family."

I set my knife and fork on my plate to signal I was finished. When I saw Gia Kubek heading toward us, I sat up straighter.

"Tasha! Vlad! So great to see you both. I hope the meal was good?"

"Perfect," I said. Vlad nodded as he chewed his last bite.

"Wonderful. I'm glad I stopped in. I'm prepared to make an offer to publish your cookbook, Tasha. When can we meet?"

"A cookbook!" Vlad nudged me with his shoulder. "Secret project, eh?"

My cheeks reddened. "You could say that."

"My schedule is open next week," Gia said. She placed a business card on the table. "Call me."

"Oh—okay. Thank you."

She smiled. "My pleasure." She pointed to Vlad. "Don't skip dessert. I recommend the New York cheesecake."

Gia left us, and Vlad turned to me. "I leave to take call?"

"You don't have to."

"I will call here. Do not want to miss a minute with you." He was sweet, but the endearment landed flat. My thoughts drifted again to the letters as he dialed his agent.

"Hello, I … I see. But—it is only November. We are still working on lines … Then there is nothing to do …"

Vlad's shoulders sagged. Whatever the news was, it wasn't good.

He ended the call and closed his eyes, pressing them shut tight. Then he set the phone down and tugged at his carefully combed hair.

"What is it?" I asked softly, laying my hand on his shoulder. "Is everything all right?

He shook his head, opening his eyes and dropping his hands into his lap. "Nothing is right. It is nightmare. They have traded me to Miami. I must be on plane at nine in morning."

I gasped. "How—how can they do that?"

Vlad shrugged. "Happens all the time. At least I am still in USA."

"But—didn't they recruit you from the KHL because they wanted you?" I didn't understand any of this.

"Da. Yes. But I am not playing here the way I played in Russia. Chemistry is off. Mixing up is not improvement."

"And they can just trade you away, with less than a day's notice? Where will you live?"

"Yes. There have been rumors this week. I am small piece in a bigger deal. My agent says we will find out in a few hours what happened."

I frowned. "So, this is goodbye?"

He turned to me and cupped my shoulders, his eyes pleading. "You must come with me."

I shook my head. "I can't go to Miami. My jobs are here. My cheerleaders are depending on me."

"They can hire new coach, no?"

"Vlad." I placed my hands over his and drew them off my shoulders to hold them between us. "I can't go with you. I'm sorry."

"At least say you will come to Miami to see? And we can talk plans for future? Football season is almost over, no? And your Worlds team—you say they can coach themselves. After Christmas, perhaps?"

His earnest plea hurt my heart.

Future. This was what I'd wanted. The whole point of dating a hockey player. A future where I wouldn't have to struggle over money.

But, thanks to Monty, I might have another option now, one where I wouldn't have to be dependent on anyone.

What divine timing.

"No. I'm sorry." I shook my head. "I can't."

His expression cracked my heart further. Vlad was a sweet guy, and one day, he'd find someone who would uproot herself in a heartbeat for him.

Someone that wasn't me.

I KEYED OPEN the door to my apartment and was surprised to find the kitchen light on. I was sure I'd switched it off when I left.

"Oh!" A figure rose up from the sofa, and I jumped so high I nearly hit the ceiling.

"Sorry! So sorry!" Monty apologized. "I texted you I was coming over. I forgot my, um, pillow?"

"You didn't." I narrowed my eyes. "'Fess up. Why are you *really* here?"

He hesitated, sliding his hands into his pockets and lifting his shoulders. "I heard about the trade and thought you might be upset, so I came over once Nana got settled with the night nurse."

"Oh." I hung up my coat and slung my purse strap over the peg next to it. "That was thoughtful of you."

"So? Did Vlad ask you to go with him?"

"To Miami?" I asked.

Monty nodded.

"He did."

"And? Do I need to find a new coaching partner?"

I studied his expression. Tense, like a little boy who wanted to know if he was in trouble. I rushed to reassure him. "I'm not going to Miami, Monty. I wouldn't leave you hanging like that. Especially after you stepped in to help me when Nate quit. And you got me a book deal."

"After the season?"

Monty's tone lacked its trademark self-assurance. I walked over to him and patted his arm.

"No." I sank into the sofa. "Not ever." I pulled a pillow onto my lap. "It's not meant to be."

His shoulders seemed to relax—or maybe I imagined it—and he lowered himself into the cushion next to mine, folding his arms across his chest. "He's a chump."

"He's not. I'm sad to see him go. But not for the reasons I should be sad." I rubbed my eyes with my fingertips. "It's confusing." My head found his sturdy shoulder, and I sighed. "Shouldn't I be sad? Like breakup-level sad?"

"You're not? You've been dating the guy for months."

"Not really. We've been going ON dates for months. Weeks, really." I thought back over our time together. "Six total, I think? Some group events. Games. Inconsistent texting. We're still getting to know each other. We're not even official."

"He never asked you to be his girlfriend? You wore his jersey to games. That looked pretty official to me."

"Nope. But those letters … and when he asked me to go to Miami, he implied that he wanted to plan a future with me. He's very sweet and very shy, I think. He told me today it's easier for him to write his feelings than to speak them."

"I don't think he's shy at all," Monty said. "I think he's toying with you. I think he wants a trophy wife he can eventually use to gain citizenship. It's clear he's in no rush to commit."

"That's a terrible thing to say." I glared up at him, surprised by his vitriol. "I'm no trophy wife."

"No kidding. Your resting face is scarier than mine."

"Hey!"

"Kidding." He held up his hands. "But he's still a chump."

"You think you know so much. If you'd read his letters, you'd know how much he cares about me. I think I broke his heart tonight."

"Words. They're meaningless unless they're backed up by actions."

"Oh really?" I huffed. "And what actions do you think would be appropriate? He's a gentleman."

Monty snorted. "Hypothetically?"

I nodded, and he shifted on the sofa, scooching back and turning sideways to face me.

He locked his eyes on mine, and his tone became earnest. "If you were my girl, I'd make sure you knew it. There would be no doubt in your mind. I would look at you like a man in love, and you'd be confident that there was no one else for me but you. Admit it. Be honest—Does he look at you that way?" Monty didn't wait for an answer. "He didn't even walk you to your door tonight. Does he even care about your safety?"

"This building is pretty safe." I felt compelled to defend my not-boyfriend. "Nothing is going to happen to me between the entrance and the apartment."

"Oh really? What about walking in to find a strange man inside sitting on your sofa?"

"You are *definitely* strange," I muttered.

"I'd certainly text you more than once every few days, and I'd call you every day, twice, when I was on the road, just to hear your voice. You think Xavier and Penny or Gabby and Noel go more than eight hours without talking to each other?"

"They're newlyweds. They don't count."

"Ask them. Ask Gabby how often she and Noel texted when they first started dating."

I didn't have to. It was constant.

"So?" I looked down at my hands. "Every couple is different."

"Yeah, but you weren't even a couple. And he kissed you like he was *obligated.*"

My head snapped up. "Ugh! You watched him kiss me?"

"Not on purpose, but I saw him kiss you after the last game, and it was ..." He seemed to fumble for words. "All wrong."

"All wrong?"

"Unequivocally. If you were *my* girl"—his voice turned hoarse, husky and ragged—"I'd kiss you like you're the only source of oxygen in a burning building. Like the air in your lungs was the air I needed to live, and I wouldn't stop until I stole all but your last breath from you. Until our shared breath became our lifelines and our souls were filled." He cleared his throat. "Hypothetically, of course."

"Of course." *I* could hardly breathe right now. Fire flickered through me like a Fourth of July sparkler.

I had to look away.

"Kisses like that aren't real, Monty. Pure fiction," I said. The way he described what kissing should be ... like it was in books and movies.

"I guess you'll never know because you only date chumps."

"Not fair." I pointed at him. "You just have super high standards. I'm realistic."

"You should be less realistic and demand better. You deserve better, Tasha. And you definitely deserve to be kissed right."

Why was he so hung up on how Vlad kissed me? Did it reveal some kind of vibe I wasn't aware of?

"Hypothetically," I said slowly, "and in the pure interest of proving you wrong, *how* would a kiss like that go?"

Monty pulled the pillow from my lap and tugged me up off the sofa so that we were standing only a few inches from each other. "Hypothetically? First, I'd look into your eyes, tell you how blue they are. My favorite color, a mirror image of my own, like the sky on a clear day."

"Cheesy," I scoffed. "Then what?

"Permission to touch your face and hair?"

"How romantic." I shrugged. "Go ahead."

Monty cleared his throat and swallowed. He held my gaze as

his hand rose slowly until his fingers were threaded through my hair over my ears. "Then I'd run my fingers through your hair from the top of your head to the ends." As he spoke, he did just that.

I was suddenly feeling warm. Way too warm. Had he messed with the thermostat again?

"And tell you how soft and stunning it is and how good it smells and how it's my favorite scent and that I even sneak some of your shampoo sometimes."

"Say what? That's my super expensive gluten-free shampoo! I wondered why it was going so fast!"

"I left two new bottles under the sink in my bathroom for you."

"This isn't very romantic."

"Then I'd step closer. Tell you how beautiful you are, not just on the outside but on the inside, too. That I admire your strength and your intelligence and your ability to do all the things you set your mind to. How you're in the gym practicing tumbling and kickouts and getting your partner-stunting back after all these years, for yourself, not because you have to prove you're better than anyone else. How you care for others and selflessly work day and night to make sure everything and everyone is okay and how unique and amazing of a person that makes you."

"Hypothetically."

"No. That's all true. And any guy who doesn't see it and remark on it and compliment you regularly—out loud, to your face—is a chump."

"Um. Thank you?"

"Then I'd reach for your cheek and hold it in my hand and tip your chin up so that we could look into each other's eyes." His voice dropped lower. He did as he described, and I held my breath.

"Then?" I whispered back. Monty's face was *so close*. His warm breath caressed my nose and cheeks and lingered on my lips.

"Then, I'd drop my gaze from your eyes to your lips and tell you how perfect they were and how much I wanted to feel them against mine. To show you with a kiss what my words claim, that you are the sun and the stars and every source of light in my world." He rubbed his thumb over my cheekbone. "Hypothetically," he whispered.

"Hypothetically," I whispered. "Then?"

"Then, I'd lean in. My other hand would come up and cup your other cheek. I'd hold you in my hands like you're the most precious fragile porcelain. And touch my lips lightly to yours."

Neither of us were moving—or breathing.

"But I wouldn't stop there. I'd trail my lips to your ear, your jaw, the side of your neck." Monty's thumb lightly traced a path as he spoke. "My lips would brand your skin in such a way that you'd have no doubt you were mine. And I'd want you to do the same to me. Sealed with a kiss would take on a whole new meaning."

"Hypothetically?" I searched his eyes. Nothing about this felt hypothetical anymore. Were these *his* feelings?

He didn't answer. Not even a nod. His lack of confirmation was sending my thoughts and heart into a tailspin.

"I've never been kissed like that before," I admitted hoarsely. "What's wrong with me, Monty?"

He snapped back to attention and dropped his hands. "What do you mean? Nothing's wrong with *you.*"

I hung my head and sank back into the sofa. "Why couldn't I ever inspire that kind of passion in any of my relationships? Or make it work with Vlad? He's a great guy, but even I can see that four months of inconsistent dates and communication are never going to sustain a relationship. It went both ways. I *wanted* to fall for him. But it just didn't happen. I'm too … icy? Prickly. Was he so afraid to even *talk* to me that he had to write letters for fear of how I might react to his spoken words?"

Monty plopped down next to me and crossed his arms over his chest. "Chump."

I sighed. "Not a chump." I rushed over to my purse and pulled out the latest letter. "Read this."

I pulled the letter out of the envelope and handed it to him. As he began to read, I closed my eyes, wanting to get the full effect of the beautiful words.

"My feelings live deep in my heart, and it is only here I can confess them, for I fear if I speak them aloud, they would lose value."

He paused, and I snuck a glance over at him.

His eyes flicked to the letter, then to me as he read the remaining sentences:

"Can you *feel* my soul reaching out to you? It cries for your love like a desert flower cries to be watered."

How had he memorized it so quickly? And the way he was reading it … like, he, Monty, meant it.

But that was just because he was a good reader, right? He couldn't possibly feel that way about me. I was love-starved and trying to grab hold of any string of affection that dangled in front of me. He was just being a good friend and looking out for me, like old times.

Right?

"Another thing?" Monty leaned forward, resting his arms on his thighs. "He's got this love letter thing nailed down. How many other women has he written to? He doesn't even use nice paper. I would never write my girl letters on cheap cardstock. Only the finest, most elegant stationery, like what my grandpa used to use to write to Nana."

"He wrote her letters?"

"He did. There's a whole bag full in her closet."

"You were snooping?"

"I was nine and looking for a place to hide. My parents didn't find me for hours."

"I bet. Anything juicy?"

"Nah. Grandpa wasn't very sentimental. Mostly accounts of his time and how much he missed her. Nothing flowery like your letters."

I held the peach card in my hand. It *was* cheap. Part of a multicolor pastel bargain set at Target.

"I should go," he said, popping up from the sofa. "You'll be okay if I leave you?"

"I'm fine. Just another breakup."

"Sort-of breakup," he reminded me. "The chump never made it official, remember?"

"Right. So I shouldn't cry about it." I sighed. "Thanks for coming over to check on me and reminding me I have worth."

"I shouldn't need to remind you, Tasha." He pulled on his hoodie and picked up his keys from the dish by the door. "But I will, anytime you need to hear it. Hug?"

I walked into his open arms and wrapped mine around his waist. "Thanks."

"Like I said, anytime. Anyone who's intimidated or afraid of your hedgehoggy prickles doesn't deserve your good stuff."

I swatted him and booped him on the nose. "Go home to Nana. I'll see you tomorrow."

He grinned. "See you tomorrow."

CHAPTER 28

Monty

On Sunday, the skies over Palmer City hung dark and heavy, threatening to storm at a moment's notice. Up in the mountains, it was snowing, but it wouldn't get cold enough here to be anything more than rain. The slow-moving system would hit us right around dinnertime.

Brenna and her event crew had outdone themselves with the decor and theming in Nana's favorite colors—red and blue—and Fyvie from the bakery had brought over a truckload of diabetic and celiac-friendly desserts from the bakery that looked more tempting than their traditionally made counterparts.

The party was in full swing when Gabby tapped me on the shoulder at the dessert table. "Kitchen. Now."

I raised an eyebrow and held up my gluten-free gooey brownie.

"Bring it with you. This is important, Montgomery."

I winced. She never called me that.

"Am I in trouble?"

"You bet your pom-poms you are."

I rolled my eyes. "Poms are for girls. I had a *megaphone.*"

"You're going to have a mega headache if you don't follow me into the kitchen right now."

"Fine, fine."

I hurried after her through the rooms to the kitchen. Brenna's catering staff were all in the dining room, so it was empty.

"Senior year of college. We were taking an online writing class because the day class got dropped and the night class conflicted with Worlds team practice."

"Yeah, so?" I took a bite of the brownie and chewed it slowly.

"We partner-edited." She leaned closer. "Do you remember?"

I shrugged and swallowed the brownie. "Not really." I popped the rest of it into my mouth.

"Well, *I* do. Because your poems were all lovesick odes to some girl you denied existed. You used phrases like 'my feelings live deep in my heart' and 'I fear to speak my heart aloud' and 'my soul reaches out to yours' or something. Phrases that somehow ended up in Tasha's love letters from Vlad."

I sucked in a breath.

Bad idea.

The brownie got stuck in my throat. I coughed it up, and Gabby ran to the fridge to get me a bottle of water.

"One phrase? I could believe it was a coincidence. Two? Still plausible, but I'd give you the benefit of the doubt. Three? Straight up PLAGIARISM. So how did a dude from Russia who speaks minimal English—and can barely read it—get access to your poetry?"

"I don't know what you're talking about," I insisted.

"Then check your Google docs." Her tone softened. "Were you trying to send Tasha messages, Cyrano-style? Or was it truly an act of your subconscious?"

What was she talking about? "Stop reading into it. Vlad asked me for help. I just rewrote what he wanted to say in a way that was intelligible."

"I knew it!" She poked my bicep. "You need to tell that to Tasha. Poor thing is wallowing in guilt about breaking things off with a guy who she thinks is in love with her."

"Guilt? She's not upset that they broke up?"

Gabby shook her head. "I think she knew it was never going to work."

"Then why did she keep trying?" I had to know.

"Have you seen her medical bills?"

I had. One morning when she was at work, I'd gone into her room to borrow her tape to wrap a gift for Nana. Her dispenser was a paperweight, and underneath was a stack of bills. On top was a payment plan stub from the hospital. She hadn't been kidding when she'd told me it would take years to pay it off. After visiting Nana, I went straight to Pasta Nacht's to ask Astoria where I could find her mother.

That was when I began typing up the rest of her recipes in earnest.

The kitchen door opened, and Noel poked his head in. "Hey, Monty. Gab—Coach texted. Our flight is leaving an hour early to beat the worst of the storm. Do you want to go home now or catch a ride with Tasha? She's going to bring Penny home later."

"I'll go now. Be right out." He left, and she turned back to me. "You need to come clean. Don't let Tasha feel any worse than she already does. And"—she poked me again for emphasis—"you may be surprised at her reaction, you big doofus."

I clutched at my heart. "Name-calling? That hurts."

She grinned. "I'll hurt you worse if you don't confess. Don't test me."

Gabby turned on her heel and stalked out of the kitchen. I sighed and followed her so I could thank Noel, Xavier, and Brendan for coming.

It began to rain shortly after, and Tasha and I helped Brenna's crew bring in the tables and chairs that were set up on the veranda. A loud thunderclap made us all jump as lightning crackled over the lake below, treating us to a stunning show of nature's uncontrollable power.

"Have you seen Penny?" Tasha asked once we were back inside. "She's not at her harp. I can't find her."

"Maybe she changed her mind and left?"

Tasha shook her head. "Who would she have left with? I watched her wave goodbye to Xavier, and if she got a ride from someone else, she would have told me."

"And you've searched the house?"

"Well ... just the downstairs. And outside. I don't think she'd go upstairs. She'd be afraid of intruding."

"Probably. But she's pregnant. Maybe she had to go to the bathroom and the downstairs ones were occupied?"

"Maybe. I hadn't thought of that."

"I'll go upstairs and check. You hang out down here in case she comes back."

"Okay."

I jogged up the main stairs to the second floor and opened the first door, a guest room. "Pen?"

No answer. I cut around the bed to the en suite bathroom. Empty.

Back in the hall, I checked the other three rooms before entering my own at the end of the hall. The door to my bathroom was closed, so I knocked. "Pen? Are you in here?"

The toilet flushed, but there was no verbal reply. "Pen? You okay?"

"I—I don't know." Her voice was low, weak.

"I'm going to open the door, okay?"

"'Kay."

I turned the knob and pushed the door open. Penny was kneeling on the floor with her head resting on the closed toilet lid and her hands on her rounded middle. The air was rancid with vomity fumes.

"Is the baby—" Tears burned my eyes. I couldn't finish the sentence.

"She's fine," she said. "I think it was something I ate."

"Can you stand? Do you want to lie down? I have a four-thousand-dollar mattress that will cradle you like a fluffy cloud."

"Can't … OOOOHmygosh!" She lifted the lid. I sprang into action, gathering her waist-length hair while she heaved.

"I got you," I murmured softly as I reached to flush the toilet. "You Palmer women and your food issues. It's scary."

"I … n-never had food issues before. S-sorry."

"Penny!" Tasha knelt beside me and hip-checked me out of her way. "What's going on?"

"I … maybe food poisoning? My indigestion has been so bad. I've eliminated so much from my diet."

"What did you eat today?"

"I had a protein bar before church. Only had eggs and bacon

at brunch. I was fine. It was probably the chicken salad I had here? But I thought I was safe because I've had it before. It's Brewski's, right?"

"Yes," I confirmed.

Tasha looked up at me. "Chicken salad could easily be the culprit. The mayo could be bad or the chicken undercooked. And with her stomach already in chaos, it wouldn't take much for it to revolt."

"But no one else is sick." I didn't understand. "Brenna's pregnant, and I saw her eating the chicken salad."

"And she's been eating that stuff her whole life. Her stomach is probably made of steel from all the fried food and junk she's consumed—Penny!—she fainted!"

"I'm fine. Just wanna close m-my eyes," Penny insisted.

"You're not fine, Pen. Monty! Get Nana's nurse."

I ran out of the room and hurried down the stairs to find Nana. Only a few guests remained; most had left when the storm started to pick up, and by this point I'd lost hope my parents would show up. "Where's your nurse?"

Nana snorted. "She's a party pooper, so I sent her off to the sunroom to read in the rain. She's checking on me every twenty minutes though."

"Thanks!" I kissed her on the cheek and ran off toward the back of the house.

I explained Penny's condition, and the nurse followed me upstairs. We reached my room, and I pointed to the open door inside. "She's in there."

I hung back by the door. I wanted to give them space but also stay close enough to see and hear what was happening.

"Penny? I'm Lily. I'm a nurse. Can you open your eyes for me? Good. I'm going to examine you, okay?" The nurse put her stethoscope in her ears and checked Penny's pulse, heartbeat, and breathing.

"Can you lift her shirt for me?" Lily asked Tasha.

I turned away to give them privacy but didn't leave so I could hear everything.

"Is she okay?" Tasha asked. "The baby?"

"The baby's heartbeat is strong, nothing amiss to lead me to believe it's stressed. No cramping or bleeding. But she's weak and dehydrated. I'd suggest taking her to the ER for fluids."

"Okay. Penny, can you stand?"

"Later."

"I got her," I said. "Tasha, go tell Brenna she's in charge. Lily, can you let Nana know what's going on? I'm going to take Penny down the elevator to my truck."

I carefully slid one arm behind Penny's back, the other beneath her knees, lifted her, and carried her out of the room. The elevator had been installed where the back servants' staircase had been, and I'd never been so glad for it. We took it all the way down to the driveway, which was a level below the first floor.

"Just a few more steps, Penny." I kept my voice calm so as not to alarm her.

"'Kay." Her head fell against my chest.

The storm hammered against the roof as I hurried through the breezeway and into the garage.

We got to my truck, I managed to press the fob twice, and the horn honked when the doors unlocked. I stretched my fingers to pull the handle to open the back passenger door but couldn't get a good grip.

"I … can do it." Penny shifted in my arms.

"You sure?"

"I'm … pregnant. My arms aren't … broken." She breathed heavily as she reached out, pulled the handle, and opened the door.

"Good job." I used my shoulder to swing the door open all the way. "Let me get you settled back here."

"L-Look at you, M-Monty. P-Protector vibes look g-good on you."

"Don't tell anyone," I whispered. "You'll ruin my reputation." Penny was stuttering, an old condition that returned every now and again when she was stressed or anxious. Since Xavier wasn't here, it was up to me to make her feel safe and take care of her until we got to the hospital.

She held up her hand in a fist and tapped the nail side of her thumb twice to her lips, the ASL sign for "secret."

"Good." I winked and set her gently on the leather seat, dragged the seat belt across her torso, and clicked it in place.

She slid the lap portion below her belly and closed her eyes. She groaned and rubbed her hand over her belly.

The back door behind the driver's seat flew open. Tasha used the running board to step up, tossed a blanket onto the seat and climbed in. Her phone wedged between her shoulder and ear, she sat down and pulled her own seat belt on.

I pressed the remote start on the fob, and the big V8 engine rumbled to life. On a night like tonight, the extra power might come in handy. I rushed around, yanked open the driver's door, and climbed in behind the wheel. The temperature outside was in the low forties, so I cranked up the heat in the back seat.

"Gotta let you go, Mom. I'll see you there." Tasha ended the call and leaned forward. "I sent you a text with a link to Palmer City General, where Penny's OB has rights. We're going there in case he needs to check on her." She shook open the blanket and laid it over her sister.

My phone automatically connected to my truck's GPS, and I pulled up the text with the location.

"You ready?" I peered at Tasha in the rearview mirror. Her expression was stoic and calm, but her eyes told a different story.

Fear.

"Mrs. Nicks's car was the only one blocking you, and I asked her to move it. So you should be clear."

"Brilliant." I hadn't even thought about that. "Thanks."

I pressed the button on the rearview mirror to open the garage door. It rattled from the heavy wind slamming against it and slowly creaked its way upward. Rain whipped in through the opening, and I caught a glimpse of how extensively the weather conditions had deteriorated.

Tasha twisted to look out the back window. "Oh my gosh. The storm has gotten so much worse. Please drive carefully."

"Count on it." Not a chance in this lifetime I'd let anything happen to either of them.

I backed slowly out of the garage, and the truck was hit by a deluge of water like driving into an automatic car wash, heavy and powerful and blinding. I flipped on the wipers and maneuvered the truck around, careful not to hit Tasha's car. Once I was clear of the remaining guests' vehicles, I cautiously navigated the long, winding driveway down to where it met Stagecoach Road.

Lightning lit up the sky, and thunder rumbled close enough to vibrate the truck. Another bolt hit with an earth-shaking crack in front of us, illuminating the dark sky and the tall pines lining our property.

"Look out!" Tasha shouted and pointed toward the front. "Tree falling!"

I'd begged Nana when I moved in to let me cut down the two trees closest to the driveway. I was concerned they'd fall and block us from getting in or out of the property. But she'd said the odds of what happened the night Mindy died could happen again were slim to none and not to worry so much.

Slim to none wasn't good enough.

But this time, I was prepared.

The tall ponderosa fell as if in slow motion, landing square across the driveway and blocking our path out to the main road.

I slammed the truck into park, headlights aimed at the downed tree, and threw my door open and jumped out of the cab. Wind and rain slapped against me as I ran back to the tailgate. I dropped it down, hoisted myself up, and crawled along the bed to the built-in toolbox. I swiped my arm across my face to wipe away the icy rain, spun the lock dial to the right, then to the left, then right again—Mindy's birthdate—and lifted the lid.

The sharp metal edges of the chain saw blades gleamed up at me. It was made for a night like this. I looped the strap holding the safety glasses over my head, and they hung from my neck. I grabbed the headlamp, stretched the strap around my head, and clicked it on. I hefted the chain saw out of the box and closed the lid. Tasha's wide blue eyes stared out at me through the rear window.

"I'm going to cut it up!" I yelled and pointed at the chainsaw.

"I'll help!" Her voice was muffled, and she spun around.

Before I could protest, she was out of the cab and running through the rain toward the fallen tree.

By the time I reached her, she was straddling the end of the tree and pulling at the branches.

"Cut here first!" Her hair blew around her face as she shouted over the storm.

"You can't be that close!" I shouted into the rain. "I got it! You can help me clear the tree away!"

"Okay!" She hopped off the tree and jogged a safe distance away.

I slid the safety goggles onto my nose and made sure they were secure over my eyes. The headlamp was bright enough to illuminate a wide swath of the tree. I flipped the switch on the chain saw, pulled back the handle guard, and yanked the cord once, twice, and it buzzed to life.

"Pull your sweater up over your face!" I lifted my own shirt to demonstrate, just in case she couldn't hear me.

Neither of us had thought to grab our jackets, and I only had one set of goggles.

Tasha nodded and complied.

I lopped off a few of the smaller branches until I was able to get a clean cut on the fattest part of the tree. I brought the saw down on the exposed trunk, and it chewed through the bark, sending sawdust onto the ground to mix with the rain. As soon as the chain saw made it all the way through, I lifted it away, and yelled, "Clear!"

Tasha lowered her sweater, leaned down, and rolled the piece away. We repeated this process several times, then worked together to pull the cuttings off to the sides of the driveway.

Once the road was clear enough to pass, we hustled back to the truck. Tasha rejoined Penny in the back seat, and I climbed into the bed to secure the equipment in the toolbox. I grabbed two of the towels I kept in there and ran back to the driver's door.

I climbed in and handed one of the towels back to Tasha. "Here ya go. I'll buy you a new outfit at the gift shop," I promised and dried my hands.

"Thanks." She smiled and dragged the towel over her face.

"Oh my gosh!" Penny said. "You guys were amazing out there."

"We *do* make a pretty good team," I said, towel-drying my face.

"We sure do!" Tasha squeezed her hair with the towel.

"You always have," Penny said, then she moaned a little.

"How are you feeling, Pen?" I asked.

"Tired. And my stomach's kinda crampy."

"We'll be there soon." Tasha tucked the blanket closer around her sister. "I never knew Monty could handle a chainsaw. Did you?" She smirked at me in the rearview mirror. "I'm kinda liking this lumberjack version of him."

I shook my head and smiled. Lumberjack, eh? I'd take it. I *was* a big manly man, after all. My eyes flicked to the rearview mirror again and I took in the vignette of sibling love, a love I had missed for so long.

Penny giggled and let her body lean against her sister. "You're the best sister, Tasha. You're always there for me."

"Aw, it's nothing, Pen. Any person in there would have helped you," she said.

"Yeah, but not the way *you* do. You know me like no one else does. Remember when I needed a job? You vouched for me to the Bevells, knowing full well I wouldn't be able to speak to customers because of my nervous stutter. And you encouraged me to take ASL as my foreign language because I'd have to speak in class with all of the others."

"Really, it was nothing, Pen. Shush, and let me tell you the tale of Lumberjack Monty."

As Tasha chronicled a play-by-play of our tree removal to Penny, my shoulders relaxed, and I let out a long, silent breath.

In a way, this whole incident felt like a redo, a second chance for me. I wasn't able to save my sister, but I *was* able to ensure Penny was no longer in danger.

Nothing would bring Mindy back, but being prepared and able to help a friend in crisis gave me much-needed peace.

I pulled up to the emergency entrance. Mr. and Mrs. Palmer were there waiting for us. Tasha hopped out and ran around to open Penny's door so their dad could help her down from the truck and into a wheelchair.

I pulled away as they whisked her inside, and I navigated to the parking garage. Once I was inside the building, I went straight to the gift shop for new clothes.

"Hey Monty! Got caught in the storm, huh?" The elderly cashier waved me over. I was a frequent customer here and knew all the staff. I usually picked up flowers or toys for the kids I visited.

"Hi, Connie. Nah. Decided to take a dip in the fountain for funsies."

"Oh, you!" She chuckled, and I grinned back. "Let me know if you need any help."

"Will do."

Not much of a selection. Scrubs, athletic gear, tacky touristy threads. I decided on royal blue Denver Edge hoodies and black unisex sweatpants. A two-pack of socks, a pair of boxers and … I stared at the women's underwear section. There were too many choices, from full-on waist-high coverage to thongs. I had no idea what Tasha wore. I thought back to our stunting. I didn't remember her having a panty line, so that would lead me to think thong, but was that for practice or every day? And the bras—sports, underwire, no underwire, pushup?

"Women's undies, huh?"

My cheeks heated. "My friend and I got caught in the rain. She's in the ER with her sister," I explained. "I'm buying us dry clothes."

"A *friend,* huh?"

"Yes, a *friend.*"

"Noted. You got a picture of her?" I nodded. "Let me hold these, and you find it. I'll see if I can figure out her size, okay?"

I passed her the bundle of clothing and scrolled until I found my favorite picture of Tasha. It was from Gabby's wedding. She'd asked me to take a picture of her standing outside the barn doors in her bridesmaid dress.

"Ooh, pretty one! Zoom in on her chest."

"What? No. Give me the clothes back, and you do the zooming."

Connie cackled with laughter. "Testing you. Good news! You passed!"

I held the bundle while she assessed the picture. "I'd say she's between a small and a medium. Since you're just friends, how about a sports bra and boy shorts? Modest bathing suit kind of coverage."

I released a breath of relief. "Yeah. Good idea."

She plucked a matching set off the wall and added it to my stack. "Anything else? Shoes?"

I looked down at my soggy sneakers. "Yeah. Whatcha got in men's thirteen and women's seven?"

"You know her shoe size!" She elbowed me. "Just *friends,* huh?"

"She was my stunting partner for sixteen years, Connie. I literally held her feet in my hands."

"Uh-huh. You want to be matchy matchy on the shoes, too? Nothing screams *partners* like twinning!"

"Just whatever you have is fine." This was taking way too long.

Ten minutes later, I'd changed into my new clothes and texted Tasha to find out how Penny was doing.

The doctor just left. She's getting fluids. They're going to admit her overnight for observation. Her OB is on the way.

Okay. I'm in the ER waiting room. I got you some dry clothes.

I'll be there in five.

I stuffed my phone in my pocket and walked toward the door that led to the unit.

When Tasha came through the door, I held up the shopping bag with her clothes. Poor thing was damp and shivering.

"Thanks! I'll be right back!"

I stayed put, waiting for her, and when she emerged for the second time, I couldn't help grinning like a clown. "Nice outfit," I teased.

She snorted and pulled on her wet braid. "You realize this isn't a cheer comp, right? We don't have to match."

I shrugged. "Too many choices on the women's wall."

She shook her head. "I'm not complaining. This is warm and soft. Let's go sit."

I followed her to an empty corner, and we placed our bags on the coffee table wedged between perpendicular chairs.

"You were amazing out there," Tasha said. "Thank you."

"Just did what I had to do," I replied. "You were totally the VIP of that operation. You have great instincts, Tasha."

"So do you. We move well together. Five months of being roommates, and we didn't bump into each other once in the kitchen."

"And cleaning up those suds felt like one of your choreographed routines."

She laughed. "Floody bubbles! That was insane."

"And fun."

"Yeah. Once I stopped being annoyed with you."

"Well, no more of that now that I'm finally out of your hair," I said.

Tasha frowned and tugged her knees up to her chest, her new shoes flat on the seat. "Yeah. No more having to listen to your shower concerts. I could hear you through the walls! I do miss the ugly old cat, though." Her lips twitched as she fought a smile.

"Have you given any thought to Nana's invitation?" I asked.

"To move in with you?"

I nodded.

"Every other minute since she asked."

"Really?" I tried not to sound too hopeful.

"Yeah. Who wouldn't want to live there? It's the most gorgeous piece of property I've ever seen. Beautifully decorated. State-of-the-art kitchen. A pool, a lake, a brook, a veranda, a gazebo, turret library, a sunroom, a mud room, a fancy parlor, a study …"

"You'd be surprised. The last girl I took out talked about building a mansion in the mountains on our first—and only—date. It was a common theme."

"Is that why you stopped dating? Gold-diggers?"

"Pretty much. I'd rather spend time with Nana and the kids. Once we're sure Penny's okay, I was planning to do a round in the pediatric oncology unit. Want to come with?"

"I'd love to, but you're changing the subject."

"Nah. I'm just done talking about it. So, you moving in or not?"

"Wouldn't it be weird for you?" She rested her chin on her knees and tilted her head.

"Why? You can have the room next to mine, if you want. It'll be like old times. The walls are thicker than at your place, but you could probably still hear me sing. I'll even take requests."

She laughed. "Old times. Like *last week*. Old times!" She was cracking up.

And I loved it.

"I'll even steal your shampoo and hide Cadbury eggs in your room."

"Hide Cadbury eggs? Where? And how did you get them out of season?"

"I have my secret ways."

"That just might be the deciding factor. Those are my *favorite*. You're a good friend, Monty."

"Yeah, I know. I hate that they make you sick, though. I might have to rethink that."

She sighed. "They don't make me sick, per se. They just, um ... give my insides a little, ah ... *boost* when things are stuck and aren't moving along on their own. Like coffee does."

Her face flamed bright red, and a look of relief crossed her features when her phone rang. She pulled it from her pocket. "It's Mom. Hi ... Okay ... Is it all right if Monty comes? He's still here ... Okay ... See you soon." She ended the call. "Mom says Penny's strength is returning by the minute. They're transporting her now, and she should be settled in her room in a half hour or so. You want to go see the kids on the way?"

"Yeah. Let me run our wet stuff to the truck. Meet you at the gift shop?"

She grinned. "See you there."

CHAPTER 29

Tasha

I took Monday off work and called my assistant coach to run the high school cheer practice so that I could sit with Penny all day and reply to Xavier's incessant texting when she was napping. He wanted to fly home, but she insisted he save his "baby daddy requests" for later in the pregnancy. The hospital released her around dinnertime, and I decided to stay with her overnight at their house.

I was late to work on Tuesday, but no one minded. I eased their minds on Penny's recovery, and by the time I'd left, the whole town was updated and praying for my sister.

I ended the high school team practice early and couldn't get to the Plex fast enough. I needed to burn off my stress, so as soon as I was stretched, I headed straight for the tumble mats and trampolines.

Monty was there with Evan, working on the timing of his tumbling passes for our routine. I joined Monty at the edge of the mat to watch Evan take off. His sequence was extraordinary. Monty had choreographed fifteen seconds of cross-mat tumbling that included eighteen flips, ten twists, and five punchbacks.

"He's going to break your record," I warned Monty. "You sure you don't want to get into the routine to defend it?"

"He's not even close. My Team USA pass was eight seconds longer, and no one's come close since."

"Don't get too cocky, old man. Another year or so, and someone's bound to pass you."

"Are you challenging me?"

I shrugged. "Do you feel challenged?"

"I do, actually." He waved Evan over when he finished his sequence. "Stand with Tasha while I prove I'm still the best."

This was going to be fun to watch.

"What's he doing?" Evan asked.

"Version 3.0 of the pass that won Team USA gold three years in a row."

"No way! He can still do that?"

"We'll see, won't we?"

Monty stalked to the corner of the mat, turned his nose up at us, and took off. He could be annoying, but he wasn't a liar. He *was* the best.

"Twenty-five flips, sixteen twists, eight punchbacks. Perfect form on the layouts. He sets a high bar." How much more could he do? Seeing him tumble like this made me want to challenge him more, push him to his ultimate limits.

Monty didn't just tumble and bounce and twist. He flew. His taut muscles flowed into one elegant move after another until he stuck the landing with the same ease he had when he stepped up to the counter to order a drink at the Coffee Loft.

"We need him on the team. Why doesn't he compete?" Evan asked.

"He's already won all the titles. He likes coaching. And the Ridgie the bear gig isn't optimal for team practices. He's only missed a handful. And he can do *that.*"

Monty finished the tumbling pass with a flourish and aimed a smirk at me. He bowed deeply to the audiences on the mats and up in the balcony who'd begun cheering him on when they noticed who it was and what he was doing.

"You don't need him, Evan. This team can win without him showing off." I held my hand up to high-five Monty as he jogged back.

"Still got it!" His hand slapped mine. "You were saying?"

"Great job." I grinned. "Now that you're warmed up, wanna throw some partner stunts? You've inspired me."

He looked up at the clock. "Evan's got three minutes left."

"I yield that time to Coach Tasha," he said. "Want me to spot?"

"Sure," I said. "Go do that pass two more times while I warm up on the tramp."

"Yes, Coach!"

"What do you want to work on today?" Monty asked.

"I was thinking about trying the partner sequence that leads into the pyramid. The Showcase is four days away, and they're all still wobbling in the same spot. I want to feel it, see if I can figure out why it's not coming together smoothly, and figure out a way to modify it without throwing the count off."

"Sounds fun."

I practiced the sequence on the trampoline. Monty and Evan watched me intently the entire time, which encouraged me to be even sharper and land as clean as I could. I didn't want to mess up or fall, especially after Monty had just proven he was still in his top form.

I didn't have any trouble with the flips, twists or kickouts, but I did have an issue during the part I'd referenced. I found myself hesitating a millisecond due to a blind spot.

"I think I figured it out!" I jumped down from the tramp and waved him onto the floor. "Evan, let me know what you think. Monty, you know how this goes, right?"

"I do. I've been working with Evan and Amelia on it. She wobbles in the same spot. Let's do it!"

We got into position, and Monty tossed me up. Due to the blind spot, I wobbled just as the girls had been doing.

When I landed on the mat, I turned to the guys. "What if, instead of a full twist, we switch it out with a half and move the full to the beginning of the sequence. That'll eliminate the blind spot and should make the rest of it flow."

"That should work," Evan said. "Let's see it."

Monty's hands gripped my hips, and I was off. It felt *good* to be back up in the air. I hadn't realized how much I'd missed it until he encouraged me to try it again.

"That looked great, Coach! I think it's going to work." Evan's expression was sheer admiration.

That felt good, too.

Every athlete appreciated a coach who gave their all. This was my all, for now. But I was motivated, and I planned to encourage at least half of our athletes—the ones who were ready—to try out for Team USA.

I couldn't stop smiling, and neither could Monty.

Evan left us with a warning. "If you two keep grinning like that, your Coach Monsha rep will be ruined."

I laughed. "Noted."

When Evan left, I asked Monty if he had dinner plans.

"I figured I'd hit the café in the main building. You?"

"I brought chicken curry stew. There's enough to share if you want some."

"Heck yeah! Thanks."

Over dinner, Monty told me he planned to bring Nana by the Coffee Loft the next day.

"Pumpkin Spice Blah-te season is almost over, and she feels cheated. Even though you or I have brought her one almost daily since it was approved."

"She knows we serve it year-round now, though. Right?"

"Yeah, Penny mentioned that when the management changed. But she likes the fall decor. Christmas stuff is already popping up around town. And Nana does not approve."

"That's true. And the music's been on the radio for weeks." An idea occurred to me. "You still have a friend at the print shop, right?"

"Yeah. Why?"

"If I send a design over, can you call and see if he can make a banner on short notice?" I put my spoon down and held my palms up. "Picture it. Welcome back, Nana Booboo!"

He laughed. "She would love that. I'll bring her crown."

"What time?" I asked. "It's a game day, right?"

"It is. We could come in the morning."

"Hmm. No. Let's time it for just before Xavier comes in for his toffee coffee. More people, a few local hockey celebrities, and Penny will be there. She's not working this week, but she'll be in to make his good-luck coffee. You can still get to the arena on time, right? Or I could bring Nana home before I head to the high school."

"That works. Great idea. She's going to love it."

"Good!" I stirred my stew. "It's a plan."

"Spit and shake on it?"

"Ew, gross, no. What are you, four?"

He waggled his eyebrows. "Only on the inside."

I snort-laughed so deeply it triggered hiccups, which made me laugh harder. That set Monty laughing, and it took a while until we calmed down.

When the hiccups finally stopped, I wiped my eyes and shook my head. "You are too much."

"Yeah, I am. But not for you, I hope?"

I looked up from my curry to find him staring intently at me, absent of his trademark cocky grin—a serious expression like the one from Saturday night, when he was describing how he'd kiss me if I was his girl.

The *zing* was back, firing like shooting stars all through me. For a moment, it even felt like I thought my heart stopped, then it shocked back to life with a grand finale of those zings. I definitely lost track of its beats, but then the pulse in my ears thrummed in earnest, and I realized my heart rate was actually sky-high.

"No," I whispered. "You're not too much for me. You're just right."

CHAPTER 30

Monty

"Look at the Christmas display in the bookstore! Disgraceful! Thanksgiving is a week from tomorrow, and it's like everyone's already moved on from it!"

"Just terrible, Nana," I agreed.

There'd been a rare open parking spot a block up from the Coffee Loft, and I thought it would be nice to take her for a little window-shopping stroll. It was turning out to be quite entertaining—for me.

"And look! Even the antiques store is draping pine over their window. What is wrong with people? I'm going to have to have a talk with Gladys. She should know better. Oh! I know! Can you get Gabby's mom to do an investigative report?"

"She's a weather woman, Nana, not a beat reporter or investigative journalist."

"Hmm. Well, she's got to know *someone* who can film this travesty."

We reached the end of the block at Prospect Road, and I pressed the button on the traffic pole to cross to the other side.

"And look! St. Mary's already has their nativity out. *Their nativity!* Not just the creche. I can see putting up the structure to stay on schedule, but the start of Advent is still over two weeks away!"

"Maybe everyone is in the Christmas spirit early this year," I offered. "You can't fault them for that. It's the best season." The signal flashed the white walking man, and I pushed Nana across to the other side of Main.

"Oh yes I can! I'm getting old. No season should try to push another season out of the way. Who started this? Do you think it was the bookstore? I heard from Clarice that people start reading Christmas novels in October. October! Before Halloween!"

"I've heard even earlier than that," I stated in my most scandalized conspiratorial tone. "Like July!"

She waved me off. "Yeah, yeah, Christmas in July is a *thing* now. But come August first, put it away until the first Sunday of Advent!"

I stopped in front of the Coffee Loft. "No Christmas here. All pumpkins and leaves and cinnamon sticks and poison coffee."

"Yes, they're the only ones on the block with any sense. All right. End of tangent. Time for some pumpkin spice and dirt cake. Tasha texted me that she made the sugar-free stuff and will have it for me behind the counter. Speaking of Tasha, when are you going to get a girlfriend?"

"That was nice of her. You're the only woman for me, Nana."

"Ha! I'm old, and we're related," she quipped.

"You're a handful, is what you are," I bantered back at her. I tapped the assistance button next to the old saloon door that hung on the exterior as a tribute to the building's history. The modern door opened slowly and engaged the chimes. I pushed Nana through the doorway and stopped just short of the queue so she could get a full view.

She gazed up at the banner in awe. "They even decorated the spiral stairs railing to the loft in twinkle lights!"

I raised my hand in the air and counted down. "Three, two, one!"

"Welcome back, Nana BooBoo!" The staff and customers cheered, and I pulled out her tiara, which I'd stuffed into my hoodie's center pocket.

"You should put this on," I said.

She grinned and set it on her head. Tasha was the first to approach her with the coveted pumpkin spice latte. We shared a grin as Nana sipped it from a new personalized orange mug that read "Nana's PSL."

"This is perfect," Nana praised. "Did you bring my dirt cake?"

Tasha nodded and pointed to a table that was set with a red tablecloth and blue and white flowers. "Head on over to your VIP table and I'll bring it right out."

"You spoil me. Can't wait till you move in!"

Tasha's lips parted to protest, but I shook my head. She hadn't decided yet, and it wasn't the time to tell Nana that, unless she was prepared to discuss the subject in front of half the town.

I wheeled Nana to the table and sat in the chair across from her. Her eyes were saucerlike as she stared at the heaping portion of sugar-free dirt cake. I sipped on the iced chocolate Tasha set out for me and watched Nana dig in. For once in her life, she seemed speechless.

Not for long, though. When she finished, she set her fork down. "It's good to be back. Thank you for this."

"It was all Tasha's idea," I admitted. "Though I probably would have thought about it if she hadn't."

"Mmmhmm." She patted my hand. "*Sure* you would have." She turned her head toward the register where Tasha was working. "I do love that girl. I wish she didn't have to work so hard."

"Working hard has made her who she is, Nana. You worked hard when you were her age."

"I did. Maybe that's why I relate to her so well. But I never had money worries. Those can choke you. Has she decided about living with us?"

"Not yet, but she's going ahead with the recipe book. She's very excited about it, actually."

"I'm glad. That was nice of you to get that going." She pointed to the entrance. "What's *he* doing here? I thought he got traded?"

I followed her finger to where Vlad had just entered with Xavier, Penny, and Noel. "He did. The Edge is playing Miami tonight."

"Well, there are coffee shops in Denver," she huffed. "Oh look! Brendan brought Kingston!" She clapped and whistled. "Kingston Brewer! You get over here and give Nana Booboo a hug!"

I rolled my eyes. Nana was a big fan of our hometown hero and was crushed when he was traded to Montana a few years ago. Behind the guys, Brenna was arm in arm with Kingston's wife, Taylor.

I waved, and Taylor tugged free of Brenna, wading through the people who had gathered around Kingston to welcome him back to town.

"Monty!" Taylor was little, animated, and bouncy, which had served her well on the cheer floor. We'd been on several teams together over the years. She hugged Nana first, and I stood up to welcome her back.

"Hey, Tay." I released her and tipped my chin toward her husband. "He's stealing Nana's Welcome Back party."

"Sorry. Believe me, I bet he wishes he wasn't! We had no idea this was happening. Thanks for your bow order, by the way." She bit her lip and glanced back over at the crowd, many of which had followed the players in from the street. Xavier was trying to get Penny through so she could make his toffee coffee. "Is it always such a madhouse here on game days?"

"You're welcome. Not usually this mad," I admitted.

Taylor pulled a chair over and sat between me and Nana. "How's your Worlds team coming along?"

I narrowed my eyes. "Are you trying to trick me into spilling our secrets?"

She laughed. "Nope. Kali's team has nothing on the FireVolts, especially our tumblers."

"What else is new?" I asked. "You should come to the Showcase Saturday, if you're still in town."

She nodded. "I think I will. I'll be here working remotely with my clients through Thanksgiving, then I'll have to figure out what to do from there. And I can't miss my team's competitions. We'd always hoped for this trade, but the timing was later than we expected. We'd almost given up."

"Seems like perfect timing to me," Nana huffed and leaned toward her. "Have you met that Vlad guy?"

Taylor's brows knitted together. "Yeah. He seems nice. Adorable accent."

Nana rolled her eyes. "He's a hottie, but he wasn't right for our Tasha."

Taylor looked from Vlad to Tasha and then to me. "Huh?"

"I'll explain another time," I said. "Come by the gym tomorrow. You can watch us practice."

"Oh yeah! I'd love to see Nate, too. I'm so proud of him." Taylor and Nate had been partners for almost as long as Tasha and I. "King! Come see Nana before she implodes!"

Kingston was significantly shorter than the other guys, and it was humorous to watch him slip under Brendan's arm and around Noel to get to our table.

"Nana Booboo." He grinned, then kissed her cheek. "It's been too long. You don't look a day older than the last time I saw you."

"Aw, stop it. You're too kind." She raised her eyebrows. "Did you get your Cityside Subs endorsement back?"

He laughed. "Nah. That's all Noel's now. Besides, he looks better on billboards than I do."

"He's not a Palmer City native," she protested. "At least Brewski's can take down that horrid Montana jersey of yours now. They should have kept your Voltage sweater up, if you ask me, no matter how proud they were of you."

He smiled. "You'll be happy to know that Uncle Quinn and Aunt Angie already have an Edge jersey in their possession and are in the process of switching them out."

"Good! And your cats?"

"Luc and Bourque are doing great, a little mad at us about the car ride, but we'll spoil them until they get over it. And I've got my cousin Drew lined up to spoil them when Taylor and I are away."

"Good man! Best cat sitter in town!"

I tuned out of their conversation when I caught a wisp of peach in my peripheral. Vlad was at the register, handing Tasha what would be his last letter. I'd told him she felt it was a clean break, but he'd insisted on one more, to thank her for being his friend and wishing the cards had been in their favor.

I'd resisted helping him until I realized this would give me the opportunity to also express what *I'd* been feeling. For once, this was a letter I felt good about and wanted to write. If Tasha ever did find out who was behind the words—and I had no plans to tell her—she'd be clear on how I felt about her.

CHAPTER 31
Tasha

The café was insanely busy and crowded. I wasn't sure if I regretted the timing I'd chosen or not. Nana didn't seem to mind one bit that Kingston had stolen her thunder.

When the players left, most of the crowd dispersed with them. Ten minutes after that, it was finally quiet. My shift was almost over, and then I needed to head out to the high school.

I leaned back against the counter and surveyed the café. Penny and Brenna had joined Nana and Monty at her table, and from the way they were looking at and rubbing their bellies, I could deduce what the conversation was about. Monty looked up and caught my gaze and made a funny face. He was probably super uncomfortable.

Out of nowhere, Gabby's hand closed around my wrist. "Kitchen!"

She pulled me toward the door before I could reply. It swung shut behind us. "What?" I asked.

She pointed to the pocket in my apron. "Open it."

"Later."

"Now."

"Why?"

"Because."

I narrowed my eyes. "Not good enough."

Gabby sighed and rolled her eyes. "C'mon, Tasha." Her eyes

flicked toward the door. "Just … I want to hear what he could possibly have to say, and if he made you feel bad, I'll get Noel to check him into the boards tonight."

"With his one kidney?" I asked sarcastically.

"Yes!"

"It's that important you'd risk a future of dialysis for your husband?"

"Just open the letter!"

"Fine." I tore open the flap and pulled it out. "Dearest Tasha." I squinted at the script, reading ahead and not believing what I was seeing. My heart thumped in my chest.

"What is it? What's it say? Why do you look like you've just seen a ghost?"

I peered up at her over the letter. Instead of looking concerned, she wore a satisfied smirk and was practically salivating.

I shook my head and shoved it at her. "Excuse me."

I flew through the door and stalked to Nana's table. "You!" I shouted at Monty, grabbing his wrist much like Gabby had gripped mine. "Kitchen! Now!"

His eyes widened, and I pulled at him as he began to stand. I didn't even bother to excuse my interrupting. I was confused, incensed, confused, elated, *confused* …

I got him through the door and pointed to the letter in Gabby's hand. "Explain that!"

Gabby's lips twitched. She set the letter on the counter and slipped back into the café.

Monty just stared at the paper. I positioned myself between him and the counter and crossed my arms. "Well?"

He paled, and his expressions twisted and morphed from one to another, like he wasn't sure how to react to being caught. I knew all his faces and recognized panic and torment, then worry. His eyebrows rose with hope, and then he blanched, as if he were in pain or was going to be sick.

I quoted the letter. "I'm 'the sun and the stars and every source of light' in your world. You said those exact words to me Saturday night. Do you think I'm stupid?"

His face scrunched, and he pulled at his hair. "No, Tasha. I think you're very smart."

"Apparently, I'm not smart enough, because I can't figure out why *your* words are in Vlad's letter."

Monty closed his eyes and recited, "I would sacrifice my happiness for yours, even if you never knew."

I gasped. "Has it been you the whole time?"

"Yeah. I'm sorry, Tasha. I was just trying to help the guy ... and express how I feel for someone who will never feel the same for me."

"Someone who would never feel the same for you? Who?" I picked up the letter and scanned the words for a clue.

"My heart is heavy with love unclaimed, but I shall be sustained by the memories you gave."

My hand flew to my mouth. "Me?" I whispered.

He covered his face with his hands and nodded.

Monty was in love with me.

Me!

His archenemy. Former partner. Verbal sparring opponent.

I set the letter down again and walked slowly toward him until the toes of our shoes touched. A surge of suppressed feelings rushed through me, and I pulled on his hands, revealing a reddened face and shiny eyes.

"I—I'm sorry, Tasha. I know you're sad about Vlad leaving. I—"

"Shut up," I whispered, pulling his face down to mine. "I'm not." I pressed my lips to his. His arms came around me, and he returned the kiss with fervor, then bent to lift me off my feet. I wrapped my legs around him as he carried me toward the empty counter, setting me on top of it for better leverage for kissing.

For the record, real-life kisses *can* be better than fiction.

When I couldn't breathe, I pulled away and looked up at him shyly. His smile was so big and genuine.

"I love you, Tasha. I always have. That's why I couldn't be your partner. I didn't think I could bear it if my personal feelings put you at risk. But that backfired in the worst way. I hurt you anyway—and worse, at that. I should have apologized a long time ago. I'm sorry. I will *never* hurt you again, I promise."

"You can make up for it by writing me more letters," I decided. "And you have to kiss me like that at least three times every day and make up the deficit when you travel."

"Deal."

"Shake on it?"

Simultaneously, we both spit into our right hands and slapped them together.

Yeah, it was gross. So what? I had a feeling we'd be sharing all kinds of germs in the future.

CHAPTER 32
Monty

Ridgie the Bear had the best performance of his life Wednesday night.

It wasn't too hard, since I only had to outdo myself.

But with Tasha watching, wearing the jersey I'd asked the equipment manager to make in haste, with "RIDGIE" across her shoulders over double zeroes, just like mine, I was pumped up more than ever. More than any national, international, or Worlds title I'd achieved.

Somehow, I'd won the heart of the girl I'd loved for over two decades. This bear's feelings were finally out of hibernation.

It seemed like forever until I could get to the family section to greet the kids—and Tasha. She hung back while I goofed around and posed for selfies. Vali was there—she'd been released from the hospital a few weeks ago—and I'd asked Kami if she and Ryleigh would host her and her parents.

Finally, it was Tasha's turn. I blew her a kiss and cast out an invisible fishing line. She laughed when I got Ryleigh and a few of the other kids to help me reel her from her seat to the aisle.

I bent my bear head down, and she kissed me on the nose. A collective "aw" thundered around us as the footage reached the jumbotron during the commercial timeout. My paws flew to my cheeks, and I tilted my head, giving them my best Bashful impression. Tasha wrapped her arms around me, a bear hug for the bear, and then we posed for Mags, who'd snuck away from her usual post by the players' bench.

I had a feeling Bailey was already working on an article about a certain lovestruck mascot for the team's website.

Play resumed, and the crowd forgot about us. I made the ASL sign for "I love you" and pointed to Tasha.

"Oooh, Ridgie's got a girlfriend," Ryleigh sang. "Can I be a flower girl at your wedding? I can provide references."

"Ryleigh!" her mother scolded her, but she was laughing along with the other Wags.

"What? It's true. I've been a flower girl seven times." She tipped her chin up at me. "You know how to get in touch if you decide to go with a *professional.*"

I patted her on the head, then pointed at Tasha and signed for her to call me.

As I turned to leave, the fans erupted. Kingston Brewer had scored his third goal of the game. Hats flew, and I changed course toward Taylor. She high-fived me, and I made a grabby motion with my hands and patted my shoulder. She grinned and scooted in front of me. I squatted, placed my paws on her hips, and boosted her up to sit on my shoulder.

Jared was not pleased.

"Me next!" Ryleigh demanded.

"You gotta be eighteen and sign a waiver," Jared told her.

He totally made that up. There was no rule against me picking up kids, as far as I knew, but there wasn't much I could do since I couldn't speak, and being purposely defiant in front of the public was frowned upon.

It was a good night. The Edge won 5-3 over the New Orleans Crescents, and a barrage of thousands of stuffed and plastic birds rained down on the ice after the final horn. The players were still celebrating in the dressing room after I showered and changed.

I was surprised to find Tasha waiting for me. "Don't you have to work at the crack of dawn?"

"Hello to you, too." She smirked. "Drive me home?"

"Of course." She snaked her arm around my waist, and I pulled her to me. "I'm glad you came."

"I love watching you work the crowd. Especially the kids. You've really taken this mascot thing to a whole new level."

"Just wait until All-Star Weekend. Those other stuffies better be prepared to be upstaged."

Tasha laughed. "I wouldn't expect anything less."

"I tend to put everything I've got into things that matter to me." We turned the corner. The hall ahead was empty. I let go of her and gestured from my head to my feet. "Are you ready for all of this? All Monty, all the time?"

She crossed her arms and raised her eyebrows. "Hmm. Maybe not *all* the time. Eighty percent? I do have three jobs, you know."

"I'll take every minute you can give me." I dropped my bag to the ground and reached for her. "And every kiss you'll take. Each one is a promise that I'll keep."

"Keep saying things like that, you might work up to one hundred percent." She walked into my arms and pressed her lips to mine.

CHEER SHOWCASE DAY at the Plex.

We'd be the last team to perform, but several of our athletes coached other teams, so Tasha and I hung out behind the curtain that separated the performance mat from the warm-up mats. The risers were packed, and it was standing room only up on the balcony.

Our phones buzzed about thirty minutes in. I checked mine to find a text from Evan: *I'm not going to make it. Fill in for me. My uniform is in my locker. Combo is 02-14-24.*

"Evan?" I asked.

She shook her head. "Nope. I've got one from Amelia. She says she's not going to make it. Everything I need to fill in for her is in Evan's locker?" Her voice rose with each word. "What does she mean, Monty?"

"I don't know. Evan isn't coming either. I think they're setting us up."

"But—why? Why wouldn't they want to perform after all the work they put in?"

I had my ideas, but I'd keep them to myself for now. "We'd better get changed and run through the routine. I'll text the group chat to see who's available to run it with us."

We hurried to the lockers. I grabbed the bag inside, and we raced to the coaches' locker room. I fished out the shirt and pants and gave the bag with the rest to Tasha.

"I can't believe she did this to me! She was just here, coaching her tiny and mini teams! I wondered why she was in warm-ups and not in uniform, but did it occur to me to ask?" She answered her own question. "No! No, it didn't, because *who drops out of the showcase an hour before they're set to perform?* No one!"

"Well, they did." I gently guided her toward a changing stall and nudged her in. "Get dressed so we can go save the show." She entered the stall and slammed the door. I slipped into the one next to hers so I could hear all her mutterings.

"Save the show? They're just darn lucky we made the routine and know the positions well enough to fill in for them! Save the show—ha! *They're* going to need saving the next time I see them!"

I smiled as I listened to her rant on the other side of the wall. Thursday night at practice, Evan and Amelia had stayed after to watch us work out. It felt incredibly freeing to tumble and stunt and goof around with combinations when you weren't under any pressure to perform.

And we *might* have snuck a kiss or two.

The jig was up. Our captains got to witness Coach Monsha at our mushiest.

Tasha was still ranting when I exited my stall to slick my hair into place and pull on my FireVolts Cheerdana.

"It's a good thing my abs still look good! Look at this! Way too much skin!" She pointed to her bare midsection. "Oh, why did I have to choose such a complicated hairstyle? I should have just gone with a simple pony and Cheerdanas! Easy! Simple! And requiring extra hair ties, of which I have *exactly enough,* thanks to Barfy! And have you seen all the colors in this eye shadow palette?" She held it up and waved it in the air. "I hope you still like glitter, because it's gonna be all over you for days."

"Just like old times." I grinned. "Can I help?"

She tapped her chin. "Yeah." She divided her hair into three sections, two at the crown and one at the back. "I don't have any clips. Can you be a human clip and hold the sections I'm not working on?"

"Sure." I stood behind her as she continued to ramble as she braided and twisted her hair, offering supportive and affirmative responses when required. Then I watched her apply her makeup. It took me back in time, and I was determined that we'd pull off our best performance ever.

She might be upset with our captains, but I planned to thank them profusely for this opportunity with my once-again forever partner.

CHAPTER 33
Tasha

"One more time!"

We'd moved through our formal rotations on the warm-up mats, and now we were on deck. The music for the performing team had just begun, so we had just over two and a half minutes to run through our own two-and-a-half-minute routine.

I clapped my hands above my head to signal I wanted their eyes on me. "Listen up, team! Dance full-out, mark the baskets, partner stunts go up. We're doing the pyramid. Make sure you're not in Monty's way for his tumbling passes. Everyone counts out loud. Set!"

The final run-through was a success. I high-fived Monty, who hadn't even broken a sweat. "Nice work, partner."

"Did you expect anything less?"

I swatted him. "Be nice."

"I'm always nice."

I made a face at him.

"Bring it in," he called. "FireVolts on three!" We formed a crowded circle and pushed all our hands into the middle. "One, two, three—"

"FireVolts!"

Our team was directed to line up, and we took our places, two by two, at the curtain.

Go time.

"Don't you dare let me fall," I whispered.

"Never." He kissed my forehead and hugged me tightly.

I still couldn't believe I was doing this. I hadn't performed in front of an audience in years. I was confident Monty wouldn't let me hit the floor, but what if *I* couldn't hit my sequences? Or got stage fright? Or forgot the dance moves?

I didn't have time to finish playing out all my anxious thoughts. The emcee announced our team, and we ran out. In the coaches' spot, just below the stage, were Evan and Amelia.

Those little stinkers!

I didn't have time to gel on that, either. "Set!" I shouted. The mat shook as we sprang into our starting positions.

The music began with a clip from "Everybody Groove," followed by a medley of upbeat hip hop clips. I led the dance group as the first basket tosses launched. Monty and his tumblers did their thing around us, and then we moved into position for our first partner sequence. That was followed by more tumble runs, standing tumbling, and high-level stunting from the basket groups. I met Monty in our spot for the sequence we'd re-configured, then it was into the pyramid, down to the floor, and the big finish. The last section included Monty's fifteen-second tumbling run, the final dance sequence, and our most high-level basket tosses.

The ending pose came too quick. We held for applause, then jumped up and started cheering for ourselves. No falls, and if this had been scored, we were confident there wouldn't have been any deductions.

I ran to Monty and jumped into his arms. He caught me and held me up so I could kiss him, but I didn't stop at his lips.

Nope.

I left bright red kissy prints all over his cheeks, chin, nose and forehead.

He carried me off the stage, laughing. Back behind the curtain, we were greeted by our conspiring team captains. They'd brought Nate and Taylor with them, probably for support because they were afraid of how I'd react.

Monty set me down, and I waved my finger in front of them.

"That could have been a disaster of epic proportions. You sabotaged the whole team!"

Evan and Amelia just grinned at me, then looked at each other. "Sorry, Coach."

"Let's not be too harsh on them." Monty was grinning, too. "They gave me a chance to remind everyone I'm still the best tumbler."

I rolled my eyes. "Extra laps at our next practice, and I am officially putting you two in charge of the fundraising efforts for the Florida trip. When we qualify, of course."

"Yes, Coach!"

"Now get out of my sight!" Evan and Amelia rushed away, and I turned on Nate. "Did you know about this?"

He held up his hands in defense. "I know nothing."

Taylor grinned up at him. "He's not mean enough to be party to something like this." She patted his arm.

"Hmm." I wasn't convinced.

"You were amazing out there, Tasha." Taylor beamed. "You and Monty should try out for Team USA. I know they'd love to have you both back. You've got the skills nailed down."

I shook my head. "I'm good. I much prefer the coaching side of this sport. Besides, I have three—"

"Jobs, we know," Monty finished. "And I'll be busy with the NHL playoffs. If Kingston keeps playing like he played Wednesday night, we've got a good chance to not just get to the final this season but to win it, too."

"Yeah, I hope so! Because …" Taylor placed a finger over her lips and checked to make sure no one else was listening. "I *really* want a baby-in-the-cup picture!"

"You, too?" I asked, smiling. Straight-up baby fever right now in this town.

She nodded.

"Congratulations!" Monty hugged her.

"Shhh!" I placed a finger over my lips. "They may not want that public yet!"

"Sorry!" Monty apologized.

"It's okay," Taylor assured us. "I don't think anyone heard us. Do you two have plans tonight? Brenna reserved the function room at Brewski's to watch the Edge play Montana. It's a big game for King. He's never played against Alexei Kriz before. It's going to be something."

I looked up at Monty. "We could bring Nana."

He grinned. "She'd love that."

"Great!" Taylor looped her arm through Nate's. "We'll see you there."

Once they were out of earshot, I turned to Monty. "And tomorrow …"

"Yeah?"

"I was thinking we could start packing up my apartment?"

"Yeah?"

"Yeah." I booped his nose. "But only if the third-floor room between Nana's and the turret library is available."

He scratched at the back of his neck and feigned consideration. "I'll have to check with the boss."

I locked my gaze on his and looped my arms around his neck. "I love that turret room. Best place to think and relax. And I'd like to move in before Christmas. Her place is a magical wonderland in the winter."

"It'll be even more magical with you there." He pressed his forehead to mine and pulled me closer.

"Double the magic," I whispered, pressing the tip of my nose to his. "Monsha forever?"

"Monsha forever," he promised, sweeping me off my feet with a kiss that made my toes tingle and my heart zingle.

Was zingle a word? I didn't care. I was being kissed like a heroine in a love story.

My love story.

And what a tale it was.

Epilogue

MONTY

Six months later

As always, the Worlds team closed out the Plex's annual cheer banquet. Tasha and I would be last at the podium to distribute awards to our athletes. We'd taken first place in every competition we'd entered and beaten every team at Summit, *the* competition in Orlando that featured teams from, well, all over the world.

The emcee called us to the podium, and Tasha and I took turns highlighting each of our athlete's attributes and contributions.

"Amelia." Tasha held up her certificate and trophy as Amelia strode up to the podium. "Your strong leadership, nurturing qualities, and initiative to think outside of the box and challenge others—including your coaches—is unparalleled by anyone I've coached or who's coached me. You've been an integral part of this team's success, to me personally, and to this gym—am I right, Lil' Chargers and Power Ups?"

The tiny and mini teams Amelia co-coached and their families stood up and cheered as Tasha finished her praise and handed over the award.

My turn. "Last but not least, Evan." I sighed dramatically. "What can I say? He's the best tumbler in competitive cheer. I'd

say in the world, but until he can best my twenty-two-second tumbling pass, unfortunately, he's just second best. Maybe next year." I grinned at him as he approached and patted his back. "You're a great leader, inspiring others to push one more time, two more times, however many times it takes to reach the goal. And I'd be remiss if I didn't point out your emotional support of your teammates on and off the mat. It was our honor to coach you this year, and we hope you'll be back."

I handed him his award, and Tasha hip-checked me away from the podium. I rubbed my hip and pretended it hurt, much to the delight of the audience.

"I have one more award." Tasha tipped her chin up and looked down her nose at me. "I think a certain coach deserves recognition, don't you?"

I feigned surprise, but we'd practiced this. I had an award for her, too.

"Mon-ty! Mon-ty!" The crowd chanted and I bowed.

"This guy"—she tossed her thumb at me—"has been a gym rat here since he was four years old. How do I know that, you ask? Well, I was here, too. And on Monty's first day of cheer camp, he was a *disaster.* We preschoolers who'd been lucky enough to have his big sister Melinda as our tiny cheer assistant coach expected so much more from him. He couldn't even do a forward roll!"

I will not cry. I will not cry. I'd cried when she'd rehearsed it. Got it all out.

So I thought.

"Well, I marched up to him at our first water break and told him just how bad he was and proceeded to demonstrate the correct form. He just needed the right teacher. Whatever I told him to do, he did. For sixteen years!" She laughed. "He may be a little cocky, a touch of snobby, and a bit self-centered at times." She looked over to me, and I bent my arms up in a shrug for the audience. "But when you need anything, anything at all, he'll be there. He takes exceptional care of his Nana." We both waved to her. She dabbed her eyes and waved back. "He's besties with dozens of kids going through treatments for childhood cancer and other conditions, and he's proven here at the gym that he can sub in for anyone, anytime."

Here was where I was supposed to wave elbow-elbow-wrist-wrist, royalty style, but instead I was losing my cool. Between her words about me and the speech I had planned for her, my emotions had a mind of their own.

"This award not only exemplifies his attributes but also his willingness to model and demonstrate them, like when he pulled in Ryleigh Spencer to fill in at a qualifying competition. Monty, Ryleigh, you made dreams come true that day for the Circuit Breakers. They hit zero, took first place, and received a gold bid to Nationals, where they took first place." She paused for applause. I leapt off the stage and ran out to Ryleigh. She put down her Lofty-size pink and blue Magic Charm shake real quick and I almost shuddered at how much sugar was in that thing. I pushed the thought aside and boosted her onto my shoulder so she could bask in the praise.

"To Coach Monty, I present the award for Best Clutch Performance." I set Ryleigh down and strode back up to the stage to rejoin Tasha at the podium. She handed me the certificate, and I leaned down to kiss her.

Then I hip-checked her away from the podium.

Gently, of course. We'd rehearsed it.

"As Coach Tasha mentioned, we met on the cheer mat the summer before prekindergarten. Even then, she was a smart know-it-all and could back up her bragging by outperforming anyone who challenged her. Best forward roll? Tasha. Best walkover? Tasha. But she wasn't just the best, she was the first. For every new skill, she was the first to ring the bell, and she'd prance in front of the team to demonstrate. And she was the first —and only—girl to steal my heart."

"Awwwwwwwww." All the athletes and their families chorused.

"It took me over two decades to tell her so, but it's the truth. I remind her every day with fancy words and love letters. I even taught myself cursive. Right, babe?"

Tasha sighed and rolled her eyes, but she was smiling. She

nodded in affirmation as the audience collectively swooned at the admission of my romantic gestures.

I grinned and continued. "What she didn't tell you about the day we met was that we partnered up for a stunt. She pushed and poked and prodded me until my form was perfect, and of course, we were the best. The only pair the coach didn't have to adjust. So I asked her to be my partner forever."

"Awwwwwwwwwww."

"We spit on our hands and shook on it. Today, I'm honored to present her with the Best Partner award." I handed her the certificate and a bouquet of peach carnations I'd stowed under the podium. Poking out of the bouquet was a small stuffed hedgehog. "There's no one better. And if she'll have me, I'd like to renew that promise of 'partners forever,' right here, right now, with you all here to witness it."

I hip-checked her one more time to push her farther from the podium, but instead of holding her hand and raising it into the air as we'd planned, I dropped to one knee.

"Tasha, will you marry me and seal us as Monsha forever?"

As I expected, gasps of *aw,* high-pitched squeals, whistles, and other such cheers became the soundtrack to my proposal.

Tasha's mouth dropped open in surprise, but she was quick to nod in the affirmative.

But instead of saying yes, a look of confusion marred her face. "Penny?"

"Huh?"

She pointed, and I turned to look behind me. Penny was standing in the wings with Xavier. She was wearing a long, flowy dress in FireVolts colors and was clutching her belly. I'd invited them, but Xavier declined, texting that Penny wasn't feeling well. But here they were.

"Say yes, Tasha!" Penny called. "My water broke! I gotta goooooo!"

"What—oh! Yes!"

I slid the ring on her finger and stood up to kiss her and spin her around.

Standing ovation, as expected. To the tune of "Mon-sha! Mon-sha!"

I set her down, and we spoke at the same time. "Hospital?"

"Yes! Wait! Nana first. And there's something I need to pick up at home," I added as we hurried off the stage.

We reached the parking lot in record time, and I stopped the wheelchair short when I caught sight of my truck.

"Montgomery!" Nana exclaimed. "Your vehicle is oozing birdseed!"

Each of the four windows were open to allow the birdseed to trickle out and down the side of the doors. The bed was filled to overflowing with the substance, and little puddles were forming on the ground alongside it.

Tasha was laughing, and I shot her a disapproving glare. She jingled her keys. "Good thing we drove separately."

"Freaking Zaki Marsch," I muttered. "Change of plans, Nana."

We followed Tasha to her car, and I drove us home, dreaming up schemes to get back at the clown who mildly inconvenienced us for the sake of payback.

He had no idea who he was messing with.

Game on.

"I'm going to be an aunty!" Tasha sang from the back seat. She held up her left hand so I could see her diamond in the mirror. "And a wife! Best day ever!"

"And an author," Nana said, pointing at the box sitting on the front stoop. "I believe your books have arrived."

I pulled into the garage and set up Nana's wheelchair as my fiancée helped her out of the car. She'd lost weight eating Tasha's food and was walking much better, but she tired out quickly.

"Get Nana settled, and I'll bring your books in," I suggested.

"Will do. Thanks." She lifted her chin for a kiss.

If she was expecting a quick peck, she was engaged to the wrong guy. I swept her into my arms, held her tight, and dipped her low.

"Get a room, you two!" Nana teased. "Whew! I need a fan after watching that. Good thing you didn't pull that move on stage, Monty."

I twisted Tasha up and squeezed her to my side. "I planned to, but someone had to get all water breaky on us."

Tasha, wearing a smile and a deep pink blush from our kiss,

shook her head as she pushed Nana into the elevator. We rode it up, and when the doors opened, I hurried toward the front of the house and out the front door.

The yellow box was heavy and bore the Tia Gia logo. I carried it inside and placed it on the coffee table by Nana's recliner.

Tasha stared at it.

Nana pointed to her sewing basket. "Monty. Scissors."

I retrieved the scissors and cut the tape along the creases.

And snuck in a soft forehead kiss before I stepped away.

Tasha continued to stare at the box.

"C'mon, Tasha. Open the box before your niece turns one!" Nana encouraged, as only Nana could.

"You do it, Monty," Tasha said. "You're the one who made it happen."

"It's all your content, Tasha." I picked up my phone. "Let's do an unboxing video."

"Okay. Give me a sec." She closed her eyes and took a deep breath. "Ready."

"Three, two, one ... go!"

With care, Tasha opened the flaps and pulled out a copy of her book. As she turned it over in her hands, her smile grew. Pure joy.

She held the cover up and locked her eyes on my phone like a deer in headlights.

It wasn't your typical unboxing video, but she could voice over it later or set it to music.

"This is amazing." She handed the book to Nana. "Have one."

Nana received it graciously and hugged it to her chest. "I'll read it cover to cover and let you know if I find any typos," she pledged seriously.

Tasha laughed. "Thanks." She turned to me. "Can we go now?"

"Grab a book for Penny, and I'll be right back." I hustled to my room and returned with a pink "Welcome Baby" gift bag.

"Aw! You got a gift for my sister's baby!" Tasha clapped. "Uncle Monty rocks."

I liked the sound of that.

"What did you get her?" Nana asked.

"I think you'll both approve." I reached into the bag and pulled out the peach onesie with a pumpkin on it. Inside the pumpkin were the words *Pumpkin Spice Spice Baby*.

Tasha snorted, and Nana hooted deep from her gut until they were both roaring. I just stood there grinning like the fool I was.

A fool in love.

I still stood by my claim that coffee was poison, but I knew how to compromise.

That laugh and smile on Tasha's face?

I'd do anything for that.

Maybe even try that vile brown liquid.

But that was for another day.

Bonus Epilogue

Tasha

July 4th

I surveyed the trays of desserts lining the counters of Nana's massive kitchen and wiped my brow. Four different options, all much-loved and highly rated selections from my best-selling cookbook. Plus Tia Gia's Lemonade Crispies for Penny. They were her newest favorite.

"I think we did it, Fyvie. So what else am I forgetting?"

Our beloved baker tucked a loose auburn curl behind her ear. "To enjoy yerself? The whole town's at Gretzky Pond for the fireworks."

I shook my head. "You go. I'll get this cleaned up." I nodded toward the entryway where Monty was sauntering in. "Help is on the way."

He crossed his arms and leaned against the arch that separated the two rooms. "If by 'help' you mean official taste-tester who also doubles as the world's best dishwasher loader and starter, then yes, I can help."

Fyvie and I exchanged a glance and burst out laughing. The

Floody Bubbles Incident, or as Monty called it, The Great Dishwasher Debacle, had spread all over town and was now an official drink at the Coffee Loft. Gabby's recipe of seltzer water with a pump of blue raspberry flavoring was an instant hit.

Monty turned his nose up at it and refused to acknowledge the drink's existence.

"I'll see yeh tomorrow then." Fyvie slipped off her apron and slung it over her shoulder. "Keep the cat out of 'ere, eh?"

Monty shook his head. "He's got free rein. I bought a big fridge for all this and future events. It's in the garage."

Fyvie shrugged. "Okay. Well, see you tomorrow, then." We each hugged her goodbye, and I walked her to the front door to see her off.

When I returned, the kitchen was empty and three trays were missing. I assumed Monty had already made a few trips with the desserts to the garage. I picked up a tray and turned—almost right into him.

"Whoa!" He raised his empty hands and scooted backward just in time to avoid wearing two dozen gooey brownies.

"Sorry!" I took a deep breath, grateful for his quick reaction.

"It's okay." He placed his hands by mine on either side of the tray. "I got this. You should go to bed. You need your beauty rest for the big day tomorrow."

I snorted. "Oh really? And you don't?" I poked his bicep, held snug by his white cotton T-shirt. "Your face might scare the children."

His lips twitched, and he quirked a brow. "Kids love me. The man and the bear. Try again."

I rolled my eyes and regretted ever telling him out loud that he wasn't too much all those months ago. He'd been pushing those limits since.

Quite adorably, of course, but the man could be *impossible.*

"I'm too tired to spar," I conceded. "Fine. You get this done, and I'll head to bed."

He set the tray on the nearest counter and opened his arms for a hug. I squeezed him tight, and we just held each other for a few moments. Then he tipped my chin up and brought his lips down to mine. A gentle brush, just enough to make contact and send a shiver through my body. "Good night, partner," he rumbled.

"Good night, partner," I whispered back, reluctantly stepping out of his embrace.

Monty never let go first.

He placed another kiss to my forehead. "I'll see you at the barn at two o'clock. Don't be late."

"Wouldn't dream of it. I love you, you big bear." I booped him on the nose.

"I love you, too." He squeezed my hand and then let it go. "Sweet dreams. Of me."

I laughed. "Of course. Good night!" I turned to leave and blew a kiss over my shoulder. He caught it and slapped it to his cheek.

He was something else.

And he was mine.

Tomorrow, it would be official.

The grandfather clock in the back hall was chiming a quarter till nine as I hurried up the stairs. It was still early, but I was exhausted after a busy week of work and wedding prep. And I still had a few things to do.

I opened the door to my room, and my eyes went immediately to the bed. On the peach duvet, leaning up against the throw pillow, was a cream-colored envelope. I grinned, knowing instantly what it was.

Since Thanksgiving, Monty had been writing me letters. At least one each week: some long, some short, some funny, some heartfelt. His Valentine letter was the first in cursive. Oddly, it was similar to my sister's handwriting. I wondered if she'd helped him learn. He'd taught himself script to "prove" his love, loyalty, and devotion. Unneeded, of course. The man was the most loving, loyal, and devoted I'd ever known.

Well, except for maybe Xavier. I might concede a tie there. No one had ever seen a cuter baby-girl dad than that guy. And he treated my sister like the royalty that she now was.

To my favorite (and only) prickly hedgehog,

So, it was going to be one of *those* letters. I grinned.

From the moment we met, I knew you were going to be a big part of my world. Most people are skeptical when we tell our story, unable to believe that four-year-olds can remember anything, never mind so clearly. Let them think what they want. We know it's true, and really, who else matters? You are my sun, and I am merely the moon, reflecting and basking in all your beauty and goodness.

I've never been afraid to love you, Tasha. I loved you as a preschooler, as a kid, as a teen, and I love the woman you've become, and are. Loving you is, and always has been, easy. Like tumbling. It came naturally, and I was good at it. But unlike tumbling, I messed up, and I will forever regret that. But it's part of our story, and here we are today. So I will work on forgiving myself for the pain I caused you.

Until I messed up, you were the only person alive other than Nana that I knew for sure loved me and wanted to spend time with me. My parents didn't love me the way parents should, and I know now that was because of their grief, but for a long time, I felt unlovable, unworthy, and unwanted.

These feelings were magnified when I realized I was in love with you. You were always pursuing other athletes—some with talent, some with money, all with charisma. But I couldn't see what they had that I didn't. I was—and still am—handsome, charming, talented, rich, and a total catch. You craved security and peace and I could give you those things—and more. I struggled to try to understand why you didn't want me.

I was right in front of you the whole time, but you didn't see me. I wanted to jump in front of you and wave my hands and shout, "Tasha, are you blind? Do you know how much money I have? How much more I'll get when I turn twenty-five (we are filthy rich now, by the way)? How much I love you?"

The answer to that question is more than life itself. And I will never, ever, ever take for granted one moment we have together.

After tomorrow, you'll be stuck with me in your sight forever. I'll be the stamp to your envelope. The sticky residue you can't remove from the price sticker on your favorite book. The sap on your Christmas tree. The marshmallow in those lemonade crispers.

I can't thank Nate enough for getting a "real" job last summer. I was going to do anything and everything it took to mend our friendship. Becoming roommates strengthened my resolve—even though I had no clue how to go about earning your trust again. By the grace of God, I did. You forgave me, and I need you to know I won't ever take that grace for granted or do anything to jeopardize your trust—or our relationship—ever again.

I look forward to our life together as official "partners forever." I even got a tattoo to commemorate the occasion.

Don't ask to see it until tomorrow night, though. It's for Wifey's eyes only.

Sleep well, my Tasha. I love you more than I could ever express with my fancy words, toe-curling kisses, or smoldering stares. And I can't wait to spend the rest of my life loving you in all the ways you deserve.

Till tomorrow,
Your Monty

Oh my heart!

The man was everything—sweet, loving, loyal, a tad insufferable … and he was *mine*.

I slid the letter back into the envelope and padded over to my open closet. There, my wedding gown hung in its garment bag. Below, in a take-out canvas tote from the Coffee Loft, my wedding shoes sat on top of a pile of similar cream-colored envelopes.

I'd decided Nana's way of storing love letters in a shopping bag was sufficient, and thus began my collection in a bag from the place that held so many of our mutual memories.

I wasn't much of a writer, but tonight, I had something for Monty.

Checking the clock, I knew I'd have to act fast. Monty always went into Nana's room at nine o'clock to say good night and read a chapter of the Bible to her. I dropped the new letter into the bag and pulled out a light blue envelope. Counting on my hunch that

I didn't think he'd break his routine, I poked my head out of my room and stealthily crept down the hall to Nana's door.

Yes! His deep voice was muffled, but he for sure was in there. I raced to the stairs and down one flight to his room and slipped the envelope under his door. Heart pounding, I ran back the way I came, took the stairs two at a time, and sprinted back to my room, closing the door gently behind me.

Mission accomplished.

Monty

July 5th

The warm summer rays reflected on the sparkling surface of Lake Moonshine. I stood on the veranda next to Nana's wheelchair with a blue envelope in my hand as we gazed out over the lawn at the reception below.

"It's her best recipe yet," I bragged. "Award-winning, for sure."

"Stop teasing the old woman and read it already," Nana demanded. "I'm not getting any younger."

I grinned. "What if she wants to keep it private?" It wasn't often that I got to hold anything above Nana's head, so I was enjoying myself dangling this carrot.

She waved her hand flippantly. "That girl tells me everything. And if it's what I think it is, I already know."

"Huh?"

"You don't think she came to me for marital advice?" Nana smirked up at me. "I lived in matrimonial bliss for decades, and Tasha married *you*. No offense, but sometimes you're a brat."

My smile widened. I wore that title with pride.

"Go on, read it," Nana coaxed. "She won't mind. And I'm dying to hear what she did with all my thoughts and recommendations."

I snorted. "All right. But if she *didn't* want me to share it, it's your backside on the kicking block."

"That's not even a thing. *Read.*"

"Yes, ma'am." I cleared my throat and removed the pale blue sheets of paper from their matching envelope. "Monsha Marriage Recipe. Prep time: Twenty-one years. Cook time: Till death do us part. Ingredients: love, faithfulness, trust, respect, honesty, communication, humility, patience, a sense of humor, loyalty, perseverance, grace, compassion, date nights, love of children, love of the less fortunate, love of our adversaries, love of God.

"Instructions: Mix all ingredients together and work them until partnership is dissolved by natural causes. Note: In case of burns or inconsistencies, always admit wrongs and strive to do better. Always forgive and offer grace when intentions are best. Offer compliments and constructive criticism, but never dole out either with a mean heart. If said heart is hurting, seek love and comfort from your partner. Balance the mixture by allowing each other's strengths to shine and pick up the slack for each other's weaknesses. Serve each other always, with joy and a happy heart."

Nana sighed. "And that girl says she can't write. That's beautiful, Monty."

I sniffed. "There's more." I shuffled the pages. Nana didn't need to hear the mushy stuff that came next, but at the end Tasha had nailed future potential conflicts and offered advice on how to handle them. She knew herself—and me—so well, and I was super impressed.

"Are you going to share it, or do I have to grab it from you?"

I mimicked her sigh. "I *guess* I can read it. But it's your head on the chopping block …"

"Ha! You got your cliché correct. Good boy!"

I held back a smile. I did love teasing her. "Always. Okay, here's the rest from Tasha: Having known you as long as I can remember, and being competitive with you for the entire duration, I can see that eking into our marriage and home. I see us potentially getting into trouble competing—don't even try to best me in the kitchen—see what I mean? Overscheduling—one event may not be more important than another, so if we're double- or triple-booked, let's talk that out. We're both workaholics, and we'll need to make time for each other beyond playing cards with Nana."

"Hey!"

"She goes on: No offense to Nana, of course. I love her like my own. But we need time for just *us*. Penny and Xavier are gifting us three weekend stays at the Honeymoon Tree House at the Top of the Falls Resort in Elk Creek Falls. Let's get those booked ASAP. And let's make some babies. We've wanted kids since we were kids. Remember how we used to 'parent' Parfait? We were awesome. And you *know* we're going to out-parent all our friends, so why wait to get started on that?"

Nana whistled, so I paused. My cheeks burned just a little, but I kept reading.

"Monty, you tell me I'm your sun. But during those years when we didn't talk, I had zero light in me. I became one with the dark. Nothing was right, and nothing *went* right. You'd always been the positivity in our partnership, and without you, there was no brightness to light my way and remind me that the world can be a wonderful place. I'm so lucky that God brought us back together and that this is my life now, with you. I'm living all my dreams, and I know you are, too. It's because we're better together. We always have been. And we always will be."

Water in my eyes caused Tasha's words to blur. I swallowed back a lump that dried up my throat and waited for Nana's reaction.

Her eyes were closed. She was quiet for a minute, and when she opened them, a tear fell from each, tracing her cheeks until they reached her jawbone and she wiped them away.

I replaced the letter in the envelope, slid it back into my inner jacket pocket, and squatted down to give her a hug. "You okay?"

She nodded. "It's a reminder that good can come from bad, if you look for it. If I hadn't had the stroke ... we may not be here today."

"Oh, Nana." I squatted and turned her face to look at me, eye to eye. "Don't say that. We would have found another way."

She shook her head. "Maybe. But I'm glad it played out the way it did. And I hope you have a whole bunch of babies for us all to spoil and love on."

I kissed her forehead. "That's the plan."

"Don't look now, but your parents are headed this way," she warned.

I stiffened. They'd been at the ceremony, and the rehearsal dinner, and all of the events, of course. My wedding was an important social event, after all. But except for a couple of handshakes from my father and air kisses from my mother, there hadn't been any other interaction with me or Tasha.

"Stand up," Nana dictated. "Wipe your tears away, and summon that cordial aloofness you got from your father. Be calm, graceful, and businesslike. You got this."

"I got this," I repeated. I was prepared for this, thanks to Nana and Tasha. Last week we'd brainstormed and visualized all of the possible scenarios involving my parents. They weren't toxic; they were just absent. Emotionally neglectful. I'd prayed that would change as I grew older, but as a certain country song goes, sometimes God's greatest gifts are unanswered prayers.

Although the little boy in me still held out hope that my prayers would be answered and they'd suddenly see me.

Like Tasha did.

"Montgomery." My dad's greeting was smooth and clipped as he stepped onto the veranda. "Congratulations again, son."

And like the handful of times before, he stuck out his hand. And like every time before, I shook it. Tasha had wondered aloud if he craved physical touch and that was the only way he knew how to offer it.

"Dad. Mom," I said. My mother hugged me, and again, her lips didn't touch my cheeks.

"Don't want to get lipstick on your face," she said, as if reading my thoughts.

"I don't care about that," I whispered, immediately regretting my words and letting the façade crack. I straightened to full height and stepped back. "Thank you for coming."

"Wouldn't miss it," Dad said. "We're incredibly proud of you and wish you and Tasha a lifetime of happiness."

I blinked at him. I'd longed to hear those words my whole life. "Uh. Thanks."

Mom patted my bicep. "So proud. And Mindy would be, too." A corner of her mouth turned up into an almost smile.

Trying not to choke up, I managed to respond. "I wish she was here."

Mom did smile now, and she turned toward the lawn, sweeping her arm in a flourish. "She's here, Monty. I can feel her spirit."

I was blinking again, but it wasn't because I was surprised this time. I quickly swiped at my eyes.

My parents didn't get to see me cry. Not anymore.

"Hey, Monty." Nana tugged at my jacket. "Isn't it almost time for line dances?"

I lifted my wrist to eye level and pretended to check my Rolex. "Would you look at that? It is. Thanks for the reminder, Nana."

"Anytime. Now give me your jacket and go find your bride."

"Apologies," I said to my parents as I slipped off my jacket and pulled at my bow tie so that it hung free. "We'll catch up later?"

I didn't give them a chance to respond as I bolted down the steps and toward Tasha, who was out on the dock posing for photos with her bridesmaids. Arywn Baughn, her dressmaker, arranged Tasha's dress each time as Penny, Gabby, Brenna, and Amelia crowded around her.

I watched from the grass as the photographer and others snapped pictures. My girl was the most beautiful, the most animated, and the most … heck, the most *everything.*

My everything.

Tasha's eyes found mine and locked into place. She grinned and said something to the ladies, then began walking toward me, her voluminous dress billowing around her in the light breeze.

"Line dance time?" she asked.

"You know it. You've got some lipstick on your face."

"I … huh?"

I took her face in my hands and pressed my lips to hers. "There. Now it's on my face."

She snorted. "Sorry. This kind doesn't transfer."

"What sort of witchcraft is that, and why haven't you used it before?"

She shrugged. "Maybe I like my lipstick on your face. Just not today, though." She winked. "Wynnie, can you help get my skirt off? I don't want to mess anything up. I plan to wear it every five years when we renew our vows."

Arwyn nodded as she smoothed out her own dress, some sailor-suit-inspired ensemble that made her look like she just stepped off the *Titanic.* "Sure thing. But let's not do it by the water?"

"Lead the way." Tasha looped her arm through mine, and we followed Arwyn to the side of the lawn, out of the way of the guests and in the shade cast by ponderosas.

The dressmaker, using some kind of hook tool, began unbuttoning the line of pearls at Tasha's waist, and the skirt began to fall. She stepped back and frowned. "Monty, can you help hold the fabric as I unbutton it? I think between the two of us we can keep it off the ground and free from grass stains."

"Sure." As I moved into place, I looked up and caught Zaki Marsch watching us. Our prank war had turned into a fun friendship. After the Edge's playoff run ended, I'd waited until he'd gone back to Canada to exact my revenge for the birdseed. I'd stolen Xavier's phone when he wasn't paying attention and scrolled his contacts. Sure enough, he'd stored Zaki's garage code. I'd snuck over to his house in the middle of the night, drained his hot tub, and with the help of my new friends at the marine store, we'd transformed it into a paradisal environment for a small school of koi that I thought looked awfully lonely at the store.

The best part was that he got to watch me set it all up. At three o'clock in the morning Montreal time.

I was expecting a pretty epic retaliation. But so far, nothing.

I waved at him. "Zaki! Come help!"

Arwyn froze. "No," she whispered. "Not him. He's a *disaster.*" Her eyes widened. "Sorry! I didn't mean to say that out loud." She smacked her forehead and groaned.

I laughed. "I'll keep him in line. It's just a dress. We got this."

Arwyn looked petrified.

Tasha tried to reassure her. "He'll be careful, or Monty will beat his butt. Heck, if he ruins my dress, *I'll* beat his butt!"

"Who's beating butts?" Zaki asked. "Hey, Wynnie-bon. You made this?"

"I did," she said tightly. "Are your hands clean?"

He held them up, palms out. "No frosting, butter, beer, or butter beer."

Arwyn snorted. "Good. Kindly help Monty and ensure the skirt doesn't touch the ground as I unhook it from the pearls. And none of your funny business or pranks, got it?"

Zaki nodded solemnly. "I think my pranking days are behind me. I'm out of ideas."

"No kidding?" I asked.

"Yeah, I think so." He sighed. We each grabbed a handful of

fabric on each side of Tasha as Arwyn returned to unhooking the pearls.

Tasha frowned but didn't comment. A few minutes later, the puffy skirt and its bustled train were in Arwyn's arms. Zaki saluted her and went back to his table.

"I'm glad he stopped the pranks," Arwyn said. "I still have nightmares of him ruining my tea gown with a cinnamon roll."

"That was an accident," Tasha reminded her.

"Collateral damage of a prank," Arwyn argued. "And no remorse. He calls me 'Wynnie-bon,' like Cinnabon. Get it?"

Tasha snorted. "I wondered about that. Well, whatever it was, he's done pranking. I overheard Xavier tell Penny that Zaki's wife got full custody of their girls, and he's devastated."

"What?" I asked. That couldn't be true. His twins were four or five years old and worshipped their daddy. "He's like the best father. Definition of 'hashtag girl dad.'"

Tasha nodded. "He travels too much. And the court *always* sides with the mother unless there are serious red flags. She gets full custody, and he can visit in the offseason."

"Visit in the offseason?" Arwyn asked. "Don't they all live in Denver?"

"Nope," Tasha said. "She moved back in with her parents in Montreal."

"That's terrible." Arwyn said what I was thinking.

I felt sick to my stomach. I turned and found Zaki, sitting at his table and chatting with some kids who were obvious fans of the star player. He was smiling, but his smile didn't reach his eyes. "Why is he here?"

"The girls are on vacation with their mother and her family. He'll be heading back up next week. It's so sad."

"It is," I agreed and pulled her to me. "Never leave me, okay?"

"Never," she promised.

Arwyn cleared her throat, reminding me she was still there. "I, um, will bring this back into the house and hang it up. If you'll just step out of the petticoats, we can see if the bottom layer of the dress needs to be steamed before you head out to the dance floor."

Arwyn handed me the bundle of fabric and untied some

strings at Tasha's back. My bride leaned on me, and I held her steady as she stepped out of even more skirts.

The dressmaker stepped back and surveyed the remaining skirt: a full, calf-length taffeta thing that was pinched into poufs like Tasha's duvet.

"Cute," I complimented.

"Yes," Arwyn agreed. "And the fabric isn't crushed like I feared. You're good to go, Tasha."

"Thanks, friend." She gave Arwyn a hug. "We'll see you out on the dance floor?"

"Maybe," she said, pulling the wedding dress skirt from my arms into hers. "Have fun out there."

I bent my arm and offered it to Tasha. "Ready to cut a rug? Er, parquet?" I asked.

"I was born ready, partner!" Tasha grinned and booped my nose.

I loved it when she did that.

"Great! One more stop." I towed her over to the bar, where Drew Brewer was mixing drinks.

He saw me coming, reached underneath, and tossed me a bag.

"What's that?" Tasha asked.

"Wardrobe change." I unbuttoned my beige vest and handed it to her. With a wink, I pulled out a custom-made vest I'd ordered from the tailor who'd made my All-Star game Ridgie suit. I held it up for her inspection.

Tasha doubled over laughing. "That's so perfect!"

The vest was screen-printed with images of both Edge mascots, Ridgie the Bear and Percy the Pigeon. I gladly took full credit for the second mascot, seeing as how it was my efforts to comedically trap it that made it a thing.

It was time to remind everyone here how awesome I was.

Not that I needed their praise or approval, but I'd wanted it when I ordered the vest.

Now I knew all that I ever needed, all that I cared about, was Tasha's approval.

I buttoned it up and took her hand. "Let's Hustle." I signaled to the DJ and led Tasha toward the dance floor. The instrumental mood music shifted into the iconic song, and we joined the Boomers already gathering.

As it faded out, we shared a grin and scooted over to the DJ's table, where we had a fun surprise in store for our family and friends.

"All right, ladies and gentlemen!" The DJ lowered the music as we stepped into position and initiated the first part of our plan. "Evan and Nate, you're needed in the center of the floor. Our bride and groom have a special treat for their guests. Let me just get them their props." He handed me a Cheerdana that said "Monsha Forever" with my and Tasha's faces between the words. Tasha got a cheer bow I'd had Taylor make special. Over the center knot was a button with the same picture. The left-side tail was vinyl'd with the word "Monsha" and the right side with "Forever." Instead of a hair tie, Taylor had glued on something called an alligator clip so that it could easily slide into Tasha's hair behind her tiara. I smiled at the absence of the hair tie, thinking of my klepto cat and the collection I'd found under Nana's recliner.

The music stopped completely, and confused faces turned our way.

The guys hurried up to us, and Tasha stepped in front of me. We hadn't practiced this, but I was confident we could pull it off.

"Don't drop me," Tasha whispered.

"Never," I promised. I placed my hands on her waist, and we waited as Evan and Nate rolled up their sleeves and squatted into position facing each other.

I held her steady as she placed a foot into each of their waiting hands and let go as they hoisted her up, dress and all, into a full extension.

Now it was my turn.

I got under the dress as the guys brought her feet together. As they held onto her heels and toes, I secured my fingers around her arches. Evan and Nate stepped away to thunderous applause, and I could only imagine Tasha's grin as we pulled off the most epic partner stunt.

Of course, I had to show off even more. I pulled her feet

together until they touched and grabbed them both with my right hand and let go with the left.

I waved to family and friends with my now-free left hand and basked in the gasps, whistles and "Montgomery, you put that girl down *now,*" from Nana.

Since it was Nana, I obliged.

Nate and Evan spotted Tasha as I brought her down and set her on the ground.

She turned and hugged me fiercely. "That was incredible!"

"You're incredible." I was getting choked up. I kissed her like it was my job and dipped her for the cameras.

I twisted her back up and reached back to take a headset from the DJ. "Now that we've got your attention, we'd like to teach you a new line dance. Fun for all ages. Can I get my assistants to the front, please?"

My bestie Britlynne had finished her treatments and had finally become healthy enough to go back to dancing last month. She followed my new bestie Ryleigh up to the DJ booth, where they retrieved bags of Monsha Forever buttons that matched the one on Tasha's bow.

Once I was certain everyone in the vicinity had pinned one to their shirt or dress strap, I waved the girls back to where Tasha and I were standing. They took their places on each side of us. After the first full rotation, they'd go out into the crowd and help those less coordinated to learn the steps.

"All right, you old folks know this tune. It's called the 'Monster Mash.' But I have some friends who make cheer music, and for a modest donation they were able to update it with new lyrics—written by me, of course—and some fun effects. Family, friends, Tasha and I, along with our talented assistants, present the world premiere of the Monsha Mash. Are you ready?"

"YEAH!"

"All right, before we hit you with the lyrics, we're going to learn the steps to the instrumental version." I spun on my heel so that my back was toward the crowd. Tasha, Brit, and Ryleigh followed suit.

I pointed to the right. "It starts just like the Cupid Shuffle. The first thing we're going to do is four steps right. No grape-vining; sorry if you're old and like that move. Step out with your right foot, then slide your left in to meet it. Three more times. Great job! Now clap and use your right foot to step back. Slide your left foot to your right. Right foot back again, but leave that left foot where it is and use it to stomp twice."

The grumblings were expected. I turned around so I could monitor their progress. "All right, watch the ladies here. We'll take it from the top so far. Right step one, two, three, four, clap once. Step back right, left, right. Stomp left, left. That's it! You're getting it!"

It wasn't pretty, but it was progress.

"Looking better! One more time, then we'll finish it." I turned around. "Right step one, two, three, four, clap once. Step back right, left, right. Stomp left, left. Bring your right foot forward to meet your left. Wave your hands in the air above your head and yell 'Woo!'"

"Woo!"

"Nice, nice. To finish it off, we're going to bring those hands down and straight in front of us and quarter turn to our left. Let your hands hang from your wrist and zombie walk for four steps. That's it. You got it! We're covering a lot of the floor here. Now, from the top."

We did six more rotations, and it looked like most people were getting it. "All right, are you all ready for the song?"

"Yeah!"

"All right! When the lyrics start, we begin. Ready?"

"Ready!"

I looked at Tasha. She grinned back and wiped the beads of sweat from her forehead.

Hmm. Maybe I should commission a personalized Cheerdana for her.

Yeah, I should. With my face and sweet nothings scrolled all over it.

Later. It was time to show off our collaboration. My words, her moves.

Fun for all.

"Get ready! And ... go!"

We were working in the gym late one night
When teammates arrived, right on time
They gathered around, with big wide eyes
And waited patiently for our big surprise

We did the Mash (The Monsha Mash)
It was a cheer gym blast (The Monsha Mash)
We did it with sass (The Monsha Mash)
We did the Monsha Mash

From our tumble mats to the balcony high
To the main cheer floor, where the flyers fly
The all-stars appeared from their respective homes
To watch all the fun from the FireVolts

They did the Mash (The Monsha Mash)
It was a cheer gym blast (The Monsha Mash)
They did it with sass (The Monsha Mash)
They did the Monsha Mash

It went on for a few more verses and ended to the expected cheers, whistles and compliments. I took Tasha's hand, and the little girls joined us for a deep, theatrical bow. Then I twisted her around for another grand dip.

"Partners forever," I whispered.

"Partners forever," she replied, gazing back up at me with the love I'd craved for as long as I could remember.

"I love you," we said simultaneously, then I lowered my lips for another kiss.

I couldn't wait to start our epic life together.

SEW MATCHA
IN LOVE
COFFEE LOFT
SERIES
KERRY EVELYN

To all the hearts starting over after losing love:
It will find you when you least expect it.

CHAPTER 1

Arwyn

My drafty sewing room had nothing on the biting wind of an early January day on Main Street in Palmer City. My brain froze with each new step. Why had I chosen to walk when I could have driven?

Oh, right. My chosen word for this year was "engage."

What had I been thinking?

Engage with nature, I could do.

Maybe.

People were another story.

The rhythm of my footfalls matched my breath, forming puffy clouds with each word I muttered just loud enough for myself to hear.

One.

More.

Step.

You.

Can.

Do.

It.

I said it over and over, passing business after business after business, their windows still framed in Christmas lights and featuring holiday displays. I crossed Prospect Road with a longing look up the block toward the bookstore on the left and the

general store on the right. A new book was always a treat, and sweet Janey and her husband, Simon, would send me off with a bag of sweets, but knowing me, with people I actually liked to people with, I'd stick around chatting and then be late for my appointment.

I plodded up the block, stopping just short of the Coffee Loft. Its line stretched out the door to its neighbor, Shanna's Soda Shoppe—my home away from home.

It was early afternoon, so the place was virtually empty. I settled myself onto the '50s-era vinyl and chrome barstool and reached underneath the counter to hang my purse on the shiny silver hook. Most of the town's children were back to school after Christmas break. Toddlers were napping, the retired crowd had long since consumed their lunch, and anyone who didn't have to be out in the biting cold was smart enough to stay inside.

Which was exactly where *I'd* be if Tasha Biddington hadn't insisted on meeting me here. Though she had a thriving meal-catering business now, she still filled in from time to time at the Coffee Loft next door, which was where she was today. It was a game day for the Denver Edge, and Tasha's brother-in-law had to get his magical coffee or something. NHL players in a small-town coffee shop caused quite a stir, and Tasha, her sister, Penny, and their cousin Gabby—also married to an Edge player—helped out before they headed to the game.

Normally, I wouldn't go anywhere near the place on a game day, but Tasha was so happy with the vintage gown I'd restyled for her wedding last summer that she wanted me to custom-make a Regency gown for her sister to wear at the Biddingtons' annual Valentine gala, so we needed to get started, like, yesterday. In this part of the state, the gala was second only to Denver's Once Upon a Dream Ball, and I'd give my eyeteeth to attend either. For now, I'd have to be content creating the gowns. But someday …

Well, a girl could *dream.*

I pulled off my soft leather kid gloves and set them on the counter. The clock above the soda fountain was just shy of the hour. I scanned the empty space and sighed contentedly, proud of my *Gilmore Girls*-obsessed friend for her accomplishments here. This place could be right out of Stars Hollow—or Disney World—

with its pastel-striped papered walls, metal accents, and candy wall. I'd designed the staff uniforms, modeled after the Dapper Dans and Main Street USA trolley singers' costumes.

Taylor Doose would be envious, no doubt.

Back when it was an ice cream shop owned by her parents and called Sundae School, it had been a second home to me. Shanna was several years older than me and was the closest thing I had to a big sister. She hadn't been interested in sewing at all, preferring to work in the ice cream shop alongside her dad. When they'd been short-staffed, I'd fill in, but my heart was always in the sewing shop upstairs.

Helping Shanna and her family transform one generation's family business to the next's dream was the least I could do after spending every day after school here for as long as I could remember. Shanna's mom refused to charge my dad for the babysitting, saying she should be paying him for my delightful company and assistance with her part-time tailoring business in their upstairs apartment.

Shanna emerged from the kitchen, adjusting the bowler hat on her head. Her expression brightened when she saw me. "Arwyn Baughn! You didn't tell me you were coming!"

I shrugged and smiled, subconsciously checking the fit of her puff-sleeved dress. "I'm a lady of mystery," I teased. "You never know where I might show up."

Shanna snorted. "More like I never know *if* you'll show up, Miss Queen of Canceling Plans."

My hand flew to my heart in mock offense, and I fluttered my eyelashes. "Moi? Cancel?"

"Well, not when it's important. You never once canceled on my girls. They miss you now that they're both in school."

"I miss them, too. Being an au pair suited me."

Shanna snorted again. "You even have a way of making nannying sound glamorous. Besides, you're from here, and you always went home each night, so technically you can't be an au pair."

I rewarded her with an exaggerated pinched face.

She grinned and didn't miss a beat. "But back to the fact that you're here, sitting on my shiny new stool. Didn't you say you'd be setting Wednesday afternoons aside for cleaning wedding gowns?"

"They are," I said, my thoughts briefly going to Wynnie's Wedding Dress Library, a gown rental side business I'd curated in my climate-controlled garage. It was a sub-business of Wynsome Designs, my made-to-order historical costume line. "But Tasha said she'd help me next Wednesday if I met her here today." I'd taken in three new dresses over the holidays, and they needed to be cleaned and mended and sorted.

"Sounds like a plan." She tipped her chin up. "Your usual?"

"You know it."

As she made my Straw-Berry Dreamy soda, the door chimed. I swiveled in my stool, expecting to see Tasha, but instead, two little girls giggled their way in, poufy sparkly princess dresses swishing under their peacoats. Two auburn braids and a single blond plait peeked out from underneath pom-pommed tams, similar to the one on my own head.

"Girls! No running!" The woman who accompanied them had a French accent, which caught my attention.

"Sorry, Auntie!" they chorused in perfect English, racing straight toward the stools to the right of me.

I lifted my gaze to their frazzled aunt, offering a sympathetic smile before I turned back to Shanna. She set my soda onto a branded cork coaster and moved down the counter to welcome her new customers.

The bell over the door chimed again, and this time it was Tasha.

"Mrs. Ridgie!" The blond ran toward her, the redhead close at her heels. "Can you babysit us when Auntie Sofi goes back to Canada?"

Our eyes connected briefly. Mrs. Ridgie? Tasha's husband, Monty, was the mascot for the Edge, the NHL team in Denver.

"Isla! Amelie! So great to see you." She bent down. "Remember, Ridgie's identity is a big secret." She looked over at me and smiled, looking happy and healthy, her baby bump just starting to show.

"Oh!" Isla turned to me, distress on her delicate features. "I'm sorry!"

"It's okay. Wynnie over there is my friend. She knows the secret."

"He shouldn't take his head off if he wants it to be a secret," the redhead observed. "He should kiss you with the bear head *on*."

Tasha laughed. "I'll let him know, Amelie." She stood. "Sofi! How lovely to run into you here!"

"Vraiment charmant. How lovely indeed!"

Tasha finally reached the counter and made the introductions. "Sofi, Amelie, Isla, these are my friends Arwyn Baughn and the owner of the Soda Shoppe, Shanna Lane. Wynnie, Sofi is Zaki Marsch's sister, and these are his girls."

I stiffened at the mention of *him*.

Zaki.

"Nice to meet you," I said. "Are you girls wearing Elsa and Anna dresses?"

"Yes!" Amelie confirmed. "*Frozen* is our favorite!"

"I love it, too," I replied.

"See, Sof, I told you she'd be perfect. Wynnie, aside from Penny's Regency gown, I—we—have another ask. Zaki is taking the twins to a con in a couple weeks, and he needs a costume."

"And all the Kristoff costumes are bad!" Amelie frowned. "None are *real*."

I narrowed my gaze, pretty sure of the ask that was coming.

Tasha grinned wider. "Remember last summer, when Zaki helped you and Monty remove my train at the wedding? And that super cute crossbody you made for me with all the pockets so I could carry my safe food and snacks off the ship to the island excursions on our honeymoon cruise? What kind of a friend would I be, when asked if I knew anyone that could help, if I didn't remind him that he knew the best costume designer in the world?"

"The world? Really?" I held her gaze.

Being Tasha, she was unfazed. "Anyway, Zaki's on his way to the Coffee Loft with Xavier and Jason for Xavier's lucky pregame toffee coffee, and I thought you could talk."

I looked at the girls, staring up at me with big, wide, hopeful puppy eyes. They seemed pretty normal. And not in the slightest overly excitable like their father.

The first time I'd met Zaki Marsch, he'd burst into the Coffee Loft like a whirlwind with his teammates, swiped a hat off one player's head and tossed it to another. Instead of reaching its intended target, it hit my cinnamon bun, knocking it out of my hand. The bun tumbled down the bodice of my gown and landed in my lap. I still remembered the sticky glaze ruining the delicate lace and beading. He'd been mortified, apologizing in rapid-fire sentences while his teammate Xavier—now Penny's husband—struggled to hold back laughter.

Zaki paid for the dry cleaning and a replacement bun—and sent a box of them to my house the next day—but that didn't stop him from making a joke of it and calling me Wynna-bun.

And it didn't stop me from making it my personal mission to avoid him.

I hadn't been able to look at a cinnamon roll since without thinking of him.

Zaki was loud, unpredictable, and utterly *not* the type of person I would befriend.

And now, apparently, I was supposed to work with him?

And Tasha—one of my very few friends—knew how I felt about him. She'd lured me here under false pretenses.

But—I needed the money. After materials, a custom-designed Kristoff costume could yield a few hundred dollars' profit.

"Fine. I'll talk to him."

"Yay!" The girls bounced, clapping in excitement. They asked what I was drinking and ordered the same. While we waited for Shanna to make their sodas, they shared that they were five and a half, loved *Frozen,* ballet, and hockey, and they were living with their daddy now because their mommy lived in Canada and had to have a big surgery.

When they received their drinks, I slid off my stool and begrudgingly followed Tasha next door to the Coffee Loft. It smelled like its usual mix of espresso, cinnamon, and whatever syrup Penny used to concoct Xavier's lucky "Toffee Coffee." It wasn't unpleasant. In fact, the smell should have been comforting, like a cozy blanket after a long day. But for me, sitting here at Tasha's insistence, it felt like a trap.

I adjusted my faux ermine collar, tugging it higher around my neck and sinking my chin into its softness, as if it could somehow shield me from whatever was about to happen. The warm glow of the shop's lights reflected off the shiny brass buttons on my lavender winter coat, a semihistorical throwback to the Victorian era. Normally, dressing like this made me feel calm, grounded. But today? Today I felt like I'd walked into an unfriendly classroom of popular middle school girls.

"I can't believe you dragged me into this," I muttered to Tasha, who was sipping a hot pumpkin spice decaf with a self-satisfied grin.

"You need the work, Wynnie. And you're *perfect* for this," she said, setting her mug down. "It's fate."

"It's *not* fate," I replied. "It's you and Monty scheming." I glared at the man sitting next to her. He crooned gibberish to the nine-month-old in his arms, their niece, Melody. The baby completely ignored her mother, who sat between us.

"Same thing," Tasha quipped. Before I could argue further, the door chimed and Xavier entered. Melody squealed at the sight of her father and stretched her arms out toward her dad.

As Monty handed the baby to Xavier, the door opened again.

Zaki Marsch. No. 87.

The only reason I remembered his number was because it was the same number as my house.

Sure. Keep telling yourself that.

Zaki, a picture of effortless confidence, strode in like he owned the place, flashing a smile and fist-bumping the guys.

He looked ... different. Still ridiculously tall and broad-shouldered, the Edge's alternate captain had an air of maturity about him. Formerly blond and clean-shaven, he now sported a trim, auburn beard, the same shade as the short curls poking out from his pom-pommed team beanie, which did not complement his calf-length wool overcoat.

Sans the beanie, he could have been cast as an extra for a Titanic film.

Arwyn Baughn. Stop ogling. He doesn't look that *good.*

He lifted his chin and caught my gaze. I quickly looked away, regretting he'd caught me staring.

I wasn't curious at all why he'd stopped dying his hair blond and had grown a dashing short beard.

Tasha smirked.

Did I say dashing out loud?

Oh no.

"Wynna-bun," he said, drawing out the nickname like it was some kind of inside joke. "Fancy seeing you here."

I straightened in my chair, trying not to glare or be distracted by his smooth voice and trace of a British accent. "You knew I'd be here."

"I'd heard," he admitted, plopping into the chair next to me like we were old friends. "But I had doubts you'd show up."

"She almost bolted," Tasha tattled.

"Well, I'm glad you didn't," Zaki said, leaning back and stretching his arm over the back of my chair. I sat up straighter. "We've got important business to discuss."

"You mean your Kristoff costume?" I said coolly, keeping my tone as professional as possible.

"Exactly." He grinned. "The twins are obsessed with *Frozen*, and I can't let them down. It's a children's con, Wynna-bun—this is serious stuff, and my girls want their dad to dress up."

I opened my notebook, trying to ignore the warmth in my cheeks. "Okay. Let's start with materials. Do you want—"

"Daddy!"

He grinned, flashing too-perfect teeth for a hockey player, and turned toward the door. "Ah. My experts have arrived!"

His daughters ran in, clutching half-finished Straw-Berry Dreamy sodas in their mittened hands. Sofi waved cheerfully and ushered the twins to us.

The little girls squealed in unison, abandoning their sodas to their aunt's fast hands to launch themselves at him.

"Daddy!" they cried again, each grabbing a leg.

"Hey, munchkins!" he said, standing and scooping them up effortlessly, one on each arm. They giggled as he spun them around before setting them down. Then his eyes landed on me, and that grin turned mischievous.

Monty sauntered over. He'd gotten the baby back from Xavier, and he had *trouble* written all over his face. "Marshy."

"Ridgie."

I suppressed a laugh at their orchestrated stare-off.

Monty rolled his eyes at Zaki's use of the mascot's name, but it was good-natured. The two had been caught up in a prank war for most of the last year. In public, they kept up the icy rivalry as the team's top pranksters. In private, they were friends. Tasha told me at their wedding last summer that he'd stopped responding to Monty's pranks, so Monty kept escalating.

A sudden wave of dread hit me. I got *that feeling* sometimes, and my gut has never been wrong.

"Hey, Pen." Monty turned toward his sister-in-law. "Doesn't Marshy still need a nanny? Wynnie's a pro with kids."

There it was. My gut was right on. *Again.*

I shuddered.

Zaki's eyes went wide, and he shot an uncertain glance at Sofi. "Yeah, so, uh, Sofi's going back to school next week," he said. "And the girls need a nanny."

"You'd be *perfect,*" Tasha said quickly. "You've been a nanny, you speak French, and the girls already like you."

"They don't even know me," I reminded her.

"They will!" Monty insisted cheerfully. "You've got all the qualifications."

I looked over at Penny, who hadn't said much and had even less to say now, as she was suddenly very interested in her mug of tea. "You knew about this?"

"She thinks it's a great idea," Tasha said, not meeting my eyes.

Zaki leaned forward. "It's not forever. Just until the end of the season."

I hesitated, my mind racing. On one hand, the idea of working for Zaki was overwhelming. He was loud, unpredictable, and frankly, a trifle intimidating. But on the other hand … the money would be a lifesaver. And the twins seemed like great kids.

As if on cue, Isla tugged on my sleeve. "Do you like ballet?" she asked, her big brown eyes wide with curiosity.

"I do," I said softly. "Do you?"

She nodded enthusiastically. "We want to learn to dance like swans!"

"Like *Swan Lake*?" I asked, smiling despite myself.

"Uh-huh! Daddy says he can be a swan too, but he's not very good at ballet. He's not *graceful* in slippers!" She giggled.

Zaki groaned, then snorted. "Thanks, Isles. Throw me under the bus, why don't you?"

Amelie climbed onto the chair beside me, holding her soda with both hands. "You speak French?" she asked, her voice barely above a whisper.

"Oui," I replied. "Tu parles français aussi?"

Her face lit up. "Oui!"

"She's fluent," Tasha said, nudging Zaki. "See? Perfect."

I looked back at Zaki, who was watching me with an expression I couldn't quite read. For once, he wasn't grinning or cracking a joke. He just looked … hopeful.

"Okay," I said finally, surprising even myself. "I'll think about it."

The twins cheered, and Monty flashed a triumphant smile as he bounced Melody in his arms. Zaki's grin returned, causing my heart to beat faster and overriding my brain, which wanted to continue loathing him. For a brief moment, I wondered if I'd just made a mistake. But when Amelie climbed into my lap to compare the shade of her red hair to mine, chattering excitedly about swans and ballet, I realized maybe, just maybe, this wouldn't be so bad.

"Can you come to our house tomorrow afternoon?" Zaki asked. "You can see the place, and we can talk about the costume."

I nodded. "I'll need to measure you."

Monty smirked, and I sent him a death glare.

The guys hung out for a few more moments while Penny snuck behind the counter to make them their coffees. After they left, Tasha walked me outside.

"I still don't know why you think this is a good idea," I said, turning to Tasha.

"Because you're amazing," Tasha said patiently. "You've been a nanny before, you're fluent in French like the twins, and you can sew while they're at school. Plus, you need the money for your house repairs."

I flinched at the mention of my house. It had been my father's pride and joy, an old Victorian tucked on the edge of town, full of charm and *problems*. The roof needed work, the heating was unreliable, and every time it rained, I prayed the basement wouldn't flood. I'd been scraping by with freelance costume commissions, but it just wasn't enough to keep an old house—and my sanity—afloat.

"Still," I protested weakly. "He's ..."

"Ridiculously handsome?" Tasha offered, grinning.

"I was going to say 'a walking hurricane,'" I muttered.

"Same thing," she replied with a shrug.

CHAPTER 2

Zaki

I'd lost track of time again.

When I saw Arwyn's older model sedan pull into the driveway to our mountain cabin, I was mid-swing with the axe, splitting another log for the firewood stack on the porch.

The rhythmic *crack* of wood splintering was therapeutic, and I'd had every intention of stopping after a dozen logs so I could shower and dress for company. Sweat soaked through my white tee, clinging to my chest and back. My athletic shorts were dusty, my socks were wet and muddy, and my team-branded slide sandals were—

Not my best look.

Not that I was trying to impress her, but Arwyn was one of those women who were *always* put together. Elegant, confident. Even when she was dressed oddly, like from another century. That took guts. And she didn't give a rip about what people thought of her … eccentricities.

And now, there she was, standing next to her car, staring at me wide-eyed like I'd just stepped out of a *How Not To Make an Important Impression* social media reel. Her cheeks turned the same pink as the puffy scarf wrapped around her neck.

I let the axe rest against the chopping block and raised a hand in greeting. "Wynna-bun! Hey! Sorry, I—uh—lost track of time." I glanced down at myself, mentally kicking every decision I'd made this morning. Fantastic.

Way to impress the one person who might actually save your backside.

A very sweet, demure, pretty person.

She blinked a few times, then cleared her throat, her hands clutching the strap of her vintage leather messenger bag. "I, um ..." Her eyes flicked at me from feet to face, and not in an approving way. "I can wait if you need to finish."

"No, no, I'm done!" I slung the axe over my shoulder and crossed the yard in long strides to lean it against the porch latticework, nearly tripping over a rogue piece of firewood in the process. *Smooth, Marsch. Really smooth.* "Welcome to the North Mountain! That's what the girls call it. They're *Frozen* fanatics. You know, the movies?"

"I'm familiar."

"Great, 'cause we kind of went over the top with that theme up here." Why was I rambling? She already knew how much I loved *Frozen*. "I'll just ... uh ... go freshen up. Just one second." I opened the front door and called out to my sister to corral the girls' dogs. The little West Highland Terriers were gated from the main part of the house, so I wasn't worried about them attacking our guest, but she wouldn't be able to work with them sniffing around.

"Sof! Wynnie's here! Can you put the pups up? Sofi and the girls—and their dogs—are in the kitchen," I explained.

"Got 'em!"

"You didn't mention dogs!" she hissed.

"We have fish, too. Out in the hot tub."

She laughed. "I heard about that. Tasha said it was Monty's favorite prank to date."

I grinned and gestured for her to enter ahead of me. Arwyn strolled in daintily, clutching a bag that looked like it belonged to Mary Poppins at her waist, with an unrushed air of importance, like she was walking a red carpet to be presented to a monarch. Then, before she was barely a meter into the house, I bolted, calling over my shoulder. "Be right back!"

Arwyn's gaze flicked away, her usual mask of calm slipping into place, but not before I caught a hint of amusement twitching at the corner of her mouth.

Good. She wasn't mad.

By the time I came back downstairs, freshly showered, beard trimmed, and wearing my favorite flannel and jeans, Arwyn was standing in the living room, holding a mug of tea and studying the fireplace like it might hold the answers to life's greatest mysteries. She'd removed her outerwear to reveal a long dress, her hair in a loose bun behind her head, with wisps floating by her ears. The golden highlights in her auburn hair caught the firelight, and the faint scent of roses wafted over from her direction. Standing very still, she looked like a painting looking at my painting.

"French." She pointed to the painting of downtown Montreal at Christmastime over the mantel. "Vintage?"

"Copy. Sorry about earlier," I said, running a hand through my still-damp hair. "Not exactly a great first impression."

She glanced over her shoulder, one eyebrow arching slightly, then snorted. "First impressions are overrated." Her lips twitched, almost imperceptibly. "This is your third."

Was that a joke?

"Riiiight." I waved to the girls, who'd looked up from their coloring books and were now giggling, their heads together, glancing at us and then back to my sister behind the counter and speaking in rapid French. Their presence gave the room a warm, chaotic hum of life, which was exactly how I liked it. It had been too quiet the last six months without them here.

When we'd separated, Viki had kept the condo by the arena, which we'd bought when we first moved to Denver. It was also close to the girls' preschool and ballet studio. I'd moved into our cabin up here in the mountains, where we spent a lot of time in the summer and escaped to when I was home for more than a day during the season.

The cabin had been a dream of mine since I was a young boy. I'd lived my first few years in Denmark, and my German grandmother lived with us until Dad was traded to a team in England. Fairy tales shaped my childhood. If Oma wasn't reading them to me, one of my sisters was. Hans Christian Anderson and the Brothers Grimm would entertain me during the day and feed my nightmares.

Some of those stories were dark and terrifying.

When I was sixteen, I was good enough to play in the Quebec junior league. My parents shipped me off to Montreal to live with my mom's best friend from when she attended McGill. City life was busy and crazy, and I longed for a quiet retreat. Mom was from a little town outside Quebec City, but it was too far of a drive for my extended family to shuttle me back and forth, so I lived with Colette and Pierre Larioux, their hockey-playing sons, Patrice and Pascal, and their daughter, Victoire.

Viki. We'd hit it off on Day 1. She'd been surprised this big dumb jock was able to speak French and English fluently and discuss the classics.

You don't grow up in a home of two sisters in the Western hemisphere without learning Austen, Shakespeare, and Disney.

The gilded picture frame, with its fleur-de-lis accents, had previously held our last family photo. I'd tried everything to hold our family together. But after over a year of counseling, Viki had determined we were no longer compatible. There wasn't anything I could have done to change her mind. But in the end, she'd been right. We'd grown up and grown apart. She didn't love me anymore, and I had to confront my deepest secret—that I loved the idea of being married and having a family more than I loved her. It wouldn't have been fair to either of us to stay in a loveless marriage. And we didn't want to set an example for our girls that it was okay.

"It's a replica," I stated. "I couldn't see spending the money for the real thing when this looks just as good."

I swung my head back to Arwyn, who patiently held up a length of measuring tape with one perfectly shaped eyebrow raised.

I tried to mimic the one-eyebrow thing, crinkling my forehead and squinting one eye, but nope, couldn't isolate the one.

"Are you okay?" Arwyn asked. "Your face is twitching."

Fail.

I waggled my eyebrows to recover. *That* I could do. "I'm fine. Why the eyebrow raise?"

She shrugged. "I wasn't expecting you to be frugal. I'm impressed."

"I don't like to waste money on things." I tipped my chin to the girls and grinned. "Except for them. Their room is an Arendelle paradise."

Arwyn's lips spread into a wide, genuine smile as she turned her head toward the kitchen. "I would love a tour sometime."

"I happen to know the two best tour guides personally," I boasted.

"I've no doubt. Ready to start measuring?" she asked.

"Daddy!"

Isla and Amelie slid off the barstools and ran to us. I squatted down, ready to catch them. They hit me like little squirmy cannonballs, and I swooped them up into my arms. I closed my eyes, inhaling their baby powder and cookie scent. I wish I knew how to box it up to take on the road with me. Someone should infuse that scent into a candle or something.

"Can we watch?" Amelie asked.

"Can we help?" Isla asked.

"I don't think—" I peered between their heads at Arwyn.

"Absolutely," she said, her smile widening. "I have two very important assistant positions I need to fill for this client. Preferably by little girls who are good listeners and experts in everything *Frozen*. Do you qualify?"

"Yes!" they squealed in unison.

I set them down, and they practically tripped over their dresses to get to Arwyn.

"Do either of you like to write?" Arwyn inquired.

Amelie's hand shot up. "I have three diaries and a book of lists I write in every day."

"Wonderful. Taking detailed notes is important to creating a garment that fits. And who is good with their hands?"

"Me!" Isla shouted. "I do crafts. I made that—" She pointed to the lumpy ceramic bowl on the coffee table. "And that!" She pointed to the cross-stitched-by-number snowman in the frame on the wall.

"Excellent craftsmanship and needlework. Okay, girls, you're hired. Mr. Marsch is expecting the highest-quality Kristoff costume, and we must meet his expectations. Are you ready?"

"Ready!"

Arwyn handed the tape measure to Isla and pulled a sketchpad from her bag. She scrawled something on it with a pencil, then handed it to Amelie. "First, we need to get your dad into position."

"I'm ready," I said, crossing my arms and leaning against the side of the stone chimney.

Arwyn clucked her tongue in disapproval. "That won't do. Take three steps toward me. Stand tall. Arms at your sides. Feet shoulder-width apart."

"Yes, ma'am." I stepped as directed and stood as instructed.

"All right. Amelie, on the pad is the outline of a person, with a line at each spot I need to measure. You can see they're lettered. The head is A, the neck is B, et cetera. I'll call out the letter, and you write the number. Isla, are you ready with that tape?"

"Yes!"

"Great! We'll start with your dad's head and work our way down."

Three pairs of eyes gazed up at me.

"Wynnie?" Isla whispered. "How do I get up there? Daddy is *very* tall."

"Indeed," Arwyn whispered back. "Ask him to sit on the sofa."

"Okay." She raised her voice. "Daddy! Sofa, please."

I crossed to the sofa and sat. Isla kicked off her sparkly plastic heels and scrambled up onto the cushion. My arms shot out to steady her and keep her from getting tangled in the tape.

Arwyn instructed Isla as she wrapped the tape around my head. "Looks good. Now pull it snug."

I winced as my daughter yanked it so tight I was sure it had cut into my skin.

"Not tight, Isla. Snug. Like this." Arwyn's fingers lightly brushed my ear. The tape loosened to a point where I could hardly feel it, like a whisper on my forehead. "We don't want his hat to be too tight or too small." Isla took the tape from her and mimicked her actions.

At least I thought she did. I didn't have eyes on the top of my head, so I couldn't swear to it in court, but it sure felt the same.

"Perfect, Isla!" Arwyn called out the measurement to Amelie, who recorded it on the sketchpad. "Now, his neck."

"Please hold still, Mr. Marsch," Isla instructed seriously. She expertly wrapped the tape around my neck. I thought about pretending to choke but didn't think Arwyn or the girls would appreciate the humor.

Arwyn squinted at the tape at my neck and called out the number to Amelie, then leaned over to check her work and praised her for her neat writing. "Great job, you two!"

My girls beamed with pride, and I couldn't help smiling with them.

This wasn't how I'd pictured the consultation going, but it was fun, and the girls were having a great time. Part of me wondered if this was Arwyn's way of interviewing *us* instead of the other way around.

I didn't care. I could tell at the Coffee Loft she was great with kids, and as far as I was concerned, the job was hers. I just hoped we were passing her tests, whatever they were.

She motioned for me to stand again, and I reclaimed the spot she'd directed me to earlier. "Isla, let's measure Mr. Marsch's waist next. He'll have to stand for this. You'll need a stool. Ah! That ottoman over there by the window." I watched with interest as she rushed over to the small footstool and brought it over, setting it on the ground at my side.

Isla climbed up and stretched the tape out in front of her. "Mr. Marsch, could you please hold your arms out?"

I raised them high, and she attempted to wrap the tape around me. Arwyn stepped in, guiding and sliding it until Isla held it in place.

"Thirty-eight!" Isla called to Amelie. "Right, Wynnie?" she whispered.

Arwyn nodded. "Correct."

They continued to measure me, and I had to admit I was having a great time. I loved how Arwyn let the girls assist. It did cross my mind that maybe I made her nervous and the less she had to touch me, the better. I'd noticed her cheeks reddening at times, like when she had to measure my hips and thighs, but I couldn't be sure if that was because of me or modesty.

When she finally stepped back, satisfied, I let out a low whistle. "That was intense. You always take your job so seriously?"

"Yes," she replied simply, rolling up her measuring tape. "Were you aware your right arm is half an inch shorter than your left?"

"I am now. Hey, you forgot my inseam," I teased.

Her eyes widened, and if I thought her cheeks were rosy earlier, they were scarlet now. I held her gaze in a challenge.

She tipped her chin up. "About that—I'll require a pair of your best-fitting dress pants for that task."

I wondered how she'd planned to handle that. I wasn't about to let Isla take *that* measurement.

"So," she continued, smoothing out invisible wrinkles in her dress, "about the nanny job ... Can we talk somewhere private?"

"Yeah." She hadn't said no. I tried not to look too eager as I moved to lean against the fireplace mantel. I addressed the girls. "I think it's almost time to decorate those cookies. Get started, and I'll join you after Wynnie and I talk, okay?"

They hurried off, and I directed Arwyn to the small room off the living area. It had been their playroom until I'd had a contractor combine their bedrooms into one big everything room upstairs. I'd bought a desk and love seat to make it look like an office, but I didn't really need one. There was plenty of space for my laptop and anything else business-related in my bedroom.

I gestured for Arwyn to sit on the love seat and pulled out the rolling office chair for myself. I sank into it and leaned my forearms on my thighs. "What're you thinking?"

"I'm thinking it's a lot to ask," she said bluntly. "Your daughters are lovely and smart, and I know we'd get along wonderfully, but you want me to move up *here,* in the middle of winter, away from town and my business for an unspecified span of time, and ... It's not exactly... practical. And you have two dogs!"

I nodded, expecting this. Tasha had warned me she'd be a tough sell. "I get it. It's a big ask. But I really think this could work for both of us. The dogs are puppy-pad trained—they won't go outside if it's too cold or snowing. You'd still have time to sew while the girls are at school, and I'd make sure that you're compensated fairly."

Her arms crossed, and she tilted her head. "Define 'fairly.'"

"How about a five thousand dollar advance?" I offered.

That got her attention. Her brows shot up, and for the first time, she actually looked surprised. "Five thousand dollars?"

"Yep. To help with your house repairs," I said, keeping my tone casual, "and for extras. The girls have ballet on Saturday mornings in Denver. They missed their dance friends last fall."

Her lips parted, and for a second, I saw something in her expression that wasn't guarded or skeptical. Vulnerability, maybe. Gratitude. And then her expression shifted. I detected anger and pride.

"Tasha told you," she said, her voice barely above a whisper.

"Don't blame her," I said quickly. "I just … She explained how much that house means to you. And I know what it's like to need help but not want to ask for it. So let me help. We can help each other."

She tucked an auburn tendril behind her ear as she hesitated. "You promise no pranks?"

I saluted her. "Scout's honor."

That one eyebrow raised again. "I doubt you were ever a scout," she observed dryly. "They don't salute. They do that three-finger thing."

"Fair point," I said, raising a hand like I was swearing an oath. "But I promise. No pranks on Arwyn." She had reason to be concerned. I'd been the recipient of multiple pranks during my first season playing in Quebec, but I'd turned that around the following year, and since then, I'd been the one pulling the best pranks on my teammates—and our mascot. But last summer, when the girls moved to Canada, I hadn't had it in me. But now that they were back … Monty had a lot of payback coming to him, and my idea factory was back in business. I'd ease myself back in, starting small, then get him good when he least expected it.

She exhaled slowly, then looked up at me, her green eyes steady. "Okay. But I have another condition, besides the no pranks, and it's a big one."

"Name it."

"It's probably a deal-breaker."

"Then it's important. Go ahead."

"It took me over an hour to drive here. Driving up and down that mountain road every day, in the winter, four times a day, is a no-go," she said. "If I'm doing this, the girls are staying at my house. It's walking distance to Palmer City Academy, which has an extended winter break—you could register them tomorrow, and they could start with the other mid-year transfers on Monday. I have the space. You can stay in my father's old room when you're in town if you don't have the time to trek them up here in between games, if you like."

That was not what I'd expected. But it made sense. And the idea of my girls staying in a cozy Victorian house, in a small town with plenty of people that I knew nearby to support them, should they need it, complete with a resident seamstress-slash-nanny, wasn't the worst thing in the world.

"And," she continued before I could reply, "I need to know about their mother—where she is, how she is, her level of involvement, how often to call her, et cetera. Otherwise, no deal."

"Okay," I said. "Deal." I lowered my head to gather my thoughts. *Just the facts, Zak. Stick to what she needs to know, not the rest of the stuff.* When I looked back up, Arwyn was staring at me intently. "Viki is in rehab—physical therapy. Earlier this week, she underwent the first of several surgeries. She's had chronic pain from a dance injury for a long time. During childbirth, her pelvic bone fractured. And a year ago, she tore her labrum. That's the muscle on the hip—"

"I know. Former ballerina here." She smiled sadly, her big green eyes wrought with concern. "Goodness, the poor woman."

"Yeah. And she hid it well for a long time. She became a pro at managing her pain. She didn't abuse painkillers or anything like that, but her quality of life has suffered. We have the resources to get her the best help in the world, but she refused to go to therapy or have surgery. When she and the girls moved back in with her parents last summer, they saw the extent of it, and her mom and dad and I confronted her at Thanksgiving." I grimaced, remembering the look of betrayal on her face. She'd thought it was all my idea as an attempt to get full custody of the girls. "If they were in Montreal, Viki would continue to put them first and not get the surgeries or focus on getting better. So, Isla and Amelie are here with me until the end of the season, or when Viki is fully recovered, whichever comes first."

"Wow." Arwyn swallowed visibly. "Okay. Thanks for filling me in. Can they talk to her if she calls?"

"You're welcome. And yes. Now tell me about this house of yours and the repairs that are needed. I have to make sure it's safe for the girls."

At that, she softened. "Oh, it's totally habitable. Just drafty and creaky and not up to the historical society's exterior expectations. And it needs a full paint job and refreshed landscaping."

Five thousand dollars sounded like it would barely make a dent in the work she needed to have done. "Okay. I can work with that. Tell me more."

Arwyn's entire face lit up as she spoke, and I could tell this house wasn't just a building to her—it was history, family, memories. And she loved it.

"It's been in my family for generations," she said, her voice warming with enthusiasm. "It was built in the late 1800s, and my great-grandmother married one of the Palmer sons—the founders of Palmer City. It used to be so beautiful. Stained glass windows, carved wood banisters, the works. It's a little worn now, but it still has the old charm."

A gasp turned our attention to the cracked-open door. "It sounds like our dollhouse, Amelie!"

I laughed. "Come on in, girls."

Amelie explained. "You were taking too long. The cookies need you. But Daddy! Show her the picture of our dollhouse first!"

I pulled out my phone and scrolled through until I found the photo they were talking about—a miniature Victorian dollhouse their mom had brought with them to Montreal.

Arwyn's breath hitched when she saw it. "It's almost exactly like it!"

The twins squealed in delight, bouncing in their chairs. "We want to live in the dollhouse!"

I laughed and held out my hand to Arwyn. "Looks like the decision's been made."

She hesitated for half a second, then placed her small hand in mine. "Deal," she said softly.

Her hand was warm against mine, and as the twins cheered, I couldn't help but smile.

Maybe this was going to work out after all.

CHAPTER 3

Arwyn

The buzz of saws and banging of hammers were not my typical Sunday afternoon soundtrack. Somehow, no permits or permissions from the town were needed for the work that needed to be done, and Montoya Construction had been available to start repairs immediately on my house. I'd had to scramble to get my sewing machine and supplies out of the front room and into the garage before Beck and her crew showed up yesterday morning. Since this whole fiasco was Tasha's idea, I called her and Penny to borrow their husbands' muscles. An industrial machine like mine wasn't easily relocated.

"Thank you again for making time for me this weekend, Beck," I said to the contractor. I'd gotten to know her pretty well while she and her crew renovated the ice cream store into a soda shop. "I don't know how I ever agreed to this. Two little girls I barely know, living here with me, and their dad here part-time, possibly. Tell me I'm crazy."

"You're crazy," she said. "But honestly, I've wanted to get my hands on this house for a long time. So much potential! Please let me know when I can spiff up and paint the outside? And do let Liam know if you want to convert the garage to a more suitable commercial space. His architect fingers are itching for a new historically modern project. Picture it—sliding barn doors, track lighting, an actual changing room instead of a quilt hanging from a clothesline …"

I sighed. "We'll save those things for the next influx of money. Probably in the next millennium at this rate."

"That's okay. We'll have this place kid-proofed in no time. And you were right, sealing off the third floor for now is the best alternative until we can redo the floors and stairs and get you a new roof."

"I hate to do it, but it's not safe up there for the girls," I admitted. "What's the most cost-effective way to seal it up?"

"Well, the back stairs are easy. There's a door already there, so we'll add a bolt and a combination lock. The front staircase is more challenging. We can seal it up with plastic to block it, but that won't keep out kids who are determined to see what's on the other side. Your best option is a door and frame at the base of the stairs on the second story. Lock it up. And we can remove it later, when you're ready to tackle the upstairs."

"Okay." I tried to picture what that would look like. It didn't seem like it would be an eyesore. I'd still have access. And it would save me money heating it.

"Great! Leave the repairs to us, and you go do what you do best. I'll call you if we run into anything that requires your input." Beck tightened her messy bun and slid her safety goggles over her eyes. "Should be move-in ready by Tuesday."

Tuesday. My stomach dropped.

I wasn't ready for this, but my dad used to say, "The only way to face a fear is head-on. Do it scared, Wyn. Then it's not scary anymore."

That had worked out well for him. Until it hadn't.

I missed my parents. I really could've used their advice on this one. Dad was six feet under and had been for almost five years. Mom checked in when she could, but sometimes it was months until it was safe for her to communicate or get word to me. I suspected she was in the CIA, and when I asked, she would neither confirm nor deny it.

I pulled on my coat and flipped up my hood to make the trek over the light cover of snow to the detached garage. Over a hundred years ago, it had been a carriage house. Then a gardener's shed. When Dad retired from the military to become a wildlife photographer, it became his workshop. After he died, I left it as it was for a long time—until I ran out of room in the main house for my collection.

I pushed the key into the lock of the windowless structure and opened the door, tentatively walking forward on the carpet into the darkness until I could grab the cord that would signal the interior lights.

Sure, I could have used the flashlight feature on my phone to find it, but what fun would that be?

"Ow!"

Step three-point-five put me in direct contact with my industrial sewing machine.

I rubbed my knee. "Sorry, Nellie." I patted its arm in apology. I'd named her after the American Girl doll who worked in a factory in New York City as a child, changing the threads on the big machines. The name was a callback to the books I loved as a child and a reminder that my favorite era of time had a dark side that the romanticism of the period often overlooked.

Reaching up and a tad forward, I caught the cord and pulled. The uncovered bulb's soft glow illuminated the immediate area and left the perimeter in darkness. I hung my coat on the rack by the door and traversed the mosaic of garage-sale carpets and throw rugs, pulling on the rest of the lights.

Monty and Xavier had moved the racks of wedding gowns and my clothes from upstairs to the perimeter, leaving the space in the back right corner for the changing area. Behind the hanging quilt were three full-length mirrors and a set of hooks for garments. Beck had installed high shelving for my hat boxes and accessories over the racks, and they brought a touch of decor to the otherwise industrial-looking space. I might keep them here permanently.

In the center of the room, Nellie sat sentry, facing the doors. Behind her, three dress forms—two female and one male, dubbed June, July, and August, respectively—formed a semicircle in front of my cutting table. To the machine's left was a four- by two-foot table I used as an extension for large projects, and to her right was the antique chest of drawers that held most of what I needed to work through Tuesday. I had to finish up Zaki's costume, and I wanted to get started on designs for Penny's gala dress, even if I wasn't yet one hundred percent certain Tasha had been serious about that or if it had just been a ploy to get me to meet with Zaki.

We hadn't revisited the topic—our communication over the last few days was centered around the upheaval she'd brought to my calm and quiet—and dare I say, gloriously boring—life. But I did plan to ask her about it, and I wanted to have a few concepts ready, just in case.

Penny was the sweetest human in the world. Her shape had changed since she'd become a mother. We'd spoken about altering the dresses she had for when she returned to playing the harp for events, but it would be nice to surprise her with something new and custom-made.

The light above the changing corner flickered, earning a deep frown from me. "You'd better get your act together before Mr. Marsch arrives," I told it with authority. I checked my pocket watch. *Yikes.* They'd be here in less than twenty minutes.

I scooted around Nellie and went straight to August, where the tunic was draped. It was a simple piece at its base, charcoal-gray wool with lighter gray fur trim at the sleeves and hem. Ribbons in shades of blue accented a maroon fabric belt to give the appearance of stripes. I'd tack it onto the tunic, give it a nice, flat knot at the side, and set in snaps to hold it in place. On the worktable sat the loose-fitting dusty blue pants, an elbow-patched shirt, a hat, and pointy boot covers to pull over his hikers.

I may have gone a little overboard with my attention to detail.

The sound of an engine and tires crunching on the snow drew me from my inspection. I hurried to the door to open it. In front of me was a shiny black minivan, *not* the kind of vehicle I'd expect from a multimillionaire defenseman. He sure meant it when he said he didn't like to waste money on things.

Zaki grinned at me as he slid the door to the back seat open. The girls were again clad in princess dresses of the same shades as the first two times I'd seen them. I wondered if all of their clothing was *Frozen*-inspired.

"Wynnie!" In less than five seconds, they'd unbuckled themselves and ran straight for me.

I opened my arms for the embrace and snuck a glance up at their dad, who was closing the van's door. He wore the same team beanie as last week, but instead of the elegant wool overcoat, he'd donned a sage puffer jacket.

Green was definitely his color.

"Amelie! Do you see the dollhouse?"

"Oh Isla, it's just as I imagined!"

I laughed. "Come on in to my temporary workshop." I let go of the girls and stepped toward the door. "Inside you'll see a lot of pretty dresses, my sewing machine, and all of my tools. It's important that you don't touch any of it, okay? There are some pattern books on the table you can look at and some drawing paper and pencils. Feel free to sketch or write while I work on your dad's costume. Okay?"

"Okay!" they chorused.

I took a deep breath and heaved the door open. "Go on in and explore. You too, Mr. Marsch."

He winked at me and followed the girls in. I shook my head and scooted around him toward August.

"Nice setup. So do you make costumes for, like, theater productions?"

I shook my head no. "Too much drama. Emotionally charged cast members who are overworked, underfed, and sleep-deprived. Directors telling actresses that they aren't the right size or shape for a dress. Having to hack up beautiful pieces and 'theater stitch' them together to fit around microphones or mend them with *staples* to make it through a scene." I shuddered. "I learned pretty quickly I'm the sew-at-home custom-order kind of seamstress."

"It's a very impressive space."

"I don't usually work here. This garage is just for storing the wedding gowns."

"I can't wait to hear more about that," he said sincerely. "Tasha explained your dress library. I think it's awesome."

"Thanks." My cheeks heated. "Um, you should check out your costume."

He followed me to August. "Wow. It looks just like the one in the movie."

I frowned. "The cartoon?"

"Better than the one in the movie."

I pressed my lips together.

"Better than the Disney World version?"

I grinned. I liked praise. "Why, thank you. You're too kind. And I'm glad, because you can get the movie version online for a fraction of the cost. You do like to be frugal, after all."

He snorted. "I spare no expense for my little ladies nor the kingdom of Arendelle."

I smiled and shook my head. "They sure do have you wrapped around their little fingers, don't they?"

He held up his pinky. "And when they have big fingers like mine, I'll be just as wrapped."

"And with that ..." I removed the tunic from August and gathered the pants, shirt, and hat from the sewing table extension and pushed them toward him. "You can change behind the quilt in the corner."

I followed him to the makeshift screen and waited. The girls were off in the opposite corner, heads together, no doubt plotting world domination.

Fjord domination?

Zaki's voice carried over the quilt. "Wow, Wynna-bun. This is softer than it looks. And I think it's a perfect fit."

"I'm glad to hear it," I replied evenly.

"Amelie! Isla! Ready for the big reveal? Can I get a drum roll?" Zaki's request was jovial and upbeat, like he was revealing something so much more fun than a costume.

I looked over at the girls. They'd paused their frantic whispering and were soon at my side.

"Ready, Daddy!" Isla called. She counted down from three, and they began slapping their thighs and humming a drumroll sound. It started softly and increased in volume as Zaki's disembodied fingers teased the quilt to the side.

He strode toward us, then stopped holding his arms out and turned in a circle. "What do you think, ladies?"

Nordic Mountain Man to a tee, I wanted to say. Instead, I deferred to the girls.

Isla held her elbow with one hand and tapped her cheek with another. "Nice. But the hair isn't working for me. Kristoff is blond, like me."

"I like the hair," Amelie said. "I think he needs mittens."

Zaki, no doubt expecting high praise from his biggest fans, held a smile, but his eyes told another story. He was afraid he'd disappointed them.

Little girls could be very hard to please.

"I can make mittens," I offered. "I don't make wigs, though."

"Mommy used to paint his hair," Isla said.

I caught his gaze. "I've never painted hair before."

"I can order a wig," he said and turned back to Isla. "Do I have to shave?"

She rolled her eyes. "Daddy. You *know* Kristoff doesn't have a beard."

"But I *like* my beard." He sighed. "Okay, but only because you asked me to."

"Yay!" Isla clapped.

"Isla! The other thing!" Amelie hissed.

"Oh! Daddy, can Wynnie come, too? She has all these pretty white dresses!"

Zaki's brow crinkled. "Sure. We could use a Marshmallow, the snow monster."

"No, Daddy!" Amelie giggled.

"Olaf?"

"We already have an Olaf!" Isla reminded him.

I tilted my head, confused. Did Zaki have a girlfriend?

"The dog," he supplied. "Laffy is short for Olaf, and Vennie is short for Sven."

"Ah!" I smiled in understanding. "Girls, I am so honored you thought of me, but this is an important daddy-daughter date."

Amelie shrugged. "Sometimes he's too much fun and I get tired. If you came, you could help me find a quiet place. Right?"

My eyes widened. For a girl her age to be able to identify the cause of stress and know what to do about it certainly was surprising.

"She gets panic attacks," Isla explained. "Sometimes I can help, but sometimes I can't. And Daddy tries, but ..."

Zaki cleared his throat. "It's, ah, new." He scrubbed the back of his neck. "Overstimulation leads to meltdowns, and that escalated when the girls moved to Canada last summer."

"So, can you come, Wynnie?" Isla asked. "We can help you pick out a snow queen dress!"

I met Zaki's gaze, my eyes asking the silent question. Poor guy looked hopeless. I could definitely help. Amelie sounded a lot like me at her age after my mother left to chase bad guys.

"A snow queen, hmm?" I squatted down to the girls' level. "Tell me what a snow queen's dress should look like, and I'll pull out a few options."

"Yay!" Amelie wrapped her arms around me from the side. "Thank you!"

Isla tapped her chin again. "Long sleeves, because it's cold. And big balloon poufs on your shoulders."

"Puffed sleeves?" I asked, rising up and edging backward until I was sitting in the armchair.

"Yes!" Amelie crawled into my lap. "And a big skirt, like a bell!"

"Okay, I have a few like that. What else?"

"A crown!" they shouted simultaneously.

"I have several. How about we choose the dress first, and then you can help with accessories?"

"Yes!"

"I'll need an assistant to help carry the dresses. Someone tall, strong. Know anyone?" I guided a giggling Amelie off my lap.

"Daddy, will you hold the dresses?" Isla sighed. "She was talking about you, you know."

He bowed. "Kristoff at your service."

I returned his grin and spun on my heel toward the opposite wall, where the petite gowns hung. I had two dresses in mind that would be a good fit—and fit me. One was a scaled-down version of Princess Diana's from the early 1980s and the other a sparkly strapless number from the early 2000s. Instead of sleeves, it had arm-length fingerless gloves with poufs just below the shoulder.

I retrieved the clear garment bags from the rack and hung them over Zaki's arm. "Follow me."

I led them to June and July and removed the gowns from the bags to set them up on the dress forms. I pinned the gloves to July at each side and stepped back. "What do you think?"

The girls each ran to a different dress. Of course. I sighed. "You want to be the tiebreaker, Mr. Marsch?"

He shook his head no, but his lips twitched.

I braced.

"I think you should try them both on," he suggested.

"You do, do you?" I smiled tightly, convinced he was making this harder on purpose for his own entertainment.

"Yes! Try them on!" the girls echoed.

"Fine," I agreed, turning back to him. "But first let me make sure your costume is set, okay?"

He nodded and continued to hold my gaze. The seconds ticked by, making the blink of time feel like eternity and derailing my whole train of thought. "Fair enough."

Compose yourself, Arwyn.

Easier said than done.

CHAPTER 4
Zaki

Arwyn was *all business* when she worked.

"Shoulders back," she said, her voice soft but firm.

"Yes, ma'am."

Every so often, her fingers would brush against my neck, cheek, or hand, and each time we touched generated a jolt of static electricity. She felt it, too. I saw a flicker of *something* cross her face before she looked away and focused on her task.

Maybe one of us needed to use a new fabric softener.

I did as I was instructed, standing tall while she moved around me, checking the fit at my chest, waist, and shoulders. Pulling here, tugging there. Using chalk and pins, which she held in the corner of her mouth. Her concentration was so intense that I almost forgot to breathe.

"Your shoulders were made for this costume," she mumbled.

Was that a compliment? I stood a little taller and puffed out my chest. "I do have pretty amazing shoulders," I agreed. "Hey, aren't you afraid you might swallow those pins?"

She glanced up at me, unamused. "No. Arms out to the side."

"Like a scarecrow?"

"Like someone with uneven arms who wants their costume to fit properly."

"Got it. No scarecrow vibes," I said, holding my arms out.

She stepped closer, smoothing the fabric of the shirt from shoulder to wrist, her brows furrowed in focus. "Hold still."

"I'm holding still!"

"You're fidgeting."

"Am not," I said, shifting slightly. "Ow!"

Her lips pressed into a thin line, and she gave me a look that could probably stop traffic. I smirked and immediately locked into position, because something about her quiet authority was strangely impressive.

Behind us, the twins erupted into giggles again. "Daddy's in trouble!" Isla sang.

"I am *not* in trouble," I called over my shoulder.

Arwyn's quiet "hmm" suggested otherwise.

Finally, she stepped back. "I've marked and pinned everything that needs to be adjusted. Please, take it off *carefully.*"

"Promise," I assured her.

I retreated to the corner behind the quilt and changed. She reached for the costume the moment I stepped out, and she returned it to the mannequin-thing. A dress form, she'd called it. And each of them had names. June, July, and August.

A strange sense of humor, but I liked it.

"Your turn." I leaned toward her. "Need any help?"

Her cheeks pinked again. I did love that reaction. As long as I was just catching her off guard—I didn't want to make her uncomfortable.

Arwyn raised her chin. "I've got it, thanks."

The girls and I were a captive audience as she removed the first dress from June and carried it behind the quilt.

"Do you want a drumroll?" Isla shouted.

"Sure!" Arwyn called back.

I held out my fist for a bump. "Good suggestion," I praised.

She pressed her little fist to mine. "I know."

I hooted. "Let us know when to start."

"Now works!" Arwyn called out.

The three of us gave it our best effort as Arwyn emerged around the quilt. The dress was big, heavy, and seemed to swallow her up. The girls and I watched as she turned in a circle, clutching the fabric at her thighs to keep it from bunching on the floor.

"I'd have to hem it, but … I'm not feeling this one," she said.

"Yeah, it's too big," Amelie said.

"Next one!" Isla called.

Arwyn removed it from July and disappeared again behind the curtain.

"Drum roll!" she called a few moments later.

This time, we were louder, and when she emerged, the girls stopped clapping and squealed.

"That one!" Isla ran to her. "With a big tiara!"

"And a fur cape!" Amelie suggested. "In case you get cold."

Arwyn looked over the girls to me, and our eyes locked. "What do you think?"

I tried to think of a snappy reply, but I couldn't speak. *Stunning* didn't begin to describe her in this dress. The top was elegant and fit like the gloves on her arm. The waistline hit just below the curve of her hip, then flared out. She'd piled her hair on top of her head, held with a pencil, and—

"It works," I managed to squeak out.

She rolled her eyes, but the tinge of annoyance was missing this time.

"Good. All right, let me get changed, and then I can take you into the house for a tour. And I'll show you girls my collection of tiaras."

The girls chatted happily while I tried to get the picture of Arwyn in that dress out of my head. She looked like a bride. Better than any I'd ever seen, including Viki. It was Arwyn's quiet confidence that leveled her up. No need to meet or outdo a trend, nothing flashy, just … calm.

I wasn't used to calm. We'd never been friends.

Chaos, on the other hand, I thrived with.

Calm had always felt lame, boring. But Arwyn made it seem classy and peaceful.

God knew I could use some peace.

Once everything was restored, we donned our coats and walked over to the house. Most of Beck's workers had left for the day, and our visit was mostly uninterrupted. The girls were excited to move into the 'real live dollhouse,' especially when Arwyn let them try on her tiaras.

"We have a home game tomorrow night," I said. "Would you like to come?"

Arwyn looked at me like I'd just asked her to suit up and join me on the ice. "I don't think so."

"Not your thing?" I asked.

She shook her head. "Loud, lots of people, cursing, fighting ..."

"Those are the best parts!" Isla interrupted. "Right, Amelie?"

My youngest daughter's eyes widened. "Um, sure."

Huh. That was new.

"Okay, then. We'll see you here Tuesday for move-in, I guess?"

"See you then." She smiled. "And good luck tomorrow night." She tucked a handful of auburn strands behind her ear, and my fingers twitched.

I slid my hands into the pockets of my puffer jacket and curled my fingers into fists so they didn't move on their own accord. "Thanks. We're playing Seattle. We should win, easy."

"Great. Bye, girls."

"Bye, Wynnie!"

Lately, I'd felt the urge to cause some trouble. Monty had it coming to him after turning my hot tub into a koi pond. Something big ...

As I drove up the mountain, it hit me. A prank so epic, the entire arena could witness it.

It was time to start paying back Ridgie the Bear for all the fun he'd had at my expense. I'd start small and warm up. Then I'd strike.

And I already knew the perfect date to do it.

CHAPTER 5

Arwyn

With the help of Beck and her crew, the girls' rooms were ready by dinnertime on Monday afternoon. The second-floor front room, formerly a sitting area, had been transformed into a winter-inspired playroom/study area. Beck had found a child-size table and chairs at a yard sale and painted them white. A shag carpet underneath the table looked like snow over the blue carpet, a fjord, if you will. The old books had been boxed up and taken to the third floor so empty shelves could be filled with their things.

I'd given them my childhood bedroom, adjacent to the sitting area. When dad died, I'd moved downstairs to the former housekeeper's room. It was spooky and lonely upstairs at night, and having all my stuff on one level was easier to manage. I'd used my old room like a closet these last few years, keeping most of my lesser-worn period clothing, hats, and accessories there. It was easy enough to move it all out to the garage for the girls.

The room was small, a tight fit for two twin beds, so Beck got creative and built a pop-out daybed into the window seat. The bedding Zaki rush-ordered had arrived earlier in the day, and I'd washed the comforters and sheets while the crew ensured the safety of the bed. A fresh coat of powder-blue paint and chevron-patterned drapes over the windows brought the formally wallpapered room into the twenty-first century.

Since the closet was tiny, Beck's dad had added a row of hooks to the wall next to the free-standing wardrobe.

All that was left to do was get my dad's stuff out of his room.

I stood in the doorway of the master suite, assessing the towers of boxes of photo equipment, prints, negatives, and portfolios that I'd moved in from the garage when I turned it into the wedding dress library. I could move them all into the adjacent dressing room-slash-closet. How much space did Zaki need?

I texted him a few pictures of the spaces. *I'm not sure where to put my dad's stuff. How much space do you need for your clothes and things?*

He texted back right away. *Maybe a foot to hang my game-day suits? A few drawers. I can live out of my suitcase, too. Don't stress, Wynna-bun. Please don't feel like you have to move anything. I'll help tomorrow.*

Okay. Thank you. Good luck tonight.

Thanks. Hey, check this out.

A few seconds later a video came though. Zaki sat at a table, ballcap backward and holding a silver Sharpie. Ridgie the Bear set down a tray of pucks next to him and moved behind him, covering his mouth with his paws. Zaki picked up the first puck, and a look of confusion crossed his features. As he held it in his left hand and began to write on it, the shape of the disc seemed to … shift. When he squeezed it, it squooshed in his hand.

It was cake!

Looks like Monty got you again! I replied. *That puck looked so real!*

It did. As did the others. It took four for me to realize they were ALL cakes.

So funny! Are you going to prank him back this time?

I really should … Too many ideas to choose from, though. Maybe you can help?

Oh no! I tapped the screen almost frantically. *I will not get involved. I know what he's capable of, and I'm very afraid.*

I'm even more capable, especially if you're on my side.

I sucked in a breath. Something about that last text made me uneasy. But not in a bad way.

Deciding to let it go, I changed the subject. *I'll see you tomorrow. Go … get a hat trick or something.*

Ah, the lady is speaking my language. A hat trick is a challenge for a D-man but not impossible. I'll see what I can do.

Just have fun! I added. *D-man means you play defense, right?*

Are you asking me to teach you the ways of hockey?

Was I? I really had no interest in the game. Or did I? Maybe I should learn, since that was his job and it would be polite to ask him about it when he stayed here.

Maybe a lesson or two, I texted back.

I'm a great teacher, you know. You might want more lessons. Do you skate?

More lessons? How complicated could the game be? Bunch of guys hitting the rubber disc into a net.

I'm decent on figure skates.

Excellent. You can come with me and the girls up to the cabin after the con and we can learn on my home rink.

Your home rink?

In the backyard.

You have a rink in your backyard?

I do.

Huh. That was interesting. How had I missed that?

Okay then. Next weekend.

Sweet! I'll pick up you and the girls after practice Saturday and have you home before my flight to New Orleans Sunday night.

That sounds a bit crazy. We can do it another time, when you have more time.

I live for crazy.

That I knew. It was what I was afraid of.

I liked my small, quiet life.

Zaki Marsch was not small or quiet.

Good thing this arrangement was temporary.

CHAPTER 6
Zaki

I put my phone away and leaned over Xavier's shoulder. He was on a video chat playing peek-a-boo with Penny and Melody, who was clapping her mittened hands together every time he revealed his face.

I missed those days. I sniffed and blinked back the hot tears that were forming in my eyes.

That used to be me. The happy guy with the wife and kids on the other side of the screen. But I blew it. And the worst part is, I didn't know I was blowing it, and when I figured it out, it was too late to save it.

Back when Isla and Amelie were little, Viki and Lauren, our goalie's wife, would bring them to home games. We'd video chat for good luck before the game, and I'd skate over to them during warmups and make them laugh.

They were here with Sofi tonight, who was flying home to Quebec City in the morning. I was going to miss her, and I knew the girls would, too. It was hard enough for them to be away from their mom.

I'd been hoping for a trade all season, and with the trade deadline approaching, moves were happening. Our team was good again this year, and I was a big part of that, which meant a trade for me was unlikely. But I wasn't giving up hope. My contract was up at the end of the season, and like I told management, I was either going to Montreal or retiring. I loved the game, but I loved my girls more. And they needed both me and their mom in their lives.

Viki and I might not be in love—we hadn't been in a long time—but I'd always thought love was a choice. After the initial attraction and excitement wore off, staying together was something you chose to do because you loved and respected your chosen one and wanted to build a life and grow old together.

We'd been teenagers when we met and started dating. Her mother had been a prima ballerina. Viki loved to dance and had dreams of following in her mother's toe shoes. She went to college and studied dance but gave it up to come with me to Colorado. She promised me her dream had changed, but after the girls were born, she became distant. I attributed it to the fractured pelvis and emergency C-section and the resulting pain and therapy afterward. But our connection wasn't the same after that. I hired a nanny, slept in the guest room, and took care of the girls when I was home so she could rest. I built her a ballet studio in the basement of the cabin, but she preferred to stay in the city, near the Wags.

I couldn't blame her, but I didn't know what else to do. And I had no idea our marriage was in danger. I thought it was a rough patch we'd work through. When the girls were three, she told me she didn't love me anymore and wanted to separate. I suggested counseling. We attended sessions for months, together and separately, but it didn't go anywhere.

Viki was done with me and this life, and I wasn't.

She stayed in the Denver apartment with the girls, and I trekked up and down the mountain.

Then, after our Stanley Cup loss last summer, she decided she'd had enough of Colorado, too, and took the girls back to Montreal.

Way to kick a guy when he was already down.

I'd put in for a trade immediately, but since we'd made it to game seven of the Stanley Cup final and I was still under contract, I was staying.

Not having my girls close by was more painful than any check to the boards, concussion, broken bone, or torn muscle. It hurt deep, and the pain surfaced in ways that went against my character and personality. It sucked the positivity right out of me, and I didn't like who I became the last six months, easily agitated on the ice, looking for fights and participating in every opportune scrum.

Turns out our rivals didn't, either. The media were already talking about ways the Seattle guys might return the love I gave them at our October meeting.

"Let's go, boys!" Dean Hathaway, aka Cappy, our captain, banged his stick above Xavier's head, causing him to jump and drop his phone.

I picked it up and waggled my eyebrows at Penny and Melody. "Uh-oh, Mel! Your daddy's in trouble!"

"You too, Marshy!" Dean swatted me in the shin with his stick. "And if it was you that duct-taped pink lace to Ridgie's jersey and shorts, nice work!"

"Busted." Xavier smirked at me and took his phone back. "Bye, Punkin! Bye, Pen!"

"See you at warmies!" Penny blew a kiss, and Xavier hurried to put his phone away.

When I'd found a large roll of hot pink lace on the driver's seat of my van—no doubt Arwyn's way of accepting my invitation to be a co-conspirator— many options floated through my mind. Taping flouncy rows of lace to the hem of Ridgie's jersey and shorts had been the idea I liked the most, and it was a good warm-up for The Big One. There hadn't been time for Monty's handler to remove it before his meet-and-greets, so some of the fans had gotten some interesting one-time photos. Arwyn had texted me that Ridgie's social media was blowing up as fans tried to guess the reason for his glow-up.

If anything, he owed me a "you're welcome."

After a pep talk from Dean and words from the coach, the lineup was announced by a hyped-up Brendan Trotter, and we assembled in the tunnel to wait for our cue to step onto the ice for warmups.

I was on the second pair tonight with Xavier. Brendan and Trask Emerson were the starting D-men, so I got in line behind them. It was always interesting listening in on their conversations. Two of the politest guys you ever met. Brendan was from Minnesota, the Land of the Helpful, and Trask was from Charleston, the Land of Manners. They even *complained* politely. They rarely got mad. Never heard more than a muttered mild curse from either of them.

Needless to say, not too fun to prank, but I did enjoy their gripes about domestic issues, like Trask's lawnmower malfunctioning and spitting grass back at him or Brendan's attempt to change his own oil on his sports car and wearing more than the car received. Today they were debating whether Valentine lights on their mirror-image cookie-cutter homes could be a thing.

Wholesome. Adorable, even. Blissfully unaware that while they were planning something sweet, at any moment their wives could drop a bomb on them and the life they fantasized they had would burst faster than the seams of a juice box in the hands of an overenthusiastic toddler, leaving behind confusion, wide-eyed panic, and pleas for forgiveness and a do-over. Anything to keep their family together.

We hit the ice and skated circles, shooting pucks at the net. Big crowd tonight, and at least a dozen signs along the sides with my name on them, asking for a stick or a puck. I tossed a few pucks over and posed for a few selfies.

When I felt I was loose enough, I picked up two pucks and glided over to my girls.

"Daddy!"

I grinned and held up the pucks. "For my biggest fans!"

Sofi rolled her eyes and pointed. "I think those ladies over there are your biggest fans."

I followed her gaze and snorted. "Bubbles, Blossom, and Buttercup?" The three women had been compared to the PowerPuff girls on a lookalike cam years ago and had run with the theme ever since. The blond-, red-, and black-haired trio had been trying to get my attention all season, but I'd ignored them. I wasn't looking to date a fan. Tonight, the blonde held a sign that read, "Marshy: Spin to win!" with their faces glued to the poster and a plastic game spinner in the center, currently pointing to her likeness.

"You know them, Daddy?" Isla asked.

"Nope." I held up the pucks. "Ready to catch?"

"Ready!"

I tossed them over, one at a time, kissing them before each throw. "I'm glad you're here. We're going to need all the luck we can get. Seattle's on a winning streak, and if they win tonight, they'll pass us for first place in the Western division."

"You got this, Daddy! I have faith in you!" Amelie called.

I grinned. "I might have to fight a little. You know I'll be okay though, right?"

"Fighting is part of the game," Isla stated. "Bruh! We *know* that, Daddy. Just win your fights, okay?"

I laughed. "Bruh! Count on it." I shot a questioning glance at my youngest sister. "Bruh?"

She shrugged. "As the oldest member of the family to be born in this century, it's my responsibility to educate my nieces in current slang."

"Uh-huh. They sound like the rookies, Sof."

She shrugged, and I skated to the bench smiling.

"Heads up, duster!"

My skates flew out from under me before I could react, landing me flat on my back.

Above me, in a Seattle uniform, was the biggest jerk in the league. Dante Leinecker smirked and skated back to his team as I pulled myself up.

Xavier skated over. "You okay?"

"Already plotting my revenge," I quipped. "Since when is he—"

"The trade went through last night. I *hate* that guy."

"You run into him already?" I asked. Xavier played with him years ago, and he constantly made passes at his sister, Daniella. And not of the hockey kind.

"Not yet," Xavier said. "But we should watch out for him." At our last game against Tulsa, Leinecker said something to Xavier that made him crazy. It took three of us to pull him off the guy. I landed a good punch, if I do say so myself.

"I won't pass up a chance to hit him for you," I promised.

He grinned. "And I'll do the same when McCrae comes after you."

"Deal, deal. Knuckie seal?" I rhymed.

It was our thing.

We fist-bumped to lock it in. Creighton McCrae had been a thorn in my side for years. The right-winger knew how to hook me on the backcheck without being detected by the linesman. Three times last game. I'd earned a ten-minute misconduct for sitting on him and punching him *Christmas Story* Ralphie style. I was strategic where I landed the punches and careful not to hurt him—I didn't want the team to incur the extra penalty kill time for blood—but it sure looked bad on the replay. The fans ate it up. Probably mortifying for him, especially when a Ralphie/Scut Farkus clip played side-by-side with our replay on the jumbotron. It almost got me a hearing with the department of player safety. But someone decided the intent to harm wasn't there, so I narrowly avoided a suspension.

What could I say? It was December, and my favorite movie was on my mind.

I was ready for him tonight. And Leinecker, too. Convenient that they were playing on the same line.

A few minutes in, their forward line matched up with Xavier and me on defense.

Seattle iced the puck, and as we gathered in the defensive right circle around Dean, flanked by wingers Noel Allaire and Kingston Brewer for the faceoff, Xavier and I mimed a plan.

I pointed to McCrae and then tapped my chest, then gestured for Xavier to take Leinecker. Xavier pointed at Noel and shook his head, reminding me about his kidney issue. Noel was married to Penny's cousin Gabby and had only one kidney. We couldn't let him get hurt.

The ref dropped the puck, and we dropped our gloves. Dean joined the scrum, and Kingston got in front of Noel, holding his stick horizontally, challenging anyone who would come toward them.

I landed the first punch on McCrae and was rewarded with a knee to the hip. "You fight like a girl, Creighton. Your sister teach you that move?"

"No, yours did," he retorted. "It was hot, too."

I laughed and launched myself at him. He twisted away, so I grabbed a fistful of his jersey, and we both went down.

"Don't talk about my sister!" I hissed. Our helmets were off now, and I rolled on top of him. His eyes widened. I grinned. "Don't worry." I patted his cheek. "I won't mess up your pretty face." It was one thing to pretend to beat the stuffing out of a helmet and a whole other thing to give the guy a concussion.

I didn't hate him. This was just business. I blew McCrae a kiss as the linesmen wrenched me off him and dragged me to the penalty box.

Xavier was already there. But he wasn't grinning like I was. "Why the scowl over the foul?" I asked. "Didn't you win?"

"To be continued." He spit blood into a towel. "Freaking Leinecker. I *really* hate that guy."

"Is Dani here?" I stretched my neck as I tugged on my returned gear.

He shook his head. "She's at home in Seattle. But now *he* is, too. She trains at their practice rink."

"Dani's a grown woman, Swanny. She can—and does—handle herself. And him."

He shrugged. "She shouldn't have to. I don't know why he's so stuck on her. She's never given him the time of day."

"And there's your answer."

He turned to glare at the guy in the box next to us. "I'm not done with him."

"We've all got your back. But let's not get ejected, okay? We have a game to win, and I promised Wynnie a hat trick."

He grinned. "You did, huh?"

"Yeah. So?"

His stupid smile widened. "Nothin'." He looked up at the clock. Fifteen seconds until we could bust out. "That means we need at least four tonight since I had my lucky toffee coffee. You ready?"

The door opened. "Let's do it."

CHAPTER 7
Arwyn

Zaki got his hat trick, and Xavier scored as well. The Edge won 5-3, and it was cool to watch the plastic and stuffed birds rain down on the ice. Hockey was definitely more exciting than I anticipated. And whew—the lingo! At times it felt like the announcers were speaking another language. The next time I streamed a game, I'd have to ask Isla and Amelie what all those words meant. We could make a game of it: I could say what I think it meant and they could correct me. Giggles all around. Like, why is it called a hat trick? I smiled, thinking of all the hats that rained down after Zaki's third goal. I never would have guessed it meant three goals in the same game.

For the first time since Tasha suggested this harebrained idea, I felt like it was going to work. Isla and Amelie loved their rooms, and as Zaki and I stood in the playroom watching them put away their things Tuesday afternoon, the pups looking on from their cozy spot in the recliner, the tension in my shoulders lifted.

"Digging the outfit," Zaki praised me. "You look very … governess."

"Daddy, she's dressed like Young Elsa!" Isla popped her head up from the bin of dolls she was setting on a shelf. "Long blue wool skirt with black ribbon trim. Matching short jacket and a white shirt with a fluffy collar. Black boots. You remember. From the movie?"

"Ah, right. How could I forget?"

I held back the urge to reveal I'd had this outfit for years, wore it often, and *didn't* make it as an inspirational piece from the movie.

"Do you think they'll be okay alone up here?" I asked. "I could sleep on the sofa on the nights you're not here."

"They'll be fine, Wynna-bun. And they've got Laffy and Vennie to look after them." The dogs yipped at the mention of their names, and Zaki grinned. "See?" He draped his arm over my shoulders. I shivered in response and looked up at him, surprised by the ease of the gesture.

And the fact that I wasn't hating it.

"How, um, do they like school so far?" The twins had started kindergarten at Palmer City Academy yesterday.

"They loved it. Thanks for the recommendation. Did you know Trask's stepdaughter Ryleigh goes there? They saw her getting dropped off and ran up to her. She had them under her wing and introduced to all the fifth graders before I could catch up."

"That's wonderful," I replied. I turned my gaze to the very large hand resting atop my right shoulder.

I'd never seen hands that big. I'd made the mittens for his costume, and they nearly reached my elbow when I tried them on.

Hands were funny things. Useful, yet also designed to comfort others.

Zaki Marsch's hand on my shoulder was comforting indeed.

"So," I said, very much *uncomfortable* with the pauses in our conversation. "Your schedule this week. Here tonight, tomorrow, and Friday, game Thursday, con Saturday, flying out Sunday?"

"You forgot skating Sunday," he teased.

"Right. Okay. Um, I guess I'll go start dinner, then?"

"I can help."

I looked at him skeptically. "Your personal chef has already been by to drop off all your prepped meals for the rest of the week. I can handle ziti and meatballs for the girls and I."

He grinned down at me. "Okay, then. I guess I'll play moose with the girls."

"Moose!" Amelie called. "Yay!"

I twisted out from under his arm and backed away as he dropped down to his hands and knees. Amelie set a reindeer headband on his head and climbed onto his back as he made a deep yet squeaky moosey call.

It was the sweetest thing I ever saw in my life. I covered my smile with my hand as Isla found a strip of jingle bells and fastened them around his neck. Zaki looked back at me and winked.

My cheeks flamed for reasons I didn't want to unpack, and I retreated down the stairs as fast as my much shorter legs could carry me.

SATURDAY MORNING CAME QUICK. We'd settled into a daily routine, with and without Zaki. He came and went as his schedule allowed.

The girls were surprisingly independent and capable for five and a half years old. They woke up to an alarm and got themselves dressed and ready for school. I helped with their hair, and they ate the breakfast the chef left for them. I walked them to school, walked home, worked until three o'clock, walked back to the school, walked them home, and played with them for an hour or so before they did their homework or other such activity in the kitchen while I prepared dinner. Then they'd take showers and we'd watch a movie together before bedtime.

Laffy and Vennie were adjusting, too. Well, it was more like I was adjusting to them. Sweet little things. They were quiet but mostly under my feet when I was home alone. If I was reading on the couch, one was on my lap and the other was behind my head. They'd run into the kitchen when their food was automatically dispensed by Zaki's app. They drank from a water fountain plugged into the wall, which I kept full. I disposed of their puppy pads as needed, laid out fresh ones, and gave them treats.

It was nice having company in the house. Sometimes, you

don't realize how lonely you've been until you're around people you miss when they're not there.

The hours of 9 a.m. to 3 p.m. had never been quieter in the history of quiet days.

Yesterday, I'd spent the morning zhuzhing up my Snow Queen dress, adding pale blue gems and snowflake appliques to the bodice and gloves.

I helped the girls get dressed for the con when Zaki called on his way home from practice and finished just as he pulled into the driveway. I told them to wait at the top of the steps until he came inside so they could make their grand entrance down the main stairs.

I excused myself to get ready. I was adding the finishing touches to my eye makeup—sparkly blue glitter and ridiculous false eyelashes—when I heard a knock, followed by the barks of Laffy and Vennie as they rocketed down the stairs to greet their master as he entered the house.

From the other side of my bedroom door, I listened in to the show. I could picture him bowing to the girls, praising their appearances, and calling them "Your Highness Majesties"—because he couldn't decide which title he liked better.

"Wynna-bun, you ready?" Zaki called when the giggle fest had died down. "Kristoff the Head Ice Maker of Arendelle is here to escort you to his sleigh-van-thing."

"Daddy! It's just a sleigh! Stay in character!"

I laughed and pulled the door open. "Ready!"

Zaki's eyes widened, which I will admit felt nice. It wasn't often my appearance had a positive effect on the opposite gender. They usually wrote me off as a weirdo for my untrendy, old-fashioned ensembles. I smiled wide, but it was more for him than from his reaction. The blond wig and clean-shaven face made him look like a caricature of his younger self, and it was adorable.

"Wynnie, you're *so* pretty!" Amelie breathed.

"Stunning, truly stunning! Isn't she *stunning,* Daddy?" Isla asked.

Anxious to rescue Zaki from having to respond, I blurted, "That's a great use of our Word of the Day, Isla, but I don't think—"

"Nope, don't think so," Zaki agreed.

My heart sank. Also, *rude.*

"But Daddy—"

"I *know* so, Isla." He blew at a lock of blond Kristoff hair. "The definition of stunning, for sure."

"Elsa! I'm Elsa today. Stay in character, Daddy!"

"Extremely impressive or attractive," Amelie recited. "Yes, it fits."

"Thank you, *Anna,*" I said in my best Mary Poppins tone. "Now, shall we go?"

The con was in a hotel convention center outside Denver, and we passed the ride there singing along to the *Frozen* soundtracks. Despite my protests that I was tone-deaf, they assigned me the part of Olaf, and we all sang our parts. And *wow,* could Zaki sing! Tasha had mentioned his karaoke performances were legendary, and after hearing him sing "Lost in the Woods," I was tempted to leave my house at night to see him on a makeshift stage at some bar.

"You should've added big black buttons to your dress," Zaki teased after I sang my heart out—a bit off-key—to "In Summer."

"But Daddy, we have—"

"Yeah, I know we have an Olaf, but Laffy can't sing, Isla," Zaki protested.

"Elsa!"

"Right!"

I didn't know what I was expecting, but after five minutes in the vendor hall, I found myself wondering why I'd never been to an event like this. Sure, I'd custom-made special-order gowns for conventions, but it never sounded like anything I'd enjoy. Booth after booth of pretty dresses and dolls and toys and games and art …

This was Nerd Heaven. Not a hedonistic parade of scantily clad dragon ladies or painted superheroes in skintight suits. This was … This was …

"Amazing," I murmured.

"Having a good time then?" Zaki asked as we stepped in line behind the girls at a cotton candy cart.

"The best," I replied sincerely. "It's not what I expected at all."

"There's a dress code and a long list of banned items," Zaki supplied. "The other ones are probably more along the lines of what you were expecting. I wouldn't bring the girls to those."

"I—" I pressed my lips shut. I *had* wondered how or if he'd shield the twins from things that were inappropriate. "I'm glad."

Zaki handed Amelie a credit card, which she presented to the vendor. "Four, please!"

I narrowed my gaze at him. "Is that allowed? What will Chef think?" I teased.

He took the paper cone Amelie handed up to him and plucked off a huge cloud of spun sugar. "I'll skate it off tomorrow at your hockey lesson."

"Hmm." Amelie handed me my cone, and I picked off a small chunk of blue from the top. "Well, I guess I can too, then." I pushed the treat into my mouth and smiled.

"You've got—" Zaki pointed to my face.

My fingers flew to my lips, in search of the spun sugar that dared to stick to my face. But I didn't feel anything.

"May I?" he asked.

I nodded and held my breath.

He grinned, and his thumb brushed against my … nose? I jumped back at the shock, and this time I was sure it was a static charge.

"How in the world?" I used my free hand to lightly swipe my face, just to make sure it was all gone.

He shrugged. "It matched your eye shadow."

"Its only redeeming quality." I laughed.

Hours later, as we drove back to my house, the girls asleep in their booster seats, I watched Zaki drive, softly singing along to 1980s rock ballads.

There was more to this guy than I ever could have imagined.

And I might've fallen a little bit in love with him today.

CHAPTER 8

Zaki

"Hockey Lesson 1: Make sure your skates and your equipment are on correctly. Let's take a look at how not to dress. Isles, you're up."

Isla skated out to me at the center of the backyard rink. "Don't be like me! Always fasten your chin strap." She nudged the dangling plastic end of it with her glove. "And make sure your laces are tucked in."

I snapped her strap together and tucked the loops of her laces in. "Great job, kiddo. Amms!"

Daughter number two joined me, sans gloves. "Always wear your gloves and a mouth guard." I pulled the items from the pocket of my jacket and handed them to her one at a time.

"Um …" Arwyn said from the side of the rink. She wore her long lavender coat and furry scarf. Her hands were stuffed into a large pocket thing she called a muff.

Needless to say, she wasn't dressed for hockey.

But that was okay. It would probably be easier to watch a game to explain how it worked.

"We'll work on it." I handed her a new mouthguard.

Her lips parted to protest. "But I—"

"You're not dressed for it. Too bad." I shook my head sadly. "Skating and shooting pucks are such great ways to shed the week's frustrations."

"I can skate," she said. "And maybe shoot. I have gloves on under this." She pulled a hand out of the muff. "See?"

I grinned. "Okay then. Hockey Lesson 2: Shooting."

"But Daddy!" Amelie protested. "You skipped a lot of stuff. And she needs a bucket."

"A bucket?" Arwyn asked. "You play hockey?"

"Helmet. Sometimes we play." She shrugged. "It's not hard. But it has a lot of rules."

"I'm sure. What are the rules for shooting?"

"Hit the puck and get it in the net."

"Okay. Got a stick for me to try?"

Isla skated over holding one of my sticks. "It's too big for you, but you can try it."

"Okay. Why is it too big?"

"Because you're short."

I watched the exchange intently. Arwyn didn't seem bothered or offended by Isla's directness.

"This is how you line up a shot." Amelie had her stick now and seemed comfortable enough taking over for me. "It's a lot like mini golf, but you need much more power."

She demonstrated, and her puck sailed straight into the net.

"Woohoo!" Isla cheered, holding her glove up for knuckies. "My turn!"

Her puck followed a similar path to Amelie's to the net, and the knuckies ritual was repeated.

"Great job, girls," Arwyn praised. "You make it look easy. All right, right hand low, left hand high, bend, pull back—and *whack!*"

The elbow of her stick made contact with the puck and slid a few feet toward the goal.

Amelie and Isla looked horrified. I held in a laugh and waited to see what they would say.

"I think I missed something," Arwyn mused.

"Daddy." Isla's tone was rueful. "You *have* to help her."

"Yeah," Amelie agreed. "That was a total hack job."

Arwyn snorted. "It was, wasn't it?"

"So bad!" Isla agreed. "But don't worry, Daddy is the best at shooting, and if anyone can help you, he can."

"Is that so?" Arwyn regarded me curiously, a hint of a smile playing at her lips. "I thought Kingston Brewer was the best shooter on the Edge? And Xavier is pretty good, too. Didn't he win a big award last year?"

"But *I* have my face on merch bags," I bragged. "That should say something, no?" I teased back.

"All right, *Marshy,* work your magic. Instruct me in the ways."

My heartbeat kicked up. The way Arwyn said that ... *Instruct me in the ways.* I didn't know her that well, but I had a feeling there were lots of *ways* I could instruct her in, if given the opportunity.

I needed a moment.

What were we doing?

Right. Hockey.

Shooting.

Okay.

I pushed off on my right skate and joined her at center ice. The girls arranged the pucks along the red line. "Do you mind if I get behind you and, um, guide your swing?"

Her eyes locked on mine. "I'm all yours."

Whew. Okay.

Did she have any idea how her words could be misinterpreted by a guy?

"All right. I'm gonna place your hands on the stick, then I'm gonna bear-hug you."

She watched attentively as I placed her hands. When I skated up behind her and reached my arms over hers, she stiffened.

"Relax," I whispered into her ear. The pompom on her hat tickled my nose. I slid my hands into position over hers.

"I'll try. It's a bit ... awkward."

"I promise to get you a better-fitting stick for your next lesson," I assured her. "You're perfectly set up for a golf swing, but this is hockey. You need to widen your stance and crouch."

She adjusted her position to the frame I'd created. "Like this?"

"Just like that. Now pull the stick back, and when you bring it down, try to imagine scooping the puck with the curve of the blade instead of hitting it straight on. You want to guide it, direct it, not see how high and far you can launch it. Not yet, anyway."

With my hands over hers, I pulled the stick back and swung it down toward the ice. It caught the puck, which sailed straight into the net.

"We did it!" Arwyn hopped up, and I nearly missed getting clocked in the chin by the Tam of Death.

The girls cheered and encouraged her to try it again, on her own.

She was a fast learner and a crack shot. One after the other, she hit the pucks into the net.

"See?" Isla asked. "It's not hard if you know what you're doing."

"Nope," Arwyn agreed. "Not too different from mini golf, which I am decent at. Or croquet. Bigger target, until you add a goalie, at least."

"You play croquet?" Amelie asked. "I love that game!"

"Me too!" Arwyn smiled. "We should set up a course after the snow melts."

"Yes!" the girls chorused.

As I watched the exchange happily, my body tingled from the aftershocks of contact with Arwyn. She sure was one of a kind. And the girls loved her.

I wouldn't be worried when I left them with her tonight for the road trip.

But I might be a little sad.

CHAPTER 9

Arwyn

Ah, the smell of new books! Nothing like it!

In an effort to *engage,* I decided to volunteer at Palmer City Academy's book fair. Most of it had been set up over the weekend, so by the time I arrived in the school library after dropping the girls off, all that was left to do was open the rolling bookshelves and tidy up the displays.

There were seven of us volunteering this morning: four moms, a grandmother, and Clarice, our town's retired librarian. One of the moms looked familiar, but I couldn't remember where I'd seen her before—long brown waves, light blue turtleneck under a white puffer vest, and jeans.

They were all wearing jeans.

I hadn't worn jeans since high school. Hopefully it wasn't a problem. I'd dressed for the part, or so I thought. Long skirt, button-down, argyle vest.

Librarian-ish.

I sidled over to Clarice, whose many years of similar outfits had inspired the look. Back in those days, if I wasn't in the ice cream shop, I was in the library.

I bent down to give her a hug. She used a wheelchair these days and lived at Mountainview Manor in their assisted living wing, but that didn't keep her from getting out and sharing her opinions of everyone and everything.

"Look what the cat dragged in!" she hooted. "Arwyn Baughn, do you realize you're out in public, where there will be ..." She paused, and her expression grew mischievous. *"People?"*

I sighed internally but smiled for her. "Yes, Miss Clarice. I like kids, remember? And I'm trying to *engage* more. Get involved a little. Get out of the house more. That's my word this year."

She huffed. "Engage, huh? Good one. Maybe you'll meet someone and *get* engaged. Maybe that hot hockey player you're nannying for. You've been alone too long, young lady."

I could only stare at her, horrified, as she cackled at my expense. "How did you—"

"There's no rock here to crawl under, and pink cheeks suit you, dear. You were always so serious, even as a tiny girl. Everyone in town knows. Just because *you* don't get out doesn't mean the news stays in. Kami! Come meet Arwyn. We've been friends her whole life."

"Until today," I murmured to more of Clarice's cackles.

The mom I thought looked familiar hurried over. "Miss Clarice, you're awfully bossy for the first day of the book fair," she chastised in a Southern accent. "I'm Kami Emerson. I think we have some friends in common. My husband, Trask, plays for the Edge."

I shook her hand. "That's where I know you from. Your daughter is Ryleigh?"

She laughed. "The one and only. She made quite a splash at Tasha and Monty's wedding. That child sure keeps me on my toes! I *loved* Tasha's gown, by the way. You did an amazing job, and in such a short time."

"Thank you." I began to relax. "That was one of my favorites to date."

"I hear you also made Zaki's Kristoff ensemble?" I nodded. "Incredible! Trask texted me a picture last night. Apparently, Zaki fell asleep on the plane and his seatmate raided his phone. They had a field day when he woke up. All the memes!"

"Yikes," I squeaked. If anyone ever got ahold of *my* phone, I'd probably die.

"He had it coming. All those pranks over the years? This was nothin'."

"I guess." It sounded like a nightmare scenario. I didn't know what else to say.

"Let me introduce you to the other volunteers." Kami linked her arm in my elbow and dragged me away from my poorly intentioned crutch that was Clarice. The old woman had the audacity to wink at me as I was led off.

I was put in charge of restocking items as the stacks and piles were picked at by each class. Occasionally, a student asked for help or advice, and I was happy to give it.

As the last class before lunch filed out at eleven thirty, Mrs. Reed, the librarian, called us all together. "Wonderful job this morning! Minimal mess and no tears. I'll call that a win! As a thank you, the PTA is providing lunch for all the volunteers, in my office, each day this week. It's already set up. Morning crew, you're welcome to stay or grab and go. If you're here all day and/or want to eat lunch with your student or students, I ask that you return before the next class arrives at twelve fifteen. Afternoon volunteers were invited to lunch, but I don't expect them to arrive until noon. And if you signed up for the morning and want to stay all day, I'll be glad to have you. Any questions?"

I leaned toward Kami. "We can eat with the kids? Where? How?"

She grinned. "Follow me."

We filled our plates from the selection of salads and breads in Mrs. Reed's office and grabbed bottles of water.

"Cafeteria is this way. The lower school students have lunch and recess from eleven thirty until noon, and upper school's is from twelve fifteen until twelve forty-five. And here we are." She tucked her bottle of water under her chin and pulled open the door.

I froze.

Waves of memories from the cafeterias of my past rose from their graves and haunted me mute.

"Arwyn? Are you okay?" Kami held the door with her whole body, waiting for me to enter.

"Oh! Yes. Sorry. How do I—"

"Find the twins? You don't. They just found you." She pointed her water bottle toward the twins and grinned.

"Wynnie!"

"You're here!"

"Come to our table!"

"Can Ryleigh's mommy sit with us, too? And Ryleigh?"

I turned my head to Kami for answers. I was sure I looked like a deer in headlights.

"Of course!" Kami said easily. "Why don't you take Arwyn to your table, and I'll see if Ry is available." She lowered her voice. "She sits with kids from her hockey team at lunch, and they usually strategize for the next game. It's very important business."

"Hockey hockey hockey, always hockey," Amelie huffed. "Rescue her from that boring stuff. We're talking about princesses at our table."

"I'll see what I can do," Kami promised.

"C'mon, Wynnie, this way. Can I carry your water?" Isla asked.

I handed it to her, and Amelie's little fingers took hold of mine and held them tightly, as if she knew I'd considered bolting. We reached the table, a long rectangle with connected stools on each side.

Isla took charge of the seating arrangement. "Everyone on this side, move down two seats. Amelie, you slide over one spot and Wynnie can sit in the middle of us. Ryleigh and her mommy can sit across."

The little girls all did as instructed. For Isla's sixth day at a new school, she sure seemed well-adjusted.

I sat between them, not sure what I was supposed to do or say. I'd never dined with a table of kindergarteners before.

Kami and Ryleigh arrived, and I realized I didn't have to do anything. Ryleigh, the fifth grader, had full command of the table. The little girls asked her questions and hung onto her every word.

"Who's your favorite princess, Ryleigh?"

"Sleeping Beauty. She's the best dancer."

"She's mine, too!"

"And mine!"

Ah, impressionable little girls.

Fifteen minutes later, Ryleigh was explaining to her captivated audience why Tinker Bell and her friends were superior to princesses because they fixed things and controlled nature. Kami and I ate our lunches, smiled a lot, and answered questions when we were asked, but for the most part, it was the Ryleigh Show.

"Thanks for a lovely lunch, girls. It's time for us to get back to the books," Kami said. "We had a wonderful time!"

"Will you come back tomorrow?" Amelie asked.

Kami shook her head. "I'm taking Ryleigh's brother to the doctor tomorrow."

"Wynnie?" Isla asked. "Can you come again tomorrow?"

"Well, I—" I began. "I'm not sure. I volunteered for today. I can ask Mrs. Reed if she needs more help tomorrow."

"Yay! We shop tomorrow!" Amelie pulled at my arm. "Will you help me pick my books? Daddy said we can each spend twenty dollars!"

"I definitely don't want to miss that!" I hugged them goodbye, then followed Kami back to the library. "Can I do that? Come again tomorrow?"

"I don't see why not. Especially with the kindergarteners. It's all hands on deck for that group. But don't you have to work?"

"I do." Penny's Valentine gown wasn't just a ploy. She and Tasha were coming by tomorrow to choose a design. "I could move some things around. Come in the mornings and stay for lunch."

"I say do it, then. You had fun this morning, right?"

"I did."

"Then it's a no-brainer."

The afternoon passed even more quickly than the morning had, and by dismissal I was filled with joy and drained of energy. I waited for the girls in the school lobby, and my heart warmed again as they ran to me the instant they saw me. Isla and Amelie looked like they stepped out of a catalog, with their tiny pink peacoats, matching ballet-themed backpacks, and shiny black boots.

When we got home, we had a quick snack and went outside to play. Though the air was chilly, the sun blazed its warmth, something I loved about living in Colorado. I rocked in the creaky porch swing as they released their excess energy on my old playset. If I could bottle up even a little of their endless fuel, I'd be better for it.

I returned to the book fair the next day and had a glorious time helping the girls spend their money. On my recommendation, they'd each purchased their own copy of *Anne of Green Gables*. I was surprised they weren't familiar with the classic Canadian story and promised to read it with them at bedtime.

They climbed into bed, propped up on pillows with Laffy and Vennie cuddled up at their sides. I'd also purchased a copy of the book. I had several copies of my own, but I thought it might be easier for us all to find our place if we all had the same edition.

"Wynnie?"

"Yes, Amelie?"

"Can we call Mommy? She might like this story. She's from Canada."

I smiled. "Of course." I retrieved her tablet from the top of the dresser. I kept their electronics downstairs with me at night. "Here you go."

I'd been in the background a few times last week when the girls had video-called their mom, but I hadn't spoken to her. I felt the anxiety creep in. Had she even had a say in who Zaki hired to take care of their girls? I suddenly felt put on the spot.

"Hi, Mommy!" The girls bent over the tablet and held up their books.

"It's story time!" Amelie said. "Wynnie is going to read to us. Want to listen?"

"It's a Canada story!" Isla said. "And you're in Canada!"

"I am. That's very nice of her." Viki sounded tired, defeated. My heart cracked for her. I couldn't imagine how much she must miss her daughters. "Turn the screen so I can say bonjour to your sweet nanny."

Amelie held up the screen and switched the view.

"Bonjour," I said. "Nous lisons *Anne … la maison aux pignons verts*."

"Mon préféré. Les filles vont adorer. Merci de le leur lire, et merci de m'inclure."

"De rien." I smiled. "It's my favorite, too."

"Wynnie speaks French, Mommy." Isla took the tablet from Amelie and switched the view back.

"Very well too, I must say. So, are we ready to start? My healthcare providers have me on a strict schedule here." She lowered her voice to a whisper. "It's almost my bedtime."

The girls giggled, but I wondered how Viki's recovery was coming along.

"I'll get started right away. Page five, girls." I waited until they were ready. "Chapter one: Mrs. Rachel Lynde is surprised. Mrs. Rachel Lynde lived just where the Avonlea main road dipped down into a little hollow, fringed with alders and ladies' eardrops and traversed by a brook that had its source away back in the woods of the old Cuthbert place ..."

CHAPTER 10
Zaki

I woke up Wednesday to a text from Viki: *Call the girls at 7:30 p.m. their time.*

We were flying to Tampa this afternoon, so that would be nine thirty. I could do that. I already planned to call them at eight.

I texted back. *Want to tell me why?*

Nope. <smile emoji> *But you've been invited to something. Don't be late, okay?*

I set the alarm on my phone for nine twenty-five. *Okay. Thanks.*

Weird that the girls or Arwyn didn't invite me, but I didn't have time to dwell on it. We'd beaten Nashville last night and had a team breakfast meeting in a banquet room downstairs. Then practice, then the flight. By nine thirty, I'd be ready for bed.

I missed my girls. I didn't get to say good night to them on game nights, and we'd had two in a row. We'd had a quick call yesterday before the game, and they told me about the book fair and lunch with Ryleigh and Kami. It sounded like they were having a great week.

As an afterthought, I sent another text. *How's the recovery going? Papé said you're doing great but how do you feel?*

Viki's dad had been as much of a dad to me as my own dad. I'd started calling him Papé and her mom Maman when we got married. It felt weird now, but it was what it was.

Fine. Slow. Painful. Could be worse.

I hate this for you, Vik.

Me too.

I was showered and lounging on the bed in my hotel room at nine twenty-seven. Close enough. I tapped the button for the group video chat and a few seconds later was rewarded with the sweetest faces on the face of the earth.

"Daddy! You made it!" Isla turned, and her nose poked into Amelie's screen. "I told you he would!"

"I'm here. What's the occasion?" I asked.

"Storytime!" Amelie bounced. "But you have to hang up and call back. Just call Isla. Because I'm going to call Mommy."

"Okay. I'll be right back then. Don't start without me." She giggled, and I ended the call to start the new one. "There you are!"

"Here I am! And there's Wynnie." Isla flipped the screen.

Arwyn waved. "Hi." I squinted to see what she was wearing. It looked like a kimono. Pink with white designs and trim. Pretty cool.

"Now say hi to Mommy!" Isla held up her screen to Amelie's. I waved at Viki. She smiled tightly, but it was more of a wince. I made a mental note to ask her parents about the care in the rehab facility.

"We're all here now, Wynnie," Amelie reported. "Daddy, you didn't miss much. So far, a red-haired girl named Anne who has no mommy and daddy—isn't that so sad?—from Nova Scotia took a train and a boat and a train to Prince Edward Island to live with a new family. A sister and brother who are old and have a farm. But they didn't want her. Guess why?"

"Hmm ..." I stroked my beard. "I can't imagine why. Is she a naughty girl?"

Amelia and Isla laughed. "No!" Isla said. "But she does talk a lot. A *lot* a lot."

"More than you two?"

They giggled again.

"Who wouldn't want a good little girl? I know! Was she very ugly? Did she have warts all over her face?"

"No!" the girls hooted.

"Then I can't imagine why anyone wouldn't want a sweet little girl. *Especially* a redhead."

"Well, Daddy, you see—" Amelie paused, her tone serious. "She wasn't a *boy*. They wanted a boy! To do farm chores." She wrinkled her nose.

"Farm chores! Can't girls do farm chores?" I asked.

Isla shrugged. "Not a long time ago. It wasn't ladylike. The ladies had tea parties. Every day! They couldn't be dirty from *farm work.*"

I held back a smile. "What kind of farm work, exactly?"

The girls looked at each other and shrugged.

"Growing potatoes," Arwyn said. "And vegetables. Apple trees. Chickens. Hay for their dairy cow. Milking the dairy cow."

"Sounds fun," I said. "Thanks for catching me up."

"Wynnie, can you start now?" Amelie pleaded. "Daddy, no more questions. Buy the book if you want to read along. I've been waiting *all day.*"

I snorted. "Yes, ma'am."

Arwyn started. "Chapter four. Morning at Green Gables."

"Wait!" The screen went awry as Amelie set it down and picked up her book. "Now I'm ready!"

"All right," Arwyn said. "It was broad daylight when Anne awoke and sat up in bed, staring confusedly at the window through which a flood of cheery sunshine was pouring and outside of which something white and feathery waved across glimpses of blue sky."

Arwyn's reading voice was controlled. Elegant. She sucked me into the town and the people of Avonlea, and three chapters flew by. I'd have to get the audiobook so I could keep up with the story since I wasn't free every night at seven thirty. Somehow, I already knew that whoever would be narrating the book wouldn't be as nice as Arwyn. I wondered if she'd ever considered doing voice work. For a woman of few words, she sure had a beautiful speaking voice.

I said good night to the girls and waited about ten minutes before I texted Arwyn.

Thanks for taking such good care of the girls. And including their mom. It means a lot.

It's my pleasure. They're the sweetest kids, and my heart goes out to Viki. I can't imagine how much she must miss them. I miss them while they're at school, and I just met them.

How much did I want to tell her about our situation? Probably the more she knew, the better she'd understand how hard it all was for all of us.

I texted: *Yeah, it was really hard to take them from her, but she needed the surgeries and time in rehab. She never would've stayed at a facility if the girls were in Montreal, and that would compromise a full recovery. Bringing the girls here was her parents' idea, and to be honest, I still don't feel good about it, even though I know in my brain it's the best plan.*

Three dots appeared, indicating she was typing. Then they stopped. I watched the phone, waiting.

Do you want to talk about it? I'm a good listener, and I promise to keep it private.

That was nice of her, but I was reluctant to bring her into the family drama. It was one thing to tell her about it and another to use her as my therapist. I got the feeling whatever I told her she'd carry like a weight, and I didn't want to put that on her.

Maybe another time, I texted back. I'd leave the door open in case I changed my mind or our circumstances changed and I had to tell her more. *Thanks.*

You're welcome.

Good night, Wynna-bun.

Good night, Mr. Marsch.

I grinned at my phone. Her humor was understated, and it intrigued me.

There was so much more about Arwyn Baughn that I wanted to know. Not just because she was taking care of my girls but because she was a cool human. She didn't care about the latest fashion or decor. She did her own thing, wearing outfits and decorating her house like she was living in another century. I wondered what she had against this one and if I could find a way to show her the present could be just as exciting as the past.

Returning "home" to Arwyn's house was night and day to coming home to the Denver apartment. I'd hand my keys to the valet, wheel my suitcase and garment bag to the elevator, and key open the door to a quiet apartment. If Viki and the girls were home, they were practicing their ballet or working with their tutor or pretending to be princesses in their playroom.

I pulled into the driveway, and the front door flung open before I could put the van in park. My girls, dressed in their plaid school skirts, navy vests, and white button-down shirts with matching tights, ran down the steps shouting at the top of their lungs that I was home. I had to scramble to get out of the vehicle before they reached it. Laffy and Vennie joined the chaos with a cacophony of delighted barks. It only took a quick scruff to each of the terriers' heads to get their tongues lolling to one side.

I scooped up my daughters and closed my eyes, inhaling their strawberry shampoo and … cookie dough?

"Have you girls been baking?" I asked. My stomach growled at the prospect of cookies.

"Yes!" Amelie held my cheeks in her hand and rubbed her nose on mine. "Your beard is tickly."

"I thought you liked my beard?"

"I do. But it's not soft anymore. But it's tickly."

"That's 'cause it's short, Amms. It needs to grow longer, and then it'll get soft again."

"Well, tell those hairs to hurry up, then!"

I laughed. "I think they heard you. Let's hope they listen."

"Daddy!" Isla leaned her head in front of Amelie's so she'd be in my direct line of sight. "It's *butter tarts!*"

"Butter tarts?" Now my stomach *was* growling. Butter tarts were one of the few cheats I allowed during the season.

If they were good.

No one made butter tarts like Maman, Viki's mom. Her recipe was the standard, to the point where Viki wouldn't even attempt them because they never came out exactly right.

"Yes!" Amelie's palms left my cheeks to push Isla's head out the way. "Wynnie asked Mommy for Mémère's recipe! And we made it!"

"You did? Mémère's butter tarts? Here?"

"Uh-huh," Isla confirmed. "And we called Mémère so she could teach us. Come in and eat them!"

"If you insist." My luggage could wait. Butter tarts!

"But Daddy." Isla's hands jerked my head so that her lips were on my ear. "Whatever you do, *don't call them cookies."*

"Wynnie said that word and Laffy and Vennie went crazy," Amelie reported. "They've been trying to steal them!"

"Well, we can't let that happen." I crouched to set the girls on the ground and looked up toward the front door. Arwyn stood on the porch, a picture of nineteenth-century domesticity. Auburn tendrils fanned out at the sides of her head, escaping from the bun that was loosely pinned on top. A blousy white shirt with fancy buttoned cuffs trimmed with lace tucked into a long green skirt.

She looked like the painting of *Anne of Green Gables* on the cover of book six.

Yeah, I was keeping up with my reading, and I bought the whole series. Arwyn was rocking the *Anne of Ingleside* look.

And it was doing funny things to my insides.

It wasn't like me to feel flustered. Or stare.

I'd have to dive into that later.

"Hurry, Daddy!"

I jogged up the steps. Arwyn stepped aside, but I shook my head. "Ladies first."

She smiled shyly and followed the girls into the kitchen. I closed the door behind me and locked it, then followed the scent of the freshly baked butter tarts to the kitchen.

Two furry blurs rushed past me, barking and begging for even more of my attention. I gave Laffy and Vennie a quick pet on the head each and turned my full attention to the girls.

"Ta-da!" the twins chorused, one on each side of the plate of cookies, waving jazz hands over them.

"Try them, Daddy," Isla commanded. "Don't just stare at them. Tell us if they're good!"

"I'm sure they're perfect," I insisted. And I would keep it to myself if they weren't.

"Here." Amelie held one up above her head. "Eat."

"Bossy." I took it from her and held it up at eye level. "Well, it *looks* like Mémère's butter tart. Or as she calls it, *tarte au beurre.*"

"Daddy!"

"Fine, fine." I took a bite into the shell. Then another, capturing the raisin filling, determined to drag out the process as long as I had a captive audience.

It was a skill, taking multiple bites of a butter tart. They were small.

"Daddy!"

I popped the rest into my mouth, chewing slowly and swallowing. "Just like Mémère's."

The girls whooped, jumping up and down, the dogs joining in their celebration.

"I told you!" Isla hugged Amelie. "We did it!"

"Well, Wynnie helped," Amelie confessed. She looked up at me. "A lot. They were hard to make."

"So I've heard." I turned to thank Arwyn, but she wasn't there.

"Where did she go?" I asked, peeking out of the kitchen.

Amelie pointed toward the living room. "At the sewing machine. She said we're all yours 'cause she needs the last of the natural light to finish Penny's bodies because she's coming tomorrow to try it on."

"Penny's bodies?" I asked.

"Yes, Daddy." Isla rolled her eyes. "The bodies. It's the part of the dress in the front that has all the pretty decorations."

"Ah," I said. "The bodice."

Isla pinned me with a look that could take down a weaker man. I prayed for her future husband. "That's what I said. *The bodies.*"

"Right," I conceded. Best never to argue with a five-year-old girl who knows more than you do.

"So, it's just me, you, and you, and the butter tarts?"

"Nope," Amelie said. "You'll ruin Chef's dinner."

"What?"

Amelie pointed to a box of aluminum foil on the counter. "Wrap it up, Daddy. You can have more later. We have a schedule to keep."

I waggled my eyebrows. "We do? Tell me more."

Isla reached her hand into the side pocket of Amelie's vest and pulled out a piece of paper. She unfolded it and began to read: "Eat two butter tarts before five o'clock. Five: Preheat the oven to 375 degrees. Five ten: Put in Chef's dinner and set the timer for forty minutes. Go outside and play until it gets dark." She looked up. "We should hurry. My weather app says sunset is in fifteen minutes!"

I crossed to the oven and set the temperature. "What's after playtime?"

Isla continued. "Five twenty-five: Come inside and wash our hands. Five thirty: Dance party. Five forty: Set the table. Five fifty: Daddy takes out chicken dinner and puts it on plates. Five fifty-five: Get Wynnie and tell her dinner is ready. Six: Say a blessing and eat." She looked up. "That's all we've got so far."

"Great reading, Isles. That's a very strict schedule. We'll have to stay focused to get it all done. And wow, you wrote all that, Amms?"

She nodded. "We made a list with Wynnie and then I copied it." She handed it to me.

My girl had better handwriting than half the team. "Very nice."

She beamed with pride.

I loved complimenting my daughters.

I popped the lids off the containers labeled "Friday Dinner" just as the oven dinged it was ready. Once the premade meals were arranged on the middle rack, I shut the door and set the timer. It was nothing fancy—baked chicken tenderloins, vegetables, and heirloom potatoes—but I liked it, and I knew the girls would eat it. I'd ordered extra food for the nights I'd be home and hoped Arwyn wouldn't mind. She had her hands full on the days I was traveling, so I figured I'd take care of dinner on the nights I was home.

"Playtime!" Isla announced. "Get your coats on!"

I set the alarm on my phone for fifteen minutes. Didn't want to be late to wash my hands before the dance party.

Playing with my girls on Arwyn's old swing set was a blast. I helped them across the monkey bars as the dogs leapt and yipped underneath. On the swings, I let them kick me in the backside while they tried to soar as high as their little legs could muster. Every few kicks to the bootie, I'd pretend they got me good and fall on the ground, thus offering Laffy and Vennie chances to use me as *their* personal playground and slobber on my face accordingly.

Performing for my girls and their dogs and being rewarded with hysterical giggles was the very definition of fatherhood joy.

The alarm went off too soon, and I'll give them credit; they were determined to stick to their plan. I washed my hands at the kitchen sink when they ran to the downstairs bathroom, and we were ready for the dance party at five twenty-nine.

"Where's the party?" I asked.

Isla shrugged. "In the front room?"

"Isla," Amelie chastised, "Wynnie is *working* in there!"

"Let's ask." Isla ran out of the kitchen, Amelie hot on her heels.

I followed them across the vestibule and into the living room that Arwyn called the front room. A row of open trifold project boards propped up by stacks of books and ottomans separated Arwyn's work area from the rest of the room. Laffy and Vennie scratched at them, barking and jumping.

Arwyn rose from the chair at her machine and faced us, gesturing to the makeshift fence. Wringing her hands, she apologized. "I hope you don't mind. I had to keep them away from my work."

"Not a problem at all. I should have anticipated that. I'll order a gate tonight."

"You don't have to do that. I—"

I held up my hand. "I want to."

"Okay, thank you."

"Daddy, the schedule!" Amelie protested.

I grinned at Arwyn. "Want to join us for our dance party?"

"I'd love to. If your dad doesn't mind."

"Not at all. I can teach you my best moves."

"Your moves are so bad, Daddy. But we're glad you're home," Amelie said.

Home. Here, at 87 Idlewild Way, it felt like *home.* Like I'd always imagined it.

On a rare occasion, Viki would drive the girls up to the cabin, but it was never like this: the homecoming my teammates who had families talked about and looked forward to.

This was the homecoming I'd been missing.

The homecoming I wanted.

The homecoming I couldn't keep.

CHAPTER 11

Arwyn

Zaki took the girls with him to practice Saturday morning after their ballet class, and the house was so quiet I almost didn't know what to do with myself. Penny wasn't due until ten for her first fitting, so I decided to strip the beds and wash the sheets and towels. I turned the television on to the classical music channel and donned my nineteenth-century housekeeping apron.

Chores were more fun in character.

The washer and dryer were downstairs, so I removed the sheets off my bed and grabbed the bathroom and kitchen towels for the first load. I headed upstairs next and paused on the landing. The girls' play space was immaculate. Every toy was on a shelf or neatly arranged in the window seat. The chairs were pushed in at the table, and there wasn't anything on the floor for me to pick up or step on. We'd cleaned up last night—and every night—before bed, but I didn't expect this level of tidiness after all the noise I'd heard while they were getting ready this morning.

Their room was just as neat. As I pulled back the comforter and blanket to remove the sheets and shook the pillows out of their cases, I thought about how easy these first two weeks had been. Sure, we were busy, but it was a *good* kind of busy. We'd settled into a routine and had even had some impromptu ballet practices to sharpen their skills for their first lesson since their recital in Denver last spring. With my experience, I was able to adjust and critique their positions and movements.

I gathered the linens in my arms and added the towels from their bathroom and walked to my dad's—now Zaki's—room. The door was open, so I dropped the girls' linens outside the doorway and crossed to the bed. I hoped he didn't mind that I was intruding.

I repeated the sequence of pulling back the comforter and removing the sheets and pillowcases. When I bundled them into my arms, I caught the faint scents of mint and eucalyptus mixed with something I couldn't place, but it felt masculine. Aftershave? Beard balm? Whatever soap he was using, it smelled really nice, and familiar. Did he always smell like this and I just hadn't noticed?

I quickly entered his bathroom, grabbed the used towels from the hamper, and hurried out of the room, revisiting the urge to snoop for the scent sources.

I wasn't a creeper.

On the floor, I rolled all the sheets and towels into the smallest bundle I could manage and carried them down the stairs. This amount of bedding and towels would have to be split into two loads, and I still had my own clothes and the girls' playclothes to wash.

I'd have to alter my laundry schedule. As much as I loved living in the past, an entire day devoted to laundry wasn't my idea of a good time.

Zaki had set up a routine with the dry cleaner to drop by and collect the girls' uniforms Thursday night so they'd have freshly laundered and pressed clothes for school and I wouldn't have to fuss with ironing. I'd told him I didn't mind, but after the first week, it hit me how time-consuming it was to take care of children full-time, on top of home care and oneself. It gave me a new respect for stay-at-home parents and those that had to balance working outside the home and most especially those that worked *from* home and were interrupted on a constant basis.

I was folding the kitchen towels from the first load when Penny arrived. I quickly finished the last two at the speed of lightning and stuffed the upstairs sheets into the dryer just as she rang the bell.

"Coming!" I set the dial, pressed the button, and ran to the front door. Spying the jar of doggie biscuits on the counter, I plucked out two, and with the same firm but cute commanding words that the girls taught me, I told Laffy and Vennie to go to their beds by the fireplace. A little more than amazed that the dogs had stopped and took notice, I called, "Be right there, Penny!" and followed them to their beds.

I rewarded them with treats and hurried back to the front door, sliding the bolt out of place and clicking the thumb turn to the left to unlatch the mechanism. "Sorry, I didn't want the dogs to scare the baby—"

I pulled open the door and grinned, surprised to see Monty behind Penny, wearing baby Melody on his chest in an elaborately tied cloth inside his open jacket.

"I hope you don't mind I brought the baby whisperer with me," Penny said, stepping inside and pulling off her scarf. "I couldn't get her to stop crying this morning, and neither could Xavier. He had to leave for practice, so I called Tasha to see if she could come stay with her while I came to my fitting, but she was still out delivering meals, so she sent Monty to meet me here."

"It's no problem." I looked outside as I shut the door behind them. Sure enough, Monty's truck was parked behind her crossover. "I can take your jackets."

Penny hung hers on an empty hook on the wall in the vestibule. "We can hang our own. I love your apron and all, but you're not a servant."

"Really, I don't mind. You're my guests," I insisted.

Penny gently extracted the baby from Monty's wrap, but the moment she was in her mother's arms, her nose twitched and she began to cry. Penny bounced her and cooed in a gentle tone while Monty removed his coat and hat, but Melody's wails only grew louder.

Monty reached for the baby, and Penny reluctantly handed her over. Once Melody was tucked back into the wrap, her crying ceased and she closed her eyes.

"I'm a terrible mother," Penny murmured. "I can't even comfort my own baby."

"Aw, Pen, you know that's not true," Monty said. "Remember what Nana Booboo said? That I'm a walking furnace? She's probably just cold. Or teething."

"Her gums are a little swollen." Penny sighed and wiped her eyes. "And I'm always cold." She turned to me. "Sorry to complain. I'm still trying to figure all of this out."

"It's no problem," I assured her. "Your gown is hanging on the back of my bedroom door. You can change in there, and then we'll go into the front room to make adjustments and discuss embellishments."

"Embellishments, huh?" Monty interrupted. "Like sequins and flair?"

"Something like that." I wasn't about to launch into all the possible embellishments of the Regency era with a guy whose only experience with design was deciding how many rhinestones to add to his cheerleading pants. "Make yourself at home," I told him and led Penny through the kitchen to my bedroom.

I would regret *that* invitation later.

When Penny opened the door and stepped out of my bedroom in the dress, I gasped. The gown was stunning, and it fit her like a glove. "Pen!" I whispered.

"You've outdone yourself," she praised. "Just needs a hem."

"Turn for me?" I asked. She complied, and I took a closer look.

"I'd be the envy of all the ladies at a Bridgerton ball," she boasted. "I can't believe I get to wear this! I've always wanted a Wynsome Design. This is stunning, Wynnie."

"There's more to come. Let me pin that hem, and we'll talk about beading and appliques."

Penny looked down at the dress. "But it's so pretty like this. And beading—if you mean hand-beading?" I nodded. "That's so expensive. Really, this is amazing as it is."

I shook my head. "I was instructed by Tasha to spare no expense. Right, Monty?" I called toward the front room.

He didn't answer. Weird.

"Okay," Penny said. "But know that it's more than I dreamed already."

I grinned. "Thank you."

It was great to have Nellie, June, my table, equipment, and supplies back in the front room. I directed Penny to stand on a small stepladder I pulled out from behind my dresser of notions. We chatted as I pinned the hem of the gown's satin and sheer overlay, which covered the center panel. The short, puffed sleeves also had a matching sheer overlay ending in a casing that I'd strung a ribbon through to tie in a bow.

"All right. Go change and bring me back the dress. We'll drape it on June here"—I pointed to the dress form—"and play with the accents."

Penny grinned. "Be back in a jif!"

A thump above my head made me jump. So that's where Monty went. Another thump, followed by a thunk.

Then barking. Lots of barking.

"Monty! You okay up there?" I called up the stairs. "You aren't traumatizing the dogs, are you?"

"Fine!" he called back. "Just—uh—doing backflips to make Melody laugh!"

He and Tasha coached an all-star Worlds team at the sportsplex, and Monty prided himself on being the best tumbler in the world. "Well, don't crash through the floor!" I yelled back. "Those boards are old!"

"Ten-four!"

I shook my head and checked my phone. Zaki had texted a picture of the girls and Ryleigh sitting on the bleachers with some other kids and a young woman who held a tablet. A few rows up, in the shadows and a little out of focus, was a group of women around my age, who I assumed were their moms. I recognized Kami sitting with Brenna Trotter and Taylor Brewer—both from Palmer City—holding little ones of various ages and pointing toward the ice.

The caption read, "Sources tell me the girls told Ryleigh about your hockey lesson and now they're plotting a group lesson for the Wags. Our social media manager, Mags, is all over it!"

I didn't know if I was supposed to text back or not, so I put my phone back on the charger and made a mental note to mention it in conversation when they returned.

Penny joined me in the front room, and we draped the dress gently over June. I adjusted the width of the form to the correct fit.

I waved her over to the table next to the sewing machine where I'd laid out various samples of laced and beaded appliques, lengths of lace and beads, and embroidered ribbons, and a few sketches of ideas I'd had for the center panel.

"These are all so pretty," Penny breathed. "I love this sketch of the harp embroidery with the bronze thread. How would you even do that on such fine material as the sheer overlay?"

"It would be set into the dress panel, and it wouldn't be too difficult. I located a harp stamp, and I'd use fabric chalk to lay out the pattern. Then it's just a matter of embroidering the stitching over the lines. The sheer is thin enough and has a sheen to it that will enhance and bring out the metallic thread underneath."

"You make it sound easy."

"It's not too hard. It took me years of trying different methods to figure out stitch techniques that worked for designs like this, which fabrics to use, and which methods I enjoyed. This will be time-consuming but also therapeutic. It gives me a chance to sit quietly and relax."

"And you can do that with the girls and dogs?" She quickly snapped her mouth shut. "I'm sorry. I just can't seem to get anything done with the baby at home."

"I understand. I used to nanny for Shanna, remember? It was tough with one, and when the second came along, it was near impossible to do anything except take care of them. But they grew and became more independent, and there were nap times. Melody won't be a baby forever, Penny. Before you can blink, she'll be in kindergarten like Isla and Amelie and able to entertain herself while you work—or play your harp."

"That's what K-Kami k-keeps telling me. B-b-but it's … hard." She sniffled and took a long breath in and out. "Sorry for breaking down again. I feel so helpless and unproductive. And then my b-big b-brute of a b-brother-in-law swoops in and calms her storm in s-seconds." She sighed.

I wrapped my arms around her, concerned to hear the return

of her stutter. "Accept the help, Penny. And don't doubt for a minute how incredible of a mom you are."

She gave me a squeeze. "Thank you."

"You're welcome. Now let's pick adornments for the bodice. You're going to be belle of the ball!"

She grinned. "Nah. But maybe the gal of the gala."

I laughed. "The gal of the gala, then!"

We were just finishing up when Monty came down the stairs with Melody and the dogs. Their nails clitter-clattered softly down the newly-polished hardwood steps as they raced each other to the bottom.

"She's napped, been changed, and had a snack of those puffy things that melt in her mouth." Monty oriented Melody so she could see Penny, and the baby reached her little sweater-clad arms toward her mother. Monty pulled her from her wrapping and handed her to Penny.

"Sweet girl." Penny bounced her in her arms and kissed her head. "You're a lifesaver, Uncle Monty."

"Yeah, I know." He grinned. "I'm going to head out if you don't need me anymore. I dropped Nana Booboo off at the Coffee Loft on my way here, and I think she's had enough time to terrorize the Riveras and their customers for one day. And we're taking Tasha out for a birthday lunch."

Penny laughed. "Go get her. And thank you again for your help. Uncle of the Year, for sure."

"Did you expect anything less?" He raised an eyebrow and grinned.

I rolled my eyes. Classic Monty.

Once they were gone, I folded the now-dry upstairs sheets, put the towels into the dryer, and topped off the dogs' water and food so they'd be distracted while I stamped the pattern of harps onto the dress at my worktable.

It took only a short time to stamp the fabric. Pleased with the arrangement, I gathered all the materials I'd need for this part of the process, including the gown, and took them to my room. I didn't want to take any chances that the dogs might suddenly learn to climb their new gate or displace it.

As I sat in my great-grandmother's comfy armchair, I thought about the picture Zaki had sent me. Most of my friends that were my age had paired up, and several were starting families or already had them. It hadn't bothered me in the least that I wasn't in a relationship or in that stage of my life. I was happy for them, and I trusted in God's plan and His timing. I'd always believed that if that was meant for me, I'd be ready if and when the right man came along.

I hadn't really ever put myself out there, though. Should I start dating? I didn't know the first thing about that. Sure, I'd been asked out plenty of times. Dances in high school, a few dates here and there when I was taking business classes at the local university. But no one I ever wanted a second date with. So I'd retreated into myself and my home and worked on building my business.

But seeing Penny with Melody, Tasha's pregnancy beginning to show, and people all around me becoming parents, I was feeling … left out? Maybe it was time to take Shanna up on her offer to set me up with her husband's best friend. I'd met him at their wedding, years ago, and he hadn't made much of an impression, nor did he seem interested in me. But he was a doctor now and too busy to go out looking for a soulmate.

Who knew? Maybe the seven-years-older versions of us were different. I'd certainly changed a lot since then. Not so much in appearance, but I had more confidence now and was mostly happy with who I was as a person. I had my faults and struggles —like going out in public—but didn't everyone have a thing they were working on?

I thought about all the pros and cons as I hand-stitched the harps and lost track of time. I didn't look up until Zaki and the girls pulled in. They came in the house and ran up the stairs so fast, I didn't even have time to tie off my stitch and greet them.

I was arranging the gown on June, whom I'd moved into my bedroom, and scrutinizing my progress when Zaki's shave-and-a-haircut knock on my door made me jump.

"Come in," I called, crouching down to fix a loose pin at the hem.

"Am I disturbing you?" Zaki leaned against the doorframe in a fitted Dri-Fit team T-shirt that strained the fabric over his biceps. His *tattooed* biceps. And tattooed left forearm …

"In more ways than one," I muttered. *Oh my.* He usually wore a hoodie in the house; I'd never seen his … arms.

They were nice arms. Strong arms. Inked with an artsy vine and his girls' names and the shapes of the places he'd lived weaved in with woodsy landscapes and team logos and a hockey stick and …

Stop staring.

Well, I couldn't know for sure if they were strong arms, and since I didn't have any plans of testing that theory, I would just happily keep assuming so in my head.

"Sorry, what?" he asked.

I stood up and tapped my own bicep. "Your shirt is ill-fitting. Perhaps a size up would fit better? I don't think I could alter that one." *Or perhaps I could turn down the heat and you can cover up so you don't distract me,* I wanted to add.

He barked a laugh as my cheeks burned, but I think I covered up the fact that I was staring—and impressed—at his, er, *strength.* Yes, strength. That was it. I drew in a long breath through my nose and let it out slowly between my lips.

"So … how was your morning?" I asked. "Do the girls need anything?"

He shook his head. "Just the sheets for their bed. We can handle making the beds, but I might need some assistance keeping them out of harm's way when I flip the furniture back to its original positions."

Now it was my turn to ask. "I'm sorry, *what?*"

"The nightstands and chair in my room are upside down, the box spring is on top of the mattress, and the shirts in the closet are hanging inside out. My cable remote and toilet paper are AWOL, and all my toiletries have been swapped with the girls'. Either you're stronger than you look or you were invaded by a prankster."

I slapped my palm to my forehead. "Monty!"

"I figured. And since I promised you a prank-free workplace, I take full responsibility and assure you the dormant prankster in Zaki Marsch has been awoken and unlocked and is ready to seek revenge for all the atrocities that have been committed since I filled his truck with birdseed last May."

Birdseed? I didn't know how to respond to that. "Um, okay?"

His mouth spread into a full-faced boyish grin that made the corners of his eyes crinkle.

Laced with mischief, it was the most beautiful smile I'd ever seen.

Oh, lordy, I could *not* crush on this guy. He was my boss, the team troublemaker—heck, he'd literally invited trouble into my house. Well, I guessed I was partly to blame for that, but—

No.

I would not become the cliché nanny who fell for her hot pro-athlete boss.

"I'm sorry, and I'll definitely help to put things to rights," I promised. "And Monty is no longer allowed in here unsupervised."

He laughed again as I charged out of the room and up the stairs. I pointed to the Lincoln Log cabin on the girls' table. "That wasn't there this morning. Check the tin for missing items."

Isla ran over to the shelf and yanked off the green plastic cover. "Here's your remote, Daddy! And toilet paper!"

Zaki made a game of putting everything back together and making the beds with the girls. Once everything was put back the way it was supposed to be, I texted Shanna.

Is your husband's BFF still single? I think I might want to meet him again.

Yes! Finally! He is. Come in tomorrow at noon. He just moved here from Elk Creek Falls and stops in every Sunday after church for a root beer float and a chat with Dylan.

Really? Which church?

St. Mary's.

Huh. I hadn't seen him there. But I hadn't been to church in a few weeks, so I easily could've missed him. Plus, he probably looked different now. Seven years, after all. *Does he wear his scrubs to church?* I typed.

Nope, he changes here before their chat.

Right. It was silly to think a doctor would wear scrubs to Catholic Mass. The dress code probably forbade it, anyway.

Okay, see you then. I swallowed, and my gut felt strange.

Can't wait!

CHAPTER 12

Zaki

Montgomery Biddington had nerve, I'd give him that. During dinner, Arwyn recounted her day and apologized again for assuming Monty would behave himself, especially while taking care of Melody. She'd thought he took the baby upstairs to sleep and play.

Which he had.

I needed an epic response. None of the old regulars would do. Itching powder in the mascot headpiece, duct-taping his bag shut —all amateur level. He'd turned my hot tub into a koi pond, for Pete's sake.

And it had to be somewhere he wouldn't expect it. Not at the rink or at the arena. Or at his house.

I was a little afraid of his Nana, and I wasn't ashamed to admit it.

At the cheer gym? The birdseeding of the truck had been done outside the Palmer City sportsplex during their end-of-season banquet. I'd had some teammates help me with that one.

Teammates … Maybe I could infiltrate the cheer team! Tasha wouldn't help me prank her own husband, but Kingston's wife, Taylor, was a former cheerleader there and knew just about everyone.

I'd have to plead my case, but King and I went way back to

when we played for the Voltage together, and I was sure I could convince him and Taylor to help me out.

"Daddy, what are you going to do to Ridgie Bear?" Amelie asked.

"I'm not sure yet, Amms. Got any ideas?" I glanced at Arwyn, who hid a smile.

"You could make him dress up as a princess!" she squealed.

"Or a snowman!" Isla suggested.

"He's probably already got plans for those things. I'm thinking something along the lines of a surprise, like what he left for us today."

The girls looked at each other, then at me. "We'll get back to you."

I laughed. I loved it when they spoke in unison.

After we all pitched in to clean up dinner, I suggested a movie night. Arwyn wanted to get back to her project, but she said we were fine watching on the bigger screen in the front room instead of upstairs.

"Zaki?" she asked, turning back to the kitchen as she approached her door. "You're off tomorrow morning, right?"

"I am."

"Is it all right with you if I went to church and then for a soda? I'll be back around one thirty."

I nodded. "Sure. Mind if we come with you? The girls haven't been since Christmas."

She hesitated, tucking an invisible strand of hair behind her ear. "Um, of course. We'll need to leave by ten."

"I'll have the girls fed and dressed by nine fifty," I promised.

"Great. Well, enjoy your movie."

"How can I not? It's *Frozen 2*. I know every word by heart. Let me know if I'm singing along too loudly and I'll turn myself down," I joked.

This time she smiled. "I will."

I watched her go into her room and then joined the girls and the dogs on the sofa.

THE NEXT MORNING, I donned a dark gray suit, light blue button-down, and a tie with shades of blue and red that the girls had chosen for me to wear the night before. They'd decided to wear their Christmas dresses, which were light blue and red plaid, and wanted me to match. Once my tie was knotted to perfection, I went to their room to see if I could help them get ready. I smiled when I saw Arwyn in a long, charcoal skirt and pale blue tuxedo-style blouse, braiding Isla's hair.

My girls had coordinated Arwyn to match us. A warm, fluttering sensation warmed my veins as I thought about how happy the girls must be here and with Arwyn.

Church at St. Mary's was exactly what I expected. I hadn't grown up Catholic, but I attended with Viki's family when I moved to Canada and then joined before we got married. It was important to Viki that our children grow up in the church. The girls had been baptized as infants, and we went to Mass as often as we could when we lived in Denver.

Arwyn preferred to sit in the back so she could be the first to leave, and that was probably a good idea since I was stopped at least a dozen times walking in. Palmer City was a hockey town. I'd lived here for a year, playing for the Voltage before I got called up to a permanent spot with the Edge. All the charm of the town was just as I remembered, and everyone here either knew me or knew of me.

With the soda shop being next door to the church, we left the van and walked the short distance. Arwyn and Amelie walked just ahead of Isla and I, the girls holding our hands and chattering about the second reading from Nehemiah.

"He said eat the fat!" Isla shouted to her sister.

Amelie craned her head over her shoulder, "And drink the sweet wine! That's soda, right, Daddy?"

"He could have meant soda," I said, "if it had been invented back then."

"He said you'll find joy in it, Daddy," Isla said. "I do!"

"Me too!" Amelie agreed.

It was always interesting to me what the girls took away from church and their school lessons. I'd have to look up that verse later and help them unpack the purpose of it.

We arrived at the soda shop, and I reached for the door handle. "Do you mind if I run into the Coffee Loft and get a Matcha Madness? I'll bring it back here if you'll save me a seat," I offered as I opened the door.

"Of course, Daddy," Amelie said.

Arwyn nodded, and I held the door as they entered. I watched them head straight for the stools at the counter. Arwyn set her Mary Poppins bag on the one farthest to the left by the old-fashioned register and helped the girls onto the stools to its right before settling on the one next to Amelie.

I hurried next door and entered the queue. It wasn't busy, but I had a feeling the crowd would pick up as the church continued to empty. Surprisingly, I didn't run into anyone I knew—or who recognized me—and I was able to get my drink and get back to the soda shop in under five minutes.

I pulled open the door and paused, surprised to see Arwyn chatting with a man in scrubs on the stool next to her. The woman behind the counter—who I assumed was Arwyn's friend Shanna—was chatting up my girls but kept looking over at Arwyn and the guy.

Did she know him? Were they friends? Was he a serial killer? Unlikely in scrubs, but you could never really know, right?

All important questions I would need the answer to ASAP.

For my girls, of course.

I couldn't have their nanny associating with serial killers.

I plastered a grin on my face and sauntered in like the famous professional athlete I was.

The man was the first to see me. He sat up straighter, and his eyes went wide.

Ah, a fan.

This was going to be fun.

I walked up to my girls first and kissed each of them on the tops of their heads. "How are my favorite girls? Enjoying your sodas?"

"I got Peach of My Heart, Daddy!" Isla held it up. "Try it."

I took a sip. "Peachy." I turned to Amelie, whose straw was poised for me to try next. "And what's this?"

"Lime of My Life!"

"Mmm, that's citr-errific!" I looked up at Shanna. "Thanks for making my girls awesome drinks and for being a great friend to Arwyn. She says great things about you."

"She's my favorite," Shanna said. "Sure you don't want an ice cream soda?" She pointed to my drink.

"Want? Yes. But my chef would go on strike if he found out I had all that sugar in one sitting." I turned back to the girls. "Your turn. Sip my Matcha Madness?"

"Ew, Daddy," Isla said. "You know we don't like that."

"But it matches your sister's dress," I protested.

"So does my Lime of My Life," Amelie retorted.

I sighed dramatically. "Fine. What's Wynnie drinking?" I whispered. "And who's that guy?"

Amelie set her drink down and cupped her hands over my ears. "Straw-Berry Dreamy. We tried that one last time. It's good. That's Adler. He asked if Wynnie was *seeing* anyone. What does that mean?"

I shrugged and turned to get a better look at the guy. In the scrubs, he could be anything from a transportation guy to a doctor.

"How 'bout I go find out?"

They both nodded profusely.

"And report back, Daddy!" Isla shout-whispered.

I straightened up and smoothed out my tie as I walked around Arwyn and offered my hand to the guy. "Zaki Marsch. And you are?"

He smiled easily. "Adler Lansing. You're really Zaki Marsch?"

"That's what my work visa says. You're a friend of Arwyn's?"

"Working on it." He grinned and glanced at her. Her lips were pressed tightly together, and she was avoiding eye contact with the both of us. "Shanna's husband is my best friend. Arwyn and I were in their wedding several years ago. We're catching up."

I stole a glance at Arwyn, who looked like she'd rather man the goal at a puck shooting contest—sans equipment.

Awk-ward. “Well, I’ll leave you to it, then.” I turned on my heel, but he wasn’t done with me.

“Zaki? I’m a big fan. Can I get an autograph? You could sign my napkin.”

I’d learned to always be prepared to scrawl my signature. Pulling a Sharpie from my suit jacket pocket, I uncapped it and waited for him to set a clean napkin on the counter.

“Can you sign it to Doc Lansing? My patients will get a kick out of it.”

I scribbled on the napkin. “You’re a doctor? What’s your specialty?”

His face lost the starstruck chump expression. “Emergency medicine.”

I winced. “That’s tough.”

He nodded. “I’ve seen some things.”

“I’m sure.” Well, this wasn’t as much fun as I thought it would be. I was hoping for a chump to mess with. This guy, while a little awkward, was a lifesaving hero.

Arwyn looked up at me and spoke for the first time since I’d walked in. “He’d like to take me to dinner on your next night off. I think that’s Wednesday?”

It wasn’t, and she knew it. My next night off was tomorrow. I got the feeling she wanted to buy time to decide whether or not she wanted to go out with the guy.

I played along. “Yeah, Wednesday, unless another meeting pops up.”

“Great.” She smiled up at me with big, grateful eyes.

It warmed my heart that she trusted me to cover for her. I also couldn’t help feeling relieved that she didn’t seem very enthusiastic about dating the doc.

I returned to the girls, who were working on activity placemats. I picked up Arwyn’s bag and set it on my lap so I could sit on the stool. The shop was filling in with people, and sitting next to the register put me in an exposed position. I looked over my shoulder to find an empty table we could move to.

But then I thought against it. My gut told me that Arwyn would feel more comfortable with three wingmen at her side.

Every so often, she'd turn toward us, catch my gaze, and look away.

After the girls had a slurping contest to finish their sodas—they tied, respectively—I slid off my stool and helped them down.

"I can bring Wynnie's bag to her, Daddy," Amelie volunteered.

I handed it to her. "It's heavy," I warned.

"I got it." She tapped Arwyn's arm. "We're done, Wynnie."

Arwyn smiled and turned back to the doctor. "It was great running into you, Adler."

"You too, Arwyn. I'll call you."

She nodded. "I look forward to it."

I bit down on my lip. Her tone didn't match her words. "We'll wait for you outside," I said.

"No need." She slid off her stool. "I can wave bye to Shanna from here."

Adler stared after her as we walked out. I held the door for her and the girls and lifted my hand in a wave.

I suddenly felt very protective of my nanny—er, the girls' nanny. I was sure Adler was a nice guy, but I didn't catch any vibes between them.

Also, Arwyn and Adler? What would their couple name be? Arler? Adwyn? Lansingbaughn? Wynnabingo? Ick.

Zakwyn had a much better ring to it. Or Wyki.

I stopped in my tracks. Where had *that* thought come from?

"Daddy, why did you stop? The car is over there." Isla tugged on my hand.

"Huh? Oh." I fished for a reason. "I think I have a rock in my shoe."

She huffed. "You can fix it at the car. Amelie and Wynnie are way ahead of us. Let's go!"

Yes, they were. My feet began walking again, and my eyes found the other half of our group, about five yards ahead of us. Arwyn walked as elegantly as she looked. She carried herself with an air of importance, like a queen, but she wasn't arrogant. Just ... poised. Confident.

But Viki had carried herself confidently, too. I'd learned that the more put-together she was on the outside, the more of a mess she was on the inside. On the days she felt the worst, she wore more makeup or tried a new hair technique. She'd dress to the nines, force smiles, and exude grace. Then, as soon as we walked through the door to the condo, she'd fall apart. Straight to bed with a heating pad and a muscle relaxer, insisting she'd be fine.

Only she wasn't.

Was Arwyn hiding pain underneath her carefully composed exterior?

And why was it suddenly so important to me that I knew if she was?

CHAPTER 13

Arwyn

Adler Lansing was just as I'd remembered. Nice but unremarkable.

That sounded mean to say, but for an ER doc, I'd have expected him to have an easier time carrying a conversation. One might think talking to people all day or night might teach you some conversation skills.

Obviously, he had them. Conversations. He had friends, and they spoke. Maybe he was shy around people he didn't know well. I could empathize with that. But trying to keep the conversation going today strained my patience and drained my energy. I'd learned over the years to seek out those with energy to give, not take.

It occurred to me that Zaki Marsch had more than enough energy to give.

I was glad when the girls were ready to leave. There wasn't anything *wrong* with Adler, per se. And I did feel for the guy. He was over thirty, and according to Shanna, he'd been ready to find someone to settle down with and grow a family for a long time now. I was sure his person was out there, but it wasn't me.

At least I didn't think so. Maybe having dinner with him would be different. In a quiet spot, with no distractions, we could talk about important things instead of trying to make small talk about soda or the weather or the priest's homily.

"Daddy? Can we go to your game tonight?" Isla asked from the back seat as Zaki parked the van in my driveway. We'd driven to church since it'd been snowing lightly when we left.

"You girls have school tomorrow, Isles," he reminded her.

"But Wynnie's never been to a game, Daddy," Amelie said. "She doesn't know what she's missing."

She had a point. I'd never been to an Edge game.

I'd also never had the *desire* to go to an Edge game.

But maybe ... maybe I should check it out. Take the girls. See what it was like. Penny would be there, and Tasha. Penny had mentioned it was Monty's birthday, so the whole family was going. I wasn't sure if Kami would bring Ryleigh and Conner, as it *was* a school night, but I could always bring Isla and Amelie home early if they got tired.

"Let me talk to your dad about it inside," I said. We climbed out of the van and crunched into the snow that had fallen on the brick walk leading up to the house. It was beginning to snow again, and although I was interested in going to the game, I didn't want to drive in a storm.

I unlocked the door and ushered them all inside. Laffy and Vennie greeted us like we'd been gone for a week, sweet things. I was glad they had each other to play with while we were gone.

After we removed our outerwear, Zaki sent the girls and dogs upstairs and motioned for me to follow him into the kitchen.

"Please don't feel pressured to take them tonight." He leaned back against the counter and slid his hands into his pockets.

He was still wearing his suit and tie.

I mentally cursed my eyes for lingering on him.

But, darn it, he looked *so good.* A far cry from his earlier years with the dyed blond hair and clean-shaven face.

I couldn't picture a more handsome man if I tried, and I did *not* like these thoughts and feelings.

I'd worn my hair down in loose waves today, and I pulled it all to one side and over my shoulder as I found the words to respond, fidgeting with the waves and twisting them into a single long ringlet.

"I think it would be fun," I said. "But it's a long drive, and my little car's snow tires aren't anything I'd trust on a slippery highway, especially with the girls in the back. Could we ride with you?"

"You can. But know there will be a lot of down time. I like to get there early, and then there's press afterward and, well, you'd be there really late."

"I see. Never mind then. Another time. Maybe your next Saturday game?"

He caught my gaze and held it but didn't say anything.

"I think you have a Saturday game after your next road trip?"

He nodded. "How 'bout this? You can ride in with me, and I'll catch a ride home with Monty. The snow should be cleared by then. He owes me after that stunt."

I grinned. "He sure does."

"You can drive the van?"

"Oh, yeah, I used to drive Shanna's all the time. And it's not as, um, *new* or sturdy as yours."

He grinned. "It does have great snow tires. I'll tell the girls." He pushed off from the counter.

"Wait!"

He paused and waited for me to speak.

"Um, silly question. What do I wear?"

He grinned. "Anything blue. Jeans?"

"I don't have jeans. Leggings? I could hem up a skirt to knee length, and I have a navy vest and—"

He held up his hand to stop my nervous stream of words. "Leggings are fine. No need to alter a skirt. You can wear one of my jerseys. It'll probably fit you like a dress."

I gaped at him. A jersey? I'd never worn a jersey from any sport. They didn't look very comfortable. "Um, okay. If you think that's best."

"You'll match the girls, and they'll love it." He laid his hand on my shoulder. "Don't overthink it and you'll have a great time."

Don't overthink it? He might as well have told me not to breathe.

I hurried to my room to text Tasha. *Please tell me you're going to the game early tonight. I'm taking the girls, and I need to know EVERYTHING.*

TASHA CALLED me instead of texting back, and she did her best to put me at ease. I didn't know why I was so anxious about taking the girls to a game. Yes, there would be a lot of people there, but I'd be busy with Isla and Amelie, and I knew who to ask if I needed help. She reminded me of those things and invited us to watch from the suite Monty purchased for the game.

His Nana Booboo was coming tonight for his birthday, and only the best seats would do.

I'd met Nancy Biddington a few times, and she was a delight.

Well, she'd scared me a little as a child, but I grew to love her once I understood her. She was good friends with Miss Clarice, who I learned was also coming to the game.

I really needn't worry.

After seeing me dressed in Zaki's jersey, black leggings, a black turtleneck, and black boots, the twins insisted on wearing their own black leggings, turtlenecks, and boots. Zaki thought that was adorable and had us pose for a mini photo shoot on the porch steps.

While it snowed.

We lasted about five minutes before we ran back inside into the warmth.

It was just as cold at ice level, where we watched the warmups, but toasty in the suite. No coats, hats or mittens needed up there, thank goodness.

Surprisingly, I found myself having a good time. At the end of the first period, Zaki was the last off the ice, and he raised his stick toward us all, mouthing the words *Happy Birthday, Ridgie!*

I got that feeling in my gut again.

There was a knock at the door, and Ridgie entered, followed by his handler, Jared, and Mags, the team's social media manager. Baby Melody let out an ear-piercing screech, and Penny hurried to a corner to shield her from the big scary bear.

"My favorite mascot!" Nana Booboo called from her wheelchair. "Come give your biggest fan a kiss!"

Ridgie looked from her to Tasha and back again. Tasha lifted her arms in a big shrug, and Ridgie clutched his heart, turning so that his head was positioned looking over his shoulder as he walked toward his grandmother.

The door opened again, this time without a knock, and the team's second mascot, Percy the Pigeon, entered holding a very large gift box, the kind where the top was wrapped separately so it could be pulled off to reveal its contents. Behind him was a cameraman.

I looked up at the jumbotron, and sure enough, Ridgie was on screen and the announcer was directing the fans' attention to our suite.

"Let's all turn our attention to Ridgie! Did you know it's his birthday? Percy has a special gift for him, but first, can we get you all to join in on singing 'Happy Birthday'?"

Everyone in the arena joined in as Ridgie danced and overdramatized his reaction. Percy set the box down on a high-top table, and when the song finished, he pulled Ridgie over to it. Ridgie positioned himself behind the box so that everyone could see his gift and pulled off the lid.

Shouts and squeals erupted from all of us as at least a dozen white birds took flight to the tune of "Free Bird" and soared across the arena. Monty stumbled back, waving his arms and falling on the ground for effect. After the birds made it safely to their trainer up in the rafters, Percy handed Monty a large gift tag that read *A Special Gift from Marshy and Percy.* Ridgie turned it toward the camera and face-pawed his forehead. Laughter and whistles erupted from the fans, and shouts of "Marshy! Marshy!" overshadowed Ridgie's birthday celebration.

Zaki Marsch had reentered the Prank War in a big way. I just hoped it would stay contained in the arena.

CHAPTER 14

Zaki

By the time I got home, it was after midnight, and I was wired. It usually took several hours for the adrenaline of the game to wear off, and it was rare if I was asleep before 2 a.m.

I crept into the house quietly and tiptoed up the stairs to cut off the dogs. I hoped the metal jingle of Laffy and Vennie's collar tags didn't wake the girls or Arwyn.

The pups dutifully followed me to my room and supervised my nighttime routine. I was used to them coming in and curling up on either side of my waist until I fell asleep, then they'd ditch me for the girls until they woke up.

It felt like I'd just fallen asleep when my phone alarm signaled it was time to wake up and get dressed if I wanted to help Isla and Amelie get ready. I threw on jogging pants and a hoodie, slid my unsocked feet into sneakers, and strode down the short hall. By the time I got to the twins' room, they were fully dressed and Arwyn was braiding Amelie's hair.

I pivoted and hid outside the doorframe where they couldn't see me, but I could see them and listened to their excited chatter about the events at last night's game. But it wasn't their words that stopped me short.

A brick wall of memories gripped my heart and squeezed as I took in the vignette, stealing my breath. These two could have been mother and daughter with their auburn hair and light dusting of freckles.

Neither of the girls had their mom's coloring. Viki's hair was dark brown—almost black—and her skin was naturally tan. The girls' skin was pale like mine. Amelie's ginger hair was from me, and Isla was blond like my mom and sisters.

Two Christmases ago, four-and-a-half-year-old Amelie cried in my lap because all she wanted from Santa was to be blond like me and Isla. I explained to her that my blond was fake and I was a redhead just like her. She'd stood on my lap and inspected the roots on my head and the morning stubble on my face. Satisfied I was telling the truth, she cried again and said red hair was ugly and my changing my red hair further confirmed that.

I told her I loved her red hair and promised her I wouldn't dye mine ever again. Viki's and my divorce had already finalized, and it would be weird to have her keep dyeng my hair anyway. Amelie had slapped her hands on my cheek and planted a wet kiss on my lips.

Now, Isla was the lone blonde. She had more confidence than her sister, an obsession with Elsa from *Frozen*, and idolized my sister Sofi, so I didn't think I'd have to worry.

"And Percy was there and he gave Ridgie the gift tag and it said, 'A special gift from Marshy and Percy!'" Isla paused, brushing her hair. "Ridgie was *not* expecting all those birdies to fly out of the box!"

"Did you hear Nana Booboo laughing?" Amelie asked. "I never heard a louder laugh!"

"And Ridgie fell on the *ground!*" Isla set her brush down and switched places with Amelie. "It was so funny!"

There was a pause as Arwyn began braiding Isla's hair, so I used the opportunity to announce my presence.

"Gooood morning, ladies," I said in my most goofy dad voice. "Need any assistance with your morning beautification rituals?"

Isla actually rolled her eyes at me, which made me grin wider.

Goal achieved.

"You can button my cuffs, Daddy," Isla said, holding out her wrists. "But leave the braiding to Wynnie. We've seen what your hands can do, and it isn't pretty."

Kids repeated the darnedest things. Xavier had said those exact words to me when we were discussing shots on goal and debating what constituted a dirty dangle.

I held back a laugh and snuck a sideways glance at Arwyn. Her lips were pressed tightly together, and her shoulders shook in a way that indicated she was holding in her reaction.

I buttoned Isla's cuffs and turned to find Amelie with her arms extended, so I buttoned hers, too. Then she raised her arms high. "Up, Daddy."

I hoisted her up and held her close. This request was happening less and less these days, and I would never deny it.

She rested her head on my chest and closed her eyes. "You got him good, Daddy. Great job."

High praise from the babe. I snuck another glance at Arwyn, whose lips were again pressed together, but this time her smile was noticeable. I caught her gaze and coughed.

Isla, not to be out-complimented, gave us a full rundown and her opinions on all of it. "Daddy, that was the best ever! When Percy brought Ridgie the present, we all crowded so close. But then the camera guy said 'Back up!' so we gave him space. Then Mr. Jared said 'you move here' and 'you move there' and we did. And then he said 'Wait!' and Miss Mags found a spot and the camera guy got a spot and everyone was guessing what was in the box, but they were all wrong! And then Ridgie pulled the lid off and we were like, whoa! He was so surprised he fell on the floor! Nana Booboo had the best laugh. And then she screamed and said, 'Don't poop on me, you pigeons!' and 'Who is responsible for this?' And then the birdies flew away. Daddy, can we have white pigeons for *our* birthday?"

I waggled my eyebrows. "Maybe. I also may have, uh, seen to it that the laces to his skates were relocated so that he was a bit late for the second intermission entertainment." I grinned, remembering Jared and Mags running around trying to find them. "So, the gift was a hit?"

Amelie lifted her head from my chest. "Oh yeah. I can't wait for *your* birthday, Daddy. To see what you get from Ridgie."

My smile faded. If things went my way, I'd be a long way out of Colorado by the time my summer birthday rolled around.

The walk to school was rejuvenating. Both girls insisted on holding Arwyn's hands, and I followed behind, a little insulted but grateful they were taking to her so well.

We walked the girls to the flagpole at the front of the school's property, and they raced inside, shouting goodbye to us. No doubt they couldn't wait to recount last night's antics with their friends.

And I realized I hadn't had much of a chance to get to know Arwyn below the surface yet, and I wanted to. As we turned to walk back home, I had an idea. "It's a beautiful morning," I said to her. "Bright sun. Want to take a detour?"

She looked up at me curiously. "A detour? To where?"

I shrugged shyly. "Coffee Loft. Then along the Creek Walk. It's been forever since I've sat on one of the swinging benches. Unless it's too cold for you?"

She shook her head. "I'm okay. Sure, that sounds nice. But the creek is frozen over."

"That's all right." I figured it might be. "I thought we could catch up and—get to know each other a little better?"

I held my breath waiting for her answer.

When she tipped her head back to look up at me, she was smiling. "I'd like that." Arwyn's arms were crossed, her mittened hands tucked under them. No muff today and no Mary Poppins bag.

I let out a long breath and dared to bend out my elbow. She knew exactly what I was asking without any words, and my heart flipped when she hooked her arm through.

An unexpected tingle fluttered through me like I'd been zapped by a faulty circuit.

This wasn't supposed to happen.

I was falling for Arwyn.

I had to be careful. We could only ever be friends. She had her life and her business here, in her hometown, and I was moving back to Montreal at the end of the season.

But ... the thought of her with anyone else—especially that doctor—had me in knots.

Her arm slid away as we approached the entrance to the Coffee Loft, leaving me with my right arm free to open the door for her. It was close to nine o'clock, and I was surprised to find that the line wasn't out the door.

I followed her inside and scanned the tables as she walked straight to the queue. No one I recognized. Good. Not that I minded, but I didn't want to be spacey or aloof if someone I knew was here and thinking I was ignoring them. That wasn't who I was.

I stepped in line behind Arwyn, and we waited quietly until it was our turn.

"Good morning, Arwyn! Zaki, right? Together or separate? Your usuals?" Marie, the owner's daughter, knew everyone after meeting them once and memorized their orders.

"Together," I said before Arwyn could answer.

"Yes, a hot vanilla spiced tea with one sugar to go, please." She turned to catch my gaze. "Thank you."

"My pleasure." I held her gaze for a beat longer than I should have, then answered Marie. "Lofty-size Matcha Madness, please."

"Coming right up!"

I pressed my credit card to the pin pad and tapped in a tip as Marie wrote our orders on cups. We moved down the counter and waited for her mom, Jannell, to make our drinks.

"Zaki Marsch! No way!"

As I turned toward the door, a quartet of young guys in Voltage hoodies, hats, and sweats were filing in. I grinned, recognizing them from training camp. None of them had made our roster, but they were good players, and their team was in first place in their division.

I transferred my drink to my left hand to reach my right out for fist bumps. "Arwyn, stay away from these troublemakers. They're bad news. Especially this guy," I teased. "I played with his oldest brother."

He grinned. "Mason Kuntz. Nice to meet you."

"So, how's it going? Volts are looking sharp this year," I complimented him.

"Yeah, I'm happy to be here. We've got a great team."

"Hit me up if you want to come to a game," I offered. "Mason knows how to get in touch with me."

Another round of fist-bumping and I gestured for Arwyn to

lead the way out. Once we were back on the sidewalk, she tucked her arm back into mine.

We crossed Main Street at the intersection and strode past the bookstore, picking up the smoothly paved sidewalk that ran southwest alongside Snowpack Creek. Swinging benches were placed alternately on each side of the creek, and we chose the closest one to settle into.

Arwyn had been quiet during the entire walk over, and I was desperate to fill the silence. As she sipped her tea inches from me, I wondered what to ask her first. I wanted to know everything. Her childhood, her family, her hopes and dreams.

"So ..." I elbowed her gently and kept my eyes focused on the frozen creek bed. "How did you become so awesome?"

She elbowed me back. "So ... how'd you become so crazy?"

"Touché," I conceded. "Sisters. I was always being bossed around by the older one—Mirette—and looking out for Sofi when I was around. It was kind of boring at home. And I had to be on my best behavior when I lived with Viki's family. So whatever hockey team I was on became my outlet for the extroverted entertainer that cries from my soul to be released on a daily basis."

She laughed. "And all are still your friends. Even their siblings, like Mason. Amazing."

"Yeah, I'm a lovable guy. My brand of torture comes from a place of love." I snuck a glance. She was grinning.

Good.

"Are your parents still in England?" she asked.

I shook my head. "They moved back to Quebec when Sofi started college. Mirette still lives in Sheffield, though, with her husband and their three kids."

"You must miss them. Do you get to see them often?" Her empathetic tone made me think she already knew the answer.

I shrug. "Not as often as I'd like. Family—all of my family—is important to me." Looking at her and knowing she was on her own made me want to include her in everything the girls and I did while we were here.

Her response cemented my sentiment. "Take in and cherish every moment, Zaki. You never know when it could be your last with someone you love."

I knew from experience just how true that was. "Your turn," I encouraged her. "Tell me everything about you. All the things that made you who you are, because from what I've witnessed, you're an amazing person, Wynna-bun. And crazy talented."

She sighed. "There's not much to tell. I'm super boring, actually."

"Run your story through the Zaki Scale of Snoozes and I'll determine how boring you are." I tapped my nose. "I have a talent for sniffing out and avoiding everything boring, you know."

"Ha!" She nudged me back with her entire torso and took a sip of her tea. "I think your sniffer is broken because I'm the very definition of plain and boring. I'm sure that's why I developed such an extensive imagination."

"Go on." I set what remained of my Matcha Madness on the trash can next to the bench. I didn't want any distraction while she told me about herself.

"Okay. I was born here. My parents met at a military ball in Colorado Springs, fell in love, and made our home their base. My grandparents were still living here at the time, but with Mom and Dad assigned elsewhere, there was no point in putting roots down. They didn't plan on having children, so I was a surprise. Mom wanted to continue serving, so Dad left active duty as soon as he could to stay home and raise me. He had a lot of money saved, so he dabbled in wildlife photography. He'd take me on walks and hikes and sold some of his photos to magazines and even a jigsaw puzzle company."

"That's pretty awesome," I said. "I'd love to see some of his work. It's all in the room?"

She nodded. "Everything I could find. Help yourself. I keep meaning to go through it all, but it's still too hard. I still can't believe he died from a snake bite."

Arwyn looked away. I wanted to comfort her. My arm moved of its own accord, circling around her back and pulling her to me. "I'm so sorry, Wynn. I can't imagine."

She laid her head on my shoulder. "Thanks. He was missing for two days. The worst two days of my life. Mom came home for a bit after that, and we grieved. But then she was off again. I don't know where she is most of the time. She's undercover and emails when she can. I think she's a secret agent."

"Wild," I said. I wanted to know more about her elusive mom, but I wanted her to smile again more. "What about the years in between? How did you come to love the fashion of the past? Learn how to make costumes?"

"My dad got a photography job at the *Palmer City Gazette* when I was in kindergarten. He spread the word that he needed after-school care for me, and Shanna's mom got the job. Shanna and I were already friends from the schoolyard—we both liked to read under the same tree next to the playground. I saw her reading there the first day Dad dropped me off for his job. I didn't want to play on the apparatus—it was too crazy, unlike mine at home, which was just for me. The next day, I brought a book and sat with her."

"And you were instant friends."

"We were. Her mom would take us to the library some days. Other days we'd play while her mom sewed—she had a tailoring business upstairs. The ice cream shop didn't bring in a bunch of money in the winter. And she taught me how to sew. I wanted to make the dresses the girls in my historical books wore. I naturally leaned to the late Victorian to Edwardian era, thanks to the stories and the way our house was built and decorated. It was easy to pretend I was the characters in those books since my house was like theirs with the patterned wallpaper and dark wood and knickknacks."

"How many years older than you is Shanna?" I asked.

"Five. It was like having a big sister."

"Must have gotten lonely when she changed schools."

"Not really. I had my books, sewing, and I'd see her after school. She got married young, though. Her parents moved to a retirement community, and she and her husband moved upstairs. They had two little ones a year apart, and I'd babysit while she worked in the store."

"That's how you became the nanny of nannies. Nice. And how did you meet Tasha?"

"I knew Tasha from school. We were in classes together growing up, but she was friends with the popular girls, and I kind of stayed to myself. One year she needed her cheer uniform altered because she'd lost a lot of weight, and Shanna's mom was hired to do the alteration. She showed me how to do that. So Tasha and I got to talking, and she told me to come by the Bevvie Bar if I wanted to hang out. We had some things in common, and over the years, most of her friendships dropped off. I'd invite her and Penny over to my house for tea and movie nights in. I rarely went out, and she had all those jobs, so when she wasn't working, she wanted to unwind. And then she got the job coaching at the high school cheerleading squad and had zero time."

I'd heard about Tasha's jobs to pay her medical bills. I couldn't imagine how hard that must have been. And for her friends, who she wouldn't allow to help her and had to watch her fight an autoimmune disease and work literally just to live.

"I like my quiet life," Arwyn confirmed. "But you're right, it is a bit lonely. I like to be by myself a lot. That's when I do my best work and my best thinking. But there are times when I just need people around, and that's usually when I'll go to the Soda Shoppe. Or call Tasha and see what she's doing, or Penny. But they're so busy now with their husbands and with Melody that it feels even lonelier."

"I get that. The last six months nearly killed me. Living alone is hard, especially when you've never had to. It feels like you've lost everything." I'd never admitted that out loud before.

She turned to me. "It does feel that way. I think Tasha noticed I was a bit off, and that's why she suggested I work for you. She thought I missed working with little kids, and she was right. A couple of kids I can handle. And I'm not afraid to be myself around them. They just want to play and be loved, and I have a lot of love to give."

"Do you?" I murmured. "How much more?"

The last sentence was out before I could stop it. Her eyes widened, and I wished I could've taken it back. She shifted out from under my arm, arranging herself sideways on the swing.

I didn't want to lead her on, but darn it, I wanted her to stay in my life. And in my girls' lives. And it was crazy to think that in just a couple of weeks, she'd made herself such an irreplaceable part of our family.

The distress on her face said it all. I hurried to make a joke of it. "Because—" I leaned in. "I could buy you a cat."

Her expression relaxed, and she laughed. "Don't you have to get to practice?"

I pulled out my phone to check the time. "Yeah. We should head back."

I stood and offered her my hand to assist her up from the bench swing. We deposited our cups into the trash, and once her arm was tucked in mine again, I dared to ask her about her date with Adler.

"So, Wednesday. I should be home by five. Are you looking forward to your date with Adler?"

She was quiet for a beat. "Not really. I should be, though, right? I mean, I'm at the age where I should want a relationship and a family and all that. But ..."

"But?" I prompted.

"Shanna said that he's ready for all that now. What if I'm like my mom? What if I don't want to be a mother or I discover after I have children that I just like taking care of little kids because I can give them back? What if I get so overwhelmed with motherhood like she did? What if I crave quiet and my own space and I can't handle the pressures of family? And a doctor's wife? Social engagements I'd have to host and charity events to attend and living life through the public lens? I would be terrible at all that."

My breath caught, because I knew exactly what she was talking about. If we dated—she and I—her life wouldn't be completely hers anymore. She would be followed online, and pictures and videos of her and the girls would become viral social media reels. Her business would blow up, and people would want to be friends with her to get to me and the team. She probably already got a taste of that, being close with Penny and Tasha.

I stopped in the middle of the sidewalk and placed my hands on her shoulders. "Arwyn." I used her full name so she knew I was serious. "I was terrified of becoming a dad. But the moment I held my girls, I was in love and knew without a doubt that despite my fears and shortcomings, I would jump through fire to keep them safe. I grew into the role and learned to be the best dad I could be because I wanted to be. You seem like you put in more than a hundred percent to things you care about. And if you wanted to be a mom, I'd bet my millions you'd give all the other moms a run for their money."

"How can you be sure?" she whispered.

"Because I see you with my girls. You put your discomfort aside to volunteer at the book fair. You read to them every night. I can't speak for your mother, but something tells me she wasn't a fan of little kids either, was she?"

She shook her head. "No."

"Then I think you're overthinking again." I gave her shoulders a light squeeze and pulled her into a hug.

"So you think I should go to dinner with him?"

I shook my head. "Can you picture a future with him? Living in your house? Raising kids, however many he said he wanted? Can you picture that, and do you like what you see?"

Her chin fell to her chest, and she turned away from me, crossing her arms and looking down at the creek bed.

"I can't. But I also don't want to let life pass me by. I don't see myself as a spinster. But I don't leave the house often, and I can't picture anyone else in my home, especially now that you and the girls are there. The loneliness is going to hit real hard when you leave."

I stepped beside her, keeping my hands in my coat pocket to prevent me from physically reaching out to comfort her again. I wanted to pull her to me, but I sensed that she needed the space. And I didn't want to offer her anything I couldn't give.

But something I *could* give her—a shot at confidence. And not just to sing adorably off-key to *Frozen* songs in the van.

"Hey. Would you want to attend the Biddington gala with me? I mean, if you're not already going?" I asked. Xavier had reserved double the number of seats this year and was still trying to fill them. I'd bought a pair of tickets but hadn't planned on attending.

"I—um." She peered up at me. "The Valentine gala?"

"Yeeeeess," I dragged out my reply. "You mentioned charity events. This could be a good opportunity to see if you hate them as much as you think you do."

"So you need a date?"

I clutched my chest. "You wound me." I grinned, but her expression remained neutral. "I don't *need* a date. I have no desire to find a date. In fact, I was going to give the tickets away or just skip it."

"What about the girls?"

"Their old babysitter in Denver is probably available. If you don't mind her spending the night here."

"I don't mind." Her eyes narrowed. "And this is purely for experimental research purposes?"

"Entirely," I confirmed. "If you hate it, we'll leave. And I was thinking we could take the girls to the cabin on Sunday."

"Hmm." She looked back out over the creek. "I *would* like to see Penny strum her harp in her new gown."

My heart rate kicked up. "So it's a yes?" I could hear the excitement and desperation in my question.

Tone it down, Marshy.

She turned back to me and smiled. "It's a yes. Thank you for asking me."

I held out my arm. "You're welcome. I promise to be the very best research help you've ever had, Wynna-bun."

She laughed. "Good."

Pretty sure I grinned like a clown the rest of the way home.

CHAPTER 15
Arwyn

Well. That was unexpected.

Me, Arwyn Baughn, Zaki Marsch's date to the Biddington's gala? Sitting at a table with pro hockey players?

That was not on my bingo card this year.

Or any year.

But we were going as friends, for research purposes, so that was totally fine.

I was totally fine.

Fine.

Super fine.

Fine and dandy.

Dandy.

Okay, I wasn't. I had just over two weeks to make a dress. Or alter one. There was that blue one I'd made for a Wendy Darling costume for a Halloween event I'd taken Shanna's kids to at the library a few years ago …

High-waisted pale blue satin brocade with a navy sash. It would make a decent enough base that I could adorn to match the theme.

Engage, Arwyn.

Yeah … this engagement was a whole new level of engaging for someone who wasn't a joiner.

After Zaki left for practice, I went to the garage to retrieve the gown, July, and a stack of Regency-era fashion books to peruse. It took two trips to get it all into the house and through the doggie gate, since the dress form was an awkward carry. I set July next to June, who was still wearing Penny's gown, and draped the blue over her.

The shape of the dresses was similar, and I debated adding sleeves to mine. Penny had opted for long, fingerless gloves to give her arms more freedom of movement. Last year, she'd played her harp as the main entertainer; this year she was just playing "The Star-Spangled Banner" at the opening. For the first time ever, she'd be able to enjoy the gala as a guest.

I'd never been, but I'd heard stories. Monty's parents' annual event went back generations and raised oodles of money for a different charity each year. It was always a different theme and location that fit the theme. Two years ago, it had taken place at a castle in Colorado Springs and carried a Renaissance theme. Last year at a lodge.

This year, the gala was taking place at Hotel L.O.VE, a massive and old resort, also in Colorado Springs. I'd been there only as a summer bride's assistant, standing by with my sewing kit to make sure there weren't any wardrobe malfunctions with a gown or bustle.

The resort was about thirty minutes from my house, so Zaki wanting to stay at the cabin that weekend didn't make sense to me. Maybe he just missed it? For growing up in a city and playing in one for so many years, his heart seemed to be in the mountains.

I was probably overthinking things again. The girls loved it there, too, and it made sense that he'd want to spend as much time as possible at his mountain home.

I wondered if he would sell it when he moved back to Montreal.

Not wanting to think about the temporariness of our situation, I flipped through my books, and several ideas began to form into a design that would elevate my Wendy dress up a few levels to Regency Ball status.

Since the fabric was already textured, adding embroidery or a lace overlay would take away from the quiet simplicity of the brocade. I'd keep the sash and create a matching satin ruffle that would emerge up from the neckline and add the same feature to the bands under the puffed sleeves. Good thing I'd saved the extra fabric! A double strand of pearls around my neck and lacy glove-clad wrists would keep the ensemble understated and still classy.

And it was especially important to me that my gown didn't upstage Penny's. I wanted her to feel like the belle of the ball.

Or the gal of the gala.

I chuckled to myself as I sketched out my plan and then colored in the design with pencils in shades of blue. As I drew, it occurred to me that it wouldn't be right to go out to dinner with Adler when I had a future date planned with Zaki.

It was a friends thing, nothing more, but … Adler didn't know that or even had to. But even so, it didn't feel right. And then if we did go out and he wanted a second date, wouldn't he naturally assume I was available for Valentine's Day, too? What if he wanted to *be* my Valentine? I didn't want to miss the gala, and I knew in my heart I'd have a wonderful time with Zaki.

Canceling was the right thing to do. I took a deep breath and called Adler, leaving a message when he didn't answer. I hated to cancel in a message, but what other choice did I have? Show up at the ER?

That settled, I went back to my drawing. I'd just finished the design when the dogs started barking.

"What is it, boys?" I asked. As I stood, they jumped off the sofa and ran to the front door. I wasn't expecting any guests, and Zaki wasn't due back until later this afternoon, so I was surprised to see that he'd returned early.

I opened the door, and he hurried inside. "Is everything okay?" I asked.

He replied as he peeled off his jacket and hat. "Big storm coming in from the mountains. The guys that live on the other side of Denver left early, so Coach called it."

"Do you think we'll get it bad here?" I asked. I hadn't checked the weather since last night.

"We might." He walked past me into the front room and flicked on the TV to the Weather Channel. "I checked the radar on my weather app and listened to predictions on the way home. There." He pointed to the screen. "Seventy percent chance it'll turn toward Colorado Springs. We'll keep watching it. But the girls might have a snow day tomorrow."

His grin at the prospect of a snow day melted my heart like wax over a flame. The flashes of the little boy inside of him always warmed my heart. His girls were lucky to have a fun dad.

I'd been lucky, too. My dad had been my hero.

"I love snow days," I said. "And I know the best spot within walking distance to go tubing. There's a big hill behind the businesses on the east side of Main Street, and the steepest part is behind the police and fire stations."

His smile widened. "Do you have tubes or sleds?"

I shook my head sadly. "If I do, they've been deflated in the basement for a long time."

"I'll run to the sporting goods store and pick up the girls on my way back. Need any groceries?"

I shook my head. "Chef has us stocked through Friday."

His smile faltered. "I leave for another long road trip Friday afternoon."

"I can cook, you know," I reminded him.

"I know. And I appreciate it. I just want to help out as much as I can."

"I appreciate that, but you forget, I'm the hired help. It's my job to take care of your girls, even if it doesn't feel like one."

He nodded, and when he spoke, his voice was low. "You're so good at it, Wynna-bun. You're going to make a great mother someday. Trust me on that."

I swallowed. "Thank you."

CHAPTER 16
Zaki

There was enough snow to cancel school and our game Tuesday night.

After a morning of tubing down the hill with other local families, we trekked home and warmed up with hot chocolate while Arwyn read three more chapters of *Anne of Green Gables*. I got the fire going in the old fireplace, and the girls snuggled up on either side of me on the sofa, with Laffy and Vennie snuggled into them. Isla's tablet leaned against the lamp, pointing at us so Viki could see the girls.

In the armchair, Arwyn seemed content bundled up in a blanket and the fur collar she liked to wear. She looked cold, though, and I couldn't help but think she would be warmer with us on the sofa.

I hadn't dated at all since Viki and I broke up. There wasn't anyone I knew or had met who lived up to the impossible standards a stepmom to my girls would have to meet. Someone who'd love them as if they were her own, was gentle and kind but knew when and how to discipline, was patient and serious but knew how to have fun. Someone who, by just being a quiet presence, could flood me with the peace that I craved but couldn't create on my own.

Someone like Arwyn.

If I planned to stay in Colorado, I would—

But I didn't.

I couldn't.

I had to put my girls first.

So why was it so hard to get the idea of pursuing Arwyn romantically out of my head?

THURSDAY NIGHT AFTER OUR WIN, the team returned to the ice to assist and support our goalie, Jason, as he and Lauren revealed the gender of their second child. I watched with the guys at the red line, wearing a new helmet since *someone* had covered my visor in some kind of cooking grease.

As Lauren stood in the center, holding their toddler in her arms, I recalled a similar moment six years ago when Viki and I were the expectant couple.

Dean had placed a puck on the ice. I pulled back my stick and hit it hard, causing pink dust to cloud around it as it slid toward the goal. A girl! I hugged Viki, the crowd cheered, and then ... Coach brought out a second puck. We'd had no idea we were expecting twins until that moment. I hit it and—pink again! I'd wanted a big family. The crowd went wild, and I remembered that feeling of excitement like it was yesterday. Viki, however, looked terrified.

Maybe I should've paid more attention to her fears. But being the positive guy I was, I didn't believe that there was anything for her to be afraid of. She had the best doctors, Chef made all our meals, and she did all the right things. Her obstetrician assured us her fears were normal and expected and told her not to watch the horror-story videos about childbirth on social media.

But the birth *was* difficult, and it changed her. It changed *us*. Sure, becoming parents was supposed to change you, but I didn't catch on that, on top of the injuries she sustained, she was experiencing postpartum depression. She was incredibly loving to the girls, and I assumed her lack of interest in me was due to exhaustion. Or fear that she could get pregnant with multiples again.

But her detachment never lessened or went away. No matter

what I did, I couldn't win back her affection. I pulled out all the stops—fancy dinners, getaways, flowers, gifts. She was always too tired to enjoy it, so she said. And still, I refused to dig deeper, thinking everything would go back to the way it was at some point, if I just waited it out.

That day never came. When she told me she wanted to separate, I suggested counseling. I was confident we could work through it. Jason and Lauren had broken up and gotten back together. They were in love and determined to find a way to make it work. And they had.

When I reminded Viki about our friends' struggles, she dropped the bomb: She didn't love me anymore.

It crushed me. I'd failed. I'd failed her and my girls. Somehow, I'd pushed her away. I'd become unlovable. I was too much and not enough.

It was over.

I switched my brain off the sad stuff so I could concentrate on being happy for my friends. Jason skated out from the bench in full gear. We banged our sticks on the ice as he made his way along the edge of the red carpet to center ice and to Lauren and their daughter. They patted his helmet and blew him a kiss, then he skated to the net and pulled his mask down.

"And now, we'd like to invite Jason's friend Gordie to the ice to drop the pucks for a special revelation!"

When we were on the Voltage, we partnered with the Palmer City Sportsplex's team for kids with differing abilities, the Flying Stars. We helped them play sports and train for the Special Olympics as part of our community volunteer work. We all still kept in touch with the kids, but mine had moved away, so I hadn't had a chance to see him grow up and spend time with him like some of the other guys had. Jason still saw Gordie regularly, and this year, the teen's high school team was undefeated. Gordie's left arm ended just below the elbow, so he needed assistance with putting on and resetting his gear, but he had cat reflexes in the net, just like his mentor.

Gordie walked along the red carpet, pulling clear pucks from a satchel and dropping them on the ice in front of me, Kingston,

Brendan, Trask, and Xavier, all former Voltage players. Then he went to stand by Lauren.

The five of us crossed over the carpet to get to the pucks and waited for our cue.

"On the count of three, shoot your pucks. One, two, three!"

I sniped it straight to Jason's left pad. Upon contact, it lit up blue. The other pucks also hit, and he had one in his glove that he dropped to the ice.

All blue!

The crowd chanted "Boy! Boy! Boy!"

The entire team skated to the net and piled on Jason, offering congratulations and some good-natured punches.

But our celly was cut short by the announcer.

"Edge players and fans, kindly turn your attention to the team bench, where our sports reporter and Jason's sister Bailey has been joined by three very special guests. Their dad, Hall of Famer Lincoln Dexter; their mom, Melinda; and Bailey's sweet little daughter!"

"Thanks, everyone!" Bailey's smiling mug was plastered on the screens. "I'm so happy to be here with my parents to get their reactions. What do you think, Mom, Dad? After two baby girl grands, there's a boy on the way!"

"We are absolutely thrilled," Melinda said in her thick Southern accent, wiping her eyes. She'd met Lincoln when he was playing in her hometown of Atlanta, and Jason and Bailey had grown up there.

"Can't wait to take all three of them skating!" Lincoln agreed. They were a hockey family through and through. Bailey was an Olympics gold medalist netminder, and sometimes I thought she loved the game more than Jason did.

"Awesome! Well ... We have another surprise for you all. You all know my husband, Lawson?" Lawson Brewer, Kingston's cousin, emerged from the tunnel and waved, wearing a matching team satchel to Gordie's. "Y'all better get back to your spots, guys. There are five more pucks to shoot. Hey brother, think you could help us out?"

Jason saluted his sister and scooted backward to the net. The five of us chosen ones returned to our positions on the goal side of the red carpet as Lawson dropped five more clear pucks.

"All right!" Bailey was up on the screen again. "Three, two, one!"

I fired my puck at Jason's blocker, and it lit up blue. The other four pucks also lit up blue as they hit their targets. Jason skated to Lauren and pulled his helmet off to kiss her.

Over on the bench, Bailey had passed her mic to her dad and was now making out with Lawson while their daughter pulled at her hair.

I'd never seen the crowd so crazy. I grinned like a loon, so happy for my friends. A new baby boy for each of the Dexter siblings.

Ridgie skated out and made a big show of giving Big Sister onesies to the little girls and blue Edge-branded onesies to Lauren and Bailey.

My heart cracked at the thought of not having any more children. Isla and Amelie would make the best, most doting big sisters.

Arwyn's face flashed behind my eyes.

What if?

She'd canceled her date last night and suggested the girls give us a ballet lesson, citing teaching a skill to others helped you learn it. Of course, I went out of my way to be the worst I could be and had all three of the girls in stitches. Arwyn gave up trying to remind me to be serious because ballet was a very serious discipline. I knew that from Viki, and I didn't want my girls to lose the fun of it if or until they were ready to study it seriously.

I'd gone to sleep with images in my head of Arwyn in her white tights and filmy skirt dancing around the front room on her toes with my girls, holding invisible beach balls, and me "throwing" mine and acting sad when no one caught it.

I loved that she was active with them as well as encouraged quiet time.

I loved that she was happy being a homebody, and I loved that I—the extroverted prankster attention-seeker—was happy being a homebody with her.

I loved who I was when I was within those walls.

I loved everything about her. And the life I was living right now.

CHAPTER 17
Arwyn

I was reading in my armchair in the front room when Zaki arrived home from Denver. I couldn't sleep, and reading wasn't really happening, either.

The girls and I had watched the first period of the game snuggled up in their bed with the dogs. When they'd fallen asleep during the intermission commentary, I switched off their television and came downstairs so I could view the rest of the game. The announcers kept hinting about a special revelation after the final horn, and I was curious.

After the gender reveals, the network had shown a compilation of other baby Edge reveals over the years, including Zaki's. The elation on his clean-shaven face when the second puck was brought out was that of a kid at Christmas who'd received the gift he'd been wanting more than anything else.

I wondered if they showed that in the arena, and I wondered if Zaki saw it. I wondered, even if he didn't see it, if he thought back to it. I couldn't imagine the heartache of being so happy, only to have it all end a few short years later.

It wasn't my business, and I wasn't sure why exactly I was waiting up. To offer him support, of course, if he wanted to talk.

Ha. He *always* wanted to talk.

But family stuff he usually kept for when the girls weren't around, so I wanted to give him an outlet if he sought one.

In the dim light of the entryway, he removed his overcoat and hat. As he turned to the stairs, he noticed me. I set my book on the end table and stood up.

"Hey," I said, trying not to be distracted by him in a suit. "Nice goal in the third. And the empty net one, too. One shy of a hat trick."

Zaki smiled, but it didn't reach his eyes. "Thanks. Did the girls stay up for the whole game?"

I shook my head. "They fell asleep a couple minutes into the first intermission report. I came downstairs to watch the rest."

He nodded, and the silence between us became loud. I scrambled for words, but none came.

Some support. I couldn't even speak.

"Well, um. Good night," I said. "I'm going to be up for a bit, um, reading. But ... if you aren't tired or want to talk ..." I lifted my hands and shrugged. "I'm a good listener."

I sank back into my chair but kept my eyes on him. He folded his hands behind his head and blew out a breath, then nodded. "Okay if I change first?"

"Of course. Want to go into the kitchen? We have sugar-free cheesecake."

This time his smile reached his eyes. "Yeah, that sounds good."

I wasn't sure if he got my Golden Girls reference, but that was okay. I hurried into the kitchen to boil water for tea and pull out the box of pre-sliced cheesecake I'd ordered from Tasha last week.

Hmm. Only one slice left. I'd forgotten that the girls and I had indulged earlier in the week. I was holding a knife and debating on how to cut it when I felt Zaki behind me.

"Last piece? I don't need any if you want it," he offered.

I shook my head. "I think we both need to eat it for this to work."

"That's what I've heard," he replied.

"Oh yeah? From who?" I was testing him.

"Just some sweet old ladies. Met one of them in person, you know."

I set the knife down. "You didn't!"

"I did. Out in LA after a game. Betty White was a crazy flirt."

Was he serious?

"I'm serious. There's a selfie on my Instagram."

"Wow," I breathed. It had never occurred to me that he must have met scores of celebrities over the years.

The teakettle whistled, and I left the uncut slice to attend to it and fixed myself a cup. Zaki sat at the round table and gestured for me to sit next to him instead of across, where I usually sat. He'd set the plate between our seats with two forks, one on either side. Apparently, we weren't slicing it in two.

"You take the first bite," I suggested. "Tell me what's weighing on you."

Zaki picked up the fork and stabbed off the point of the cheesecake slice. "I'm happy for my friends." He slid the fork into his mouth and pulled it out clean. I watched him chew, slowly, quietly, no slurping or weird noises.

My misophonia appreciated that.

"But?" I prompted.

"But I can't fight off the feeling of massive loss. My family is broken up. I don't see a path to having more kids. When we get back to Montreal, we'll share custody again, and I'll miss even more than I do now." He dropped his head. "And then I feel worse for thinking those things. I have two beautiful girls. So many people can't have children or never get the opportunity to. I can't be ungrateful or upset. I have blessings that people would die for."

I used the side of my fork to cut into the back corner and scooped the cheesecake onto the tines. "Your feelings are valid, Zaki. Your life hasn't gone as you planned. You fell in love as a teenager, set high expectations for your career and personal life, and achieved most of them. Then you got blindsided. You never saw that coming. You couldn't ease into it or prepare for it. It was there one day and gone the next." I stuffed the fork into my mouth and fought back tears, thinking about the glass-encased flag on the mantel over the fireplace.

"Like your dad," Zaki said quietly. He set his fork down and reached for my hand. I let him take it and watched as he rubbed his thumb lightly over my knuckles. "I'm guessing the sting of it never goes away."

I shook my head. "It doesn't. But listen—we both still have so much to be grateful for. We both get to do what we love. We have great friends—distance won't change that, only the frequency of seeing them. And your girls—they're the best gift. I saw your face on the screen when they played that montage. The size of your grin equated to how amazing of a dad you wanted to be, and are."

He gave my hand a light squeeze, still holding it, while his other hand cut into the cake for another bite.

I didn't say anything as he thought over my words. I didn't know how to convince him just how great of a father he was. When he spoke, there was pain in his voice and a touch of anger.

"What you didn't see was the terror on Viki's face." He let go of my hand and his fork and rubbed his palms over his eyes. "She was so scared, and I didn't notice. And when she told me, I didn't validate any of it. I didn't listen to her 'what ifs,' and I refused to consider anything that might go wrong. Why would it?"

I wasn't sure if that question was rhetorical, so I took another bite of cheesecake.

Two bites left.

I set my fork down. I didn't want to finish the cake before the talk was done.

Zaki's hands covered his eyes, and his elbows rested on the table. Should I reach out and comfort him like he'd comforted me? I wanted to. From what I could tell in the short time I'd known him, he welcomed and craved physical touch.

I went for it.

Pushing my chair out from the table, I stood up and moved into place behind his chair. Then I wrapped my arms around his shoulders and rested my head against the side of his.

Zaki's head shifted as it straightened up and his hands closed around mine.

I found words. "You couldn't have known," I whispered. "You were young and on top of the world with your whole future ahead of you. You can't carry that guilt, Zaki. It's eating you and preventing you from moving forward."

I closed my eyes and absorbed the warmth of his cheek against mine. We stayed like that for some time, and then he spoke.

"How is it that someone you barely know can know you so well?" In a swift move, one of my arms was over his head and we were twisting—no, he was twisting—and then we were standing, inches apart, and my hands were inside his, resting on his chest. "I feel like you know my heart, Wynnie. I want to know yours."

"I—" How did I answer that?

Honestly, of course. I couldn't lie.

"I think you already know it." I dared to look up and catch his gaze.

"I think I do, but—it's complicated." Those blue eyes shone with unshed tears. How long would he continue to avoid things that he knew would make him happy?

"Everything important always is," I reminded him. "That's what faith is for. If I didn't believe everything would work out when Dad died, it wouldn't have. Sure, I struggled. I still am struggling. But I find a way to do what makes me happy." I squeezed his hands. "There is *always* a path to happiness, Zaki. You just have to dare to veer off the path *you* paved to take it."

He crushed me into a bear hug and held me for a long time, his head resting on mine, our hearts beating in sync through my kimono and his hoodie.

Like with the children, I wasn't going to be the one to break the hug.

When he did step back, his face was streaked with tears, but he was smiling. I reached up to wipe them, but he caught my hand and pressed my palm into his cheek. The soft scruff of his beard tickled my skin, and I smiled back.

"You, Wynna-bun, are a treasure, you know that?"

"You give me too much credit." I'd only been speaking from my heart. That came from a higher power. I never had decent words off the cuff.

"Go get some sleep," he said. "The girls will be up in a few hours. Actually, you sleep in. I'll get them up, ready, and take them to school."

"Well, okay ..." My gaze flicked to the almost-gone cheesecake. "But first ... cheesecake?"

He lowered my hand and snagged my fork, cut a generous bite of it, and held it up. "Airplane?"

"Really?" My eyes rolled heavenward. I loved his playfulness, but ... *airplane?*

"It's fun. See?" He made a whirring sound and traced a flight path through the air between us. "C'mon, Wynna-bun. Take a chance. Have some fun."

"Take a chance, huh?" I tilted my chin up. "You'd better not miss the runway."

His eyes gleamed with mischief, and he made no promises. "Airplane, coming in for a landing!" His whirring was louder this time, and I laughed as his "plane" made a smooth landing in my open mouth. "I never miss important shots."

I tried not to choke from laughing as he made a show of scooping up the last bit and airplaning it to his own mouth.

"I'll clean up, Wynna-bun." He tugged me in for another hug. "Thank you."

"Anytime," I said into his hoodie. "Good night, Zaki."

As I crossed the kitchen to my room, I snuck a glance over my shoulder. The tender look on his face as he watched me set my insides on fire.

Had we just stepped into new territory?

It sure felt like it.

CHAPTER 18
Zaki

After being in the depths of despair—a phrase my girls picked up from *Anne of Green Gables* and had been using at least twice daily—last night, I went to sleep with renewed positivity and a big dose of hope.

And heartfelt pleas to never dye my hair again, lest it turn green like when Anne tried to rid herself of her unwanted red hair.

Arwyn hadn't disagreed when I told her she knew my heart, and she hinted that I knew hers. I could read what she wasn't saying. We had feelings for each other that were crossing the lines of friendship. With her intuitive inclination and me wearing my heart on my sleeve, I was sure she was able to read into my expressions.

In my soul, I knew we could be good for each other, and I wanted to find out. The tricky part was exploring that while she was working for me. If it didn't work out, the girls and I would be crushed. And if it did work out, would she move to Montreal?

There was only one way to find out.

However, I had to be careful not to come on too strong and scare her away. I lived my life big, and she was showing me how living small could be the best way of all.

As I helped the girls get ready for school, I told them Arwyn was sleeping in. They humored me as I tried to braid their hair, but despite my best efforts, it was a major fail.

"Daddy?"

"Yeah, Isles?"

"You go make Wynnie breakfast in bed. Then she'll be awake and can fix our hair."

I snorted. "It doesn't look that bad."

Amelie shook her head sadly, holding up her barely-held-together braids. "Daddy! You used *zip ties*. It's an abomination."

I barked out a laugh deep from my gut. "That's a big word."

"Daddy, all the girls will think Wynnie doesn't care about us if our hair is a mess. And that's not true. She *has* to do our hair." Amelie's last sentence came out as a whimper.

"Okay, Amms, no need to cry," I said quickly. "You girls go knock—gently—on Wynnie's door and ask for her help. I'll make pancakes."

"Yay!"

I followed them down the stairs and into the kitchen. Arwyn's door opened, and I was relieved to see her sitting up in bed, reading the book she'd had last night.

I snuck at least a dozen glances as I warmed up Chef's pancakes and set up a tray for Arwyn. Pancakes, syrup, hot tea, napkin, fork. As an afterthought, I added a scoop of strawberry ice cream on top of her stack of pancakes. I carried the tray to her room just as she finished Amelie's second braid.

"What's this?" she asked.

I shrugged. "An apology for waking you up?"

"Not necessary." She grinned. "But I'll take it."

"Daddy, I want ice cream on my pancakes!"

"Me too!"

"Okay, okay!" I laughed. Arwyn climbed back into her bed, and I set the tray over her lap. "Enjoy."

"Oh, I will."

We grinned at each other. I reluctantly turned away and joined the girls. From my seat at the table, I could see into Arwyn's doorway. Each time she caught me looking at her, I winked and she quickly averted her gaze.

But each time, her smile grew wider.

AFTER I WALKED the girls to school, instead of heading home to drive straight to practice, I picked up drinks at the Coffee Loft and walked back to the house. I didn't want to bother Arwyn if she was already working, but I craved seeing her again.

The front room smelled like roses and hot glue. Arwyn liked to burn a candle while she worked, and it made the place even more cozy.

She was bent over a pile of gauzy fabric at her worktable and was gluing something to it. Her hair was piled on top of her head the way she liked to wear it. A few strands of hair on each side of her face had escaped, framing her ivory complexion and making her freckles stand out.

I stood awkwardly at the doggie gate with the drink carrier, waiting for her to notice me and look up.

"New dress?" I asked.

"I'm actually making something for you. Per the girls' request."

"Oh really?" I stepped over the gate and set the drinks on the coffee table and petted each of the dogs on the head.

"Mmhmm." She still hadn't looked up. "A tutu. The girls have decided to teach you ballet during your video calls on the road."

"I see."

"Be sure to act surprised when they give this to you tomorrow and oversee the packing of it."

"I'll be over-the-top grateful."

"I knew you wouldn't disappoint."

"Never. I brought drinks. Not sure if yours is still hot though."

"Thanks."

"Anything I can help you with?"

She shook her head. "Just give me a minute to finish gluing the sequins on the ribbon trim."

"Sixty, fifty-nine, fifty-eight, fifty-seven ..."

Arwyn let out a small, amused exhale as she leaned back in her chair and looked up at me. "Done. I'm all yours. What's up?"

All mine? Her gaze lingered on me a beat longer than usual, and suddenly, the air in the room felt … different. *Charged.*

"I, uh, brought you tea."

"You said that," she reminded me. "Thank you."

"You're welcome." I bent to pull it from the carrier, and when I straightened up to hand it to her, she was standing.

Close.

Her eyes flicked to my mouth for the briefest second, and my heart did a stupid somersault.

She reached for the tea, but I held onto it. If I let go, I didn't trust myself not to take her in my arms and kiss her with all the fervor that had been building.

I needed to back away. But I couldn't. Not when she was looking at me like that, all serious and quiet and beautiful in a way that made me want to memorize every detail. My pulse hammered in my ears as I leaned in just a little closer, close enough to feel the warmth of her breath.

And then—

"Rrrorroough ruff!"

Arwyn stepped back, eyes wide as the dogs jumped off the sofa and ran to the front door. I turned to follow her gaze out the front window.

Montgomery Biddington was marching up to the porch, holding the gift I'd left on his doorstep on my way home last night.

Well, that had backfired.

Or not.

I probably shouldn't be kissing my nanny, anyway.

Arwyn hurried to the door and opened it. Monty handed her the metallic-blue-wrapped box. "Hope I'm not interrupting anything important." He turned to shoot me a smirk. "But I had to return this gift."

I joined Arwyn and the dogs in the vestibule. "Sorry, no returns."

He lifted the lid, revealing the egg-filled nest inside. "Birds are gross. My wife is pregnant. We have a cat. No birds. And where is their mama? Did you kidnap them?"

I laughed. Arwyn looked up at me, and I winked. "They're not real, Monty. I do have a heart, you know."

"Then use it more often." He glanced from me to Arwyn and back to me again. "Good luck on your road trip. I'll see you both at the gala."

He spun on his heel and marched back to his truck.

Use my heart.

I wanted to. More than anything.

This road trip could not have come at a worse time.

But—the Olympic break would start when I got back. Since I wasn't playing—I'd declined, citing child-care issues—we could extend the Valentine weekend at the cabin, if Arwyn was amenable to it. I'd even find a way to bring along all her sewing equipment if she asked.

CHAPTER 19
Arwyn

Zaki's short road trip to California over the weekend felt longer than usual. Why couldn't I stop thinking about him?

Kami picked up the girls Saturday afternoon for a sleepover. The house was so quiet, even with the dogs. I kept myself busy, taking them for a walk along the creek. I finished both Penny's gown and mine with the Edge game on for background noise. They won 5-2, and I debated texting Zaki to congratulate him.

By midnight, I was still wired.

Uneasy, even. I hadn't been alone in the house in weeks.

California was an hour behind, time-wise, and Zaki would be up for a while since it took him hours to come down from the adrenaline high.

My heart overruled my brain, and with the dogs on either side of me for moral support, I sent a message:

Great game tonight. You were amazing anchoring that first PK.

He texted back right away. *Thanks. Look at you, talking hockey.*

I smiled and tapped out my reply. *When I framed it as its own language, it became easier to pick up.*

Ha. It really is. The bubble popped up with three dots, indicating he was tapping more words. *So, watching hockey by yourself on a Saturday night. You sound like a fan.*

I wasn't alone, I typed with a grin.

Oh no?

Nope. Laffy, Vennie, June, and July were here rooting for y'all, too.

No August?

Nah. He doesn't like hockey.

How do you know?

Hmm. How *did* I know?

I laughed softly as the answer came to me. *Watching players get slammed into the boards reminds him of the time I knocked him over. He's still recovering emotionally from that.*

A trio of laughing emojis was my reward.

I loved that he understood my humor. Most people didn't.

One game down, two to go, then over two weeks off. You must be excited to spend all that time with the girls.

Instead of texting me back, my phone rang, signaling an incoming call. I accepted and held the phone up to my ear.

"Hi," I greeted him. "Everything okay?"

"Hey. Yeah. I just—" He paused.

I waited.

"I had an idea I wanted to run by you. I was going to call you tomorrow, since we're off, but you're up, so …"

"Spill," I demanded. His uncertainty made me curious.

"I was thinking I'd take the girls to the cabin over the off weekends, but then I had another idea, because I want to spend the time with you, too. If you want to spend time with me, er, us."

"I'd like that a lot," I said softly. "I have next weekend free, since I finished both gowns. But that's a long drive from the gala the following weekend." Had he changed his mind about going?

"We can stay until Tuesday morning, since Monday is a holiday."

"Right, I forgot about that. More hockey lessons, then?"

"And more ballet lessons. You remember I have a studio in the basement."

I laughed. "I do. Don't forget to pack your tutu."

"Not a chance."

"You're a great dad, Zaki." I smiled to myself, remembering how my own dad would go along with any kind of play I suggested. Mom was more down-to-business. She'd taught me how to take care of myself and find purpose in the things I loved.

My eyes began to burn with the hint of tears to come. I missed them both so much.

"Why so quiet, Wynna-bun?" Zaki's tone was buttery soft. Concerned but interested.

"I was remembering what it was like to have parents," I confessed.

"Ah. When was the last time you saw your mom?"

"A little over a year ago, when she came home to get the rest of her stuff and sign the house over to me. She's had an apartment in Washington, DC, for as long as I can remember and decided to make the move permanent."

"That must have been hard for you."

"Not hard. Just sad." I swiped at my eyes with the end of my sleeve. "I'd been living by myself for years at that point."

"You're incredible, Wynnie. You know that, right?"

I chuckled at the awe in his voice. "You're sweet. I've just done what I needed to do. Like you. I couldn't imagine moving to a new continent when I was fifteen and living with strangers. The very thought of it is terrifying."

"All I could think about back then was hockey. I just did what I needed to do," he echoed.

I settled back into my pillows. "You've created a wonderful life for yourself and your girls, Zaki. They're smart, friendly, fun, well-adjusted, and able to navigate redirects with ease. Many adults can't do that."

"Yeah. I'm proud of those little sass-tots."

"Sass-tots?" I giggled. "I've never heard that one before."

"That's what our housekeeper in England called my sisters. Isla and Amelie take it to another level, though. If Mrs. Litherland ever met them—" He whistled.

"I'd love to hear more about your life there," I said.

"Are you sure? It's after midnight over there."

"I'm sure."

"All right. If you fall asleep while I'm droning on, I promise to forgive you."

I snorted. "Good, because I heard you can be a bore."

He groaned, deep and theatrically.

"You sound like a dying moose, Marsch."

"Your words speak daggers! Oh, the wound you've inflicted to my heart! How can you be so cruel as to insult me so? And who told you that? I must prank them appropriately."

I was full-on laughing now. "I'll never tell. Start talking."

He sighed dramatically. "Picture it. A breezy summer day in Copenhagen. My parents were visiting Dad's family before he had to return to Sheffield for training camp. My older sister, Mirette, was obsessed with *The Little Mermaid.* As the famous statue came into her sightline, I gave my mother a swift kick—so my dad tells it—breaking her water right there on the promenade."

I yawned. "Ouch."

"I'm boring you already, eh?"

"Not at all. Go on." I turned my face away from the phone as the next yawn hit.

"I was born later that day. We stayed in Denmark for a couple more weeks and then went home to England. South Yorkshire is a beautiful place, Wynnie. You'd love it. Rich history, rolling hills, rugged moorlands, lush gardens, wetlands, birdwatching, castles . . ."

Castles. I like castles. I drifted off to sleep to visions of mermaids and castles and a tall, kind, ginger-bearded king ruling over the land with the sweetest little princesses by his side, blowing a kiss to an auburn-haired maiden on horseback and whispering, "Sweet dreams, Wynna-bun."

CHAPTER 20
Zaki

The Olympic break was flying by. Our first weekend at the cabin was medicine to my soul. Arwyn had picked up enough hockey knowledge and lingo and chirping to play two-on-two with the girls and me. She and Amelie gave Isla and I a run for our money.

After the girls went to bed, we'd sit by the fire and talk. And the more we talked, the harder it was not to lean over and kiss her. But I refrained. I had to be sure that she was sure about starting something because I couldn't open my heart to breaking again. If the season ended and we parted as friends, I could handle that.

But if we became more and she didn't want to come with us back to Canada …

The possibility of not having her in my life—in *our* lives—stole my breath and not in a good way. It strangled my lungs and crushed my heart.

What didn't hurt my heart was my decision not to play in the Olympics. Denmark didn't have a chance at winning, and it felt good to give the opportunity to a younger guy. And the quality time I gained with my girls and Arwyn—that was more important than anything.

The morning of the gala—Valentine's Day—the girls woke me up by jumping on my bed and kiss-bombing my face. I returned

their greeting with tickles, and while we tousled, I noticed Arwyn in the doorway, in her kimono, holding some sort of … crown?

Luckily, Isla and Amelie tired quickly. As they lay on me gasping for breath, I asked them if all the kisses meant that I was their Valentine.

"Of course you're our Valentine, Daddy!" Isla huffed. "There's no boy at school that's as good as you." She hopped off the bed to retrieve the crown thing from Arwyn.

I laughed as she placed the homemade circlet of glittery construction paper on my head. "Good. I'm happy to be your Valentine. But …"

"What, Daddy?" Amelie asked. "Don't you like your King Valentine crown? I cut it out and wrote 'King Daddy' and Isla glued on all the sparkles."

"I do. I feel very loved. And very dashing. But … does Wynnie have a Valentine?"

I met her gaze. She raised her eyebrows, and I grinned.

"Of course, Daddy," Amelie assured me. "Laffy and Vennie are her Valentines!"

As if on cue, the dogs barked to confirm, and we all laughed.

Arwyn made pink heart-shaped pancakes for breakfast, and we ate a few cookies that were left over from the batch the girls decorated for their class party the day before. I brought them to ballet and snuck out to run quick errands to the print shop and florist.

I doubt they even noticed I was gone.

When we returned home, I set the girls up with a Barbie ballet movie on the sofa and asked Arwyn to come upstairs with me.

I took her hand and led her up the stairs and into my room, to the overly large closet where all her father's photographs were stored.

"Close your eyes."

"Should I be afraid?" she challenged.

"I hope not. No-pranks promise, remember?"

She pinned me with a narrow gaze.

"Okay, bad example. Trust me, okay?"

"Okay."

She closed her eyes, and I snuck over to the far side of the bed where I'd stashed the bag from the print shop. Inside was a box with two large hardcover coffee table books. I laid each book on top of a stack of her father's boxes.

I guided her over to stand by the first book. "You can open your eyes now."

Her eyes flickered open and then went wide. "Is this—? When did you—?"

"It is. A book of all your dad's wildlife photos. I found some DVDs with the images on them and I made a book."

"This is ... This is amazing." Page after page of animals native to Colorado filled the book, from the fish swimming in Snowpack Creek to a bear roaming up in the mountains.

"And ..." I gently turned her to the next book. "A family scrapbook."

She gasped. On the cover was a holiday portrait of Arwyn as a little girl in a fancy holiday dress, held jointly by her parents, each in their dress blues. "Where did you find these?"

"In the box labeled 'Family.' Your dad was pretty organized."

"I didn't know. I—I couldn't look at them. I was too afraid. It was too painful. But now, here, in this book—somehow, it's different."

She spun around to face me. Her eyes were filled with tears ready to spill over. "You've given me the most amazing gift." Her face crumpled as she spoke. "How can I ever thank you?"

"Wynna-bun, this is me thanking you. For taking care of my girls. For loving them. For welcoming us into your home, even when you didn't like me."

She laughed. "I *really* didn't like you."

"Don't I know it! I've never been more thankful for good references." I grinned.

"I was right to be afraid you'd turn my life upside down," she said. "But I never imagined it'd be a positive upside-downing."

It was my turn to laugh. "Unlike Monty's prank."

She sniffed. "Yeah. I'm rooting for you in that prank war."

"Good. Because I might need your help."

"It would be my pleasure." She wrapped her arms around my middle. "Thank you again for the books. I love them."

I held her tightly to me. "I'm so glad you do." I closed my eyes and concentrated on committing this moment to memory. The softness of her body against mine, the rose-scented silky hair with its fly-aways caressing the underside of my chin, the security of her arms against my back.

I couldn't remember the last time I'd felt this appreciated, this comforted, this ... loved.

It took a whole lot of willpower to let go. "What time is Penny picking you up?"

"I'm meeting her and Tasha at the salon at eleven, then we'll grab lunch at Brewski's. Do you need me to pick anything up while I'm out?"

I shook my head. "Nope. Have fun." I gave her shoulder a squeeze. "See you in a few hours."

She gathered up the books and nodded. "Bye, Zaki."

I joined the girls and watched Barbie do her swan princess thing as they attempted to imitate the characters on the screen. When it was over, I made them lunch and took them outside to play.

We were still outside when Arwyn pulled into the driveway. The girls ran to the car to greet her.

"So pretty, Wynnie!"

"Can you do my hair like that?"

"Mine, too!"

Arwyn's hair was elegantly gathered and secured at the back of her head in a loose bun, and ringlet curls framed her face, tumbling out from a headband of three evenly spaced pale blue satin straps. Over her right ear, three ribbon roses in shades of blue seemed to hold the straps together.

It wasn't too different from her usual updo, but without a strand out of place, it gave a more elegant appearance, understated and refined.

Stunning.

She smiled up at me as the girls followed her into the house, asking questions about the process and planning their own future Regency tea party.

The doorbell rang, signaling the babysitter was here. The girls tugged her inside and introduced her to Arwyn. After a quick tour of the house, she took the girls upstairs to play so we could get ready.

I'd debated shaving my beard and leaving sideburns, as was the fashion of the times, but decided against it. Arwyn liked my beard, so if that meant losing a mark for not being historically accurate, I didn't care.

The "kit" I'd ordered included everything I needed to transform into a fine Regency-era gentleman. I'd opted for the trousers instead of breeches—I hoped Arwyn didn't mind. The starched white shirt had a stiff, high collar, and I was glad I'd ordered a size larger than I needed. I buttoned the waistcoat, watched a YouTube tutorial to arrange the cravat, and pulled on my tailcoat, tucking a light blue handkerchief into the pocket. Lastly, white gloves. After holding Arwyn's hand, I understood the reason for them.

Skin-to-skin touching made a person *feel things*.

When I was satisfied with my appearance, I strolled down the hall to face the critics.

"Daddy!" Amelie saw me first. "You look like a prince!"

"Almost," Isla said, frowning. "You need your King Valentine Crown."

I laughed. "I'm afraid that's against the gala's dress code, girls. But I'll happily wear it if you want to take a picture."

"Oh, yes!" Amelie agreed. "By the fireplace. Let's go get Wynnie! Daddy—get her flowers!" She picked up her tablet and headed for the stairs. Daisy bouquet and corsage in hand, I followed her and Isla, with Trudy, the babysitter, bringing up the rear.

Arwyn wasn't ready yet, so the girls took turns posing me by the fireplace, with and without the crown, with and without them in it.

Then I caught a cloud of pale blue out of the corner of my eye. I twisted up from the girls to get a better look.

I didn't hear anything. I didn't see anything in my peripheral. I was sucked into a dream state where all I could do was watch.

Arwyn floated into the room in her fancy blue gown with that elegant updo, and the only word that came to my mind was *thief*.

She stole my breath, my thoughts, my heart.

"Thief?" she asked.

Uh-oh, I hadn't meant to say it out loud.

"Daddy, Wynnie didn't steal anything," Amelie pulled at my coattail. "Why did you say that?"

"Well." I scrambled for something corny and hopefully light. "Our Wynnie looks so beautiful, she stole my breath away."

The girls giggled. "That's silly, Daddy. You're still breathing," Isla pointed out. "More pictures!"

By the time the girls were done with us, I was sure I could fill another photo book.

CHAPTER 21
Arwyn

I couldn't stop looking at him.

Forget Darcy or Bingley or even Mr. Knightley—Zaki Marsch was *the* Regency dream guy. Dressed to the nines in his perfectly tailored kit, the man should have been a supermodel. When I was squished up against him, the hard muscles of his arms and thighs burned through my cloak and gown and made my skin hot.

There were eight other people in the limo—beautiful people—and I couldn't take my eyes off the man next to me.

Occasionally, I forced myself to turn my head. Xavier and Jason, who'd been away representing the USA, were back from the Olympics, just for the night, and Zaki hung on to their every word. They'd played their qualifying games and now had a few days off during the women's qualifiers. Penny shone in her new gown, and Lauren glowed in her fifth month of pregnancy. On the other side of Penny, Gabby and Noel's faces were glued together, and his hand rubbed her belly like it was a genie's lamp. I had a feeling there would be another announcement coming soon. On the other side of Zaki, their new teammate Flynn and his fiancée, Meggie, were quietly taking it all in.

"Look!" Penny pointed out the side window as the car turned on to the winding road that led to the resort. "It's like a winter wonderland!"

Brenna Trotter, our town's premier wedding planner and wife of Edge defenseman Brendan Trotter, had told me about this place in the winter. But her description did the actual scene before me very little justice. The massive exterior with its intricate towers and balconies was bathed in warm, golden light that dazzled in a display of elegance unmatched by anything I'd ever seen. Behind it, the towering silhouettes of the Rockies framed the classic Mediterranean-style buildings. Strings of twinkling fairy lights connected the old-fashioned streetlamps, creating an enchanting and inviting ambience.

Inside, the gilded and marble lobby dripped with wealth and luxury. Outside the ballroom, I removed my cloak at the coat check and handed it to Zaki, who gave it and his overcoat to an attendant. Sadly, formal manners dictated he give over his top hat as well. We proceeded to the step-and-repeat backdrop for photos, which made me a little uncomfortable, but it wasn't too bad.

The ballroom … The ballroom was right out of a Regency novel. Ornate chandeliers, gilded mirrors, and nineteenth-century furniture sets were arranged throughout the space. Long banquet tables stretched from the door to the dance floor, set with towering topiaries, fine porcelain dishes, gleaming silver, and gilded candelabra.

"This is the best research ever," I whispered to Zaki as we walked arm in arm to our seats. "There are too many distractions for me to think about the crowd, and no one I've met so far seems fake or insincere."

"There are a lot of great experiences outside your comfort zone, Wynna-bun. But give it time—the fake and insincere part," Zaki murmured into my ear. "Hang with me, and you'll get your fill."

I frowned. "Surely, anyone here who's a fan is sincere about it."

"You'd think so. But my photo and autograph are commodities. Most people don't care about the player; they care about the status of being with the player or the autographed item they can showcase or sell. And keep your guard up—they may try to get close to you since you're close to me."

"I hate that for you," I said. "How do you decide who you can trust?"

"You keep your net wide but your circle small. Family, long-time teammates. Teammates' families. That's about it. And you nurture those relationships when you get split up. I've known Jason and Kingston since the minors. When Kingston went to play in Montana, we got together when the teams played each other. And he invited us up there to visit. Lauren and Viki are still close, and she's been a good friend even when Viki started to pull away. We don't let the people we care about quit."

I turned his last sentence over in my mind. I knew what he was referring to, but it was his marriage that jumped to the front of my mind. It was admirable, the way he'd tried to save it. But ultimately, Viki had quit him.

"Sometimes you have to give up things, Zaki. Things that bring you down. Things you can't fix. It's not always quitting. And it's okay."

He pressed his lips together and nodded. We arrived at our table, and he pulled my chair out for me. On my other side was Flynn, whom I hadn't said more than a hello to. Across the table were our other limo-mates, and within minutes, Zaki and Gabby, the most extroverted of the group, started a conversation we could all participate in. I didn't even notice when Penny disappeared.

Promptly at seven o'clock, the soothing sounds of classical music stopped and the emcee welcomed us all. He spoke about the charity, introduced Mr. and Mrs. Biddington, and passed the mic to Monty, who spoke about the silent auction, whose proceeds would benefit children in local pediatric cancer units. Then we all stood for Penny's rendition of "The Star-Spangled Banner."

By the third course, I was having a great time getting to know Zaki's teammates and their significant others. Tasha and Monty stopped by to say hello. Tasha's belly bump looked adorable under her ribboned empire waistline.

After dessert, members from the local symphony took the stage and performed popular classic and modern selections. Couples took to the dance floor, and Zaki turned to me.

"Arwyn," he said, his voice low but carrying easily over the lilting strains of the symphony. He offered his hand, absent of the white gloves. "Would you grant me the honor of a dance?"

The question was simple, friendly. But his eyes ... his eyes said something more. Bright, hopeful, playful, and a touch mischievous, they locked onto mine with a fervent intensity. My pulse quickened, and heat crept into my cheeks as I nodded. I'd have been content to watch from the sidelines, to quietly melt into the background on a settee in the corner and soak in the atmosphere and lose myself in the romance of it all—for research purposes, of course.

But the way he looked at me made it impossible to refuse. His grin—oh, that grin—lit up his face, boyish and unguarded. I laid my hand in his, feeling the warmth of his touch even through the fine fabric of my lacy glove.

"If the gentleman has determined a dance to be part of the lady's research," I began, grateful my voice sounded stately—and far steadier than I was feeling—"then how is the lady to refuse?"

Zaki tugged me up from my seat gently and tucked my arm into his. "Splendid." Then he bent to whisper in my ear, his warm breath coaxing goosebumps to make an appearance. "How's my impression so far?"

"Of?" I teased. Above us, the chandeliers glittered like the stars in my eyes, illuminating the grandeur. The melody of the strings on stage summoned me like a piper as Zaki guided me through the dancing couples into the center of the dance floor.

"You wound me. My impression of a gentleman, of course. I risked my reputation watching clips of Regency films on the plane. Tell me I didn't waste my time?" In one swift motion, he placed my free hand on his shoulder, his right hand settled lightly at my waist, and the left held mine firmly but gently.

"Smooth move," I murmured. "You learned that from a movie clip?"

He waggled his eyebrows. "Not that one. That's all Marsch. Impressed?"

I fluttered my eyelashes. "By your roguish move and charm? I'm on guard, for sure."

His expression changed from teasing to serious. "You never have to be on guard with me, Wynna-bun."

I swallowed, surprised by the intensity behind his statement. "Noted."

The symphony transitioned to a waltz, and his expression lit up again. "I should warn you," he said softly, "I'm an expert dancer."

He guided me effortlessly, confident and smooth. I clung to him, relishing the strength beneath my hand on his shoulder and grateful for the lacy fabric of my glove, which was surely absorbing the clamminess.

Was there anything this man couldn't do? It was as if the music flowed through him, and I relaxed into the rhythm of the dancing, not needing to count and putting my trust in him completely to lead.

"Where did you learn to dance like this?" I asked. "You're a natural."

"I was born waltzing," he boasted.

"Really?" I challenged, my brow knitting.

"It's you, Wynna-bun. You're making me look good," he countered.

"Hmm." I wasn't convinced, but if he didn't want to tell me, it was easy to assume he'd learned to dance with his ex, and I for sure wasn't going to bring her up during this perfect moment.

"Look at me, Wynn."

"It's not a paso doble," I protested. "No eye contact required." But my eyes found his again, and the warmth radiating there blurred my thoughts. For what it was worth, we *could* have been dancing the paso the way he was looking at me.

"I can dance that, too," he challenged. "Do you want to see my best matador moves?"

Whew.

Okay.

"Maybe another time," I squeaked. If he kept talking like that, I'd lose my ability to form coherent thoughts, never mind witty replies.

As we box-stepped and twirled, the room and the people blurred around us, the hems of their gowns swept the polished wood, and the very small space between became charged with an electricity that made my breath catch each time his hand adjusted slightly at my waist or our eyes met for just a beat too long. The song began to build to its crescendo, and he pulled me just a fraction closer, enough to catch the scent of his soap or shampoo or—

The instruments quieted as the music changed to an upbeat but slow cover of Maroon 5's "Girls Like You" in the style of the Vitamin Strings Quartet, and I relaxed against him, daring to stretch my arm up past his shoulder to cup the back of his neck.

His look of surprise at my forwardness made me regret the action, but I didn't retract, waiting to see what he would do.

Nothing. He did nothing.

Oh my.

I turned my head to my left to catch my breath and jumped when I felt the hair on his cheek graze mine. "Three dances in a row." He clucked his tongue, the soft vibrations causing an encore from my goosebumps. "Scandalous. People will talk."

"What shall we do about it?" I whispered back.

"I'd like to keep dancing with you. If there's room on your dance card?"

There was no dance card, of course. But if there had been, I'd have let him write his name on every line. But he had a point—three dances with the nanny *was* probably pushing the friend-zone line.

Gah! I couldn't deny my attraction to him or that my heart cared about him more than it should.

I couldn't deny that when I read my historical novels, I pictured his face on the hero.

And I couldn't deny that, had circumstances been different and he had plans to stay in Colorado, I might take a chance on something more than friendship.

"I'd like to keep dancing with you, too," I said.

So much for restraint.

"I'm glad. It feels like I'm in another world, dancing here with you."

"Pretending to be in the past can help medicate a present that isn't well," I said softly. "It's meant to be an escape. A temporary one, of course. We can be in this world of nineteenth-century finery but not *of* it."

"Yes. I should escape more often. Maybe you'd join me? I'm sure there are Regency balls and galas one can attend regularly?"

"I, um—yes. The closest is Once Upon a Dream Ball in Denver, but there are countless others." His head was still bent next to mine. I slid my hand from the back of his neck around to his lapel and moved in closer so that we were almost nose to nose. "Why?"

"This elegant world of the past suits you," he said. "You have a timeless quality about you, fitting in here like you were born for the era, not in the chaos of the modern world."

I smiled, warmed by his words. "You're surprisingly poetic for a rough-and-tumble defenseman who pranks his friends for fun."

The glint of mischief I loved returned to his eyes. "What can I say? I see beauty, deep to the core, natural, effortless beauty in front of me, and I can't not comment."

My breath hitched, and for a moment, the world truly did fall away.

His gaze dropped to my lips, just for an instant, before returning to my eyes. It was barely noticeable, but it sent a rush of heat through me.

"Arwyn," he said, his voice so low it rumbled. "There's something I want to tell you. But I'm not sure if I should."

I opened my mouth to respond as the final note of the song hung in the air. Applause erupted around us, shattering the fragile bubble we'd created and giving me time to formulate a response.

I stepped back and somehow pulled my hands together to join in the clapping. Zaki's hand lingered at my waist before he brought his fingers to his mouth and whistled.

My mind spun with questions I wasn't ready to ask and feelings I wasn't ready to name. The emcee announced the orchestra's break and handed control over to the DJ, who began to play a blend of upbeat music.

And still, I couldn't speak.

Brendan appeared next to Zaki, and they appeared to exchange some sort of signal.

"Stay here." He winked. "The show's about to start."

"The show?" I echoed.

"No idea," Brenna said from behind me. I turned, and she shrugged. "They're up to something. All we can do is wait and hope not to be part of it."

I was sure I looked like a deer in headlights. "Excuse me?"

The blond ringlets framing her face bounced as she chuckled. "Just a hunch."

I followed the trajectory of her gaze, and sure enough, Zaki and Brendan were jogging up the side steps of the stage, each with a mic in hand. They'd removed their tailcoats, rolled up their sleeves, and donned dark sunglasses.

I gulped.

But he'd said I could trust him. He knew I was as introverted as they came and I preferred to be anywhere alone than in this crowd.

With every muscle in my body, I resisted the urge to run.

Also, I couldn't have. His teammates and their significant others were beside and behind me, making an exit impossible.

"How's it going tonight?" Brendan shouted into his microphone, and the crowd cheered. "Marshy and I have a surprise for you all. Now, Monty, I know you weren't expecting this, and we do apologize for any inconvenience this may cause."

Zaki explained. "You see, I gave you a very heartfelt and thoughtful birthday present. Two, actually." He tapped his heart and turned to Monty, who was now at the side of the stage, eyebrows raised coolly, but inside I would bet he was seething. "I went out of my way after the bird release to drop the second gift off on your doorstep. And you *returned* it. It hurt, man. It really hurt."

He made a sad face and paused, the guests all *awwing* and further fueling his act.

"So," Brendan said again. "He decided to try a little harder. During the band's break, we arranged to bring you …"

"Karaoke!" Zaki announced.

"Oh my!" I laughed.

"Look at Monty." Penny giggled. "I think these two will have to double their donation if they want to attend next year!"

"At least!" Brenna agreed.

"So, do I have any requests?" Zaki asked the audience.

"I have a request," Brendan replied. "I'm in the mood for some ABBA."

"ABBA, huh?" Zaki asked. "I didn't know Monty liked ABBA."

"Only one way to find out," Brendan suggested. "Let's, ah, *take a chance?*"

Brenna snorted and leaned into my ear. "This is *gold!* Save my spot while I get my phone!"

Brendan wrapped his fingers around the top of his mic. "Take a chance, take a chance, take a chance." He repeated the phrase over and over as the music filtered in.

Zaki watched him pace the stage, hyping the crowd with his free hand and getting the guests to join in his background vocals. Then he turned to face the audience and hit me straight on with the first line of the song. It was like he was speaking to me directly, telling me if I changed my mind, he'd like to be the first in line.

But it was just a song, right? A song Monty didn't like, a gag to prank him back?

An explosion couldn't have touched the magnetism keeping our eyes locked. I clapped along, mouthing the background lyrics, but no sound came out. There was a line about being all alone when the pretty birds had flown, which was enough for the audience to believe he was referencing the prank war, but I'd bet my business the lyrics were a veiled message to me.

He couldn't get me off his mind?

He dreamed about being alone with me?

He knew I was afraid of starting a love affair?

I stopped clapping and fanned my face. *A fan!* I should've brought a fan! Why hadn't I thought about bringing one to hide behind?

Because you don't need to hide when you're with him.

The realization struck me like a puck to the face. Stopped me short. Hurt a bit.

Okay, a lot.

A lot a lot.

As I watched him ham it up on stage, a fire burned inside me.

It started as that warm glow in my cheeks, then moved down to my chest and fanned out all over, setting my nerves on fire. And when the song ended, he handed Brendan his mic, jumped down from the stage, the sea of people parting, and strode straight toward me like a man on a mission.

He must have seen the panic on my face, because he slowed as he approached. "Join me for a walk in the gardens?"

I nodded. "Let's go."

We fled the stifling ballroom and retrieved our outerwear from the attendants. I tucked my arm in his, and we followed the signage to the doors that led outside. The cool blast of air stung my face, but I welcomed it.

It wasn't just my skin that needed cooling.

"Wow." Ahead of us, the still waters of the lake shimmered, the lit fountain in the middle spraying water and sending out ripples that caught the moonlight and reflected the warm glow of the windows from inside the main building. More trees adorned with the same fairy lights we'd seen in the front of the building created a canopy over our heads as we slowed our paces, traversing a curvy stone pathway, guiding us through the manicured landscaping toward the lake. Ornate iron benches peppered the path, tucked into the bushes to offer privacy to their canoodling occupants.

"It's so lovely," I breathed as we reached a small unoccupied gazebo, just off the main path in an alcove of pines. Adorned with the fairy lights that illuminated the single bench inside, it seemed magical, otherworldly, unmodern, and—

"Perfect spot." Zaki peered down at me. "Shall we?"

I nodded, and we continued in the direction of the gazebo.

I stopped just short of the steps. I needed to ask him *the thing*. "Wait, before we sit …"

"Yeah?" We faced each other, and the slight breeze blew my carefully coiled tendrils across my face. Zaki reached up to tuck them behind my ear. The gesture was gentle, tender. His roguish charm made my stomach flutter.

"You … Back in the ballroom, you said you had something to tell me. And then you sang that song and invited me out here. Am I … Am I to believe that you … that I … that we …?"

"Wynnie … Wynna-bun … I'm falling for you. I've tried not to, but it's happening fast and easily and completely. I can't stop it. And I don't want to. Because I think you're falling for me, too. Am I right?"

Well now, he didn't mince words, did he?

Okay, Wynnie Wynna-bun. You can be direct, too. Out with it.

My heartbeat drummed in my ears, so loudly the nighttime sounds around us faded away. But instead of panic, I felt peace. Out here, in this setting, dressed for the past but very much living in the present, I could be myself.

I could be myself with someone who wanted me to be me.

"Yes," I whispered. "And I don't want to stop it, either."

Those beautiful blue eyes held mine as I tipped up my chin. When Zaki's lips touched mine, every muscle in my body went weak. I reached up to take hold of his face, to keep it in place, just in case he thought of pulling back from the most perfect kiss ever. I closed my eyes and let him lead.

Oh lordy, what have you done? If this doesn't work out, you'll be spoiled for any other man because surely, no one else can kiss like that.

His hands were around me, pulling me into him. One thing was certain: Zaki Marsch had a way of making the ordinary feel extraordinary.

Suddenly, a series of bright flashes forced me to close my eyes tighter.

Fireworks?

"That's not fireworks," Zaki murmured, turning me away from the light and tucking my head protectively into his chest. "It's paparazzi."

CHAPTER 22
Zaki

I knew it would happen eventually. I never expected it to happen *the first time we kissed.* I'd been so caught up in the moment, I'd forgotten what a high-profile event this was.

I'd forgotten my celebrity status.

When I was with Arwyn, I felt normal. She didn't want anything I could give her, not material things or to travel. She was happy in her home, doing her thing.

Though she looked shaken up, Arwyn assured me she was fine, and we went back in to the gala. She went to the ladies' room, and I perused the silent auction in an effort to avoid conversations with people who wanted things from me. I won a VIP ticket package to the Colorado Ballet, which the girls would love, and it came with a behind-the-scenes tour that featured time with the set and costume designers.

When we arrived home, she went straight to her room, and Trudy and the girls were up before we could talk about the kiss. I prayed we'd have a chance to discuss what happened before she went on social media.

The next morning after church, we headed out toward the mountains. The drive up to the cabin was lively. Arwyn had shared the songs from *Anne of Green Gables: The Musical* with the girls and sang along to it with them. As I unpacked the van, I found myself humming about being the lost Lady Cordelia DeMontmorency.

That Anne sure was wild.

It was an unusually warm day for February, and I was disappointed to find my backyard rink slushy. I'd have to test the ice before skating.

After delivering all the bags and gear where they needed to go, I joined the girls at the counter that separated the kitchen from the living area while Arwyn unpacked Chef's lunch. She'd brought her white apron with the ruffles and wore it over a blue cardigan that brought out the lightness in her eyes. A plaid skirt, in colors similar to the flannel I had on, peeked out from under the apron.

"Anything we can do to help?" I asked.

She shook her head but smiled as she placed my plate in front of me.

"Look, girls—just what I wanted! Salmon with a side of salad. Can you say that fast ten times?"

I took a bite and winked at Arwyn as the girls accepted the challenge.

"Salmon with a side of salad. Salmon with a side of salad. Salmon with a slide of salad! Salmon with a slide of slallad! Slammin' with a slide of slallad!"

"Nice try," I commended them. "Slammin' salmon makes it sound so much better."

Arwyn placed their plates of sandwiches and fruit on their placemats and then came around the counter to sit in the stool next to me to eat her grilled chicken salad. The girls were ignoring us, still trying to outdo each other and beat the tongue twister, so I took the opportunity to check in.

I leaned away from the girls and spoke low. "Are we okay?"

She nodded. Her lips twitched, then spread into a small smile. "I am if you are."

"I'm better than okay," I assured her. I took a bite of salmon and chose my words carefully. "There are pictures. From the gala. And a video. If you see them, just scroll past, okay?"

I didn't think her ivory complexion could get paler, but it did. All color drained from her face as she pulled her phone out of her pocket and pulled up social media. She went directly to Instagram and typed in my handle.

Photo after photo, plus reels of us kissing by the gazebo, some with captions—favorable and unfavorable—but a common theme throughout.

The Nanny That Stole His Heart. Is Marshy Marriage-Minded? Hot for the Help! Puck Bunny or Black Cat for Denver's Most Eligible Dad?

After a few seconds, all I could see was red.

Before our relationship could even have a chance, it was hit with this test. This was not how it was supposed to go. I desperately wanted a chance for our love to grow privately—not on social media, in front of the world.

"Excuse me, girls. I think I left something in the car." Arwyn slid off her stool and speed-walked to the front door.

"Daddy, can we help her find it?" Amelie asked.

"Yes, let's!" Isla agreed, and before I could answer, they were off and running out the door.

I followed them and watched from the window. I needed to call Viki.

"So, you and the nanny, huh?" Viki sounded upbeat and happy.

"Me and the nanny." I sighed. "If she'll even have me after this. Sorry I didn't tell you. I caught big feels, and last night was so fancy—I couldn't hold back."

"I'm happy for you. But"—she blew out a breath—"does this mean you're staying in Colorado?"

"What? No."

"Her life is there, Zak. If she's someone you want to be with, does she know that you'll put the girls first?"

"She knows. And honestly? I'm pretty sure she'll put them before me." I opened the door to get a better look, and the dogs almost tripped me trying to get out there. The girls were inside the van. The trunk was open, and Arwyn was pulling out blankets. When the girls emerged from the back, she wrapped them each in a blanket and closed the trunk.

"I'm glad. But Zak, if you want to stay in Colorado—"

"I don't. And if that's a dealbreaker, that's a dealbreaker. We'll part as friends at the end of the season."

"Even if she's the one that completes you?"

On top of the tree trunk I used to split logs, Arwyn had the girls' Anna and Elsa dolls and was performing some sort of skit. The girls giggled as they watched. I reached back inside to snag the dogs' leashes from the hook just inside the door.

"Even if."

"You could miss out on the love you've been looking for your whole life. I'm sure the girls would understand."

"Seriously, Vik?" It angered me that she even thought that. "If Arwyn is the person I want, she wouldn't want me to give up my girls."

"No," Viki agreed. "She wouldn't."

"I gotta go. The girls will call you tonight."

"Bye, Zak. Good luck."

I shoved the phone in my pocket and jogged out to the dolls' stage on the tree trunk. The dogs sensed me and met me halfway. I snapped on their leashes and walked them back to the girls.

"Don't let them run away," I whispered to the girls. "Call for me if they get antsy."

I nodded to Arwyn and went back into the house. I was debating whether to put in a call to the PR team when my phone rang.

Monty.

"Looking to hire me to perform at your next party?" I joked.

"Not unless I decide to throw a grad party for Clown College."

I rolled my eyes. "What do you want, then?"

"What I want is for my wife to speak to me. Security failed big-time last night, and Tasha isn't the easy-to-forgive type. She can't get hold of Arwyn. I suspect she's with you and not answering her phone because of all the publicity. I need to apologize to her. And if you've got a brain in your head and a heart that cares for that sweet girl, you'll put out a statement about this madness."

"Hold on." I closed the door and went back to my spot at the front window. "You think me saying something will end this? What kind of statement?"

"Seriously? The *only* statement. You love her, right?"

"It's been a month, Monty. I hardly know her. I just kissed her last night, for Pete's sake."

"Yeah, no brain in *your* head. Well, you may not know it, but the rest of us do. It doesn't take long to fall in love when you *know.* It's instant. Boom. Life changed."

Instant? That wasn't how it was with Viki. I was living with her family for a year before I even asked her out. Our feelings had grown gradually, and ...

"Monty—how did it switch for you? You and Tasha were friends for a long time before you fell for each other. How did you know those feelings were real and not just ... convenient because of all the time you spent together?"

"Convenient? Look, Marsch, I didn't call to become your therapist. If you're referring to your ex—your high school sweetheart-turned-hockey-wife, yeah, I think you have an argument for convenience. Especially if you were friends first. But there's nothing *at all* convenient about loving Tasha. Never was, never will be. She's my rose *and* my thorn. And I can't live without her. So let me apologize to Arwyn so my wife will speak to me again."

"I—okay."

As I turned to the door, Laffy and Vennie began barking in earnest. I hurried to open it and investigate.

Horror stopped me dead in my tracks. Arwyn, waving the Anna doll, stood between the dogs and the stump. The girls were trying to pull the dogs backward, but the Westies strained at the leashes.

Barely visible in its surroundings coiled a prairie rattler.

I pocketed my phone and ran as fast as I could, scooped up a dog and a girl in each arm and carried them back to the house. Amelie screamed as Vennie's leash slipped from her grasp. He wiggled out of my grip and bolted in the direction of the snake.

I had to protect the girls. I hurried them to the safety of the cabin so I could help Arwyn before it was too late.

CHAPTER 23
Arwyn

Amelie's scream cracked my heart.

There was no way I was letting that serpent hurt her dog.

Once Vennie's leash slipped, I turned my back on the snake and ran straight for the dog. I reached him in seconds and scooped up the wiggling, agitated bundle of fur. "There, there, it's okay, Vennie." I bounced him like a baby and soothed him the only way I knew how as I backed my way toward the porch, keeping my eyes on the vertical pupils of the prairie rattler.

Why on earth wasn't that snake hibernating? Had the warm weather enticed it out of its den?

Vennie continued to growl. "Shh, you're fine. You're fine."

Another step backward.

"Arrr rrah rah rah rah!"

I struggled to contain him in my arms. Thinking fast, I reached for the hem of my apron and pulled it upward. Somehow, I was able to swaddle him in the fabric.

But while I was busy wrapping him up, I lost track of the prairie rattler.

I scanned the yard and the driveway, listening for the sound that would give away its location.

I felt Zaki behind me. A quick glance at the porch confirmed Zaki's axe was leaning by the door.

"Take the dog." As I turned to hand off Vennie, the stupid man grabbed the axe and ran straight for the snake.

"Zaki, no! It's venomous!"

"I know! Go inside!"

"I will not!" I couldn't let him get bit. It was too far to a hospital.

I had to get Vennie to safety first, then I was going after the rattler.

"Girls!" I opened the door a crack and squatted to their level to dump Vennie out of my apron. "Amelie! Bring the dogs into the kitchen and make sure their gate is latched. Isla, run to the bathroom and bring me the biggest towel you can find. Hurry!"

Isla was back in seconds, bless her little heart. I grabbed the towel and slammed the door shut. "Stay inside and don't come out until your dad or I tells you it's safe, got it?"

"Got it!"

"Good girl! And don't worry, 'kay?" I shouted into the door as I took off after her dad.

"Okay!"

Zaki had chased the snake down the gravel driveway toward the turnoff to the main road. I ran at him as fast as my button boots could carry me.

"Don't let it get away!" I slowed to a stop next to him, panting to catch my breath. The combination of the running and the elevation was making me lightheaded.

"Whoa!" Zaki's axe-free arm reached out to steady me. My eyes flashed to his. "What do you think you're going to do with that towel? Yell *torro torro* and expect it to charge you?"

I held up the towel and laughed. It hadn't even registered that it was red. "I—I don't know. Cover it?"

"Not a bad idea. You think snakes can see color? Toss the towel on its head, and while it's distracted, I can slice it."

I cringed. "Okay. Let's do it. But fast. The girls are so upset." I took a deep breath and tried to keep my voice even. "And Zaki—don't get bit. Isla and Amelie need their dad."

I spun on my heel and ran for the snake. When I was within a few feet, I snapped the towel to entice it. The head lunged forward, and I tossed the towel, lifting a prayer that the center of it would land on the head, momentarily blinding it.

The towel hit its target, and the long body whipped and whooshed. Zaki's axe came down once, then again. A third time. The tail went still, and I turned away once I was sure it was no longer a threat.

"Wynna-bun, are you okay? Talk to me."

But I couldn't. One foot in front of the other. As I neared the house, though, I realized I couldn't let the girls see me in my current state. They didn't know about my dad, and I didn't want to upset them any more than they already were.

I turned toward the back of the house and picked up my pace.

Zaki's boots crunched the gravel behind me. "You have to go inside. They have to see we're both okay. Then you can disappear if you need to. I'll give you space, I promise. Just tell them you're okay first."

My feet halted. He was right.

He pulled me to him for a quick but firm hug, then with his arm at my back, guided me to the front door and pushed it open.

"Daddy! Wynnie!"

Zaki bent to hug the girls, and they climbed onto him. As he stood up, they reached over to hug me.

"Are you okay? Is the snake gone?" Isla asked.

"He's gone," Zaki confirmed. "And he can't hurt anyone anymore."

"Daddy!" Amelie gasped. "Did you unalive the snake?"

"Sadly, yes." His face sombered. "It was a threat to my girls. And *no one* threatens my girls."

"But Daddy," Isla squirmed. "Snakes are God's creatures."

"And God gave mankind the authority over them." Zaki pressed his forehead to each of theirs.

"Well." Isla leaned back in his arms and tapped her chin. "I think I will need to practice running faster. I don't want to hurt snakes. At least not until I'm a big girl."

Zaki laughed. "How about you just yell for me next time?"

"Why, Daddy?" Amelie asked. "Wynnie was handling it. She takes good care of us, you know."

"I know." He turned to me. Three pairs of pale blue eyes were upon me, and I couldn't help but smile back.

"I could never let you get hurt." I sniffed.

"Hey, girls, how about a ballet lesson in the studio? I've been practicing my glissades, but I don't think they're any good. I feel like a sideways frog."

Amelie giggled and patted her dad on his shoulder. "That's okay, Daddy. We can help!"

"Great! I'll meet you downstairs in five minutes." They ran off, and he turned to me. "Take as long as you need. Call me if you want my support. I'm sorry, Wynna-bun. It's been quite an afternoon."

I nodded and turned to the stairs to go up to my room. I had a lot to think about.

I pushed the snake and my grief for Dad to the back of my mind. It was times like this I wished my mom was around. I knew she missed him, too. But she was an expert at compartmentalizing, and I'd never seen her fall apart emotionally.

The social media ... Yes, I could think about that.

When you stacked it next to Zaki or one of his girls or dogs *dying* ... It couldn't even be a thing, could it? It bothered me, yes, but it was me who decided how it made me feel.

Over the last two years, I'd watched Penny go from unknown small-town harpist to Wag to world-renowned musician, thanks to Xavier's job and familial connections. I wasn't looking to advance my career or become famous.

I was looking for love.

Well, that wasn't true. I hadn't looked. But it had found me.

Zaki and I had attended the gala as friends and left as more.

And now, I had to decide what that *more* was.

This sweet, kind, burly, hockey-playing mountain man at heart loved his family fiercely, and his generous heart was everything I didn't know I needed.

A glutton for torture, I pulled out my phone and again searched his social media. A new image was trending. A simple blue square with a red border wasn't anything extraordinary, but the white text inside of it was.

A Statement from Zaki Marsch:

To all the fans who were happy to see me find love again, I thank you from the bottom of my heart. The woman in the pictures is everything to me and I love her. I will do everything to protect her and my girls. Please respect our privacy, and if our relationship is to grow to something more, you know I'll share it with you. Well, if that's okay with her. Because I'm smitten, she's in charge, and I don't care who knows it.

CHAPTER 24

Zaki

I saw Arwyn enter the studio while in the throes of repeated dégagés while the girls planned their next mode of torturous ballet drills for me. I clumsily danced over to her, spinning into a very badly executed pirouette. I ended with a curtsy, holding out the edges of the tutu she'd made for me. When she smiled, I relaxed and dropped a knee to the floor for an over-the-top ending pose.

"You love me?" She held up her phone. On the screen was the statement I'd posted regarding our relationship.

"I do." I glanced back at the girls to make sure they were still deep in their plotting and took Arwyn's phone. I set it on the floor and took her hands in mine. "I love you, and I'm so sorry for what happened last night, Wynnie. I should have been more vigilant."

She smiled. "Monty called me. He said he was to blame for all of it because his security was incompetent and I should go easy on you and will I please forgive him so that Tasha will speak to him again?"

I laughed. "We've caused quite a stir."

Arwyn smiled and reached for my hand. I stood up and let her pull me out of the room and around the corner until my back was against the wall.

"I had Monty put me on speakerphone, and I told Tasha there

was nothing to forgive." She reached up and wrapped her arms around my neck, her fingers twirling the short ends of my hair. "There was no intent to harm."

"Not an ounce. So ... we're okay?"

"Almost."

"Almost?"

"Are you forgetting the kiss-and-make-up part?"

"No. I was just dragging it out to make you want me more."

"Oh really? Playing hard to get, huh?"

"Trying. It's not working too well, though, is it?"

She shook her head. "Big fail. You should just kiss me and concede."

"I can't argue with that." She closed her eyes, and I lowered my lips to hers, savoring their softness for a beat before I put my heart and soul into a kiss that was meant to be remembered.

Too soon, she broke the kiss. "What will we tell the girls?"

"Those who kill snakes together stay together?"

She snorted. "Can you ever be serious?"

"Wynna-bun, I've never been as serious as I am right now. I love you. And I want us to be together."

"I hear a 'but' coming."

"But I can't stay in Colorado."

"That's okay. I can't, either."

"You can't?"

"Not if you and the girls aren't here. I'm kind of attached. Because I love you, too."

I laughed and pulled her in for another kiss, a deeper one. "I'm so glad I skipped the Olympics."

She pulled my face back to hers, and we picked up the kissing. At some point, I heard giggles and whispers.

"Is Wynnie going to be our stepmom?"

"I hope so! But—you don't think she'll be mean, do you?"

"Oh. Yeah, stepmoms can be mean. What will we do if she's mean to us?"

"I don't know. Lock her in a tower?"

"We don't have a tower."

"We'll have to take her to a castle, then. Xavier has a castle! I'm sure he has a tower!"

"Yes, let's ask him!"

It was hard to keep my lips from laughing, so I gave up trying.

Enough was enough. I pulled Arwyn to me and turned us to face the little plotters. "Wynnie doesn't have a mean bone in her body, girls."

Isla rested a hand on her hip and tilted her head. "Daddy, she helped you kill a snake."

"Because she loves you," I protested. "Requirement number one of a *good* stepmom."

"Daddy!" Amelie hopped with excitement. "There's a list of requirements for a good stepmom?"

"There should be, don't you think? Why don't you girls go make one? Add 'must love children' on the first line."

"Daddy, the first line is for the title of the list." Amelie shook her head and turned to her sister. "C'mon, Isla. We have work to do!"

"That should keep them busy for five minutes." I turned back to Arwyn, unable to stop the smile tugging at my lips. "Now, where were we?"

Her eyes sparkled as she whispered, "I believe we were in the middle of—"

"This," I finished for her, my voice a low murmur. My gaze dropped to her mouth—soft, inviting, and begging to be kissed. Slowly, deliberately, I slid an arm around her waist, pulling her close, feeling the warmth of her body against mine.

Her lips parted, a silent invitation, and I swooped her up into my arms. Her surprised chuckle dissolved into a gasp as I claimed her mouth with mine. The kiss was slow at first, tender, exploring, until the spark ignited into something more urgent. I shifted her in my arms so I could cup her cheek, and deepen the kiss, pouring every ounce of longing, hope, and promise into that moment.

When we finally pulled apart, her cheeks were flushed, her breath was shaky, and her eyes were locked on mine. I smiled, brushing a stray strand of auburn hair from her face. "Losing myself—then finding myself with you—is finding home."

She melted in my arms, her lips curving into the kind of smile that made me want to kiss her all over again.

Epilogue

ARWYN

Four months later

The June day was warm, and by the time Zaki arrived with the RV, it was nearly stifling.

The Edge had lost in the Stanley Cup final to the Miami Ice Cats for the second year in a row, and now Zaki and the girls would be moving back to Montreal. His agent was hopeful the team there would sign him, and he'd found an apartment near Viki's parents' house to live in until I flew up there and we could go house-shopping.

House-shopping. I looked around my front room. Could I really leave? I still hadn't decided on when I'd join them in Canada or what to do with my house.

This was my family's home. It was where I grew up, where my dad grew up. Where *his* dad grew up. I'd never sell it.

With the money I'd earned from taking care of Isla and Amelie —which Zaki wouldn't let me refuse to take—I'd fixed it up, repainted it, and let Beck and Liam have a field day redesigning the interior of the garage. When I moved to Montreal, what would become of my wedding dress library?

I still had so much to sort out.

Instead of flying, Zaki decided it would be fun to drive to

Quebec, stopping along the way to see the US. Flynn and Meggie were getting married in Maine at the end of July, and I planned to meet them up there.

From my sewing machine in the front window, I watched the girls and pups go inside the RV. This would be a fun adventure for them. Amelie had been making lists for weeks. What to see, what to pack, what to do.

I lost track of how long I stared at the RV. When the girls exited it and headed for the house, Zaki was right behind them.

"Wynnie!" Amelie was first in the front door and almost tripped over her green princess dress running to me. "Come see it!" She opened the doggie gate and let Isla in, then ran over to me.

"Yes, come see." Isla took my hand and pulled at it.

"Okay." I looked up at Zaki, and he waggled his eyebrows.

Silly man.

With an almost-six-year-old tugging each of my hands, I let them pull me out of the house and to the RV.

Then they let go and ran up the steps, disappearing inside.

So much for my tour.

I looked back at Zaki, and he shrugged.

I walked the remaining distance and ascended the stairs slowly. Amelie was waiting between the front seats. "This is where the driver sits"—she pointed to each in turn—"and where the navigator sits."

I turned toward the main living space, where Isla stood by the sink. She gestured to the loft over the front seats. "Up there is where me and Amelie will have our quiet time. And here"—she pointed to the table and booth-style benches—"turns into our beds!"

"Very nice," I said approvingly.

"But," Amelie said, "we can sleep up there, too. If we have a *guest*." She looked at her sister.

"I see. Like your aunt Sofi," I filled in.

Amelie grinned. "Sure. Follow me."

She led me past the bathroom and to the main bedroom at the back. "This is Daddy's room." She walked around the bed to the side wall, which featured a freestanding closet and a built-in set of drawers under the window. "These are fake drawers. Pull here."

I approached the small dresser and pulled at the side as instructed. It swung open, barely missing the corner of the bed.

"The top is fake, too." Isla joined us and lifted the surface upward and over to the left side.

I gasped. It was a sewing machine table.

"But—why?" I asked.

"We won't need a nanny anymore," Zaki said. I spun around. I hadn't heard him enter. "But we need you. Will you come with us?"

Amelie pulled at her braids. "It's a bend in the road, Wynnie. Like when Anne had to leave Green Gables, the place she loved the most in the world, to follow her dreams."

Her perception and wisdom were right on.

A bend in the road, indeed.

"I—don't know."

"We got you a gift!" Isla opened the closet and pulled out a small blue leather box and lifted the lid. Inside was a beautiful cameo brooch.

I ran my finger over the smooth faux ivory silhouette and coral base. "It's beautiful. Zaki Marsch, are you bribing me with jewelry?"

He shrugged. "It was their idea. I told them you couldn't be bought, though."

I laughed. "I do love it."

He smiled. "What if I throw in the bed and sleep on the benches? This whole room would be your space."

"Zaki, you're six-foot-three." I looked around the room. "And it would be selfish of me to take all this space."

He shrugged. "It's selfish of us to try to steal you from your home. The floor works, too. Wynna-bun. I'll sleep outside in a tent every night if it means you'll come with us."

I stared at him, mouth gaping. "You want me to come with you that much?"

"Yeah. I do. I mean, *we do.* Right, girls?"

"Daddy. Stop messing around!" Isla shouted. "It's secret weapon time. Ugh."

I held back a laugh as she handed the blue box to her father and ran to the bed. She and Isla climbed up and held hands, then began jumping up and down and giggling.

I turned back to Zaki, and for the second time, I gasped. He was down on one knee and was lifting the velvet that held the cameo from the box. He set it on the bed.

Underneath was the most beautiful daisy-inspired antique ring I'd ever seen. A pale yellow center was framed with petal-shaped diamonds, with more diamonds set into the band.

"Daisies represent innocence, loyalty, and a fresh start. In England and Scotland, they represent the sun. And that's what you are to me, Wynnie—my sun. Shining brightly, casting your light on my world. I love you with all my heart and promise to do everything to make you happy. I'll always fall short of Gilbert Blythe, but I'm better-looking and taller. And I passed your mom's extensive background check. What do you say? Will you marry me?"

"And will you be our stepmom, Wynnie?" Amelie asked. "We made a list of all the requirements of a super stepmom and you check all the boxes!"

"And could you be our tour guide? And navigator, too?" Isla asked. "Daddy is not an expert on America."

"Hey now!" Zaki protested. "I've been to every major city dozens of times."

"Hockey arenas don't count, Daddy," Amelie huffed. "We want an adventure. We want to see the *sights!*" She turned to me with pleading eyes. "And I need you to hold me tight when it's too much."

Amelie hadn't had a full-on panic attack since they moved in. I'd adopted Monty's I-let-go-first hug policy the minute I'd learned of it. To think I'd made a difference touched my heart in ways I couldn't fully process.

"Yes, I'll go." I smiled at the girls. "And yes, I'll marry your dad."

"Yay!"

Engaged. What a prophetic Word of the Year that turned out to be.

The girls cheered as Zaki stood and folded me into his arms and we sealed our new promise with a kiss.

Our new *adventure.*

Bonus Epilogue

ZAKI

"Let it goooooooooooooo, let it gooooooooooooo!" I sang along with Isla and Amelie and our howling pups to their favorite Disney anthem. Beside me in the RV's passenger seat, my beautiful fiancée, Arwyn, added her slightly off-key alto to our chorus.

Our trip so far across the US from Colorado to Maine had been fun, exciting, and filled with memories for the next coffee-table photo book I was secretly creating. My agent had called to tell me Montreal had offered me a three-year contract for half a million more than I expected to get. Even Monty's going-away prank couldn't dampen my mood.

Somehow, the guy had switched out our sheets. On Arwyn's bed was a screen-printed photo of him wearing only his cheer shorts and flexing his Tim Tebow-size guns. And the girls' *Frozen* sheets were replaced by a Ridgie the Bear pattern.

Day 2's first stop found us at a Walmart purchasing replacements.

I had big plans for when we arrived in Maine and two epic surprises for Arwyn that she would one hundred percent not see coming.

I turned in to Disney's Fort Wilderness in Florida as the song reached its crescendo. Once we were hooked up to our campsite, Arwyn and I had a special announcement for the girls.

Isla and Amelie had asked Arwyn if she could teach them to make "pretty summer ballgowns." She'd been over-the-moon happy to give them lessons in design and basic sewing. The girls had worked together to create lists of features for their dresses, and Arwyn had helped them sketch them out. We'd visited multiple sewing and hobby shops across the Midwest on our way to Florida, and earlier this week, the original Elsa- and Anna-inspired gowns were completed.

And just in time, too.

"Girls?" I poked my head up into the loft above the front seats. "Instead of exploring the campground tonight, how about you put on your new *Frozen* summer gowns and we go explore Royal Sommerhus at Epcot?"

I covered my ears to protect them from the deafening banshee-decibel screams emitting from their little mouths.

A short time later, we boarded a resort bus to take us to the theme park. Isla and Amelie made fast friends with a little girl dressed in Elsa's blue dress, and soon the whole bus was singing along to "Let It Go."

I wrapped my arm around Arwyn and leaned down to brush my lips against her forehead. "Having fun yet?"

She chuckled. "Fun is something that's never lacking with you Marsches. Did I bring my Tylenol, though? Yes, yes, I did." She grinned up at me and puckered her lips.

I happily obliged the request.

We reached the park and scanned our Magic Bands to enter.

"Maps!" Arwyn power-walked to the brochure stand that held maps in every language. She and the girls each grabbed an English version while I pulled it up on my app.

"It's very far away," Amelie said, her voice laced with disappointment.

"It's only half a mile, Amms," I encouraged. "Just a little longer than your walk to school."

"But Daddy." Isla pointed to the stroller rental. "Why walk when we have a Sven to pull a sleigh? Daddy, will you buy us a sleigh? And pull it?"

I laughed. "Sure. But it's a rental, and I'll have to push it."

She rolled her eyes. "I know that, silly. That's what imaginations are for! And no crazy driving, please."

"Your wish is my command, Queen Elsa." I saluted to her giggles and turned toward the rental line.

A few minutes later, the girls hopped into the double stroller, and we were on our way. I zoomed them through the front of the park—we'd have a full day here later in the week—and we made it to the Norway pavilion in record time. The thatched roof, wooden beams, and snowflake details on the exterior made it feel like we'd wandered straight into Arendelle.

"Wow," Arwyn breathed. "It's even more beautiful in real life. Like a Scandinavian fairy tale."

"That's 'cause it *is* a Scammnayvienne fairytale, Wynnie," Amelie said. "Sven! Pull over and park!"

Once they were out of the stroller, I wheeled it over to stroller parking and rejoined the ladies at the Lightning Lane queue. We were right on time and scanned in. The girls clutched their autograph books to their chests like treasures, their bubbling chatter filled with reminders of what to tell Elsa and Anna.

Cast members dressed in traditional Norwegian attire pointed us to the scanners and ushered us onto the path to the Sommerhus. The queue wound us through a cozy, rustic, cottage-like setting with walls adorned with rustic Nordic decor. The colorful rosemaling, framed family portraits, and tapestries brought the animated world to life. Isla and Amelie took their time, pausing every few feet to point out relevant and important details like a painted wooden lunchbox, copper pots, woven baskets, carved trolls, leather snow boots, homemade skis, and antique jewelry.

The line slowed as we reached Anna and Elsa. Each of the immersive meet-and-greet spaces reflected their unique personalities and roles from the movies.

Finally, it was Isla and Amelie's turn, and they took off like cats pouncing after their prey. Anna crouched and held out her arms, and the girls almost bowled her over.

"Watch," Arwyn whispered. "Anna won't let go until the girls do."

"Just like you," I replied. "Were you a Disney princess?" I slid my arm around her waist and pulled her into me.

She shook her head. "Only in my imagination."

"Then you shall be one in my imagination, too." I waggled my eyebrows. "Jasmine, I think."

She swatted me playfully, and we turned back to the girls. Anna's character's bubbly personality and warm, joyful vibe was a perfect impression. She chattered while signing the autograph books and reacted appropriately when the girls informed her they'd helped to make their dresses. And chattered even more while taking pictures with Isla and Amelie, both together and individually.

"Hey! Parents! Yoohoo!!" Anna bounced and waved. "Come take a picture with us!"

"Daddy and Wynnie aren't married yet." Isla frowned. "Is that okay?"

"It's okay with me. Waaaait a second. Is your dad a fixer-upper?" Anna whispered loud enough for us to hear.

The girls giggled. "No!" Amelie said. "But he does fix things. Mostly his hockey sticks." She sighed dramatically. "Every game, he has to tape the bottom part to keep it together."

I held back a laugh. Kids!

"Excellent!" Anna clapped. "So shall we get Grand Pabbie to perform the ceremony? We can dress your dad and Winnie in big green leaves and—"

"No!" The girls were laughing harder than during a tickle fest.

"All right. Just the picture then. Gather around." Anna opened her arms, and we took about a thousand pictures with her.

I was glad I'd purchased the photo package.

Quick hugs and waves goodbye and we moved through the space to Elsa. Her vibe was understated, serene, and elegant. The colors surrounding her were cool and calming, with soft blues, silvers, and whites. The decor of snowflake patterns and icy accents created the feel of a frosty yet welcoming winter wonderland.

After a long hug, Elsa straightened out and gracefully shook out the sheer cape attached to her dress. Isla attempted to do the same but couldn't quite get it right. Elsa gave her a few tips, and she had it perfect after a few tries.

We joined the girls for photos once again, and Elsa greeted us. "I hear congratulations are in order."

"Thank you," Arwyn and I replied.

Looking straight at Arwyn, she asked, "And you've known him more than one day?"

Arwyn laughed. "Yes."

Elsa smiled. "Wonderful. When you're settled, may we chat? I've heard the royal dressmaker of Arendelle is retiring, and my sources tell me you are the most talented in the land."

Arwyn blushed. "I'd love to, if these princesses here will lend me out."

Elsa grinned at the girls. "I'm sure we can work something out."

This was some pretty awesome make-believe.

We took a thousand more pictures with Elsa and exited the attraction in The Fjording, an immense gift shop.

As is the Disney way, I learned.

It was a good thing I had millions. The shop was stocked with Anna and Elsa costumes, accessories, and toys, plus stuffies of Olaf, Sven, and other characters. There were *Frozen* books, puzzles, and collectibles and Arendelle-inspired home goods and apparel.

"Wynnie, let's twinnie." I pointed to a wall of Norwegian winter wear. "Sweaters?"

She laughed. "It's a hundred degrees outside."

I clutched my heart. "And I thought the woman was a planner." I shook my head sadly and pointed to a red-and-ivory patterned sweater. "These will be cozy for a Montreal Christmas Eve. Or any night, actually."

She nodded. "True. Let's get them. And matching sweaters for the girls, too. And a Viking helmet and sword for you."

"I love how you think!" I brought my lips down to hers. "So you want to play Viking, eh?"

"Ha! Speaking of the girls—" Arwyn seamlessly changed the subject and stepped away to scan the store. "Where are they?"

I looked past the clothing into the next section of the store. "There!"

"Daddy! Look at us!" Amelie called.

"Take a picture of the big ugly troll, Daddy!" Isla hung over one of its arms. "And help me sit on this!"

Nearly reaching the ceiling of the shop, the carved statue of the mythical Norwegian troll was posed in a crouched, slightly hunched position, as if ready to spring into action. Its shaggy hair and bushy eyebrows gave it a wild, primal look. The creature peered at us with an expression that was both mischievous and friendly. The wide grin, exaggeratedly bulbous nose, and expressive eyes felt like they were looking into my soul. I shuddered.

Arwyn and I helped the girls up to sit on each of the troll's arms, then we stepped back to take pictures.

"All done! Please get us down. We have some serious birthday shopping to do!" Amelie pleaded, and thus began the shopping spree of their young lives. Arwyn and I followed them around like human shopping carts, holding all the things their hearts desired.

Did I spoil them? Yes.

Did I like spoiling them? Yes.

Was I glad the gift shop offered a service to ship the gifts back to the resort? You betcha.

Did I plan to spend $2,183.48 in a theme park gift shop? Nope. Nope, I did not.

After a late, improvised dinner of Norwegian cheese and snacks, I pushed the stroller leisurely toward the front of the park to look for a good fireworks viewing spot.

As the show began, I pulled Arwyn to me. "Thank you for today. I think it was their best day ever."

"You don't have to thank me, Zaki. You didn't force me to be here." She tapped me on the nose. "I loved every minute. Those girls are treasures, and as much as you spoil them, they never act spoiled."

"They are a lot, though."

"They are. And you are, too." She turned in to me and pressed her body to mine, winding her arms around my neck. "But it's a *good* a lot. And I can't get enough of it."

"I can't get enough of you," I said softly. "I can't wait to marry you, Wynna-bun."

She grinned up at me. "Me either. First stop in Montreal after we drop the girls off, we'll find a church and set a date."

"Think they take bribes? I want to marry you as soon as possible."

Arwyn snorted, then startled as the first booms rumbled in the sky. She pulled my head down to hers and whispered into my ear. "I can't wait until we can make our own fireworks."

A growl worked through me, coming from deep within as my mouth crashed down on hers for a passionate and thorough kiss. "Fireworks are for amateurs," I breathed when we came up for air. "I'm aiming for supernovas and nuclear reactions."

I delighted in her reaction, a responsive shiver that prompted me to hug her tighter. As the fireworks faded into smoky clouds against the dark sky, I had one more thing to say. "See?" I whispered. "The universe already agrees—you're my supernova."

Isla & Amelie's List of Requirements for a Super Stepmom

1. Lets us call Mommy whenever we want.
2. Gives us big long hugs!
3. Makes the best heart-shaped pancakes for breakfast.
4. Likes to play dress-up with us.
5. Can braid our hair like Elsa and Anna.
6. Reads us stories.
7. Lots of dance parties.
8. Smells like cookies or flowers.
9. Fixes boo-boos with sparkly Band-Aids and magic kisses.
10. Loves Laffy and Vennie and pets them a lot and gives them treats when they are good boys.
11. Helps us with princess puzzles.
12. Knows how to build castles with blankets and pillows.
13. Likes glitter.
14. Knows all the Frozen songs and sings them really loud with us.
15. Likes to color and does the itty-bitty tricky parts for us if we need help.

16. Is not scared of monsters.
17. Lets us lick the spoons when we are making butter tarts.
18. Doesn't let snakes get us.
19. Helps us with our ballet.
20. Knows all the fun park spots and takes us there often.
21. Paints our nails soooo pretty with sparkly polish.
22. Likes to jump in puddles with us when it rains.
23. Ice skates with us and takes us to watch Daddy play hockey.
24. Lets us eat extra strawberries.
25. Likes to do crafts and will teach us how to make pretty dresses.

SUN, SEA, &
BLUEBERRY
TEA
KERRY EVELYN

To my Blueberry Tea Crew!
Britteny, Debbie, Denise, Jane, Kaity, Sarah, Shanna, Tabbi, & Valerie

Author's Note

Welcome to Crane's Cove!

I can't wait for you to meet your new friends in Maine! If you're new to Crane's Cove, get ready to have an amazing time with a cast and setting you won't want to leave!

There are a lot of characters to get to know between the Denver Edge Hockey players and families and the Crane's Cove crew. But not to worry—little Amelie Marsch has made lists for you! You can find them at the end of this story, just before the recipe section.

I had so much fun writing this story, especially the twins' summer camp shenanigans. Having spent many years teaching kindergarteners and first graders in multiple formal and informal settings, it was hard to pick and choose from the endless fountain of memories to share. The real fun begins when the grownups aren't around—and when the kids act like little grownups themselves, emulating what we model—like our big words, expressions, list-making, and pranking—and reminding us that learning is fun and fun is important.

Happy reading! I'm so glad you're here! Or "hee-yah" as we say in New England!

XOXO!
Love, Kerry

Chapter One

ZAKI

I'd been *harboring* a secret for weeks, and as I steered the RV down the winding coastal road in Downeast Maine, the irony of the word made me chuckle. A secret, tucked away like a pearl in its oyster shell, safe and secure in the very place we were headed.

Crane's Cove in late July stretched before us in all its postcard-perfect glory. "Postcard perfect" was Arwyn's description, and she was right. Every vista in the Acadia National Park vicinity was a picture worthy of sending to loved ones. To my right, the ocean shimmered under the late July sun, its waves rolling lazily toward the cliffs below and breaking gently against the rock face. The lighthouse on the water appeared to float in the distance, a silent, steadfast guardian anchored to the Cove's seafloor. To my left, the entrance to the Cliff Walk Resort came into view, a welcome sight after today's long hours on the road.

I stole a glance at my fiancée, curled up in the passenger seat, her soft smile indicating that she already felt the pull of the seaside town's salty air. In the seats behind us, twins Isla and Amelie, dressed in their Elsa and Anna *Frozen* ballgowns and tiaras, chattered away with their little Westies, Laffy and Vennie, who occasionally yipped in agreement.

My girls had turned six yesterday, and it blew my mind how much they'd developed over the last year. As they grew, so did my

doubts about doing the whole parenting thing wrong. First the divorce, then sharing custody. This past year had been the most challenging—being apart from them for six months when their mother took them back to Montreal last summer. After that, they were apart from their mother for seven months while she healed after multiple surgeries. All the back and forth and hurting hearts had been hard, and I knew it would have been so much harder if Arwyn hadn't come into our lives just at the right time. I'd fallen for her—hard and fast—and so had the girls.

They were so excited to attend the summer camp the resort offered, and Arwyn and I were excited for some much-needed time alone. A week in this charming town to romance her. A week to celebrate Flynn and Meggie's wedding. A week to—if all went to plan—ask my Wynna-bun to change up our wedding plans.

For the very best reasons.

Even so, I had doubts about that, too. Arwyn hated to be put on the spot. She was a thoughtful planner by design, and we'd made big, complicated plans that she'd been over and over, constructed and deconstructed and put back together again. Plans A, B, and C. There were contingency plans for contingency plans. Breaking my news to her might break her trust. And then what?

I just knew this was one of those times I had to trust my gut.

I exhaled slowly and turned in to the resort's entrance. Over my professional hockey career, I'd played in front of thousands of roaring fans, faced down the toughest players in the league, skated into overtime battles with everything on the line, and pulled off the most epic pranks. But nothing—*nothing*—felt as thrilling as what I was about to do tomorrow.

A welcome sign directed me to pull into the main lodge's circular drive to check in. When the passenger door aligned with the front doors of the lodge, I set the RV in park. Before I could turn the engine off, a sandy-haired man about my age in a well-worn Cliff Walk visor appeared at the side door and knocked.

"Permission to come aboard?" he shouted through the window and grinned. Laffy and Vennie barked a greeting from their crate between the girls' seats.

I unlocked the doors and lowered Arwyn's window. "Welcome aboard!"

"Hey, that's supposed to be my line! Welcome to the CW!"

He opened the door, and I exited my seat, offering my hand. "Zaki Marsch. This is my fiancée, Arwyn, and our girls, Isla with the blond braid and Amelie with the auburn braids." The pups howled. "Laffy's the ivory dog, and Vennie's gray."

"Call me Wynnie," Arwyn insisted, unbuckling and turning her chair around to face him. "There will be a test." She laughed.

The man chuckled. "JC Crane, resort manager." He shook our hands, then turned to the girls. "Pleased to make your acquaintances, your majesties. It's not often we host royalty here at the Cliff Walk."

The girls giggled in their booster seats. Their obsession with Disney's *Frozen* was going on four years now.

Isla tossed her single braid over her shoulder. "Pleased to meet *you,* Mr. JC!"

"The pleasure is all mine. You're going to love our camp. My oldest daughter, Bianca, just turned six, and she can answer any and all of your questions about everything. I often go to her myself for answers."

Arwyn snorted, and my grin widened. "Oldest daughter? How many do you have?" I asked.

"Three. Bianca, Stella, and Lilly. Plus Vera, our snooty cat. I'm tragically and delightfully outnumbered."

"All designers," Arwyn observed. "Is your wife in the fashion industry?"

He shook his head. "Caroline is an interior designer and a fashion expert. And she was very against the names I chose if we had boys. Sadly, Nomar, Pedro, and Papi Crane were just not to be."

I laughed. "All Red Sox players." I shook my head. "Love it."

JC adjusted his visor. "Thanks. I appreciate that. And it's fun being a girl dad. I get three makeovers a week!"

"Girl dads rock!" Amelie bounced. "Are you a good hair-doer, or do you try your best with zip ties like my dad?"

He laughed. "I'm not allowed to touch my girls' hair. Stella said I'd need professional lessons before I came near her again with a brush."

The girls giggled, and JC turned back to Arwyn and me. "We've got you all set up in Cabin 21, also known as Salt Mist Cottage, in our new expansion off Blueberry Lane. By Friday, most of the new cabins will be occupied by your teammates and their families. Should be a fun time."

"Totally. Thanks for putting us all together," I said.

"Anything for Flynn and Meggie. She's worked here at the resort since she was a teenager. They met when his team at the time was playing the Acadia Harbormasters, and it was love at first sight for those two. That dude was so smitten and didn't care who knew. He'd come to town to visit every chance he got, and he's worked here for a month or so every summer since, in between hockey camps and visiting his family. Of course, if I was from Vermont, like him, I'd come here every chance I had, too, just sayin'." He flashed his wide grin again. "No shade to Vermont. I'm just a coastal guy through and through."

Now it was my turn to snort. Flynn had stated on more than one occasion that unless you loved to ski and/or grow your own crops, Vermont probably wasn't the place you'd want to settle down in. We planned to make a few stops in the state on our way to Montreal for teddy bears, maple syrup, and cheese.

"He's a great guy and a heck of a player," I said. "I haven't spent much time with Meggie, but she seems like the perfect match for him."

"For sure," JC agreed.

"She's incredible," Arwyn praised. "And an angel with animals, I hear."

JC nodded. "She's been invaluable to my brother Easton as his assistant the past few years. We're sure going to miss her when she joins Flynn permanently in Colorado."

"From the way Flynn talks about Crane's Cove, I have no doubt he'll retire here," I said. "I give him eight, maybe ten more years on the ice if he can keep from getting injured."

JC grinned. "At least. All right, I won't keep you all any longer." He pointed out the front window. "Follow this driveway back to Cliff Walk Lane and follow that road until you come to the fork at the Fitness Center. Turn right and then take another right onto Blueberry Lane towards the new cabins. Circle around until you find the driveway marked twenty-one. Your key code was texted to you this morning."

"One-four-three-one-four-three!" Isla blurted.

JC laughed. "You got it. And you can always change it if needed. If you have any trouble, just call the main number and we'll get it fixed." He handed Arwyn the folder he'd been carrying. "Here's your personalized Folder-O-Fun. Camp starts at 9 a.m. sharp. Anything else I can do for you?"

Arwyn and I shook our heads. "Nothing I can think of," I said.

JC saluted us. "Then I'll leave you to it. Have fun, girls!"

"We will!" Isla and Amelie chimed.

Once he left, I followed his directions to a canopied lane that led to the circle of new cabins. Flynn had recommended we book in this section of the resort where they were set up in a circle, facing each other wagon-style. In the center was a playground, a covered pavilion with grills and picnic tables, a grassy area, and a kiddie splash zone.

As we rounded the circle clockwise, Isla read their names. "Sea Glass Haven, The Gull's Nest, Moss and Moose ... What's a chall-let, Wynnie?"

"It's pronounced sha-lay," Arwyn said with a smile.

"Oh!" Amelie exclaimed. "It's French!"

I grinned. They were fluent speaking their mother's language. Reading and writing it would come later.

"Driftwood Loft, Tidepool Hollow, Cranberry Knoll. I know it's knoll and not kah-nole from our fairy house art class!"

"That was so fun!" Amelie agreed. "Are we almost there?"

"Almost," Arwyn assured her. "According to the map in the folder, it's almost all the way around."

"Okay." Isla sighed. "Blueberry Hill Getaway. Sandpiper Sanctuary. Maine Squeeze Honeymoon Hideaway, Lighthouse Lookout ..."

"Here it is, girls!'

"Finally!" Isla huffed. "Oooooh, it's pretty. Salt Mist Cottage!"

It was. Tucked under branches of tall trees and framed by lush greenery and wildflowers, this place looked like it was pulled right out of a storybook—or one of the girls' picture books. The cedar shingles and crisp white trim give it a classic charm, but it was the peace and quiet that hit me first. No car horns. No city hum. Just birdsong and the distant sound of a boat horn. Any doubts I had about this being the perfect place to spill my secret were completely erased.

I recalled the photos of the property from the website when we booked. Inside was the perfect mix of cozy and quaint. A total Pinterest dream, Arwyn called it, with its big windows and throw pillows. Master bedroom on this level and a cozy loft with bunk beds and a pullout sofa upstairs, which was a step up from the sleeping bag I'd been nesting in during the trip. Occasionally, we'd stayed overnight at hotels along the way, but like I told Arwyn, I would have slept outside in a tent if she insisted.

"Wynnie, can I have the map later?" Amelie asked. "I want to make a list of all the cabins in my vacation diary."

Arwyn twisted in her seat to answer Amelie. "Of course. I'll leave the folder on the kitchen counter. You can look through it whenever you're ready."

"Thank you!"

I parked the RV in the driveway and hurried outside so I could open the main door on the other side for my ladies and the pups. They greeted me with grins, and after the twins went running off, each holding a Westie on a leash, I held up my hand to block Arwyn's way.

"Toll, please." I puckered my lips.

She laughed and leaned down for a kiss.

As our lips met, I caught her around the waist and pirouetted her to the ground. "I love you."

"I love you, too." She nodded toward the cottage. "Shall we go in?"

"One more kiss. The girls are still walking the dogs." I spotted them out of the corner of my eye. I'd instructed them earlier to take Laffy and Vennie to the tree line but not go into the woods. "We can let them go in first. More smooch time."

"I like how you think." She lifted on her toes, and when our lips connected, a contented sigh rippled through me.

This was going to be the best week ever.

Chapter Two

ARWYN

Monday morning, I woke up to a melodic chorus of birdsong through the open window. A slow smile took hold of my lips and spread until they were stretched into a wide grin.

This place was *heaven.* Salt Mist Cottage was roomy with a cozy vibe and decorated with a vintage seaside theme. Shiplap in the main areas, Victorian wallpaper and fixtures in the bedrooms and loft. The master bath even had a clawfoot tub! And this resort—*this resort!* It had everything I loved—charm, nature trails, horses, and the ocean. The seafood at dinner last night had been everything the reviews promised and more.

The whole town was made for romance and nostalgia. Piney Point Road jutted out at the end of the Cliff Walk's private beach, bisecting the crescent-shaped cove and marina. From drone pictures, it looked like a heart.

Living in Colorado my whole life, I'd only seen the ocean a handful of times when my father was working on special assignments. Dad was a soldier turned wildlife photographer, and I loved every moment we'd spent exploring together. He died several years ago, doing what he loved.

I dressed quickly in an ivory cotton top with puffed short sleeves and pulled out a skirt I'd made from thrifted handkerchiefs. When Zaki purchased the RV for the cross-country trek,

he'd had the bedroom in the back renovated with a sewing machine console and cabinets for all my supplies. I'd been teaching the girls how to sew. We were making our dresses for the wedding as we traveled. Just a few more weeks and I'd be Mrs. Zaki Marsch!

Everything was set: a beautiful church in Montreal, a gown made from my mother's and grandmothers' dresses, and *Frozen*-inspired dresses for Isla and Amelie that they'd designed and "helped" me sew. The only thing missing would be my mother. She had a highly classified job with the military overseas and couldn't get away, but she said she'd try to stream in if she could.

It'd been that way since I was six. Mom was brilliant, spoke several languages, and was an intimidating figure with her trademark tight auburn bun, cat-eye glasses, and stern expression. I missed her, of course, but she was saving the world.

Humming to myself as I twisted my hair up into a loose bun, I was thankful to the birds. The extra minutes before the alarm trilled gave me more time to run through and visualize today's plans. I pulled tendrils over my ears and twisted them around my fingers. My diamond daisy engagement ring caught the sunlight streaming in and reflected on the mirror.

Once I was ready, I left the room and tiptoed up to the second-floor loft, glad that the shag-covered steps were new and didn't squeak. Water pooled in my eyes as I took in Zaki in the pullout and the girls in their bunks, still adorably asleep. Laffy and Vennie snoozed at their feet. The girls' beds had drawer steps to access the top bunk, which the dogs loved to climb but refused to descend.

My family, I thought. *How had they become my whole world so fully and quickly?*

Zaki held the sheet at his waist, his biceps peeking out from a thin white cotton tee. He was smiling, and I wondered if he was pretending to be asleep for the girls' benefit. Stubble poked up around his trim auburn beard, turning my thoughts to our goodnight kiss, when it lightly scraped my skin. His unruly ginger hair, which I'd discovered had become quite untamable in the summer humidity, lent him an extra air of boyishness. And those blue eyes—fathomless.

In the top bunk, Amelie was tangled in a mess of covers, her arms straight up next to her head. On the bottom, Isla was tucked in exactly as I'd left her the night before. I'd be surprised if she'd moved an inch.

"Psst."

The Westies' heads popped up. I shushed them and turned back to Zaki, who'd opened his eyes and was waving me over. I crossed over to him, and he caught hold of my hand, tugging me closer. I sat on the mattress, and his arms closed around me, pulling me down until my head rested on his massive chest.

"Good morning," he whispered into my hair. "Don't wake them up just yet." His low, rumbly morning voice held just a touch of British accent, which made me all swoony.

"Not a chance if this is the alternative," I whispered back. "I can't wait to marry you and wake up in your arms every morning."

"I can't either. Remember that thought later, okay?"

I raised my head and studied his face. "What are you up to? You better not be planning any pranks, Zaki Marsch!"

He just grinned back at me, so I kissed his nose and shook my head.

The girls began to stir, and Zaki stole one more kiss as I attempted to extract myself from his arms. The alarm clock on the end table separating the pullout from the bunks trilled, and I was standing up straight when Isla's eyes flicked open.

"Mornin', Isles," Zaki lazily greeted her. He folded his arms behind his head. "Ams, you awake up there?"

Amelie sprang up to a sitting position and blinked several times. I chuckled softly. This girl always had a hard time falling asleep. Like mine, her brain insisted upon making lists as soon as her head hit the pillow. It was hard to turn that off.

"Wynnie!" Isla greeted me. "It's camp day!"

"I need my new camp diary!" Amelie shouted. Laffy howled with her. "Daddy! I left it in the RV!"

"We can grab it before we walk over," Zaki assured her. "Are you ready to get ready?"

"Yes!" Both girls scrambled out of bed, and I walked over to assist Laffy to the ground. The bunk was low but still an impossible jump for a little dog.

We had plenty of time to get ready and for the girls to eat breakfast, but they moved at warp speed. Thirty minutes later, we were saying goodbye to Laffy and Vennie and locking the cottage door. I'd found the perfect sun hat in Charleston—wide-brimmed straw with a black ribbon around the base and a hole in the top for my hair to poke through. It fit my vintage Edwardian-inspired style and was functional, too.

Amelie retrieved her diary from the RV and fell into step with Isla, just ahead of us.

"It's my turn to read cabin names," Amelie insisted. "Pinecone Perch … Twilight Retreat … Winking Lobster Lodge! That's funny!"

"Look!" Isla pointed. "There's a lobster hanging next to the front door. And it's winking!"

We all laughed, and Zaki squeezed my waist, pulling me closer to him. The walk through the resort's grounds was lovely. We followed the signs to the stables, then turned toward a covered pavilion, much like the one by our cabin. JC and Meggie were there, each holding tablets. Two girls about Isla and Amelie's age sat at the nearest picnic table sculpting Play-Doh.

"We're the third and fourth ones here!" Isla squealed, taking Amelie's hand in hers. They ran straight for the pavilion, causing all four pairs of eyes to look up.

"Meggie!" The girls ran toward the tall, athletic brunette, who'd styled her long hair in a fancy braid. I gave Isla two days before she asked me to do her hair that way.

For the billionth time, I thanked God for sending her to us.

Meggie opened her arms and bent down to embrace the twins. "Look at you two! Jean shorts and *Frozen* T-shirts!" She lowered her voice. "This is really Isla and Amelie, right, not fake girls pretending to be them?"

Amelie giggled. "It's really us. You can't wear princess dresses to *camp*, Meggie."

"Just making sure it's really you." She gave them another hug. "How is your trip going so far?"

"Great. Where's Flynn? Isn't he helping with the camp kids?" Isla asked.

"He's in charge of the rising sixth graders," Meggie replied. "You'll see him around." She leaned in close like she was going to reveal a secret. "They start their day at the pool. It's *freezing*. Way too cold for me. But not for someone whose job is on ice."

Isla giggled. Amelie smiled and pointed to the girls at the table. "Can we talk about Flynn later and make friends now?"

JC barked a laugh, then cleared his throat. He strolled over to the sandy-haired girl who was obviously his mini-me. "This is my daughter Bianca and my niece Paisley."

"She's my cousin!" Bianca beamed. "And look—my other cousins are almost here." She pointed to a spot behind us, where a boy and a girl were running at top speed toward us. "Hallie and Harlan are twins, too!"

Several yards back, a woman in her early thirties with suntanned skin and long dark hair held hands with a police officer who could have been Craig Melvin's doppelganger, dimples and all. His name badge read D. Saunders.

JC introduced us with an amused grin. "Damon is my wife's sister's husband Matt's cousin, and Shelby here is my bestie since forever."

"Matt's my dad!" Paisley chimed in.

"Nice to meet you all," I said.

"Pleasure's ours," Damon drawled in a Southern accent. "Welcome to Crane's Cove." He turned to Zaki. "Sorry about your Cup loss. You sign with Montreal yet?"

"Still deliberating," Zaki replied. Anyone who followed hockey was on edge wondering what superstar Zaki Marsch was going to do. His agent had been in talks with Montreal for months, and they'd made a fair offer, but Zaki was seriously considering retirement if he couldn't go back to Denver. He really didn't want to play for any other team, and the Edge would sign him back in a heartbeat. But with Viki, his ex, living in Montreal and now recovered from her surgeries, he'd rarely see the girls if he returned there since they'd be sharing custody again in a few weeks.

Shelby tipped her chin toward Isla. "Like I tell my kids, let it go and give it to God."

"Spoken like a true pastor's daughter." Damon grinned. "Such wisdom!"

Shelby rolled her eyes. "Or too much *Frozen.*"

"There's never too much *Frozen!*" Isla insisted.

A quick glance at the adults, their lips twitching like mine, confirmed that they'd all seen more than their fair share of the popular movie. Zaki and I stayed to chat for a few moments until more campers began to arrive. We hugged the girls goodbye and strolled hand-in-hand back to the main lodge. We had a breakfast date planned at the Cliffside Diner.

At the reception desk, the assistant manager, Jordan, handed Zaki a set of keys. "The golf carts are parked around the side. Yours is pale blue with a white awning."

We thanked him, and a few moments later, we were cruising leisurely down Cliff Walk Lane toward the main road and the ocean. I held on to my hat and basked in the early morning sunshine. The air still held a bit of the crisp overnight chill to it, but the sun was warm on my skin.

When the traffic was clear, Zaki crossed and turned left. The diner, a refurbished train car, was just up on the right. We pulled into the parking lot and found a parking spot. Zaki ran around to help me down, and I let him.

I loved his chivalry.

His hand guided the small of my back as we walked to the entrance. He pulled the door open. Inside, it was just as I imagined. A counter with vinyl stools cut a third of the car in two. Booths lined the front windows and a built-on extension that ran at a right angle.

"Reserved for Officer Saunders," I read on one of the stools. "Aw. Damon has his own seat."

"That man's a hero!" Two booths down from the door, a little old lady with a pouf of white hair grinned at us. Across from her, a woman a few years older than me hid a smile behind her hand. "And he's my grandson."

"We just met him and his family at camp drop-off," I said,

walking up to the booth and extending my hand. "I'm Arwyn. You can call me Wynnie. And this is my fiancé, Zaki."

"Daisy Mae Saunders. Call me Meemaw. I know all about *you,*" she said, waggling her eyebrows at him. "And your team. Your goalie is from Georgia and will be here later this week. I'm going to meet him."

This time, the woman across from her couldn't hold in her laugh. "I'm Lanie. Meemaw here is obsessed with Jason Dexter. And his sister, Bailey. It's kind of my fault. I might have gotten her into hockey."

Meemaw raised her brows and turned back to Lanie. *"Might have?"*

Lanie threw her hands up. "Okay, okay! I take full responsibility." She looked back to us. "I'm a physical therapist at the sportsplex outside Boston. My best friend, Sarah, is a trainer for the professional team that's based there."

"And let's not leave out the fact you dated Alexei Kriz before he was traded to Palmer City." Meemaw smirked.

"No way," Zaki said. "Small world. He's a great guy."

Lanie's face flamed. "Very small." She took a sip of her iced tea. I noticed blueberries floating in it. How interesting.

"And now she's married to my grandson, Matt. They have two beautiful children and—"

"Daisy Mae!" Zaki and I turned toward the source of the voice. Behind the counter, a woman with curly gray hair piled high on her head shook a pen in Meemaw's direction. "I will not have you scaring away new customers!"

Meemaw waved her off. "Sadie, if they scare that easily, they need a faintin' couch and a fan."

Zaki snorted, and I did a terrible job holding in my laughter.

Sadie shook her head. "Sit wherever you like. I'll be right over."

"It was great meeting you both," I said.

"We'll see you again." Meemaw winked. "It's a small town and a short week."

"Gotta love the small-town grapevine," I said to Zaki as we settled into a booth around the corner. The window offered a view of the lighthouse in the cove. "I wonder what she knows about everyone else coming in for the wedding."

"That's something I loved about living in Palmer City," he said. "That feeling that everyone knows you and has your back. You'll miss that in Quebec." He stretched out his arm over the tabletop to take my hand. "Remember, if I sign with Montreal, you can fly back to Colorado whenever you miss it. And we'll spend a month there every summer with the girls."

"Zaki," I said gently. It was time to truth-bomb him. I knew he worried about me adjusting to city life. "Home is wherever you and the girls are. My house in Palmer City is just a dwelling now. It'll be empty with you three and the pups not in it. Going back won't ever be like it was before you were there."

He squeezed my hand. "You say that now, but ..." He looked out the window, and it became clear to me what was really bothering him.

"I'm not going to leave you because I miss my town and my friends. Not now, not ever. When I make a promise, I keep it. I'm not *her*, Zaki."

"I know." He smiled. "I'm sorry."

"It's okay." I squeezed him back. "Sadie's coming."

"Welcome to the Cliffside Diner." She handed us the menus. "Can I get your drinks while you look over the menu?"

"What is it that Lanie was drinking? With the blueberries?" I asked. "I don't see it on the menu."

"Ah!" Sadie smiled. "We're testing a new blueberry iced tea. It's Molly Dalton's latest healthy food experiment. She's selling the tea leaves at Seaside Stories—the gift shop a few doors down—and we're serving it up to locals with the berries to try to entice them to buy it. Antioxidants and blah blah blah. They have it at the resort, too."

I grinned back at her. "I'd love to try it."

"Got it down for ya. And for you, hockey guy?"

Zaki flashed his teeth. "Ice water, no lemon, please."

"Be back in a jiff."

Zaki and I had a lovely breakfast. I splurged on buttermilk crepes with fruit and whipped cream, and he had the Mainer omelet with lobster, tomatoes, mascarpone, and freshly chopped dill. We said goodbye to Meemaw and Lanie on our way out, our bellies and hearts full.

"How about a stroll on the beach?" Zaki asked, pointing to an entrance to the Cliff Walk, a paved walkway that stretched the length of the cliff. "There's a stairway to the shore a little ways down."

"Sure." I tucked my arm into his and sighed. "It's so beautiful here."

"*You're* beautiful," he said, bending down to sneak in a kiss on my cheek and dislodging my hat.

I laughed. "Did you know that lighthouse is a guest suite?" I asked. "Meggie said she and Flynn will be staying there the night of the wedding. There's a tour of it online."

"Oh yeah?" Zaki asked. "That sounds cool."

We reached the steps marked "Private Beach. Cliff Walk Resort Guests Only." He gestured for me to descend first. It was a long way to the bottom, and I had to hold up my skirt to avoid tripping on it.

The beach was buzzing with activity. A rental shack, covered in colorful buoys, seemed to be the hub of activity. Kayaks, floats, and loungers dotted the sand and sea. Families splashed in the water and built sandcastles.

"I'm glad the camp has a beach day tomorrow," I said. "The girls will love this."

"They sure will." Zaki stopped to scan the beach. "Let's go over there. See those boulders in the shade of the cliff? Looks like a good place to sit."

"It does." A nice, private area to sit and enjoy the ambience was just what I'd been thinking.

We removed our sandals—Zaki insisted on carrying mine—and made our way down the beach to the rocks. Zaki dropped our shoes at the base of the boulder and helped me up onto it. When he hesitated, I patted the rock. "Come sit."

He shook his head. "I think I'll head to the shack and get us bottles of water. Gotta stay hydrated. Be right back." He blew me a theatrical kiss, complete with a bow, and jogged off with a grin. I pulled my small sketchbook and a pencil out of my satchel and began to draw the lighthouse on the water.

Zaki returned with the waters, but he still didn't climb up. And he looked *really* nervous.

"Is everything okay?" I asked. "You look like you're going to be sick."

He shrugged and reached up to me. "Come on down for a second?"

"Okaaay." I set my sketchbook and pencil down and took his hands, then carefully slid off the rock and onto the sand. He turned me so that my back was to the shack and the sea was to my right. "You're acting *really* strange."

"So, normal then," he assessed.

I shook my head. "Not your normal strange. Different strange."

"Well … I had an idea. Hear me out?"

I regarded him curiously. "Of course."

He swallowed. "Will you marry me? Right here, on this beach, in Crane's Cove? Sunday morning?"

I blinked up at him. "Hmm? Here? What about our church wedding in Montreal?"

Zaki bent forward, pressing his forehead to mine. He spoke earnestly. "We can still do it. Have a marriage blessing ceremony when we get to Montreal. We won't have to change any plans, just the priest's words. I don't want to wait any longer, Wynnie. When we get to Quebec, I'll only have two weeks before the season starts. The girls will be with their mom. If we get married here, the remainder of the summer can be our honeymoon."

"And you wouldn't have to sleep on the floor of the RV for the rest of the trip," I teased.

"Yeah, I definitely feel like I haven't gotten my money's worth out of that king bed." He waggled his eyebrows roguishly. "But there's something else. A bigger reason."

"There is?"

He nodded. "Turn around."

I pivoted slowly and squinted at the figure walking toward me. My heart raced, and I took off in a run, arms out and ready to hug.

"Mom!"

Chapter Three

ZAKI

I let out a long breath and waved to Arwyn's mother, who was now jogging toward us. It had been over a year since they'd seen each other.

As I watched their reunion, I couldn't have been happier. When Mrs. Baughn had called me for a video chat after Arwyn emailed her about my proposal, I'd never been more nervous in my life. This woman was most likely a CIA operative or something similar, and I knew I was about to get grilled. She introduced herself as "Baughn. Alyce Baughn." I laughed so hard, and she didn't crack a smile. After over a half hour of questioning, she'd finally smiled but insisted on meeting me before the wedding.

Not because she didn't approve—I'd emailed her before I proposed to ask permission to marry her daughter. She'd done a full background check before she gave her blessing. She wanted to see her girl and meet me and the twins. It had been my idea to move the wedding up so that she could be there for it.

But I still worried how Arwyn would take it. Was I being too presumptuous? Too eager? Too—*Zaki?* The last thing I wanted to do was add to any wedding nerves or doubts that she had. I sure had enough of those for both of us. Not about our love or commitment to each other. I worried that I'd mess it up, like I had my first marriage. I'd grown up and learned a lot since then, but at the core, I couldn't

change who I was. Wanting the best for those I love and for them to experience life to the fullest was both my strength and my weakness.

They walked arm-in-arm back to me, and I held out my hand. "Great to finally meet you, Mrs. Baughn."

"Call me Alyce." Her grip was firm, just what I'd expect from a military professional. "We have a lot of work to do. Where are you with the planning?"

"Mom, I haven't even said 'yes' yet!" Arwyn smiled.

"Well, tell the man 'yes'!"

"I …" She looked from me to her mother. "I haven't finished my dress. There's so much to do! Where? How? The girls?"

I held up my palms. "Here, on Sunday. Morning ceremony, then brunch on the beach. The team will still be here. Montgomery Biddington booked a private jet to fly in our friends from Colorado that aren't already here for Flynn's wedding. I've already booked accommodations for them all. My parents will drive down from Quebec City on Friday. They'll stay in our cabin overnight with the girls on Sunday so we can stay *there.*" I pointed to the lighthouse.

"What? Oh my gosh! How?" Her eyes were wide. "I don't understand. And what about your sisters?"

"Sofi will be driving down with Mom and Dad. Mirette and her family can't get away, but they've extended their stay in Montreal so the girls can have more cousin time." My older sister lived in England with her husband and kids. "Flynn and Meggie are leaving Sunday afternoon, so they don't need their second night. And …" I pulled out the ring box that had been burning a hole in my shorts' cargo pocket. "Our rings were ready early, so I had them shipped here."

"Wow, I … yes! Yes, let's do it!" She jumped into my arms, knocking off her hat.

I blinked back tears, I was so happy. Hugging her close, I whispered, "I thought you might want your mom here, so …"

"This is the best gift, Zaki. Thank you." She pressed her lips to mine, and I didn't care that her mom was a yard away. I kissed her like she should be kissed. Long, deep, and tenderly.

She pulled away all too soon. "I need to know everything

you've planned so far. Names, places, contacts, everything. Then I need to make lists. Separate them by day. When do you want to tell the girls? And who is going to marry us?"

I shrugged. "The pastor from the church up the road. Or the assistant pastor. They said they'd get back to me."

She blinked at me, then turned to her mom.

Alyce laughed. "Don't worry, Wyn. We've got this. I'll fly someone in to conduct the ceremony if I have to." She patted Arwyn on the shoulder, then checked her watch. "I should go check into my room. We have an appointment with the wedding planner in an hour."

"In an hour?" Arwyn squeaked.

"In the conference room," I supplied. "Can we drive you back to the lodge, Alyce?"

She shook her head and gestured to the steps at the other end of the beach. "I'll walk back. It's a beautiful day."

Arwyn stepped out from my embrace to hug her mother. "I'm so glad you're here."

"Me too, sweetie."

We hurried back up the steps to the golf cart. I'd underestimated how long it would take to get from the beach to the diner and back to our cabin. I left Arwyn in the vehicle while I ran into the RV to retrieve the folder that had all the plans and a brand-new legal pad for Arwyn to write notes and make lists.

We made it to the conference room with five minutes to spare. Alyce was already there, chatting with JC and a woman with curly blond hair.

"There they are! The happy couple!" JC grinned. "Arwyn, Zaki, this is my sister and our event planner, Molly Dalton."

"Of the blueberry tea!" Arwyn's face lit up. "I'm going to need to buy a crate of that before we go."

Molly grinned. "Thanks!" She gestured to the table. "Shall we get started?" We sat down, Molly and JC across from Arwyn and I, with Alyce at the end. "All right. I've confirmed with the church, and the assistant pastor, Ryan Engstrom, will marry you at 11 a.m. on Sunday, on the beach. He'll meet you today at camp pickup. His daughter, Nicki, is in camp with your girls. I'll need the guest count by Thursday so we can plan food and chair setup. Here's the catering menu and ..."

The meeting flew by in a blur, but when we left, Arwyn looked relieved.

"So all I really have to do now is finish my dress? They're taking care of everything else?"

"That's all," I said, as we walked into the dining room. "I need to run out and do a few things. I'll meet you at camp pickup, okay?"

"Okay. Wait—you need to eat, too."

"I ordered my food to go. Enjoy this time with your mom." I kissed her and said goodbye. "I'll walk the dogs while I'm at the cottage, so no need to rush back."

I had a bunch of phone calls to make. But first, the lobster roll on the toasted split hot dog bun was calling my name.

PICKUP TODAY WAS at the stables, and as I rounded the corner of the barn, I saw that Arwyn was already there, speaking to a tall blond man holding a towheaded toddler. I checked my phone. I was ten minutes early. When had she gotten here?

I stopped for a minute to take in the full scene. A few feet from them, a teenager with Down syndrome was instructing Isla and Amelie as they helped him brush down a dappled gray with a black mane. The rest of their age group was standing at the fence of the pen while a younger boy—I guessed around thirteen or fourteen—held the reins of a brown horse with a white diamond on its muzzle while he took their questions. A ponytailed girl sat atop the beast, sitting primly in the saddle as the boy pointed to her helmet.

I walked toward the girls slowly with a finger over my lips so they wouldn't shout a greeting when they saw me and startle the horse. They grinned and waved, causing Arwyn to turn around. Her face was glowing with happiness, and I wanted to think I was the reason—or at least part of the reason—for it.

"Zaki!" I gave her a kiss, then turned to the man as she introduced us. "This is Dr. Ryan Engstrom, the assistant pastor from Crane's Cove Congregational Church."

Ryan shifted the boy to his left side and shook my hand. He was a beefy guy, built like an offensive lineman. "This is Ned."

"Nice to meet you, little guy." I shook the toddler's hand.

"Zaki hockey!"

"Yes, sir, are you a fan?"

Ned smiled again, then buried his face in Ryan's chest. "He's shy, but he loves to skate and hit pucks. I thought he'd play baseball like me and his older brother—that's Noah out there in the pen with the kids. And his sister Nicki plays softball—she's the one on the horse. But Ned has zero interest."

"Maybe it'll come later," I replied.

"Maybe. So, Sunday morning is a go, I hear. I was just telling Arwyn about the procedure. We don't need to do a rehearsal, unless you want to. With a wedding the night before, you'd have to do it a few days prior, but we can figure that out if you want to do it."

I shook my head. "We can skip it. My girls know what to do with the flower petals. We won't have a formal wedding party, just our girls and the dogs. We're going to write our own vows. What do you think, Wynna-bun?"

She nodded. "I agree. We're here this week for Flynn and Meggie. I don't want to take any time or attention from them or their events."

Ryan pressed his lips together. "Just because your wedding is small and last-minute doesn't mean it's not as important."

"I know," Arwyn said. "But we'll be having a second wedding in Montreal. It's too much to ask—"

"Wynnie," I said firmly. "It's not. I told you. I've spoken with everyone. They understand. They're all getting an expenses-paid weekend away and are thrilled to be here. And they sure won't miss the party we're going to throw in Montreal when we get there, either."

"Okay. It just seems like … a lot."

"And you would do it for them if it was the other way around," I reminded her.

"True," she conceded.

Meggie emerged from the barn with a cowbell, striking it five times to signal the hour—or the end of camp. She set it down on a table next to a plastic bin and called all the kids over to her. The girls gave their brushes to the boy and ran to her.

Parents and babysitters filed in around us as we waited for our children. Noah released the other kids, and soon the lot of them were standing in a huddle, each with one arm extended into the center.

"Count us off, Bianca," Meggie said.

"One, two, three!" Bianca shouted.

"Sandpipers!" the kids cheered. Then they turned towards us parents and began to sing to the tune of "Eight Days a Week."

We're the pipers, yeah Sandpipers
We don't have nothin' but fun, yeah!
Five days a week!
Five days a week, we luh-uh-uh-uh-ove it!
Five days a week, is not enough to strut our stuff!

Apparently, each child had come up with their own special walk to strut, which they demonstrated as they filed into a line. Meggie handed each of them a large mesh tote bag and sent them off.

"Daddy!" Isla exclaimed with glee as she and Amelie reached us. "We have a song! Did you like it? Did you see us brushing Slade? He's such a nice horse. That's Mocha in the paddock. Can you buy us a horse?"

"Please, Daddy? Jamie said we did such a good job brushing her!" Amelie begged.

Before I could answer, Ryan's daughter caught up with them. "Daddy, can Isla and Amelie come to dinner with us? Please?"

Amelie chimed in. "They're going to the milk jug stand for hot dogs and ice cream! And Hallie and Harlan are going, too! They're cousins!"

Crane's Cove was starting to sound like a Lilo and Stitch cartoon with all the cousins. Was *everyone* here related?

"I thought Hallie and Harlan were cousins with Paisley and Bianca?" Arwyn asked, as if reading my thoughts.

"They are," Nicki said. "That's the *other* side of the family. My mommy and Auntie Shelby are sisters."

As Ryan tried to explain all the connections, my head started to swim. I didn't need to worry, though. I'd bet a year's salary Amelie would go home tonight and draw out family trees.

"Please, Daddy? Wynnie? Can we go? And can we bring the pups? Jamie is bringing his dog, Rodeo." Isla pointed to the golden retriever who was sitting calmly by a set of mounting steps. "And Hallie said her dad might bring their old dog Fenway, too. After work. 'Cause he's a policeman."

"We-ell ..." I looked at Arwyn.

"Sure. Is that Dockside?"

Ryan nodded. "Best ice cream in town!"

Arwyn's face lit up. "That's what I heard. I was reading about a flavor of ice cream they have that I'd love to try. Blueberry coffee crumble."

I cringed. "That sounds ... interesting."

She laughed. "I know!"

Chapter Four

ISLA

Today was beach day at camp!

Amelie and I were so excited! We put our bathing suits on under our clothes like Meggie told us to, and then we packed the beach bags she gave us with a towel, sunscreen, and a change of clothes. We all had a different color bag. Together, our bags made a rainbow! Mine was baby blue. Amelie's was mint green. Paisley got light purple, Bianca yellow, Hallie pink, Harlan orange, and Nicki's was red. There's another boy in our group. His name is Archer, and he's Harlan's best friend. He's Paisley's friend, too, from where she lives. Their mommies are best friends. So many best friends! He got the white bag. Harlan said he's the cloud! We all laughed, even Archer, because that was funny.

Meggie has two groups. We were all in Group 1. Sometimes we did stuff with Meggie. Sometimes we did stuff with Noah. He's her assistant. Sometimes we do stuff with both of them and then Group 2 and Group 1 become one big group, called the Sandpipers. Jamie is Noah's cousin, and he helps at the barn to assist Kat, who's the boss. She's old—almost thirty-three—and she's going to have another baby, so she needs a lot of help. She's married to Easton, who's Mr. JC's brother. He's a veterinarian and helps take care of the horses.

It's a lot of people. I'm glad Amelie makes lists. I don't think she spelled all their names right, but that's okay. Wynnie calls her writing "invented spelling" and says it's part of the learning process.

We ate our breakfast really fast today because we wanted to get to camp early. Last night at dinner, me and Amelie and the girls and Harlan and Archer made a plan for the beach. We'll set up our bags in rainbow order so they're easy to find and spread out our towels in a circle like how our cottage is. Then we can build a sandcastle in the middle. Noah said he has a *lot* of sand toys to bring!

We were going over the plan when Mr. JC ducked under the pavilion.

"Hey, hey, boys and girls!"

We looked up at him. Meggie was handing him a clipboard. That was weird. Where was her tablet?

"Amelie," I whispered. "I think she lost her tablet!"

"Oh no!"

"She didn't lose it," Bianca interrupted. "She doesn't bring it to beach days 'cause it might get sand in it."

"That's very smart!" Amelie praised Meggie.

"Shh!" Harlan shushed us. "My uncle is waiting for you to stop talking."

I looked up. Mr. JC was staring right at us.

"Sorry!" I whispered.

He smiled.

I knew I liked him. I smiled back.

"As you all know, Meggie is getting married on Saturday." We cheered and clapped because that is important! "And she has some things to do this week to get ready for it. So I'll be filling in so she can go to her appointments and stuff." He rubbed his hands together like my daddy does when he thinks he's going to announce something we think will be fun. "Who's ready for the beach?"

"Me!" we all shouted. All sixteen of us!

But not Noah. He looked a little nervous. I wondered why. It was just the beach.

I shrugged. Maybe he didn't like sand.

"So here's how it's going to go. Noah and I will each drive a group in one of the big golf carts. The beach stairs are steep, so we'll have to be careful. A section of the beach will be roped off for us, and there will be a rope with buoys in the water. You're not to go under or past the rope. It's there for your safety and so we can keep track of you. It's a big beach, and we don't want to lose anyone. Any questions?"

I raised my hand. "Are you a lifeguard?"

He nodded. "Both Noah and I are trained lifeguards. Hallie?"

"Uncle JC, does my mommy know that you and cousin Noah are taking sixteen kids to the beach *by yourselves?*"

Mr. JC nodded solemnly. "She does. And as you might have guessed, she'll be joining us there." He grinned.

Hmm. That was interesting.

Hallie rolled her eyes.

Mr. JC laughed. "You look just like your mom when you do that." He patted her head. "You don't need to worry. I run this whole resort, remember? How hard can a day at the beach with sixteen kids be?"

"Jordan helps you run the resort," Harlan clarified.

"And Mommy says he does a way better job at twenty-four years old than you did," Hallie accused.

"She's right. But I'm thirty-two now and a grown man." He bent down, picked her up, and flipped her upside down. Hallie squealed like the baby piggy at the zoo!

"Put me down, Uncle JC!" She sounded mad but she was laughing. We all were!

"Say you're sorry for doubting my awesomeness."

"I'm sorry!"

"And tell me I'm your favorite uncle."

"You're my favorite uncle!"

Mr. JC turned her right side up and set her on the ground. "Anyone else have a question?"

"Mr. JC?" Archer raised his hand.

"Yeah?"

"I'm a good swimmer. I win all the races."

"That's great, Archer! So I know you'll do a great job helping to keep all the kids within the ropes, and call for me or Noah if you see anyone in trouble."

"Yes, sir!"

"Awesome." He adjusted his visor. "If there's no more questions, let's go!"

We followed him and Noah on the long walk to the main lodge. It was going to take forever to get to the beach!

When we were finally buckled into the golf carts, I leaned over to whisper to Amelie. "We need to prank him."

"Why do you want to prank my dad?" Bianca whispered. She was sitting on the other side of Amelie. We were in the back row.

I pointed to Mr. JC. He was singing along to some old song. Hallie and Harlan were riding with him in the front. "Because that's what you do when someone new joins the team. It's the official welcome."

Archer turned around. He and Paisley and Nicki were in the middle row. "I've never heard of that. We don't prank anyone on my teams. It's against the rules."

I sighed. "Camp isn't a kids' sport, Archer, so don't worry. My daddy is a *professional.* And he's the best prankster on his team. We get pranked, too. It's all just fun."

Archer didn't look convinced.

Amelie backed me up. "We won't break any rules, and we won't hurt anybody. We can bury him in the sand and give him a mermaid tail. Or change his water for ocean water."

"Like an April fool!" Paisley shouted.

"Shh!" Bianca hushed her. "He can't suspect!"

"Right!" Paisley agreed.

"So how do we do this with Auntie Shelby there? She has eyes on the back of her head!" Nicki worried.

"Very carefully. And maybe we can get Hallie and Harlan to distract her."

"Good idea," Nicki agreed.

"I have an idea!" Bianca whispered. "My dad will eat *anything.* We could trade out his snack for something yucky! It won't make him mad at all. He always tries Auntie Molly's gross healthy food experiments. And some he likes!"

We all covered our mouths so he wouldn't hear us giggle.

"Ooh! I know what we can do!" Nicki lowered her voice. "My Mommy helped Molly make the sandwiches for lunch today. We can choose peanut butter and jelly or turkey and cheese. What if we"—she cupped her hands around her mouth—"combine his! There's always extra."

"That'll work!" I said. "Bianca, you take an extra PB&J. Paisley, you take an extra turkey. Hallie and Harlan can grab onto their mommy's hands and show her something they found—or lost. Bianca and Paisley will combine the sandwiches—we can eat the extra bread. Then they can switch it out for one of his sandwiches!"

"I can distract Mr. JC," Archer offered. "I'll throw my Frisbee super far, out of the zone, so he has to go get it!"

We talked more about the plan, and the only thing left to do when we got to the beach was tell Hallie and Harlan. Bianca filled them in as we walked to the area with the ropes.

It was such a fun morning! We swam and played in the sand. When it was lunchtime, Noah spread out two really big blankets and unpacked the coolers of food and drinks onto a table that popped up from a bag. Hallie and Harlan pulled their mom away. Archer threw his Frisbee, and Mr. JC ran to get it. Me and Amelie and Nicki asked Noah lots of questions so he wouldn't watch what Bianca and Paisley were doing.

We all took our food to the blanket for Group 1. Mr. JC came back with Archer's Frisbee and plopped down next to Bianca. "This my lunch?" he asked, pointing to the sandwich, chips, and apple next to hers.

She nodded, then turned her face away.

Don't laugh! Don't laugh! I silently yelled at her.

I looked past the blanket. Mrs. Shelby had just returned to her foldy chair behind Hallie and Harlan and was staring at JC.

She knew!

I held my breath.

Mr. JC slowly unwrapped his sandwich. All of us were watching him. Well, not Group 2. They were on the other blanket with Noah.

"Smells great!" Mr. JC said. We held our breath while he took a big bite.

We all stared at him while he chewed. His eyebrows went up,

and the bump in his throat moved up and down a lot. I covered my mouth and tried not to laugh.

He finally swallowed it all. We waited to see what he would say.

"Well. That was delicious! Who here has ever tried peanut butter, jelly, mayonnaise, cheese, and turkey?"

None of us raised our hands.

"You should." He rubbed his belly and took another bite. Again, he struggled to swallow it. Bianca was right. Her dad *would* eat anything!

"Who can I thank for this ah-mazing sammie?" He looked at each of us. When his gaze landed on Paisley, she broke.

She laughed and laughed, and the rest of us had to join in. Mr. JC was just pretending to like the sandwich!

"Great prank, kids!" he praised. "You sure got me good!"

Amelie and I high-fived each other. "Daddy is going to be so proud!" she shouted.

I grinned at her. "*So* proud!" I agreed.

Chapter Five

ARWYN

Tuesday flew by way too fast. Zaki and I went to apply for our marriage license. When we returned, he brought in my sewing machine from the RV and Mom helped me set up a workspace in the dining area. We moved furniture to block it off from the pups. I was running low on thread, and I hadn't yet purchased the beads, lace, or embroidery thread I needed because I thought I'd have a whole extra month to construct the gown.

There wasn't a shop in the Bar Harbor area that had what I needed, so Wednesday morning, I climbed into Mom's rental car to drive to Bangor. By the time we returned to the resort, members of Flynn and Meggie's wedding party had begun to arrive. Zaki knew several of them from the league, and it would have been rude not to greet them, but the interruptions added up. Zaki ordered us lunch from The Lobster Trap, and the owner, Denise, delivered it herself. Turned out she was a big hockey fan and wanted to congratulate Zaki on the Edge's Cup run.

After we ate, Zaki left to run errands. Mom settled into a chair at the end of the table with her laptop while I sewed. Usually, I liked the quiet while I worked, but I only had limited time with her before she went back to who knows where. I wasn't very good at initiating conversations though, and sometimes I blurted out questions or thoughts before I could think them through.

Often, they were unexpected and/or off-topic, and I'd learned early on from other kids laughing at me to keep them to myself.

But there were so many questions I wanted to ask her. Why *this* particular week for vacation? Are you on a secret assignment close by? Why was your job more important than your family?

But instead, I asked a safe question. "Did you really have an hour-long video chat with Zaki? He's been known to exaggerate."

She typed for a few more sentences, then closed her laptop. "I did. I had to make sure he'd take good care of my girl. He's already got a family to support. How do I know he can give you all the attention you deserve?"

"Why?" I blurted before I could think. "I've been taking care of myself for years." *Didn't Dad and I deserve your attention?* I wanted to ask.

Mom raised her eyebrows. She didn't speak for a good, long minute. "And you've done a wonderful job taking care of yourself. You have a reliable support network and caring inner circle. Marrying Zaki isn't the problem I see. Leaving your home, your friends, and everything you know and love to move to a new place—a city—where you'll have to build a support network from scratch seems like a mountain to climb for a quiet introvert who prefers a cozy reading nook to a Wags Night Out."

I frowned. A few months ago, that was one hundred percent true. "I've changed," I said. "Zaki—in his big but gentle way—has encouraged me to tiptoe out of my shell. He's given me the confidence to leave the house and open up more. The Edge wives and girlfriends are amazing, and I'm sure the spouses in Montreal will be, too. And his family is only three hours away in Quebec City. It's going to be fine."

"And the girls? Taking on the role of stepmom? Partnering with their mother to help raise them? No doubts there?"

I pressed my lips together and fought back the hot tears that were burning at the back of my eyes. "Why are you bringing all this up? Don't you think I've thought of it?"

"It's my job, Wyn. This is what mothers do."

Do mothers also leave their husband and six-year-old daughter to pursue a lucrative career as a spy?

But I didn't say that. I couldn't. And had the roles been

flipped, I knew I wouldn't have been so harsh on my dad. But the truth was, I worried about my mom. Not that she wouldn't come home but that she couldn't. That she'd die somewhere alone and I'd never see her again.

I swallowed hard, locked eyes with Mom, and spoke firmly. "I will do everything I can for those girls—and any children Zaki and I have—to ensure they grow up happy, healthy, and feeling supported."

She smiled. "I know you will." Her smile fell as she turned to gaze out the window. "Cherish every moment, every milestone. You won't realize how fast they're going until you wake up one day and your child is driving you to the airport."

I sucked in a breath. Did Mom have regrets?

"Do you—" I took a deep breath while I found the right words. "Do you wish you hadn't worked so much when I was growing up?"

Six months ago, I wouldn't have dreamed of asking such a question. I'd always just been happy enough with Mom visiting. No expectations, no disappointments.

When she didn't answer right away, my doubts crept in. The last thing I wanted to do was ruin our visit. "I'm sorry, Mom. That wasn't fair of me to ask you that now, when you've come all this way."

"Don't apologize, Wyn. The truth is yes, and no. Do I regret missing out on watching my only child—my sweet girl with a bigger heart than anyone I ever knew—grow up? Yes. But my facility with languages and logistics makes me invaluable in my line of work. If I hadn't been out there, doing what I do … Well, let's just say there are a lot of people who wouldn't be alive or free or—" She swiped her eyes and gave a little smile. "And had I been there, I'm not sure you'd be the same person you are today. You've got my analytical brain and your father's tenderness. You're perfect, in every way, and I have to continue to work to protect you—and others—from afar. But I promise to try to come home more often, if you want me to."

The satin slipped from my hands, and I stood up slowly and walked to Mom. I wrapped my arms around her from behind and leaned my head against hers. "Yes. Whenever you can. I love you so much, Mom. And I'm so glad you're here with me now."

She nodded and twisted to give me a firm strong hug. "Me too."

We held each other, both of us silently weeping until her phone rang. She excused herself and walked into the bedroom to take the call and I went back to work at my machine. By the time the girls returned from camp, I'd only just attached the scalloped trim to the skirt. It would take me all night to bead and appliqué the bodice. And the long, over-the wrist sheer sleeves ... They would be the first thing to be scrapped. While required for our church wedding in Montreal, I wouldn't need them here on the beach. And I could save the train for the Montreal ceremony as well. As I stood at the table gazing upon the pieces and willing the panic not to set in, those familiar strong arms enclosed me from behind.

"Wynna-bun," Zaki said, the nickname evoking the cinnamon bun accident that once made me think I'd hate him forever. Funny how life worked. He trailed his lips along the shell of my ear. I shivered, and he squeezed me tighter. Weighted blankets and snug hugs always helped to slow my heart rate.

"I'll never finish in time," I whispered. "And especially not if I have to attend all the pre-wedding events. Like dinner tonight and activities after."

"It doesn't have to be perfect. You could wear a sundress. Save the fancy for Montreal. I want to marry *you,* Wynnie, not your dress."

I sighed. "I know. Okay. I think I've decided to skip the sleeves and train. But there's still so much to do."

"*Sew matcha* to do," he teased, referencing my profession and his favorite iced pre-workout drink.

He was corny like that.

The pun worked, and I laughed.

"How about I take the girls to the arts and crafts activity tonight?" he offered.

I laughed again. "You don't have any idea what it is, do you?"

"Not a clue."

I slid out from his embrace and walked into the kitchen for

the Folder-O-Fun on the counter. The Wednesday schedule was right on top. "'Crochet Corner: Join our Head of Security, Jack Dalton, as he teaches beginner and advanced crocheters. Learn a chain stitch or a cat stitch while you lounge on our back deck. Dessert, coffee, and tea included.'" I caught his gaze and lifted my eyebrows. "I have to take them."

"Or I can learn how to crochet. From a *man.*"

I chuckled. "By all means, go for it then."

"I've heard about that guy. He was a Green Beret, and if he can crochet, so can I."

I set the folder down as the back door banged open. Isla and Amelie ran inside, followed by my mother, with both Westies on their leashes.

"Thanks for picking them up from camp, Mom," I said. "Girls, head right on up to the shower and—"

"We know!" they chorused.

The girls were loving Camp Cliff Walk. Each night at dinner, they recounted their day animatedly and reenacted their favorite moment with gusto. My favorite so far was their impression of JC when they pranked his sandwich. Today was day three, and they had their routine down. Breakfast, camp, shower, dinner, after-dinner family activity, bedtime story. We'd set a goal to finish the Anne of Green Gables series by the end of our trip and were just about at one of my favorite parts in *Anne of Ingleside.* Isla and Amelie had been captivated by Anne's five-year-old twins, Nan and Di. We'd had many a lively discussion regarding the fictional twins' choices, adventures, and trouble with other little girls.

Tonight's dinner was for the wedding party and out-of-towners. There would be another one Friday night at the beach after the rehearsal in the church. Then the wedding on Saturday, and before we knew it, Sunday would be here in a blink.

The panic started to set in again.

Stop it, Arwyn. You're a professional. It doesn't have to be perfect.

But I wanted it to be.

While Zaki carried my gown into the bedroom to keep it safe overnight from Laffy and Vennie, I tidied up, placing everything I needed to customize the bodice in a bin for when I returned after dinner. If it had been any other project, I would have brought it to the arts and crafts event to work on, but I wanted to keep the fine details of my gown to myself and Mom—and also far away from messy desserts.

Dinner was animated, as I expected it would be. The hockey players, Flynn and Meggie's family and friends, and past teammates of Flynn's from when he played in New England filled the dining room. To be truthful, I was glad to be going back to Salt Mist Cottage afterward. I needed to recharge in a quiet space.

"Can I make you some tea?" Mom asked.

"Yes, please," I said. "There's a box of blueberry tea leaves on the counter."

"On it. Hey," she called. "Any preference on which mug? These are so interesting. *Decaf? No Thanks, I Like My Sanity. Sea-ze the Day. Berry Sweet Mornings Start Here. You Mocha Me So Happy. Steeped in Love. Cliff Walk Cafe: Where Every Sip Is a Story. You're My Cup of Tea. Perk Up, Buttercup?*"

"No preference," I said. "You pick for me. Molly said every mug at the resort is different. I think it's cool."

The master suite had a sitting area, and I sat on the love seat to work on the bodice. It was finally hitting me that this gown was for *me*. I'd restored, redesigned, and reworked wedding gowns for others. Designed and adorned and constructed others from scratch, but this one—*this one*—was just for me. And I'd get to wear two versions of it.

Another gift of Zaki's spontaneity.

Mom joined me and set out tea on the thin, rectangular coffee table. I read the mugs she'd chosen: *You're My Cup of Tea* for me and *Sea-ze the Day* for her.

That was Mom, all right.

I loved spending time with her. We swapped stories from town and her travels that we couldn't share over email or in short phone conversations.

It was a little past eight thirty when Zaki and the girls returned. I set my work aside, hugged Mom goodbye and wished her a safe walk back to her room in the main lodge. I hurried upstairs and arrived just as Isla and Amelie were settling into their beds. Zaki handed me my copy of *Anne of Ingleside*—we each had one—and I began to read.

Chapter thirty-four always made my heart smile. I remembered being a little girl and how every feeling from love to shame seemed amplified. Rilla felt deeply embarrassed at the thought of carrying a cake through her town, even though no one understood why. When she was five, she once saw an old, shabby woman named Tillie Pake being teased by boys while carrying a cake, and the memory stuck with her. The boys even made up a mocking rhyme about it. Since then, Rilla connected carrying cakes with being undignified and unladylike, and the idea had taken root in her young mind.

"Wynnie?"

"Yes, Amelie?"

"You carry cakes. And you're a lady," she observed.

"I've never carried a cake," Isla remarked.

I smiled. "Remember when Dove told Nan she wasn't really Nan?" They nodded. "We talked about how sometimes kids—and grown-ups—make up hurtful stories to amuse themselves or to gain attention or because they're feeling badly about something and want to hurt others so they aren't the only ones hurting."

"That's not nice *at all,*" Amelie huffed. "It's just mean."

"We would never do that," Isla said matter-of-factly.

"I'm glad," I replied. "Let's find out what happens next."

Within minutes, the girls were giggling along to poor Rilla's cake-carrying plight, which resulted in its unfortunate end, and I reluctantly closed the book after just the one chapter. "It's been a long day. Maybe tomorrow we can squeeze in two chapters," I said. "We only have seven left."

Zaki and I tucked the girls in and headed back downstairs and out to the front section of the wraparound porch. He lit the citronella- and lemongrass-scented anti-mosquito tiki torches, and we cuddled up on the porch swing.

"It's kind of like how I imagine Prince Edward Island to be," I said. "Minus the red cliffs, of course, but stunning in its own way. I'm so glad we're getting married here." I tucked my head into the curve of his neck and closed my eyes, content and consumed with joy.

His voice rumbled against my head as he spoke. "Me too. Four nights from now, we'll be husband and wife and staying in that lighthouse."

I twisted my neck to kiss his chin. "Ninety-six hours."

"Ninety-six times sixty ..." He paused to work the math out in his head. "Five thousand, seven hundred, sixty minutes."

"That's all?" I teased.

"Well, if we sleep for eight hours each these next three nights, you can knock twenty-four off the ninety-six, which is only seventy-two hours and ... four thousand, three hundred, twenty minutes!"

"But who's counting?" I asked.

"Me," he admitted. "Still too long." He lowered his lips to mine for a quick kiss and grinned.

"That's all I get?" I pouted.

"Are you saying that kiss was unsatisfactory?"

I held in a laugh. "Incredibly disappointing."

"I'll have to remedy that."

And he did.

Chapter Six

ZAKI

After dropping the girls off at camp on Thursday, Arwyn and I were just short of the main lodge when my phone rang. The Swan Lake tone signaled the call was from Viki, my ex-wife.

"You should take that," Arwyn said. "I'll meet you inside."

I nodded. "Okay."

Viki and I had a good relationship post-divorce, and she and Arwyn had gotten connected through video calls with the girls. When Viki's schedule allowed, she joined us via video chat for the nightly bedtime readings.

"Hey, Zak. Just two quick things. I know you're busy."

"It's fine. What's up?" It was unusual for her to call; she almost always texted, so I knew this had to be important.

"Did you sign with Montreal yet?"

I let out a frustrated breath through my nose. "Not yet," I said shortly. "But I will. I told you, they're still working out details. I—"

"Don't."

Huh? Had I heard her right? "What do you mean, 'don't'?"

"Don't sign with them, Zaki. Stay in Colorado. You love it there, and they need you. There's no way you'll even get close to winning a Stanley Cup with the Saints. I—"

I cut her off and tried to keep my tone even. "Some things are more important than winning a Stanley Cup. Like my kids. No chance I'm signing any contract that keeps me away from them. Last fall was the worst time of my life with the girls in Montreal with you while I stayed in Colorado. And you know what that feels like, because they haven't lived with you since December."

"I know. I've done a lot of thinking over the last month. Lauren and Jason visited with their kids last weekend, and I realized how much I missed them and all my friends in Colorado. We practically grew up there, you and me. This last year, being home … It's not the same as it was before we left. All last fall, the girls told me more times than I could count how much they missed Denver. I couldn't have imagined they'd feel displaced at only five years old. It was all they knew. Their friends are there, their ballet school, everyone they know and feel safe with. And Arwyn has her business there. It makes more sense for me to go back than for all of you to uproot your life on my account."

I leaned back against the lodge, stunned. "Are you serious?" My tone was soft, laced with hope, vulnerable. This was the last thing I'd expected.

"I am. Lauren told me about the townhouses under construction in her neighborhood. It's equal distance from Palmer City to Denver. Only thirty minutes to the girls' school. Isla and Amelie are my world, too, Zaki, and I want them to be happy most of all."

"Wow. I—I don't know what to say."

"Say you'll call your agent and restart talks with the Edge."

"Yeah. Yeah, I will." I sank to the ground and stared out into the trees. My head felt foggy, like I was in a dream.

"One more thing," Viki said.

"Yeah?"

"My parents feel weird about going to your wedding Sunday. Can you call them and tell them they're being ridiculous?"

"Why do they feel weird?" I'd moved in with Viki and her family to play hockey when I was sixteen. Our moms were best friends, having been roommates in college. I was just as close to her parents as I was to my own.

"Zak, if you can't figure that out on your own … Never mind. Just please call them again and tell them how much you're looking forward to seeing them and that the girls miss them, whatever you need to say. They should be there."

"Yeah, I can do that."

"Call your agent first."

"'Kay. Vik?"

"Yeah?"

"Thank you."

I ended the call and pulled myself to my feet, walking in a daze to the dining room. Before I called my agent, I needed to know what Arwyn thought.

She was sipping blueberry iced tea when I sank into the chair across from her. "I have some big news." I quickly filled her in.

Her eyes went wide as I relayed the conversation. "And you're sure she won't change her mind?" Arwyn asked.

I shook my head. "I don't think so. But maybe I should wait on signing anything until she buys a place?"

Arwyn reached for my hand. "Whatever you decide, I'm with you."

"I know."

After breakfast, we headed to the stables for a trail ride and picnic lunch. The shady uphill path through the trees was lined with evergreen and white birch. The scent of the ocean blended with the pines, creating a fragrance that I was growing to love.

Up ahead, the weather-distressed red barn and fenced-in paddock were quiet, unlike the other day when we picked up the girls. As we drew closer, a pregnant woman with a long brown ponytail emerged, followed by Jamie and Rodeo.

"Hi!" she greeted us. "I'm Kat Crane. You must be Arwyn and Zaki?"

I nodded. "We are. Hey, Jamie."

The boy grinned. "Uncle Easton and me got your horses saddled. Buttons for you." He pointed to Arwyn. "And Elvis for you." He pointed to me.

"I can't wait," I said.

"We selected the horses based on the riding experience you shared in your waivers," Kat explained. "It's not an exact science, so if you require a change, we can bring a different horse out to you."

She motioned for us to follow her as a tall, bearded man in a western hat led an impressive black horse out of the barn. Jamie ran to him to take the reins, and he disappeared back inside.

Kat gestured to the horse. "The picnic lunch you ordered is in the pack strapped to Elvis here. Buttons will be out in just a minute. She's got a blanket on her back. The trail map is on the CW app, as well as our contact info, if you should need any assistance."

"Thanks," Arwyn said.

I looked into the barn. Six stalls on each side at this end of it. Tack room, office and supply area farther down. "Nice stables."

"We like 'em," Kat said with a smile.

We mounted our horses, and I gestured for Arwyn to lead the way to the trailhead. The trail itself was too narrow to ride side by side, but I didn't mind. Watching Arwyn ride had me grinning like a fool. I'd convinced her to buy a pair of jeans just for this purpose. She rarely wore pants, always dressing in old-fashioned or ultra-feminine dresses. I loved her style, but when she realized her old riding pants would need to be replaced, I suggested jeans instead. She'd get more wear out of them—potentially.

The trail wound upward through the back of the property and opened into a meadow. "Hitching post over there." Arwyn pointed.

I pulled up next to her and dismounted. She swung her leg around and over Buttons's back, and I was right there when her feet hit the ground. Taking her hand, I tugged her to a nearby tree and backed her up against its ample trunk. Before she could protest, I rested my arm on the tree above her with my palm flat against the bark, and bent to kiss her, using my free hand to trail my finger along her cheekbone and tucked a wayward strand of hair behind her ear. Just a quick brush of my lips, but I wasn't done yet.

"We're alone," I said huskily. "Like *really alone.*"

Arwyn replied in a singsong voice. "Whatever shall we do about it?"

"I can think of a few things."

"Oh yeah?"

"Mm-hmm." I nuzzled her nose.

"Like what?" She maneuvered her head, trying to catch my lips.

I pulled away. "Collect berries. Climb trees. Picnic lunch."

She smirked. "Or?"

I twisted us around so that my back was against the tree now. She melted into me and sighed. I took the opportunity to pull off her sun hat and reach for the hair claw that held her auburn waves on top of her head. I tossed the hat like a Frisbee, clipped her claw to the hem of my shirt, and ran my fingers through her silky hair.

"I can't think of anything else." I rubbed the scruff on my chin, pretending to think.

"I can." She cupped my face in her hands. "Can you guess?"

"Maybe. But I'll hear your ideas."

"If you stop teasing me."

I grinned. "But I *like* teasing you."

She laughed. "Oh, I know. Close your eyes."

"I prefer to keep them open." I planted a kiss on her nose.

"Then I guess there's nothing to do but pick berries and—"

"Okay." My arms closed around her, and I cut off her sentence with a light kiss on the tip of her nose. Her eyelids fluttered as her hands found my hair, and only then did I close my own eyes, wanting to block out the nature sounds around us so I could concentrate fully on Arwyn.

Gone were the snorts of the horses, the tweedles of the birds, and the rustling of the leaves. The soft touch of her lips, her rose-scented hair, the tickle of flyaway strands against my neck, the way we fit against each other … It all consumed me.

Until the sound of kids singing pulled us from each other, and we reluctantly headed back to the horses. A camp group passed by us and continued up the trail as we collected the picnic lunch and blanket from Elvis and Buttons.

I followed Arwyn into the meadow, where she spread the blanket over the tall, lush grass, next to a sprinkling of wildflowers.

"The pink and purple are lupines," she said. "The yellow ones are goldenrod, and that's Queen Anne's lace next to the daisies."

I sank onto the blanket next to her and began to unpack the

soft-sided thermal cooler. "Flowers 101," I teased as I passed her the hand sanitizer. "Will there be a quiz?"

She nodded as she rubbed her hands with the gel. "High stakes. A kiss for each correct answer."

"I should study, then."

Arwyn laughed. "You do that. Oooh! Blueberries!" She opened the container and popped a few into her mouth. "They're so sweet here. Small, but sweet."

"Like you," I cooed. "Teeny and delicious." Her giggle was music to my ears as I quickly sanitized my hands and scooped up a handful of blueberries. "Open wide!'

"You're going to—oh!" A blueberry hit the tip of her nose. She caught it on the bounce in her hands.

"I am," I said. "Try again?"

"If you insist." She parted her lips and tilted her head back. I lobbed a blueberry toward her, and it hit its target.

Arwyn chewed it and grinned. "Nice shot."

"I *am* a professional."

"With a puck."

I shrugged. "I'm good at hitting targets."

"Your turn." She pinched the first blueberry between her thumb and index finger.

I leaned back on my elbows and opened my mouth toward the cloud-speckled blue sky. The sun was brighter than I was expecting, forcing my eyes to close against the light.

Instead of a blueberry, it was Arwyn's mouth that met mine.

Another kissing session?

Way better than lunch.

Up here, alone in the meadow, it felt like we were in another world, and I could tell from the fervency of her kisses that she wanted to make every minute count.

Arwyn pulled away and smiled, waiting for me to make the next move. As I drew near her again, her smile faltered, and she breathed in a slow, steadying breath. It whooshed out in a soft sigh, and I patiently pressed my lips to hers once again. But this time, I deepened the kiss so that her next sigh would be all mine.

Lunch could wait.

After we tucked the girls into bed, I kissed Arwyn goodbye, grabbed my Edge cap, tossed it on backward, and took the resort shuttle to Paddy's Tavern. Flynn's bachelor celebration was already in full swing when I arrived.

It looked like every guy in town had shown up. I recognized Ryan, Easton, Damon, and Matt at the pool table—I'd met him at pickup yesterday—and a cluster of professional hockey players in a lively darts tournament. Flynn's dad and uncle sat at the bar, and his brother and cousins were on the small stage attempting to sing a rock song I think was from the 1970s.

I loved a good karaoke night.

I finally spotted Flynn at a round high-top table in the corner with our Edge teammates, Xavier Schwan and Trask Emerson, and his bestie from when he played in Boston, Taz Houlihan. I'd known Taz since we were kids. He grew up in Palmer City, and his sister was the assistant trainer for the Voltage. Taz was one of those kids we called an "ice rat"—if he could've lived at the rink, he would have.

Flynn, ever stoic, wore an expression that was hard to read. But from the way the other guys were leaning in, I surmised whatever they were talking about was important.

Maybe I could help.

I beelined for the table, and when I reached earshot, I heard him loud and clear. I had no doubt he was talking about the big commitment he was about to make.

"But how do I *know* it's going to work?" He looked up just then, and our eyes locked. He paled, probably thinking about my divorce. His relationship with Meggie had begun when they were teenagers, just like mine and Viki's.

So given my history, I had a unique perspective the other guys at the table didn't.

I pulled an unoccupied stool from a neighboring table and joined them, folding my arms on the tabletop before I spoke. "You can't ever know for sure. But what you *can* do is listen.

Check in—often. Not just ask if she's good. She'll always say yes. Get the details, and let her talk all of them out of her. Then ask if she wants advice or help. Don't offer it without asking first. And be affectionate. Hug often. Make her morning coffee when you're home. Add whipped cream and sprinkles for flourish. Find other ways to constantly show her she's your world."

"And if I do all that and she still wants to leave me?" Flynn rubbed the back of his neck. "Wait … did you do all those things?"

I shook my head and thought for a minute before I responded so I could form my racing thoughts into something constructive and helpful.

"I was young. I did everything I could think of at the time. Ultimately, it wasn't enough because you can never control everything … especially another person. When she told me she didn't love me anymore, I knew I would never be able to fix that, no matter how much effort I put in or tried to change. I'm a lot. I'll never stop learning and growing to be the best man I can be, but I can't change the core of who I am. I strive to be better today than I was yesterday, and that's all I can do." I lifted my chin so I could lock eyes with him. "I assumed she'd always be there, because she always was. And when she said she was fine, I assumed she was telling the truth. If you ever hear Meggie say she's 'fine,' always assume the opposite."

"You know what they say about *assuming*," Taz interjected. "The first three letters make an—ow!" Xavier cut him off with an elbow to his bicep.

I smirked. "It's true. Never assume. Instead of worrying and wondering, take action. Communicate. Meggie is leaving her home and her veterinary assistant job for you. She's put off her dream of becoming a vet herself so she can support you. That's a lot for you to carry on your shoulders. I get that. She may regret her choices at some point, like Viki did, but that isn't anything you can control. What you *can* control are your words and actions. Making her feel valued, showing your gratitude, and showing up for her."

"Do you wish you had done more of that?" Flynn asked. "If you had, do you think you'd still be together?"

I still felt bad for not being what Viki needed, but I knew in my heart our separation was better for both of us. "Not anymore," I confessed honestly. "After she filed for divorce, for the longest time I wished I had. But it wouldn't have helped. Ultimately, we wanted different things, and by that point, neither of us were willing to give something up for the other. We thought we were each other's person at the time, but then we grew up and realized we weren't right for each other. In retrospect, we probably never would've gotten together in the first place if I hadn't been living in her house. And then I met Arwyn, and it was different. That woman saw the worst of me before she saw the best of me, and she gave me a chance. I'll never take her love for granted. It's a work in progress, but it's growing every day. She's my forever."

"The forced proximity trope," Jason Dexter, our goalie, said from behind me. "Twice."

All our heads turned to stare at him.

"What? I'm well-read. Y'all know that."

We exchanged a round of cheerful chirps, aimed at Jason and his confession that he read romance novels.

"Don't judge." He elbowed me. "I know about you reading the Anne of Green Gables series."

"With my *daughters,*" I retorted.

"Mm-hmm. Sure." He took a sip of the water bottle he'd brought with him. "And if Arwyn asked you to read them just because?"

My cheeks heated. I was glad for my ginger beard. "Yeah. I'd read them."

"And would you have read them for Viki?" Jason pushed.

I shook my head. "Unlikely."

"Exactly my point. You"—he pointed to Trask—"went hard chirping at me reading Lauren's favorite book when we were dating. That book was key to me getting a second chance when I blew it with her. And yet here y'all are, chirping me again now for taking an interest in my wife's interests. And I couldn't care less." He turned to Flynn. "If Meggie asked you to spend a weekend watching Hallmark Christmas movies, would you?"

"Heck yeah," he said.

"Point made." Jason grinned.

"Unfair ask," I insisted. "Bro's from a tiny town in Vermont. He grew up in a Hallmark movie."

Jason sighed heavily, like my comment wasn't worth responding to. I grinned at him.

"Let me try," Trask said. "Kami's got her PhD in environmental science. She was finishing it when she met me, and then she planned to move back to her family's bee farm in the South Carolina Lowcountry and start a career as a research scientist testing and analyzing swampy dirt. She put that on hold. For me. Because we talked about it. The career of a professional athlete isn't very long. We all know there are expiration dates on our bodies playing such a physical sport. I'll retire before I'm forty, and she can have a long career after that. And right now, she's happy being a hockey mom to our kids. They're growing so fast, and she's there for every minute of it. You can't ever get that time back. If she was traveling around the world sampling dirt, she'd miss a lot of it."

Like Arwyn's mom did, I thought. How had she felt about missing Arwyn growing up? My girls were the same age Arwyn was when her mother left.

"So every summer," Trask went on, "she chooses a vacation location or a research project—just for her—where she can dig to sample and analyze dirt. Sometimes we make it a family affair, for fun and to teach our kids about the environment and cool things like why citrus thrives in the South and apples don't."

"I don't know Meggie too well," I said. "But from what I can see, she isn't being coerced to marry you and move to Colorado. She doesn't appear to be marrying you for money or out of convenience—"

"Hey now," Xavier warned. He was smiling though. His marriage of convenience to Penny had worked out far better than either of them could have imagined.

"Sorry, Swanny." I grinned back at him. "Meggie's different from Viki, Flynn. I know it, and you know it."

"Yeah. You're right. Thanks, guys."

"Anytime," I said.

Jason pointed to the small stage by the bar. "Looks like it's about to get loud."

"Uh-oh," Flynn said. "I don't know who's worse. You or JC."

"JC?" I angled my body toward the stage. Sure enough, JC had the mic in his hands. The beginning chords of "Don't Stop Believin'" began to play.

"You gonna let him show you up, Marshy?" Taz instigated. "You know you can't resist."

Once JC started singing about the small-town girl in her lonely world, a cluster of women appeared out of nowhere and began singing along.

All hopes of finishing our conversation dashed, I grinned at Taz and hopped off my stool.

It was time to introduce Crane's Cove to Quebec's pride and joy.

Celine Dion.

Chapter Seven

ARWYN

Friday morning, I woke up early to finish my gown. After an entertaining breakfast of Zaki recounting and overperforming "Because You Loved Me," complete with pulling me up from my chair and waltzing me around the kitchen to the chorus, he walked the girls to camp.

I watched them go, shaking my head and feeling warmth from my head to my toes. In two days, we'd be an official family, and I was overcome with the best emotions.

I retrieved the bodice and skirt from my closet and moved the furniture to block the dogs, apologizing to them for the fourth day in a row. Mom would be here any minute to help me pin the waistband of my dress to the skirt, sew it, and reinforce the seams. I'd opted to keep the bodice separate from the skirt. It was long enough to cover the waistband, and this way, I could tie on a train with a sash for our church wedding. The dress was heavy and needed a good steaming but was otherwise completed.

I couldn't believe I'd done it! No sleeves, no train, minimal puffs at the shoulders, and about three quarters of the embellishments I'd planned, but it was finished.

And just in time, too. Our friends from Colorado would arrive at the resort any minute now. All that was left to do was affix a ruffle to the hems of each of the girls' dresses, but that would take no time at all.

"It's beautiful," Mom said, pulling me in for a hug. "I love how you used pieces of my gown and each of your grandmothers'. It's like a bit of them are here with you. And you added in your own flair to the bodice and hemline. And, of course, the trademark Wynnie puffed sleeves. It's brilliant work. They'd be so proud of you."

"Thanks, Mom."

"You're welcome. I'm glad you decided to get married here. Jumping into things like that isn't like you, but it's good for you. You'll have a great story to tell and beautiful memories. As the Wayne Gretzky guy said, 'You miss one hundred percent of the shots you don't take.'"

I laughed. "Like I said, I've changed. Not too much, but Zaki's good about easing my anxiety so I'm not afraid to experience new things and go off-plan."

"I can see that. You complete each other. He's your lobster. Full steam ahead!"

"Ha!" I chuckled. "Just not in a lobster pot!"

Laffy and Vennie howled, and it took me a second to realize they weren't just laughing along with us. I turned my attention to the front door. I grinned when I saw the mop of blond curly hair and hurried to let Molly in. Behind her was my friend Brenna Trotter, a hometown girl who'd married a hockey player. Her husband, Brendan, started with the Voltage, the minor league team based in Palmer City, then moved up to the Denver Edge. He and Zaki were good friends.

"I'll walk the dogs," Mom offered, swiping a tear from her eye. "You get this wedding planned, okay?"

"I've never seen you cry," I said, touched. *Not even when Dad died.*

"I must be getting sentimental in my old age." She called the pups to the back door, and I raced to the front.

"Hey!" Molly greeted me. "I brought reinforcements!"

Brenna grinned and flicked her long blond hair behind her shoulders. "I wanted to rush over before all the girls arrived. They're bringing in a mini bachelorette party this afternoon."

Oh my. That was unexpected.

I hugged them both and gestured for them to sit on the couch.

I sat across from them in an armchair, the only other piece of furniture that wasn't cluttered with sewing supplies or being used to block my work area from the Westies.

"You look like a deer in headlights!" Molly chided. "Not to worry, everyone gets the jitters."

"It's the people," Brenna told her. "Wynnie's an introvert."

"I'm right here, Bren," I said, maybe a little too sharply. I gave a nervous chuckle to try to soften the comment. "Sorry. That came out harsh."

Brenna waved me off. "No worries. Let's get these details finalized. Oh! And I brought favors." She reached into her tote bag. "This one's for you. What do you think?"

I unwrapped the bundle of tissue paper she handed me. It was a circular salt-dough ornament. I brushed my fingers over the tiny starfish glued to the sand on the bottom third of it. Textured white paint outlined the sand above and blended with an ocean blue. The top crescent was painted royal blue and punched with a hole for hanging twine. *Arwyn & Zaki* was calligraphed over the paint.

"It's beautiful," I breathed. "How did you have time?"

"I got to work as soon as Zaki called Brendan. Tasha and Penny came by to help shape and bake them, and I did the calligraphy on the flight here."

"Wow. Thank you." I wrapped it back up in the paper. "But don't you have a wedding this weekend at the barn?"

Brenna was a wedding planner and owned a barn venue in Palmer City. Her weekends were booked a year in advance.

"Sure, but my assistants can handle it. It wouldn't feel right if I skipped your wedding to work."

"But—you've already RSVP'd for the Montreal wedding," I protested.

"Wynnie," she said firmly. "This is what friends do. We all want to be here. For *both* weddings."

"I—thank you."

We spent the next twenty minutes with Molly going over the plans for Sunday morning. When the kitchen clock struck noon, I turned to it and caught movement in the windows.

Brenna beat me to the back door and pulled it open. They

were all here—Shanna, who was like a big sister to me; Penny and Tasha, sisters to each other and my closest friends from back home; plus three of the Edge Wags—the pro sports nickname for wives and girlfriends—Kami, Taylor, and Lauren. All were armed with tote bags, except for Tasha, who wore her two-month-old daughter Nanette on her chest and carried a covered cupcake pan.

"Monty asked if he could volunteer at camp, so I've got the baby," Tasha explained.

I rolled my eyes. "Of course he did. And no one's complaining," I assured her. "She's the sweetest!"

"Bless his heart," Kami cooed in her Southern accent. She and her husband, Trask, were from South Carolina. "That Monty is something else. The rest of the guys took all the kids for a nature walk on the trails. That flight was long, and it'll do 'em good to get their wiggles out before Meggie and Flynn's rehearsal and the bonfire tonight."

"I made the girls new bows!" Taylor handed me two pale blue gift bags. A former all-star cheerleader, Taylor had a booming cheer bow side business in addition to counseling current and retired pro athletes full-time. "They can wear them Sunday if you want to save their tiaras for the Montreal ceremony."

"Thank you," I said, touched. "Knowing them, they might wear both."

"If anyone can pull that off, it's Isla and Amelie," she agreed with a chuckle.

She joined the other women in the kitchen, and all I could do was watch and smile in wonder as all eight women took over the cottage. Caterers from the resort arrived with tri-level stands for sweet and savory bites. Every spare chair and stool was procured, and by the time my mom returned with Laffy and Vennie, the porch was set up for a proper tea party.

"Now for the finishing touch!" Kami announced. She wrapped a feather boa around my neck and perched a fancy wide-brimmed hat on my head. "And I brought you some lavender honey from my family's bee farm."

"Wow." I sniffed. "This is so nice of you all. You didn't have to—"

"We wanted to," she insisted. "You're a blessing to us,

Wynnie, and we're so happy for you. Now go sit in the comfiest chair out there. You can't miss it. It's the one with the 'Bride to Be' sign taped to the window behind it."

I'd never been the recipient of a big fuss like this. I felt so loved.

Taking a deep breath, I strode purposefully toward my designated seat and pushed away all the insecurities that wanted to steal my joy.

I was getting married in two days!

Chapter Eight

AMELIE

It was Friday, our last day at Camp Cliff Walk, and Mr. JC was filling in for Meggie all day again 'cause she's getting married tomorrow! In the morning, he took us on a big yellow bus to Acadia National Park to see the harbor seals. He said he was friends with one of them, but I couldn't be sure if he was fibbing or not. But she did bark at him when he called her Pepper.

Mr. JC barked back, and we all laughed. He told us to try it because barking like a seal wasn't as easy as it sounded. Then Bianca told us that her Auntie Molly had the best seal bark and it sounded real! Hallie and Harlan told us they heard it and it was definitely the best. Then we all tried. We were not very good *at all,* but we sure had fun and we laughed a lot!

It was more fun than potato sack races and ziplining and even the mini sticks game we played with Flynn's group during our sports rotations yesterday. His group was our partner group. We each got paired up with a big kid for sports and some other activities. Me and Isla were on the same team, and we won!

On the bus ride back to camp, I added harbor seals to the "Animals" list in my camp diary. I had so many lists! My favorite one was all the new words I learned from our new friends, like bubblah—that's what they call a water fountain you drink from; pockabook—a purse!—jimmies, which are chocolate sprinkles, and fluffahnuttuh. Those were sandwiches with peanut butter and marshmallow Fluff. So yummy!

When we got back to the pavilion, Monty was there! That man was so silly. He and my daddy are friends. They prank each other *a lot*. Once, Monty made our hot tub into a koi pond! That was after Daddy filled his truck with birdseed.

Monty even pranked our RV. On the first night of our trip, me and Amelie's *Frozen* sheets were Ridgie the Bear sheets! Ridgie is Daddy's team mascot, and Monty is the guy in the suit. Then, when Wynnie pulled back the blankets to go to sleep in her bed, her blue sheets were gone and there was a white one with Monty's picture on it instead! It was as big as him—and he was only wearing shorts! He should have been here yesterday for the Oreos we brought for the kids. Daddy helped us scrape out the cream and fill them with white mint toothpaste. It was really funny when the kids took their first bite. And Noah almost threw up!

Daddy and Monty were so crazy! Their prank war gave me an idea.

I would tell Isla and the other kids during the afternoon snack. Group 1 always sat at the picnic table closest to the barn. I waited until Mr. JC and Noah went to talk to Kat and Jamie in the paddock. Monty was helping give Group 2 their snacks so no grown-ups could hear me. "We need to prank Flynn and Meggie!"

"Oh! Yes!" Isla agreed. "How?"

"Remember Rilla carrying the cake?" She nodded. "We're reading a book, and the little girl carried a cake." I explained to the kids about Rilla from our story. "And we can hide the cake tonight!"

Paisley looked unconvinced. "What's tonight?"

"It's the rehearsal dinner party on the beach," Bianca said. "Remember? For the wedding?"

"Oh yeah! I forgot that was tonight! I have a new dress! And a new one for the wedding, too!" she beamed.

"You're all going to be there, right?" Everyone nodded their heads. "Good. Rehearsal cakes are small, so me and Isla can carry it. We need a place to hide it on the beach."

"I know!" Bianca said. "I can get the key to the shack from my daddy. There's a snack freezer in there. We can put it on top."

"And we can leave a clue on the table!" Hallie said. "How about … 'Roses are red, violets are blue, we love you so much, so we had to prank you!'"

"Oooh, that's perfect!" I exclaimed.

"My sister is so smart," Harlan said. "She can write the poem, and at the bottom she can write a really small sentence that says where it is so they don't worry."

"Yes!" I said. "Shh! Monty is coming!"

We all got super quiet and smiled up at Monty. He raised his eyebrows and leaned down onto the table, putting his chin on his hands and sniffing. We giggled.

"I smell trouble," he said. "Eight kids going silent, all at once? *Very* sus."

"We're just being polite," Isla said. "It would be rude if we kept talking when you came over."

Nice! I thought. Isla was a quick thinker.

"Mm-hmm," Monty hummed. He stood up and stuck out two fingers, pointed them to his eyes and then toward us. "I'll be watching you. And tell your dad I enjoyed the crocheted splattered egg on my windshield."

I held my breath until he was far enough away, then Amelie and I burst into giggles. Last night, Daddy had asked Jack to help him connect the long white and yellow yarn strings he made to form a sunny-side-up egg. We thought that was silly but didn't ask what he planned to do with it!

After sharing the story with our friends, we got back to talking about the cake prank. By the end of snack time, the plan was all set.

Flynn and Meggie were going to be so happy they were so loved by us kids!

"BE careful going down the steps in your dresses, girls!" Wynnie led us down the wooden stairs to the beach. Isla was behind me, and Daddy last.

Wynnie worried too much. Me and Isla had lots of practice with stairs in our princess dresses. Tonight, we were just wearing regular sundresses. Piece of cake!

I giggled. *Cake!* It was almost time for our prank!

The sun was setting, and the beach was getting dark. Wynnie took my hand, and we followed Daddy and Isla past the shack to the end of the beach where the party was. A big fire and lots of tables were spread out in the sand. Behind the tables were more stairs that went up the rocky wall. A DJ was playing old-people music.

We had to leave Laffy and Vennie at the cottage. That made me a little sad, but Daddy said they could get lost and that would make us sadder.

"Our friends are over there!" Isla said. "At the bounce house!"

I stretched my neck to see where she was pointing, and I saw them. "Can we go over there and play?"

"Sure. Just be careful," Daddy said.

Isla and I let go of their hands and ran for our friends. This was going to be so fun!

Hallie was standing on the bounce house step holding the flap open for us. "Take your shoes off and come inside!"

Isla and I kicked off our *Frozen* Crocs and crawled up onto the step and into the bounce house. It was the big kind that had a bouncy room and tunnels to a ball pit and a rope ladder to a slide and even a tunnel underneath! We followed Hallie through the bounce room and crawled through a circle opening to get to the ball pit. All of our new friends were already there.

Isla and I jumped in, and Harlan and Archer moved to stand in front of the entrance tunnels to block other kids from coming in.

"Okay, people!" Isla shouted. Everyone looked at her. I was glad she was taking charge. She was good at that kind of thing. She lowered her voice. "There are two assistant camp counselors watching the kids' area, so we have to be careful they don't hear us. Hallie, did you bring the note?"

Hallie reached into a pocket on her dress and pulled out a piece of paper. "I did!"

"And Bianca, you got your daddy's key to the shack?"

"It's in my pocket!" she confirmed.

"Okay." Isla waited for everyone to lean toward her. "The cake is on a table with the gifts. In a little bit, everyone who is coming should be here, and that is usually where they go first. Right, Amelie?"

"Right!" I said. "And it's usually decorated like a tuxedo. For the groom. Because the bride gets to pick the fancy cake on her wedding day."

"I saw it," Bianca said. "It *does* look like a tuxedo!"

"Good!" Isla said. "And it's close to the shack, so we can move it quick. But we need a distraction."

"I brought my Frisbee again," Archer said. "I can throw it into the water and get grown-ups to help."

Paisley piped up. "I don't know. They might not want to get their clothes wet."

"That's true," Nicki agreed. "You could throw it at the fire. It's just a Cliff Walk Resort one, right? Meggie or Mr. JC would probably give you a new one."

"That's a good idea," said Isla. "And you should cry when it burns. Then all the grown-ups will feel bad and try to make you feel better, and they won't even think about the gift table!"

"I can try," Archer said. "I'll fake cry if my eyes don't work."

"Good," Isla nodded. "Let's play until it gets dark. Then wait for my signal, okay? I'll yell 'wheeeee!' and go down the slide. Then meet me in the tunnel underneath it."

"Okay!" all the kids shouted.

We bounced and climbed and slid down the slide so many times! There were other kids there, including some of Group 1's little brothers and sisters. Archer's mom, Sarah, was there watching his little sister, so I told Isla we needed to distract her, too. Paisley said she would tell her about Archer's Frisbee and try to lead them toward the fire.

Just after dark, Isla climbed the slide. I was right behind her. "Let's do this together," I said.

"We can race!"

"Yes!" We got into position and sat at the top next to each other. "Ready?" I asked.

"Go!"

"Wheeeeeeeeeeeeeeeeeeeeeeeeeeeeeeeeeeee!" Isla was so loud!

We landed at the bottom and ran around to the tunnel and snuck inside. Only Group 1 was in there and none of their brothers and sisters. Isla reminded them of the plan, and then we were off!

Bianca raced to the shack. Archer and Harlan ran to get his Frisbee. Nicki and Paisley ran toward the fire. Hallie came with us.

The music changed just then to a dance called the Cupid Shuffle, and so many of the grown-ups went to the dance floor. What good luck for us!

Isla and I reached the gift table. There it was, the tuxedo cake, in a white box with a clear plastic screen on top so you could see it inside! We got on either side of it and slid our hands under the corner of the cake's box. Once it was clear of the table, Hallie set the note down and put a rock on top of it so it wouldn't blow away.

We were almost to the shack when the wind blew really hard.

"Look out!" Bianca yelled.

I looked up. Archer's Frisbee was coming straight at us! And so was Archer!

Isla screamed. I screamed. Archer ran right into us. The cake fell to the ground. I fell on top of it. Isla got bumped and fell, too.

"Quick! Throw the Frisbee toward the fire!" Harlan hissed to him.

Archer recovered the Frisbee and gave it another toss, and it hit the pretty wedding arch that was set up near the fire. Someone's big dog ran after it and crashed into the arch, and it fell toward the fire. Then it was burning!

I'd squooshed the cake! The arch was on fire.

Everything kept happening so fast!

And it was all my fault.

My heart began to beat so fast it hurt. "Isla," I whispered. "I need to go. *Now!*"

Her eyes went wide, and she grabbed my hand. She knew what to do when my panic came.

But she held onto me too tightly. I had to pull away.

I ran and ran until I got to the stairs.

"Amelie! Wait!"

But I couldn't.

I just couldn't.

I ran and I ran and I ran until I reached the stairs. *Up up up,* I chanted inside my head for each new step.

When I reached the top, I took a deep breath to look for cars, then ran some more.

Chapter Nine

ZAKI

One minute I was trying to outperform Monty with my Cupid Shuffling, and the next I was helping to pull the arch from the fire and shucking off my shirt to help tamp out the flames.

Was that the best idea? No. But it was the first thing I thought of.

Behind me, Rodeo and another dog were barking, kids were crying, and around me, shirtless hockey players and Monty—who were taking my lead—were working to stifle the burning flowers covering the arch. Within a few minutes, the flames were out, and it looked like the structure was still intact. It would just need a new paint job.

I grinned at my teammates with pride. Don't let anyone ever tell you that a hockey player won't give the shirt off his back for a good cause.

"Zaki!" I barely registered Arwyn's voice as I stood and wiped soot from my face with the back of my hand.

I turned, my satisfaction transforming into concern when I saw the terror on her face.

"Zaki! The girls are missing! We have to *go!*"

"What? How?"

She pointed to the resort's head of security, talking into a radio. "They ran off! Jack is calling all staff to look for them, and Damon is coordinating with the police!"

"I don't understand. They were just in the bounce house. We waved to them just before the Cupid Shuffle. Where did they go? There are two staff members monitoring the kids' area."

"Two teenagers who are *very* panicked right now. Hallie said something about a prank gone wrong and Amelie falling on the cake, and Zaki—they're *gone!*"

I scanned the beach and tried to stay calm. There wasn't enough light to see much of anything. "They couldn't have gone far. Amelie probably wanted to hide because she was embarrassed." I couldn't wait to hear how she'd fallen on the cake, which was supposed to be on the gift table.

Arwyn shook her head. "Hallie told Damon she saw them running up the stairs. He took off after the girls, then told her to tell Jack, then me, everything she knew. It sounded like Amelie had a panic attack. *C'mon!*"

She didn't wait for me. As I ran after her toward the stairs we'd just descended about an hour ago, I pulled on what was left of my short-sleeved button-down.

Had the girls crossed the busy road to the resort? Or had they turned right onto the Cliff Walk toward the diner? I prayed they didn't go left. The only thing going that way separating them from a rocky fall off the cliffside was a short metal guardrail.

Don't think the worst.

The girls had spent the first five and a half years of their lives living in Denver and Montreal. They knew how to walk and cross busy streets.

But those streets were well-lit, the traffic was slower, and they always had an adult holding their hand.

Arwyn stopped running just short of the stairs. "Go ahead of me. You're faster!"

I looked up. Flynn was almost to the top, followed by Meggie and two of her bridesmaids. A quick glance down the beach revealed figures ascending the other set of stairs that led up toward the diner and shops.

I sprinted up the steps, taking them two at a time. At the top, two police SUVs with their lights flashing blocked the road.

Damon was helping an officer set up a roadblock with cones as another policeman held up traffic with a stop sign on a pole.

I had no idea what to do next. Follow Flynn and the ladies across the street? Turn right and meet up with the group at the next set of steps?

Arwyn caught up to me just then, panting. Through her gasps for air, she called out to Damon. “Which way?”

Damon turned toward us. “We think they ran up to the resort! I didn’t get up here in time to see if they crossed, but these guys here came from two different directions and didn’t see them. We’ve got a search party getting together along the road, just in case.”

Arwyn’s phone rang as we crossed the street. “It’s Meggie!” She answered the call and said “mm-hmm” three times. “We’ll meet you there!”

“Where?” I asked, frantic.

“She thinks they might be hiding in the barn. She’s sending one of the security guys to meet up with us and drive us there.”

Up the lane, I could just make out a golf cart heading for us. “I can’t believe they’d get that far so fast. And in the dark.”

“They’re your girls, Zaki. Don’t you know how fit they are? They skate lightning-quick and are super strong from ballet. Did you forget they each either won or tied for first place in all the kindergarten running races on field day? Amelie even set a school record in the twenty-yard dash.”

Despite my panic, I couldn’t help but beam with pride. I’d watched them run those races and was so proud of them.

But running from their *problems* was not okay.

Being a parent is hard. When we found them—and I knew we would—I’d have to find a way to reassure them they were safe and loved but still let them know what they did was wrong. If this was all a result of a prank gone awry, as Hallie said, they would have to apologize. But was that enough of a consequence for six-year-olds?

I gestured for Arwyn to hop into the front seat of the golf cart, but she shook her head and sat in the second row with me. She squeezed my hand and called her mother to explain the situation.

“Someone’s already checked out the cottage, and there are

staffers searching the area. Meggie thinks they went to the barn. Can you think of any other place they might hide?" Arwyn closed her eyes and squeezed my hand harder. "Okay. We'll see you there."

She turned to me. "Jack already called her, and she's almost at the barn. She said she told him exactly what she thinks of the camp staff's negligence and recommended more rigorous safety training."

It hadn't even occurred to me yet that the staff had fallen short of keeping our girls safe.

The stables loomed ahead on the path, lit by old-fashioned streetlamps. As we neared it, I jumped out of the golf cart and ran at top speed for the open barn door. All the lights were on inside.

I stopped to listen at the entrance, heard the sound of my girls crying and froze.

Chapter Ten

ARWYN

When the golf cart slowed to a stop, I slid out of my seat and walked to Zaki. He was standing at the entrance to the barn, shoulders slumped with his hands in his pockets. In the distance, I heard the girls crying. Why hadn't he gone right to them?

"Hey." I slipped my hand into one of his pockets and took hold of his fingers. "Are you okay?"

He shook his head and wiped his eyes with his other hand. "Why did they run? Why didn't they come to me? What do I say to them?"

I rested my head on the singed shoulder of his shirt. "You remind them that you love them more than anything. That nothing they could ever do or say would make you stop loving them. That it's okay to make mistakes. Reassure them you know they weren't trying to hurt anyone but always try to think about what can go wrong when they plan a prank. That there will be consequences—in this case, the cake, the arch, and a bunch of shirts."

He smiled. "Thank you."

"Anytime."

We walked hand in hand past the horses to the tack room. Isla and Amelie clung to Meggie, crying into her dress as she sat on a bale of hay. Standing off to the side were Flynn; two of Meggie's

bridesmaids, Maddie and Mellie; and my mom. Laffy and Vennie sat leashed at her feet, tails wagging.

I let go of Zaki's hand and approached the girls, giving each of their backs a light rub. "You're okay. Your daddy is here." I glanced up, and there he was, wearing a soft, protective expression. His eyes held the kind of warmth that cocooned you like a weighted comforter—gentle and secure—but I caught that hint of pain that was tearing him up on the inside. The slight lift of his brows, the way he pressed his lips together—everything about him on the outside radiated quiet reassurance and an air of maturity he didn't often reveal in public.

Meggie nudged them off her lap and stood. Zaki crouched and opened his arms. They ran to him with tears clinging to their lashes and streaking down their cheeks, and he lifted them off the ground. Their little legs closed around his waist, and I noticed their bare, dirty feet. They'd come all this way with no shoes?!

"Daddy, I pranked wrong and ruined the cake!" Amelie wailed. "And then the fire!"

"It was my idea, too!" Isla cried. "All the camp pranks started because of me."

"Daddy! Your shirt!" Amelie cried. "Did you burn in the fire?"

"No. I used my shirt to help put it out." He reached around Isla and poked a finger through a hole where a button used to be. "It's a new style. I kinda like it. Natural air-conditioning. What do you think?" He sat down on the hay bale and settled a girl on each leg so that they faced each other.

I'd tell him later what *I* thought.

My eyes couldn't help but linger—just for a second—on the way Zaki's shirt clung in places and hung loose in others, its hem scorched, collar frayed, and little holes scattered across the fabric like confetti. He should've looked ridiculous. But sitting there, with both girls curled into him, their cheeks streaked with tears, he looked like the hero of an action movie—messy but solid and steady. There was a rawness to the moment, rugged and tender, and it hit me low in my chest. That sharp, quiet ache of love I could never quite name but always felt like falling and finding home at the same time.

The girls weren't impressed with his antics. Isla and Amelie just stared at him, incredulous. Then they laughed.

I let out a long breath.

They were going to be okay.

Mom handed me the leashes. "I'll run back to the cottage and get them shoes," she whispered.

"Thanks," I whispered back.

"I'll wait outside," Flynn said. "Glad they're okay, Marshy." He clapped Zaki's back.

"I'll be out in a few minutes, Flynn," Meggie said. "Please call Kat and tell her to let everyone at the party know they're okay." She turned to us. "My friends and I were telling the girls about the time we got trapped in the tunnel underneath this barn. It's been filled in, so it's not a danger anymore. But we were missing for a long time, and no one knew where we were. The whole town looked for us, just like they were looking for them. Everyone was so scared and worried that something bad might have happened to us."

Amelie wailed louder. "I am so bad! I'm so sorry, Daddy! We ruined the wedding."

"And everyone is mad at us! Our new friends are never going to want to play with us again." Isla sniffled.

"Hey," Zaki said. "Whoa, whoa. Hang on a second. Listen, my sweet little pranksters. You did not ruin the party, just the cake. No one's mad at you. I promise. Mistakes happen, and believe me —this one is going to be a story we'll tell for years. The arch will be okay. It'll just need to be repainted for tomorrow."

"Can we help?" Isla asked, lifting her head to look at Meggie. "I'm a good painter."

Meggie nodded. "Of course."

I sat down next to Zaki. "First things first—I know you're both very upset, but are you okay? Can I look at your feet?"

Isla sobbed, "I cut my toe, Wynnie. It hurts a little. But we *did* ruin the party, didn't we?"

"No, sweetie," I assured her. "It just stopped for a little bit so everyone could look for you and your sister. How are your feet, Amelie?"

"Dirty."

I held in a chuckle.

"I'll get the first aid kit," Maddie offered.

"And some nice warm, soapy towels," Mellie added.

"Thanks." I stroked Amelie's hair. "I know you got scared. That's okay. You know you can come to us, right?"

She hung her head. "I didn't think. I just ran."

"And I ran after her because I didn't want her to be alone," Isla said.

"You're a great sister," I said, reaching over Zaki to squeeze her hand.

Zaki echoed my observation, then gently told them all the things I'd suggested at the barn door just moments earlier.

Maddie and Mellie returned and insisted on washing the girls' feet—and their faces. Laffy and Vennie yipped their approval and tried to help. The girls laughed, and I had to pull the dogs away while Mellie bandaged Isla's toe.

When they were all cleaned up, Meggie knelt in front of the girls. "Do you know what's more important than parties, wedding arches, bonfires, or even cakes?"

"Cake's pretty important," Isla said.

Amelie nodded seriously. "Really important."

Meggie laughed lightly. "It is. But it's not as important as your family and friends. No matter what happens, no matter how big of a mess things turn into, your parents and family and us friends —who are like family to you—are always going to love you. Forever and ever. That's not going to change, no matter how many cakes you squish or how many arches you set on fire."

Zaki agreed. "Just like I said. And you know, you're not the first ones to cause a little cake chaos. I once tripped over a plant and landed on top of *the* actual wedding cake at a teammate's reception. I was stuck in frosting up to my elbows."

The girls giggled. "No!" Isla exclaimed. "Did you hide?"

"Nah. But I did make several phone calls to local bakeries and offer them a lot of money to bring a new cake. And then someone told me that only the top layers of the cake were actually cake and the rest of it was fake and frosted for decoration. The *real* cake everyone was going to eat was a sheet cake in the kitchen!"

"Oh, Daddy!" Amelie giggled. "You got lucky!"

"Yep. And you know what? We all laughed about it later. Just like Flynn and Meggie will. What matters is that you're safe and that you promise to always tell us when something goes wrong, okay?"

"We'll always help you," I said. "There's nothing you can't tell us. We're a family, and family sticks together—even when things get messy."

Amelie smiled. "Like when Vennie got into the peanut butter because I thought Isla covered it and Isla thought I covered it but nobody covered it and he made a mess in the RV?"

Zaki grinned. "Exactly like that."

I smiled too. "Now, how about we head back to the party? Molly texted me that Sadie from the diner is frosting a new cake just like the one you crushed. Apparently, she has a backup in the walk-in refrigerator, ready to be frosted if needed."

Isla clapped. "Really?!"

I nodded. "Really."

"We got lucky, too, Daddy," Amelie said.

"You did. Let's go back to the party. And no more pranks tonight, okay?"

"Okay!"

"Group hug?"

"Group hug!"

Chapter Eleven

ZAKI

After another apology from the girls to Flynn and Meggie, we returned to the party. The girls' fears about their friends being mad at them were erased when they all ran to give them hugs and told them how glad they were to see them unhurt. Every one of those kids had something nice or encouraging to say, and within minutes, they were playing like it hadn't happened.

We left the party earlier than we'd planned. The girls would need a full night's sleep so that we could meet up with Molly at dawn to repaint the arch.

The girls and I snuck out early the next morning so we wouldn't disturb Arwyn before her already-too-early alarm. When we arrived at the yard off the main lodge Saturday morning, JC was there, too, and we made it an entertaining time for the girls, hoping to erase whatever bad feelings might remain in their little hearts. After we sanded the wood, JC did his best impression of Bob Ross, exaggerating his paintbrush strokes and earning endless giggles from the girls. My parents brought in breakfast from the diner, and Alyce joined us all. JC's parting words to the girls was that the burning arch fiasco would be remembered as a "happy accident."

Later that afternoon, we took a shuttle from the resort to the church for the 5 p.m. wedding ceremony. The wedding arch, freshly painted and flowered, was set up on the church lawn, where the ceremony was to take place. Meggie and Flynn's woodsy rustic theme was a perfect fit for what I knew about her, featuring burlap table runners, lantern centerpieces, and a s'mores bar, which we'd made the twins promise to stay away from unless a grownup was there to help.

After the nuptials and bridal party introductions, guests mingled, enjoying the perfect weather. While the band—Harbor Lights, a popular country pop group—took a break and the buffet dinner was being set up, Arwyn, the girls, and I headed toward our table to retrieve their sweaters. The warm day was cooling off, and there was a bit of a chill in the air.

"Zaki Marsch!"

I turned and grinned. Daisy Mae Saunders—er, *Meemaw*—was headed straight for us. It was hard to believe she was over ninety years old from the way she moved.

"Well, well, look who's here! My two favorite fire-starters! That was exciting last night, wasn't it?" The girls' eyes went wide, and Meemaw laughed. "Oh, I'm just messing with you, sugarplums. Weddings need a little drama—it keeps things interesting. Why, back in my day, a wedding wasn't complete without a chicken running through the reception or a cousin fainting during the vows. And good it happened at the rehearsal. Tonight should be perfect."

"I'm pretty sure you've caused your fair share of chaos at weddings too, Meemaw," Arwyn quipped.

Meemaw clutched her heart, as if offended. "Me? Chaos? Never! I'm a perfect guest. It's not my fault if my dance moves were so impressive they once knocked over a punch bowl or two." She winked, and the girls giggled.

Arwyn turned to the girls. "Isla, Amelie, meet Daisy Mae Saunders. You can call her Meemaw."

"I'm glad you two are laughing," she told the twins. "Don't trouble your hearts at all about what happened last night. When you've been to as many weddings as I have, you learn that it's not about perfection—it's about the stories you'll tell later."

I lightly patted my girls on the back. "See? Even Meemaw thinks a little chaos is part of the fun."

Meggie and Flynn strolled over. She smiled warmly at all of us and addressed the girls. "For the record, I'm so glad you're here. This wedding weekend—and this whole amazing week—wouldn't have been the same without you."

"Really?" Amelie said.

"Really," Meggie confirmed.

Meemaw leaned in conspiratorially. "Now, who wants to help me sneak an extra slice of that cake after everyone's been served? I've got a feeling this one is going to be better than last night's replacement!"

Amelie twisted around to look at me. "Can we, Daddy?"

I laughed. "As long as you only take one slice each."

Meemaw grinned. "Stick with me, and I'll teach you how to snag cake and avoid getting caught. First rule: Always smile and act innocent. Second rule … I'll tell you that later. How about you tell your parents to go dance and I'll keep an eye on you for a bit? Have you tried my deviled potatoes yet?"

"Deviled potatoes?" I asked.

"Tater skins stuffed with creamy Southern potato salad. Try a bite, and you'll want the recipe, sure as I know these girls want to know my secret."

"Daddy, Wynnie, please go!" Isla begged.

"I guess we're out, Wynna-bun."

Arwyn slipped her arm into mine and led me toward the dance floor. "Molly said she's one hundred percent trustworthy, kind, and capable."

"I believe that," I said.

As the sun set over the church grounds, its rays cast the dance floor in a golden glow. The music slowed, and couples began swaying together.

I pulled Arwyn into my arms and lowered my head so that we were cheek to cheek.

"I could dance like this all night," I sighed.

"Me too."

I closed my eyes, and we melded into each other, swaying to several songs and forgetting about everything—and everyone—else.

"Daddy!" Isla tugged at my suit jacket, and her lips fell into a disapproving frown, like a teacher who'd suffered through one of my schoolboy pranks. "Meemaw says to tell you you're not married yet and you should leave room for the Holy Spirit."

"What does that mean?" Amelie asked.

I barked a laugh. "I'll tell you when you're older. Right now, it means you two get to dance with us. May we have this dance, princesses?"

"Both of us at the same time? And Wynnie, too?" Isla tapped her chin.

"Of course. My arms are big enough to hold all three of you. Each of you girls stand on one of my feet and hold on to my waist, and Wynnie will stand behind you. Like a sandwich."

The girls giggled as they climbed onto my feet and tried to balance. Once they were secure, Arwyn positioned herself, and I hugged all three of them to me, leaving a little bit of space for the girls to breathe. Being the little wigglers they were, they quickly decided the family dance wasn't for them and asked if they could go dance with their friends, who, from the looks of it, were doing some kind of dance-off by the stage.

The music stopped, and the band took the stage again. Apparently, they were from Crane's Cove and good friends with all of the locals here.

"Macy! Sing 'Meant to Be'!" JC shouted from the other side of the dance floor. He'd sung a duet with her earlier and wowed the crowd.

Show-off.

The lead singer smiled out on the crowd. "I was going to start with something more upbeat. What do you think, friends? Should I take JC's request?"

The guests cheered. I wasn't familiar with the song, but right now, anything slow meant more time holding Arwyn.

"It's our song," Taz said, squeezing Maddie to his side. "Right, babe?"

Maddie blushed and nodded, then turned her face into his chest like she'd rather be anywhere else.

They reminded me of a couple I knew very well.

I kissed the top of Arwyn's head, sure that she could sympathize with Maddie.

"All right, then," Macy decided with a conciliatory smile. "As some of you know, this song is very personal to me. I wrote it as I was coming out of a hard time. I hope it inspires you that no matter how challenging life can be, there's happiness waiting on the other side. You just have to claim it and take it."

"Good advice," Arwyn whispered. "May I have this dance?"

"I'm supposed to ask that," I teased. "Do you plan to steal my dance moves, too?"

"Nope, just your heart," she replied.

"No can do." I shook my head.

"No?"

"You already have it."

"And you have mine." She tilted her chin up, and I met her lips with a slow kiss. Then I tightened my arms around her and focused on the words of the song.

I'd become steady like the shoreline, safe and sure
You were wild like the waves, crashing through my world
Never thought our paths would cross this way
But God had a plan, and He made us stay

I didn't see it coming, but now I understand
Love works in ways that we don't have to plan

You're the fire, I'm the calm
You're the storm, I'm the dawn
Somehow, we fit like a melody
You make me brave, I hold you close
With faith, we found the way to go
It's crazy, but it's pure and clear like a morning daisy
You and me were meant to be

From the moment of my darkness, you took my hand
We didn't know forever was part of God's plan
Now with two little hearts running at our side
Love looks a lot like faith in real life

I didn't see it coming, but now I understand

Love works in ways that we don't have to plan

As she repeated the chorus, some of the guests started to sing along.

Through the bonfires, through the rain
Through the laughter, through the flames
We were never lost, no, we were found
God was writing love all around

She sang the chorus again and I tried to commit every word to memory. Then the last two lines came, and I almost lost my composure.

I was steady like the shoreline, safe and sure
You were wild like the waves … and I love you more.

Wow.

Those lyrics could have been written for Arwyn and me. I was the wild waves upon her shore, and she provided a loving home for the girls and I when we were the most lost. And the morning daisy bit? How had I never heard this song before? Daisies had become our thing. I tipped Arwyn's chin up so I could look into her eyes. A silent promise passed between us.

Meemaw sniffed behind us, breaking the moment. "Oh, I'm not crying. There's just too much love in the air, and it got in my eyes."

Molly was with her, and she grinned. "Sure, Meemaw. Want me to grab you another blueberry sweet tea to help with that?"

Meemaw winked at her. "Make it a double."

Chapter Twelve

ARWYN

The morning sun glowed golden over the cove, casting a warm shimmer on the gentle waves lapping playfully at the shore. A scattering of boats bobbed lazily in the distance, their sails white against the horizon. The sky, a brilliant powder blue, stretched endless and cloudless, and the salty breeze carried the trademark refreshing scent of the Atlantic. Seagulls squawked overhead, their cries mingling with the rhythmic and steady hush of the tide. In the water, the lighthouse served as a silent witness to the day's promises.

Blooming beach roses and sun-dried seaweed blended with the salty air, while the occasional puff of warm wind carried a faint scent of blueberry scones from the diner. The breakfast treat called to mind that fateful cinnamon roll that ruined my dress during a game of coffee shop keep-away. I would have kept avoiding Zaki forever if our friends hadn't intervened when he needed a nanny for his girls. I'd done something I'd vowed to never do—judge a book by its cover or, in this case, a pro athlete by his playful disaster. Zaki was loud, excitable, and held a firm air of self-confidence—everything I was sure I'd dislike.

I'd been wrong, of course. He *was* all those things, but he was so much more. He'd broken my prejudicial stereotypes, led me into the unknown, and encouraged me to be vulnerable. I was no longer terrified of how much space he took up or how loud and crazy he could get. He inspired me to take risks, let my hair down —and even, on occasion, wear jeans.

I chuckled to myself at that last thought. My younger self wouldn't have believed it, nor the fact that I was hopelessly in love with a sporty guy. Especially one as impulsive as Zaki. But I'd learned impulsivity wasn't always bad; it often led to beautiful discoveries, picture-perfect moments, and unforgettable memories.

Like yesterday, when he showed up after the tea party with a silver daisy-chain tiara. It was the perfect accessory for my hair since I'd decided to save my great-grandmother's veil for our church wedding.

The bodice was reimagined from my mother's early-nineties gown. I'd kept the puffed sleeves but toned them down and removed much of the lace appliqué over the satin, keeping it to the heart-shaped neckline and down the center. The full skirt from the early 1960s had only reached my ankles, but once I added the scalloped trim, it grazed my toes at full length. I'd use fabric from the skirt of Mom's dress to make the train in the coming weeks.

I'd secretly embroidered a daisy at the nape of my neck, where Zaki liked to brush soft kisses when I wore my hair up. I shivered, thinking of the kisses we'd share later and what he might think when he found the floral symbol of our love.

In my hands I held two bouquets of salt mist roses and daisies. Yesterday morning, after the arch painting, the florist arrived and our moms helped each of the girls construct and tie one half of the bouquet, which I would give to them to keep after the ceremony. One bouquet was wrapped in pale blue to match Isla's dress and Amelie's in mint green to match hers. They'd worn their hair down and opted to wear both the tiaras and Taylor's bows, which wouldn't surprise anyone that knew them.

As I followed them down the wooden steps, my gaze swept over the small crowd of friends and family, seeking out and finding Zaki. Our eyes locked across the distance, and my fingers gripped the railing just a little tighter with my non-bouquet hand to keep my balance. Last night had been the first we'd spent apart since the road trip began, and his absence in the cottage kept me awake.

He wore a tailored tan suit that hugged him in all the right places—familiar, like his usual pre-game attire, but softer somehow, and the absence of his tie made it feel more intimate. Instead, his crisp white shirt was open at the collar, its first two buttons undone, just enough to make my pulse speed up. The jacket clung to his broad shoulders and those strong, safe arms I knew so well, its fabric stretching just slightly across his chest with one single shiny button holding it all together. His typically tousled auburn hair was parted to the side and coaxed into a style that tamed his curls but still gave off an air of playfulness.

Oh my. I couldn't look away. Straight twenty-first century dapper he was, and I nearly swooned. This was the man I loved—dashing, unpredictable, and one hundred percent Zaki—and in mere minutes, one hundred percent mine.

When he turned to speak to Ryan, we lost the connection, and my heart hammered with its absence and the anticipation of closing the distance between us.

Framing him and the pastor was a natural arch constructed of driftwood, adorned with wildflowers in soft blues, creams, and blush pinks. I could just make out a sprinkling of daisies tucked into two nautical knots, one on each side. Did the structure belong to the resort? The church? Or had someone made it for us?

When I reached the bottom of the stairs, Zaki's eyes were on me again. I slid out of my shoes and stepped onto the sun-warmed sand to begin the walk toward him down the short aisle. Flowing white sashes fluttered gently, knotted to the aisle-side chairs and connected by daisy chains. Ahead of me, Isla and Amelie scattered shiny seashells and rose petals on either side of my path. The sparkles caught the sunlight, adding a touch of magic underfoot.

Off to the side on a teak platform, Harbor Lights provided the soundtrack. That was a fun surprise! Macy's two brothers strummed acoustic guitars as she finished up the lyrics to the wedding version of "Ordinary" by Alex Warren.

Laffy and Vennie sat proudly at Zaki's feet, each wearing a

circlet of coordinating wildflowers around their necks. He handed their leashes to the girls, and they turned to join their grandparents in the front row off Zaki's shoulder. On the bride's side of the aisle were my mom, Shanna and her family, including her parents who babysat me after school when I was young and gave me my first job. Our mutual friends were scattered on both sides, and the sheer number of them who traveled to be here for our last-minute nuptials brought tears to my eyes.

The tears spilled over as I met Zaki's gaze again. It was intense and felt like it reached my soul.

"I'm the luckiest guy in the world," he whispered. "I'm marrying you twice."

"You are. But I am, too. I'm glad I said yes."

"Both times?

"Both times."

The song ended, and Ryan welcomed everyone to the ceremony. Our guests sat, and I noticed Mom wiping at her eyes. Twice in two days! She really was getting sentimental in her (not very) old age. "Our bride and groom have written their own vows. Go ahead, Zaki."

He didn't hesitate for a beat. "Arwyn, from the moment we met—the second time—I felt something shift in me. I chalked it up to friendship, but it was more than that. A connection I couldn't explain. A feeling that you may be the key to my complete healing. I couldn't explain it, and I dare not speak it. But then, after a time, I saw the way you looked at me and my girls—with your soft, kind, observant eyes that reflected your gentle, loving heart—and somehow, it hit me like a puck to the head that you were about to brighten our world.

"You stepped into the chaos of the twins' giggles, crazy dogs, and life under a microscope with an ease and poise that you didn't think you had in you, but you wanted to be there for us. I knew we'd each found the missing parts of ourselves. Your quiet strength and my loud chaos have only ever brought out the best in each other. When you told me you loved me, I felt more joy than I could have imagined. And you didn't just love me—you *saw* me. You listened when I didn't have words. You steadied me when life kept threatening to knock me off-balance.

"I promise to love you and protect your heart with the same fierceness I protect Isla and Amelie. I'll make you laugh when life gets too heavy, hold your hand when you feel alone, give you space when you need it, and never stop choosing you—ever. You are my safe place, my unexpected joy, my forever adventure, my lighthouse beam in the storm. Together, wherever we end up, we'll build our home on a solid foundation of love. And I promise, no pranks in the house."

There was a jaunty quirk to his lips, and then they spread into a wide grin. I couldn't help but smile back. He'd spoken all the words I'd hoped to hear, wanted to hear, needed to hear.

Words that told me I was wanted and that I *fit*. With him, with his girls, and in their life.

Ryan prompted me to speak my vows, and I swallowed the lump that'd been growing steadily since Zaki's first sentence. I'd worked all week on memorizing my words, but I was nervous I'd forget something important.

"Zaki, you came into my life like an unexpected check to the boards. I'll admit, your chaos was not something I wanted to be around. But as I grew to know you, you didn't seem so chaotic. You aim to live life to the fullest, and I admire that. At home, your persona was comforting, grounding, and everything I could ever have hoped to find in a life partner.

"I didn't expect love to look like what we've created, but every bit of it is perfect. You're steady like a well-brewed cup of tea, bold in your convictions, and gentle in the way you love. You've taught me that love isn't always fireworks—it's warm hands holding mine, it's being known and accepted completely, and it's showing up every single day and being present in a way I've never been. I promise to love your girls like they've always been mine. I promise to make space for you when you need it, to keep choosing you over and over, and to keep showing up with open arms. I promise I will be there waiting at the end of every road trip and be there for you in any and every other way you need me. Always."

And now he was crying, too.

"I believe the girls have something to say," Ryan said.

"Yes, we do!" Isla replied.

"It's in my wedding diary!" Amelie explained.

She had a wedding diary?

As the girls approached us, Zaki pulled a small, sparkly book from his back pocket and handed it to her. She turned a few pages.

"Macy, can we please use your microphone?" Isla asked. "The people in the back need to hear this."

There was a tittering of laughter as Macy brought the mic over and handed it to Isla.

"Thank you," she said into it. "Amelie is going to hold her diary, and we are going to read our parts. We would like to thank Hallie and Harlan's mommy Mrs. Shelby for helping us write the rhymes at camp and for fixing Amelie's spelling. And for copying it perfectly when we were done onto the pages so it's easy for us to read it better. She's a writer, you know."

"A very *good* writer," Amelie emphasized. "She helped us make all of our ideas fit." She looked up at Ryan. "Can we start now?"

"Take it away, girls," he said.

Isla began. "'We Love You, Arwyn!' A poem by Isla and Amelie." She looked up at the guests. All eyes were fixed on them. "We used to be a team of five. Just Daddy, us, and our silly doggies! But now there's you, and that's just right, like Olaf warm-hugging Elsa tight."

She paused, then Amelie read from the book. "You're kind like Anna and smart as well. You read us lovely stories to our friends we tell. You braid our hair and sing a little flat, but you know we don't care about that." Amelie tossed her hair over her shoulder and turned to me. "Right?"

"Right," I assured her with a broad grin.

"My turn again," Isla said. "You bake cookies, you read to us at night, and you *always* make the wrongs feel right. You're patient, fun, and super cool—and we're so glad you help us with our school!"

Amelie read the next quatrain. "We love you so much and now you can see, you're the perfect match for our fam-i-ly! Thanks for marrying Daddy and joining our fun family crew. We're so glad you said 'I do!'"

The audience clapped and whistled. "She hasn't said that yet," Isla fretted in a loud whisper.

"But she will," Amelie whispered back. "Right, Wynnie?"

"You bet!" I assured her. There was no doubt in my mind.

When the applause ended, Ryan bent forward. "Girls, do you have the rings?"

They reached into the pockets I'd sewn into the seams of their dresses and handed him the two boxes. He removed the rings and handed the boxes back to the girls. When they were back in their seats, he continued the ceremony.

"Zaki and Arwyn, having declared your love through your vows, we now come to the exchange of rings—symbols of the unending love and commitment you share. These circles are reminders that your love has no beginning and no end. As you wear these rings, may they constantly remind you of the promises you've made today. Zaki, please take Arwyn's hand, place the ring on her finger, and repeat after me."

Zaki slipped the ring on my finger and lifted my hands to his lips, brushing a light kiss over my knuckles.

I'm pretty sure our new Crane's Cove friends in the back row heard my swoony sigh.

Zaki repeated Ryan's words. "Arwyn, with this ring, I give you my heart. I promise to love you, honor you, cherish you, and stand by you in all seasons of life. This is my promise to you."

Ryan said the words again, and it was my turn to make the promise. I gently pushed Zaki's wedding band onto his finger. "Zaki, with this ring, I give you my heart. I promise to love you, honor you, cherish you, and stand by you in all seasons of life. This is my promise to you."

"Beautifully done," Ryan whispered for only us to hear. "Ephesians 4:2-3 calls for us to be completely humble and gentle; to be patient, bearing with one another in love. To make every effort to keep the unity of the Spirit through the bond of peace. Marriage is a beautiful time when two souls start to share one heart. Now, Zaki, do you take Arwyn to be your lawfully wedded wife, to have and to hold, in joy and in sorrow, in sickness and in health, to love, honor, and cherish in all the days and ways to come, for all the days of your life?"

I expected Zaki to grin, but the expression on his face was that of pure sincerity. "I do."

"And Arwyn, do you take Zaki to be your lawfully wedded husband, to have and to hold, in joy and in sorrow, in sickness and in health, to love, honor, and cherish in all the days and ways to come, for all the days of your life?"

"I do."

Zaki didn't wait for Ryan to pronounce us wed; I heard the words as my now husband's hand cupped my cheek and his lips met mine in the tenderest of kisses, the kind that set butterflies loose and rendered every muscle weak.

The guests cheered, and Isla and Amelie returned the two halves of my bouquet to me for our journey together up the aisle. We bent down to wrap our arms around them and squeezed them in a warm hug that Olaf himself would be envious of.

Epilogue

ZAKI

After a fun—and prankless—party on the beach, Arwyn and I climbed the wooden steps to the awaiting carriage at street level. Elvis the horse stood proudly in front of the nineteenth-century double-seater, ready to be driven by Easton, who was clad in a suit with tails and a top hat. Our luggage for our overnight stay was inside. We'd travel in the buggy down the road to the marina and board a boat to the lighthouse. Isla and Amelie would walk there with my parents, Alyce, and our guests for the big send-off, then ride in the carriage back to the resort with their camp friends.

After helping Arwyn up into the rig, I climbed up beside her and rested my arm on top of the seatback. She settled in against me, and the moment her face turned toward mine, I stole a kiss. The journey to the marina was all too short, and moments later we were disembarking to say goodbye to our friends and family.

We hugged the girls goodbye first. "Bye, Daddy! Bye, Wynnie!" Isla waved as she sprinted to the carriage.

"Don't fall in the water," Amelie advised, then took off after her sister.

I laughed as Easton gave them boosts into the carriage. They settled on the forward-facing seat to await their friends, who were just coming into view on the Cliff Walk path.

My dad shook my hand and pulled me in for a hug. "Enjoy

your night. We're so happy for you. You deserve all the happiness in the world, and so do the girls."

"Thanks, Dad."

I hugged my mom next. "I'll have my phone on if there are any issues."

"We'll figure it out," she said. "You enjoy your night with your bride. We'll see you after breakfast."

Arwyn finished hugging her mom, and we switched places. "Alyce," I said. "I'm so glad we could do this while you were stateside."

"Me too," she said, and hugged me close. "You take care of my girl, okay? Otherwise ..."

"You'll take care of me?" I quipped.

She laughed. "You know it."

I grinned and released her. "I promise."

"I know you do. Now get out of here."

"Yes, ma'am."

Hours later, as the sun set, Arwyn and I stood on the lighthouse balcony, arms wrapped around each other. The only sound was that of the rhythmic crash of the waves—a perfect lullaby for the first night of our forever.

I turned to her. "Wynnie?"

"Yeah?"

"I still can't believe you're mine. You're a lighthouse, steady; a light in the darkness, guiding me home. And I'm a tidal wave, restless and unpredictable. But somehow, we work. Standing here with you ... It feels like we've been heading toward this moment forever, even if it's only been a handful of months. You, me, the girls—it's ... everything."

"Well, technically," she teased, "I'm only officially yours as of today. Even though you stole my heart months ago."

I chuckled. "Best day of my life, second only to the twins entering this world." I bent my head toward hers until our foreheads were touching and whispered, "Here's to forever, Wynnabun. Whatever comes next, we've got it covered—together."

Our lips met in a slow, tender kiss, and she pulled away too soon to echo my sentiment. "Together." She kissed me again and then frowned, but her tone was light and teasing. "It's so strange without the girls here to tuck into bed and read a story to. Whatever will we do with ourselves tonight?"

I played with a curl that had escaped from her updo. "Oh, I don't know. I can think of a few things."

"Hmm. Can't collect berries or climb trees here. The time for a picnic lunch has passed. So I assume you have something else on your mind?" she teased, recalling my lines from the meadow.

"Maybe. Wanna cuddle on the couch? No kids or dogs to battle us for cushion space."

"I like how you think."

"Maybe a PG-13 movie?" I suggested.

"Scandalous."

"And then …" I let my words trail off and flashed a mischievous grin.

"And then?" Arwyn's eyes narrowed, challenging me to voice my thought.

I went for it. "You want to make a baby?"

She pulled my face down to hers and kissed me more firmly than ever before.

Taking that as an affirmative, I swept her into my arms and carried her across the deck and inside. Above, the beam from Crane's Light swept the sea, a beacon for our future together.

Forever started tonight.

Thank you for reading my Coffee Loft Collection!

You can find a mini printable of Amelie's Camp Diary, plus other bonus content, on the Freebies page at my website. To receive the password to my bonus library, sign up for my newsletter at KerryEvelyn.com/links. There, you'll also find the deleted prologue to *Sew Matcha in Love*, fun puzzles and printable activities, coloring pages, and a bunch more recipes!

Amelie's Camp Diary

For a fun printable mini book, download the Bonus Epilogue.

This Journal Belongs to:

Amelie Marsch

Pictures by Isla Marsch

Cliff Walk Kids Camp
July 27-31, 2026

Group 1 Sandpipers

Meggie
Noah
Me
Isla
Bianca
Paisley
Hallie
Harlan
Nicki
Archer
Sometimes JC

Families

Bianca
Stella
Lilly
Mommy Caroline
Daddy JC
Cat Vera

Paisley Saunders
Rhett
Mommy Lanie
Daddy Matt

Hallie Saunders
Harlan
Theo
Mommy Shelby
Daddy Damon
Cat Buster
Dog Fenway

Kat Crane
Easton
Little Charley
Katie (coming soon!)

Nicki Engstrom
Noah
Ned
Mommy Jane
Daddy Ryan
Dog Astro

Jamie Dalton
Mommy Molly
Daddy Jack
Dog Rodeo
Turtle Tutty

Archer Miller
Aurora
Mommy Sarah
Daddy Zach

CW Grownups in Charge

JC: Manager
Jordan: Assistant Manager
Caroline: Hospitality
Molly: Event Planner
Mellie: CW Kids
Kat: Horse Trainer
Easton: Vet
Meggie: Assistant Vet
Jack: Security

Field Trips

Marina
Beach
Hike to the Meadow
Trail Ride
Acadia National Park

Fun Snacks

Ants on a Log

Peanut Butter on Celery
Apple Snail

Gummy Worm Mud Pudding

Grape Caterpillars &
Ladybug Tomatoes

Cracker & Cream Cheese
Pretzel Spiders

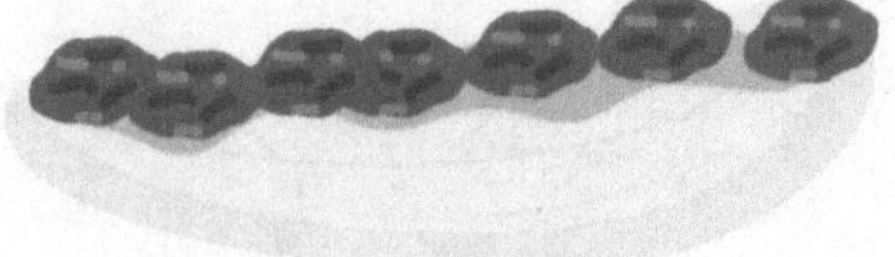

Crafts

Nature Paintbrush Trees
Button Life Preserver
Red Solo Cup Lighthouse
Popsicle Stick Bird Feeder
Yarn Dreamcatcher

Animals: To Eat

Codfish
Haddock
Scrod
Lobster
Shrimp
Oysters
Clams
Cow
Chicken
Turkey
Pig

Animals: Alive

Dogs
Horses
Squirrels
Chipmunks
Butterflies
Dragonflies
Fireflies
Mosquitos
Ants
Seagulls
Tadpoles
Hermit Crabs
Harbor Seals

Horses

Mocha
Buttons
Slade
Elvis
Mack
Bolt
Chopper
Dottie

Pranks

Yucky Sandwich
Oreo Toothpaste
Saltwater in JC's Stanley
Cake Taking

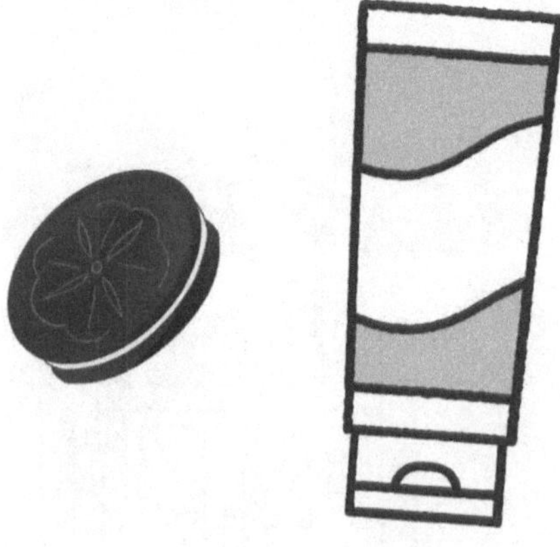

New Words

Bubblah
Pockabook
Fluffahnuttah
Jimmies
Clickah
Cellah
Wicked
Townie

Recipes

Toffee Coffee

Ingredients:

- 1 scoop coffee ice cream
- 1 tbsp butterscotch chips
- 12 ounces hot coffee
- whipped cream
- salted caramel sauce
- 1 tbsp toffee candy crumbles

Instructions:

1. Scoop the ice cream into a mug.
2. Add butterscotch chips.
3. Pour the coffee slowly to melt the ice cream and butterscotch.
4. Top with whipped cream.
5. Drizzle the caramel sauce and sprinkle Heath bits on top.

Toffee Sugar Cookie Fudge

- 1 1/4 cup dry sugar cookie mix
- 1 14-ounce can condensed milk
- 1 cup white chocolate chips
- 1 cup butterscotch chips
- 1/2 cup toffee candy crumbles

Instructions:

1. Combine sugar cookie mix, condensed milk, white chocolate chips, and butterscotch chips in a large pot and mix well.
2. Warm pot over medium heat and stir until mixture is melted and gooey.
3. Line an 8x8 baking dish with parchment paper. Pour mixture into the dish evenly.
4. Top with candy crumbles, pressing them lightly into the mixture.
5. Refrigerate until solid.
6. Slice as desired and serve.

Irish Cream Brownies

Ingredients:

Brownies:

- 1 box 9x13 pan fudge brownie mix (or your favorite homemade brownies)

Frosting:

- ¾ cup unsalted butter, softened
- 3 cups powdered sugar
- 1/3 cup Irish cream liquor

Ganache:

- 3/4 cup semisweet chocolate chips
- 5 tbsp heavy cream
- 1/3 cup Irish cream liquor

Topping:

- 1/4 cup semi-sweet chocolate chips
- 1/4 cup sprinkles mixture (green, orange, white)

Instructions:

1. Prepare brownies according to package or recipe instructions and cool completely.
2. For the frosting, beat the softened butter on medium speed until fluffy. Stir in Irish cream and mix well.
3. Slowly add the powdered sugar, a little at a time, until completely mixed. Beat mixture until soft and fluffy.
4. Spread the frosting over the cooled brownies and refrigerate while making the ganache.
5. For the ganache, combine the heavy cream and Irish cream in a saucepan over medium-high heat and bring to a boil.
6. Remove immediately from the burner and pour over the chocolate chips. Do not stir for 5 minutes.
7. After 5 minutes, whisk the mixture until it's smooth and pour it evenly over the frosted brownies.
8. For the topping, arrange the remaining chocolate chips and sprinkles over the ganache.
9. Let the brownies cool at room temperature for 30 minutes.
10. Refrigerate until set. Cut to desired size and serve.

Xavier & Penny's Wedding Cake

Caramel Buttercream Coffee Cupcakes

Ingredients:

- 1 box of coffee cake mix
- 4 cups powdered sugar
- 1 stick unsalted butter, softened
- 2 tbsp heavy cream
- 1 tsp vanilla extract
- 1/4 tsp sea salt
- 1 bag butterscotch chips
- 1 bottle salted caramel sauce
- 1 tbsp toffee candy bits

Instructions:

1. Prepare your favorite coffee cake recipe and divide into 12 cupcake liners. Cool completely.
2. To make the buttercream, whip the softened butter. Add half of the powdered sugar and whip on high speed. Gradually add the remaining powdered sugar, whipping on low speed until incorporated. Add 1/3 cup salted caramel sauce, vanilla, heavy cream, and salt. Whisk until desired consistency is achieved. Transfer to piping bag and add tip of choice.
3. Core out a small area in the center of each cupcake and pipe in the buttercream.
4. Frost the cupcakes with the remaining buttercream.
5. Drizzle caramel sauce over the frosting. Sprinkle with butterscotch chips and toffee candy bits.

Nana's Pumpkin Spice Latte

Ingredients:

- 1/2 cup brewed coffee
- 2 cups 2% milk
- 2 tablespoon pumpkin puree
- 1 tablespoon sugar
- 1 tablespoon vanilla extract
- 1 teaspoon pumpkin pie spice for coffee, split
- Whipped cream
- 2 cinnamon sticks

Instructions:

1. Add milk, pumpkin puree, and sugar to a saucepan over medium heat. Slowly heat the milk until hot. Do not boil.
2. Remove from heat and whisk in coffee, vanilla extract, sugar, and pumpkin pie spice.
3. Top with a dollop of whipped cream and dust with pumpkin pie spice.
4. Garnish with 2 cinnamon sticks.

Tasha's Pumpkin Spice Coffee

Ingredients:

- 8 ounces brewed dark roast coffee
- 1 teaspoon vanilla extract
- 1 tablespoon sugar
- 3 1/2 teaspoon ground cinnamon
- 3/4 teaspoon ground ginger
- 3/4 teaspoon nutmeg
- 1/2 teaspoon ground allspice
- 1/2 teaspoon ground clove
- 1 cinnamon sticks

Instructions:

1. Add vanilla extract, sugar, and spices to coffee.
2. Stir well.
3. Garnish with cinnamon stick.

Monty's Key Lime Protein Shake

Ingredients:

- 2 cups ice
- 1 scoop vanilla protein powder
- 3/4 cup unsweetened almond milk
- 1/2 cup freshly squeezed lime juice
- 1 tablespoon lime zest
- Pinch of salt
- 1 crushed graham cracker
- 1 slice lime

Instructions:

1. Combine ice, protein powder, almond milk, lime juice, lime zest, and salt.
2. Blend until smooth.
3. Top with graham cracker crumbs and garnish with lime.

Tasha's Recovery Soup

Ingredients:

- 1 tablespoon extra-virgin olive oil
- 2 stalks celery, diced
- 2 large carrots, sliced into 1/4-inch disks
- 1/2 cup kale, thinly chopped
- 1 large zucchini, chopped
- 8 cups chicken bone broth
- 2 chicken breasts
- 1 teaspoon ground turmeric

- 1/2 teaspoon ground black pepper,
- 1 teaspoon ground ginger
- 1 ½ teaspoons dried thyme
- 1 tablespoon fresh parsley, chopped
- 1 tablespoon fresh cilantro, chopped
- 1 pinch sea salt
- 1 splash lemon juice
- 1 tablespoon zest of orange
- 12 ounces gluten-free egg noodles

Instructions:

1. Add all ingredients except the egg noodles to the Crockpot and heat on high for 30 minutes.
2. Reduce heat to medium and cook for 2-4 hours.
3. Add noodles 30-60 minutes prior to serving.

Tabbi's Dirt Cake

Ingredients:

- 2 large (or 3 small) boxes Jell-O vanilla pudding
- 3 cups of milk
- 2 8-ounce boxes cream cheese, softened at room temperature
- 16 ounces Cool Whip
- 1 package of Family-Size Double Stuffed Oreo cookies
- 1 package gummy worms

Instructions:

1. Remove cream cheese from refrigerator and set on counter for 30-60 minutes until softened.
2. In a food processor, crush up half the Oreos and layer onto the bottom of a cake pan.
3. Mix the pudding and milk, adding one package of cream cheese and half the Cool Whip until smooth.

4. Add in the remaining package of cream cheese and Cool Whip.
5. Layer mixture onto the Oreos in the pan.
6. Crush the remaining Oreos and sprinkle over top of cake.
7. Garnish with gummy worms and serve chilled.

Penny's Just Peachy Tea

Thanks to Shanna for this one!

Ingredients:

- 3/4 cup water
- 3/4 cup lemonade
- 1 bag mint tea
- 1 bag peach tea
- 1 tbsp honey

Instructions:

1. Add boiled water to mint and peach tea bags.
2. Add honey and let steep for 3-5 minutes.
3. Add lemonade.

Serve hot or over a full glass of ice.

Pasta Nacht's Gluten-Free Dairy-Free Fettuccine Alfredo

Ingredients:

- 1 package gluten-free fettuccine noodles
- 1 tbsp avocado oil
- 1 tsp salt
- 2 tbsp butter substitute
- 1 tsp minced garlic
- 4-5 ounce firm tofu

- ¼ cup oat milk
- 2 tbsp canned coconut cream, unsweetened
- 2 cups chicken broth; split
- 3 tbsp gluten-free flour
- 2 tbsp nutritional yeast
- Italian seasoning to taste
- Black pepper to taste
- Optional: Chives to garnish
- Optional: Grilled chicken breast

Instructions:

1. Prepare pasta according to instructions. Add 1 tbsp avocado oil and 1 tsp salt to the water prior to boiling.
2. In a blender, add the tofu, oat milk, 1 cup chicken broth, and coconut cream and mix until smooth.
3. In a small saucepan, melt the butter substitute over low heat. Add the minced garlic and sauté for 2-3 minutes.
4. Add the flour, yeast, and 1 cup chicken broth to the saucepan and stir until combined.
5. Add the blended mix to the saucepan and stir until combined. If the mixture becomes lumpy, add chicken broth as needed, remove from heat, and return to the blender to smooth.
6. Add Italian seasoning and black pepper to the mixture as desired.
7. Serve sauce over pasta or mix together.
8. Add chicken if desired and serve.

Tasha's Gluten-Free Gooey Brownies

Ingredients:

- 1/4 cup cocoa powder
- 1 cup coconut sugar
- 1 1/2 cups almond flour
- 1/4 tsp salt
- 1/4 tsp baking soda
- 3 tbsp avocado oil
- 1 tsp vanilla extract
- 1 large egg
- 1 egg yolk
- 2/3 cup dairy-free chocolate chips

Instructions:

1. Preheat oven to 350 degrees.
2. Line an 8x8 baking dish with parchment paper.
3. In a medium bowl, mix the almond flour, cocoa powder, salt, and baking soda until fully blended.
4. In a large bowl, use a mixer to beat the sugar and oil until blended. Mix in the egg, yolk, and vanilla. Beat until just combined.
5. Add the mixture from the large bowl and hand mix until blended.
6. Fold in and evenly distribute the chocolate chips.
7. Pour the mixture into the dish and use a rubber spatula to spread it evenly.
8. Bake for 24-28 minutes until center achieves desired gooiness.
9. Let cool completely. Slice and serve.

Tia Gia's Gluten-Free Dairy-Free Lemonade Crispies

Find Tia Gia's signature lemonade recipe in One Margarita *by Kerry Evelyn*

Ingredients:

- 6 cups gluten-free crisped rice cereal
- ¼ cup lemonade
- 3 tbsp plant butter
- 10 ounces Marshmallow Fluff or mini marshmallows
- 2 tbsp lemon zest, split

Instructions:

1. Melt the butter and Fluff (or marshmallows) in a saucepan over medium heat and stir until completely melted.
2. Stir in the lemonade and 1 tbsp zest. Remove from heat.
3. Pour cereal into a large bowl. Stir in the liquid mixture.
4. Grease an 8x8 pan (or 9x12 pan for thinner treats) with plant butter or aerosol plant butter spray.
5. Pour the mixture into a baking dish and spread evenly.
6. Garnish with 1 tbsp lemon zest.
7. Cool in refrigerator for 30 minutes before serving.

Matcha Madness

Prep time: 3 minutes | Servings: 1

Ingredients:

- 1 cup ice
- 1 cup almond milk
- 1 banana

- 1 tbsp organic Japanese matcha powder
- ¼ tsp ground turmeric

Instructions:

1. Add all ingredients to a blender.
2. Blend until pureed.
3. Serve cold with a smoothie straw.

Zaki's Favorite Butter Tarts

H.M. Shander's recipe!

Prep time: 10 minutes | Cook time: 20 minutes | Servings: 24

Ingredients:

- 2 eggs
- 2 c of brown sugar
- 2 tbsp vinegar
- ½ tsp vanilla
- ½ c butter, melted
- 2 c raisins
- 1 sleeve of frozen tart shells

Instructions:

1. Beat the eggs well.
2. Add in sugar, vanilla, and vinegar.
3. Stir in the melted butter and raisins.
4. Fill the frozen tart shells three-fourths full.
5. Bake at 350 degrees for 20 minutes.
6. Cool and enjoy. This freezes nicely.

Straw-Berry Dreamy

Prep time: 2 minutes |Servings: 4

Ingredients:

- 14 oz Mountain Dew
- 1 pump Torani strawberry syrup
- 1 to 2 tbsp vanilla creamer
- whipped cream
- 1 strawberry, sliced

Instructions:

1. In a large glass, add Mountain Dew and strawberry syrup.
2. Using a muddler or spoon, mix together.
3. Pour into four 4-ounce cups. Drizzle with vanilla creamer in each cup.
4. Top each with whipped cream and garnish with a strawberry slice.

Shanna's Soda Shoppe Favorites

Recipes contributed by Shanna Johnson

Lime of My Life

Prep time: 2 minutes | Servings: 4

Ingredients:

- 14 oz Sprite
- ½ pump Torani lime syrup
- ½ pump Torani vanilla syrup
- 2 tbsp creamer

- optional: 4 thin lime slices
- optional: graham crackers, crushed

Instructions:

1. In a large glass, add Sprite, lime syrup, and vanilla syrup.
2. Using a muddler or spoon, mix together.
3. Pour into four 4-ounce glasses. Drizzle creamer into each glass.
4. If desired, sprinkle with graham crackers and garnish with a lime slice.

Peach of My Heart

Prep time: 2 minutes | Servings: 4

Ingredients:

- 14 oz Sprite
- ½ pump Torani pineapple syrup
- ½ pump Torani peach syrup
- optional: 4 gummy peach candies

Instructions:

1. In a glass, add Sprite, pineapple syrup, and peach syrup.
2. Using a muddler or spoon, mix together.
3. Pour into four 4-ounce glasses.
4. If desired, garnish with gummy peach candy.

Sunflower Bakery's Cinnamon Rolls

Submitted by Shanna Johnson

Prep time: 2 hours | Cook time: 20-25 minutes | Servings: 1-2 dozen rolls, depending on thickness and size

Ingredients:

Dough

- ¼-oz package of active dry yeast
- 1 c warm milk (between 105-115 degrees)
- ½ c granulated sugar (and 1 tbsp for the yeast)
- ⅓ c softened butter
- ½ tsp salt
- 2 eggs
- 4 c flour

Filling

- ½ c cinnamon sugar
- ½ c brown sugar
- 3 tbsp cinnamon
- ½ tsp nutmeg
- ⅓ c butter, melted

Icing

- 3 tbsp butter
- 2 c powdered sugar
- 8 oz cream cheese
- 1 tsp vanilla

Instructions:

1. In a small mixing bowl, add the warm milk, yeast, and 1 tbsp sugar. Whisk well and set aside until it is bubbly and foamy. This usually takes about 10 minutes.
2. In a large separate bowl, add sugar, butter, salt, eggs, and flour. Mix these well by hand or using a stand mixer with dough attachment.
3. Once the yeast mixture has finished, pour it into the large mixing bowl. Mix until well combined.
4. Spray a clean large bowl with nonstick cooking spray and place the dough into the bowl. Cover and let rise in a warm area for an hour, or until dough has doubled in size.
5. After the dough has doubled in size, roll it out onto a floured surface until it is approximately ¼-inch thick, in a large rectangle shape.
6. Now prepare the filling by combining the sugars, cinnamon, and nutmeg into a bowl. Mix well.
7. Spread melted butter over the cinnamon roll dough and be sure to cover every inch of the top. You can melt and use more butter if you need to. While the butter is still wet, sprinkle the seasoning over the top until it is well coated and no longer soaks into the butter.
8. Starting on the long end, slowly roll the dough down to the bottom edge. Pinch the seam slightly to avoid it coming apart. Using a sharp knife, or unflavored dental floss, cut the dough into 1½-inch slices.
9. Preheat the oven to 350 degrees. While it is preheating, prepare a 9x13-inch baking pan or cookie sheet with nonstick cooking spray. Place the cinnamon rolls onto the pan, cover with plastic wrap or a damp towel, and let rise for another 30 minutes.
10. Bake cinnamon rolls in the preheated oven for 20-25 minutes or until golden brown.
11. While cinnamon rolls are baking or cooling, combine icing ingredients and beat well until combined and fluffy. Spread on top of cinnamon rolls and enjoy.

Molly's Blueberry Tea

Ingredients:

- 2 ½ c blueberries, split
  - 1 c to make juice
  - 1 c to dry out
  - ½ c fresh blueberries for garnish (optional)
- ½ c orange zest
- ½ c black tea, loose leaf
- ½ c dried hibiscus leaves
- 1 cup dried hibiscus leaves

Instructions:

1. Use a potato masher to press 1 c blueberries in a flat-bottomed bowl. Add 1 tbsp water and mash until purple juice begins to rise to the top. Strain the mixture to yield ½ c blueberry juice and set aside. Save the leftover blueberry mixture for pancakes or pie!
2. Bake 1 c blueberries and orange zest in a single layer on a cookie sheet in the oven for 7-8 hours at 170 degrees F.
3. Mix dried blueberries, orange zest, tea, and hibiscus leaves in the blueberry juice to coat. Add up to 1 tbsp water if needed.
4. Spread on a cookie sheet in a thin layer and let dry completely in the sun or bake for 2 hours at 170 degrees F. Break up any leaves or berries that are stuck together and let dry out overnight if any moisture remains.
5. Use a mortar and pestle to mash and break large bits of the dried mixture into finer pieces. Then, spoon 1 tbsp of the mixture into nylon tea bags.
6. For hot tea, place one teabag in a teacup and add boiling water. Let the tea steep for 4-5 minutes and remove the teabag.

7. For iced tea, place two teabags in a tall glass and add boiling water. Let the tea steep for 4-5 minutes and remove the teabags. Let the tea cool naturally. Once fully cooled, add a scoop of ice and garnish with fresh blueberries.

Meemaw's Deviled Potatoes

Taking Daisy Mae's Southern Potato Salad to a new level!*

Contributed by Shanna Johnson

Ingredients:

- 1 bag baby gold potatoes
- 3 large eggs, hard-boiled, peeled, and chopped
- 1 c mayonnaise
- ½ c sweet pickle relish
- 1 tbsp yellow mustard
- 1 celery stalk, minced
- 1 tsp salt
- 1½ tsp onion powder
- 1 tsp black pepper
- ½ tsp dried dill
- ¼ tsp cayenne pepper
- ½ tsp smoked paprika

Instructions:

1. Place potatoes in a large pot and cover with cold water. Cook on medium-high heat until boiling. Cover and lower to medium-low heat. Cook for about 15 minutes.
2. In a large mixing bowl, whisk together the mayo, mustard, pickle relish, and minced celery. Add the eggs to the bowl and seasonings (except for paprika).
3. Drain the potatoes and let cool until warm. Slice each potato in half, carefully scooping out the centers and leaving a little bit of potato along the edges. Add the

scooped-out potato bits to the bowl and mix well. Use a potato masher if needed.

4. Blend the mixture in a blender or food processor until creamy.
5. Scoop the mixture into a frosting bag and pipe into the potato halves.
6. Sprinkle paprika and serve.

For more story-related recipes, check out **Kerry's Novel Eats & Treats,** ***a curated collection!***

Acknowledgments

First and foremost, thanks to God for connecting me with the most amazing bookish people as I continue to pursue my life's work. The life of an indie author challenges you in ways you could never imagine. It's easier when you have such lovely friends and fierce cheerleaders in your corner to keep reminding you why you're doing this and encouraging you to keep going when you hit the lows.

This story would not be what it is without my amazing Blueberry Tea Crew! God has blessed me with the most wonderful people. These incredible readers that are friends and readers-turned-friends and I have been collaborating for months to make this story the absolute best it can be for fans of my worlds and new visitors. Britteny Williams, welcome to the beta crew! You have fit in seamlessly and have so much to offer. I'm so glad you took a chance on me! Author Debbie Hyde, I appreciate your support and all that you do for indie authors. You bless us so much! Denise Ridgely, my angel-on-earth friend! I'm so glad you found my books and my words can give you a sweet escape from the sadness you see every day. Jane Litherland! What can I say? My SYS from Sheffield, across-the-pond-hockey buddy, radiant rhyming reviewer extraordinaire, I can't imagine my life before you were in it. Kaity Norris, I'm so glad we became friends! You inspire me so much and I can't wait till your book is out so you can inspire all the kids that need to know they are meant for so much more. Sarah Graves, I miss you so much. Thank you for being there for me for all these crazy years, through homeschooling shenanigans and cheer comps and everything in between. We must plan something the next time you're in town! Shanna Johnson, your effortless ability to read my mind and articulate the vibes I can't put to words will always astound me. Your friendship is a gift, and I can't wait to support your dream! Tabbi Cagle, your eagle eye, fun-loving perspective, and crazy memory of my characters continues to enrich my stories and delight readers. You think of the coolest things and connections, and it's so fun! Valerie Hills, my dear SCBL con buddy, I can't wait to hug you this summer. Thank you for your years of love and support and for all the time you've given to me and the people in my head. I could write pages of gratitude to each of you! My deepest thanks to you all!

To author Melissa J. Sweet, thanks for helping me dig deeper, down to the puddles of mush. The way you see and understand character—with empathy, intuition, and eyes that can see into their souls—makes you an incredible writer and critique partner. I'm so grateful to the bookstagods for crossing our paths!

To Monica Cobine, Gail Silva, and my mom, Judy, thank you for "Gamma reading" and sharing your invaluable insight and catching those stinkin' typos!

To Korin Adamites, thank you for all the things, including the bajillion perfectly timed reels that make me laugh when I want to cry.

To Stephanie Harrell, thank you for regularly reminding me of my worth. Especially when I forget or stubbornly refuse to acknowledge it.

My SSCGs! Love you so much, sweet little group o' mine! Thank you for your endless support, spot-on advice, and the not-always-wanted truth bombs. I'd have quit years ago if not for you.

Thanks to BookNookNuts for squeezing me in last-minute—again! I appreciate you tons and am so grateful to have worked with you on all of my projects. You are amazing, and I love you bunches!

Much thanks to my editor, Chris Kridler, for always challenging me to dig deeper, think harder, and write better. You make my brain hurt in the best way! I'm so grateful you push me beyond the easy and into the heart of the story and characters. Thanks for never letting me get away with lazy writing, even when I try to sneak it past you like my cat hiding hair ties under the couch. And, wow, the formatting of this book (and all the books in this series)! I love it so much and am so blessed to work with such an amazing person and incredible talent.

To my hubby and kiddos, I love you so much. Y'all inspire me and give me endless material to include or shape into something unique in my stories.

To Lucy, my delightful writing partner—I promise to pet you after each sprint if you stay off my keyboard.

If you are reading this and happened to have been a Sandpiper at Camp Massasoit in the summer of 1985, hello! It's so funny what sticks with us, isn't it? Do reach out to say hi and let me know if I got the lyrics wrong! I also remember partial verses about seeing Lloyd every day at the pool and telling Jeff we thought crafts were really cool. I don't have a lot of memories from my time there, but the ones I do have are vivid. Singing the song and hating the group changing room. Loving buying candy and hating walking on the beach. Loving that there was an actual pool, so we didn't have to swim with the fishies or get stuck on the other side of the lake in a boat at the previous camp I'd attended (that actually happened—one of the counselors had to swim back to shore)!

Finally, much thanks to C.L. Rain for inviting me to be a part of the *Banter and Blushes: Splash of Romance* anthology, Sophea Chan who formatted the anthology, and to my fellow storytellers, Tia Marlee, Dineen Miller, Kaci Lane, Jess Hansen, Leah Busboom, Christine Sterling, and P. Harlow—it was a pleasure working with y'all, and I hope our stories bring as much joy to readers as this collaboration brought to me.

Enjoy 3 Seasons of The Coffee Loft!

WINTER COLLECTION

J.P. Sterling *Pardon My French Press*

Tia Marlee Bean *Wishing for a Latte Love*

Kimberly Krey *Java Hearts & Cupid Darts*

Kimberley Montpetit *Wake Me Up Before You Cocoa*

Ginny Sterling *May the Froth Be with You*

Carly Greer *Frappe to Know You*

Katie O'Connor *Cappuccino Mugs and Fire Fighter Hugs*

H.M. Shander *Living La Vida Mocha*

Audrey Carnes *Caffeine Kisses and Winter Wishes*

Kerry Evelyn *That Thing You Brew*

Kaci Lane *Brewin' Up Love*

R.S. Jonesee *Love You a Latte*

FALL COLLECTION

J.P. Sterling *No More Mr. Chai Guy*

Ellie Hall *Don't You Forget About Tea*

Kerry Evelyn *Pumpkin Spice Spice Baby*

Susanne Ash *Beanful Wishes*

Tia Marlee *You Mocha Me Crazy*

Mel Walker *Grounds for Romance*

Tracy Broemmer *Soy Into You*

Meg Easton *Spiced Chais and Secret Spies*

D.E. Malone *A Café Au Lait Kind of Love*

Kimberley Montpetit *Snow Is Falling, Cocoa Is Calling*

H.M. Shander *It's a Brewtiful Day*

Bella Greene *Espresso Your Love*

MOUNTAIN BREW COLLECTION

J.P. Sterling *Truly, Madly, Steeply Brew*

H.M. Shander *Mountain Beam Dream*

Leah Busboom *Mission: Imbrewable — A Frothy Fiasco*

Susanne Ash *All You Need is Macchiato*

Tia Marlee *A Brewtiful Kind of Love*

Kerry Evelyn *Sew Matcha in Love*

Kimberley Montpetit *Cocoa Kisses & Mountain Misses*

Books by Kerry Evelyn

Crane's Cove

Love on the Edge (Matt & Lanie)

Love on the Rocks (Easton & Kat)

Love on the Beach (Damon & Shelby)

Love on the Fly (JC & Caroline)

Love on the Heart (Jack & Molly)

Love on the Brain (Ryan & Jane)

Love on the Island (JC & Caroline's destination wedding novella)

Crane's Cove Chronicles

Cat's Paw Cove: Moon Mist Manor Miniseries

Christmas at Moon Mist Manor (Matt & Lanie)

Love Overrules the Lawyer (Javier & Rachel)

The Beachcomber's Buccaneer Bounty (Drake & Leda)

Palmer City Voltage

Love on the Ice (Alexei & Ginny)

Cruising on Ice (Kingston & Taylor)

Christmas on Ice (Trask & Kami)

Sparks on the Ice (Noel & Gabby)

Melting the Ice (Gemma & Zander)

Celebration on Ice (Jason & Lauren)

Crushing on Ice (Brendan & Brenna)

Palmer City Voltage: The Complete Series Box Set

The Coffee Loft: Denver Edge Hockey Romance Miniseries

That Thing You Brew (Xavier & Penny)

Pumpkin Spice Spice Baby (Monty & Tasha)

Sew Matcha in Love (Zaki & Arwyn)

Sun, Sea, & Blueberry Tea (Zaki & Arwyn's road trip novella)

Coffee Loft Collection Box Set

Once Upon Academy

The Swan & the Phoenix (Reggie & Nettie)

Collections

Crane's Cove Box Set 1

Crane's Cove Box Set 2

Small-Town Christmas

Nonfiction

City Nights (How I Met My Other Anthology)

Fenway: A Beacon of Hope (How I Met My Other 2 Anthology)

The Believer's Journal for Everyday Faith

The Advent Experience Keepsake Planner

How to Binge-Write Your Novel

Kerry's Novel Eats & Treats: Unforgettable Favorites from Sweet and Savory Stories

About the Author

Kerry Evelyn writes heartwarming sweet romance filled with small-town charm and unforgettable characters chasing their happily-ever-afters. Her books have won multiple awards, including a Reader's Favorite gold medals in Romantic Comedy for *That Thing You Brew* and *Pumpkin Spice Spice Baby*, as well as a silver medal in Christian Romance for *Love on the Brain*. This *NSYNC fanatic is fueled on faith, Dunkin' iced coffee, and a love for people, including her amazing family, and a passion for storytelling that brings readers back for "just one more chapter." Kerry loves (in ever-changing order) books, boybands, cats, hockey, sweet drinks, taking selfies, traveling, and the madness of getting the stories in her head onto the page. Find out more and sign up for her newsletter at KerryEvelyn.com/links.

Website: KerryEvelyn.com
Reader Group: Facebook.com/groups/CranesCoveCrew
Spotify: tinyurl.com/KerryEvelynSpotify

facebook.com/KerryEvelynAuthor
instagram.com/KerryEvelynBooks
tiktok.com/@KerryEvelynAuthor
pinterest.com/KerryEvelynBooks
amazon.com/Kerry-Evelyn/e/B077LWTYXJ
goodreads.com/kerryevelynauthor
bookbub.com/authors/kerry-evelyn

www.ingramcontent.com/pod-product-compliance
Lightning Source LLC
LaVergne TN
LVHW041050080826
845145LV00007B/1519